MAGICALLY MATED

LIMITED EDITION SHIFTER ROMANCE

LIV BRYWOOD

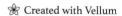

EXCERPT FROM CAPTIVE OF THE BEAR CLAN

As Draven sprouts fur and his features begin to distort and morph in that disorienting way, I think about what an amazing creature he is. He's all man and all bear at the same time. It's sexy.

My mind drifts to the kiss I shared with Kaval this morning, and I can't help but wonder what it would be like to kiss Draven. They're both such fascinating guys. I get the feeling that I may be getting myself into a whole different kind of trouble hiding out in the woods with these sexy shifters.

An emotional storm is brewing out here.

Even though I haven't really had much time with Stone, there's definitely some kind of connection there. I suspect we may share a mutual attraction too.

Finally, I pull my attention back to the task at hand and utter my incantation. The aura-bubble coalesces around me. I focus on keeping my breathing even as I pour energy into it, carefully and steadily, like blowing a huge gum-bubble. Thirty seconds later, it's fully formed and reinforced. Draven roars a warning and begins his charge.

He's coming on fast, and even though I'm confident my shield will hold, I can't stop the nervous flutter in my belly. My heart starts pounding. Adrenaline courses through my blood. It's a normal reaction when a six hundred-pound bear is charging at you full speed. Regardless of your magical abilities, that's some scary shit. Primal instincts run *deep*.

When he's about ten feet from me, he launches himself through the air, claws ready to tear through the barrier. I reflexively raise my hands in front of my face and squint my eyes shut in anticipation of the impact, but there is only silence. I open my eyes apprehensively and see Draven two feet in front of me, suspended in mid-air with a dumb, surprised look that I've never seen on a bear's face before.

"Aha. Success." I jump into the air in triumph.

I'm so excited that I lose my concentration. My energy falters, and suddenly Draven is falling toward me. I turn to run, but I'm too slow, and his massive arm knocks me to the ground.

Luckily, my reflexes are fast enough to soften my fall with my hands, so I don't end up with a mouthful of earth.

I push myself up on an elbow and look behind me. Draven's enormous paw is covering most of my ass, and my skirt is slightly ripped where his sharp claw tore through it. His claws and fur disappear as his paw shrinks back down to a human hand, so it covers only one cheek now. Draven gapes up at me naked and dumbfounded, and then notices the placement of his hand and jerks it back. His cheeks flame. As he stands, he turns his head away to avoid my eyes.

CAPTIVE OF THE BEAR CLAN: CHAPTER 1

MINERVA

The night breeze stirs my hair into a wavy tussle as I speed along the moonlit road which curves around the mountainside like a lover. Looming huge on the horizon, the moon—a blue moon—dominates the sky, robbing the stars of their light.

It's all a matter of perspective, of course. The moon only seems brighter. We'd learned in school that the stars are really suns, burning a million times brighter than the moon on its best night. But then again, I'd also learned that perspective and reality can sometimes intertwine—if one is a witch.

There are many witches in my hometown of Bonfire Falls. I am but one among the many, like the stars above. And to be honest, I'm not one of the brighter ones. To some witches, magic comes easily. Me, not so much.

But that's fine with me. I don't need to be like Azealia, a powerful witch capable of bending time and space to her will, to be happy. Tonight, all I need to be happy is a song I can dance to, some cute guys, and lots and lots of booze.

It's my twenty-first birthday, and tonight is my party.

The blue moon is most auspicious in many ways. I'm trying not to think too much about magic tonight, though. Rather, I'm hoping that some socializing will help me forget how lonely I am.

In a small town like ours, it can be hard to find someone to date and even harder to find someone you can trust. People are always snooping into your business, and sooner or later the truth comes out. Let's just say I don't have a good track record of picking trustworthy people.

I round the bend, and the moon disappears behind an outcropping of boulders. Shafts of silvery light dance across uneven terrain until they're blocked by the mountain. Darkness envelops me. I really don't care much for this particular stretch of the road which includes a cluster of old knobby pines jokingly called the Twilight Zone. Plenty of stories in high school were traded about how someone's cousin or neighbor had gone missing because their car got a flat right in the heavy copse of pines. Pure nonsense, but there is a palpable sense of evil about the place. Some of the older witches claim it was the place where a terribly sinister witch met her end, but I don't believe them.

Still, I roll up my window as I pass through the darkness. The problem with being a witch is your sixth sense is more enhanced than the average human's. You can never be sure if it's just your imagination or something really is out to get you.

Thankfully, I drive out of the copse and back into the moon's wonderful grace. I pull off the main road and take the serpentine rock-strewn trail that meanders up the rest of the way to the coven's meeting spot. Even though I don't have a lot of friends, the entire coven is going to show up to my party because it's tradition. I've certainly showed up for a lot of parties dedicated to people I didn't like.

There won't be many people I'm really close to at the party except for my best friend Arianna, and—if he shows up—my friend Kaval.

Arianna is a witch like me, and we've been friends since grade school. She and I are the same age, but where I'm cautious and try to keep my emotions bottled up, she tends to just explode all over a situation. While she's not gifted enough to hold any real power in our world, she can enthrall a room with her stories. However, she tends to be aloof, and she's hard to get to know, so I'm her only real friend.

Kaval... Kaval is another matter. He's a Bear Clan shifter, and that's where the complications start. While the war between the witches and the shifter clans ended long ago, and a truce was established here in Bonfire Falls, there's still a lot of lingering tension and prejudice between the groups. In an effort to establish more common ground, our schools were integrated, which is where I met Kaval—which is quite fortunate, because he skipped class more often than he attended.

I smile when I think of him, the perpetual rebel without a cause. If he wasn't sneaking away from school to smoke pot, he was dropping Mexican firecrackers down the toilets. The only class he went to regularly was Shop, and that was just an excuse to work on his bike.

With his riding leathers, tall, powerful build, and overall 'don't mess with me' demeanor, a lot of people were intimidated by Kaval. Not me, though. I've always been able to see past his exterior at the teddy bear inside. Kaval would never hurt me, at least not physically. He's always been there for me, in his own way. One time, a guy grabbed my ass in the lunchroom. Kaval knocked all of his front teeth out with one punch.

I pull my battered pickup to a halt next to a line of other vehicles. Most of the coven is already here, but I have a right to be fashionably late to my own party, don't I? Besides, I had a hell of a time picking out an outfit.

Looking down at myself, I think I did all right. I've chosen a tight, body-hugging black skirt paired with a puffy-sleeved blouse that shows just the right amount of cleavage. A faux corset is laced around my midsection, giving me a sleek figure and providing a place to keep my phone. The skirt stops at mid-thigh, leaving a brief patch of smoothly shaven skin before my striped stockings start. Hiking boots complete the look, because heels would've just been stupid in this rough terrain.

My hair was another matter. I almost went with pigtails, but tonight is about becoming an adult. I decided to put my hair up into a topknot and let it fan out down my back. A leather choker with a pentagram—which is not the same as a Satanic symbol, thank you very much—adorns my throat. I play with it idly as I follow the beaten trail toward the sounds of music, laughter, and the occasional loud clink of glass bottles being properly disposed of.

I walk between a pair of shoulder-high conical pillars carved from a single solid boulder and enter the coven's retreat property. Flames leap ten feet high from a massive bonfire. Witches from my coven twirl and prance around the fire, dancing to the rhythmic beat of loud music. A couple of elders approach me to pay their respects, then they quickly excuse themselves. I'm not a particularly powerful witch, so they won't be staying for my whole party.

"My" party might be a bit of a misnomer. I put my hands on my hips and glare at the party guests. No one has even noticed my arrival other than the elder witches of our coven, and they just wanted to get their obligatory pleasantries out of the way so they can go home and sleep. Even my supposed BFF Arianna hasn't even looked in my direction.

My good mood is starting to fade even before something ice-cold shocks my shoulder. I shriek and leap nearly a foot into the air.

Deep, baritone laughter greets my semi-amused scowl when I turn around to find Kaval there. He's holding two beers in one of his massive hands and has another wedged between his forefinger and middle finger.

"Happy Birthday, Minnie," he says, finally calming down.

"I'll forgive you for that if one of those beers is for me." I arch a brow. One of those had better have my name on it.

He extends the third beer to me. It's already open and foam dribbles over the rim.

Taking the cold bottle, I stare up into his beautiful face. His big expressive brown eyes and dazzling smile melt my heart. It should be illegal to be so damn sexy. Friends aren't supposed to be this hot.

Kaval is big, even for a Bear Clan shifter. His shoulders are so wide that he has to turn sideways to get through most doorways. He's wearing his leather riding jacket tonight. It's sexy as hell.

Beneath the jacket, a tight white t-shirt does little to conceal the hard knots of muscle on his torso. His denim jeans, which are ripped in the knees, do nothing to hide his massive package. I swallow and look away. I shouldn't be staring at him like this. He's my friend. We've never been anything more than that. I wouldn't want to ruin what we have by becoming lovers. It's not worth the risk.

"You're looking good, Minnie." His gaze rakes up and down my body.

"Oh yeah?" I do a little twirl for him. "Do you like my outfit?"

Kaval whistles loud enough that several of the party guests turn and notice me for the first time.

"I love it." His stare intensifies.

There are times when I'm almost certain he's attracted to me, but I could be projecting my own desires onto him. I certainly have thought about being with him—every girl in town has—but Kaval doesn't do attachment. He's lover material, not boyfriend material. We're alike in some ways because I avoid attachments with other people too. It's much safer that way. You can't get your heart broken if you don't give it to anyone.

He shakes his head as if he's coming out of an enchantment.

"I have something for you." He reaches into his back pocket and digs out a wrinkled piece of orange paper. "Happy Birthday."

"What is this?" I ask, laughing. My hand is tiny compared to his. I retrieve the paper. I unfold it to find a greeting card. On the cover, glitter-embossed candles adorn a towering cake. "It's so fancy. Thank you, Kaval."

I lean up and kiss his smooth cheek. He blushes and quickly looks around to see if anyone is looking. I don't know why he cares, but I don't question it.

"Kaval..." My fingers brush my lips. "Did you shave? You never shave."

"I shave," he says defiantly. A second later, his massive shoulders sag a bit. "Well, not all the time. Once in a while. Anyway, open it."

I open the card. The flickering bonfire illuminates a handwritten note. I squint, but it's hard to decipher his handwriting.

"What does it say?"

"It says you have a hundred hours of free labor at Claws," he says with a shrug.

"Oh..." I laugh. "I see. One hundred hours of free labor at the Claws and Steel Garage." He owns the best car and bike repair shop in town. I twirl a strand of hair around my finger and give him a coy smile. "So... what kind of labor will you be performing?"

I intended the line to be flirty, but he thinks I'm being serious.

"Well..." His forehead scrunches as he ponders his response. "Y'know, your truck could probably use a tire rotation. Maybe an oil change. You should probably replace your battery terminals because that gets a lot of folks in trouble in the winter time, and—where are you going?"

Car repairs? Seriously? He's cute, but sometimes the man can be as dense as an oak tree.

"I'm going to grab another beer." I chuck my empty bottle into a metal trash can. It shatters on impact. "Thanks for the present."

I leave Kaval there scratching his head. I don't want him to see my disappointment, so I quickly slip into the crowd.

It takes me a few minutes to get through a crush of well-wishers who have finally decided to greet me. I end up doing a Jell-O shot, a Jaeger bomb, and a slippery nipple before I finally get a beer.

My mind is buzzing. So is my body. Moonlight pulses through me. I draw strength from the moon's luminous presence. I don't even drink the beer. I'm entranced by the sight of the bright white orb hovering in the night sky.

Kaval's probably still waiting for me. I tear my eyes away from the moon and spot him talking to Arianna.

She's leaning in close, and she's running her fingers along his forearm. Her wide, dewy eyes bat up at Kaval. Even though I can't hear her what she's saying above the din of conversation, her intentions are obvious.

What the hell is she doing? I turn my back for a minute, and she goes after my... my... what? My friend? Why am I so angry?

The bottle in my hand shatters. Curious faces turn my way. I stand there not bothering to check for blood. Had I really been squeezing it that hard?

I want to squeeze Arianna's throat instead. Look at her with those tight booty shorts and crop top, rubbing her tits all over Kaval. Can't she tell he's not interested? She's staring at me, her eyes wide. Not so flirty now, are you?

Something bounces off my cheek. I glance around as pine needles, twigs, and even a black beetle have been swept into a slow-moving vortex which is whirling around my body. I hadn't even realized I was using magic. It's never come to me so easily; it must be the rage. I can't stop it from bubbling up inside of me.

Arianna's supposed to be my best friend. How could she? How dare she!

I lift my hands up to my midsection, instinctively summoning my newfound power. A spark appears between my palms. It flickers faster and faster until it extends into a luminescent orb the size of a bowling ball. Pine needles blacken to ash when they fall anywhere near it, but my hands are unharmed. It's like I'm the source of the heat. It's as if I'm pouring my soul into this deadly sphere, and I'm powerless to control it.

The darkness inside me knows this sphere is meant for Arianna.

How could she?

How dare she!

She must *burn.*

I give in to my rage and send the ball of energy sizzling across the ground toward her. People panic and start running. The use of magic outside of sanctioned coven rituals is strongly discouraged. I could get into a huge amount of trouble for this, but I can't stop it. This isn't normal magic. This is dark magic, terrible magic, destructive magic—the kind of magic that can kill.

As the sphere moves above the earth, it leaves a blackened trail beneath it. Any second now, it's going to smash into Arianna's face, and she won't be so pretty anymore.

Arianna. My best friend. The girl who'd spent the night at my house and shared a bathtub with me when we were children. The girl who gave me a pad at just the right time in high school. I don't want Arianna to be hurt, but my shadow side doesn't care.

I try to call the sphere back to me, but it's too late. The energy has been released, and I realize it's feeding off my anger. Try as I might, I can't control my rage. I can't stop it, but maybe I can redirect the energy and punish her another way.

Without really knowing how, I force the sphere to release most of its power directly into the earth. A blast of energy extinguishes the bonfire and knocks everyone to the ground. Arianna and I are the only ones left standing.

I can't let her go unpunished. My anger and my desire to see her hurt changes. It shifts as an overwhelming desire to humiliate her rages through my soul. The remaining energy from the orange sphere explodes toward her. It tears her provocative outfit into shreds. She screams as her naked body is tossed through the air. She slams—back first—against a tree. Hissing streams of energy wrap around her flailing limbs. The magical bonds completely secure her to the rough bark, while leaving her naughty bits exposed.

That should teach her.

Panting, I'm suddenly very weak. Chaos spreads through the circle as people scramble to their feet before running toward their cars. Several of my fellow witches remain frozen in place. They're caught in a time distortion which was caused by my powerful magic. To my dismay, Kaval is also frozen in place, his eyes wide with fear.

"Oh, Kaval." I ignore Arianna who is struggling against my magical bonds. She pleads with me to release her, but I don't care. This was all her fault and now Kaval probably thinks I'm a monster. "I'm so sorry."

Before I can reach his prone form, a tall witch steps into my path. Her ice-blue eyes flash as if illuminated from within. Her blood-red lips curl into a wicked grin.

"So much power," she hisses. "Come, my sisters, let us dine."

She's not alone. Two other women advance toward me. They float over the ground as if propelled by magic. Their placid demeanor makes them all the more terrifying amid the chaos.

Her sisters have the same eyes, but they're different in other ways. The shortest one has darker skin and a sort of roughness to her features that reminds me of my friend Stone. Her other sister is quite beautiful, but poisonous vipers can be beautiful too.

It's too much for me to take. I don't know how I summoned such powerful magic before, but I can't seem to do it now. Now that I need it, it's gone. The only thing I know right now is that I definitely do not want these women to capture me.

Screaming, I leave my poor frozen Kaval behind. Fueled by terror, I run into the forest in a terrorized, mad dash to get away from the truest form of evil.

CAPTIVE OF THE BEAR CLAN:
CHAPTER 2

MINERVA

P ine branches scratch my face as I dash madly through the forest. I stumble over rocks and fallen limbs. A sharp pain in my side grows worse each time I draw breath, yet I must keep running. I don't know why, but I feel that my death is certain if I fall into the clutches of the three strange witches pursuing me.

Despite a head start, the three witches keep pace with me. While I have to duck under tree limbs or bend them aside, they're using magic to clear their path. Protruding limbs wither into dust at their behest.

Magic... I still can't believe what I've done. My mind whirls with the fallout of my assault on Arianna. I've never felt such rage, such boiling black hatred. Witches have to be wary of falling into the abyssal darkness of their own souls, particularly if they are powerful. Am I already losing myself to the pull of dark magic?

I hit my foot on a jagged stone and tumble into a pile of fallen pine needles. Scrambling, I make it to my feet and keep running even though my foot now throbs with pain. I cry out in agony with each footfall. My misery only serves to make the pursuing witches more gleeful.

"This is fun," giggles the witch with red lips.

The sinister yet cheerful tone in her voice urges me to run faster. I thought I was familiar with the woods around the coven's ritual grounds, but I'm so turned around now that I can't find any of the landmarks I would normally use for navigation.

The moon is hidden behind the canopy of trees making it useless for navigation. Only splashes of spotty silver hint at its existence. Some part of my panicked mind tells me to run toward a road, to get to where there are people, but I have no idea which way to go.

Bursting through a dense thicket, leaves and twigs tangle into my hair and claw at my clothing. It's as if the forest itself is enchanted. As if it's conspiring to help the witches capture me.

I run up a short hill. When I reach the crest, I'm confronted by a sheer cliff over fifty feet high. My heart sinks. I start to run parallel to it, hoping to reach the woods which is nearly a hundred yards away. The tall witch casually steps out of the tree line to block my path.

Undaunted, I turn around and run the other direction, but her companions have already cut me off. I'm trapped. I stand between the three witches. Sweat pours down my face.

"Leave me alone!"

They close in on me.

"I'm afraid we can't do that." The witch's red lips curl into a cruel smile. "We need you alive. We need your magic."

My magic.

It's the only option I have left. If I could level an entire coven then maybe I can blow these three witches right off the mountain.

I try to summon the same level of anger and rage that I'd felt earlier, but it's not working. All I can feel is fear. I'm afraid of these witches, but I'm also afraid of summoning the dark magic which simmers in my soul. It's dangerous, but what choice do I have?

I hold my hands up and try to push past the fear. For a moment, a small spark appears between my palms. The witches slow their advance. I can feel them summoning their own eldritch talents to protect themselves.

Suddenly, my spark dies as quickly as it was born. No amount of desperation will bring it back.

"Come on," I shout in frustration.

I manage to recapture some of the anger and the spark flares back to life. This time, the globe is only the size of a golf ball. Frantically, I toss it at the lead witch. With an amused smile, she spreads her palms wide, creating a webwork of glowing eldritch energy like a cat's cradle. The sphere hits the strands and gets stuck like a fly in a spider's web.

"Not much power left, eh?" She closed her palms together and snuffs my spark. "You expended too much attacking that trollop—though I've been wondering why you just didn't kill her. If someone went after my man, I'd rip her to pieces, one limb at a time."

"She's weak." The tall witch wrinkles her nose. "She'll never agree to help us."

"Help you?" I ask, suddenly hopeful. Maybe they don't want to hurt me after all.

"Oh, she'll help us," says the short, dark skinned witch. "She has no choice."

"I just want to go home," I whimper.

All three of them find this quite amusing. Their sadistic laughter echoes off the cliff.

"Home?" The red-lipped witch sneers. "How can you call any place home when it's polluted by the filth of shifters?"

"Bears and wolves... disgusting," hisses the tall witch. She sends out a stream of spittle to emphasize her loathing. "And those dragons... pretenders. They cower on their tiny patch of turf because they fear our power."

"But the war is over." I shake my head. "We live in peace. Some of them are my friends."

"Friends?" A scowl blackens the red-lipped witch's lovely face. "Like the long-haired wannabe biker? His death will be slow and painful."

That sets me off. While I can't seem to access my magic, I have no trouble summoning my rage. I forget that it's three on one and that they have an advantage because they understand how to control their magic. I don't. All I know is that they've just threatened Kaval, so I'm going to make them pay.

"Don't even think about touching him," I snap.

With a snarl, I charge at the red-lipped witch. All three of them are caught by surprise, unable to believe I would go on the offense.

Years ago, Kaval taught me how to throw a punch. I ball my fists and let my rage flow into them. My solid right cross connects with the witch's jaw.

As she tumbles onto her ass, her eyes glaze over. I recover my senses enough to make a break for it. Their angry shouts echo into the abyss. I run for all I'm worth toward the tree line. Maybe if I retrace my steps, I can make it back to somewhere familiar.

Ahead of me, the forest looms. Its friendly darkness is

ready to shield me from the witch's sight. But, when I am less than a few steps away, I feel a telltale tingle on my skin. Magic is afoot.

The knobby trunks of two massive pines suddenly bend and shift like modeling clay, smashing themselves together and cutting off my escape.

I skid to a halt and risk a glance over my shoulder. The short witch is kneeling. She's attending to her injured friend while the tall one is standing a dozen feet away with her eyes focused squarely on me.

"Oh god, oh god, oh god..." I choke out. I search for a way around the magically warped trees. I spot an opening and dash toward it, but the trees twist themselves into an impenetrable barrier.

"You can't run from your fate," the tall witch hisses.

Her sister has risen to her feet. She flings off the assisting hands of the small witch while she fixes me with a sinister glare. "You *will* help us destroy the shifters once and for all, whether you like it or not."

I can't run from them. Even if they hadn't closed off my escape route, I'm exhausted and barely able to draw breath into my tortured lungs. My heart hammers in my chest. My injured toes swell inside my boot.

My magic is of no help either. I can only summon meager amounts, not enough to protect myself.

With nothing else left, I reach into my boot and withdraw a short-bladed silver dagger. It's mostly ornamental, meant for ceremonies as a focus for magical energy, but the edge is real enough.

I draw it out of its sheath. The three witches stop their advance. Their eyes narrow. Now I'm a threat. They didn't see it before, but I have other ways of protecting myself. Ways that have nothing to do with magic.

"Come on," I shout. I'm trying to sound angry, but I fear rattles my vocal chords. "You think I won't cut a bitch? Huh?"

The red-lipped witch chuckles a melodic sound. She rubs her sore jaw.

"I'm sure you would—if you could hang on to that knife," she says.

"It's getting so, so heavy..." The tall witch's words cast a spell over me.

Despite my best effort, the tip of my knife begins to droop. My hand aches with the effort it takes to hold onto it. The weight seems to increase with each second.

"So very heavy," says the short witch. "Wouldn't it be so much easier just to drop it?"

"Just drop it," says the red lipped witch.

"Drop it," says the tall witch.

"Drop it," they all say in unison.

With a cry of frustration and fear, I lose my grip on the knife. It falls to the dirt.

Clutching my hand, which is cramping terribly, I back away from the three witches with a whimper. I can't fight them. They're too strong.

"Stay away from me," I shout while holding my hands up defensively. "I won't help you kill anyone. I can't. My magic doesn't even work when I want it to."

"That won't be a problem," says the red-lipped witch. She turns her beautiful yet cold eyes on the tall witch. "Seize her."

I crouch, expecting a physical attack, but the tall witch just smiles. She spreads her arms out at her sides, palms facing toward me, and then she swiftly closes her hands.

The earth buckles and shakes beneath my feet. I nearly stumble again as a twisted, dirt-encrusted tree root shoots up between my feet and instantly snags itself around my right ankle.

Screaming, I try to pull free, but another root explodes from the earth. Then another and another. The hard, scratchy tendrils take all my limbs prisoner, entwining themselves about my body like living serpents.

Desperately, I struggle against their grip. I actually manage to take a few steps until I reach the end of their slack. Then I'm held fast while the roots slither around my arms and legs, stretching me out spread eagle until I'm unable to move at all. Now I know Arianna's terror.

"Let me go," I shout as a tendril snakes around my waist.

The roots are extending, almost as if they are growing around my body, binding me tighter. In between futile struggles, I glance up to see the red-lipped witch approaching.

Panicked, I lose all rational thought and just flail as much as I can. It's pointless. I can't budge more than in inch in any direction.

Finally, I hang there sobbing as the witch stops. Her face is just inches away from my own. I can't stand to look into eyes filled with cold malice, so I turn my head away.

"Make her look at me," the red-lipped witch commands.

The roots stretch up from my shoulders, extending around my throat and forehead. A crackling sound fills the air as the roots tug at me. I can't fight their strength. They pull my face up and force me to meet her gaze. The witch brushes her fingers over the red mark on her jaw—she's going to have a nasty bruise—and then her eyes narrow.

Viciously, she slaps me across the cheek. I see the blow

coming, but I'm helpless to avoid it. My face stings where she struck me, but her rage is not sated. Her nails dig into my chin as she clamps down on my jaw. She squeezes until I fear she'll draw blood.

"You hit me," she says through gritted teeth. "In the face."

"Scar her," hisses the short witch. "Unpretty her."

"Cut out her tongue," the tall witch demands, looming closer. "She can serve our purposes without it."

"No, please," I say weakly. "Just let me go. I'll never help you kill innocent people."

"Shifters aren't people," hisses the red-lipped witch. She releases my face and then pats my cheek. For some reason, the gentle pat is more humiliating than the slap. "They're no better than the animals they turn into, eating their own shit, and rutting about like dogs in heat."

"I think she lets that big one stick his cock in her," says the short witch.

"Oh, yes," purrs the tall witch. "I bet she lets him put it anywhere he wants."

"Have you been sucking off shifters, bitch?" The red-lipped witch sneers. "You're not worthy of the power you wield."

"Shut up," I snap. How dare they talk to me this way.

"Oh no, we made her mad," says the tall witch. "Better not talk trash about her hairy shifter biker boyfriend."

"Yeah, you'd better not," I say, a grin breaking out on my face, because I can see something they cannot. "Because he just might hear you, and he'll be pissed."

"We don't fear shifters." The red-lipped witch sneers.

"Besides, what's he going to do?" snaps the tall witch. "I don't see him around. Where is he?"

"Breathing down your neck."

Kaval looms up behind the witches, slapping his palms onto the heads of the tall and short witches. With a grunt, he brings his arms together, and their skulls connect with a sharp crack.

Both women crumble in a heap. They're temporarily dazed. Because the tall witch is unable to concentrate on her magic, the roots and tendrils binding me slacken, loosening their grip.

The red-lipped witch snarls. Twin balls of flame appear in her palms with an ease that makes me envious.

"Kaval, look out," I cry as she sends one of them hissing through the air at his massive back.

Despite his bulk, Kaval nimbly ducks beneath the witch's missile. The sphere explodes against a tree trunk. When the smoke clears there's a smoldering hole big enough that someone could put their head through it.

Undaunted, the red-lipped witch flings her second energy sphere, but Kaval skips to the side. Strangled, unarticulated rage gushes from her throat as she sends another sphere and another at the massive shifter, but each time, he's just a bit quicker.

"You missed," Kaval taunts in a sing-song voice.

The witch is frustrated. She has expended a lot of her energy, but her sisters are beginning to regain their senses.

"We have to get out of here," I say.

I squirm to escape the tangled roots. Though they no longer grip me like a conscious thing, they are still entwined around my body. Kaval dips into a crouch, scoops me up in his arms, and then stands up, ripping the roots right out of the ground. Though I am still wrapped up in their scratchy embrace, at least I am no longer tethered in place.

Kaval takes off for the tree line at a dead run, his long legs eating up the distance in a mere fraction of the time it took me. As he runs, his body sprouts thick tufts of fur. His already massive arms increase in girth, and soon I feel like a mere baby tucked into the mountain of solid muscle that makes up his chest. The angry shouts of the witches fade into the distance as I cling to him. Trees flash by in the moonlight and soon we can't hear them at all.

CAPTIVE OF THE BEAR CLAN:
CHAPTER 3

KAVAL

I get asked all time by people what it's like when I'm in my bear form. To be honest, the biggest difference is the smell. Some people might think their sniffer is pretty damn good. They might be able to tell the difference between one fancy-ass cologne and another. That's so cute. Good for them. My shifter senses are way beyond that. I can tell you exactly what was in the cologne down to every last molecule. I can tell you where the lavender was grown. I can tell you where they distilled the verbena. My nose never fails me.

Right now, even though I can't see them, I can still smell the witches who are pursuing us. Their scent is rancid sweat mixed with some hoity-toity, hundred-dollar-a-bottle perfume. If I'm spending a hundred bucks on a bottle of something, it had better be scotch.

Anyway, I can smell the witches who are tracking us through the forest. I can smell deer bounding out of my way. I even catch the scent of a distant bonfire. It all gets filtered through my senses. I sift through what's important and what's not.

By far, the most intoxicating scent in the forest is Minerva's. I memorized her scent a long time ago. I inhale the phantom fragrance when she's not around. I try not to think about her too much, but I can't help it.

She's clinging to my back. It feels so good to have her riding me, to have her draped across my furry body. I'm in my bear form, but I wish to god I could be human right now. She feels so good—too good. I shouldn't be thinking about her like this.

It's not that I'm hard up. I get plenty of tail, but this thing I've got going for Minerva... I don't know what to call it, but it ain't just about sating my lust. It goes deeper than that. But it would never work between us. I'm not the right guy, so I've never crossed that line with her. But man, do I want to. Not a day goes by that I don't think about her spread out beneath me. Lips parted, eyes rolling back in her head. The things I want to do to her...

I shake my head. In the short term, I'm a real fun guy to be around. Everybody loves a bad boy. But, sooner or later, I rub most folks the wrong way. They want to go through life never questioning the assholes in charge, the same assholes who are fucking them day in and day out while they work nine to five. Fuck. That.

I'm in business for myself. Don't answer to no boss but me. Some folks have a problem with that. They think I'm trying to separate myself from society. Well, I am. Screw the status quo. I live life on my own terms, and anyone who doesn't like it can suck my ass.

Minerva's not like the others. She's always accepted me for who I am. Sometimes, she'll even tag along with me when I'm up to shenanigans.

Our friendship shouldn't have happened, but it did. When the Universe screws up and brings a guy like me and a girl like her together, well, who am I to question it?

"Kaval, where are you taking us?" Minerva asks.

"A cave," I reply, using a combination of growls and snorts—the bear clan language. Being a witch, Minerva can understand it, and I can understand her—well, sometimes I can understand her, if you catch my drift. *Women.*

"A cave?" she asks, as if aghast at the idea. "Are you kidding me? How is going to a cave going to—we need to tell the coven, maybe your people as well."

"I'm afraid that ain't gonna work now," I reply.

My cave hidey hole is set on one of the steeper sides of the mountain with a seventy eight percent grade. Ain't nobody but a shifter gonna be able to make it up something that steep. It starts off as a narrow split in the cliff side but expands into a much more spacious living area where even I can stand up straight. It's not ideal, but it's unknown to most folks and hard as hell to get to even if you do know the way.

I set her down just inside the entrance. I use my sharp claws to help get her untangled from the tree roots. She's got a few scratches, but the bleeding has already stopped. Her clothing is far more ragged than her skin. In the process of freeing her, I cause a bit more damage to her shirt. I get frustrated with a particularly curly root and rip it off with a quick jerk that also takes her entire top with it. Oops!

She has on a sexy-as-hell lacy black bra and one of those fancy waist cincher things underneath. A corset? Not sure what they call those things. I usually just want to take them off.

"Kaval!"

"Sorry." I'm not really that sorry, because this is as close to naked as I've ever seen her. She looks pissed though, so I shift back to human form for better manual dexterity.

She's still lying on the floor as I crouch down near her legs. She cringes back for some reason. You'd think she'd be less afraid of my human form than of my bear form.

"Man, they really did a number on you. You're lucky I tracked you."

"I'm so glad you're alright." The warmth and sincerity in her tone does something to tighten my chest... that is, until she gets all uppity. "But, ah... Aren't you cold?"

"What? I'm too busy to be cold." I put my hands on my hips. "Do you want me to help you get untangled or not?"

"Well, yes, but—"

"Good, then be quiet for a minute and let me work."

I step over her entwined legs. I'm facing toward her toes for better leverage. I bend at the waist and start tugging on the roots from this new angle. "Yeah, that's much better."

"Oh god..."

"What's wrong?" I ask, finally pulling the vine free. I turn around and show it to her, smiling ear to ear. "See, it's a big one."

"It's a big one all right. Haven't you realized that you're naked?" Minerva asks, covering her eyes with her hand.

I look down at myself. Shit. I didn't even think about the fact that I've been waving my junk in her face. I've become so comfortable in my own skin that it feels natural to me, but of course Minerva's gonna be creeped out. Witches aren't in the habit of walking around in the buff. Shifters are. Just one more way we're totally different.

"Shit," I say. "I'm sorry, babe. Look, you wait here while I go put some clothes on."

"You have clothes out here?" Minerva asks, suddenly perking up. "Don't tell me you have a secret bachelor pad in there with internet and hot running water."

"Uh, naw, it's just a cave," I say, shrugging. "I wasn't

thinking about comfort; I was thinking about safety when I picked this place. I have a stash of clothes here. Once I'm dressed, I'll tell you it's safe to come all the way inside."

"Oh boy," Minerva says, sitting down with her back against the wall. She buries her face in her knees and sits there still as death.

She's really been through a lot tonight, and I'm afraid it's not over yet. I squeeze through a tight spot that leads into the main chamber of the cave. My eyes adjust to the low light, and I easily locate the stone box sitting undisturbed in the back of the cave. I run my fingers over the intricately sculpted lid, the stylized bear and representations of trees. My friend Stone made it for me years ago. He's a bit of an odd guy for a bear shifter, an artist. Most of us are into hardcore physical labor. It keeps our bears in check. But Stone's different. Not in a bad way, just different.

I lift the heavy lid and move it aside. I find denim pants, a denim shirt, and a leather jacket. After pulling it all on, I grab a pair of brand-new boots. They're a little tight because I haven't broken them in yet. Other than that, I'm pretty comfortable when I come back to check on Minerva.

She hasn't moved. She's still sitting with her back against the tunnel wall. I come up next to her and offer her my hand.

"Minnie?" She doesn't stir. "Minnie, it's okay to come in now."

Minerva sighs and looks over at me. Tears stream down her face. I reach out and take her hand. She doesn't resist as I pull her into the main chamber with me.

She just goes with the motion and buries her face in my chest. I put my arms around her, to comfort her of course, but I'm caught up in how good it feels. Haven't I dreamed of this very moment so many times? But not like this.

Still, I can't help the warm feeling spreading through my chest. Minerva, whose scent I can never forget, whose heart I can never have, is so close that I can feel her heart beating. It's almost more than I can stand. I have to kiss her. I mean, I don't have to, I want to... but should I?

I have a lot of girls I can call up for a good time, but none of them are Minerva. She's the only woman who has ever been able to listen to me without judgment. She's the only person who has been there for me every time I needed a friend, no questions asked. If I try to push our relationship further, I could lose my friend. I sure as hell don't want to do that.

"It's all right," I say while patting her back.

"Kaval," she says in a weak voice. "Do you think I'm a bad person?"

"What? No." I pulled back so I can look her in the eye. "You're a wonderful person."

My words have the opposite effect. Her face scrunches up and she seems on the verge of tears.

"If I'm a good person, why did I try to kill my best friend tonight?" she asks.

"Uh, about that," I say, clearing my throat. "Now that you've been, uh, 'outed' as a powerful witch, you're going to have big orange crosshairs on your back."

"What?" She looks up at me with wide, gorgeous eyes. Realization dawns. "You mean people are going to bother me for magical help so much I turn into a hermit like Azealia?"

"No." I chuckle. "I mean, yes, maybe, but that's just the tip of the iceberg. A witch as powerful as you doesn't come along too often. It's going to upset the balance. Basically, if you look at it, witches and shifters are basically in a cold war. Your power is like giving the witches a nuclear bomb. That's gonna make some folks uncomfortable."

"So, what are you saying, Kaval?" She pulls away from me fully. My body remembers the touch of her skin and my heart breaks a little, but I try and keep my expression neutral.

"I'm saying that you're in danger." Hearing it out loud terrifies me. It makes it real. "You need to hole up here for a bit until things calm down."

"You want me to stay in this cave?" she asks, arching an eyebrow. "You have to be kidding. And I can't just withdraw from my life. I have a job. I have commitments."

"If you don't hide for a while, you're not gonna have a life," I say firmly. "Those three witches who were hunting you were pretty damn powerful. At least stay here until we figure out who they are and how we can take them out."

"Take them out?" Minerva frowns. "You make it sound so easy, but you're talking about killing someone. That's not right."

"You almost killed Arianna tonight. Was that right?" I snap back. Immediately, I regret it. She doesn't get mad, but her entire body wilts like a dying flower.

"I can't believe I wanted to hurt her so much," Minerva says. Her eyes well up with tears. "It's like I couldn't control my rage."

I nod and put my hand on her shoulder.

"I'm not a witch, but from what I understand, it's really easy for a witch to go bad. The more powerful she is, the easier it is to, ah... y'know, go bad," I finish lamely. I'm not good at comforting people. I don't know how to do all the touchy-feely emotional stuff. It's not my thing, but I'm trying. I hate seeing her like this.

"I suppose I can stay here for a day or two," she says grudgingly.

"Great." I grin. She glares at me until my smile turns into a frown. "Uh, I mean, not great. But we have a plan now, right? I'll go hunt some food. You hang out here and try to get comfortable."

Even in human form, my sniffer is pretty good. One of the reasons I picked this cave was because it's downwind. I can smell four, maybe five, of my bear clan brethren on their way up the steep slope. One of them stands out from the others—Flint.

Flint is the leader of our clan. He's a massive and graying mountain of a man in human form and a terrible monstrosity when he shifts. His body is a road map of scars because some wounds are so grievous even a shifter has a hard time healing from them. Years ago, a dozen of his underlings grew jealous and they tried to kill him. They wanted to install one of themselves as clan leader. They lured him into a depleted copper mine in the hopes he wouldn't be able to escape. They were right about one thing; he didn't escape. He didn't need to. He killed them all before they had a chance to flee.

"What's wrong, Kaval?" Minerva asks, noticing my worry.

"It's Flint and other shifters from my clan. They're upwind from us. I don't want them to know you're here. I'll go out and hopefully get rid of them."

"Why should I worry if Flint knows I'm here?" Minerva asks.

"No particular reason, but it'd be best if nobody knew you were here."

Leaving her behind, I squeeze through the narrow entrance and stand in the moonlight. Four large shadows move up the slope, covering the terrain with the speed and agility that only a shifter can have. The biggest one, Flint, reaches the cave entrance first. He crosses his tree trunk-sized arms across his barrel chest and glares down at me.

"Kaval," he says in a low growl. "Bring me the witch."

"I don't know what you're talking about—" A hard slap across my jaw staggers me, and I barely even saw Flint move.

"Don't play games with me, boy," he says as his backup makes it to the top of the hill. The others spread out behind him. "Bring me the witch, and quickly. She cannot be allowed to return to Bonfire Falls. With her power, she could be the end of us all."

"Are you kidding me, Flint?" I ask while holding my sore jaw. "She's not a threat to anyone. Shit, Minerva can barely even control her magic."

"Then she's even more dangerous," Flint says. "I'm only going to ask you one more time, Kaval. Bring. Me. The. Witch."

The other three bear clan shifters bunch up around him, flanking me. They're ready to pounce at a moment's notice.

"If you want her, you have to go through me," I snarl.

"Kaval, stop."

We all turn to see Minerva standing in the moonlight holding her tattered blouse closed with one hand. She shakes her head at me. Her bottom lip quivers.

"I can't stand the thought of you getting hurt because of me."

"Who says I'm gonna get hurt?" I ask with a wink. I snap my head forward and catch the closest shifter right on the bridge of his nose. It splatters with a nice wet pop. He falls backward down the hill.

Minerva screams at me to stop, but it's too late. I kick one of the remaining two in the chest, and he waves his arms wildly to avoid taking a tumble like his buddy with the broken nose. But then the other one grabs me from behind, and Flint lays into me a few times. It feels like a building is getting dropped on me every time he hits me.

They tackle me to the ground and pummel me pretty good. I've gotten my ass whipped before, but this is one of the top ten worst times. I'm not in any shape to stop them when they wrap a thick chain around my torso, legs, and neck. They're not just binding my human form; when I shift, my neck gets bigger, and I risk strangling myself if I change into a bear.

But I can still cuss and bitch, and I let them have it while they pull Minerva's arms behind her back and bind them tightly.

"You chicken shits," I sputter. "Leave her the fuck alone."

I get a kick for my troubles. Minerva cries out for me to stop as they continue to bind her arms. The bastards force her elbows together and tie them as well, which has to suck.

She continues to plead for mercy as Flint stomps and kicks my chained form through the dirt. When I get out of this, I'm going to fucking kill him.

Finally, they shove a dirty rag into Minerva's mouth and tie it into place with some rope. They cross and tie her ankles as well, and Flint tosses her over his shoulder like a sack of potatoes. The other three struggle to lift me up. It takes three of them to hold my flailing form, but they manage to fall into line behind our clan leader.

We're in deep shit, and we're probably as good as dead.

CAPTIVE OF THE BEAR CLAN:
CHAPTER 4

MINERVA

I t's hard to tell where you're heading when you're bouncing along on the shoulder of a massively built bear clan shifter. I quickly learn to keep my head turned to the side to avoid smacking my nose into Flint's back as he walks.

His hand is holding on to the backs of my thighs, and I feel like a mere toy in his hands. I've really made a mess of things. First, I nuke my own birthday party and almost kill my best friend—I wonder if she's still tied to that tree, naked and scared—and now I've gotten the friend I make googly eyes at in trouble with his own people.

After what feels like an hour of swift hiking, we come upon a rustic, ancient cabin. Moss encrusts the swollen timbers making up the outer wall. I wonder how long it has been here, tucked away deep in the mountains. It reeks of history and enigma. What is this place?

Flint carries me inside. There is a main living area and a few branching doors, but I'm in no position to see where they lead. The bear clan leader deposits me with surprising gentleness on the floor next to a thick wooden post that looks like the trunk of a tree. In fact, I think it is a tree that grew through the floor of the cabin and was carved into this shape. I'd be fascinated by it if I wasn't freaking out.

One of Flint's minions ties my neck to the post with a tight leash. I'm already having trouble breathing with this stupid rag shoved half way down my throat. I have to keep my back perfectly straight, straining for purchase with my bound hands, or I'll suffocate. If I knew how to control my magic, I would blast the shit out of everyone here. Except Kaval, of course.

They dump him on the floor next to me and then padlock his chain to the post. As Flint leaves the room, Kaval continues to berate his clanmates between bouts of frenzied struggling.

"You fuckin' punks," he bellows. "You ain't shit without big bad Flint around, are you? Lemme out of these chains and we'll see how long you last."

To their credit, the bear clan shifters do their best to ignore him. However, that means their attention is on something else—me.

I don't like the way one of them is looking at me. My ripped blouse came all the way off during the struggle, and it's not like I can cover my exposed cleavage with my arms tied behind me. The bear shifter's eyes roam all over my body. I shudder to think of what would happen if I were alone with him in such a state.

Kaval's angry protests cease when Flint comes back into the room. Flint squats down in front of me and reaches for my face.

"Don't hurt her, Flint, please," Kaval says. I'm not used to hearing him beg. He really must care about me. That gives me some comfort. At least one person is on my side.

Flint unties the rope holding the rag in my mouth and

carefully extracts it. I cough and sputter a bit before glaring up at him.

"What do you want with me?" My voice is horse, and I desperately need water.

"I need you to answer a few questions," he says in his slow rumble.

"What kind of questions?" I ask cautiously.

"She doesn't know anything, Flint, just let her go," Kaval says.

Flint doesn't even glance at him.

"There are tales of rogue witches who have a particular dark magic..." He's staring at me with gray eyes set deep into in a scarred and monstrous face. "A magic so dark, it can destroy the very soul of another witch and steal her magic."

I'm not supposed to tell witch secrets to anyone, least of all shifters. However, I get the feeling he will find out one way or another. Maybe already suspects that the stories are true and he's just looking to confirm his suspicions.

"Such magic exists," I reply. "It's forbidden, of course, but it can be done."

"And such magic can only be stolen by another witch?" he asks.

"Yes," I reply quickly, hope making my heart pound in my chest. "Yes, it only works with another witch. You have to be able to use my magic to control it. Shifters can't control it. Dragons? Maybe, but not shifters. You can't take my magic, so just let us go."

"I wish I could," he replies, rising to his feet. "For what it's worth, I'm sorry. But the greater good requires... sacrifice."

"What?" I have no idea what he's talking about. Does

he think he can sacrifice me or something? Burn me at the stake and steal my magic?

Kaval goes into a thrashing fit. Chains rattle, his muscles strain, and I'm starting to believe he's actually going to break free when Flint lays him out with a fist to the temple.

"Kaval!" I shout as he crumples into a heap. "Stop hurting him. Please."

Flint seems remorseful, but he heads toward the exit, not even looking at me when I continue to shout.

"Hey," I bellow. "Let me go. You can't use my magic. You're not a witch."

"No, but I am," says a voice that seems hauntingly familiar. I turn to see a waifish, dark-haired girl stepping out of the shadows. I remember her, a somewhat nerdy girl who kind of kept to herself.

"Rebecca?" I ask. "Is that you? Where have you been? Everyone thought you ran away to California."

"That's what I wanted them to think," she says with a cold smile. "All of the bullying twats who enchanted my deodorant to smell like cow shit, who tied my shoelaces together and made me break my front teeth, all of the stupid cows who stood by chewing their cud while it all happened. I made them all think that I had run away. But I didn't run away. I ran toward my fate."

"What are you talking about?" I ask. "Why leave at all? I know some of the girls were mean to you, but—"

"Some of the girls?" Rebecca snaps. "Try all of them. Everybody always had a snide comment or a minor curse to throw my way. They made my life miserable because they had magic on their side. There was no way to ever be safe as long as they could cast spells from a distance. Magic shouldn't be allowed to exist. It should be stripped away from all witches."

"Rebecca..." I don't know how to respond. I had no idea how much she'd been bullied. "I'm sorry you went through all of that."

"Oh, you're sorry?" she scoffs. "That's rich. They left you alone, for the most part. You were always weak with magic, never a threat. And you had your big, bad shifter bodyguard to protect you. Well, he doesn't look so big and bad now, does he?"

I glance over at Kaval, who is trying to wake up. His eyelids flutter, and a low groan escapes his throat.

"Useless," she says with a sneer. "I wasn't just goofing off for the last year, Minerva. I've been studying forbidden magic. I was training to drain Azealia of her magic, but you're even more powerful. You can give me the strength I need to wipe out the witches of Bonfire Falls forever."

"You can't," I gasp. "Not every witch in town was cruel to you."

"No, but they didn't help me, either," Rebecca says. "Fortunately, I found an ally in Flint. He knows magic is a threat to everyone, even other witches."

"He wants war," Kaval says. He groans as he sits.

"Kaval, are you alright?" I ask, wincing at the way his eye has swollen shut.

"I'm fine," Kaval says. He turns to address the other witch in the room. "Rebecca, is it? You can't trust Flint. He's been hankering for another war ever since there's been peace. He'll use you and cast you aside if it helps him achieve his goal."

"Once I absorb Minerva's power, no one will ever cast me aside again," Rebecca says. "After all the witches are dead, I'll be the only one with magic."

"Rebecca," I plead. "Don't do this. You can't kill the whole town."

"Why not?" she asks. A look of sheer confusion crosses

her face. Her hands clench at her sides. Suddenly she whips them up in front of her, stretching her arms as if she's trying to bury her nails in my chest. Black magical energy crackles around her hands. It breaks free and streaks toward me.

I close my eyes, turn my head, but I can feel a well-spring of power build in my belly. A glimmering aura of protection erupts around my body. Rebecca's shadowy beam of pure anti-life is stopped, dispersing into a spray of shimmering light.

Rebecca drops her arms and the beam ceases. She growls in rage and frustration and then raises her hands again. I cringe, but once more, the aura springs up around me, protecting me from the terrible energy.

Rebecca laughs. She ceases her attack once more and turns partly away from me.

"Oh, she's good," she mutters, seemingly to herself. "Instinctively protecting herself, body and soul."

"Give it up, Rebecca," I say boldly, hoping I can bluff my way out of this. "You can't get through my shield."

A guttural cry of rage erupts from her mouth. She turns in a half crouch and brings both hands up in a circular motion. This time, when she summons the magical beam of shadowy light, it's twice as wide as before. It spears toward me, but again my aura surrounds my body and stops her magic.

Rebecca cries out in rage. She takes a few staggering steps forward. The aura bends and buckles under the assault, but it does not breach my orb of protection.

She looms over me. Her hands are mere inches from my aura as she pours every ounce of willpower into the spell.

Finally, she relents, only to erupt into a screaming fit loud enough to wake the dead. Rebecca turns toward an old wood stove in the corner and points her hands at it. Instantly it's crushed like a tin can, crumpled into an unrecognizable mess.

"Looks like your plan has a slight flaw," says Kaval, laughing. "You're not powerful enough to get the job done."

"Shut up, shifter scum," Rebecca shouts.

I fear for a moment she'll vent her wrath on his help-lessly chained form, but instead she faces me.

"You know, Minerva," she says in a pleasant tone. "I always kind of thought you were mostly all right. True, you didn't lift a finger to stop them from bullying me, but then again you never actively participated. Plus, you loaned me a pencil once when we were juniors. That should count for something."

"Please, Rebecca," I beg. "Just let me go. I'm not really a powerful witch. I can barely even control my magic. If I could just give it to you, I would, and I mean that."

Rebecca shakes her head, clapping her hands over her ears.

"No, shut up, shut up, shut up," she hollers. "People don't just give up their power. People don't give up anything. All they do is take. I'm tired of them taking things from me."

"Then let's go confront them, Rebecca," I say. "Listen to yourself. You've driven yourself crazy with all of these thoughts of revenge. Maybe they can apologize, and—"

"Crazy?" she says, her eyes go wide. Her whole body is trembling. Her tone is low and threatening, "Did... you... just... call... me... crazy?"

"Rebecca, I'm—"

"Shut up and die," Rebecca shouts, throwing her hands in my direction.

A thick, black ray of violent energy streaks across the

cabin. It refracts against my aura and blasts a hole in one wall. She doesn't quit. Shouting and straining, she tries desperately to break through the shield, but it's impossible. She's not powerful enough. When she finally drops her arms, she stands there, panting.

I can't let her see it, but throwing up a protective wall is draining my magical reserves. There's a limit to how much longer I can block her magic.

Rebecca stands and stares at me intently. A wet clump of hair has fallen across her left eye. She brushes it away as she tilts her head to the side.

"You're looking tired, Minerva," Rebecca says with a zealous gleam in her glazed-over eyes. "I'd say you're running low on power."

"In your dreams," I say defiantly, but Rebecca shakes her head and wags a finger at me.

"Ah ah ah," she says slowly, ticking off her words with her wagging finger. "Nice bluff, but you're losing it. I'm going to get through your precious aura, Minerva."

Snarling, she unleashes her dark energy once more. The assault is different this time, less intense, but something I suspect she can sustain for much, much longer.

"I just have to keep going until I wear... you... down." A mask of rage darkens her features.

I'm bound and helpless, unable to flee, with only my aura to protect me.

An aura that is fading fast.

CAPTIVE OF THE BEAR CLAN: CHAPTER 5

DRAVEN

I'm wiping down my massage table in preparation for my 1:30 appointment when my friend Josie, fellow masseuse and aromatherapist at Crystal Springs Spa, pokes her head in the room.

"Hey, Draven. Mrs. Cavendish again, eh? Isn't that like her third booking with you this month?"

"Fourth, actually," I say, not looking up from the table.

Josie chuckles. "Well, well. Maybe your last appointment didn't quite satisfy her *particular* needs..."

I glance up and find Josie staring at me with a strange look that is part mischief and part expectation.

"Yes, well, there's really no quick fix for chronic back pain, Jos. You know what a long, slow process it can be. But I do believe we've made some good progress in our last few sessions."

I turn my attention to the side table and my selection of oils, selecting several for a blend that I believe will be effective in relieving Mrs. Cavendish's lumbar issues.

"Ha. Oh, sweet Draven. What I mean to say is, maybe you didn't quite scratch the particular itch the old widow was looking to get scratched." She raises her eyebrows at me, expecting something, though I'm not quite sure what.

I scrunch my face in confusion. "I really don't think it's a matter of itchiness, Jos. You should know back pain goes much deeper than the surface. It's about releasing tension in the right places, finding the meridians where stress and trauma originate from and coaxing the body's energies back into balance by applying pressure to the proper points. What do you think about a chamomile, lavender, and rosemary blend?"

She shakes her head and sighs, then lets out a full-bodied laugh. "Well, Draven, I think that will do just fine. Blend all you like, but I think she might be more interested in a little 'essence of Draven,' if you have a snowball's chance in hell of catching my meaning." She looks at me expectantly again, waiting for me to catch up.

Her implication dawns on me, and as understanding blossoms, an embarrassed rush of heat creeps up my neck. I hope I'm not blushing too visibly.

"Oh, c'mon, Jos. She's just a nice woman seeking relief for her back pain. Get your mind out of the gutter."

She scowls at me doubtfully, then her face softens into an expression of something like disappointment.

"Honestly, Draven, for all your skill as a masseuse, your inability to pick up on the most blatant signals is astounding." She glances down and to the side.

I turn away from my oil blend to consider her for a moment. Her downcast eyes and crossed arms give me the sense that something is troubling her beyond her perception of my denseness regarding the purity of Mrs. Cavendish's motives. I am about to ask her if everything is okay when I catch a snippet of passing conversation from two of the spa's shifter security guards as they move down the hall towards the back entrance of the building.

"—Some kind of *massive* awakening at a coven-kegger last night, like next-level magical amplitude. Birthday girl was outputting *unreal* energy. Practically blew the whole party apart," one of the shifters says.

Minerva's birthday was last night. I move closer to the door to hear better.

The other shifter, who's voice I now recognize as Louie's, lets out an impressed whistle. "And Flint captured her? Musta been tough."

Captured? What the fuck?

"Nah, she didn't even put up a fight," says the first shifter, who I'm pretty sure is named Marcus. "Kaval on the other hand... He came raging outta his cave like a madman, put a real hurt on Cheever and Briggs before Flint and the rest finally pinned him. They got him and the witch tied up back at the clubhouse." The conversation fades as they pass through the rear exit.

I turn to Josie. She has also overheard the news and looks mildly intrigued but doesn't seem finished with the thread we were on before the interruption.

"Hey, hang on a minute will ya? I gotta go check something," I say.

She shrugs and smiles weakly. I think I see disappointment flash across her face again but can't be sure. I take off down the hall toward the exit, hoping to catch Marcus and Louie. I pause before passing through the door, composing myself and putting on what I hope is a semi-casual, disinterested demeanor.

I emerge into the bright mid-afternoon light and find the two security guards leaning against a concrete retaining wall in their matching uniforms—black short-sleeve polos, black pants, and black mid-height combat boots. Lou is shaking out two cigarettes from a pack. He produces a silver lighter from his back pocket as Marcus takes one cigarette and places it in his mouth. I give a nod as they notice me. I stroll toward them.

"Got an extra smoke?" I ask. I don't smoke, but I need a way into this conversation.

"Sure thing, Draven." He lights Marcus' smoke, then his own. He shakes out another cigarette and holds it out to me. "Haven't ever seen you light one up. Thought you were all about holistic living these days. You know, yoga, meditation, essential oils, vegetarian diet and all that? Fuckin' weird, as a bear, if you ask me." He looks over at Marcus, who chuckles and shrugs noncommittally as he exhales smoke.

Lou looks back to me sympathetically. "No offense though, bro."

I give a good-natured chuckle and shrug as I take the offered cigarette. "What can I say? I still have my vices."

He holds the flame out to me, cupping his hand to protect it from the non-existent wind. I pretend to take a puff.

"You know, our ancestors *have* always been omnivorous, but there were also whole clans who thrived almost exclusively eating roots and berries, only using the spring-run salmon each year to beef up after hibernation," I say.

They certainly didn't eat fucking hamburgers off the greasy griddle of The Ursusspool five nights a week, I avoid adding.

He and Marcus share a brief, bemused look and shrug, suddenly fascinated by their cigarettes.

"So, I heard some shit went down at some coven party last night," I say casually.

They both lift their eyebrows and nod excitedly.

"Hell yeah some shit went down. That hot little witch Minerva had some kind of awakening. She started shooting off some epic fucking magic, like serious time-bending, earth-scorching shit," Louie says.

"No shit? Bet that ruffled some tails." I strain to keep my concern from showing. My inner bear is alert and in protection mode. It doesn't care about hiding anything. My bear wants me to shift and run off to protect her.

"Damn right it did. A bunch of elder witches turned on her, but Kaval was there and charged in all alpha-bear and fucked 'em up. He carried Minerva off to his cave Ursus-style. He probably gave her a taste of the *Big Furry,* if he was smart." Louie gives Marcus an elbow and they chuckle conspiratorially.

An intense heat blossoms in my chest and my stomach tightens. I realize that my hands are in tight fists, the cigarette crunches between my fingers. I force myself to relax. My bear wants to sprout claws now and smack these fuckers across the face with them.

I stay silent. I'll let these fuckers run their mouths and tell me everything they know, but I'm not about to join in on this toxic male shit.

Marcus and Lou stop grab-assing and Louie continues, "Somehow, Flint found out about the whole ordeal. He pulled his crew together to go and find this Minerva chick. He's got some crazy idea about using her power for something or other, I don't know. Anyway, they surrounded Kaval's cave and told him to give up the witch. Kaval comes out full Grizz, spitting venom and swingin' hard, but he's outnumbered ten to one. Eventually, they pin him and take him and his little witchy fuck-buddy back to the clubhouse. Got a couple burly bastards there guarding them, I hear."

Shit.

"Fuck, man, that's wild. What do they want with Minnie anyway?" My bear insists I ask, and for once, I don't mind losing an argument with the beast. After listening to this, I don't care that much about keeping the concern out of my voice.

"Ha, Minnie?" Lou smirks. "Fuck if I know. You should stay out of it, Draven. Flint's on high alert, and judging from how he hog-tied Kaval, I'd say you'd be smart to steer well clear of this."

I can't tell if his look is more an expression of concern or an implied threat, but I don't really care to find out.

"Don't worry about me, guys. You know me, cool as a cucumber. I don't mess with clan shit if I can help it." I drop my cigarette and crush it under the rubber heel of my sandals. "Thanks for the smoke. I've gotta run though. I've got a booking soon. I'll see ya."

I turn back toward the door and try to maintain a casual pace. My bear is urging me to shift and run to rescue Minerva. My skin crawls as my primal instincts try to take over. I resist the urge to shift.

"All right, Draven. Be good brother," Lou calls after me. "And give my regards to Mrs. Cavendish. Send her my way if she's still having *back problems* that you can't handle."

Lou and Marcus' laughter is cut off as the door closes behind me.

Josie leans out of a room on the right and raises her eyes at me in question. "What was that all about?"

"I'll explain later, I promise." I give her the sweetest, neediest smile I can muster. "Can you do me a solid though?" She shoots me a suspicious look, raising one eyebrow. "Cover Mrs. Cavendish for me? I'm not feeling well."

"Draven, no way. We already went over this, she isn't even here for the massage. I really don't think I'll be a satisfactory stand-in for you, at least not with this client."

"Oh, c'mon Jos. I wouldn't ask if I didn't feel terrible. I

swear on my claws I will buy you all the spicy-tequila pickle backs you want next time we go to The Cave. But right now, I need you." I plead with my eyes until her scowl softens. Relief begins to bloom in my chest. I'll have to find a way to pay her back later.

"Fine, but you should know I intend to get *very* drunk on your dime this weekend." She makes a feeble attempt at a friendly smile, but whatever was bothering her before has not gone away.

"Thank you."

I give her a friendly thump on the arm before I start running down the hall. I hear her muttering something about a horse's ass. I shrug. I don't understand her at all.

I race out of the spa and jump into my car. I zip out of the parking lot onto the main road. My bear is growling at me to race down the dirt road to the bear clan clubhouse, shift in mid-air at the front door, and just start ripping throats until I get to Minerva.

My skin is hot, and fur is already sprouting up my arms. My muscles bulge as adrenaline surges through my veins. My bear begs me to shift, but my human brain fights back. Even in my elevated state of aggression, plunging into the clan's den without backup will not end well.

I skid to a halt at the turn-off that would take me toward the clubhouse. I'm aching to exorcise my demons all over the faces of Flint's thugs. I look off in the direction of the clubhouse, then back towards town. Back to the clubhouse, then to town.

Fuckkkk.

I let out a mighty roar and race off toward Bonfire Falls. I can't do this alone. I need backup.

I come screaming into the dirt lot outside Kaval's place, the Claws and Steel Garage, dirt and rocks kicking up in my wake. I jump out. I can tell from the silent, closed hangar door that Kaval isn't here, so I race around to the rear of the building. I take the stairs two at a time up towards Stone's studio. I bang on the door like a madman. I can feel the thumping, rhythmic bass of the electro-funk Stone favors when he's working, but no answer comes.

"Stone, open up," I shout, still pounding on the door.

Still no answer. I try the knob and step through the flimsy, creaking door into the smell of pulverized marble. My fellow shifter stands in the center of the room, carefully chiseling the life-size ass of a naked man with a massive marble cock.

"Stone," I yell over the music.

He jerks his head up and stares at me, mouth open in surprise, which quickly turns to anger.

"What the fuck, Draven? You could've ruined this whole fucking sculpture. Do you have any idea what a block of marble this size cost?"

"Sorry, brother. I tried knocking, but you were clearly engrossed in this man's ass, and I simply could not wait." I gesture down towards the sculpture's huge stone penis. "Guess we know this one's not a self-portrait," I say, grinning.

"Oh, fuck off, you hippie. Maybe I made it for you so you could finally get some," he snaps back, smiling. "What's so fucking urgent anyway?"

"It's Minerva."

Stone's smile drops away, replaced by a grim expression of concern. "What's wrong?"

"There was an incident at her coven party in the woods last night. She had some kind of awakening and magic'd all over everybody. Some witches tried to mess with her, but Kaval was there and shifted to the rescue. Fucking Flint got word of it, though, and rounded up his goons to go and get them. Ambushed Kav at his cave, and now they've got both of them tied up at the clubhouse."

"What does Flint want with Minerva?" Stone asks, anger momentarily giving way to confusion.

"I don't know. Some half-baked scheme to seize control of the town, I'm sure. We can figure that out later. Right now, we're going to get Minerva and Kaval."

"Fucking right, we are. What are we expecting at the clubhouse?" he says, jumping right on board as I hoped he would.

"Dunno yet. Marcus and Louie spilled the beans while I was working at the spa. They said Flint's got a couple shifters guarding them. I thought about storming the place myself, but my less-furry half thought better of it, so I hustled on over here."

He claps me on the shoulder and gives me an approving smile. "That was a smart move, my friend. Let's go, we can scheme on the way."

He grabs his keys and turns toward the door, then pauses and turns back to his desk, rummaging about in a large chest underneath. He emerges with a large metal mallet.

"Better to have it and not need it, than need it and not have it. Right? You wanna grab something? Dealer's choice," he says, sweeping his arm over the room full of sculpting tools in invitation.

I grin and extend the long, razor sharp claws on my right hand. "No thanks. You know I prefer to go *au naturel*."

We race down the dirt road toward the clubhouse in Stone's yellow door-less Jeep, kicking up dust in our wake as the wind whips through our hair. Stone pulls the jeep off the road into a pullout about half a mile from the clubhouse.

For the rest of the way, we stalk slowly and quietly on foot. We stop about twenty feet from the edge of the woods so we can see the rear entrance where two of Flint's shifters stand guard.

"Any ideas?" I whisper, as I rack my brain for some semblance of a plan.

My bear is still growling for violence, urging me to shift and charge the place head-on. My human half struggles to contain my bear's rage. We need to use caution and strategy, not brute force. I manage to swallow most of my desire for immediate gratification, but bloodlust remains. My bear wants revenge on anyone who dared to hurt Minerva.

Stone's face is screwed up in concentration, nose scrunched, eyes squinting, fingers tapping rhythmically against his thigh as we squat behind a large felled tree. He doesn't appear to have heard me.

"Stone? You there."

"Shhh, I'm thinking," he hisses, waving me off with one hand.

I raise my hands in surrender and shut my mouth to let him work. If anyone can scheme up a solid rescue plan on short notice, it's Stone.

"So, there's two by the rear entrance, one out front. I'm thinking there will be one inside keeping an eye on Minerva and Kaval, and maybe one or two drinking at the bar in the basement. That's my guess anyway," Stone says. I can almost see the gears of his mind turning.

"Sounds reasonable." I'm not sure if he's right or not, but we're about to find out.

"We need to take these two at the back out quickly, get inside, barricade the basement door, and then from there I think we'll probably have no choice but to take the other two straight on. Once we're inside, I'll go straight for the front door to take the man outside by surprise. You take the man in the room and to try free Kaval quickly so that big bruiser can help us clean up whatever mess is left over."

"Okay, sounds good. But how are we taking these two chumps out before they make a big stink?" I turn toward Stone expecting a response, but he's already making his way out of the woods towards the two shifters and the clubhouse.

Well shit, I guess we'll just figure it out on the fly then.

I stay hidden in the woods waiting for the right moment to strike.

Stone approaches the men with one hand raised in greeting. "Hey fellas, you're Flint's boys, right?"

The shifters exchange a suspicious look, but they don't seem too alarmed. Stone gets closer to them and speaks more quietly. I can't hear what he's saying, but I see him point toward the front of the clubhouse and gesture wildly with both arms.

All three of them start moving around to the left side of the clubhouse, making their way toward the front. Stone slips the mallet out from his waistband behind his back.

I figure this is as good a sign as any, so I finally stop restraining my bear. I strip off all my clothes and leave them in a pile behind the tree. My ribs creak, and adrenaline courses through my veins as fur sprouts across my body. The woods around me pulse with scents and tiny movements. My vision blurs and warps, my hands swell and sprout massive claws as I assume bear form. I rear up on my hind legs to my full eight-foot height.

I take off at a silent sprint across the field, quickly closing the distance to where Stone is squaring off with Flint's men. By the time I reach him, Stone's fighting off several bears. We're outnumbered, but Stone's doing a good job of keeping them occupied.

Rather than focus on tearing out their throats, my bear agrees with my plan to free Minerva. I help Stone knock out the rest of the bears, then we head for Minerva and Kaval.

They're tied to a post in the corner of the large room. Minerva is gazing wide-eyed at me.

"Draven?" she whispers.

"I'll get these chains off in a second," I communicate through grunts. In my bear form, I can't speak, but I can rip chains to pieces. I do exactly that, freeing her.

Her hair hangs disheveled around her face, which is streaked with dirt and makeup. Her shredded blouse reveals enough of her cleavage to set my heart racing even faster, if that's even possible.

Even if I hadn't caught a glimpse of her expression, I would have smelled her fear. My bear tastes the scent of her and longs to soothe her. But beneath the fear on her face is something else. Awe. Intrigue. Lust, maybe?

Kaval clears his throat. I remember that Minerva and I are not alone and that the job isn't finished.

"That you, Draven?" Kaval grunts.

I nod my furry head. With my claws, I tear through his restraints.

"Who was that with you? Was that Stone?" Kaval rubs his wrists.

I glance over my shoulder. Stone's gone. I hear bones cracking outside. I nod at Kaval then jerk my head to the side to indicate that we need to move our asses.

Without another word, he's suddenly in his massive bear form, kneeling so Minerva can mount him.

As she straddles his enormous furred back, my lips involuntarily curl back into a snarl, and a low guttural sound issues from deep in my throat. Kaval turns toward me and begins to snarl himself, but Minerva gently strokes his cheek and shoots me a sympathetic, pleading look. I shake my great head, clearing away the tension, and nod toward the front door. Now is not the time to get territorial.

Stone's outside. He tosses the last of Flint's goons into a heap of broken, wounded shifters. He grunts in acknowledgment as he sees us emerge from the cabin. He ambles over to sniff Minerva. His bear likes her scent because it rubs its head all over her chest. Kaval snaps at him half-heartedly, and we all exchange brief looks of mutual understanding. We've never talked about it, but we all have feelings we can't ignore when it comes to Minerva. We just don't know how to deal with it without blowing up our friendships.

Stone takes the lead. It's time to get the hell out of here.

The three of us race through the forest on all fours, just as our ancestors have done for thousands of years. Except for this time, there's a beautiful witch riding one of us.

CAPTIVE OF THE BEAR CLAN: CHAPTER 6

MINERVA

My heart is pounding and wind whips my messy hair back from my face as we race through the thickening forest. Sunlight is slowly fading. A shroud of shadows covers the woods, but the heat of the day lingers. My shirt clings to my back which is wet with sweat.

I've got to get this damn corset off.

Moisture builds along my thighs where they grip Kaval's broad, fur-covered back. Where our flesh touches, electric currents arc back and forth between us, generating heat. It feels good, bouncing along, straddling his muscle-bound form. Each impact of his broad paws against the earth sends a jolt of sensation up through my pussy. I can't help but rub against the enormous muscles in his back which bulge with effort as he runs.

Effort expended on my behalf.

His power radiates up my thighs, through my stomach, and into my chest where it blooms with an intoxicating, warm sensation. I lean forward, gripping the fur at his shoulders tightly to hold myself close.

A few paces ahead of us, Stone's massive, furry bear ass leads us deeper and deeper into the forest. I can't help but be in awe of the power their bear shifter bodies exude.

I have no idea where we are going, but I don't care. I hope they take me as far away from that awful clubhouse as possible.

The chaos of the kidnapping and my subsequent rescue has left me utterly disoriented. I should be terrified. I'm a witch who can't control her magic, all alone in the woods with three hulking bear shifters, with no one around for miles. But I find it oddly comforting. I know my guys will never hurt me. They saved me. I don't know how I'll ever repay them for their bravery.

I glance behind me and see Draven's enormous form keeping pace several paces behind us. His shaggy head stays oddly still as his massive shoulders chug up and down like giant, hairy pistons. His tongue lolls comically out of the side of his mouth from the effort it takes to run for miles.

Although we're all fleeing frantically into the darkening woods, I am overcome with a sense of primal satisfaction. I realize that my best friends will do anything for me. They risked their lives. They betrayed their own kind to save me—a witch. We should be sworn enemies, but we're not. We're so much more than that, and nothing will ever keep us apart.

Draven seems to be smiling. It's hard to tell when he's in bear form.

A deep inner tranquility emanates from Kaval, even though he's showing signs of physical exertion. We've been running for a long time. I hope we stop soon. I'm exhausted, and I haven't slept in over twenty-four hours.

Fighting Rebecca sapped all of my strength. Fortunately, she gave up on trying to steal my magic right before I used the last of my energy to stop her. She has no idea how close she came to capturing my soul. I shudder at the thought.

All three shifters are exercising their most primal aspects, and I feel almost kin to them as we race into the darkness.

I replay the rescue. They fought so hard and risked their lives for me—*me*. I don't understand this connection we have, but I won't ever question it again, not after tonight.

A deep, ecstatic gratitude blossoms in my chest. All three of my saviors turned against their own kind to come to my rescue—that's how much they care about me. They chose me over their clan.

A pang of guilt strikes my heart. What have I done to warrant such sacrifice?

I'll find a way to return their loyalty and devotion tenfold, though I am not sure how I'll accomplish this. That will have to be a problem for another day.

After we've put several miles between us and the bear clan clubhouse, Stone slows the pace to a walk. Kaval pulls us up alongside him. As Draven brings up the rear, Kaval lowers himself to the ground, indicating that I should dismount. I reluctantly swing my leg to the ground. I wasn't quite ready to leave the warmth and safety of his strong back, but he needs to rest.

Most of the thick brown fur covering all three men begin to disappear, their faces condense back into their human forms. Paws shrink and claws retract into normal human fingers. The process is disorienting to watch and difficult to follow. There is undeniably something highly erotic about it, though. They seem to be both bear and human simultaneously, their features distorting, both aspects seeming to clash and swirl together. It calls to mind a great wrestling match between man and beast, one filled with relentless, primal violence, yet destined to end in a peaceful draw. And then, just like that, three distinct, beautiful men stand before me, all staring intently into my eyes, naked as the day they were born.

Heat rushes up my neck. All three men seem utterly unfazed. They're all comfortable in their own skin.

I've already seen Kaval in his birthday suit. His chest is hairier than the other two, his shoulders broader. I try to avoid looking below his waist, straining to keep my eyes up, but I can't help but take a quick glance at his huge cock. I ache with desire. I hope they can't smell my arousal, but they probably can.

My cheeks burn as I try to look anywhere but down.

Kaval's skin is somewhat darker than the others. It's a deep olive tone, bordering on caramel. Dark stubble has already started to appear on his strong jaw. His dark, wavy hair hangs down just past his shoulders. Strands of hair cling to his cheeks and forehead. He's sweaty from exertion. If we were alone, I don't know that I'd be able to control myself right now. The urge to kiss him intensifies with each passing second.

All three men glisten in the moonlight.

Draven's soft, blue eyes reflect his warm, gentle nature. He gazes at me as he pulls back his long light brown hair into a high, loose knot. He's leaner than Kaval, but the bend of his arms exposes rippling biceps and triceps. He has a Sanskrit character tattooed on the inside of his right bicep. I'll have to ask him about it later.

His abs ripple as he reaches his arms over his head. He arches back slightly, just enough to accentuate the jut of his pelvic muscles. Again, succumbing to temptation, my eyes drift down, and I see that his cock is *also* thick and lengthy, and absolutely picturesque.

I know before I even look that Stone will be sporting a similarly impressive package. It's so not fair. Why are my best friends so damn sexy? Why can't they be ugly? Temptation triggers terrible impulses. I've managed to suppress them so far, but how much longer can I hold back?

Stone is thinner than both of the other men, but he's chiseled. His thin frame reflects a wiry strength evident in the bulging veins of his forearms, which are sculpted through his constant use of a hammer and chisel. His close-cut blond hair exposes an intense, intelligent face. His large brown eyes remind me more of a deer than a bear, but his silver nose and eyebrow rings shatter the impression of innocence. He chews his full, plump lips as his active mind works.

As I survey the naked and glistening men, something stirs deep within me. A shiver runs up my legs, through my back, and leaves the crown of my head tingling. For a moment, I'm nearly overcome by a primal, cavewoman-like urge to draw all of them down into a mass of flailing, sweaty limbs where we can unleash our deepest animalistic instincts.

I shake the thought away as Kaval turns toward Stone.

"So, were you leading us in any particular direction, or did we just run six miles into the woods with no destination?" Kaval's voice is full of tension.

"What? No, 'Thank you for saving our lives, Stone. We're so eternally grateful for your brilliance and grace, how in the world will we ever repay you?'" Stone replies with mock offense and confusion on his face.

"Hey, don't forget to throw a little 'eternal gratitude for Draven' in there too, okay?" Draven flashes a charming diplomat's smile.

"I would have found a way out of there," Kaval grumbles. His face hardens, and I can see he's struggling with the shame of needing to be rescued. Part of me hurts for him and his wounded pride, but another part of me wants to groan. *Men's egos are so ridiculous. Sometimes they're as fragile as a sparrow's egg.*

To break the tension, I grab Stone and Draven around their necks, one in each arm. I hug them hard.

"Thank you guys so, so much. I can't believe you went up against the bear clan for me. I don't know how I'll ever repay you." I pull myself away before I start to get to teary-eyed.

When I see their awkward looks, I realize I've just hugged two very hot, very naked men. My cheeks flame. Thank Goddess I don't have fire magic or we'd all be incinerated right now.

"Of course, Minnie," Draven says. "I'd choose you over the bear clan every time."

"Same," adds Stone.

I'm touched by their sincere looks of devotion. I don't know why, but they seem so loyal to me even though I really didn't think we were even that close. I mean, we're friends, but they risked their lives without hesitation. That's more than just friendship, isn't it?

"Yeah, yeah, great. Okay. Everyone's very thankful and all, but that doesn't change our situation," Kaval says, breaking up the gushy emotion party in his typical macho fashion. "It's getting really damn dark, and we're out in the middle of the damn woods. It won't take Flint much time to get a search party together. I'd rather not be out in the open when they come looking for us."

"Yeah, I second that." I look at Stone, then Draven. I hope one of them has a plan.

"Well as it turns out, I did not lead us on a grand, galli-vanting run to nowhere," Stone says. A mischievous smile curls up the corners of his mouth. "This guy—" He points at his own chest with his thumbs, "—has a secret cabin not too far down that path." He gestures to a narrow deer path to our left.

"No shit. Right on, my man, very cool." Draven flashes Stone a hang-ten signal.

"I never doubted you." Kaval smiles and claps him on the shoulder with his massive hand. He gives Stone a friendly bro-shake. Stone grins.

"C'mon, let's get a move on, guys." Kaval lets go of Stone and immediately charges down the path as if they're going to race. Kaval's wide shoulders snap branches with ease as he goes. "Get the lead out," he calls over his shoulder. "Get those thumbs out your bums and put foot to dirt."

Draven, Stone, and I share a surprised look. We burst out laughing, shaking our heads as we start down the path.

"Yes sir, Captain Kaval, sir," Stone shouts, snapping up to perfect straight-backed posture and raising his hand in a crisp, mocking salute. "Right behind you, sir."

Beneath his lighthearted demeanor, I can see his mind working out potential courses of action. Stone is always scheming up something. His artist's mind is never at rest. I secretly hope he'll come up with a plan to get us out of this mess.

Draven laughs good-naturedly and gestures for me to walk ahead as we start up the path after the others.

"Hey, Minnie," he says. I turn back to see expression pinched by a genuine look of concern. "Are you okay? I heard a little about what happened last night. It sounds like you've been through a really traumatic experience."

"It's been a pretty messed up twenty-four hours, but I'm okay. I think I'm probably still in shock, honestly, but I feel all right. I can't wait to get to Stone's cabin to get a little sleep."

He puts both his hands on my shoulders and looks deep into my eyes. My knees go a little weak despite myself.

"I understand," he says. "Just know, if you ever need to talk about anything, my heart and mind are at your disposal."

God, he's so fucking sexy. Wait, his heart? What does that even mean?

Thankfully, his serious, caring expression, which is melting my icy witch's heart, softens into a more light-hearted smile.

"My masseuse's hands are yours to command as well," he adds casually. I can't tell if there are sexual undertones to the offer, but I want to believe that he's trying to tell me more than he's saying, but I've never been good at reading guys.

I'm pretty sure he's offering me more than just a massage, but who knows? I can only hope that he wants to put his big hands all over my body.

Another shiver shimmies down my spine. I need to stop thinking about what I want his hands to do to me, but I'm so good at conjuring up elaborate, Draven-fueled fantasies.

"Thanks Draven, I appreciate everything you're doing for me. And I just might take you up on your offer some time." I hope I've struck the right balance between genuine gratitude and playful flirtation. "I guess we'd better catch up to the others before Kav freaks out."

We both smile and share a chuckle as we start up the trail again.

We catch up to Kaval and Stone. We've been walking for a few minutes when a clammy, creeping feeling crawls up my spine. I'm probing my subconscious trying to identify the origin of the feeling, and then it hits me.

"Whoa, hold the fuck up." I stop in my tracks so fast that Draven bumps into me from behind. "Why in the world are we walking this way?"

Stone gives me a puzzled look. "Because this is the way to my cabin? Didn't we cover this?" He looks to Kaval and Draven, who shrug. "Am I missing something?"

"I've heard about this part of the forest. From what I hear, this is an absolute no-fly zone. Nobody goes here. You're telling me your cabin is on this cursed, godforsaken land?" I ask Stone in disbelief.

He shrugs. "Some people say that it's cursed, but I've never had any problems out here. I actually find it quite peaceful and inspiring to be in such a secluded place." He looks rather pleased with himself.

"Well, I don't know how it is with shifters, but I'm a witch. I don't mess with cursed land. We have a bad history with that shit, so unfortunately, I think this is as far as I go. There's some bad juju out here, and I want exactly *no* part of it." I cross my arms in defiance.

All three naked men roll their eyes and share brief looks of exasperation, but I can tell they're not going anywhere without me.

"Easy now, Minerva," Stone says. He raises his hands like he's trying to placate me. "Those rumors are a bunch of wolf scat. There *is* one other person besides me that lives in this part of the woods. She's an old, *old* witch, powerful, yes, but we have something of an understanding. She leaves me to sculpt and roam the woods for inspiration in peace, and I don't hunt on her land or stray too close to her dwelling."

I give Stone a suspicious, doubtful look, but his earnest gaze assures me that he speaks the truth. If Stone says it's safe in these woods, I know I can trust him. The creepy sensation dissipates, and I feel safe again.

As I look around at all three men, a feeling of peace and security washes over me. They all gaze back at me for a moment, and I get the sense that I can trust them all with my life.

I also get the sense that they're looking at me *very* intensely. I don't know what to make of their looks. I know what I want them to be about, but I try to push those thoughts aside for now. I can't believe I'm even thinking about anything but sleep right now.

My eyes droop.

"Alright, I'll trust you," I say through a yawn. "I don't love the vibes here, but if this is the way to your cabin, so be it. Let's go."

Further on down the path, another trail forks off to the right. I feel a strange pull and sway a step in that direction. A magical boundary, the likes of which I have never sensed before, stops me cold. The power emanating from whatever lays at the end of the path is so intense that it bends the air above and in front of me. Trees shimmer like in a mirage. I nod toward the path.

"That's the way to the witch's place, isn't it?"

"Yes. How did you know?" Stone asks.

"There is a powerful magic emanating from something in that direction, unlike anything I've ever felt. Whoever this witch is, she is powerful indeed."

I shudder a little, wondering what terrible things she is capable of and how she would react if she knew another powerful witch was so near her territory. As I wander, an old tale floods forth from my memory. The three guys all stare at me with curiosity.

"You know, now that I'm thinking about it, one of those rumors about the cursed woods was about a witch.

Azealia. Supposedly she was one of the most powerful witches ever born, capable of magic not thought to have existed for millennia. The story goes that she had a lover, a soulmate from many lives past... Or so she thought.

"One day, she saw him in the meadow by the stream near their cottage kissing a younger woman from a neighboring town. Her rage and despair were so great that she cursed them both, turning her lover into a crow and the young woman into a trout, so they could never meet again. The people of the town heard what she had done, and they were horrified. No one would speak to or go near her, so she fled to an isolated cabin in the wilderness, and she was never heard from again. I wonder..." My gaze rests on the path. Could Azealia be down that path?

Kaval gently steers me away from the forbidden trail and back toward our path to the cabin.

"Come on, Minerva," he says. "We've got to keep moving. Flint's probably out looking for us already."

"And you need some rest," Draven says, taking my other arm. "You've had an incredibly difficult couple of days. Let's go."

"Yeah, we all need some rest." Stone leads the way forward. "In the morning, we'll figure out how to resolve this whole mess. I've already got a few ideas cooking, and I have a feeling that by morning I may have a fully half-baked scheme on my hands."

CAPTIVE OF THE BEAR CLAN: CHAPTER 7

MINERVA

We arrive at the cabin. It's a small, charmingly rustic structure set in a little clearing near a stream. As we enter Stone's small living room, I am overcome by a wave of exhaustion so powerful it nearly knocks me to the ground. Draven and Kaval are still supporting me, and suddenly I feel a floating sensation as Kaval lifts me effortlessly in his muscular arms.

I'm mumbling about witches and shifters all being after me, worried about what I'm going to do, as my consciousness slips toward the oblivion of sleep.

After I hit the warm, soft bed, I hear reassurances of protection from all three of the guys. I can hardly keep my eyes open, but before I slip into sleep, I catch one last glimpse of the naked, chiseled bodies standing at my bedside. They're looking down at me with concern and loyalty written across their beautiful faces, and I think I see something else there too. Something like hunger, or... lust, maybe? The sight of their three large cocks makes me swoon, and I wonder if it's just a projection of my own desires. Tomorrow should be interesting. But tonight, I dream. And what sweet dreams I think they will be, falling asleep with these three watching over me, their hungry bear eyes grinning.

Hours later, I blink my eyes open and squint against the sunlight pouring in the room.

I'm in a strange room.

The events of last night come rushing back. I'm so thankful for my friends and all the help they've given me. If it weren't for them, I'd still be at the bear clan's clubhouse being attacked by Rebecca.

Leaning back on my elbows, I take in my surroundings. It looks like a man's room with brown and gray colors. I briefly remember coming to Stone's cabin last night. He has gorgeous oak walls, and one wall is entirely made of stone. The dark antler chandelier hanging from the ceiling adds to the rustic vibe Stone seems so fond of.

Or maybe that's just bear shifters for you.

I absolutely love the large window overlooking the green forest. Morning fog clings to the branches and sends a tingle down my spine.

I stretch my arms, expecting the weakness from last night to return. It doesn't. My magic is stronger this morning.

Feeling the magic flow through me gives me further strength to face whatever comes my way. Plus, my friends make it worth fighting back instead of running away from everything I've ever known.

I hunt for my shoes. I'm ready to figure out what my next move is going to be.

Voices echo outside the bedroom door. I can't make it out, but it sounds like they are arguing.

I roll my eyes. *Great.*

I stroll toward the kitchen. The closer I get, the more the male voices start to talk over one another. The scent of coffee drifts toward me.

At least they were smart enough to fix that before their bickering commenced.

Kaval grunts about frying sausages and bacon, while Stone and Draven keep naming off eggs, pancakes, omelets, hash browns, and crepes. It's a wonder I can hear anything over their boisterous discussion.

"I make the best crepes," Stone argues.

I am a little irked by their indecision about what to fix for breakfast. It's such a simple matter, yet I can't help but smile. I fight to keep a straight face as I address the crazy men.

"Guys." They don't seem to hear me over their rowdy rambling.

"Hey, guys!" Now I'm almost shouting to be heard.

They all stop talking and glance my way, appearing surprised I've been standing there without them noticing.

"Why are you all bickering like school children over what to make me for breakfast?" I ask, raising my eyebrows in disbelief.

Silence greets my question. I huff with annoyance.

"That's way too much food. You don't have to make all that for me. Why don't you just make a little bit of each item? That should end the chaos you have going on in the kitchen. Right, guys?"

They look at each other and all three agree with nods. They seem ashamed that I caught them this way. Who knew resolving an argument could be so simple?

"Yeah, you're right, Minerva. We need to work together to come up with a plan, not argue over breakfast," Draven says. "We're wasting time squabbling with one another. We need to brainstorm and come up with a plan today."

I sigh as I make my way to the coffeemaker.

"Whoever made the coffee, thank you so much." I grab a mug. A small bear is etched on the side. I squish my nose and smile slightly. It's so adorable.

I grab the pot and pour black coffee into the mug. Inhaling the delicious aroma, I take a big, loud sip. I hate burning my tongue, so they will have to deal with my slurping until it's cool enough to drink like a civilized person.

I pull a stool up to the kitchen island. After taking a seat, I rub my hands along the smooth chestnut table.

It's gorgeous.

As the guys cook, I sip the remaining dregs of coffee.

"I could make blackberry crepes. I'm pretty sure I still have the stuff to make it from when I was here a couple of weeks ago." Stone rifles through the pantry.

"You guys make that. I'll scramble us some eggs," Draven says as he gently puts a carton of eggs on the counter. The fridge is well-stocked from what I can see. Stone seems to have everything in this cabin of his.

Kaval decides to fry sausage and Draven is already cracking eggs into a frying pan.

I catch Kaval staring at my lips before he turns away to get some sausage patties out of the freezer.

"Hey, Stone? How come you have so much food up here?" I warm my fingers against the steaming mug.

"I don't know." Stone shrugs his shoulders. "I just come up here sometimes to get away from everyone and concentrate on my art." He continues working on his crepes without glancing my way.

"That seems really cool," I whisper.

For some reason, I feel like he's hiding something or there's something else to it. I let it go and watch Stone line the counter with cooking ingredients and a mixing bowl.

He seems to know what to do without looking at a recipe. When he adds applesauce to the ingredients, I raise a brow.

"Applesauce?"

"Yeah, it's better than vegetable oil. It makes it moist." Stone glances up at me before continuing to add ingredients.

"Oh, I didn't know that," I say, observing him cook a little longer.

"So, does anyone have any ideas about what our next move is?" Draven asks. "We can't take on all the witches plus the bear shifters. There are too many of them."

"Minerva can't fight them since she can't control her powers. So, where does that leave us? The three of us plus one witch who can't command her magic won't be enough. We need something else." Kaval's brow furrows as he concentrates on flipping the sausages. Sizzling, popping sounds come from the stove. Stone grabs the fruit he's going to use in the crepes. My mouth waters. Man, that sausage is making my stomach growl.

"Maybe there's another way. Minerva needs a teacher, someone who can help her control her power," Stone says as he cuts blackberries in neat little pieces before tossing them into a bowl.

"Yeah, but all the witches who could have helped me are trying to steal my soul and use it for themselves," I say, shaking my head and rubbing my hands over my face.

It feels so pointless. We're going around in circles because there really aren't many options. We need luck on our side. Maybe I shouldn't drag these three into my mess. They're only in this situation because of me. If I wasn't around, they would have nothing to worry about.

"Okay, but there's got to be someone else who can help

you figure out how to control your powers. Between the four of us, we can come up with someone who can help you." Draven's gaze locks with mine. The determined expression on his face shows me how much he cares.

"We could ask the dragon shifters for help. They have some magic. Maybe they can help Minerva," Kaval says.

Draven and Stone look at Kaval like he's crazy.

"I don't think they would want to get involved with witches and bear shifters if they don't have to," Draven says. "And it might backfire. They might want her powers for one of their own selfish reasons. They might not be any different from the bear shifters and witches who are trying to capture her magic. We'll just be adding more to the list of people who are after Minerva's powers."

Stone is quiet but nods his head along with Draven's point about the dragon shifters.

"Yeah, I guess that could happen," Kaval says. "We wouldn't want to take on all of the dragon shifters either." He turns off the stove. He uses tongs to move the sausage into a bowl and covers it with a paper towel.

I grab a bottle of water from the fridge. I'm still thirsty. I pop open the bottle and play with the cap while I try to come up with some ideas. I don't want them to think I can't put my own ideas on the table. We are all in this together.

I run through some possible options, but none of them make sense. I can't think of any ideas that will work.

"Well, what about the reclusive witch? We could see if she would help us. Would someone as powerful as her be able to help you, Minerva?" Stone asks. He stops cooking and watches for my reaction.

"Uh, I'm not sure. I've never met her, and she might not even want to help. I don't even know if I can cross her magical barrier. I felt how strong it was. I don't know if I could control my powers enough even to attempt getting past it."

And even if I could get past, would I want to talk to the witch? There are several ways that could go wrong. I don't want any of my guys to get hurt in the process either. I've never felt such a powerful magical boundary. I don't even know if I can cross it. Doubt creeps in. This might be a terrible idea.

"That's not a good idea," Kaval says. "What if Azealia isn't willing to teach her? We could be putting her in danger all over again. There's no way we are doing that."

"Yeah, I second that," Draven says. "Azealia is supposed to be very powerful. She's probably stronger than Minerva, even if Minerva was able to control her powers. There are too many variables that could go bad if we go down this route. Maybe we should come up with another plan that doesn't involve another powerful witch."

"Those are all valid points, but what else can we do?" Stone asks. "Minerva needs someone with a witch's experience and expertise to understand how to control her powers. Anyone else might try to influence her for the sake of their people or vengeance against others. Azealia might be powerful, but she lives alone. We have less of a chance of being betrayed by her than anyone else, especially considering she was betrayed by her ex. Azealia might be our only hope. And worst-case scenario, she's only *one* witch. We might be able to take her on if we have to, or we can create a diversion to get us all out safely."

"I don't like it. Too many 'what ifs', if you ask me." Kaval shakes his head and paces.

"Do you have a better idea, Kaval?" Stone's voice gets

louder as he speaks. "We don't have a lot of options. I'm not going to risk those witches or bear shifters figuring out where we are, so we can't get help from any of them. They could try to kidnap Minerva all over again."

I hate that I'm making them fight. I don't want them to argue with each other.

"Stop fighting." I put up my hands to stop them. "I don't like seeing you guys fight."

They immediately stop their dispute; each of them looks exhausted. Did they even sleep last night?

Kaval rakes his hands through his hair and exhales a long breath. He nods his head gently.

"We just want to make sure you're safe," Stone says softly.

"I know, I just don't want you to fight over me."

Kaval gently places his hands on my shoulders. He gazes into my eyes.

"We'll do whatever it takes to protect you. Even if that means arguing with each other once in a while. We care about you, and we want to resolve this before it escalates into an all-out war between the witches and bear shifters. Both sides want you, but we can't let that happen," Kaval says.

"We'll all back you up, Minerva. You can count on us," Draven says gently.

"We'll go with whatever you decide," Stone adds.

I don't know how the reclusive witch will react when she sees me, let alone how she'll respond when I ask her to help me. I don't trust witches. Hell, even my own coven betrayed me. What would make Azealia any different?

Although, the more I think about it, the more I think we have more in common than I initially thought. We're both powerful witches. We've both been betrayed by people who we thought we could trust. Maybe I can convince her to help me by sympathizing with her. It's possible, isn't it?

I don't know if I can do this, but as I glance at each of my guys, I realize that I am not alone. As long as I have these men on my side, I'll be able to get through anything.

"I know some of you guys don't completely agree with this plan, but I think it's the best one we've got. There's not a whole lot of options to choose from at this point. I want to try it. As long as you guys back me up, I'm willing to try anything," I say with utter conviction in my voice.

They all nod slowly before they take turns pledging their loyalty to me. My newfound confidence makes me all tingly. I have no idea if this plan will work, but it's the best one we can come up with. It's also the only one that makes sense given the situation with the other witches and bear shifters.

I've got three guys on my side, but I know I'll need more help. I need to learn to control my powers and stop whatever plans the witches might be brewing up while we are hiding out. It's only a matter of time before they figure out where we are. And it's not like we can all live out here forever anyway.

I have to get Azealia to help me. I hope she's willing to hear what I have to say once I do come face to face with her. Otherwise, she might just smite me right on the spot.

"Look, guys, I just wanted to say that I'm grateful for all your help and loyalty to me. Not a lot of friends would have stuck by me through everything that's happened. I'm just glad I have you." I take a moment to look at each of them individually. I want to make sure they know how much their help and friendship means to me.

"We're willing to do whatever it takes to make sure you are okay and that you keep your magic. It's your magic and no one else's. They'll have to get through the three of us before they get near you." Kaval's tone is gruff and protective.

"We are all in this together," Stone says.

"Yep, we can always work on Plan B if things don't work out," Draven says.

I smile, and we all start putting our breakfast together. It may be a little cold, but I don't care. After fixing this fantastic breakfast for me, I'm going to enjoy every last bite of it.

However, as I eat the delicious crepes Stone fixed, I can't stop feeling this warm, fuzzy feeling in the pit of my stomach.

Or is it my heart?

I don't really know. Relationships are so hard for me. I feel like I can never read the guys. I don't know what they're thinking. But I don't need to know. They already proved to me that they aren't trying to use me for my powers, unlike everyone else in my life. All three of them have my back, which is a nice change after having to do everything on my own all the time.

But I don't want them to be in danger. I can do this without them. I can go to Azealia on my own and see if she'll help me. Having people I can count on is amazing, but I don't want them to get hurt.

I scrutinize each of them carefully, as they dig into their breakfast.

If only we could all be together as more than just friends...

No, they probably wouldn't be interested.

Yet, I wonder what it would be like to be in a relationship with all three men. It's crazy and fast, but I can't seem to stop thinking about it. I trust them more than anyone else, so it seems natural to feel this way.

Maybe one day, when all of this is over, I'll be able to

take each one of them aside to ask them if they'd be willing to be with me. It could ruin our friendships, but I need to know. The love I've been searching for my entire life could have been right in front of my face the entire time.

CAPTIVE OF THE BEAR CLAN: CHAPTER 8

KAVAL

I can't stop thinking about Minerva's lips blowing on her steaming coffee this morning. She does the simplest things, yet somehow, she makes them so damn sexy. It made me want to take her on the kitchen table and do all sorts of dirty hot things with her.

I try to ignore how much I want her, but it only makes me think about her even more. I can't stop obsessing about those plump lips of hers. I want to peel off that tank top Stone gave her and get more than just a glimpse at what lies underneath. She probably has a perfect set of tits. I want to suck on her nipples and squeeze her curvy ass.

I've always been an admirer of her jaw-dropping beauty. With her silky brown hair, mesmerizing eyes, and that cute, pert nose of hers, she's a knockout. I want to lick those tantalizing freckles across her nose, along her neck, peel her clothes away to follow the trail hidden beneath.

I hold back a groan. My bear is growling to taste her.

Shaking my head, I try to expel her from my thoughts, yet she lingers. Being near her makes me want it all.

Maybe we can have something now that we're in this secluded cabin together. I just need to figure out how to get rid of the other guys.

I make a deal with my bear. I'm going to keep thinking dirty stuff about Minerva—I can't help it—and he's going to back off until we figure out how to have her. I'm trying to be a gentleman, but I'm not sure if I know how to be one.

As everyone finishes eating their breakfast, I continue my sexual musings about Minerva. Images of her naked limbs tangling with mine flash through my head. In my fantasies, I'm running my hands across her smooth skin and cupping her firm breasts. My imagination grips me. My lust is driving me crazy. I want her in bed, against the wall, on the kitchen counter. Anywhere I can have her. I'm not picky.

My cock is rock-hard against the zipper of my jeans.

My desire for her has always been there, but after being cooped up with her less than a day, I'm already feeling the familiar stirrings get stronger by the hour.

Eventually, I try to think up an excuse to get her alone. Maybe we could go outside for fresh air, or I could ask to talk to her about Azealia, privately.

Maybe she feels the same pull? I have to find out by getting her alone. My bear urges me to do it now, but I tell myself I need to restrain myself at least a little.

Draven and Stone end up bickering about who's going to wash and dry the dishes after everyone's done with their breakfast.

While they are distracted, I approach Minerva.

"Hey, Minerva? Can I talk to you in private for a second?" I ask.

"Yeah, sure." She slips out of her chair and follows me into the living room.

"What's up?" She bites her bottom lip, making it difficult to concentrate. I look away from her intoxicating lips and focus on her green eyes instead.

Okay, that's not any better.

My bear is loving this. I'm struggling to remember words. I'd planned to say words. Now I just want to growl and paw her in a very nonviolent manner.

"I just wanted to know if you were okay. Are you really sure about trying to get Azealia to help you?" I ask.

"Kaval..." She frowns, probably thinking I'm against the plan.

I interrupt her. "You know I'm not happy with this plan, but as I said before, I'll go with whatever you decide. I'll back you up if this is what you want to do, you know that." I look her right in the eyes to make sure she knows I mean my words.

"Yeah, I know," she says, and her face softens.

"Good. I just want to make sure you're going to be okay when you face Azealia. I know it's going to be another hectic experience, especially after everything you've already been through. You know you can talk to me about how this is making you feel."

"Thanks, Kaval. I really appreciate everything you've done for me." She smiles.

"You don't have to thank me. We all care about you." I place my hand on her shoulder. I can't seem to stop touching her in some small way, even to add comfort.

"Although..." She frowns and looks outside the window.

"What?" I ask her, dropping my hand. I cross my arms and give her all my attention.

"Well, I would feel safer facing Azealia if I was able to do an extra protection spell. That way I'm not completely defenseless when I face her. I'm just missing some herbs that I need for the spell," Minerva says.

"Okay, let's go out in the woods and see if we can find those herbs," I reply. Outside, the sun is bright. It's a beautiful day to go outside and look for those herbs she needs.

"Alright, it's a plan."

If Minerva can create an extra protection spell against Azealia in case our plan doesn't work, at least she'll have the extra protection. We need all the help we can get right now.

I don't want anything to happen to Minerva. I'd put my life on the line to make sure she's safe. I know Draven and Stone feel the same way too.

But now that I have this chance to be alone with her, I'm not going to waste it. This could be my chance to see how interested she is in me. Is it just friendship or something more?

Minerva and I tell Draven and Stone that we're going to search for some herbs in the woods to help her create a protection spell.

"Shoot. I forgot that I don't have my bag to put my herbs in." Minerva's face falls.

"I think I might have something to help," Stone says. He goes into the hall closet and comes back with a nice bag.

"Aww, thanks. This is a beautiful satchel." She smooths her hands over the bag and glances up at Stone with appreciation in her eyes.

"Yes, I know. I have great taste," Stone says, looking smug.

"Okay, we'll be back soon. It shouldn't take too long, unless Minerva is slow at finding those herbs." I smirk at her, and the others laugh at my lame joke. "Thanks for your purse, Stone."

"Ha, ha. Very funny." She shakes her head at me and smiles.

I'm glad I can still make her feel better, even though we're in this situation. I don't even pay attention to whatever shit Stone says to me about calling his satchel a purse. I only have eyes and ears for Minerva.

"Actually, there might be a lot of herbs available in this area since hardly anyone lives around here." She shrugs.

Draven swiftly turns his laughter into a serious expression. "'Bye guys. Be careful out there."

"Yeah, be careful. There shouldn't be anyone out there, but you never know. Keep your eyes peeled." Stone frowns, waving us off.

We both go out the back door, and Minerva clutches the satchel while I glance around the woods looking for anything out of the ordinary. Birds chirp above our heads, giving us background music. Grass and sticks crunch underneath our feet. Squirrels scamper up trees and bees buzz around nearby wildflowers.

We stroll along the woods a little while longer before Minerva bends over to examine some green herbs. I'm not sure what they are since they all look the same to me.

As she gently sets them in the satchel, sunlight shines directly on her beautiful brown hair, bringing out the reddish hue.

I think she's more stunning with the sun caressing her hair and pale skin.

I shake my head to clear those arousing thoughts before they get out of hand. I'm barely able to hide the evidence of my erection from Minerva.

While she tries to show me the difference between angelica root and frankincense, she tells me all about the herbs she needs for her spell. However, I can't keep up with her enthusiastic ramblings about odd herb names like amaranth and acacia. I nod, but really, I can't stop watching as excitement lights up her face. I could listen to her all day and never get bored.

After she runs out of steam, she asks how my work has been going. I tell her about how I love to work on motorcycles more than the other vehicles in my shop.

"There's something about working on a custom motorcycle that gets me so energized that I look forward to going to work each morning. I don't know what it is. I just feel more passionate about them." I shrug, feeling a little embarrassed that I admitted that to her. I've never told anyone about my secret obsession with custom bikes. I start looking for an herb she showed me earlier, but all the plants look the same.

"Oh, no," she gasps.

I swiftly turn around and check to make sure she's okay.

"What's wrong?" I ask her when I don't see anything.

"Your shop. I can't believe I didn't think about what all this means for your shop. For Draven's job at Crystal Springs. I mean, how are you guys going to get your lives back once this is all over? Ugh." She hides her face with her hands.

I lightly put my hands on her shoulders.

She drops her arms to her sides and looks up at me.

"Hey, it's okay. We all don't care about that shit. We only care about you. We all want to protect you. I want to protect you from those witches and bear shifters." I'm trying to calm her down, but I do truly mean each word.

She nods. "Yeah, I know. It's just, this whole thing sucks."

"Yeah, it does. But, hey, at least you won't have to worry about me keeping my job. I own Claws & Steel Garage, and whoever doesn't want my services can kiss my ass." I try to lighten the mood.

It works. She lets out a little giggle. The corner of her mouth lifts. We smile at each other before she turns around and starts looking for more of her herbs.

Her face turns serious as she crouches to look more closely at some herbs on the side of the hill.

"I don't want to ruin your lives along with mine, especially when I can't control anything that happens," she says. "This is part of the reason why I want to ask Azealia for help. I don't even know how to cast or conjure on command like normal witches. I feel like a failure. Why do I have to be so different?" She flushes and looks away.

"All you need is more practice. You'll get a handle on your magic. And maybe if Azealia isn't so bad, she can help you cast spells and hone those kick-ass powers of yours. With Azealia's help, you can do all the casting and conjuring you want without much effort. I believe in you."

She smiles softly. Her green eyes sparkle in the sunlight. She's got the most mesmerizing eyes I've ever seen. She slowly stands and puts more herbs away.

"You know I'll support you no matter what happens, right? Whatever choice you make concerning Azealia, I'll be there for you." I brush her hair out of her eyes and smile gently at her.

"Thanks. I know this is frustrating and crazy, but I feel like Azealia is the only witch who can help me. I'm desperate enough to ask for her help. I'm not even sure if she will help me, but I have to at least try to make this all right. I don't want to constantly be looking over my shoulder waiting for other witches to try stealing my soul. I need this for myself."

"You know I'll support you in whatever you decide no matter what happens."

"I know. But it's been really great not having to do this alone." She smiles and squints against the sun's rays.

I see the look in her eyes. I sense that she might be as romantically interested in me as I am in her, yet she turns away. We both walk along a narrow trail nearby.

We find the last herb, but she can't reach it. It's too high up the side of a cliff. I scramble up the cliff and pluck several stems. I climb down to where she's waiting. As I pass the herbs to her, our fingers brush.

She sucks in a breath and her cheeks go pink.

Interesting.

I can't help thinking about kissing her. My bear has been growling for it so loudly that his growls are ringing in my ears.

I know I shouldn't try to pursue a relationship with her, especially with everything she has to worry about right now, but she's too irresistible. The need to kiss her is so overwhelming that I can't stop myself.

Her breath quickens, and I catch her staring at my lips. I know I have to take the chance and just kiss her this time. I can't seem to stop myself from slowly moving closer to her. She leans in and licks her lips. I suppress a groan and lose all control.

Grabbing her by the waist, I tug her to my chest. I slowly tilt my head to make sure she wants this. She doesn't move away as I softly press my lips against hers. She responds immediately, pressing closer and wrapping her arms around my shoulders.

I try to keep the kiss gentle, but she drags her hands through my hair. My bear growls as her mouth opens, inviting me to take more of what she's offering me. I slide my tongue into her warm mouth. I taste blackberries and then just Minerva as we explore each other's mouths.

Her kisses are sweet and innocent, more enthusiastic

than skilled. Yet, her reaction makes me harder than I've ever been before. She erases all thoughts from my mind as I caress her tongue with mine.

She emits a soft moan that fires my blood. Her hands cling to the back of my neck as I slip my fingers underneath her shirt. I meander up her back until I meet her bra strap. I pull her hard against my chest. Both of us are breathing hard. She moans again when I suck her tongue and then nibble on her bottom lip. Kissing her is addictive, but I don't want to let go.

As I start to run my hands around and over her breasts, she gently breaks the kiss and backs away.

Shit! I went too far.

Our ragged breath echoes through the quiet woods. Birdsong and scampering squirrels bring sound back into my consciousness. We're not alone anymore. All the creatures of the forest seem to be at play. They're oblivious to our passionate kiss.

I gaze into her eyes. She slowly steps back without saying anything about the kiss.

"I think we should head back before the others come looking for us. They might get worried." Minerva doesn't look me in the eyes as she picks up her satchel and continues on the path back to the cabin.

I can't wipe the smile from my face. She feels the same level of passion. She may want to deny it for now, but she can't deny it forever. Maybe the timing is just wrong. She's already got so much on her mind. She needs to focus on controlling her powers and figuring out how to stay safe when she faces this Azealia witch. A relationship is probably the last thing she needs right now.

I should stop this madness before it gets out of control. I still don't think she should try to go get help from Azealia. We know nothing about her. She could be dangerous. If the rumors are true, she's already used her magic to destroy the people who betrayed her. I don't see another way to help Minerva, but I don't like our plan.

If she wasn't so determined to see the reclusive witch, I'd try to stop her. But she's convinced it's the only way, so I'm going to support her no matter what. But I swear, if Azealia hurts a single hair on Minerva's head, I'll kill her. Powerful witch or not, I'll find a way.

I'm willing to wait for Minerva. Now isn't the right time to try to figure things out about how she feels about me. I don't want to put pressure on her to do anything that might make her uncomfortable. I can wait for her. I'd wait forever if that's what it took to be with her.

CAPTIVE OF THE BEAR CLAN:
CHAPTER 9

MINERVA

After preparing an infusion of acacia, lavender, and rosemary to balance and focus my magical energies, I leave Kaval and Stone back at the cabin and head upstream toward a little clearing. Draven is off meditating or doing yoga, Stone thinks, and a flash of Draven stretching shirtless in a meadow pops unexpectedly into my head, his bare, muscular chest glistening in the sunlight.

God, I just made out with Kaval only an hour ago, and I'm already drooling over the idea of a shirtless Draven. What is wrong with me?

Kaval. I can't believe after all these years we finally kissed. I've been attracted to him for such a long time, but I never really thought he would be interested in me.

He's always had one girl or another around, and they were always the trashy, badass-biker-chick types covered in tattoos and piercings. I always figured I was too innocent for him, but maybe not. The way he grabbed me by the waist and pulled me to him earlier, that wasn't something he would do unless he's been thinking about me for a long time. He's impulsive but not that impulsive. There was hungry desperation in the way our tongues danced and whirled around one another. We both wanted it. A lot. There was electric chemistry between us.

I wanted him to throw me down on the mountainside, strip off my clothes and make love to me. I wanted to ride him in a field of wildflowers and let my screams of pleasure echo across the woods.

Damn, I have to stop working myself up like this.

Ever since I started spending time with my three guys, I've become a slave to my own urges. I don't know if it's the magic messing with me or what, but it seems like I'm constantly teetering right on the edge of losing control. *Which is exactly what you're out here to fix,* I remind myself.

I wade out into the stream and prepare to recite the incantation for my protection spell. I speak the words while focusing my energy and visualizing the protective aura I wish to conjure.

Sacred herbs, bitter and tart.
Steady my soul, steel my heart.
Fortify me against the winds,
Against all those that wish me harm.

As I speak the last word, a nearly invisible shield of energy encircles me. It parts the waters of the stream so that it flows around me. My feet and legs are protected from the rushing water.

"Woohoo!" I shoot my fist in the air, excited over my first real success as a witch.

My glory is short-lived, however, as a chill runs up my spine. I get the sense that I'm being watched. A rustling sound catches my attention. It's somewhere in the field to my left. I spot movement out of the corner of my eye.

My instincts take over, and the protective aura suddenly drops. The stream surges unobstructed around my ankles once again as I whirl to my left and unleash a bolt of energy at the intruder.

A shout of alarm issues from my target as he flies backward. I feel a pang of guilt when I see Draven flail and disappear into the long grass in the field.

I run towards him, shouting as I go.

"Oh my god, Draven, I am so, so sorry. I had no idea it was you. What are you doing out here? Are you okay?"

He's still laid out, rubbing the back of his head when I reach him. He pushes himself up on one elbow and lifts his head to look at me. His gaze is so gentle and sexy. There isn't even a hint of anger in his bemused look.

"I'm fine. Don't worry. It's really my fault anyway. I shouldn't have snuck up on you like that," he says as I reach down to help him up. "It's just that I saw you standing in the stream, and my curiosity got the better of me. I couldn't help it. I wanted to watch you work for a minute." He smiles sheepishly, and a blush creeps up his neck.

"It's okay. I'm actually really happy you're here. I could use your help with something, if you're willing."

"Anything." His quick response is so earnest, I could probably ask him for my heart's deepest desire, and he'd move mountains to try to make it happen.

"Great. I'm working on casting my bubble of protection. I would love to see how it holds up against a charging shifter." I'm a bit apprehensive about asking, but I need to test my magic.

"I don't know about that... I don't think it's a good idea. What if I break through and accidentally hurt you? I don't think I could live with myself if something bad happened to you because of me," he says, his face solemn.

"Don't worry about me. You don't give me enough credit. I've been practicing, and those herbs Kaval and I fetched this morning are powerful. I was holding off an entire stream before you got here and broke my concentration. I'm pretty sure I can handle one bear-shifter. Especially a *vegetarian* one." I give him a teasing smile as Draven's mouth draws into a playful frown.

"I'd like to see you try to get through my protective aura, vegi-bear," I taunt.

"Ha! Okay, Minerva. Let's do it. But don't say I didn't warn you."

"Awesome. Now, go stand over there, and make sure you wait at least thirty seconds after I speak my incantation before charging. I need time to work my spell up to full power." When he starts walking away across the field, I call after him, "And no holding back! I don't want you making any excuses later. I don't want you telling the others that I only stopped you because you didn't *really* try to break through."

He smiles and shakes his head, clearly doubtful that my spell will stop him. He pulls his shirt over his head, revealing his tan, muscular chest and chiseled abs.

Sadly, he turns away from me and toward the forest as he starts undoing his belt and slipping off his jeans.

The view of his tight, plump ass in the middle of this picturesque meadow really is nothing to be disappointed about, though. I find it difficult to take my eyes off him.

I should be focusing on my breath and directing all my energy toward my core in preparation to cast the spell, but how can I not stare at the beautiful naked man across the field from me?

He unties his long, light brown hair and shakes it out

so that it falls across his muscled back. He shoots me a devilish smile just before he starts to shift. I get the sense that I've just been treated to a private performance.

Maybe his 'masseuse's hands' comment yesterday was something more than just friendly kindness.

As Draven sprouts fur and his features begin to distort and morph in that disorienting way, I think about what an amazing creature he is. He's all man and all bear at the same time. It's sexy.

My mind drifts to the kiss I shared with Kaval this morning, and I can't help but wonder what it would be like to kiss Draven. They're both such fascinating guys. I get the feeling that I may be getting myself into a whole different kind of trouble hiding out in the woods with these sexy shifters.

An emotional storm is brewing out here.

Even though I haven't really had much time with Stone, there's definitely some kind of connection there. I suspect we may share a mutual attraction too.

Finally, I pull my attention back to the task at hand and utter my incantation. The aura-bubble coalesces around me. I focus on keeping my breathing even as I pour energy into it, carefully and steadily, like blowing a huge gum-bubble. Thirty seconds later, it's fully formed and reinforced. Draven roars a warning and begins his charge.

He's coming on fast, and even though I'm confident my shield will hold, I can't stop the nervous flutter in my belly. My heart starts pounding. Adrenaline courses through my blood. It's a normal reaction when a six hundred-pound bear is charging at you full speed. Regardless of your magical abilities, that's some scary shit. Primal instincts run *deep*.

When he's about ten feet from me, he launches

himself through the air, claws ready to tear through the barrier. I reflexively raise my hands in front of my face and squint my eyes shut in anticipation of the impact, but there is only silence. I open my eyes apprehensively and see Draven two feet in front of me, suspended in mid-air with a dumb, surprised look that I've never seen on a bear's face before.

"Aha. Success." I jump into the air in triumph.

I'm so excited that I lose my concentration. My energy falters, and suddenly Draven is falling toward me. I turn to run, but I'm too slow, and his massive arm knocks me to the ground.

Luckily, my reflexes are fast enough to soften my fall with my hands, so I don't end up with a mouthful of earth.

I push myself up on an elbow and look behind me. Draven's enormous paw is covering most of my ass, and my skirt is slightly ripped where his sharp claw tore through it. His claws and fur disappear as his paw shrinks back down to a human hand, so it covers only one cheek now. Draven gapes up at me naked and dumbfounded, and then notices the placement of his hand and jerks it back. His cheeks flame. As he stands, he turns his head away to avoid my eyes.

"Oh man, I'm really sorry." He reaches down and helps me up. "You told me not to hold back, and I didn't want to insult you by not taking you seriously. But maybe I took it too far. Shit, I really could've hurt you." Fear clouds his eyes.

I laugh and shake my head.

"No, that was great. You only got through because I was so excited that it worked that I lost my concentration. My barrier stopped you cold. And you were really coming for me, I could tell. Thank you for believing I could do it. I appreciate your faith in me. It means a lot." I gaze into his beautiful blue eyes.

He smiles and we maintain eye contact.

I am suddenly intensely aware of his nakedness. It takes every ounce of strength to keep from looking down at his cock.

The meadow is silent. The only sound is our heavy, synchronized breathing.

His eyes flicker down to my lips so quickly it might not have happened, but it did. I realize I'm biting my lower lip and rolling up onto my toes. The urge to kiss him, to throw myself on him and taste his full, pink lips, is impossible to ignore.

I know it's wrong, but even a witch has her limits.

Maybe if he would just look anywhere else but right into my soul, I would have a chance.

But he just keeps on gazing into my eyes. I can't take it anymore. I don't know what tomorrow will bring, or if any of us will even be around to regret anything.

Fuck it.

I carefully close the short distance between us and lift my chin. He tilts his head and leans down toward me. Our lips meet in a wet, passionate embrace. I slip the tip of my tongue tentatively out of my own mouth, and he caresses it delicately with his own.

The kiss takes on more urgency. Our hungry mouths succumb to each other as a gentle desperation comes over us. He wraps his arms around me, pressing me hard against him.

His huge, hard cock presses into my thigh. I reach between us and take it in my hand, gently stroking it up and down in a slow, twisting motion. As our mouths open wider, our tongues plunging deeper. His hands slide down the small of my back to cup my ass, and he squeezes, pressing me into his hard, naked body.

His cock presses against my skirt and slips between my thighs. I'm not wearing any panties because the one pair I have is drying on a clothes line back at the cabin. His cock brushes briefly against my swollen clit. In that moment, I want nothing more than to yank my skirt off and mount him right here in the meadow. I'm desperate to feel his big cock slide into my wet, throbbing pussy, but somewhere in my rational brain, I hear a voice tell me that this is not the time.

I groan.

All my problems come rushing back. I remember the coven, Flint, and Azealia. I force myself to disengage my mouth from his. I'm gasping for air and delirious with pleasure. He looks at me hungrily, but our temporary madness is waning.

"Whoa," he says, catching his breath.

"Yeah," I say, looking down at his still-hard cock. I involuntarily bite my lip. "Um, I think I need to go. Like, now."

"No, wait," he says. I half-fear, half-hope he is about to reach out and pull me back to him. Instead he asks, "Where did that come from?" The hungry expression on his face is replaced by one of bemusement.

"Actually, I've wanted to do that for a really long time," I confess, feeling both embarrassed and relieved.

This whole 'sharing your feelings' thing might not be so bad after all.

"Really? I've wanted to kiss you for years. I've had a huge crush on you for a long time, but I didn't want to screw up our friendship by trying anything. Besides, I always thought you and Kaval had a thing."

"We never... Well, actually it's just recently become

kind of complicated. I don't... I can't really explain it right now..." I ramble, wondering why the right words seem so difficult to come by.

Draven smiles sympathetically.

"It's all good, Minerva. You don't have to explain anything to me. I just want you to know, I like you. I really, really like you. I think you're smart and cool and funny and fierce. You're sexy as hell too. I would love to spend some more time with you, if you want. No pressure. It's just that I think we have a powerful connection. I'd love to explore that and see how deep we could take it. I mean, wow, that kiss was incredible."

I chuckle and return his sympathetic smile.

"I know what you mean. 'Wow' is a good word for it. I want to spend more time with you too, but I feel like we can't focus on our relationship until this magic situation is a bit more settled. I'm already having a hard enough time concentrating on focusing my power. We're going to have to be razor sharp to have a chance at facing both the witches and the shifters. Not to mention whatever happens with Azealia."

Disappointment flashes across his face briefly, but he smiles sweetly and nods.

"I hate to have to agree, but you're right. This isn't the right time." His smile turns more mischievous. "But, if you ever need to talk, or if you need a stress-relieving make-out session, you know where to find me. My door is always open."

He starts to walk away but then turns back and raises his hands, fingers wiggling.

"My masseuse hands remain at your disposal, m'lady," he says, winking at me and bowing gracefully before continuing on across the field.

I giggle but feel a pang of regret as he bends to grab his clothes. Maybe I shouldn't have pushed him away.

I sit down in the grass to compose myself while my mind replays our intense kiss. Draven's touch was strong and passionate, but there was an erotic and delicate nature to him as well. He was deliberate and precise without being careful, whereas Kaval was reckless and wild, his body surging with barely-restrained power bordering on aggression. They're so different, and yet I want them both.

A shiver moves through me. My fingers drift toward the part of me that demands satisfaction. I'm dripping wet and thick with need.

Both of the guys are so hot, so loyal, and our connections are so strong. There are unique aspects of both of them, and they drive me absolutely crazy in different, irresistible ways.

My eyes close. My finger works against my clit as I bask in the warm sun.

God, if only there were a way to have them both.

CAPTIVE OF THE BEAR CLAN:
CHAPTER 10

STONE

Cramps in my lower back make me feel like a victim of the Inquisition on the rack. I can't move. I got bored sitting around the cabin, so I retreated to the small working area I use when I come out to the cabin. There's a long wooden table, a thick stump I use for taller projects, and a hammock hanging between two trees. I use that when I'm trying to brainstorm a project.

Right now, I'm in a shed because I can't stand to have anyone watch me when I'm working. It's a thing. I don't know how to explain it, but I can't work when anyone's looking.

I'm contemplating the marble slab sitting on the work bench. I don't want to mar its perfect ivory surface with the wrong cut, but I need to strike it to make the first cut. That's the only way I'll be able to reveal the sculpture dwelling within. That first cut is always the hardest. I have to wait until I'm sure of what I want to accomplish with the piece.

The trouble is, I can't decide on what to make out of it.

Artist's block, I suppose. I chuckle. Artist's block indeed. Perhaps I should have gone with Kaval and Draven to snoop around town.

We have so little information to go on. It drives me crazy not knowing who or what might be coming after Minerva next. Draven and Kaval were right, we have to find out what's happening in Bonfire Falls before we can truly plan our next move.

Minerva's still working on controlling her magic so that she can protect herself in case Azealia tries to attack her for going into her territory. She's scared, so I don't want to push her, but it feels like time is running out. We can only hide for so long before someone finds us.

Kaval thinks that the witches or the bear clan have formed search parties. He's trying to figure out what's going on. Draven's looking for clues as to the identity of the witches who'd attacked Minerva. We still don't know who they are. Minerva didn't recognize them.

This all makes me so angry. Minerva is sweet and gentle and doesn't deserve to be hunted. Not at all. I wish she'd never come into her power. Of course, then she wouldn't here with me at my cabin. All alone. Just the two of us...

I shake my head in a vain effort and return to my task.

Spears of golden sunlight enter through cracks in the shed's walls, aiding the feeble flickering light of multiple oil lamps. I built this shed as a studio space for the cabin but never managed to find the time to lug a generator up here.

It's difficult being an artist. People expect you to just be able to 'turn on' your ability at their command. This can lead to hurt feelings and confusion when you say, "No, I can't have that sculpture of a grizzly bear finger-fucking

Lady Bird Johnson by Friday." People want the weirdest shit sometimes.

Time is a major issue for artists. Creating art takes inspiration. It takes experiences beyond the pale of normal existence. It does not take a deadline and a vague promise of compensation dangled as bait. Everyone is so concerned with money that it becomes next to impossible to find inspiration. It's not like I'm going to make a million dollars as a sculptor, and in some people's eyes, I suppose that means it's a waste of time.

But not Minerva.

My back pain fades away as her image fills my mind. Sweet, kind Minerva. When others mocked me in school, she would come to my defense. She'd tell them to stop picking on the weird boy who was always staring out of the window.

She had been attractive back then, to be sure, but as an adult woman, I almost can't bear to look at her. It's as if the kindness within has been reflected without, and I often feel as if I could fall into those soft brown eyes and never climb back out.

Suddenly I know what I'm going to carve—Minerva, the good-hearted witch, who also happens to be my best friend.

There's a certain school of thought that says pain fuels an artist's talent. It's true that you can feel Van Gogh's torment though his brush strokes and Picasso's arrogance in the alien features he scrawls upon faces. I have a feeling that one will be able to see this sculpture when it's done and feel my longing.

Under normal circumstances, it would take a sculptor several days to create what I have in mind. A combination of my greater strength and dexterity as a bear shifter, and a zealous desire to finish the work and present it to Minerva, means that I will be finished long before that.

Rapid tap-tap-taps echo off the narrow walls of the shed as I remove unnecessary bits of marble block.

Tap-tap-tap. A protrusion that could be an outstretched arm appears.

Tap-tap-tap. The beginnings of a woman's head and figure appears.

Tap-tap-tap. The snarling maw of a giant bear appears.

"Well, that's interesting." I love it when something unexpected appears in the marble.

Sweat pours off my body, stinging as it drips into my eyes. Bits of marble detritus and white dust soon adhere to my damp flesh.

In many professions, you start off small and wind up big, like building a brick wall. The first layer can be done by hand, but the tenth layer requires a crane or elevated platform. In sculpting, you start off with a big hammer and chisel and work your way down to smaller ones.

By the time I'm working on the details, the chisel I use is barely half the width of a pencil. The tip barely takes off a millimeter of stone at a time—less if I'm careful.

As I carve the waves of Minerva's windblown tresses, every detail has to be perfect.

I finish at last with the chiseling and sit back for a time to survey my work. Minerva's astride a massive, roaring bear. Her face seems both joyful and confident, like she was born to be right where she is.

The sculpture's shape and many of its details are now complete, but there are chisel marks and some unevenness upon its white surface. Using a file, I begin to soften the rougher edges of the sculpture, gradually reducing the chisel marks until they are all but invisible even when viewed from mere inches away.

I take a few steps back and gaze upon the fruits of my labor. The bear's fur has many whorls and ruffles, but Minerva is the truly striking part of the piece. My eyes are drawn to her face. I can't look away.

I shake my head. Obviously, my judgment on this matter is not to be trusted. I'm biased by feelings that I don't dare share with her. Our friendship is too important to cross that line. So, I don't. Instead, I suffer in silence and pray that my art will heal the longing in my soul. Until I can share my heart with her, I'll keep my feelings locked up inside.

Although I can't tell her the truth about how I feel, I can share this statue with the world. I pore over it closely once more and find a few flaws in my most recent polish. Using a narrow, fine file, I scratch at the underbelly of the bear to remove a contour that I'm suddenly displeased with. This must be perfect in every detail.

At last, I circle the statue and inspect it closely. I don't find any major flaws, but there are a few imperfections, like a slight disproportion in the bear's feet. However, I'm not sure how to fix this. I had to make certain the base could take the weight of the finished statue.

The marble weighs over two hundred pounds, but I scoop it up in my arms like a sack of groceries. I already know who this belongs to. There's only one person in the world who is worthy of this work.

I pause. Isn't this just the most ridiculous thing in the world? Carving the sculpture is one thing, but actually making it a gift is going to be terribly forward—isn't it? Maybe I shouldn't even let Minerva see it.

Yes, it's for the best if she doesn't. I'm lucky enough to

be her friend. It would be greedy of me to have these ludicrous romantic fantasies and expect her to share them.

Perhaps it's my distracted state of mind, or perhaps it's the marble dust lingering in the air, but I don't smell Minerva's approach. I don't hear her either. She's suddenly just there, standing behind me.

"There you are," she says, pushing the rickety shed door open fully. "I'd wondered where you'd gotten off to."

"Minerva," I say, turning around and trying to use my body to block her view of the sculpture. "I didn't hear you coming."

She steps inside of the shed. Today, she's wearing one of my borrowed t-shirts that reaches past her knees. Her hair is wet. Her skin is soft and glowing from a recent bath.

Now I can smell her. Sweet and sultry, she's intoxicating. Blood courses more quickly through my veins. Despite my vow not to do anything to jeopardize our friendship, I'm tempted to do just that.

Minera cranes her neck to see around me.

"What are you working on?" she asks.

"Oh, ah… It's nothing." I am unable to stop her as she steps around me to feast her eyes upon the finished sculpture.

"Oh my god…" Minerva says, her mouth going agape. Her brown eyes rapidly scan the statue. "Is that… Stone, is that *me*?"

"Ah," I stammer. "Well…" I scratch the back of my head.

"It's beautiful," she says, bending over and putting her hands on her knees to get a closer look. Relief floods through me like a cool mountain stream, washing away the tension so quickly I almost collapse.

"Thank you," I say. Before I lose my nerve, I add, "I made it for you."

"You made it for me?" she asks, enchanting me with those eyes once more. "Thank you. It's wonderful."

"You're welcome," I say as blood rushes into to my cheeks. Why is it suddenly so hot in here?

"Of course," she says, turning back to peer at the statue, "I didn't expect that you'd carve me without any clothes on."

"Ah..." I'm suddenly unable to think. My mouth races to fill the void, much to my chagrin. "Clothes are difficult to sculpt, and anyway nude subjects were a staple of classic era sculpture—"

"Relax," she says, laughing. "I'm fucking with you. You always were so serious, even when we were children. But I've always admired your talent. I hope you never stop sculpting."

"I—you have?" I ask, licking my suddenly dry lips. "That's... I've always adored you, Minerva. Always." I'm word-vomiting all over the place, but I can't help myself.

"That's so sweet." She encircles my waist with her arms.

"Wait, I'm all sweaty and covered in dirt."

"That's okay, this is your t-shirt anyway." Her breath is warm on my chest. Her hands spread out over my back, feeling the ripples of my muscles. "Wow, you're in pretty good shape for an artist. I could run my hands all over you."

I'm too shocked to do anything but stand there like an idiot. She's touching me. *Minerva.* How is this possible? How much marble dust did I just inhale? This must be a hallucination, but if it is, it sure as hell feels real.

My hands start roaming down her back. I trace the

curve of her spine. I cup her beautifully shaped ass, scarcely able to believe what I'm doing.

She doesn't seem to mind. In fact, she lets out a little gasp, stares up at me with what I really hope is the same passion I'm staring at her with.

"Minerva." I draw her tighter against me. Her hard nipples poke through the thin membrane of the t-shirt.

My body responds as well. She doesn't recoil when she feels my cock press against her body. I lean in, our eyes close, and our lips meet. For a very long time, I've dreamed of this moment, and now that it's happening, I never want it to end.

We explore each other's mouths. Her taste is something I'll never forget, sweet agony and wild honey. She's the ultimate aphrodisiac.

All too soon, she breaks away from my embrace and abruptly hides her mouth behind her hand.

"I—I have to go practice my magic," she says, not looking at me.

"Minerva..."

I'm frozen in place. I want to say so many things to her. I want to ask if the kiss meant as much to her as it did to me, I want to take her in my arms again and never let go, but all I do is watch her retreat out of the shed.

Slowly, I sink to my knees in the dust and stone chips. I'm emotionally drained.

During the process of making the sculpture, I'd been high on the thought of giving the statue to her. Then once the sculpture was done, I got cold feet. Fate took that decision away from me. I can't believe she saw it.

I can't believe we kissed.

Really, really kissed. I've often dreamed of what it would be like to be in a relationship with Minerva, but I've been afraid she would reject me.

Of course, she's beautiful, and I want to express my feelings physically, but it's so much more than that. Ever since I met Minerva, every sketch, every painting, and every marble sculpture had been accompanied by the often-unconscious thought of what she might think of it. Literally every project has been driven by a secret desire to please her. I never let on until now.

A rueful grin spreads across my face. Minerva is my muse. I don't know how I never saw it before, but it's true. I need her the way plants need rain. She fuels me.

But I also want—or maybe I need—something more from her.

I want her heart. I want her to feel the same way about me. I need her to care about me as much as I care about her. Before the kiss, I'd have thought that a relationship with her was impossible. After all, I'm not a burly alpha male like Kaval. I'm also not laidback, cool, and in control, like Draven. Both of them are far more experienced than I am with the opposite sex. I've dated and I'm not a virgin, but I'm not an expert like Kaval is. I don't know how to touch a woman in all the right places the way Draven does.

With those two around, I guess I'd always assumed I wasn't even in contention. Maybe I've been wrong the whole time. Maybe, just maybe, there is hope for me yet. Maybe a relationship between Minerva and I isn't as far-fetched as I thought it might be. We could have a future together, if we stay alive long enough for it to happen.

CAPTIVE OF THE BEAR CLAN: CHAPTER 11

MINERVA

The cabin is perfectly quiet as I try to refocus my energy on the spell building in my hands, but once again it fizzles out.

"Damn it." I don't want to be too loud. I don't want to attract attention to my failure and frustration. Although, Stone is out in his shack, so he might not hear me. Wait a minute. He's got the hearing of a bear. Of course, he's going to hear me.

As much as I enjoy his company, I need a moment to gather my thoughts. That sculpture really is the most beautiful thing I've ever seen. Not because I'm the subject —I'm not that conceited—but because when I look at it, I can feel everything he felt when he carved it.

The memory of kissing him, feeling the knots of muscle beneath his shirt and his stiff cock in his jeans, sends a sputter of sparks flying from my palms. They land on the edge of the fur rug. I dash to stamp them out. When I smooth out the fur to brush away embers, I laugh.

It's faux fur, of course.

I get back on my feet and prepare to conjure the beginning of a protection spell once more. It's impossible to get Stone out of my mind. If I'd stayed, how far would I have taken it? I try to tell myself it wouldn't have gone that far, but my gut knows I'm lying.

If I told anyone what happened over the last few days, no one would believe that I didn't plan on kissing all three of them. I swear I didn't. Yeah, they're all incredibly sexy and undeniably sweet, but controlling my power and avoiding capture should be my first priority. That's what a sane person would do. Clearly, I've lost my mind.

With a frustrated sigh, I focused on the palm of my right hand. A little ball of energy flickers to life and then sputters out. Apparently, I'm worthless as a witch when I'm horny. What a joke. I've read about the entire history of witches. There were witches in the past that thrived on their sexuality. They used sex magic to control the world around them. Why couldn't I be one of them? If the longing sparked by three forbidden relationships was enough to fuel my magic, I'd already be more powerful than even Azealia.

This is useless.

I let out a sigh of defeat and walk into the en suite bathroom of my borrowed bedroom. I splash cold water on my face. If it doesn't help me hone my focus, then maybe it might help my hormones simmer down.

I stare at myself in the mirror. A few days of rest up here with Stone, Kaval, and Draven did me good. All signs of stress have disappeared from my face. Good food and fresh mountain air will do it every time.

"Minnie, are you decent?" Stone calls from the hallway.

A smile automatically blooms on my face. I know what he means, but my thoughts are far from decent. Heat floods my body completely, undoing any effect the cold water had on me.

I walk out of the bathroom and open the bedroom door for him.

"I am. Are you?" I ask with a smirk. My eyes quickly flicker to the visible bulge in his jeans.

"What do you think?" He winks. "I came to see how your magic is coming along."

"It's not." I frown. "I really thought I was getting the hang of it, but now I can't conjure more than some flyaway sparks. Not very useful, considering I need it to fight for my life."

"I didn't get good at carving marble right away either." Stone offers an encouraging smile. "I really had to work at it. I found that I have to be in a certain mindset to produce the art I want to produce."

"Like what you did today?" A smile of pure admiration spreads across my face.

"Exactly." He chuckles. He almost looks embarrassed. How can someone be sexy, intimidating, charming and cute all at once? It's so not fair.

"So, the trick is to know how to get yourself into the headspace to be successful?"

"Somewhat. It's easier to develop your skills if you're in the right headspace, but you still have to practice relentlessly."

"I guess magic and art have a lot in common."

"I've always considered magic an art form." Stone shrugs. "Congratulations, Minnie. You're an artist."

"If you say so. I can't paint or draw for shit, so I have to get really good at magic." I laugh, feeling lame.

"I can't paint to save my life." Stone leans in like he's about to tell me government secrets. "I can't draw either."

"Don't worry, I won't tell the art police." I snicker.

"Good. They'll put me in art jail, and I'll be stuck lumping Play Dough together for the rest of my days." Stone laughs.

"Don't worry." I give him a reassuring smile. "I'll smuggle in rocks and charcoal when I visit you."

We're still laughing when Stone suddenly goes ramrod straight.

"What is it?"

He lifts a finger to his lips.

"I hear movement," he whispers.

Cold fear fills me from head to toe. I move closer to Stone and wrap my hands around his thick forearm. He pulls me against him as he strains to listen to sounds my ears can't detect. A few tense moments pass, then Stone lets out a sigh and laughs.

"It's Draven and Kaval." He chuckles. "They're bumbling around in all directions. If I had to guess, I'd say they're throwing anyone who might have followed them off their trail."

"Smart thinking," I say, still feeling uneasy.

"I know, I'm surprised they thought to do that," Stone teases. He rubs my back in large circles, bringing warmth back into my body.

"Play nice," I murmur. "They might hear you."

"I'm sure they can." Stone grins. "Come on, let's get a fire started."

I follow him out to the main room. He stacks logs in the sooty mouth of the fireplace.

"Want to try lighting the fire with magic?" Stone looks to me.

"I don't know... What if I burn the place down? It's a wood cabin after all."

"You'll be fine." Stone waves a hand nonchalantly. "Just try to find that headspace I told you about."

I nod and step up to the fireplace. I close my eyes and take steadying breaths. I imagine calm seas, blue skies, and flowering fields, but that does nothing to help me gather my magic.

My frustration rises. I feel like a failure. How is it possible that I'm an incredibly powerful witch, yet I can't do the simplest of magical spells? What kind of sick twist of fate is this?

My temper snaps. My palms burn. I open my eyes and gasp when I see a fireball hovering an inch above my skin.

It singes my flesh. With a panicked jerk, I launch the fire into the fireplace. It hits the wood which bursts into flames.

I stare at my smoking palms. Why did my own fire burn me? It doesn't make any sense. Magic shouldn't harm the witch who created it. This is some bullshit.

"See? That wasn't so hard," Stone says.

"I think I popped a blood vessel." I groan. "It only worked once I got angry."

"We'll work on that." Stone gives me a reassuring smile. "Maybe Draven can show you some meditation techniques."

"Yeah, maybe." I sigh. I shouldn't feel as defeated as I do. I technically got the spell to work. I did what I was supposed to do.

Kaval and Draven walk in without knocking first. Waves of relief crash over me. I never worried about them while they were gone. Shifters can take care of themselves. But now that they're in front of me, I realized I missed their presence.

"What took you so long?" I ask as I walk into Kaval's arms. He envelops me in a hug. When he releases me, I give Draven a warm hug as well.

"We had to keep it casual." Kaval gives me a small

smile. "If we walked around looking shifty, we would've looked suspicious. Blending in was key."

"Didn't anyone attack you for freeing me?"

"Nah, people are too focused on finding you to care about us. The only people left in town are the people who are willing to look the other way to maintain peace," Kaval says.

"What did you find out?" I ask.

"When we got to town, we immediately went to the pub to get a drink," Draven says.

"You weren't supposed to mention that," Kaval growls.

"It's what everyone would've expected us to do. I also had to check in with Josie at work," Draven says.

"As long as you didn't draw any unnecessary attention, I'm happy. What did you find out?" Stone asks.

"It isn't good." Kaval shakes his head. "They've got search parties crawling the mountain range looking for Minnie."

"What?" Panic makes my voice come out an octave higher than it normally does. Three pairs of concerned eyes shift to me.

"There's nothing you need to worry about," Draven says. "You're not alone in this, remember?"

"Right." I nod and suck in a shaky breath.

"We won't be able to stay here forever, though," Stone says. "This place is pretty secluded, but Flint and his goons will smell us before long."

Stone's right. I've been hiding here on borrowed time. I need to make a decision. I can't rely on Kaval, Stone, and Draven for everything. It simply isn't fair of me to put that on them.

"I'm ready to go see Azealia," I blurt out before I can change my mind. The three of them turn to look at me.

"Are you sure?" Kaval asks.

"Absolutely. I need to get better with magic as fast as I can."

"Okay." Stone nods. "We'll go first thing after sunrise."

"Actually, I think this is something I should do by myself." I'm already anticipating their protest.

"Absolutely not," Kaval says.

The others echo his refusal.

"Just think about it for a minute," I say. "Azealia was betrayed by a lover. I think she'll be more willing to work with me if I show up alone versus showing up with three male companions. We don't know how she feels about shifters either. She could sense you then decide to smite you into ash without a second thought."

"She can easily do the same to you," Draven says.

"Can you protect me from a vengeful witch with the ability to reduce living things to dust in the blink of an eye?" I ask.

"No one can stop a force of nature like that." Kaval shakes his head.

"Exactly. My risk level doesn't change whether you're there or not. Besides, with so many others looking for me, I need to be able to fend for myself if we get separated."

They all open and close their mouths, struggling to come up with a counter-argument.

"You know I'm right," I add.

"Just because I can't poke holes in your logic don't mean I accept it," Kaval says.

"Congratulations, you're a male." I chuckle.

"Very funny." Kaval rolls his eyes.

"I don't like it either," Stone says. "But I think we have to do it her way. It makes the most sense, has the lowest risk, and the most practical option."

"Exactly." I grin triumphantly. "It's settled then."

"Fine." Kaval sighs. "At least let us walk you to that

magic boundary thing. You shouldn't be walking through the forest for that long alone."

"I'd like that." I smile.

"Can we sit for a spell? I've been on my feet all day trying to keep this lug out of trouble." Draven hooks a thumb toward Kaval.

"Bullshit." Kaval shakes his head and plots down onto the sofa. "I was watching your back more than you were watching mine."

"All three of you worked very hard today." I smile sweetly. "You all deserve some time off your feet."

The three of them make their way to the sitting room. Three plush armchairs await them. I feel tempted to make a Goldilocks and the Three Bears joke, but I fear it's a tad too on the nose. Besides, the bears in that story are a mama, a papa, and a baby. Not three burly, devastatingly sexy men.

"Tea or coffee?" I ask them.

"You don't have to." Draven offers me a kind smile.

"You've barely let me lift a finger since I've been here. Let me at least pull my weight." I fix Draven with a begging stare until he relents.

"Tea, please," he says.

"Coffee," say the other two.

I get to work in the kitchen as I listen to them talk about things in town and potential plans to deal with the search parties. It's hard to plan without knowing their precise movements, so everything they come up with is hypothetical at this point.

I set three steaming mugs on the coffee table.

"Nothing for you?" Stone asks.

"Oh." I blush. "I wasn't even thinking about me. I think I'll make myself some tea as well."

I make my way back to the kitchen and put another

kettle of water on the stove. I watch Stone, Kaval, and Draven talk and joke with each other. All of them look so handsome in the glowing light of the fire. My heart does a funny flip, so I look away.

I'm in deep shit, aren't I? I can't believe I'm falling for all three of them. Going to see Azealia isn't the only decision I needed to make. I have to figure out what to do about my guys.

I've never really done the relationship thing before. I've never met anyone I've wanted to commit to fully. No one ever really seemed to get me. I've always been fine with that until now. Now, I look at three gorgeous men. They all understand me in a way no one else ever has.

If I were completely rational and capable of taking my emotions out of the equation, the solution would be simple. The stakes are too high for me to allow myself to be distracted by the idea of a relationship. However, I've never once considered myself a rational being and I'm not about to change that now.

Yes, I want a relationship.

But with who?

I adore them all.

Kaval might look gruff from the outside, but inside he's one of the sweetest people I've ever encountered. He absolutely can break the jaws of anyone who comes after me. I've never once doubted my safety when he's around. And he's just so... big. In every sense of the word. He could fuck me into exhaustion and still be up for more. I'd be a ragdoll for him to play with every night.

Draven is one of the gentlest souls I've ever encountered yet has no problem tearing people apart if they pose a threat to me. My eyes flicker to his perfect hands. In an instant, I'm transported to a tranquil, clean place that smells of lavender. Draven's hands roam my body, sending me deeper and deeper into a state of perfect relaxation. He could keep my stress at bay.

Stone. The way he sees the world as a work of art is unlike anything I've ever come across. I could sit and listen to him talk about light, shadow, and the soul for days on end. I let out a soft sigh as I think back to that sculpture. If he treats stone with such care, imagine how he would treat a lover.

Warmth floods my body. I turn my back to the three men in the sitting room in an attempt to get myself under control. I want all of them. I can't possibly choose between three perfect shifters.

What if you don't have to? The thought whispers through my mind. At first, I immediately reject it, but I can't shake the idea now that it's taken root.

Is that possible? Do bears mate for life or do they have multiple partners? Oh my God, was it rude to even think about that? This is hard enough to work through without making an ass of myself.

Even if I decide I want all three of them, what would they think of that? How could that ever work?

I'm getting ahead of myself. I pour myself a hot cup of tea and take slow, deep sips. It doesn't help.

"The fish should've come up river by now," I hear Kaval saying. "I'll go out there and rustle up some dinner."

"Can I come?" I ask before I realize what I'm saying.

Kaval looks at me with a surprised smile.

"Sure. We can even work on those protection spells if you like," he says.

Really, I just want a moment in the quiet forest to think. And I kind of want to see Kaval in action as a fisherman bear.

"Sounds good." I finish my tea and place my mug in

the sink. Kaval grabs a woven net to haul any fish he catches.

"We won't be long," I say to the other two with a smile.

I follow Kaval out into the night and make a silent promise to myself that I'll keep my hands to myself. No matter how much I want to touch Kaval, he's off limits, at least until this is all over.

CAPTIVE OF THE BEAR CLAN: CHAPTER 12

KAVAL

I'm not a nervous person. Once you get to be my size, there's nothing much that's scary. That's why I have no problem going down to the river to get fish after dark. Nothing could sneak up on me. On the off chance someone sees me and still decides to attack, he won't stand a chance in hell. A claw to the gut, and I'll be done with him.

Unless that bastard Flint and his merry band of assholes finds us. That could be a problem. It would be nearly impossible for them to sneak up on us. Stone and Draven would hear them coming too, so I have nothing to worry about.

I let Minerva take the lead as we walk. It's not that late, but it's late enough for the moon to be high and the fireflies to be out. They like Minerva. They hover behind her shoulders as she walks, making a short cape of flashing lights. I don't think Minerva notices. I decide not to tell her. If she moves, she might chase the fireflies away. Maybe they sense her magic or something?

I don't know much about magic. I didn't have to take

any classes on it in school since bear shifters don't have any. Maybe the fireflies are just inexplicably pulled to her like I am.

I reach out and touch Minerva's shoulder or waist when she needs to turn in a certain direction. The river isn't far, but we're moving slowly. After the sun sets, it's smart to move slowly and make as little noise as possible in the forest. You never know what's lurking in the dark, especially now that there are search parties coming after us. I hated being away from Minerva during the day, but I'm glad I went to town. The information I learned might just save our lives.

Luckily for Draven and me, none of the people who want us dead were in Bonfire Falls. They were all out hunting us. Ironically, we were perfectly safe in town.

Still, everyone in town did act strangely towards me and Draven. They knew we were being hunted. No one ever said anything explicitly, but I think Flint might've told them that Stone, Draven, and I are traitors. That would keep anyone from helping us.

If that's the case, Flint didn't think it through. As white-picket-fence as it sounds, Draven and I are pillars of the community. I run an essential business for fuck's sake. I don't really think of my garage as a business. I think of it as a fun activity people will pay me to do. But every car in town comes through my shop. Without me, there's no one to repair their rides.

Draven makes it his mission to be on friendly terms with everyone. I never got that. I mean, having people smile at you on the street sounds neat and all, if you're into that, but I'm not. I'd rather have a close band of ride or die brothers, than a bunch of superficial acquaintances.

Minerva and I find a great spot just above the rapids. She settles onto a rock to watch me. I only have the light of the moon, but my vision is better than a human's at night. I can easily see her, and she's looking at me with desire in her eyes.

It's nothing like the pitying looks Draven and I got when we were in town today. I fucking hate getting looks like that. I'm sure as hell *not* used to it. I've never had reason to be pitied in my life. At least those pitying looks told me what side Bonfire Falls was really on. After all, I've fixed everyone's car, bike, or ATV at least once. That counts for something.

What has Flint ever done for the community? When he's not tearing it up as a bear, he's drinking. All I ever see him do is drink at the clubhouse, drink at the bar in town, and drink at home. Oddly enough, I've never seen him drunk. The guy must have the tolerance of an elephant. I bet his bear liver helps him stay alive.

I used to have a respect for Flint. Sure, we were never friends, but his nasty scars told one hell of a story. I don't know the story personally. I don't think anyone does. Even I don't have the balls to ask him about it. Some things you just leave alone. But those scars must've come from a hell of a fight.

Or a war.

I don't know if Flint fought in the war against the witches. Taking recent events into account, I'm going to guess not. He wouldn't be in cahoots with that crazy red-headed mess of a witch if he had. That chick was off her fucking rocker.

I get it. Being bullied sucks. Well, actually, I don't get it. No one was ever stupid enough to pull that shit with me. I was as big as I am now in my early years. Only back then I didn't care enough to control my shifting or my strength.

Once, I got so pissed that I shifted in the middle of

class. I knocked over a vat of some kind of acid that ate through the floor and then the ground below it.

Minerva was my lab partner that year. She thought the whole thing was hilarious. After some tinkering, chemistry came easy to me. Relationships, well, those weren't so easy.

The day I nearly wrecked the lab was the day Minerva and I really became friends. It was also the day I fell in love with her. If I'd known then that I'd be hiding out with her in a cabin and walking through a firefly-lit forest, I wouldn't have messed around with other chicks under the guise of preserving the friendship between Minerva and me. I would've asked her out properly, took her on a real nice first date, and done all that prom bullshit that always seemed so stupid to me. I fucked up. I should have told her how I felt a lot sooner. I was a chicken-shit.

Even though I dated other girls, I never let any of them into my heart because I'd saved a huge part of it for Minerva. It was hard watching her date other guys, but my consolation was that she didn't seem to care about them all that much. She was doing to guys what I was doing to girls. Looking back, it seems like such a waste. We could have been together this whole time.

I return my attention to the river. Fish are swimming right into my net. It's almost too easy. I go on mental auto-pilot and immediately, I'm back to the moment she kissed me. I still can't believe it happened. It takes all of my willpower not to kiss her every moment I'm with her.

Even now, as she leans back to stare at the circle of fireflies around her head, I want to grab her and kiss her. But I refrain. Minerva's been in an unusual state of mind. She's been traumatized. She's been stressed. Her whole life has been turned on its ass and thoroughly fucked beyond recognition. It's better to let her set the pace. The last thing I want to do is freak her out and cause her to back off.

Also, it's not like we're living in the roomiest accommodations. Don't get me wrong, I'm damn grateful we're able to have a place with a roof, kitchen, and running water to live in while we're in exile, but it's not conducive to getting laid.

If Minerva and I start something, it'd be difficult for me to do every dirty thing I want to do to her without weirding out Stone and Draven.

Getting Minerva into my bed is my strongest desire. It's all I can think about. But I'm smart enough to know that fucking up the dynamic between myself and the guys I'm relying on is not a smart move. Especially not for Minerva. If the three of us don't work in sync, we can't protect her to the best of our abilities.

We all need clear heads to get this job done right.

Unfortunately, the best way for me to clear my head involves burying my *other* head deep inside Minerva. I could sure as hell use the release.

Fucking hell, I need to get a grip before Minerva realizes how hard I am. At least it's dark. Should shift into my bear form to fish. That will help. Cold river water will help too. I just need to keep it together.

I love rivers. I don't even think that's part of the bear thing. Okay, it might be. Either way, rivers are the only water I like. The ocean is too salty. Pond water is too slimy. Rivers are where it's at.

"Can you see the fish in the dark?" Minerva asks. She scoots to the edge of the boulder and twists her body so that her feet dangle in the gently rushing water.

"Absolutely." As if on cue, a shiny silver shape breaches a small rapid. "It'll be a piece of cake."

"I make a damn good angel food cake," Minerva says. "I should make it for you guys."

I didn't have a sweet tooth. Not one bit. But I'd eat anything Minerva put in front of me.

"That'd be great." I grin. "I'm gonna do the bear thing now. Is that cool?"

"Totally." Minerva smiles. "It's fascinating, watching you shift. No matter how many times I see it, I still think it's amazing."

Her words sent a bolt of pride through me.

I strip down. I already have a limited amount of clothes at the cabin. There's no sense in destroying a perfectly good pair of jeans during shifting. I watch Minerva rake her gaze over my naked body. Her eyes rest on my cock which is fully hard. It's then that I see it, that flash of hunger in her eyes.

I give her a sultry smile before shifting into my bear form.

My desire to fuck Minerva is briefly overshadowed by the instinctual need to catch all those fucking fish. I charge into the river and find the perfect position. Those stupid fish will flop their way right into my jaws. It's almost too easy, but it beats fishing the traditional way. I hate that shit.

It doesn't take long for the first fish to sail into my mouth. I chomp down, making sure it's dead, before tossing it onto the riverbank near Minerva's boulder.

"Whoop!" She cheers and claps.

I catch more fish than we need. Minerva cheers me on the whole time.

I like this way too much. I'm already getting ahead of myself in terms of my relationship with Minerva. All we did was kiss. It meant the world to me, but what if it didn't mean anything to her? I have to talk to her about it. Now is the best chance I'll get.

"I think you've got enough," she calls to me, laughing. "Is there a freezer at the cabin? We're going to need to store almost all of this."

I grunt back to her. It's my bear's way of laughing.

As plod out of the water, I shake myself mostly dry and shift back. I'd rather not have a serious conversation with Minerva completely naked, though the way she's looking at me sets my blood on fire. I quickly pull my jeans on and drag my shirt over my head.

"I hope you don't expect me to carry any of those," she teases as she points at the fish.

I walk over to the boulder she's perched on. She's up high enough to look me in the eyes. Her skin is silvery in the moonlight.

My plan to talk to her goes right out window. Driven by pure want, I take her face in my hands and kiss her. It's better than talking about my feelings. I'm not good at that crap. I do much better when I show them.

When she pulls me closer to the boulder, I lower my hands to her waist. I slip one hand under her shirt where I reach one perfect breast. I squeeze her gently. When I stroke my thumb over her nipple, she lets out a sigh that drives me wild. I can smell her arousal; I'm drunk on it.

I don't realize she's reaching down until I feel her dainty hand press against my groin. Even through the denim, it's enough to elicit a growl from deep in my throat. I extend my claws and start to tear through her shirt.

"Wait!" She gasps.

I pull back immediately.

"What's wrong?" I hope I didn't spook her.

"I need to tell you something," she says.

"You can tell me anything." It's hard to focus on my

words when every inch of my body is screaming to fuck, but I make it work.

"With everything that's happening, I don't want to be tied to one person," she says. "It could complicate everything."

"I know what you mean," I say, though I'm not sure that I do. Either way, I'd do anything for her and do anything to have her. "If a no-strings type of deal is what you want, I'm all for it."

Of course, I want more than that. I want so much more. But what she wants is more important. *She's* more important.

Until Minerva, I never felt serious about any woman. They were for fun and fucking, nothing more. But with Minerva? I really see a future with her. I've always seen a future with her, but now I'm finally ready to do something about it.

"Really?" A huge smile spreads across her stunning face. That smile is the reason enough for me to agree to a casual relationship. Though, the tricky thing with not committing to anything is that neither party is ever sure exactly where the other stands. It's a sacrifice I'm willing to make, for now.

"Really," I repeat.

"Thank you," she sighs with gratitude. "I love being with you. You need to know that. I think this is the best way to do things for now."

I can see her logic, kind of. I'm sure I'd understand better if I could think straight.

"Now, where were we?" she purrs.

All other thoughts fly out of my mind. She pulls me onto the boulder next to her. There's plenty of space for us to roll around together.

I crush my lips to hers, invading her mouth with my

tongue. My hand returns to its previous position on her breast. Her nipple is a hard, sensitive nub under my thumb.

"You're making me so wet," she whispers.

Holy shit.

I'm in physical pain from how much my cock is straining against my jeans. As if she can read my mind, her hand travels down to unbutton my jeans. My cock springs free. I wriggle out of my clothes and toss them off the boulder.

"I knew you were fucking huge," she murmurs as she wraps her hand around my cock.

Primal need tears through me. I lick and kiss my way down Minerva's neck before sinking my teeth into the soft place where her shoulder joins her neck. She digs her nails into my back and yelps. I'm afraid I hurt her.

"Do it again," she commands when I release my bite.

So much for thinking I hurt her.

I oblige and bite her again. As much as I want to tear every shred of clothing from her perfect body and fucking ravage her, I hold back. She's in control here. I'll obediently wait for her orders.

She pulls away from me and stares at me with eyes that are filled with primal, even animalistic, lust.

"Take me, Kaval. Fill me with your cock," she commands.

That's all I need to hear. With a snarl, I start tearing at her clothes.

CAPTIVE OF THE BEAR CLAN: CHAPTER 13

MINERVA

I don't have time to be surprised with myself. If Kaval had magic, I'd accuse him of putting a spell on me. It's so rare that I'm the one who initiates sex, but I can't resist him. He's driving me insane with desire, turning me into some wanton creature I've never been before.

As he rips the clothes from my body, I'm whimpering and begging him to fuck me. I can't even believe the words coming from my mouth. This new aspect of myself snuck up on me, but I can't say that I hate it.

I used to love teasing a man until he was desperate for me. With Kaval, I already knew he wanted me just as much as I wanted him, we just never did anything about it. Recent events have really put things in perspective. It seems so stupid now that we spent so many years dancing around each other.

At any given moment, Flint and his bears or those horrible witches that tried to steal my magic could descend upon us. Without full control of my magic, I'm basically defenseless. Except for my three shifters, of course. But even they have to sleep. One well-planned ambush, and Kaval and I might never get this chance again. I have no intention of wasting any more time.

The shirt I'm wearing is one I borrowed from Kaval. He tears it open, exposing the bra I'm wearing underneath. As he strips me, a violent urge overcomes me. Before I know it, I'm pulling him to me and enveloping him in a deep, passionate kiss. For just a moment, nothing else exists except our lips. I savor the feel of them against mine.

How have I let so many years go by without doing this? I must be crazy or a masochist.

I've talked myself out of making a move on him at least a dozen times since we've known each other. I always had him in the back of my mind as someone I could seriously date. But I didn't enjoy dating and neither did he.

Until now, I didn't see the point in risking our friendship. Now, I understand how stupid and cowardly I was being. I should've taken this chance a long time ago. Though, I can't imagine another time it would have felt this right.

I've always trusted him to protect me if something were to happen, but now I can see just how fearless and brave he truly is. He waited until the time was right too. He didn't push me. He was patient, and I love that he waited until the timing was right for us.

I pull away from him to gaze into his warm eyes. Kaval is regarded as somewhat of a rebel. If we were in a stereotypical high school movie, he'd be cast as the rebellious bad boy that all the girls want but are too scared to go after. But he's never been bad with me. I think I'm the only person who truly knows about his soft side. I know him better than most people. I know the real Kaval, who he really is inside.

"Are you okay?" he asks with a gentle smile.

"Yes." My voice is a breathy whisper.

"Good, because there's something I've been dying to do."

"Do it," I challenge.

I'm not sure what I was expecting, but I certainly wasn't expecting him to slide between my thighs and pull my knees apart. He nibbles the inside of my thigh. His mouth on my flesh is the sexiest thing I've ever seen. Watching him lick me sets off another round of naughty thoughts. In all my years of dating, no man has ever awakened my wanton side. I'm alive in a way I've never been before, and it's all because of him.

I'm ready to feel him slide inside me. I try to pull him up by his shoulders, but he just chuckles and blows a breath across my pussy. Before I can try to move him again, his tongue strokes the length of my slit. I give up immediately. This so much better that what I was trying to get him to do. I really should let him take the lead.

"Holy shit," I gasp and fall back against the boulder. His rumbling laugh vibrates against my core. My pussy clenches in response.

In the woods, far away from anything and everyone, I don't hold back my moans and cries of ecstasy. His hands grip my thighs. He holds me steady while he slips his tongue inside me.

"You taste amazing," he groans.

While he continues to lash his tongue against me, I drag my hands up from my belly to my breasts. I rub and pinch my incredibly sensitive nipples. My entire body has transformed into a single raw nerve. Even the gentle breeze skittering over my skin feels erotic.

He moves his tongue up to my sensitive pearl and slowly swirls circles around it. My back arches instinctively. My hands fly from my breasts to entwine into his hair. My hips rock subconsciously, directing the way his tongue hits my clit. He goes still, content to let me use his face and tongue as I see fit. His hands travel up my body to my breasts, which he plays with as I ride his face.

Within minutes, pleasure explodes through me as his clever tongue brings me to orgasm. I'm a shuddering mess when he rolls onto the boulder beside me. He has the sexiest, most self-satisfied smirk on his face. He wipes my juices off his chin then sucks them from his fingers.

"Oh my god." My voice is husky and almost unrecognizable.

"Don't get too relaxed," he warns. "I'm not finished yet."

He positions himself between my legs, his rock-hard cock is so big that I'm intimidated. As if he realizes my concerns, he fills me slowly, opening me to the sensations of pleasure and pain as he stretches me to my limits.

It's amazing.

I've never had someone as big as him. It takes my body some time to adjust to his length and girth. He's patient and gentle while he waits for me to relax around him. Once I'm comfortable, he picks up the pace.

The surface of the boulder is cool against my back in contrast to the heat radiating between us. I stare up at him and can't help but be amazed by what I see. A huge, sexy, beast of a man sliding his cock in and out of my pussy against the backdrop of a moonlit forest. Not even in my wildest fantasies could I have pictured something so incredible.

I reach out and run my hands along the bulging muscles of his arms and across his chest. The Greeks and Romans had nothing on Kaval, that's for damn sure.

"You're so fucking tight," he groans.

Hearing those words from his lips sends me into a whole new kind of frenzy. I claw at his hips, pulling him into me as deep as my body will allow.

He lets out a feral roar as he pounds his hips against mine.

Another orgasm builds swiftly. When it crashes over me, he moves his hand down to swirl his thumb over my clit to keep it going for longer. I place a finger in my mouth and bite down in a feeble attempt to quell the pleasure-drenching screams that threaten to erupt from the depths of my soul. If we weren't still in hiding, I'd let the whole world know how much I love this.

His pace quickens. He wraps his arms around my back and pulls me against him. He's thrusting faster, deeper, harder, and I know he's close.

Suddenly, a shudder ripples through his body. It's so violent that his claws pop out and graze my skin. It doesn't hurt. In fact, it feels amazing.

He lays by my side and cuddles me against him. I never imagined he'd be one to cuddle, but then again, I never imagined us like this either.

When we've both have a chance to catch our breath, he smiles and kisses me softly.

"We should get cleaned up and head back," he says. "The others are waiting."

I want to stay here forever. I don't even think I can move, but I have to. The other guys are waiting.

I let him pull me to a standing position. My legs are wobbly as I take my first tentative steps. He scoops me up and carries me right into the river. It's not very deep, so I have to kneel down to completely wash my body. I wash my hair for good measure, too. Bears can scent other bears, and I don't want them to smell his scent all over me. I don't want them to find out about us like that. Besides, there is no *us*. This was probably just a one-time fling. No strings. Isn't that what we both agreed to?

Damp, refreshed, and shivering, I stand up in the river.

"I swear that moonlight has a way of bending around to you make you even more beautiful," he says.

"Thank you." I give him a shy smile. "Witches have a thing for moonlight and water."

He opens his arms, and I rush into his warm embrace. He wraps me in his arms and pulls us back onto the boulder. We use its natural shape as a sort of loveseat. I lay my head on his chest and listen to his heartbeat. It's powerful and steady, like him.

I almost wish what just occurred between use changed the way I feel about Stone and Draven, but I want them just as much as I want Kaval. Now is as good a time as any to talk to Kaval about my idea, but I don't know how to ask him. It's not like there's a roadmap for this situation for me to follow. A witch falling equally for three shifters probably hasn't happened in the history of ever, so of course it has to happen to me.

A jolt of fear hits me as I realize there's always a chance that he could refuse. What if he hates me for even considering it? If I lose him as a friend, I don't know what I'll do. Not only that, but he's the brute force in our makeshift family. If he leaves, Draven and Stone could probably still protect me, but we wouldn't be as strong. Kaval makes us stronger. The four of us must stay together, at least until this is over.

Wow, how fucked up am I? I'm putting one of my dearest friendships in jeopardy, but all I can think about is affects my safety. It's not right. What about Kaval's feelings?

You know what? I'm just going to forget about this idea. We'll never make a four-way relationship work. It's too crazy. It's too impractical. It'll never work. I should just be happy with what we shared tonight and let that be the end of it.

Even as I finish that thought, a deep pang of longing resonates within me.

"That's not the expression I hoped to see on you," Kaval says. I look at him with wide eyes.

"What?" I stammer.

"Come on. You've clearly got something on your mind," he says. "Didn't you like it?"

"What? Oh god, yes. It was amazing. You're amazing."

"Then what's the with the face? You look like you just bit a lemon." He chuckles.

"I've just been thinking about things."

"About being hunted?"

It's an easy lie to claim, but I can't bring myself to tell it.

"No." I sigh.

"Then what is it?"

"It's complicated."

"Minnie, you can tell me anything." He hugs me closer. I believe him. I take a deep breath.

"Okay. The thing is, I'm falling for you. I think I've been kind of falling for you for years, but right now I'm *really* falling for you," I say in a rush.

"That's perfect." He's beaming at me again.

"There's more," I say. "The thing is, I'm also falling for Stone and Draven. I know it's totally crazy and probably stupid, but my ultimate fantasy is to work things out so that somehow, I can have all of you."

There, I said it. Any moment now, Kaval will push me away and tell me I'm insane or call me something worse.

"Oh." He sounds surprised, which is to be expected. "You mean you want all three of us to share you?"

"Yes." A deep blush colors my cheeks.

"I've heard of people doing stuff like that before. I've never thought much about it myself," he says.

He doesn't sound horrified. He said it in a tone that makes me think he might actually be considering it. He hasn't said no yet. He hasn't pushed me away and denounced our friendship. I take this as a good sign.

"If you want to take some time to think it over, I understand," I say.

He sits quietly for a moment, looking out at the moonlit river. When he turns back to me, he's smiling.

"I don't need time. I want you. I've wanted you forever. There's no one on this earth like you, and I'd do anything to have you, even if that means sharing you with Draven and Stone."

For a moment, I think I'm imagining things, but after I blink a few times and give my head a little shake, he's still looking at me with that smile.

"You're serious?" I ask. It's too good to be true.

"I'm serious. If that's what it takes, you're worth it."

I'm stunned. He wants me... *me!*

I lean in to kiss him.

"You're amazing," I whisper.

He shrugs off my praise with a sheepish smile.

"What do Draven and Stone think about this?" he asks.

"They don't know about my idea," I admit. "You're the first one I've talked to about it."

"I'm honored," he says. "Thanks for coming to me first. I know I'm going to share you, but it means a lot that I came first."

"You're welcome. Just, do one thing for me..."

"What?"

"Don't taunt the other guys about it."

"I won't, Minnie. I wouldn't demean what we have by turning it into a competition."

"Thank you."

I settle back in his arms as a warm and fuzzy sensation moves through me. I never expected him to agree. This whole evening has been filled with the most intense surprises, I'm both completely relaxed and totally excited about the future. We need to leave soon, but I want to hold onto this moment for as long as I can.

As I curl into Kaval's side against the chilly forest night, I feel better about my situation. If Kaval agreed to share me, perhaps the others will too. Maybe my fantasy will come true.

CAPTIVE OF THE BEAR CLAN:
CHAPTER 14

MINERVA

W hen I wake up the next morning, my body is still humming with pleasure. I'm alone in bed. The guys are sleeping in the living room. I didn't have the guts to invite Kaval to stay in the bed with me last night. I'm not ready for our secret to get out yet.

Besides, I have other things to worry about. Today is the day I'm going to meet Azealia. My mind fills with dark thoughts. Anxiety has twisted my stomach into knots. There's nothing that could possibly tempt me into having breakfast.

The sun isn't up yet, so I take a few moments to mentally prepare myself for what I have to do today. I lift my hands above my face and attempt to conjure a little ball of energy, just for practice. As usual, only a few sparks fly from my fingertips before fizzling out in tiny puffs of smoke. I've tried to learn to control my magic, but it's pointless. I need a teacher. I need Azealia.

"Perfect," I mutter sarcastically to the ceiling. "Azealia

will fall on her wrinkly old ass in shock after seeing what I can do."

I refuse to wallow in my failure. Instead, I push back the covers and swing my legs over the side of the bed.

A pleasant ache rests between my thighs, serving as a reminder of last night's fling with Kaval. A shiver of desire runs down my spine. I'm already wet just from the memory. I immediately snap myself out of it. I can't afford to be distracted today. I have to stop thinking about the way Kaval slid his thick cock into me last night. I can't keep replaying that exact moment over and over in my mind. It's distracting as hell.

Speaking of woods, despite the dip in the river, I smell like I slept on the forest floor. I'm not sure what Azealia will do when she meets me, but I doubt she'll wants a smelly, strange witch showing up on her doorstep.

Does she even have a doorstep?

I hop into a steaming shower. With a little help from a detachable shower head, I deal with the lingering memories from last night and emerge ready to focus on the day ahead.

The other three are already awake when I step into the main room.

"Coffee?" Stone gracefully slides a mug filled with rich coffee across the kitchen island. I don't know how he manages it, but not a single drop spills as it comes to rest.

"Thanks. I'm really going to need it," I say in an attempt to make light of the daunting task I face.

"Want some breakfast? I make a mean omelet. Do you want the works?" Kaval asks from his position in front of the stove. The scent of eggs, peppers, and bacon make me salivate. Okay, maybe I am slightly hungry.

My stomach churns.

Okay, maybe not.

"That sounds amazing, but I'm going to have to pass." I glance at the contents of Kaval's frying pan and my belly roils. "I'm scared that my nerves will make me puke up anything I eat."

Kaval and I share a look brimming with desire so hot I'm surprised I don't singe the wooden table I'm touching.

"I have an idea," Draven says.

The suddenness of his words breaks the spell between Kaval and me. Draven pushes away from the table and walks over to his bag. He pulls out three little vials.

"Are those potions?" I ask.

Potions used to be a lot more mainstream in covens, but nowadays, hardly anyone has the time to brew something for three days under the light of a very specific moon. Our magic is efficient enough.

"Kind of," Draven chuckles.

He uncaps all of the vials and passes them, one by one, in front of my nose. I recognize the scents of lavender, eucalyptus, and lemongrass.

"I picked these up from the Scented Muse Parlor yesterday," Draven explains. "I figured you might need them."

"Thanks," I say with a grateful smile. "Lemongrass is nice."

"It's energizing." Draven collects a few drops of the fragrant oil in his hand. He rubs his palms together as he approaches me. "May I?"

"By all means."

I tie my hair up in a bun, exposing my neck. Draven gets to work immediately. His skillful fingers draw the stress right out of my body. The lemongrass, plus the coffee I'm sipping, is making me more alert and prepared for what I'm about to face.

I catch Kaval's gaze. He looks torn. I think back to the

conversation we had last night. I can't believe he agreed to share me with the others. Now he looks like he might regret that decision. He's gripping the handle of his frying pan so hard I fear it's going to break and send chunks of scalding egg everywhere. I give him a wink and a sly smile to ease him. It works. He grins back and resumes cooking.

I still have to talk to Stone and Draven to see if they'll agree to my little arrangement. As much as I want to know what they'll say, I put it out of mind for now. I have to focus on Azealia and controlling my powers. I inhale more lemongrass to enhance my clarity. I'll find a way to make this all work out. I don't know how, but I'll think of something.

"Try not to tense your muscles for a while," Draven says. "And avoid stressful situations."

I swivel around and fix him with a look.

"Did you really just tell me to avoid stress?" I bite back my laughter.

Draven realizes his error and bursts out laughing.

"Sorry. It's a habit."

I have to admit; I feel much better now. Lemongrass and laughter did the trick.

LESS THAN AN HOUR LATER, the four of us are walking through the forest. We haven't reached the magical barrier yet, but I can feel it humming through the air like static before a big storm.

"You don't have to do this," Kaval tells me for the twentieth time since we've left Stone's place.

"Yes, I do." I sigh. "You know I do."

"I know, but that don't mean I have to like it," he grumbles. I link my arm through his and give him a squeeze.

"I have to side with Kaval on this one," Draven says. "This place gives me the creeps."

"The magic is designed to dissuade anyone from coming too close. But I think this magic is extra effective against shifters," I say.

"Fantastic," Stone says.

We reach the fork in the path where the barrier is working at full force.

"How are you going to get through it? Will it open for you because you're a witch too?" Kaval asks.

"I don't think I'm that lucky. I'll have to use magic to get through. I learned the spell to bypass barriers in high school... Not that I was ever able to do it." I can't help the bitterness in my tone at that admission.

"You got this." Stone gives my shoulder a squeeze.

"Right." I take a shaky breath and attempt to focus my mind against the barrier. I lift my hands, imagining a needle-sharp spiral of air whooshing forward like a drill. Sweat beads on my brow as I increase my efforts. When I'm out of breath and feel like my heads going to fucking split, I step back.

"Did anything happen?" I ask.

"I thought I felt a light breeze," Kaval says.

"Shit!" I rub my temples in frustration.

"It's all right," Draven says. "Let's try some breathing techniques. They might help you focus."

Honestly, I don't buy into the whole yoga-meditation-holistic shit. But the lemongrass made me feel better, and I don't have anything more to lose.

"Why not." I shrug.

Draven guides me through a series of breathing techniques. Apparently, I've been breathing wrong my whole life.

With his guidance, I focus my body and mind once

more on my goal. I take a deep breath, and when I release it, energy flies out of me right into the barrier. I sense a gap and dash forward. I slide through the barrier before the spell falters and the magical wall reforms.

"It worked!" I yell.

"I knew you could do it." Draven tries to force a smile, but they all look nervous now.

"Be careful," Kaval says. It's the first time I've ever heard his voice shake.

"I will."

I decide it's best to walk away quickly before I become too aware of the fact that I'm completely separated from my protectors. If I let my nerves get the better of me, I'll never learn what I need to learn.

With a wave and a smile, I turn my back on them and walk down the path toward the witches' house—or lair? Who knows? She might not even be here anymore.

Already, I feel lonely. It's only been a few minutes, but I miss my guys. I've grown so used to their constant companionship. I can't wait to get back to them. I should've had breakfast. The lemongrass Draven rubbed into my neck and shoulders has faded away. I can't smell it anymore.

I long to look over my shoulder, but I stop myself. If I see them, I'll want to run back to them.

"There's nothing to be afraid of," I tell myself.

My voice sounds strange to me. It's too loud and too sharp. It's then I realize that the forest is completely silent. Definitely not normal.

Usually, when forests are quiet, it means that a predator is on the hunt. Technically, I'm being hunted, so this isn't completely unexpected. For the first time I wonder: Could the parties tracking me break through the magical barrier? That barrier was challenging to me, but I bet a talented witch like one of the Elders could bypass it without lifting a finger.

The forest grows darker as I walk. Trees loom over me, and their branches claw down to scrape my skin and tear my clothes. I notice carvings on some of the trunks. Runes, symbols, and other images that I don't understand. Wards maybe? I didn't know of a witch that still used wards. But, if Azealia's been here for a while, it makes sense that she uses older methods of magic.

Something rustles above me. Fear grips my heart in its icy hands as I look up. Perched on a branch, barely visible against the deep green of the thick canopy, is the biggest raven I've ever seen. I feel compelled to stop walking. I can't explain it, but the last thing I want to do is walk under the branch bearing the raven.

What was that stupid rhyme about ravens we all had to learn in kindergarten? I thought it was bullshit at the time, but now I'm not so quick to dismiss it. Does a single raven mean good luck or death? It's one of the two.

"If you're indicating that I'm about to meet a bloody and painful end, can you give me a clearer signal?" I ask the bird.

The branch bends under its weight, it's that fucking huge. It can't be a natural animal. Perhaps it's Azealia's familiar. A lot of witches still have familiars, though I don't. I always liked the idea of a little kitty or something to keep me company. A black cat's a bit too stereotypical for me, though.

The raven barks something that sounds eerily like human laughter then takes off from the branch. It swoops low over my head. I'm hit by a gust of wind so biting that I think the bird actually hit me.

"What the fuck," I say under my breath.

It takes several minutes for me to compose myself

enough to continue down the trial. As I follow the thinning path, I don't run into any more ravens or forest creatures. When the path starts to disappear entirely, I worry I've somehow gone the wrong way.

I'm about to turn back when I hear the gentle burble of running water. I must be near a stream. At the very least, I can stop for a drink before reorienting myself.

But it's not a stream. Not exactly.

I push through a thicket and stumble into a picturesque clearing. In the center of the clearing is a cottage that looks like it was pulled straight out of that sleeping princess movie. Its white walls are covered in vines bursting with blooming roses in white, red, pink, and orange. It looks like a sunset is growing over the house. A watermill rotates lazily as it picks up water from a crystalline spring.

I suddenly understand why every heroine lost in the woods recklessly runs into the first building they see.

I walk through wildflowers which are sprouting throughout the clearing. The wooden door to the house has a tiny window near the top with intricate ironwork latticing in front of it. There's a black door knocker in the shape of two fish with their tails tangled together. I use it to knock on the door.

The door flies open immediately. In the door frame is not the old crone I expected to find, but an elegant woman. Her age is difficult to pin down, but she's definitely older than me. Her white hair cascades down to her feet. Her skin, webbed with faint fine lines, still looks velvety. Her eyes are unsettling. Her retinas have the same color and shine as a silver coin.

"Why are you here?" The words sound more like a snarl than speech. Her black robes are simple yet elegant. I'd even say fashionable, cut to flatter her willowy figure.

"I need your help. You're Azealia, right?" My voice carries a confidence I sure as hell don't actually feel.

She laughs and moves to slam the door in my face, but I catch it.

"Are you Azealia?" I ask in a more demanding tone.

"How dare you?" Air swirls around her, carrying with it pieces of grass and flower petals. Her eyes shine brighter. I realize now that she has so much magic swirling inside her that it shines out of her eyes. "Who's asking?"

"You need to listen to me," I beg her. "I'm being hunted by the Elders of my coven. They want to steal my magic."

"Witches have wanted to steal mine too. I managed without anyone's help. You'll do fine."

"I can't wield my magic. I don't know how. Please, I need you to teach me how to master it. If you don't, I'll be dead before dawn."

"You're being dramatic." She sighs.

"Azealia."

The sound of her own name makes her pause.

"How do you know my name?"

"Everyone knows your name." I give her a deferential nod. "You're the most iconic witch of our generation. Everyone tells stories about how powerful you are."

"Don't they have anything better to do?"

"Besides drink, dance, and fuck? No, not really." I chuckle.

Azealia's face hardens. She clearly doesn't appreciate my attempt at humor.

"I realize that you came all the way out here to be left alone, but I wouldn't have disturbed you unless it was urgent. My entire coven has betrayed me. I can't go home. I can't even set foot in my town. Greedy Elders, a pack of bear shifters, and a revenge-obsessed witch are after me. And who knows how many others are after me?"

"Why are you so special?" Azealia lifts a pale brow.

"I'm not," I say. "I can't even do magic right. I got really angry at my twenty-first birthday party a few days ago. I accidentally launched a fireball the size of a meteor at my best friend."

"Did you kill her?"

"No. I redirected it at the last moment. Instead, I ended up binding her to a tree trunk." I wince at the memory. No doubt Arianna hates me now. I can go ahead and consider that bridge burned. No pun intended.

"Interesting." Azealia sizes me up.

"I've put people I love at risk. They've gone out of their way to save me. If I don't figure out how to control my magic, I won't be the only one who dies. If you won't do it to help me, do it to save the lives of innocents that just want to do the right thing. There are people I love, people I'm trying to protect, and I can't do it without your help. There's been enough injustice in the world, don't you think?"

It's a cheap shot, and I know it, but my words strike a chord with Azealia. No doubt she's remembering the injustices she was subjected to.

"Who do you love?" She narrows her eyes.

"I love... three shifters." I'm shocked as I say it, but it's true. It's not a lie. I just realized that I love them—all three of them. I've loved them for years, but this is the first time I've admitting it to anyone, including myself.

"Shifters?" Her eyes widen.

"Three bear shifters turned their backs on their clan to protect me," I say. "They don't deserve to be punished for their goodness. They've done everything to protect me. Please help me protect them in return."

"Are you certain they are as good as you say?" Azealia's upper lip curls back slightly.

"I am. The love we have is magical. If I could figure out how to harness that love, it could be even stronger than yours." I hope she doesn't take that as an insult. I don't mean it that way at all, but it's the truth. The key to unlocking my power is by finding a way to harness my love.

Azealia goes silent as she ponders my request. I want to squirm under her heavy gaze, but I will myself to hold still.

"All right."

"Really?" My breath catches in my chest. The burdens I've been carrying for the last few days lighten a little.

"Come back tomorrow," Azealia says.

"Thank you so much! You won't regret it. I'll listen to everything you say and—"

Azealia shuts the door in my face. I don't care. I practically run down the path because I can't wait to tell the guys. This is exactly what we need if we're ever going to stop the people who are trying to capture my magic. For the first time since this started, I have hope. Real, genuine hope, and I can't wait to share it with my guys.

CAPTIVE OF THE BEAR CLAN: CHAPTER 15

MINERVA

Azealia's been kicking my ass every morning from sunrise till noon for the last three weeks. I thought she'd start me off easy at first, but nope. On my very first day with her, she asked me to levitate *all* of the water out of the pond next to her cottage. Naturally, I couldn't do it. I conjured the spell over and over until my magic stores were depleted. Only then did she let me rest. Once I was energized enough, she'd make me do it all over again. This went on for three days before I finally made the surface of the water ripple.

Of course, that wasn't enough to satisfy Azealia, but that didn't stop me from being proud of myself. That was the first time I conjured magic with any semblance of purposeful control. It was a big freaking deal. That night at the cabin, all four of us had a celebratory dinner. I felt a little stupid at first, but the guys were so sweet and supportive. Honestly, they were all so wonderful.

After dinner that night, Kaval had his own surprise for me. We returned to our special boulder and, as a reward for doing so well with my magic, he licked my pussy for over an hour until I could barely see straight. He had to carry me back to my room. He didn't even ask for anything in return. Pity. If he'd asked, I would've accommodated him.

Now, Azealia had me working on conjuring controlled magical orbs. I never levitated all of the water, but Azealia admitted that she never intended for me to. It was simply an exercise to get me used to expelling large quantities of magic and build up my stamina.

Not going to lie, I'm still kind of pissed about that. I've never said that to her face, of course. No matter how sore I am or how grumpy I am at the end of a lesson, I always thank her. She's giving me my life back. My profuse thanks seems to have little effect on her, but that doesn't stop me. Sooner or later, I'm going to win her over.

As I left her clearing after a grueling lesson with fire-balls—my hair still smells burnt—I walk through the forest and back to the boundaries of the magical barrier. As always, Kaval, Stone, and Draven wait for me on the other side.

Getting through the magical barrier became easy for me after the first week of lessons. Parting the barrier is one thing I can do effortlessly now, and I'm damn proud of it. When I pass through, all three guys are looking at me with approving smiles, but something about Draven catches my eye today. I'm not sure what it is, exactly, but I'm into it.

Living in the cabin for the last three weeks has allowed me to become much closer to all three shifters. I'm much closer to Kaval, for obvious reasons. Now, I feel like I'm ready to push my relationship with Draven forward. I intended on getting close with him sooner, but Azealia's magic lessons take up so much energy.

The four of us walk back through the forest to the

cabin, chatting companionably amongst ourselves. I skill-fully isolate Draven and speak to him in a quiet voice.

"You know, you and I haven't spent that much time together one on one," I say. "I think we should hang out this afternoon. What do you say?"

"Actually, I do have a place in mind that I've been wanting to show you. I think you'll like it. Especially since you've been working your ass off with Azealia."

"Sounds good." I grin.

When we get back to the cabin, I take a quick shower. I always work up a sweat during Azealia's lessons. Before my hair is even dry, Draven and I are out the door to his mystery location.

Kaval and Stone are washing and drying dishes. Kaval catches my eye as I leave. He gives me a knowing look. Stone just smiles and waves. Hopefully, if I can make progress in my relationship with Draven today, it'll be Stone's turn soon. I don't want to rush any of the relationships, but I'm getting impatient and greedy. I want all of them. Each of these men are so wonderful, they all deserve special attention, but today, I'm going to focus on Draven.

A knot of anxiety twists in my stomach. What if he's not interested in me? What if he is, but doesn't want to share me with Kaval and eventually Stone? I know I'm asking a lot, but my fear of rejection is just as prominent as it would be in a monogamous relationship.

Even though I already have Kaval, trying to make progress with Draven is like courting an entirely new suitor. I'm comfortable with Kaval. I know he's mine for life. However, that doesn't lessen the new-relationship butterflies coming to life in my stomach. Draven might not be so easily convinced that a four-way relationship could work.

I'm nervous. If this doesn't go the way I want it to, then I will have really fucked up the house dynamic. This has to go right.

I don't know where Draven is taking me, but the one thing I don't expect is for him to lead me to the garden behind the house.

"Hate to break it to you, Draven, but I've seen the garden before." I chuckle.

"I know." He smirks. "That's not what I wanted to show you. Though, while we're here, look how nice the herbs are doing."

He gestures toward the neat rows of herbs we planted not long after we realized we'd be staying at the cabin for a while. Each herb and flower have been specially selected based on either their magical properties or their culinary usefulness. Thankfully, most herbs do both.

"Wow." My eyes go wide as I realize how lush the garden has become. "I didn't think herbs grew so fast."

I've never been much of a gardener. When I needed to purchase herbs for spells, I went to a local store and bought them pre-dried. Though, if I'm being honest, I've only done that maybe twice. My botany-based spells have been crappy most of my life, just like my conjuring skills.

"They don't usually grow this quickly." He smiles mischievously.

"What's your secret then, Mr. Gardener?"

"This." He gestures to a plant in the back corner of the garden that I've never noticed before.

The plant isn't distinct in any way. It's short and green, like every other plant in the garden. However, from the center of the plant sprouts a thick green stalk that rises about two feet into the air. At the end of the stalk is a massive white flower that almost looks like it's glowing. The bloom is the size of my head.

"What is that? I've never seen such a pretty flower."

"It's called a Green Thumb," he says. "It has magical properties. This plant boosts the growth of all plants around it within a certain radius. I've had the seed for a while. I've been waiting for a good reason to plant it. Our herb garden in exile seemed like a good place."

I've literally never heard of this plant before. I feel like it's something every decent witch with a garden should know. Then again, this is the first time I've ever had a garden.

"That's really cool," I say. "Everyone should have one of these in their garden."

"Want to know the sad part?"

"The plant has a sad part?"

Draven takes out a pair of clippers from his back pocket.

"The flower stops the plant from affecting its neighboring plants. Once the flower blooms, it sucks the life out of the plants bolstered by the Green Thumb."

"That's a shame." I frown.

"Not really," Draven says as he clips the flower. "The Green Thumb is a very clever plant. It gives a small amount of energy to the nearby plants. Once the plants grow, the Green Thumb has a ton of lifeforce to harvest to grow its own flower."

"Are you telling me this plant is gardening other plants?"

"That's exactly what I'm telling you." Draven chuckles. "I'm taking advantage of the Green Thumbs natural cycle, and to do that, I need to take it's only bloom."

"You're making it sound so evil," I tease.

"It's not my fault the bloom is too beautiful to resist." He holds the huge bloom up to my face. Silky petals stroke my cheek. For the moment, I'm speechless.

That's one of my favorite things about Draven. He's so open and honest about what he feels that he can say the cheesiest thing and still make it sound sincere and totally swoon-worthy.

He takes the flower and tucks it into the small side pouch he carries. For a short while, we clip herbs together in comfortable silence.

"I have a confession to make," he says.

"What?" I furrow my brow.

"I left the cabin last night."

"What?"

"I went to see Flint. I thought that if I sat down with him and talked to him one on one, he'd leave you alone. Flint refused to see reason. In fact, the only reason why he didn't send his clan after me was because I came in a respectful manner."

"I can't believe you did that," I say in awe.

"I know. It was stupid of me. I made sure I wasn't followed, I swear. I'm still sorry for risking it." He looks distressed.

I take one of his massive hands in both of mine.

"Don't apologize for trying to solve this mess peacefully. What you did took so much bravery. I'm proud of you. Of course, it was also incredibly dangerous. I almost wish you hadn't gone."

"I had to. I wanted to do my part to keep you out of safe. Unfortunately, I failed."

"No, you didn't. You're one of the reasons why I'm alive right now. Don't be angry with yourself that you couldn't solve a centuries-old conflict with a few words at a table."

"Then what am I supposed to do?"

"Help me gain control over my powers. Once I have that, I'll be safe for the rest of my life." I give his hand a squeeze.

"You'll never be in danger long as I'm around."

The air hums with the palpable energy drifting between us. When our eyes lock, my belly drops. Before I can stop myself, I close the short distance between us and kiss him. Something between us snaps and catches fire.

His hands are in my hair instantly, holding my lips against his. I open my mouth for his probing tongue. My hands wind themselves around his shoulders. I take hold of his shirt, twisting the fabric.

When his lips leave mine, I almost cry out in protest. Instead, I let him trail fiery kisses down my neck.

"I want you," I murmur in his ear.

That's all he needs to hear.

He grabs me by the waist and pulls me against him. As he works me out of my shirt, he guides me toward the ground. We kneel in front of each other. Right now, he's the only thing that exists in my world. I don't even care that I'm bare-breasted in the garden just beyond the kitchen window. The other guys might catch us, but I hope they're still cleaning up the kitchen like they were when we left earlier.

I lift Draven's shirt off his body and take a moment to marvel at the solid lines of muscle in his chest. He's not as large as Kaval, but he's still a big guy. I lightly trace a finger from his chest, over his abs, and down to the button of his jeans. The outline of his hard cock is pure temptation.

I undo his jeans and push them down. Draven finishes taking them all the way off before pulling my pants off. He takes extra care sliding off my panties. Every gentle touch of his fingers against my skin just deepens my desire for him. How can someone so big and strong, someone capable of killing someone if he's provoked, be so gentle?

He pulls me to him. His cock slides between my thighs and brushes against my slit.

"I've wanted you like this for so long. I can't even remember a time I didn't ache for you," he whispers before gently nipping my lobe. "I'm yours. Use me."

Use me? Damn, that's hot.

After that little speech, he doesn't need to do anything else to get me ready. I'm slick with wet heat and shivering with desire. I gently push against his chest. He takes my cue and lays on his back in the rich garden soil. I straddle him. I slowly lower myself so that just the head of his cock is touching my pussy. I rock back and forth, teasing him. He lets out a shuddering moan. Feral need sparks like fire in his eyes. I can see how much he wants to be inside me, but I know he'll wait.

Slowly, so painfully slowly, I lower myself onto his stiff cock. I let out a long moan as I adjust to the size of him. I already knew he was well endowed, but having him inside me pushes me toward a whole new level of pleasure. He's stretching me, filling me so completely that I'm ready to lose my mind.

As I ride him, Draven moves his hands over my body as if he's trying to memorize every detail. The blatant adoration of his gaze only adds to my arousal.

"You're not a witch," he says with a smile.

"Oh?" I bend forward so that my hair brushes against his chest. "What am I?"

"A goddess," he murmurs.

He thrusts up into me. I lower myself down onto him, taking his cock deep inside me. This is so different than the fast and wild sex I share with Kaval. With Draven, he's slow and deliberate. He allows every inch of my body to fully awaken to pleasure. I'm taking everything I can get from him, and he just wants to give me more.

He admires my body as I ride his cock. His hands

travel up to my breasts where his thumbs caress my nipples. I let out a gentle sigh and tip my head back.

When Draven puts his hands on my back and pulls me down, I go with him. He lifts his head from the earth so that he can take one of my nipples in his mouth. He strokes the sensitive nub with his tongue so slowly that it's complete torture.

I adore every moment of being with him. I bask in the sensations of his gentle lovemaking until energy coils around my core. With my hips, I coax him to go faster, to drive harder. He flips me onto my back and buries his cock to the hilt.

He grabs my wrists and pins them to the ground over my head. I'm surprised and incredibly into this sudden change in temperament. I never knew he could be so dominant. I love seeing this side of him.

I lift my legs and drape them over his shoulders so he can fuck me deep. Twitches of pleasure spark along my clit. The length of his cock brushes against my sensitive nub while he fucks me. Within seconds, my body clenches and my limbs begin to tremble.

My eyes roll back as I'm hit with wave after wave of orgasmic pleasure. I'm sent tumbling over the edge when I feel his swell inside me. He comes with a mighty roar, still thrusting until every last drop of his seed fills my womb.

Thank Goddess I know which herbs to use for birth control because all of this sex wouldn't be possible without it. Shifters don't get any diseases, so I have nothing to worry about there, but a baby would be a huge problem right now. I definitely want kids, but now is not the right time.

When we're both finished, he rolls over and pulls me against his chest. We lay in the dirt in a spent, sweaty tangle of limbs. The sun warms my skin and makes me drowsy. Draven strokes my hair. I'm so relaxed I could fall asleep in his arms.

"I know I'm not the only one you're interested in," he says nonchalantly.

My eyes fly open in surprise. I try to lift my head, but he keeps me in his arms.

"It's okay," he says. "It doesn't bother me."

"Really?" I blink in surprise.

"Really. I briefly lived in a higher consciousness colony where no one wore any clothes. Everyone slept with whoever they felt desire toward. They considered it a totally holistic way of living. I ultimately left the colony because the people were too out there. It was like they weren't living in a normal reality. It got too woo-woo for me, but I'm not a stranger to the idea of sharing a lover. Besides, you're special enough that if the only way for me to have you is to share you, then that's completely fine with me."

"That's amazing. You're amazing. Why didn't you tell me this a long time ago?" I ask.

"I never thought this could happen between us."

"Why not?"

"Because you're beautiful and perfect. You could have any man in the world. Why would you want me?" He blushes.

"Because of who you are, Draven."

It's on the tip of my tongue to tell him I love him, but I wait. I still don't feel free enough to love my guys the way they deserve to be loved. As soon as I can prove to the others that I can defend myself, we'll be free to let our guard down and truly love each other. Until then, I have to be content with our current arrangement.

I kiss him softly. A huge weight has been lifted off my chest. I'm so lucky. Two wonderful men have agreed to share me, but what about the third? Will Stone be on board too? I need to know, and there's only one way to find out.

CAPTIVE OF THE BEAR CLAN: CHAPTER 16

STONE

Ever since Minerva kissed me, I've been in a non-stop flurry of inspiration. It's like I've had ten espressos, shot-gunned three energy drinks, and then did a line of coke. Not that I'd know from experience. Cocaine and bears? Are you kidding me? That's a terrible idea. It's up there in the top ten worst ideas in existence. A shifter on cocaine is a terrifying notion. We're already like bears on steroids that never miss leg day.

No, shifters and drugs do *not* mix.

I've been going to the studio at night to work. The marble I used to carve my masterpiece is the only marble I brought out here. Lucky for me, the forest has an endless supply of wood. As an added bonus, I don't need extra tools. My claws work just fine.

I've made nine wooden figures so far, ranging from about two feet tall to taller than me. Bears are the easiest thing for me to do, obviously. Bears carvings are also my best sellers.

Some of my woodwork is on display inside of the clubhouse. I wonder if Flint destroyed them now that he thinks I'm a traitor. That would be a shame. But I guess it doesn't really matter. I don't care about any of my sculptures as much as I care about the one sitting in my studio. The one of Minerva. She asked me to hold onto it until the impending magical battle is over. I'd protect this sculpture with my life, it means that much to me.

When I'm not working, I keep it covered with a sheet to preserve its pristineness. Every morning before I start sculpting, I take the sheet off. I stand there, staring at it, soaking up the inspiration that almost physically radiates from the sculpture.

More than once, I've wondered if it has magical properties because the subject is a witch. Did I manage to accidentally capture some of her magic? I hope not. I wouldn't want to take anything from her. I only want to give.

I don't possess any magic. However, I've heard that in rare circumstances, an ordinary person, or a shifter in my case, can feel something so deeply and so strongly that it generates magic.

Of course, I have no proof that it's ever actually happened. It could be a rumor for all I know. Most likely, the idea stems from stories told by humans to make them feel less ordinary. It's probably just another myth.

I carefully use a claw to shave off a sliver of wood from my current project. This one is also a depiction of Minerva. It won't be as precise as the marble one, but I decided to do it in case my sculptures really do contain magic. I'm carving a wooden rendition of Minerva completely mastering her magic. She's been progressing so well lately. I feel that this is fitting. And who knows, maybe it will help her.

It's a long way from complete, but I've been working on it every day.

I wipe stinging sweat from my eyes and turn back to

the carving. If anyone asks, I tell them I'm going to the shed to escape the heat. It's not a total lie. Every time I look at Minerva's marble twin, tingling warmth fills my body. It's a fraction of the fire I felt when I kissed her, but it's enough to make my furry butt hot.

Apparently, I'm just a soulful artist infatuated with his muse. I turn back to the marble sculpture. I reach up and touch Minerva's perfectly rendered face. Her pouting lips and seductive smile send my bear into a frenzy.

What was I thinking, making this sculpture so sensual? And why the hell is a slab of marble turning me on like this?

I think it's time to go back inside. A cold shower might be the only way to stop my burning desire for her from working its way toward my cock.

As I traverse the short distance between the studio and the cabin, I hear Kaval and Draven's voices. They're getting louder by the second. I inch closer to listen in. They never fight like this, so I'm curious to find out what's going on.

"I still don't know what to make of it, but I'm sure as hell not going to complain," Kaval says.

I assume he's talking about our sudden exile.

"Neither am I. If Minerva wants us both, I'm happy to oblige," Draven says.

Wait, what? What the hell are they talking about? Wants them both to do what?

"I guess if we're both fine with sharing, we should set ground rules," Kaval says.

"I've already given that some thought. I'm willing to go along with whatever Minerva wants. Even if she wants both of us at the same time," Draven says.

"I never even thought of that," Kaval says.

"We'll cross that bridge when we get to it," Draven says.

"No use worrying until it's happening, I guess," Kaval says.

"Exactly."

Now I'm really confused. What's going on? What would she want both of them to do at the same time?

"What about swapping stories?" Kaval asks. "What if you do something she likes that I don't do? Or vice versa."

"I think she wants both of us because of our differences. It would be disappointing if we both did the same things to her," Draven says.

What things?

Seriously, what the fuck are they talking about? They're not... They couldn't possibly be talking about... Are they both *fucking* her?

What. The. Fuck.

No, that can't be right. I must be hearing this out of context. But what else could it be?

"She's got the most divine pussy, hasn't she?" Kaval's voice is low and rumbling.

Holy shit, they are.

My heart sinks. I thought she wanted me, but she's already with them. I'm too late.

"I think about it every waking moment. Actually, I dream about it too. So, I'm always thinking about it," Draven chuckles.

Well, I guess that fucking settles that. I'm pissed. It doesn't bother me that Minerva is fucking both of them. What bothers me is that she hasn't asked me to join them.

When we kissed, I felt a spark. I thought she did too. I've been waiting to bring it up, but I never found the right time.

Maybe she was going to talk to me about it but that

crazy sculpture I made scared her off. Maybe she thinks I'm too obsessed with her. I mean, I am, but who wouldn't be?

I should just talk to her. That'll clear everything up. But how do I approach the subject without sounding like a massive douchebag? I can't just say 'hey, I heard you're fucking the other guys. Do you want to fuck me too?'

I have to get her alone first. I can't bring this up in front of the other guys. It would be awkward and weird.

I try to act normal as I stroll into the kitchen. The scent of meatballs, pasta, and marinara makes my stomach growl. It's not my bear's jealousy; I'm simply hungry.

"Hey, Stone." Draven nods cordially.

I jerk my chin in response.

"Are we having spaghetti?" I ask.

"I made veggie balls for myself." Draven grins. "Want to try one?"

"Absolutely not." I snort. "I'll stick to the traditional ones. Where's Minerva?"

"She wore herself out practicing magic all afternoon. She's asleep now," Kaval says. "I'm going to wake her in a bit. She needs to rest so we decided to get everything ready for dinner."

"Right." I nod. "She's lucky to have us at her beck and call."

Normally, I'm not that snappy. Fine, maybe I *am* wildly jealous.

"It's the least we can do." Draven shrugs.

I'm not sure if he misses the sarcasm in my tone or if he's choosing to ignore it. Knowing him, it's likely the former. I take a breath and reel in my jealousy. There's no point in making my friends my enemies. After all, they did nothing wrong. If Minerva wants them, then who am I to stop her? I just wish I could talk to her right now. I hate having to wait.

Several minutes later, she pads out of her room. Her hair's a mess, and she has sleep in her eyes. She's gorgeous. I almost melt into a puddle on the floor.

I wonder if she'll go to one of the other guys. I don't know how I'll keep myself together if she sits in one of their laps or plays with their hair. I don't want any visual reminders that I've been left out of their threesome.

She sits next to me at the dinner table.

"Hey, Stone. How's it going in the shed? You've been in there a lot recently."

"It's fine." I grit my teeth. If she knew I was carving another image of her, what would she think? Would she be flattered or run from me?

Conversation flows throughout dinner, but I hardly hear anything that's being said. I'm barely aware of what I'm eating. All I can think about is what I should say to Minerva. I'm so fixated on trying to come up with a way to approach her that I don't realize I'm the only one left at the table.

"You done, dude?" Draven asks.

Everyone else has already gotten up. Kaval's washing dishes, while Minerva's packing up left overs.

"You hardly ate," Minerva says. "Are you feeling okay?"

"I'm fine."

"Want me to pack it up for later?" she points at my plate.

"I'll wrap it up."

"Maybe you should've had the veggie balls instead," Draven teases.

I cough out a laugh as I rise from the table. I wait for Minerva to finish what she's doing before approaching her.

"Do you want to see the wood sculpture I'm working on?" I ask. That isn't what I planned to say, but it doesn't matter. I just need to get her away from the other guys.

Minerva smiles and nods eagerly. She grabs my hands and practically drags me out of the kitchen. Thankfully, none of the guys move to follow us.

Once we're in the shed, I show her my recently finished projects. I avoid showing her the wood carving of her. I still don't know what say to her. I want her to know I'm interested, but I don't want to sound desperate or, god forbid, whiny. It's a delicate balance that I could easily fuck up. I'm an artist, damn it. I'm better with my hands than I am with my words.

"Can I see the marble one again?" Minerva asks. "I just love it so much."

Despite my jealousy, her words warm my heart.

"Of course," I smile.

I pull the sheet off the sculpture. She gazes at it with doe-like eyes as she walks over to it. She briefly runs her hands over her marble arms before moving on to examine the bear. I watch her silently.

I must have an intense expression on my face because when she looks up, she frowns.

"Are you okay? You look like you have something on your mind."

This is as good a moment as any. I should tell her exactly how I feel, but I can't get my mouth to move. I stand there like an idiot instead.

She turns her attention back to the marble bear. She gazes at it softly, I'd even say lovingly. As she runs her hand over the textured fur, I wonder who she's imagining —Kaval or Draven.

I swallow back the bitterness that rises in me and force myself to speak.

"I heard Kaval and Draven talking earlier," I say. "They were talking about you. Fucking you, specifically."

Okay, that came out in the worst possible way.

Thankfully, Minerva doesn't look offended. Instead, she gives me a smile that's somewhere between sad and pleading.

"Would you believe me if I told you I planned on talking to you about that tonight?"

It sounds too good to be true, but I know Minerva. She's not lying.

"What were you going to say?" I ask.

"That I think you're amazing and incredibly talented..." she says slowly. That's the beginning of a rejection if I've ever heard one. "And I want you."

Wait, what now?

She wants me? *Me?*

My breath hitches. My cock swells in response to the look in her eyes. I can't believe what I'm hearing, so again, I'm mute.

Minerva must assume that I still need convincing, so she keeps talking.

"The way you see the world is incredible. I could listen to you talk about light, shape, and color forever. The way you describe seeing a sculpture in a blank slab of marble is like some kind of superpower. Don't even get me started on the art itself." She gestures toward the sculpture. "I mean, look at this. It's perfect."

"Thank you." I'm still too shocked to say anything else. I can't believe she really feels this way.

"I want you, Stone. Being with you satisfies me in a way the others can't," she says. "Each of you brings new meaning into my life. I've talked with them about it. They've both agreed to share me, but I want you too. If that's something you're willing to consider, I'd be honored.

If that's not your style, I completely understand. It won't change how close we are. I swear."

I can see now that she's nervous. Maybe even more nervous than I am. She opens her mouth to say something else, but I raise a hand to stop her.

"I'm in."

"Really?" Her eyes widen.

"Really."

"In that case..." The hopeful glimmer in her eyes suddenly shifts to something hungry and mischievous.

She slips out of the loose shorts she wore to sleep in earlier. They fall to her feet. She steps out of them and kicks them away. My eyes sweep up from her delicate ankles, along the length of her graceful legs, straight toward the vee between her thighs. She's not wearing anything under her shorts.

My cock is rock hard and throbbing.

She turns around and steps onto the marble base of the sculpture. The sculpture has it's back to us. She bends over the marble rump of the bear and spreads her legs, exposing her glistening slit. She glances over her shoulder.

"Take me, Stone. Make me yours."

"Minerva..." My cock's in my fist. I slowly stroke it.

"I feel so terrible for making you think I don't want you too." She gives me the sexiest pout. "To make up for it, I'll let you do whatever you want to me."

"Whatever I want?"

"Anything," she whispers seductively.

I want to rush forward and push until her until my balls are smashed against her clit, but I don't. I take my time, admiring every part of her. Perhaps, I'll sculpt her in this position one day. I'd keep the sculpture for myself, of course. Maybe Minerva will even pose for me.

The marble base puts her at just the right height for me to fuck her, but I'm not ready just yet. Her limbs quiver in anticipation. I drop to my knees and push her thighs further apart.

I lick a slow circle around her pussy. She jolts and releases a soft whimper. Her thighs tremble as I tease and torment her with my tongue until her knees buckle.

With one arm wrapped around her waist, I hold her in place over the marble bear. I slide a finger into her sopping wet pussy. She's more than ready for me.

I grab her hips and bury my cock all the way to the base. She groans and grips the bear with white-knuckled fingers. A shuddering moan bursts from my lips. Her wet walls cling to every inch of me as I thrust in and out of her. She doesn't hold back and spreads even wider for me. She doesn't hold back her cries of pleasure.

"That's right, sexy little witch. Let them know what I'm doing to you," I whisper in her ear.

It's naughty and dirty and erotic. It's more than I could ever dream of. She's mine too, and I want the others to know it.

The very notion that they might be listening to us makes me harder. In response, she clenches tighter around me. When she tosses her head back, I grab a fistful of her hair. My grasp is firm, but I have no intention of causing her pain. She lifts her upper body off of the marble bear.

She's small enough so that I can see over her shoulder. She's playing with her nipples as I fuck her. I pull out long enough to grab my cock and rub it directly against her clit. Her honey coats my cock. I slam back into her and pump faster and deeper. I want her to make her come harder than she's ever come with anyone else.

"Oh, fuck," she whimpers while pinching her stiff

nipples. I release her hair and wrap one arm around her waist to hold her steady. My other hand reaches around to stroke her sensitive pearl.

Her body begins to tremble as her orgasm builds. I release her, allowing her to bend over the marble bear. This time, I bend with her. I completely overpower her body. I dominate her, pin her in place, and make sure that every stroke hits her in just the right spot.

Her legs tremble. Her breathing comes in little huffs. The ache inside me builds. I'm desperate for my own release, but I hold myself back. She needs to come first.

With a strangled cry, she clenches around me. Vibrations of pleasure ripple across my cock as she comes. I bury myself deep inside and come harder than I ever have before. My toes literally curl, and I fight to maintain my balance.

When our ecstasy subsides, neither of us can move. She rests her cheek on the cool marble, her eyelids fluttering. I ease off of her so she can breathe. I stroke damp strands of hair away from her face.

"Is that how you expected an artist to fuck?" My voice is husky and deep.

"So much better." She sighs dreamily.

"Good."

I slide out of her, but still hold her tightly.

"You're my muse, Minerva," I whisper as I gently help her to stand upright.

Her legs are still wobbling, so I hold her against my chest. Our hearts pound in perfect harmony. I've waited a long time to be with her, and now I'll never have to wait again.

CAPTIVE OF THE BEAR CLAN:
CHAPTER 17

MINERVA

I'm sitting in the grass outside of Azealia's cottage. I'm supposed to be meditating, but I can't focus. My life has been full of surprises lately. I don't even know where to begin. I still can't believe that all three guys have agreed to a relationship with me. I'm officially the luckiest woman in the world.

Despite all of the shit I've been through this month, I've never been happier. How weird is that? I'm almost grateful that I went completely psycho at my party. Because of that, I've finally forged a relationship with Kaval, Draven, and Stone.

Next time I see Arianna, I'll be sure to thank her for trying to seduce Kaval. That'll totally piss her off. She deserves it after the crap she pulled at my party. To think, I used to consider her a friend. Why didn't I see her for who she really was? I guess I was blind.

In a weird way, I have Rebecca to thank too. If the bear shifters didn't have her on their side, they never would have kidnapped me.

I'm sorry Rebecca was bullied by other witches, maybe

I should have tried to stop them, but I didn't want to get in their crosshairs. Besides, I don't think Rebecca would've turned out any different. That level of twisted is something you're born with; it's not something you learn.

I shake off any trace of guilt. Rebecca's not my problem anymore. It's going to take more than one witch to set her straight. I can't save everyone. I can only save myself... and the guys.

My thoughts drift into a more positive space as memories from the past few days come rushing back. I really hope Azealia can't read my mind because it's dirty as hell these days. I can't help it. Now that all three of the guys have agreed to be in a relationship with me, life is sweet and so, so sexy.

When one of them makes love to me, I don't even think about all the other bullshit going on in my life. Which is exactly why I make sure I'm getting stuffed by one of them as often as possible.

The only other thing I've been doing is attending my lessons with Azealia. When I'm not here in the clearing outside of her cottage or practicing at home with my shifter lovers, I'm either bent over, on my back, or straddling someone. It's a damn good life.

"Stop thinking about sex and focus," Azealia says.

I jump. Dammit. She *can* read my thoughts.

"Always could," she chuckles. "Why do you think I agreed to take you on?"

"Because you knew I'd be a good student?"

"No, because you were a lovesick puppy, and if there's one thing I can't stand, it's lovesick people."

"What happened to you?" I ask softly. "I've heard rumors..."

"Focus on your magic," she snaps, effectively ending our conversation.

Oh well, maybe one day she'll decide to talk about it.

"Don't count on it," she says.

Dammit. Stop reading my thoughts.

I will once you master your magic.

"What the hell?" I jump to my feet. "I heard you in my head."

"That will get easier in time."

"Will I be able to read other people's thoughts?"

"Maybe," she says. "We won't know how it manifests until you're more proficient with magic."

"I'm not sure that I want that skill," I say.

"Trust me, I wish I could turn if off sometimes. Like when you're thinking about Kaval. That boy is filthy."

"I know." I grin.

She tosses a small ball of lightning toward me.

I easily diffuse it with my own magic.

"You're improving at an alarming rate. Who else is helping you?" She narrows her gaze.

"The shifters I live with will help me practice."

"I see." She pauses before speaking again. "I think it's time we complete your training. Bring them here tomorrow."

"DID she say why she wants to meet us?" Kaval asks the following morning as we approach the magical barrier.

I part it with ease and let all three men pass me before I let it seal again.

"She says she wants me to complete my training."

Unlike the first time I walked this path, the birds are singing, little furry critters scuttle through the underbrush, and the sun shines down through the thick canopy. The smell of wildflowers is pungent in the air.

Now, every time I smell wildflowers, I get aroused. The sweet scent reminds me too much of the first time Draven made love to me.

I look over at him and he gives me a knowing smile. It seems that the smell gives him pleasant memories, too.

His eyes dip briefly down before returning to my gaze. He winks.

I glance down quickly. Sure enough, my hardening nipples are visible through my shirt. I steal a glance at Draven's groin and lick my lips when I see the outline of his cock. I meet his gaze once more and wink back.

Within moments, all three of them are giving me bedroom eyes. I want sex, and they can smell it on me.

With a pained laugh, I come to a halt on the path.

"Guys, we have to get it together. I really want Azealia to respect me. That's going to be much harder if I show up too turned on to concentrate."

"Fair enough." Stone chuckles. "Speaking of Azealia, are you certain her idea of completing your training doesn't involve slaughtering us? I'd feel pretty crappy if I had to kill the second most powerful witch in Bonfire Falls."

"She's the first most powerful, not the second."

"Not from where we're standing," Kaval says.

They're all looking at me with the kindest smiles. My heart melts at the sight of them.

When we reach the clearing, I give them a moment to take in the picturesque sight. I knew Stone and Draven would appreciate it, but I'm surprised to see Kaval starting at everything with an awed expression.

"What?" Kaval asks when he catches me watching him. "I can like beautiful shit too."

I stifle my laughter with one hand and offer him the

other. Together, we walk to the cottage with the other two in tow.

Azealia answers the door before I can knock. She takes a moment to examine each of the shifter males I've brought with me.

"So, you're all fucking each other?" she asks.

Behind me, Stone snorts. Draven sputters out a surprised cough. Kaval stays silent but a smirk forms on his lips.

Too taken aback by the straightforwardness of the question, I hesitate before I answer her.

"I mean, we all have sex, but the guys aren't in to each other."

"No dicks touch," Kaval confirms.

All three men share a chuckle at my expense.

"Oh." Azealia lifts her brows in surprise. "Very well then. Let's get to work."

"What are we doing today?" I'm happy to change the subject.

"We're going to mimic what it'll be like to face a manic witch and her shifting henchmen," Azealia says. I now understand why she wanted me to bring the guys.

Azealia instructs them to shift and then attack me. They're hesitant at first, but I assure them that it'll be helpful.

Once they're shifted, Azealia starts launching spells at me in rapid fire. I dodge and deflect while keeping Kaval, Stone, and Draven at bay. I use aura shields, windshields, and even fire shields to protect myself while shooting off concentrated balls of lightning, fire, and ice. I still have a little trouble conjuring a ball of pure, invisible energy but I can manage.

When I'm out of breath and ready to collapse, Azealia stops.

"Congratulations." She's not even winded. She's been sitting around in her cottage for years, yet she can outpace me. Damn, that's impressive. "If Rebecca and Flint ever catch up to you, you can handle them."

"Why wait for them to find me?" I ask when I catch my breath.

"Why indeed?" Azealia smiles.

I turn to the guys, who have shifted back into their human forms. Luckily, I told them to bring a change of clothing beforehand, so Azealia wouldn't have the pleasure of seeing them naked. They may be willing to share, but I'm not.

They quickly dress and join me and Azealia.

"Are you suggesting what I think you are?" Stone asks.

"Yes," I say. "I have the chance to end this, so why don't I? Let's start with Rebecca and give her fight she's looking for. I know I can defeat her."

"She's an unrefined witch who acts on her rage," Azealia says. "Her magic is undisciplined. I'm confident you can out-magic her."

I beam under Azealia's praise before turning back to the guys.

"What do you say?" I ask.

"If you'd asked me three hours ago, I would've said *hell no*," Kaval says. "But now that I've seen what you can do against actual magic, I think Rebecca won't know what hit her. However, I don't like the idea of you facing off with her without backup."

"I'm in, but only if you let us come with you," Draven says.

"I agree," Stone says.

I hesitate. This is my fight. I shouldn't put them at risk in order to solve my problems.

If anything happened to any one of them, I'd never

forgive myself. I'd buy land right next to Azealia, build my own little cottage, and live out the rest of my life in angry, miserable solitude.

"I'm not angry and miserable," Azealia grumbles.

"Sorry," I whisper.

The guys give us confused looks, but we don't bother to explain the mindreading stuff. I'm still working on it anyway.

"You guys can't come with me," I say to Stone.

"I don't know why you're refusing to let us go. It's not like you can get back to the clubhouse on your own," Stone says.

I open my mouth to argue, but I realize he's right. I have no idea where the clubhouse is from here.

Kaval laughs. He's clearly satisfied that I don't have options.

"There's no way around it. We're coming with you," Draven says.

"I think that's wise. You should accept help when it's offered," Azealia says.

"See? The old witch is on our side," Kaval says. "No offense," he adds when he notices Azealia's withering glare.

"Looks like I'm outnumbered here." I sigh.

"You always have been." Stone winks.

When the men decide to return to their bear forms, I turn to thank Azealia.

"You've done so much for me. I don't know how to repay you."

"You'll find a way," she teases.

"I'll come back and visit you."

She shakes her head and waves the idea away, but I know I'll see her again. Although she'll never admit it, I think she likes having the company.

I CLIMB onto Kaval's back. He's the biggest of the three bears and therefore the most comfortable. I lay low on his back and hold onto his thick fur as he gallops through the forest. When the trees get too thick, I hide my face in his fur to protect me from slashing branches.

Draven is ahead of us. Stone follows behind. When I can lift my head, I periodically look to either side of us to make sure we aren't being flanked by other shifters.

When we reach the clubhouse, we agree that it will be far more intimidating and confusing if we come through the front door. Kaval goes first, charging in with a mighty roar. I slip in after him. Stone and Draven watch my back and sides.

Some of the shifters in the clubhouse change form before they attack us. Some don't.

I use my magic to ward off the ones in human form. Fire keeps them at bay nicely.

"Remember that you're in a wooden building," I remind them. "I'd feel *so* bad if you forced me to burn it to the ground."

The human shifters who are attacking me backed off, only to be incapacitated by Kaval.

Stone and Draven fend off other bears with ease. I'm barely breaking a sweat.

We move through the clubhouse in the direction of the room Kaval and I were held in. Surely, Rebecca will be there.

Lucky for me, I don't have to move that far. Rebecca flies through the door, a flurry of red hair and rage.

"You bitch." She looks at me, her expression crazed. Her voice exasperated. "You're ruining everything."

She tries to hit me with an energy blast, but I deflect it

back at her and knock her off her feet. Kaval moves to strike her, but I extend a hand to stop him.

"She's mine."

Kaval snorts and takes a few steps back so that he's in line with the others.

I trust them to keep the other bears off my back while I deal with Rebecca. She seems to have an endless amount of energy. Has she been practicing too?

She fires off massive spell after massive spell and keeps going long after her magic stores should've been depleted. However, what she has in raw power she lacks in control and focus. Azealia spent hours teaching me both of those things. Half of Rebecca's spells don't even hit me.

In fact, she's doing far more damage to the clubhouse than my bears and I have done.

"Give it up," I say. "You'll never beat me."

"Yes, I will." She has wide, desperate eyes. "I'm better than all of you. I'll make you all pay."

I wish she'd get tired. Maybe, if she got tired, I'd be able to talk to her. After all, she's just a teenager. No matter how many spells of hers I deflect, she keeps coming and coming.

When I look into her eyes, I don't see a person shining out. I just see hatred and insanity.

I realize what I have to do.

"Cover me," I order my three bears.

They surround me to protect me from physical harm while I construct a magic shield around all of us.

"What are you doing?" Rebecca shrieks.

Even now, she doesn't let up. She launches lightning bolts, ice picks, and spikes of pure, crackling energy at my shield, but to no avail. She only stops when she realizes I'm performing a binding spell, with her as my target.

A binding spell falls into the gray area of magic. I

wasn't stealing her magic and taking it into myself. I wasn't trying to steal her soul. No matter how insane Rebecca is, I'll never stoop that low. Instead, a binding spell removes magic from a witch and encases it into an object.

As I weave the spell, I look for something I could bind her magic too. On the floor a few yards away, I spy a pendant. It's a brown disk strung through with black leather. It must have fallen off one of the bears during the fight.

I continue weaving the spell with one hand while I levitate the pendant with the other. Rebecca sees what I'm doing and tries to snatch it, but I'm too quick. The pendant flies through the shield and into my waiting palm. I take a moment to look at it. The pendant looks like a wooden coin. On one side is a carving of one of Bonfire Fall's many scenic waterfalls. On the other side is a bear.

I smile to myself. It's very fitting.

Rebecca screams and begs until her voice is raw and scratchy. Her screams are so violent, they shake the walls and knock over furniture.

I can physically see the magic draining from her body as I finish the spell. The pendant in my hand begins to glow and burn so hot that I almost drop it.

"Please," Rebecca says. "I'm nothing without my magic. Please, don't take my magic."

"This is for your own good," I say. I really mean it.

Rebecca needs help. As long as she has her magic, she'll never get it.

She falls to her knees, weak and weeping. Her red hair doesn't look as vibrant.

Her skin is pale and waxy. The pendant stops glowing.

Rebecca's magic is gone.

I use the black leather strips to tie the pendant around

my neck. Maybe one day, I'll take Rebecca's magic for myself, but right now I'll leave it in the pendant for safe-keeping.

Maybe I'll even give it back to her one day. If she ever stops being a fucking psychopath.

I lower my magic shield.

I'm tempted to say something to Rebecca, but I know there's nothing I can say that she'll listen to. If she's going to turn her life around, she has to figure it out herself.

"Shit."

A gruff voice behind me makes me jump and spin around.

Flint!

My three bears roar.

Kaval stands up on his hind legs ready to brawl.

Flint shifts back into his human form and stalks toward us.

My bears and I bare our teeth. We're still ready to fight.

Instead, Flint surprises us by lifting his hands in surrender. I tap each of my bears to calm them down.

"Never in all of my years have I seen power like that," Flint says with awe in his voice.

"We have no problem unleashing it on you," I say.

"I know," he says. "That's why I'm not stupid enough to continue this fight. It was a fool's errand anyway. If anyone comes after you from here on out, you can be damn sure I didn't send them."

I look to Kaval, Stone, and Draven for guidance. One by one, they all nod. They believe Flint, so I do too. I trust their judgement.

"All right," I nod. "We've done what we came here to do. We'll leave now."

I turn on my heel and stride away from the wreckage I

caused. Once all four of us are outside in the crisp mountain air, I smile.

"Holy shit, I can't believe I did that," I say.

All three guys grunt in acknowledgement. Kaval positions himself so I can climb onto his back. Once I'm settled, I put his flank.

"Take me home, please." I lean forward to rest my head on Kaval's shoulders.

As the three of them dash through the woods back to our cabin, I look up at the stars shining between the treetops. For the first time since this shitshow started, I'm starting to think we can win this war.

CAPTIVE OF THE BEAR CLAN: CHAPTER 18

MINERVA

The movement of Kaval's body underneath me is more akin to a rocking horse than a rodeo horse. Surprising, considering in this shifted form he's over eight hundred pounds of pure muscle.

I use what's left of my magic to weave a spell that basically straps me to his back using ribbons of energy. I'm exhausted. My limbs are heavy and sore, but not in a bad way. If I had to guess, I'd say it's like the ache people get when they finish running marathons. I feel good. Accomplished.

The wooden pendant containing Rebecca's magic presses against my chest. It's warm. I thought it would be hard to carry it, but her magic isn't the issue. It was the way she was using it that was wrong. Magic isn't inherently good or bad. It's all about the witch's intent.

Relying on the energy straps to keep me balanced on Kaval's back, I let my eyes drift close.

I hope I can convince the guys to make me a huge dinner. They're probably hungry too. However, fighting off the bears and containing Rebecca's magical powers did more than just sap my strength. It took up most of my magic. To replenish my energy, I need to eat. I bet I could devour more than all three of the guys—combined.

I listen to the sounds of the forest rushing by and dream about eating every single thing we have in the kitchen. I want mashed potatoes the most. If I eat an entire bowl of them, is that carb loading? Should I have done that before blasting my magic muscles? I need to ask Azealia about that next time I see her. If carb loading works, then bring on the cake.

My sleepy thoughts blend from mashed potatoes to literal mountains of whatever meat Kaval can cook on a grill. Which is every meat. I'm so glad he froze all the fish he caught at the river a few weeks ago. We still had three or four whole fish left. I'm ready to eat all of them.

Do we have alcohol at the cabin? I want nothing more than to eat and drink myself into a recovery coma. Oh, what I wouldn't give for a large pizza right now.

I involuntarily let out a moan into Kaval's neck.

I know he feels it because he laughs beneath me.

"Don't judge me. I'm thinking about food," I say.

I think I mumble. Or maybe I'm just think the words. I'm too tired to tell. I'm not even aware of my body anymore. Do I have arms? Hell if I know.

I bury my face in Kaval's soft fur and allow myself to doze off.

A SICKENING CRACK WAKES ME. I don't know where we are or how long I was sleep, but I'm suddenly thrown sideways off Kaval's back. The energy restraints I conjured earlier fizzle away as I panic. His fur disappears from under me. I can't see anything, but I know I'm still moving.

No. Not moving. I'm falling.

I hit the ground hard. My back slams into a gnarled tree trunk. When I hit the ground, my head slams against the sharp side of a rock. Stars explode behind my vision. Nausea hits me like a freight train. I suck in a breath, but my lungs won't cooperate. The wind's been completely knocked out of me. I make a series of gagging, rasping noises while I try to recover.

When I am finally able to draw breath, I suck in more dirt than air. I choke on the thick soil.

A shrill female voice rings through the air. "Find her."

Shit!

The witches have found me. How did they find me?

Where's Kaval? Stone? Draven?

I want to cry out to them. Surely, they're looking for me. I open my mouth and prepare to scream with everything my damaged lungs can muster, but at the last minute, I stop myself.

What if they're hiding, waiting for the right moment to pounce on the witches and tear their throats out? I hold my scream in, but then nausea rears up inside me once more when a terrible thought occurs to me.

What if the witches have already hurt them?

No way, I tell myself. Even if those witches did get the drop on us, the three shifters still have the advantage. They might not have magic, but their brute strength is enough to stop a bullet train.

One of the witches sends up a ball of light as bright as the sun, but it's icy cold instead of hot. It illuminates the surrounding forest. I try to look for the guys, but the light hurts my eyes. I raise a hand to shield my sensitive retinas.

"There is she!" One of the witches wails.

Rapid footfalls crunch across the forest floor. I brace

myself for a punch or a kick, but what comes is so much worse.

Just like the night of my birthday party, thick roots sprout from the ground and immediately go for my ankles and wrists. I tried to keep them at bay, but my magic reserves are far too low and, on top of that, I think I have a concussion.

This time, the roots are coated in thorns. With one hand bound, I use my free hand and wildly attempt to claw at the roots. All I succeed in doing is tearing my palm to shreds. The witches dim the blinding orb of light. It's then that I notice something not right with the thorns. I can now see a thick black liquid that smells of overripe berries and decay.

Witchbane.

I instinctively recoil, even though there's nowhere for me to go.

Witchbane is the equivalent to silver for werewolves. Large doses are fatal, moderate dosages completely block all magical abilities. The thorns pierce my skin. Fire spreads through my veins with agonizing speed.

The witches didn't know I'd just come from the clubhouse. If they did, they'd know my magic was weak and they wouldn't have bothered with the Witchbane.

Or perhaps they did know and decided to use the Witchbane anyway to add to the pain. That seems more likely.

Now, there are thorny roots wrapped around both ankles and both wrists. I scream in pain as I'm hoisted off the ground. I writhe at first, but that only makes everything worse, so I stop moving completely.

Now I can see the witches that have hunted me down.

It's the same three that nearly killed me the night of my party. The red-lipped one sneers at me.

"Caught you, little mouse," she says.

"Let me go." It's the most pointless thing I can say, but I don't know what else to do.

"Oh, no, no, no," the darker one says. "Why would we do that? We've been working so hard to find you, haven't we sisters?"

"You've been quite the slippery prey," the tall willowy one says. "We felt the disturbance you caused at the club-house. I must say, your work against those filthy creatures was impressive. I thought you were a weakling that couldn't control her magic."

"It was a burst of luck." I decide the smartest thing I can do right now is play down my abilities. Maybe I can convince them that I'm not worth hunting. They already know that's not true, but I don't know what else I can do. I can't fight back. I have no idea where Kaval, Stone, and Draven are, or if they're even still alive.

The thought brings tears to my eyes. If they're dead, I don't think I could bear living. If they're dead, these witches should just kill me now.

"That's bullshit and we all know it," the red-lipped one says.

She conjures a ball of crackling energy in one hand. I know what she's going to do. I close my eyes and brace for impact. When she launches it, the faintest aura shield flickers to life around me. Instead of completely deflecting the orb, like it normally would have, it absorbs it. Some of the shock makes it into my body. My muscles go stiff, unable to handle the surge of pure electricity moving through them. My heart feels like it's in a vise grip.

"Whatever you're going to do, just do it already," I say through gritted teeth. I feel weak and hopeless. I just want them to do whatever it is they're going to do.

"No." The willowy one's smile reminds me of a feral

animal. "We want to play first. We've earned that." She nods to the red-lipped one, who approaches me slowly.

She lifts one pale hand, showing off her long, pointed nails that look like bird talons.

She draws a nail beneath my collarbone. It feels like a knife slicing my skin apart. Blood spills down my chest. It feels like I'm dying, but the Witchbane might be affecting my mind. Maybe she didn't even slice me. I don't know. Reality is blurring.

"She's fading," the red-lipped one says in an amused voice. "We have to do it now. It won't work if she's unconscious."

"That's a shame." The dark one pouts. "I wanted to cut up her pretty face."

"We can take her back to our place," the willowy one says to her sisters. "That way, we can keep her as a plaything forever."

Goddess, no.

"Excellent idea, sister," the dark one says.

The red-lipped one saunters back to stand with her sisters. They join hands, the dark one in the middle. The other two raise their free hands, drawing in power from the trees, the moon, and the stars.

When they start to chant, dread fills my soul.

They're going to take my magic, and I'm powerless to stop them.

"Kaval!" I scream with everything I have. "Stone! Draven!"

"Don't bother calling for your beasts," the dark one says. "They can't help you now."

Why? Oh, god, are they dead?

Losing my magic will destroy me, but I might be able to survive it if it the guys are still alive. Without them, there's no reason to live.

I hang from the roots like a rag doll as the witches weave their spell. Black matter, the opposite of light, reaches toward me. I can't bear to look at it. When it touches me, my body feels like it's being pierced by the fingers of Death himself. It hurts. It *burns*. And then, it feels like my very lifeforce is slipping out of me. A white light from inside me bleeds into the black.

The witches cackle in triumph.

Is this what Rebecca felt when I took her magic from her? Maybe death would be better.

I am a hollow shell when they're finished with me. I can barely hold my head up.

The red-lipped one comes at me once more. I don't see her hand move, but I feel her stinging slap against my cheek. She quickly slaps the other cheek.

She smacks me over and over, cackling as she does it. The fight is completely drained out of me. I'm just about willing to accept any fate they bestow upon me when a deafening roar cracks through the forest.

Kaval!

I can't see him, but I can feel the vibrations of his massive paws colliding with the earth through the roots that bind me. He strikes a witch. I can't see which one, but I hear her bones crack and her shriek makes my ears ring.

Two more roars.

Stone and Draven aren't far behind Kaval.

At this point, all I can see are blurry shapes swarming through my field of vision. I feel magic crackling in the air. My magic. The witches really have stolen it, and now they're using it against the men I love.

As I hang above the forest floor, I vow that one day I will take my magic back, and I will kill them.

One of the restraints around my ankles snaps. I roll my head and look down. Stone is there, carefully cutting around the poison thorns to break the roots. I don't know if Witchbane is toxic to bear shifters, but I'm glad he's not taking any chances.

He rises up on his hind legs to work through the roots around my wrists. When he frees the first one, he moves so that I can support my weight against his sloping shoulder. I grip his fur and bury my face into his bear neck. He smells like home now.

One more slash of his claw and I'm free. My weight drops.

He catches me as best as he's able to in his bear form. With some difficulty, I'm able to get onto his back.

He roars, signaling in the bear language for the other two to retreat. He takes off at a sprint. He's the fastest of my three bears. Without having to look behind me, I know that Draven follows Stone, and Kaval brings up the rear. No doubt he's taking a few last swipes at the witches before we disappear into the woods.

Naturally, the witches give chase. I can hear them screeching and swearing behind us, but they have no chance of keeping up with the bears.

I cling to Stone as he takes sharp turns through the trees. He doubles back a few times. He's trying to confuse the witches. If they can't see us, they will have to rely on scent. That won't do them much good if our scent is in every direction.

I have no idea how long we've been running. I might have lost consciousness a few times.

By the time we make it back to the cabin, I've never been so happy to be home. I remain on Stone's back as he carries me into the living room. He lines himself up with the plushest couch and crouches down so I can easily slide off.

Every bone, muscle, and joint in my body screams in

pain. I let out a noise that's meant to be a scream, but it really comes out as something guttural and broken.

My magic is gone. I cling to the tiny kernel of hope that the witches didn't take every single drop from me, that if I sleep for long enough, I'll feel it coming back.

But I know that's not true.

My magic is gone.

Wait—Rebecca's pendant!

I can harvest the magic from the pendant and use it to take my own magic back.

My hand flies to my throat. I search for the wooden pendant, but my neck is bare. The pendant must've come off when I was knocked from Kaval's back.

Even if the witches didn't get their claws on it, it will be impossible to find it in the forest.

The last bit of hope I've been holding on to slips away.

I give in to the pain and the trauma. I'm vaguely aware that Kaval, Stone, and Draven have switched back into their human form. They try to comfort me, but right now, not even they can sooth the deep sense of loss pulling at my soul.

I grab one of the couch pillows and hold it against my chest. As I cling to it, I break down crying. Sobs wrack my tender body, but the pain doesn't even matter anymore.

I just discovered how to wield my magic, and now it's gone. I'm nothing without it now. I'm not a witch anymore. I've lost everything, and not even love can save me now.

CAPTIVE OF THE BEAR CLAN: CHAPTER 19

KAVAL

Hearing Minerva cry like that is the worst thing I've ever experienced. I'd rather suffer a hundred deaths than hear Minerva cry.

Draven sits on the floor next to the couch, murmuring soft things to her. I'm glad he's taking the lead right now. He and Stone are much better with their words than I am. Right now, she needs a shoulder to cry on, and Draven's good at that stuff. He's much better than I would be. I just don't have the right words.

Besides, I'm too fucking pissed to be a calming influence on anyone.

"You're shaking the chandelier with each stomp," Stone tells me.

I look up at the antler chandelier. It's trembling and swaying. I want to rip it down and shatter it.

I should've gotten to her faster. Maybe I could've stopped those power-hungry magical bitches from laying a hand on her if I'd moved a little faster.

The trio unleashed their binding roots on me and the other two before going after Minerva. It felt like an entire tree was pinning me down. It took way too long for me to claw my way free. Then, I had to release the other two. I could've taken those witches on my own, but I couldn't do that and release Minerva at the same time. I needed their help.

At least we escaped. That's what really matters. Minerva's still in one piece. Even though she lost her magic, she's still alive. But she's dead inside. I smell her pain.

I can't imagine what that must feel like to lose something so precious. I know she's devastated about losing her powers. Just the thought of losing my shifting ability makes me shiver. If I ever lost my ability to shift, I'd feel like half a man. I wouldn't wish that on anyone. Now, Minerva's living that hell.

"I'm going to cook something," I say with a grumble.

I'm a good cook. My mama always taught me the best thing to do for a person in pain is to feed them. Minerva hasn't eaten since before we went to train with Azealia. If anything, it won't make her situation worse. It might even help.

I open the fridge and take out a bunch of vegetables, courtesy of Draven, and some meat. I get to chopping and slicing. Wielding a knife, even just a kitchen knife, makes me feel better. I make a simple broth, pour in the meat and vegetables and let it simmer.

"Let's get her cleaned up," Stone says.

"Minerva, darling," Draven says. "Can you sit up? You have a lot of scratches we need to clean."

She lifts her head from a pillow which has been thoroughly soaked with her tears. She nods.

Draven helps her sit upright. I go to the pantry cupboard and pull out a first aid kit, which I pass to Stone. I continue to heat the stew while they clean her up with gentle hands. They soothe her with soft words.

There's no light in Minerva's eyes. It's almost as if she's just a body without a soul.

I fumble with the knife as I recall something Minerva once told me. When a witch steals another witches magic, she steals her soul too. I grip the knife so hard that the handle cracks. I don't even care that it pinches my skin.

Those bitches are going to pay for what they did. They're about to get what's coming to them.

"I'll be back," I say to the others. "The stew's on the stove. Check it in ten minutes."

I stride over to the couch and plant a kiss on the top of Minerva's head.

"Where are you going?" Draven asks.

"To fix this."

"Whoa, hold on there." Stone leaps to his feet and places a hand squarely in the middle of my chest to stop me.

I want to snap his arm, but that won't help anyone. Besides, I like the guy. He's a friend. You don't snap your friends' arms. Even my bear agrees. My bear knows as well as I do that we're a family now.

"Where are you going?"

"To talk to Azealia," I say. "She's an older witch. She might know a way to get Minerva's magic back."

"That's not a bad idea," Draven calls from his place at Minerva's side.

She's dozing off even though she's still sitting up. Before I do anything else, I walk over to her and gently pick her up. I carry her into the bedroom and lay her down. Hopefully, she'll be able to get some decent sleep.

I stroke the hair away from her face and make sure she's tucked snugly under the covers before leaving the room.

I feel better knowing she's somewhere safe, comfortable, and warm.

"Good thinking." Stone nods when I return. "Now, about going to see Azealia. We're going with you."

"No way. Someone has to stay here and look after Minerva," I say. "Besides, Azealia tolerated us on her land once. I don't think she'll take too kindly to all three of us barging into her cottage. It's better if I go alone."

"Fair enough," Draven says. "But what about the barrier? Minerva had to lift it for us last time."

"At this point, I'm so pissed off that I could move a goddamned mountain," I snarl.

"Easy there." Stone lifts his hands. "We aren't doubting you. Just whatever you do, make sure you come back in one piece. Minerva will be devastated if anything happens to you, and honestly, I'd be pretty bummed too."

"I can handle myself," I say, but I appreciate his concern.

"All right, off you go." Draven waves me off. "We'll keep an eye on Minerva and finish your stew."

"Thanks." I nod. "I'll be back soon."

Without another word, I stride out into the night.

WHEN I REACH the barrier surrounding Azealia's territory, every nerve in my body is humming. I want nothing more than to turn around and go anywhere but straight ahead. Whatever magic that old witch uses is damn effective. I know I can't turn back. I have to get through somehow, for Minerva's sake.

In the end, I decide the best way to get through the barrier is the good old-fashioned way. With brute force.

I shift into bear form so I can take advantage of the extra limbs. I charge full speed at the barrier. It's like colliding with a giant boulder. It's solid and extremely heavy but not impossible to move. I put one paw in front of the other. My progress is slow and painful as I make my way down the forest path. It feels like I'm swimming in a pool of setting concrete.

An annoying raven swoops overhead and caws repeatedly.

I pay it no mind.

The sky starts to lighten by the time I force my way into the clearing. I hope Minerva's still asleep. The last thing I want is for her to wake up and start worrying about me.

Azealia is standing in her doorway looking furious. Before I can even speak, she launches a magic spell at me. When it hits me, I drop to the ground. It's a magical energy net, and it's pinning me in place.

"What the hell, Azealia?" I growl. "I thought we were cool."

"It's almost like I put a barrier there for a reason."

"It's almost like I wouldn't have forced my way through it if it wasn't an emergency," I growl back, knowing full well that she can understand the bear language. She lifts one brow. I guess that's as much interest as she's going to give me.

"We were ambushed," I say. Even speaking is an effort with the barrier still in place. "Three powerful witches hunted us down in the forest after we took down Flint and Rebecca. They stole Minerva's power."

Azealia's freaky eyes grow wide.

"That's terrible."

"Yeah, it's pretty fucking terrible. Minerva's crushed. I've never seen her like this before," I say.

"I'm sorry that happened, but I don't understand why you're here."

"You need to help her."

"I don't need to do anything." She narrows her eyes. "I already helped her, remember? I spent precious hours teaching her how to master her magic. Now that her training's complete, I have no desire to be a part of your world any longer."

"Please." I strain against the magical netting. "Don't you understand that I love her? I'll do anything for her, and that includes dragging you out of here with my teeth."

"How can you possibly love her?" Azealia says. "You allow her to be shared with other lovers."

"What part of *I'll do anything for her* wasn't clear?" I ask. "She's worth it. Even if I have to share her, she's worth it. I won't leave here until you agree to help me."

Azealia looks at me for several minutes. I'm not sure what she's looking for, but eventually her mouth shifts into something that resembles a smile.

"I'm moved by your dedication. If more men were like you..." A look of hollow longing fills her eyes. For a moment, they don't shine anymore. When she looks at me again, she's back to normal. "I know a spell that might work. I'll go with you to help Minerva."

Minerva

When I wake up, I'm in my bedroom. I'm so confused. I could've sworn I was just on the couch a moment ago.

My body is far too hot. I look down and see that I'm firmly tucked under the covers. I wiggle to free an arm then rip the covers off me. When I sit up, everything rushes back to me. Every ache and pain hits me at once with such force that I fall back into the sheets.

A hollowness tugs at my soul. I acutely feel the loss of my magic. It's like having a gaping hole right in the middle of my body.

I hate it.

I slide out of bed. I walk over to the window and crack the shutters. It's daytime. It was nighttime when we made it back to the cabin. I must've been asleep for some time.

I leave the bedroom to check on Kaval, Stone, and Draven. I don't have any memories of them being injured, but everything in my head is a jumbled mess. I need to know that they're safe.

Stone and Draven are sitting in the living room in silence. Draven reads a book while Stone stares at the window and sips on a cup of coffee.

"Hey." My voice is hoarse and doesn't sound anything like my own. Stone and Draven immediately leap to their feet. Their handsome faces are filled with worry.

"How are you feeling?" Draven asks.

"Like shit." I try to laugh, but it sounds hollow.

"Let me get you some food," Stone says. "I can make something breakfast-y, or Kaval started making a stew for you last night, but you fell asleep."

"The stew sounds nice." I probably need something nutritious right now, though sweet buttery pancakes sound divine. I look around and notice that someone's missing. "Where's Kaval?"

"He went to see Azealia."

My eyes widen.

"What would possess him to do that?" I ask.

Draven and Stone suddenly look toward the door.

"You're about to find out." Stone shoots me a smile.

Kaval comes through the front door and, much to my

surprise, Azealia follows behind him. He immediately crosses the room and pulls me into his arms. I sink into his embrace, taking in his scent and the solid feeling of his muscles.

When I pull away from him, Azealia is giving me a look.

"You look like hell," she says.

"I feel like hell." I laugh dryly. "What are you doing here?"

"Your Romeo, or I guess one of your Romeos, sought me out," Azealia says. "He told me what happened. I'm very sorry to learn that your magic has been taken from you."

Just hearing the words out loud brings tears to my eyes.

"It's horrible," I say with a whimper. I know I sound like a pathetic child, but I can't help it. I miss my magic. Without it, I don't feel like a person. I don't feel like anything. "I just want it back."

"I know." Azealia steps forward and brushes my hair away from my face. She wipes away one of the tears slipping down my cheeks. It's a mothering touch that I'm not expecting. I cry harder. "Don't despair, little witch. I can help you."

I look at her with wide eyes.

"You can?" I sniffle.

"Yes. It's a difficult spell, but not impossible," she says. "You see, it's not possible to take away the entirely of a witch's magical essence. Regardless of whether you have your powers, you are still a magical being. You were born that way, and nothing can erase that. Do you understand me?"

"I think so," I say.

"I want you to picture starting a fire with flint. You

need to make a spark first before the fire catches. This spell acts as the flint. It makes sparks that can reignite your abilities," she says.

Hope lights up my soul.

"That would be amazing. How do we do it?"

"It's better if we go outside," Azealia says. "It's a volatile spell, not without risk. I'd hate to damage your home."

"What's the risk, exactly?" Stone asks.

"If the spell doesn't take, a number of things can go wrong," Azealia says. "It can generate fire both outside and within the subject, it can fracture minds, it can even stop hearts."

Kaval, Stone, and Draven give me a look.

"I want to do it," I say. "I'm strong enough to handle it. You're the most talented witch of a generation, probably of all time. If anyone can do it, it's you."

"There's no need to flatter me," Azealia smirks.

She herds all of us outside but makes the guys stand near Storm's studio.

She tells me to stand in the middle of the clearing. I do as I'm told.

My nerves start to rise when Azealia lifts her hands to the sky. Dark storm clouds bursting with lightning block out the blue sky above. She draws the lightning into herself, and I suddenly understand just how powerful this spell will be.

I can't turn back now. If this is the only way to get my magic back, I have to see it through. I close my eyes and wait for Azealia to cast the spell.

When she does, it's almost as painful as having my magic ripped out of me.

I do my best not to scream or even show a hint of pain. I didn't want to put the guys through witnessing that.

They've already seen me weak and broken down enough for one day.

Slowly but surely, the pain ebbs. I'm filled with light. I'm practically bursting with it. My whole body heats up as energy surges through me. My feet lift off the ground. For a moment, the entire world stops existing.

All I can feel is the magic that surrounds me.

When I touch back down to the ground, I feel alive again. I feel whole.

I open my eyes. Azealia smiles at me. Kaval, Stone, and Draven are smiling too.

"It worked." I'm grinning like a fool, but I can't help it.

I take in a breath and conjure a small ball of energy. It hovers over my palm with ease.

The joy of having my magic back gives way to the throbbing need for vengeance. Azealia warns me that it won't be as easy as defeating Rebecca and the bears. I need all of the magic I can summon. I'm going after those witches, and they're going to burn.

CAPTIVE OF THE BEAR CLAN: CHAPTER 20

MINERVA

I lay the ashen amulet on the table before me and purse my lips. The twisted white willow artifact will help me against the coven, but it won't be enough. Neither will the distilled frog's semen or the ball of beeswax, or even the soft mass of orb weaver spider's web I collected while confronting a childhood terror. No amount of preparation, charms, or spells can save me from their combined might. I need more power.

Now that I know what I'm about to face, three witches with terrible magic, there is only one way to gather the power I need to defeat them—sex magic.

I put my face in my hands and sigh. How can I convince the guys that this is the only way? I know Draven will be on board no matter what, and maybe even Stone, but will Alpha male Kaval agree to it? So far, he hasn't been willing to sleep me with if the others are joining us.

The tangle of our relationships is complex enough already. Asking them to do this will only further complicate things.

I sigh and stand up. It's the only way. There's no use putting it off.

I find the guys in the kitchen speaking in hushed tones. While I don't catch every word, I definitely hear Azealia's name spoken several times.

Kaval spots me first and pats Stone on the shoulder, silencing him.

When Stone turns an annoyed glance his way, Kaval points toward me. All three sets of eyes land on me at once. It's so overpowering, I stumble over my words when I try to speak.

"Um, I need to ask you guys something... Um, you see, it turns out the only way to strengthen my powers to face off with the witches is with a tantric... Um...." my voice drops to a whisper "...orgy."

"What did you say?" Stone asks, tilting his head to the side.

"She said orgy," says Draven as if it's no big deal.

"An... orgy..." Kaval says. He's silent for a moment, then that big, beautiful roguish grin splits his face. "I'm in."

"You are?" My heart hammers and my knees go weak.

"I am, too," says Draven, nodding his head. "If this is what Minerva needs, then she should get it, period."

"It's the logical choice," Stone says in deadpan seriousness.

We all stare at him and laugh. After a moment of confusion, he smiles.

Draven sweeps me off my feet and carries me into the living room where a welcoming fire blazes in the hearth. He sets me down gently, and we're standing face to face.

After he tucks a strand of hair behind my ear, the back of his hand slides down my cheek. I shiver in anticipation. He leans in and presses his lips to my neck, tenderly leaving a trail of kisses across my throat and over my jaw until he reaches my lips. I capture his with mine and the keep deepens.

Stone and Kaval undress me. I let them move my limbs this way and that until I stand naked before the fire.

I moan softly into Draven's mouth when someone—I think it's Kaval—plays with my pussy from behind. Kaval's fingers tickle my ass. It's shockingly erotic.

I let Kaval take control. He uses his arsenal of skills to make me feel amazing. I find myself on the verge of coming already. They hold me up to keep me from melting into a puddle in front of the fireplace.

My eyes flutter. Through my lowered lids, I spot Stone standing awkwardly by himself a few inches away. He's naked and erect, but he seems unsure of what to do next. Draven notices my gaze and pulls away from the kiss.

"Come, master sculptor," he says as he circles to stand behind me. He puts his hand on my shoulders. "Put those artistic hands to good use."

Stone moves forward, flashing a grateful smile to Draven before focusing his eyes on me.

Kaval kneels behind me. He slides his hands up between my thighs. As he spreads my pussy lips with his fingers, the evidence of arousal coats him skin. I'm dripping wet, and he knows it. Slowly, my body responds, opening like a flower to welcome him.

"Touch me, Stone."

He reaches out and cups my breasts in his hands. He brushes his thumbs across my nipples. I gasp with pleasure. A mix of relief and arousal floods through my body. The tension between us is gone, and only desire remains.

His thumbs tease my nipples, rubbing and pinching until the engorged peaks tingle with sexual energy. It's magical, but it's not magic. Not yet. But it will be soon enough.

We move as one toward the floor. The soft shag carpet welcomes all four of us. I end up on my knees as Kaval continues to slide his fingers into my pussy. While Stone sucks and squeezes my tits, Draven takes hold of my hair and firmly pulls my head back until I am in the perfect position to accept his kiss.

It's like being in heaven. It's dark outside, but I'm bursting with pure sunlight. All three of them are so focused on me that it's overwhelming, intoxicating. It's everything I've ever wanted, and more.

Kaval works one, two, then three of his fingers into my pussy, pumping in a steady rhythm designed to concentrate my desire into a cone of power. It swirls and spirals into ever tightening circles until I'm taut with the need to come.

When I finally shatter, I scream into Draven's mouth. He presses hungry kisses to my lips, reveling in my pleasure as if it were his own.

I collapse against Kaval while my body shivers. I slide into his lap.

"Please," I say. "Give me your cocks."

"Do you want them everywhere?" Kaval whispers in a naughty tone.

"Everywhere?"

His fingers graze my ass.

"Everywhere."

"Yes," I whisper.

I'm willing to try anything with them because I know they'll make the experience amazing. I completely trust my guys enough to give them access to the one place I've never been touched.

Kaval uses his hand to collect natural lube from my damp pussy. He inserts the tip of his finger into my ass. It's shockingly sexy and feels deliciously dirty. I love every second of the way he's stretching me slowly. He's past the first knuckle, then the second. I writhe in his lap.

Stone and Draven each take hold of my arms to steady me. Kaval works his entire finger into my ass, and then gently fucks me with it. I know what he's after. His goal is to stretch me enough to accept his cock. The thought has me excited but a little skeptical. He barely fits in my pussy. How is he going to take my ass?

I trust Kaval not to hurt me, but he may be on a fool's mission. Still, it feels incredible, so I let him keep going until I'm spread wide and trembling with lust.

"She's ready, guys," Kaval says. "Set her down."

Stone and Draven lower me onto Kaval's swollen cock. There's pressure and just a hit of pain as he drives past the tight muscles and takes control of my ass. Groaning, I slide down the entire length of him.

I'm surprised at both how easy it was and by how good it feels. I'm so incredibly horny that they could do anything to me and I would be ready for it.

Kaval leans back on the floor. His arms wrap around my waist to insure I don't slide off of his cock.

Stone kneels in front of us. His swollen, veiny cock is in his hand. He guides it into my dripping wet pussy. I gasp. My eyes go wide as he fills me with every last inch of him. Now I have both of their cocks inside of me at once, and the feeling is pure ecstasy.

Draven's standing over me. He takes hold of my chin and turns my head around. His throbbing cock is right in my face. Greedily, I take it in my mouth, making sure to look up into his beautiful eyes. He's impossibly hot. He works so hard to give me what I need. I want to please him, so I relax my throat and take him deeper.

Stone begins pumping his hips, sliding his cock in and

out of my pussy. Kaval's short but powerful thrusts awaken nerve endings I never knew I had.

The feeling of both of them fucking me at once is as intoxicating as any drug could possibly be. I just came a few minutes ago, and I'm already tensing for another earth-shattering orgasm.

I pull my mouth off of Draven's cock to scream as rippling waves of pleasure wrack my body. It's just as intense as the first one, and I know it won't be the last.

When I'm able to regain my senses, I take Draven between my lips and give him the most amazing blow job he's ever had. I reach up and cradle his heavy balls. He's close. I want him to come. I need to taste him.

As I play with his balls, Draven gasps. His eyes flutter shut. His hand goes on the back of my head, he's using it to steady himself. His knees rest lightly on my shoulders. I love bringing him to the brink and then backing off before he can come. He enjoys the tease. He's told me as much.

I pull back to kiss his swollen, purple head. I gently lick it from the underside to the top, teasing him a bit before taking it into my mouth once more. I pump my head in unison with the men pumping their cocks into my ass and pussy.

I deepthroat his cock, letting him hit the back of my mouth. The rhythmic gurgling from my packed throat joins the chorus of wet sounds filling the room.

"Oh, god... I'm going to come!" Draven groans.

He tries to pull away, but I don't let him. I hold him in place with a firm grip on his balls. I look into his eyes as he comes in my mouth. There's no way to avoid choking a bit, but I manage not come all the way off his cock as I swallow the massive, delicious load. A bit is dribbling down my chin, but I lick up every trace of his seed while he strokes my hair and gazes down at me.

I'm in the middle of cleaning his shaft when the relentless pounding of my ass and pussy sparks another orgasm. It comes out of nowhere, and it's the biggest one yet. I turn my face to the side and scream. My body is throbbing as it fills with magical power. Instead of letting it dissipate, I capture this ecstasy in my soul. Magical power swirls around my heart. It's there for when I need it later.

All three men are still hard. It's not over. Not even close.

Kaval toys with my breasts, while he pounds my ass. He's still holding me in his lap. I think he's waiting for Stone to get closer. Draven is standing over us while stroking his cock.

Out of nowhere, Stone gasps.

"I'm going to come!" he says through gritted teeth.

Hot spurts of liquid fire accompany his moans. Kaval jerks his hips and heat fills my ass. Draven groans. I quickly capture him with my lips and take the magic generated by their simultaneous orgasm. The intensity of their energy forges mine into a pinpoint of enormous power. It coalesces around my clit and forces me over the edge.

I cry out. Another orgasm slices through my body like summer lightning. I capture the charge in my soul. This is the strongest magic in the world. It's not just sex magic, it's love magic. It's more potent and indestructible. It won't fade with time. It will only get stronger, like our love.

We lay in a pile. My head rests on Kaval's belly. Stone lays across my thighs with his chin propped on his hand so he can gaze lovingly at me. Draven is lying beside me. My arms are thrown across his naked chest, our hands intertwined.

"I love you," I say suddenly, no longer afraid to admit it.

"Who?" Stone asks. "Who are you speaking to?"

Draven chuckles.

"She's speaking to all of us," Kaval says.

"I am. I love all of you, so very much. I can't imagine my life without any of you in it. In fact, I don't want to."

"I love you, too," says Draven.

"I love you, Minnie." Kaval's belly vibrates the back of my head when he speaks. "And I don't mind sharing you at all."

"Really?" A smile spreads across my face. "I'm so happy to hear that."

"Monogamy is just societal bullshit anyway," Stone says. "I'm with you until the end, Minerva. I love you. I always have and I always will."

We're all silent for a moment, basking in our love.

"Did it work?" Draven asks. "Did you draw in the magic?"

"Oh, it worked." I giggle before becoming serious. "I'm ready to face them now. I'm ready to end this once and for all."

Laying there between their warm bodies, I feel completely loved and totally fulfilled. With the love of these three bear shifters supporting me, I know I can't lose.

CAPTIVE OF THE BEAR CLAN: CHAPTER 21

MINERVA

I n the morning, our giddy, post-orgy energy contrasts oddly with our solemn pre-battle rituals. However, none of us can seem to keep a straight face. The guys can't help themselves. They're either giving me sexy, furtive glances, or they're playing footsie with me under the breakfast table. We're all in the best mood we've been in since this all started. I think we just want it to last a bit longer before the real battle begins.

Everyone's still pleasantly groggy from last night's pleasure-induced delirium. We were up half the night because none of us wanted it to end. I wish we could hide in Stone's cabin forever, but it's not realistic. I'm ready to go into battle. I'm ready for this to be over.

After breakfast ends, a grim, business-like tone comes over all of us as we set off to accomplish different tasks. Draven is in the garden burning sage as he meditates. Kaval is out near the shed tinkering under the hood of Stone's old Jeep, which we're taking into town. The clashes of hammer and chisel echo from the studio where Stone is working. We're not sure, but it seems like his statues contain some sort of magic, so he's chiseling a victorious battle scene.

I sit at the kitchen table, surveying my magical supplies. I don't want to leave anything behind, so I'm bringing everything. I gently place the various items into the satchel Stone lent me to gather herbs. With Azealia's help, I've enchanted it, warping the space within so that it can hold an infinite quantity of small items.

A cornucopia of magical ingredients goes into the bag. Each has been carefully selected to amplify energy or aid in the casting of a particular spell.

Small jars of frog legs, pickled slugs, newt tails, maggots, squirrel eyes, hawk feathers, and bluebird eggs sit in one section of the bag. Leather pouches containing ground lavender, rosemary, thyme, marjoram, frankincense, and lemongrass sit in another. Sprigs of holly, hazel, and laurel take up little space.

Azealia even gave me a stick of *palo santo* that she collected while visiting a medicine man in Peru. The stick sits next to several sage bundles.

I tie several herb pouches to my belt for easy access along with a small but sharp ritual dagger.

I place small wicker dolls in the bag. I don't enjoy poppet magic at all, but I'm not holding anything back. These witches are hellbent on destroying the dreamy life that me and my bears have stumbled into. I'll do everything in my power to make sure that doesn't happen. We all will. I can sense new desperation in the guys. They want to guard our newfound happiness. I know that if it comes to it, any of us would die to preserve the unity of our family.

My hand caresses the cool, thumb-sized hunk of crystal quartz resting against my chest near my heart. Azealia gifted it to me during our training, hanging it around my neck ceremoniously to focus and amplify my energy.

As I tuck the last few odds and ends into my bag, I glance up and notice that all three men have abandoned their tasks. They've returned to the cabin, and they're watching me intently.

"You guys ready to go kick some witch butt?" I hope I filter most of the anxiety out of my voice.

"Hell, yeah." Kaval smiles. He fists his hands and holds them up. "Bring it on."

"If violence is what they want, we'll give it to them." Draven's face is a mask of determination.

"In order to carve out something beautiful, first you must hack away the excess." Stone gives a grim smile, shrugs and holds up his large mallet. "So, let's go carve up these hags."

I scrunch my face into an exaggerated frown of mock-offense. "Stone, I'm shocked. You know 'hag' is actually a very offensive term within the witch community. Very nineteenth century of you."

"My apologies, your witchy grace." Stone bows in feigned remorse. He can hardly keep the mirth from his tone. "Please, forgive me. I am but a humble shifter and know nothing of your witch ways."

All four of us laugh loudly, briefly cutting through the pre-battle tension.

"I suppose we can make an exception, considering these particular witch-bitches have tried to kill us several times. Let's go show these hags what real power looks like," I say.

We pile into the jeep. Kaval's driving, I'm in the passenger's seat, and the other guys are in the back.

Wind whips through the windowless Jeep. It fans my hair into a halo around my head. The sun is hidden behind a cloak of gray that covers the sky from horizon to horizon. Warm air, heavy with the promise of rain, increases the tension. I can use that tension. It's good weather for magic.

Kaval pulls the car to a stop just down the street from the apothecary that the witches operate near the center of town. It's still early enough in the day that the streets are quiet but not empty.

A postman walks down the sidewalk towards us, canvas bag slung over his shoulder. When he sees us, he stops. Kaval nods a greeting. I guess the postman considers it a warning, because he looks nervously from side-to-side before turning and walking off briskly in the opposite direction. Kaval turns back to me and the others and gives a shrug.

When I start toward the Three Sisters' Apothecary, Draven, Kaval, and Stone all move to follow. I turn and stop them with a look.

"Look, I know I can't convince you to leave this to me. I know that there's no way you'll leave me to face these bitches alone."

"Damn straight," Kaval growls.

Draven and Stone nod.

"And I get that, I really do. But I need to try to handle this myself. I need to show everyone how strong I am. If you're there to back me up, they might not think I'm strong enough when I'm alone.

"As long as there remains even a shred of doubt about my power, there will always be some witch or witches who'll think it's worth taking a shot at me. I need to make a statement. I want to make an example out of these evil bitches, so that no one else ever even thinks about trying to take my power. After today, people need to believe that I'm untouchable. I want the whole coven to cower in fear."

All three guys exchange doubtful looks. They're clearly hesitant.

"Besides, I couldn't live with myself if my weakness put you guys at risk. So, please, you can stay close, but don't interfere unless it's absolutely necessary. If things start to go bad, then of course I want you to back me up, but I really need to try to do this alone."

Kaval bristles and shakes his head. He's clearly against the idea. Stone looks fearful, as if he's already envisioning my grisly destruction. Draven steps forward, putting his strong masseuse's hand on Kaval's massive shoulder.

"We understand, Minerva. We'll honor your request." Draven's honest smile warms my heart. "But we will be watching. We're not going anywhere until it's over."

Kaval crooks a finger to my chin and interrupts Draven. "And as soon as something goes wrong, we will tear out their goddamn throats." For a split second, the face of his bear flashes. It's as if he's ready to shift at a moment's notice.

"Thank you." We embrace in a quick group hug.

"Good luck," Stone says. "And please. Be careful."

At that, I turn and head toward the apothecary while fighting off thoughts that this might not be the best idea. Not having my men at my side is jarring, but I know I must try to do this alone. I remind myself over and over that they will be nearby, ready to jump in at a moment's notice.

CAPTIVE OF THE BEAR CLAN: CHAPTER 22

MINERVA

I position myself on the street in front of the apothecary. A small crowd has started to gather just down the street, far enough away to be out of the impending action but close enough to see it happen.

Breathing deep, I close my eyes and channel energy down through my palms, building a small ball of electricity between my hands. When it is softball-sized, I take aim at the front door of the apothecary.

I unleash the ball of energy, sending it crashing through the door. It's accompanied by a deafening boom of thunder. The door disintegrates into ash, and the windows on the ground floor are blown out by the shockwave. I'm fairly certain that most of the contents of the shop have been destroyed in the blast, and that anyone inside the shop will have been alerted that there is a very angry witch outside.

My three targets come bursting out of the shop one after the other, eyes wide in shock, hands raised, poised to cast.

The tall ringleader does a double-take when she sees

me standing brazenly in the middle of the street, hands still smoldering from the attack. I watch as her anger and disbelief morph sickeningly into hunger and delight.

"Look, sisters. The bear-lover has delivered herself to us. What a divine treat. And here I thought we would have to hunt you down in the filthy, bear-infested woods. And where are your disgusting shifters, witch-whore?" She spreads her arms and looking around to her left and right. "Left them to guard the cave?"

Her sisters cackle.

"Actually, yes. I left them behind. I told them there was no need to trouble themselves with you." I keep the nervous shake from my voice. "We all agreed I could handle you three *hags* by myself."

The poisonous insult lands with the desired effect. They involuntarily flinch at the word, their faces shifting back to shock and anger.

"You little bitch," says the shortest of the three. Spittle flies from her mouth. "How dare you!"

She unleashes a wild, massive bolt of electricity in my direction. I jump out of the way. It strikes the ground behind me with a terrible crash that leaves a smoking, three-foot-wide crater in the street.

By now, a large crowd has gathered at the end of the street.

"Hey, you witches better be paying for that. Our tax money pays for these roads," someone yells.

The tall witch shoots a withering look over at the crowd. They step away from the concerned citizen. He gulps, eyes widening in fear.

As the tall witch snaps her outstretched fingers shut into the shape of a puckered mouth, the man's mouth begins to disappear. He's left with a patch of solid skin where his lips used to be. His eyes dart around in panic as people continue to distance themselves from him.

The tall witch turns her gaze back towards me, eyes narrowing in anger and determination.

"You are brave for coming here, witch. Brave, but stupid. I know your bear-men are here somewhere. I can sense their filth. But they will be of no help. Your power is already ours. Relinquish it to us willingly, and we will spare your life. Even better, join us, and help us to rid this once-great town which has been blighted by shifters." A mad glimmer flickers in her eyes. When I don't respond, she shrugs. "Or die fighting us and take comfort knowing that your disgusting lovers will follow close behind. The choice is yours. Either way, the bears die."

"Enough talking." I swirl my right hand in a 'come here' motion, drawing the breath out of the short, stocky witch's lungs as she opens her mouth to speak. I guide the air into a small glass vial in my other hand and plug the top with a cork, bending over the vial and speaking quickly into my hands. "Sigillum, spiritum, mortem." I seal the witch's breath in the vial, preventing her lungs from taking in any more air.

I tuck the vial into my belt as I look up to see the short stocky witch clutching at her throat. Her sisters look over at her, mouths open in shock. I briefly consider trying the same move on them, but they quickly realize their peril and snap their mouths shut. The sister of medium height with short hair rushes to the aid of the short one while the ringleader turns her focus to me.

The tall witch waves her hands in a figure-eight shape in front of her and raises them towards the sky. The ground under my feet trembles.

I dive out of the way as a sharp spire of stone pierces the street where I had been standing only a moment ago. I race down the street as more stone spikes crash up through the earth. Avoiding them is becoming more challenging with each passing second.

I pull a bottle of dragon's breath oil from my satchel and hurl it back at the tall witch. As I'm dodging another deadly spike, the oil lands right at her feet. It unleashes a deadly explosion. Flames lick the sky.

The tall witch leaps high into the air. She avoids the destruction and lands gracefully on the side of the building like a spider.

Thankfully, I am given a moment's respite from dodging the relentless spikes. I immediately go on the offensive. I summon another ball of electric energy. I hurl it at the tall witch, but she's already running along the side of the building towards me.

My attack misses. It crashes into the wall. Bricks and dust rain down on the sidewalk.

The short-haired witch, desperately trying to force air into the mouth of her sister, looks up and lets out a shriek of surprise.

Unfortunately, she sees the threat in time to erect a small protective dome of energy over her and her sister. The gasping witch drops to her knees, and her face turns red as she suffocates. I want to end her suffering, but I can't let up now. They would never show me mercy.

I start in their direction. Their vulnerability forms a shroud of fear around them. I don't care. Let them cower.

I'm ready to strike, but I'm forced to play defense again as the tall witch shatters the windows on either side of her. A barrage of glass shards race toward me.

I conjure a protective aura-bubble. The shards stop mid-air. I absorb their energy and send them hurling toward the tall witch.

She jumps off of the side of the building to avoid the barrage. When she lands, she rolls to break her fall.

I pull the pouch of ground marjoram off my belt and dump it on the ground in front of me, spreading it in an arc with my foot as I grab some enchanted dirt from of my satchel.

While speaking an incantation, I rub the herb between my palms. I plunge my hands into the concrete street. Because of my magic, it's as pliable as mud.

I grab the earth and breath energy through my clenched hands. I twist hard while willing the earth to obey.

Just as the tall witch is about to rise, viscous concrete from the sidewalk swallows her hands and feet. It spreads up her arms and legs, covering her inch by inch, consuming her. She screams and screams until the sound is swallowed by the earth.

I'm starting to think I'm actually going to win. My heart races. I suspect that my eyes glimmer with a wild madness. I'm radiating with power, unstoppable, and ready to destroy my enemies.

A bolt of energy shoots past my head, catching me unaware. I whirl to my left to see the short-haired witch grinning wildly.

"What are you smiling about?" I demand. "Your sisters are already dead. You're next."

My confidence swells as I prepare to deal with her.

She throws her head back and cackles, a terrible, high pitched sound.

"Oh, the young are so blind," she says.

I notice a thick green vine retreating back toward her. It holds the glass vial containing her sister's breath in its curled tip.

She laughs again, closing her outstretched hand into a

fist. The vine tightens, crushing the vial with a loud pop. She directs the released air back to her kneeling sister, who gasps in relief as oxygen floods back into her lungs.

Together, they release the tall witch from her concrete grave. I'm shocked. How is she still alive? How is that possible? I buried her in concrete.

The three witches turn towards me. Their eyes narrow.

"All you did was make us mad," the tall witch snaps.

A lump of fear settles in my throat. My magic is still powerful, but I've already expended a good deal of energy. I'm right back where I started when the fight began. I've lost the element of surprise. I've lost half of my energy. And they seem to just be getting started.

For the first time since this began, fear coils around my heart.

"It looks like you've learned some new tricks since we last met." The tall witch's face contorts into sneer. "Too bad you're a traitor to the coven. Your power is formidable. You would have made a worthy ally. But no matter, you can take comfort knowing your power will not be wasted. We will make better use of it than you ever could have."

The witches began chanting in unison, weaving their hands through the air. Thick vines shoot up through the earth to surround me.

I deflect one, two, three... but they keep coming.

One wraps around my right wrist. I pull my dagger from my belt with my other hand. I'm about to slash the vine when another one wraps around that wrist. It pins my arm to my side and squeezes so hard that I'm forced to drop the dagger.

Vines wrap around both of my legs. I'm immobilized and trapped as the witches advance on me.

Now their eyes glimmer madly as they sense victory.

They float toward me and stop ten feet in front of me. Their palms thrust forward as they unleash a coordinated barrage of energy toward me.

My protective instincts kick in. I erect a crude energy bubble that stops the brunt of their power-absorbing attack, but I can feel their magic straining against the barrier. My raw power won't hold off their coordinated efforts long.

I'm going to lose. I'm tempted to give in, to let them have the power they so desperately want. Even if I could defeat them, I'd never truly be safe. Other witches or shifters or even dragons will always sense the power within me and want it for themselves. They'll want me to use my power for their own ends.

Draven, Kaval, and Stone have been the only ones who have had no ulterior motives. They're not motivated by power or greed. They only want my love. I must fight back. I must do this for them—for us!

I fight against their growing power. My shield is faltering, but I press on. I have to. It's the only way to save the men I love.

As if summoning them with my thoughts, three brown bears come racing down the street. The witches are caught off guard, but they react quickly. They turn and send bolts of energy at the three charging bears. My bears dodge their attacks.

My power surges. The close proximity of my lovers awakens the sex magic I kept locked in my heart.

The distraction gives me a chance to direct my energy into breaking the vines. I struggle to break free, but their magic is tenacious.

The fastest bear, who I recognize as Stone, breaks off from the others and loops around toward me. He slashes the vines with his sharp claws, freeing my hands and feet.

"Thanks, Stone." I rub my wrists where the vines have left raw, red rings.

Stone nods his big bear head.

"I need a favor," I say. He looks at me with huge brown eyes, and I can tell he's ready to do anything. "Think you can get me a strand of each of those hags' hair?"

In response, he raises his massive head and lets out a mighty roar.

I'll take that as a yes.

"Great, I'll whip up a little cover for you." I rummage through the satchel and find a large bundle of desert sage.

Draven and Kaval are keeping the witches busy, moving at their blinding top speed, drawing the fire away from me and Stone.

I light the sage. I let it burn for a moment then blow out the flames, leaving the end glowing and billowing smoke.

I whisper into the burning end of the bundle, "Fumo nebulus."

I take a deep breath and push it out slowly over the glowing embers.

Smoke pours out in great billows now, creating a massive cloud that engulfs all of us. I'm counting on Stone's nose to guide him toward the witches' hair.

In preparation for his return, I draw a chalk pentagram on the ground and pull out my wicker dolls from my bag, placing them on the ground in front of me.

Amid the sounds of crashing spells and great roars of rage from one or another of the bears, I hear high-pitched squeals of pain from somewhere in the smoke cloud.

Soon after, a massive shape looms up in front of me. A pang of fear shoots through me before I realize it's Stone.

He holds large, distinct clumps of damp hair in his mouth, which he drops next to me.

I can't help but laugh.

"Jesus, Stone. I only needed one strand. Did you leave any hair on their heads?"

He shrugs his massive bear shoulders, charging back into the fray.

I pull out a strand of hair from each clump, tying each one around the neck of one of the wicker dolls. I set each of the dolls down on a point of the pentagram forming a triangle and place the burning bundle of sage in the center.

I stand and hold my hands out above the makeshift altar just as one of the sisters finally conjures a cleansing wind and clears the smoke away.

I look up and lock eyes with the tall witch. Her mouth curls into a twisted smile.

I see that Draven is down on the ground a short distance away, one of his front legs is bent at a sickening angle, broken.

My eyes widen in concern then narrow in rage. They hurt my guy. They're going to pay for that with their lives.

The tall witch's smile fades as she glimpses the dolls arranged on the ground in front of me. The moment stretches out between us. Time bends and slows.

We're both aware of the other witches battling with Stone and Kaval. The huge bears dart forward, swiping their massive paws while the witches throw spells wildly. Asphalt, bricks, and dust fly as the witches destroy the street. With every misplaced spell, they destroy the surrounding buildings.

A look of horror passes over the tall witch as she looks up from where the poppets sit. She opens her mouth to speak. I don't know if she's about to beg for mercy or cast some desperate spell against me. I don't wait to find out.

We maintain eye contact as I speak the word that seals her fate. "Ignis."

The wicker dolls at my feet burst into flames.

The tall witch screams and looks over at her sisters. Flames explode around the feet of the three witches. These aren't ordinary flames. It's magical fire with blue and purple hues. It's beautiful and terrible—and deadly.

Within moments, their screams and the crackling of the flames are the only sounds in the town. Everyone looks on in horror as azure fire consumes the legs of the screaming witches. Their faces contorting in agony. It's terrifying, but I can't look away.

They brought this on themselves. I wonder if I should feel some sense of remorse or pity. I don't. I feel only a faint exhilaration, a rush of adrenaline at my victory.

I watch silently as the consuming flames rage. All three women have dropped to the ground. They're rolling and flailing desperately, howling in agony. But the flames only spread, and soon they are engulfed from head to toe.

Eventually, there is no movement.

No screaming.

No flames.

The still-smoking bodies of the charred witches are all that remains. With a flick of my wrist, wind shatters them into ashes. The breeze carries them into the forest where they will be returned to the earth to be purified.

The crowd is silent. They are horrified and fascinated by my power.

One by one, members of the coven step forth and drop to one knee, a signal of submission. I hope my show of force has been enough to dissuade any future threats. I don't want to do more violence in the future, so I'm glad they all saw how capable I am of defending myself.

Stone and Kaval rush to Draven's side. They sniff his leg and nuzzle him with their huge noses.

I rush over to my three men as they shift back into their human form.

Stone and Kaval kneel beside Daven. His leg is still at an award angle, so I use my magic to heal it.

"How's it feel?" I ask.

Draven climbs to his feet. He tests his leg by putting weight on it.

"It's back to normal. Are you okay Minnie?"

"I've never been better."

"Are they dead?" he asks.

"Gone from this earth forever."

"Good."

I look around at my three brave lovers. My heart swells with joy. We're finally free to love each other without fear of being attacked.

"Let's go home," Kaval says.

Home. I love the sound of that.

CAPTIVE OF THE BEAR CLAN: CHAPTER 23

MINERVA

From my seat inside the Bonfire Falls Steakhouse, I have a great view of the miniature waterfall behind our table. For the first time since the magical battle, we're out in public together. I've caught a few curious glances and several people glaring, but I don't care. Witches and shifters should be allowed to love each other. I'm sick of the prejudice in our small town. I want to change it, so I'm hoping to lead by example.

This is my favorite restaurant in town. Authentic French cuisine cooked by a famous chef is exactly what I need to fuel my night. An expensive bottle of Bordeaux will help loosen us all up. We deserve it after everything we've been through.

I can't believe I'm here, alive, and safe with my men.

Despite Kaval's protests, we all dressed in formal attire. He's wearing a clean denim jacket and new jeans. It's not a tux, but he looks perfect just the way he is. I wouldn't expect anything more from him.

I'm wearing a crimson dress with a scandalously low

neckline. Kaval can't stop stealing glances at my cleavage, neither can Draven or Stone.

Draven wasn't exactly excited by the restaurant, but I had called ahead to make sure they would prepare a scrumptious vegetarian ratatouille for him. He's modeling the proper way to utilize a crisp linen napkin. Kaval frowns and stuffs his napkin into a ball in his lap.

"Close enough," he mutters.

"That's not how you do it," Draven says.

"How am I going to wipe my face if it's in my lap?" Kaval narrows his eyes. "Answer me that, Mr. Fancy Pants."

"It's not to wipe your face, it's to keep food from staining your clothes." Draven has a Zen-like smile on his gorgeous face.

"Huh." Kaval furrows his brow in thought.

Next to him, Draven is pure hipster chic, in a button-down tan silk shirt and skinny jeans. He's so ridiculously hot. Our waitress could barely take our order because she couldn't pull her eyes off of him. I wanted to stab her in the face, but I restrained myself. I mean, who wouldn't stare at Draven?

Stone is fascinated by the intricately carved arches partitioning the restaurant, but he's holding my hand under the table. He's wearing an Armani suit and tie. I can't decide if he looks like a fashion model or an international spy. Both are sexy in their own way.

Actually, scratch that. He'd be a lousy spy because he couldn't blend into a crowd. He's too sexy and people would remember him.

My men take good care of me.

We bought a beautiful new home in the center of town. The hallways often echo with my cries of passion. No matter how much sex we have, I always seem to want more. Fortunately, there are three of them, so if one is tired, I have two more to play with.

Underneath my dress, I'm wearing a corset, garter, and stockings set. I'm looking forward to seeing how the men react to this little number. They haven't seen it yet, but they will. I'm tempted to skip dinner and order in pizza instead.

When the food finally comes, we devour it. I'm still hungry for something, but it's not anything I could order in this restaurant. It's something I can only have at home.

I lick my lips and smile at Kaval.

"Do you want dessert?" he asks.

"Oh yeah."

"What do you want?" He hands me the dessert menu.

"The only dessert I want... is the three of you."

"Check please," they all say in unison.

We all stare at each other and burst out laughing.

Once the bill has been paid, we head home.

It's a beautiful two-story, Victorian-style home with plenty of space for all of us. Stone has his art studio, Kaval has a big garage to work on his private vehicles, and Draven has a wonderful garden in which to meditate and do yoga.

Our master bedroom is dominated by a giant circular bed that we had custom made. It's large enough to accommodate all of us. I love this bed. We've already spent many, many nights breaking it in.

I shake my hips a little more than is necessary as I fumble with the keys to our front door. Of course, we all want to tear each other's clothes off, but it's fun to make them have to wait.

"I think she's doing this on purpose." Stone arches an eyebrow.

"I think you're right." Kaval gives my ass a quick slap.

"Quit screwing around, Minnie, so we can start screwing around."

"You're so impatient," I tease as I finally unlock the door. "Look at that, I got it open."

"You little tease." Draven unbuttons his shirt. "You're going to get it tonight."

"Oh, honey, you haven't seen anything yet."

I sway my hips from side to side as I slowly walk up the stairs. After taking a few steps into the bedroom, I slip my dress over my head and toss it over a chair.

The men gasp. Their gazes sweep up and down as they take in the sexy lingerie. A low growl rumbles through Kaval's chest.

When I reach the bed, I drop down on all fours and crawl to the center of the mattress. I make sure they get a great view of my ass.

As they struggle out of their clothing, their cocks are already getting hard. Kaval swears as he rips his shirt off. He's so impatient, but that's just Kaval. It's who he is, and I accept each of my guys, flaws and all. Nobody's perfect, but they're pretty damn close to it.

I cup my hands under my breasts and lift them as an offering to my men.

They scramble over each other to get to me. Kaval crushes his lips against mine. His familiar taste sends a tingle throughout my entire body.

Gently, he lays me back against the pillows. He runs his mouth down my neck and leaves a trail of kisses until he reaches my breasts. He takes my nipple in his mouth and suckles on it, flicking his tongue over and around the tip. It feels absolutely amazing.

Draven is nuzzling my legs. He leaves his own trail of kisses up the insides of my thighs. I shudder as his hot breath blows over my clit. My pussy is damp and ready for his tongue.

As Kaval continues to ravish my nipples and breasts, Draven licks my pussy. He starts out with gentle licks which become rougher and more tantalizing.

Eventually, Draven sucks my clit between his lips. The sensations are incredible. To be pleasured by two men at once is a fantasy come true.

Stone kneels next to my head and strokes my hair. Instantly I reach out and take his massive cock in my hand. His veined, throbbing flesh is as hard as iron. He moves closer and I take him into my mouth. He's salty, sweet, and all mine.

I moan softly, closing my eyes as I take the tip of Stone's cock deep into my mouth. Just the tip is already too much. Giving him a good blow job will take a bit of effort on my part, but of course I know I'm up to the challenge.

Kaval starts doing more than suckling my nipples. He bites them, gently at first, but then he gradually increases the pressure. It's sort of like being under a very hot shower stream. It feels good, but there's a part of you also wondering if it's too much or if you're going to get burned.

I take Stone's cock out of my mouth for a moment until I can adjust to what Kaval's doing to me. It's painfully sexy. I love it when he gets like this. He loves to test my limits, but he never goes too far.

As if on cue, Draven buries his face in my pussy and does his absolute best to passionately eat me to an instant orgasm. I come hard; my screams echo off the bedroom walls before I mute myself with a mouthful of Stone's cock.

My hand strokes along his shaft as I slide my lips and tongue in one smooth motion. When I swirl my tongue around the tip of his cock, he throws his head back and gasps. His hand is holding the back of my head, helping to support and guide my gurgling blow job.

Kaval goes back to sucking my right nipple while pinching my left nipple—hard. I cry out around Stone's cock, but again it feels so good. I don't want him to stop.

With slow, careful effort, I'm able to take Stone's entire shaft inside of my mouth and throat. I suck him passionately until he comes. He gasps as his eyes flutter closed, and his entire body trembles. He drops to the bed beside me and gives me a look of pure adoration.

Draven traces lines around my clit with his tongue. I moan softly and put my hand in his hair. He's so good at this. His nimble tongue works its way inward until it brushes ever so lightly against my swollen clit.

I cry out and my legs shake as an orgasm threatens to consume me.

"You taste so good, Minerva." His breath is hot on my most sensitive skin.

Just the sound of his voice pushes me over the edge. Multiple orgasms wrack my body, and I'm convinced I'll die from this exquisite pleasure.

When he finally pulls his mouth away, I'm left laying naked on the bed. Three handsome faces gaze at me with love in their eyes. It's not just love, it's desire and longing and hunger.

I roll onto my stomach and lift my ass in the air.

"Who wants me?" I ask in a teasing tone.

Stone moves in first, rubbing the tip of his cock against my juicy pussy. I want him inside of me so badly that I jerk my hips back. I slide his cock into my pussy and sheath him perfectly.

"You're so big," I gasp as he fills me with deep strokes.

I moan softly as he falls into the perfect rhythm. My

hands clench the bedsheets into rumpled disarray as he starts pumping his cock into me.

Stone puts his hands on either side of my ass and really gets a grip. He grinds into me with precise strokes. He fucks like an artist with impeccable skill. My screaming orgasm mixes with his grunt of release. He fills me with his heat. He pulls out with a wet pop and caresses my lower back before getting to his feet.

Draven takes his place almost immediately, prying open my already quivering pussy with his nimble fingers. He pushes the head of his cock inside to claim me.

"I know you need more, my love." He strokes my hair.

"Oh, yes," I pant. I'm an animal when I'm with them.

Draven starts off with slow, sensual strokes. He withdraws most of his cock from my body before driving back inside. He pays attention and really knows what I like. The angle and speed are perfectly balanced. Just like him.

Tension builds in my pussy. I want to come again.

"Harder, Draven!"

Draven's thighs slap against my ass as he thrusts even harder.

I bury my face in the mattress and scream as a massive orgasm blasts through my body. He grunts and finds his own release. We lay there panting for a moment. He's still inside of me as he strokes my hair.

Eventually, Kaval growls and Draven pulls out. I struggle back up to all fours and look over my shoulder at Kaval.

"Lay down," he whispers.

I flop onto my back and spread my legs wide. Kavals wicked grin sends a fresh wave of desire skittering through my pussy.

With an animalistic snarl, Kaval surges into my pussy. I cry out in ecstasy as he drives into me like a wild beast.

It feels good to have him take charge of my body. No matter how rough he may seem, Kaval will never hurt me. He loves me, just like Draven and Stone love me. And I love all of them.

I lose all control as Kaval comes inside of me, setting off a thunderous wave of ecstasy throughout my entire body. I sigh as my lust is finally sated.

Later, we're all cuddled up together in the bed. I'm in the middle of my guys, Kaval, Draven, and Stone. I think I've loved them all for as long as I can remember. Now our love is official and out in the open. There's no place I'd rather be than right here with my men. We're finally home. I'm so ready to start a family with them.

CAPTIVE OF THE WOLF PACK:
CHAPTER 1

IRIS

As I walk through the dark forest, I scan the shadows for the hundredth time. I'm holding a magical orb of light which illuminates every tree, bush, and flower for ten feet in every direction. But it's not enough to keep my heart from racing.

The shadows outside the circle are a living, breathing horror. I gulp a deep breath and try to slow my thundering heart. A cold shiver runs down my spine. Towering branches block the moonlight. I'm completely shrouded in darkness except for the small amount of light my orb gives off.

Every hoot of an owl and every flutter of a leaf makes me jump. I stop for a second to listen for footsteps. The snap of a twig makes my heart pound so hard my whole chest vibrates. The forest is quiet except for the occasional caw of a bird or the incessant buzz of insects.

I can't shake the sensation that an unseen stalker is lurking somewhere in the darkness.

Although I sneak away from the Dark Magic Academy

every night at midnight, tonight feels different. I'm supposed to be meeting my friends from the small town of Bonfire Falls soon, but I might not make it on time, or at all.

Another shiver ripples through my body. The feeling of being watched intensifies.

Briefly, I consider my options. I don't want to lead anything negative toward where my friends are waiting. I don't know what I'm dealing with yet. I don't know if the person stalking me is another witch or a shifter, but it doesn't matter.

Malevolence rolls off the unseen force in waves. Dark magic swirls in the shadows. It feels like a thousand little spiders crawling across my flesh.

No matter what, I mustn't get caught. I'll be in trouble if that happens. If my stepmother Lexus finds out that I sneak out to visit wolf shifters every night, she'll never let me leave the Academy again.

Every day at the Academy is hell. Being able to sneak out to see my friends each night is the only way I manage to survive. I hate the Academy and everything for which it stands. Lexus is a monster, but nobody realizes just how evil she can be. If I tried to tell anyone, no one would believe me. So, I stay silent.

The thought of seeing my friends sends a fire through my body, a fire that burns brighter and hotter lately each time I'm near them. When I picture them in my mind, it calms me. My heart settles, and warmth replaces the cold shiver of unease.

The forest is completely silent again. I don't know if I'm being paranoid or not. I've never sensed a presence like this before, so what could it be... or who?

I feel it following me all the way to the waterfall. I

could have turned back, but I didn't. I'm not about to let whatever it is win. It could all be a figment of my imagination, because whatever it was had ample chance to attack me, but it didn't. So, I'm probably overreacting to being in the woods alone at night.

When I arrive at our spot, my eyes light up. Remus and Torak are already in the pool at the base of the waterfall. They're playing and splashing around until they see me. They walk out of the water to greet me with wide smiles. I can't stop staring as rivulets of water drip down their broad chests and chiseled abs. Unfortunately, they're both wearing swim trunks.

"Hey, guys. How's the water tonight?"

"Come see for yourself," Remus calls.

I smile because he's looking at me with enough hunger in his eyes to make my knees buckle. His gaze sweeps down to take in my curves. I chose a gauzy white dress for tonight. It's not the most practical thing to wear for a hike through the forest, but I like to dress up for my guys.

My gaze drops from his face to his lips. I wonder how they might feel pressed against mine and how they might taste.

I shake my head slightly and brush off the idea. These are my friends. We've been friends since we were young, and it would be weird to be intimately involved with any of them. Still, the thought lingers in the back of my mind.

A splash draws my attention to the pool. Torak wades into the waist-deep water. I'm awestruck by the sight of his naked torso glistening in the moonlight. His muscular arms are built to hold a woman close to him. I picture myself pressed against his brawny chest, which has a hint of hair that runs down the center and disappears into the water. I groan softly, thinking about what the water might be hiding.

Remus gives me a funny look.

"Are you coming in tonight?" he asks.

"I didn't come all this way to watch you have fun without me." I grin. "I'll be there in a second."

I hesitate, suddenly too shy to undress in front of them. We've swum together since we were kids, but now that we're older, it's different. Very different. The young boys I've known my whole life have become sexy men with incredible bodies. The sight of them invokes fantasies that will never come true. But I can't help but think about them. Maybe it's my hormones gone wild.

The night is warm and perfect for a swim in the cool, clear water. Besides, it's not like I'll be completely naked. I have a bikini underneath my dress. I quickly pull off my dress, fold it, and set it on a rock next to the pool.

Remus and Torak walk closer to the edge of the water as if hypnotized. Their eyes are glued to me as they take in every curve of my body. I smile at them. A rush of familiar warmth fills me when I see the bulges that their swim trunks can't hide.

Although I still think it'll be weird if any of our friendships turns sexual, I like their reaction to me. It's natural to at least think about it. In a weird way, I wish we weren't such close friends. They're so sexy.

Liquid fire runs up and down my spine. Butterflies flutter in my stomach. The drum of my heart is very different from what it was on my jaunt through the woods.

Rather than jump in like the men, I walk into the pool like a goddess. The water slowly envelops me. I close my eyes as cool water caresses my bare skin. When I lean back to let the water surround me, all of my stresses and worries drain away.

"Where's Nyx?" I ask.

"Late as usual, but he'll be here eventually." Remus looks me over again.

I shake my head and sigh. Nyx is never on time. I used to get frustrated about it, but now I just expect it. He lives in his own version of time.

Torak comes up behind me and splashes me. I turn around to splash him back, but I'm drenched a second time as Remus sends a shower of cool water over my head and down my back. The game is on.

When we tire of the horseplay, we float around the pool, talking and laughing as if none of us has a care in the world. Outside of our little paradise, we're surrounded by danger. But here, we're safe. For now, all is well.

As we float, I can't help but notice Remus and Torak's fine bodies.

Remus has the arms of a bodybuilder, strong and athletic. Every muscle in his chest is well-defined. I'd love to lick the lines along his skin, but that would be totally weird.

I sneak glances at him as we drift around in the water and chat. My thoughts start to wander. I can see him pulling me tight against him, touching me in every way. I imagine how he would taste, how my mouth would cover his, and how I would breathe in his essence.

Then, my attention turns to Torak. He's also well built. But aside from that, he's incredibly smart. His ability to solve almost any problem awes everyone he meets. He's talented and everyone respects him. He's the brains of our little group.

As I contemplate his physical and mental attributes, I find that I want to feel his arms around me. I want to feel his hands on my skin and his lips pressed against mine.

If my fantasies ever come true, it would change the

dynamics between us forever. It would surely affect all of our relationships. Not just my relationships with them, but their relationships with each other too. Falling for any one of them could hurt our friendships.

But what if it didn't? It's so tempting to think about the possibilities.

Either way, I guard my fantasies. No one ever has to know about my secret desires. I shouldn't think these things anyway, but I can't seem to stop.

Remus and Torak circle around me. Every so often, they float close enough that their hands and bodies brush against mine. I think it's an accident, but what if it isn't? Is it my imagination? I know it's crazy to think about my friends like this, but I do.

As Remus stands in a shallow part of the pool, I spot a bulge in his trunks. Maybe it's not all in my head after all.

Torak then drifts closer. His fingers lightly graze my bra. My nipples instantly harden. An immense ache overcomes me. My desire for him—for them—is getting worse every night. I live for these men. If I didn't have them in my life, I'd have nothing. That's why I can't ruin our friendships.

Suddenly, Remus stands up and announces he's brought a beach ball to toss around. I'm relieved to be ripped away from my thoughts.

My feet touch the bottom of the pool as we toss the ball around, laugh, and have fun. I wish moments like this could last forever.

A dark cloud of anxiety looms over my head as I think about returning to the Academy. My stepmother, Lexus, makes my stomach churn. Just being in her presence makes me sick. I can't stand her. I don't know why my father ever agreed to marry her. I hate my life, which is probably why I fantasize about my friends. I dream about a future without Lexus, and in these dreams, I'm always surrounded by my guys.

A sense of unease hovers over me for a moment. I shrug it off, banish it, and decide I'll enjoy this moment with my friends. I won't think about anything else until I have to. I just want to destress and enjoy the moment.

After a while, Remus and Torak stop their horseplay and glance at an area beyond our paradise. I hear someone approach, so I turn to look. Both men move to stand in front of me, ready to protect me from danger.

We sigh in relief as Nyx steps through the foliage. The tension in my body is carried away on a breeze as I climb out of the pool to greet our friend.

"Sorry I'm late. I had a delivery, and it took a lot longer than usual."

"Do you think you could have made any more noise?" Torak rolls his eyes.

"I didn't want to sneak up on you guys. I didn't want you to kill me because you thought I was an intruder. I would like to live another day, meet up for another secret rendezvous, you know, the usual." Nyx smirks. His lips are plump and sexy as hell. I can't look away.

Torak and Remus smile and nod.

Although no one ever bothers us at our special spot, we're all aware of the possibility of ever-present danger. We don't let our guard down. Witches and shifters roam the forest looking for trouble. I just hope they never find us. My magic is strong, but others are stronger.

Torak and Remus begin to toss the ball back and forth again, leaving me to talk to Nyx.

"Who were the deliveries for?" I ask.

"You know."

I close my eyes briefly and heave a heavy sigh. "I wish you didn't have to work for Howlers MC. I've heard a lot of things about them, and none of it's good. I don't want you to get hurt. Or worse."

Nyx touches my face gently and caresses my cheek with his thumb. "I promise I'll be very careful. I always am. After all, I've lived this long, right?"

"I do worry. I worry a lot. I care about you so much. I don't think I could bear it if something happened to you."

Nyx leans in closer. I think for a minute that he plans to kiss me. I know I shouldn't want his lips on mine so much, but I can't stop the desire. It's an odd turn of events. We're friends. So why would I want more? Isn't friendship enough?

I shake off the thought.

He kisses my cheek gently. I'm disappointed and relieved at the same time.

"I care about you a lot. More than you know," he says. "That's why I'm always extra careful when I go on runs. I want to be around to protect you. I know Remus and Torak would protect you too, but I also want to be here for you. Besides, we always have a lot of fun together. I won't miss out on that for the world."

Nyx kisses my nose and then runs to the crystal-clear pool. "Last one in is a rotten witch."

When he jumps in, he splashes so hard that he completely drenches the other guys. They laugh and splash Nyx as he emerges from the water.

As they swim around together, I can't help but envision Nyx's lips against mine. This isn't the first time I thought he would kiss me. We've been in a lot of situations like this before, but always at the last minute, he turns away or kisses my cheek like I'm his sister.

Why am I disappointed? Why do I want more?

It must be nerves. I don't want Lexus to catch me sneaking out. She'd have a fit, or worse. Honestly, I don't know what she'd do if she found out I was meeting three wolf shifters in the middle of the night. Thinking about the possibility of being caught makes my stomach clench.

I sit on one of the rocks for a few minutes to watch them play. They're my best friends. I'd do anything for them. I'd give my life to protect them.

I don't know when it happened, but my love for them has changed. I still adore them as friends, but now I want more. The summer heat and fear must have cooked my brain. No, it's not that. I just love hanging out with them. I can be myself. I can be serious or silly and they're okay with it. I'm a witch, not a shifter, but they don't care. To them, I'm the same Iris I've always been.

I banish my darkest thoughts before jumping into the pool to join a game of volleyball. Nyx is on his own against Remus and Torak. I join Nyx, and the next match begins.

The sound of our laughter bounces off the rocks around the waterfall. It echoes throughout our little oasis. For a while, my world is perfect.

All too soon, the time comes for us to leave.

I hug each of them a little longer than I normally do. I love the feel of their bodies pressed against mine. I kiss each man's cheek and breathe in their scent as they stand in front of me.

"I'll see you tomorrow?"

"Of course," Remus says.

"Absolutely," Torak says.

"I'll be here," Nyx says.

With a heavy heart, I watch them walk into the woods.

Reluctantly, I trudge back to the Academy.

Once again, unease grips me. I sense eyes, unfriendly eyes, boring into my back as I walk. I glance around and behind me constantly, but all I see is the forest. I distract myself and try to laugh off my concerns, but I don't know which is worse: the trek back to the Academy or my suspicion that an unseen follower is watching my every move.

As I recall our fun night together, I push my worries aside. Memories of the boys' shenanigans gradually shift to thoughts of Nyx, Remus, and Torak. I can't stop thinking about the way they looked as they stood in the pool. Moonlight glistened off water droplets as they streaked down their bodies.

I smile as I contemplate the "what ifs". What if I could kiss Nyx and actually feel his lips explore mine? What if I could touch Remus' bulge to find out exactly how big he is? What if Torak's fingers could do more than casually graze the outside of my bra and send electricity through my body? What if I took a chance and asked them to be with me?

None of this could ever happen for one simple reason: I couldn't possibly choose between them, and if I can't have them all, then it's not fair to choose just one man.

I wrap my arms around myself to ward off the sparks of worry that tingle up my spine. The long walk from the waterfall seems to pass in an instant. The Academy's imposing stone building is a black fortress against the night sky. Dread steals my happiness.

My anxiety intensifies, and my heart plummets when I spot movement by the Academy's entrance.

Lexus stands with her arms crossed. A scowl darkens her face as I approach.

There's no point in running since she's already seen me. As long as she doesn't find out I was with my friends, I might be able to get out of this alive. She hates shifters with a fiery passion. She considers them inferior animals, and she'd love to see them all destroyed.

"It's rather late for a walk." Her deceptively sweet voice chills my soul. "Where have you been?"

I fist my hands at my sides. I don't know what to expect, or if I can even defend myself against her magic, but I'm not going down without a fight.

CAPTIVE OF THE WOLF PACK:
CHAPTER 2

IRIS

My stepmother's eyes glimmer in the darkness. I struggle to keep my nerves under control. I can't show fear. Words jumble in my brain as I try to come up with a reasonable explanation for being outside—and dripping wet—at three o'clock in the morning. I have to lie, but what lie will she actually believe?

Lexus watches me intently as she taps her blood-red fingernails on her crossed arms. Impatient, she waits for me to answer her question.

How much does she know? I don't want to give anything away.

Did she have anyone follow me? Probably not.

She hates shifters. If she knew I was in their company tonight, I don't think she'd be this calm.

"I was out for a walk in the forest. It was too hot in my room. I couldn't sleep, so I took a stroll to help me relax." I manage to stay calm enough that my voice doesn't shake.

Lexus picks up a lock of my still damp hair. "Took a walk in the woods, did you? Did it rain?" She arches her perfectly drawn eyebrows, cocks her head, and purses her bright red lips.

I draw a deep breath as I face Lexus. "I found a pool on my walk and I took a dip."

"Really?" Lexus narrows her eyes. "Why do you lie to me? You know I know the truth. Where were you?"

"I told you." My heart's in my throat. "I went for a stroll in the woods because it was too hot in my room."

"Is that so?" She pauses so long that I think we're done. But we're not. "Who did you meet while you were out on this walk?"

My eyes squeeze shut. "I didn't meet anyone." I glance back at her and scan her face. She must be a bluffing. She couldn't possibly know about the guys. "I went for a walk. I was alone. It was too hot."

"Yes, yes, I know. It was too hot in your room, and you wanted to cool off to sleep."

My smile trembles as I nod.

Lexus tugs on my hair, enough to make me wince. "Since you can't be trusted to stay in your room and tell me the truth of your whereabouts, you're grounded. You're confined to the Academy until further notice. If you leave, you must be accompanied by another witch."

My vision turns red. I may be afraid of my stepmother, but I won't be spoken to like a ten-year-old child.

"I'm an adult. I don't have to answer to you. I'll leave the Academy whenever I choose, without an escort."

"Of course, dear. You're an adult, and you can come and go as you please. But I worry about you. A lot of accidents happen at night, and I wouldn't want anything bad to happen to you. It would completely devastate your father... and me, of course."

Lexus' smile could freeze a polar bear. Her gaze is as sharp as her nails.

"I'm sure you're very concerned." I flash a perfunctory smile. "However, I can take care of myself. Now if you'll excuse me." I step past her. "I'm finally tired. I'm sure I'll be able to sleep now."

"Of course. Sweet dreams. Don't let the bed bugs bite."

I highly doubt I'll sleep at all tonight. If I'm lucky, the buzz in my stomach might calm down by the end of this century. That woman is salty ice on an open wound.

I hurry to my dorm room before I blurt out anything I might regret. I don't like confrontations. My stepmother frightens me, but everyone has a limit. Lexus has almost pushed me to mine. Part of me wants to turn and tell her exactly what I think about her, but I know that's not going to help anything.

I wish my father was here. I wish he wasn't working all the time. If he could see the way she talks to me, he'd understand why I don't like her. It's not even about the things she says, it's the *way* she says it.

As soon as I reach my room, I push the door firmly shut and lean against it. My knees are suddenly weak. I'm not sure I can even make it to my bed.

Finally, my heart calms down and I can breathe normally.

Let her play her games. At least I know she isn't what she seems. I know she doesn't care about me, but she wants something from me. I just don't know what it is. Whatever it is, she won't get it.

I have to learn to control my emotions around Lexus. I'm sure she doesn't care that I loathe her, but she does enjoy my fear. She revels in the power she has over me. I won't let that woman break me. One day, I'll get out of here. Until then, she can't take what I don't give her.

After brushing my hair and teeth, I sink blissfully into

my bed. I'm almost asleep when Lexus' words pop into my head.

"A lot of accidents happen at night, and I wouldn't want anything bad to happen to you."

The more I ponder her words, the more they sound like a threat.

My real mother's car accident happened at night. I always wondered what really happened. Something seemed off about it, but I've never been able to prove anything. It's been years, but I still miss my mother every single day. She was nothing like Lexus. My real mother was loving and kind, and she only used her magic for good, never evil. Not like Lexus.

My stepmother's words continue to haunt me. Did she have something to do with my mother's accident? Is she *that* evil?

Although I despise and fear Lexus, I don't want to believe she's responsible for my mother's death. Still, it's strange that Lexus would suddenly become part of our life just a few days after my mother's burial. I try to remember how Lexus came into our lives, but I can't recall the details. It seems like one day she wasn't there, and then the next day, she was.

My eyelids become so heavy I can't keep them open. The rest of the night consists of dreams about my time at the pool with my friends. I hear the rush of the waterfall, my friends' laughter, and the songs of nocturnal animals.

My skin tingles at the memory of Nyx's, Remus', and Torak's warm bodies pressed against mine as they hugged me goodnight. My body turns into an inferno as I picture their muscular bodies as they play in the pool. My fingers ache to touch them.

All too soon, I wake up. My dreams fade into reality.

I hang around my room all day. Truth be told, I'm still concerned about my encounter with Lexus.

Once again, her thinly veiled threat pops into my head, followed closely by the thought of my mother's death. There's no way she's responsible. Her appearance the week after the funeral is just a coincidence. The issue is simply that I don't like her. Anything more is too horrible to imagine. However, my gut has never been wrong before. Right now, it's telling me to not trust Lexus —and for now, I'm listening.

Lexus is a supernaturally beautiful woman with black hair, violet eyes, and a perfectly proportioned face. But her outer appearance veils the truth. From the moment I met her, I could sense darkness and evil beneath her attractive facade.

Even at a young age, I knew she wasn't what she seemed. Over the years, the darkness inside her has grown. My father didn't notice, but he's not around much anymore. If he saw her every day, he'd see the shift.

I still can't believe my father introduced her to me only a week after my mother's funeral. A week! That's the worst part of this whole situation. I don't know how she got her claws into my father so quickly, but it makes me wonder if she knew him before the accident.

When she first came into our lives, Lexus treated me very well. That was part of why my father finally married her. He didn't know how to raise me, and her presence helped to relieve his burden. He hurt terribly after my mother's death, and Lexus knew exactly what to say to make him feel better. I don't like to think of the other way she may have tricked him into marrying her.

I shudder and sit on the floor by my window.

Little by little, my father started to rely on Lexus more and more. She slowly took over our lives, and now I'm stuck here in her academy of dark magic. Maybe she's not as evil as I imagine, but I don't know. What I do know for sure is that I don't like her, and I absolutely don't trust her.

It has nothing to do with her marriage to my father. Something's off about her. It bugs me, like an itch I can't reach. One day I'll figure her out. Until then, I'll have to keep my guard up.

Sneaking out to meet up with three guys isn't even the worst problem. If she ever found out they were wolf shifters, she'd lose it. Lexus despises wolf shifters. She doesn't like shifters in general, but she has a particular hatred toward wolves.

Some witches don't like shifters, but Lexus takes her hatred to a whole new level. She founded the Academy to train witches to fight a war with the shifters. It's a war I would hate to see unfold. My childhood best friends are shifters, and I don't know what I'd do if anything happened to them. I've never dreaded a war between witches and shifters as much as I do now.

Worst case scenarios creep into my head. I envision finding the men I care about dead in the forest. Tears course down my face, and my soul shatters at the thought. I've already lost my mother. I couldn't stand to lose my best friends as well.

I do my best to swallow my fear.

War is unlikely to happen, I remind myself. There are too many people who want to keep the peace between the shifters and the witches. The peacekeepers outnumber the warmongers. Even Lexus has limited influence because most witches are against a war.

What would any of us gain from a war anyway? Why does Lexus push for it?

I can think of two reasons. First, Lexus is fanatical in her hatred for shifters. Her ideal world entails complete annihilation of every last one. Second, she craves power. She's been able to mobilize plenty of witches who are willing to wage war on shifters. She doesn't need an army; she only needs enough magic to destroy shifters forever.

Her lust for total domination knows no bounds. She wants other witches to serve her desires. Once she gets rid of shifters, I don't know who she'll go after next. Humans? The world? She'll have both magical and political power behind her if she gets her war. My father is very influential in the world. With my mother gone, Lexus can tap into that influence.

The more I think about it, the more I realize that Lexus had good reason to kill my mother—if she killed her. But without proof, I'm just a sad girl with a dead mom, three off-limits friends, and a lot of suspicions.

Lexus is evil. I know I'm right, even if I don't have solid proof yet. But without proof, I can't tell my father. I can't tell anyone. I've never even told my guys about my suspicions. If Lexus found out I suspected her true motives, who knows what she would do?

The thought sends a chill through my body.

I pull my legs up to my chest, press my lips to my knees, and shut my eyes. I'm afraid of Lexus. I can't tell anyone about this. It's too dangerous to even see my friends for a few days. I don't want Remus, Nyx, or Torak on her radar.

No one can help me. I don't know how to win against Lexus. I can't confront her about my mother's death or a possible war because she'd just laugh at me, or worse. If I ask her about my mother's death, she'll deny it and likely tell my father about the accusation. She'll also double her efforts to make my life a living hell. I don't want to find out what she's truly capable of.

Tears well up in my eyes.

I definitely can't meet my friends tonight. I can't lead Lexus to them. It's too dangerous. I can't even talk to her about the guys because she'd kill them instantly if she ever found out how close we all are.

She tries to isolate me. I don't have any witchy friends because of her. She'll use anything she can to drive a bigger wedge between father and me. She'd definitely use my relationship with the guys against me.

Maybe I should talk to my father first.

No. Lexus has him wrapped around her finger. He's completely devoted to her. She snaps her fingers, and my father jumps to do her bidding. She's a saint in his eyes. If I voice my suspicions, I'll look wicked and petty. Without proof, my father will never believe me, and the distance between us will become an uncrossable, bitter chasm. For now, I'm stuck in the shadows with suspicions, fear, and not a shred of proof.

I shake my head.

I don't want a war.

I don't want to use my magical power against shifters.

I only want to hang out with my friends. It seems like such a simple desire, but nothing about my life is simple.

A defeated sigh escapes me. I have no choice but to wait for a few days. This will blow over eventually. She can't ground me forever. If fact, she shouldn't be able to ground me at all. I'm twenty-one. I'm not a child, even if she still treats me like one.

I settle into a comfortable chair in my room. I force myself to take my mind off Lexus. She doesn't get to control my day. Instead, I purposely turn my thoughts back to last night.

When did my feelings for them change?

I've always loved them as friends. They've always been my closest companions. We share everything. They know most of my deepest, darkest fears. They know all my secrets except one. I should have told them about Lexus, but I never had the courage to do it. I didn't want them to laugh at me. I doubt they would have, but I didn't want to risk it.

I know I'll need to stay away from them to protect them, but I won't let Lexus steal them from my memories too.

I don't want to think about the stepmonster anymore, so I grab a bottle of nail polish to freshen up my nails. They're chipped from splashing around in the water last night.

As I paint my nails, my thoughts drift back to the guys. If any of us were to cross the line that separates friends from lovers, who would it be? Nyx, Remus, or Torak? They're all equal in my eyes, so how could I pick just one?

I shouldn't think about them this way, but I'd rather not dwell on other things. I'd much rather think about my guys than about Lexus.

I blow my nails and wait for them to dry.

If Lexus wants to come after me, that's one thing. If she wants to target Nyx, Remus, and Torak, that's another. I can't let that happen. Until Lexus is no longer suspicious of me, I can't put them in danger. As much as I want to meet them again, for their safety and mine, I have to stay home tonight. If Lexus wants to punish someone, she'll have to punish me, not my guys.

CAPTIVE OF THE WOLF PACK:
CHAPTER 3

NYX

"Geronimo," Remus screams as he leaps off the side of the cliff. As he falls past the white froth of the waterfall, he straightens his body and plunges into the water. A wave engulfs Torak and me. Torak throws his arm over his face.

Already wet, I stand there, hands on my hips, and stare at the moon. The cheerful yellow orb has drifted quite a bit since we arrived at the waterfall, but there's still no sign of Iris.

Remus surfaces and swims closer to me.

"Are you all right?"

"She's late." I chew my bottom lip.

"Yes, she is." Remus glances at Torak.

He shrugs.

"She's never late." I dive in the pond then swim to the shallow water. As I wade onto the rocky bank, I shake off water like a wolf.

Torak covers his eyes with a grunt.

Iris has never been late to meet us at the waterfall. I'm

worried. My wolf paces in my chest. He can't wait to see her tonight, and neither can I.

"Well, maybe she couldn't get away from the Academy or her stepmother tonight," Remus says.

"Yeah." Torak dries off his face. He turns a puzzled expression toward me. "You know she has to sneak out and come see us, right? Maybe she finally got caught."

"Yeah, maybe you're right." My gut clenches.

I consider their explanations, but my wolf is having none of it. He huffs and snorts, anxious to see Iris no matter what the logical explanation is for her absence. Until I see Iris with my own eyes and I'm absolutely certain that she's safe, I won't be able to put this out of my mind.

It's not easy to put Iris out of my mind anyway. All I seem to think about anymore is her. I've never told Remus or Torak that I want Iris, but I do. I've wanted her for years. I don't know if it's her innocence or the fact that she doesn't have a malicious bone in her body—and to be fair, it's one hell of a body—but Iris lives in my heart, and I don't think I can get her out. I don't even want to try.

Iris has always been sweet and kind to me, even when I've acted like a bit of an alpha male jerk-off. Because she's so kind, I don't know if there's more between us. I hope we're more than just friends, but I don't know for sure. I've never talked to her about how I feel. I'm not big into talking about my feelings, so I don't even know where to start.

Iris is special, so special that I don't want to mess up our friendship. What if I make a move and she shoots me down? I can't take that kind of rejection, not from her.

When it comes to rejection, I don't get it very often. I'm twenty-three and I keep myself in great shape. I have the type of confidence women secretly admire, even if they don't admit it. I'm the guy people love to hate. I can make a woman drop her panties just by looking at her. And until recently, I took full advantage of this power.

But something's different now. Other women don't interest me at all. I only think about Iris now, and I don't know how this happened. It snuck up on me. One day we were just friends, and the next, I wanted more.

I'm not afraid of anything, but I'm terrified about telling Iris how I feel. I value our friendship. I sound like a dork, but it's true. I don't want to lose her as a friend because I'm greedy for more, and I don't want a quick fling either.

Before I can make a move, I need some sort of sign that she wants more than friendship. I'd hate to ruin our relationship or make it awkward in our little group. I don't know what the other guys would do if they found out how much I like Iris.

I glance over at Torak and Remus. They're my good friends too, fellow wolf shifters, but sometimes they don't pick up on stuff like I do.

Remus is intelligent, an expert herbalist who could teach even the old witches in Bonfire Falls a thing or two about protective elixirs. He won't assume the worst has happened to Iris because his brain doesn't go there. He thinks everyone is as good-natured as he is. He doesn't see all the evil in the world the way I do.

Torak's not any better. He's a reasonably intelligent man, but his head is often in the clouds. He's closer to man than wolf because he likes to write and perform music. Most wolves prefer howling to singing, but not Torak. He shifts with us from time to time, but he's usually in his human form. He doesn't roam the woods in wolf form the way I do. I love my feral side. I embrace it, but Torak? Not so much.

"She isn't coming," Torak says. "If she was, she'd be here by now. Why don't we come back tomorrow night?"

"That sounds like a good idea." Remus nods and turns to me. "What do you think?"

"We need to check the Academy. It's the only way we'll know what's going on with Iris."

Remus' eyes widen.

Torak's mouth gapes. "The Academy? You must be out of your mind."

"Shifters aren't welcome at the Dark Magic Academy." Torak shakes his head. "What if one of the witches decides to shove a lightning bolt up our asses just for looking over the wall?"

"Yeah, it's too dangerous. There has to be another way," Remus says.

They're probably right. It probably is too dangerous. Still, my wolf can't shake the feeling that Iris might need us.

"You're right, it's dangerous. That's why I should go alone. I'll figure out what's up with Iris, and then I'll come back and let you guys know what's up."

Torak glances at Remus and shrugs.

Remus rubs his chin. "Maybe I should go with you. Two is stronger than one."

"Two is stronger than one, but one is easier to conceal and hide than two." I slip my shirt over my head and struggle to pull it down across my damp skin. "I have a much better chance of not getting caught if I go alone."

"He's one sneaky bastard." Torak nods toward me. "He's our best bet."

"Well, all right." Remus purses his lips and grimaces at the moon. "It's pretty unusual for her to be late."

"Good. It's settled then." I pull on my riding boots. "I'll let you guys know what I find out."

"Agreed." Remus cocks an eyebrow at me. "One more thing."

"Yes?"

"Be careful."

I nod.

My wolf wants free, but the Academy is all the way on the other side of town. My Harley is the best bet for at least the first part of the journey. I hurry out to the small parking lot where I left it and hop on. I kick her to life. I rumble out of the gravel lot and pull onto the black pavement of the highway. The cops are more likely to be at the donut shop at this hour than at speed traps, so I open the throttle all the way.

My bike's a beauty. She's all black paint and shiny chrome. Normally, I inspect her for any sign of the slightest smudge on her chassis, but I don't have time to think about that right now. I'm worried about Iris. I'll worry about my bike later. If that doesn't show how much I care, I don't know what will.

As I ride, the moon peeks through the leaves and silver light slashes down to illuminate the road. I wonder if the nearly full moon is a good omen. Wolf shifters draw power from the moon. It makes it easier to shift. But all that light will make it easier for someone to see me too. It's a double-edged sword.

I exit the side road and head toward the Academy.

Wolf form is usually the best method of travel, but I have a lot of ground to cover, and I don't want to waste a single second. Something's not right, but I'm going to find out what's going on.

The dark road that leads to the Academy coils up toward the imposing structure. I swallow. My neck tingles.

Dark magic is present. I may not have magic, but I can sense it when it's this strong.

Fear doesn't stop me, but the Academy's gate does. A huge stone wall flanks the gate. I can't pick the lock. It would be too noisy. I need another way in.

I hide my ride in the bushes next to the road. I head across the street. I jump up and grab the wall, and then haul myself over.

I crouch and begin to shift. My skin burns. My hands sprout black, and my toes extend to form black claws. With a crunch and a spark of pain, my face elongates into a canine muzzle with sharp, pointed teeth.

I drop to all fours, fully one with my wolf. Although I can't see her, I scent a guard near the gate. My wolf hears distant conversation. Even at this hour, some witches are still awake.

The Academy is about a half mile or so from the road. My wolf traverses the distance in less than a minute. I lope through the trees until I reach edge of the main building then creep toward the dormitory.

If a witch spots me, I'll be hurt, maybe killed.

I know which room belongs to Iris. I've followed her back several times to make sure she got home safely. Her second-floor room has distinctive heavy crimson drapes over the window. Faint light peeks out from the edges of the curtains.

I shift back into human form. I pick up a small pebble and toss it at her window.

She doesn't appear.

I throw another pebble.

Again, no one appears.

I pick up a rock and toss it.

The rock spirals through the air.

It thuds against the window much louder than I'd intended.

I cringe.

I look around as discreetly as I can manage in case I've raised an alarm.

Iris pushes the drapes aside and whispers, "Who's there?"

"It's me. I'm coming up." I climb the stone façade. When I reach her window, I put my hand on the glass. I'm so close to her, and yet so far away—story of my life.

"You have to leave." She opens the window a few more inches before glancing over her shoulder. "If Lexus catches you..."

"I wanted to make sure you're okay." I lean in and try to peer past the crimson curtains.

"I'm fine. But I probably won't be able to see you, Remus, or Torak, for a little while, okay?"

"What?" I suppress a growl.

My curiosity and my need to protect Iris, get the better of me. I shove the window open and crawl inside.

My entrance is less than graceful.

While Iris stifles a shout of surprise, I manage to entangle my feet into the curtains. They rip from the wall and collapse on top of me. I struggle to free myself.

"Whew, I almost panicked." I wriggle out of the curtains and stand to my full height. I crack my neck.

Iris's face flushes bright red, and her jaw drops open.

"What's wrong?" I take a step toward her, and she takes a step back.

Iris shakes her head. "You're naked."

"Naked?" I look at myself. It's so natural for shifters to be nude that I didn't consider it. I grab a pillow from her bed and hold it over my crotch. "Sorry. So why can't you see me—I mean, see us—for a while?"

Iris's face scrunches up, and she puts her arms across her chest.

"My stepmother, Lexus, she caught me sneaking in the other night." Iris shakes her head and stares at the bedroom door. "I'm sorry, but I can't meet you guys. I need to lie low and not draw her attention or ire."

My lips twitch with what could be a snarl. I already hate Lexus' guts. This only solidifies my opinion of her.

"What did she do?"

"She freaked out."

"Shit."

"Yeah. So I can't leave for a while. Just a few days. Maybe a week. I don't know how long it will take her to calm down."

"A week?"

"I don't know." She gnaws on her bottom lip. I want to kiss her to make her stop worrying. I hate seeing her like this, so I don't want to pile on more stress.

"All right, fine." I sigh. "I don't like it one bit, but I understand. Tell you what, I'll wait for you at the waterfall every night. If you don't show up in a week, I'm coming back to find out if you're okay."

Iris smiles. She seems genuinely happy that I'm there in her bedroom for the first time.

"I'm lucky to have someone who cares as much as you do," she says.

"I've always cared about you—always."

My heart thunders and my palms sweat.

She's standing here, so lovely and perfect, and all I want to do is kiss her. Despite my fear of rejection, I lean toward her, intending to kiss her beautiful mouth.

A noise in the hallway makes me pull up short.

We turn to look. The door knob rattles.

I leap toward the window and climb out.

Iris mutters a quick spell to make the curtains float back into their proper position.

I don't go far. I flatten myself against the wall beneath her window. I want to hear what's about to happen, and I want to be here to protect her if she needs it. Her bedroom door creaks open and someone walks into her bedroom.

CAPTIVE OF THE WOLF PACK: CHAPTER 4

IRIS

"Damn, damn, damn," I mutter.

I fling open the door to find pretty boy Oscar standing there. He's another witch, but I can't stand him. He reminds me of Lexus. He's just too perfect. Sometimes I wonder if he's using a glamour to look that good. It totally turns me off. I don't dare open my mouth in case something rude flies out.

"I thought I heard a male voice in your room. I was worried, so I decided to check on you," Oscar says in that nasally voice I can't stand.

"I'm fine. I was just practicing a voice-masking spell, which is likely what you heard. Besides, I can guarantee that I'm perfectly capable of taking care of myself." I'm not quite able to keep the snottiness out of my voice, although I'm pretty sure that Oscar is oblivious to it. He doesn't seem to care about anything other than his own good looks and his status as Lexus' favorite student.

Oscar pushes past me as if he has the right to barge into my room. He looks around as if expecting to find a hot naked man lurking in the corner.

He notices the open window and jaunts over to look out. My hands shake as I pray to all that is good in this universe that Nyx has already slipped away.

"There's nothing out there." Oscar announces, as if I'd asked him to make sure there's no boogey man hanging around.

"I know that." I roll my eyes.

"You shouldn't have your window open, especially at night."

As he closes the window, I resist the urge to push him out of it. Usually I'm not a crazy evil bitch, but he's getting on my damn nerves.

"You don't want to give bad spirits the chance to sneak into your room," he says.

I'm pretty sure the only bad spirit in this room is him.

"The only bad spirit brave enough to come into my room and bother me at night is you." He doesn't seem to hear me, so I add, "I'd destroy any threat to me, including *bad spirits*, if they dared come in here."

"Don't be too confident. I think you need a man and a powerful witch like me to protect you from all that is evil in this world."

Oscar tosses his long blond hair out of his face. His bright blue eyes seem to look through me. He licks his lips and grins. All the other females in the Academy drool every time he does that. I usually gag.

He's trying to charm me, but he's failing miserably. He moves closer to me and puts his arm around me. As I lift his arm to remove it, I suppress a shiver of revulsion.

I distance myself by walking to the door. I pull it open and look at him expectantly.

"Lexus said that you haven't had the chance to see much of the world outside your father's house and this Academy," Oscar says, oblivious to my cue to leave. "You don't know all the terrible things out there that could hurt you. I'm a couple of years older than you, and I know what's out there. I wouldn't want anything to happen to you."

Oscar's oily charm is gross. I don't know what the other girls see in him besides a pretty face, but he completely weirds me out. It takes all of my self-control to not punch him. I squeeze my eyes shut. I count backward from ten in Latin.

I summon a civil tone. "I appreciate the thought, but I don't need a man in my life to protect me from bad spirits or anything else. I certainly don't need another witch to take care of me. I appreciate that you and Lexus are so concerned about my well-being, but right now, I only need sleep. I'm exhausted. If you'll kindly excuse me, I'm going to bed."

"I'll be happy to stand guard to make sure you're safe tonight. War is imminent. You never know who might sneak into your room and take advantage of you. Those shifters are sneaky creatures."

I hope he doesn't hear the low growl in my throat.

Oscar is a very weak witch, despite his ego, and I can cast a mind-controlling spell on him. Technically, I'm not supposed to do that, but sometimes, a woman has to do what a woman has to do. Oscar will never know what hit him.

I mouth the words silently, implanting the idea that he should never come near my room again. Oscar's demeanor instantly changes.

"Okay. Well, I have to go."

"So soon?"

I shut and lock the door behind him and heave a sigh of relief as his footsteps fade down the hallway.

"On his way to tell Lexus about our discussion, no doubt." I clench my teeth so hard my jaw hurts.

I rush to the window to see if Nyx is still around. I push open the window and look out. Glowing eyes indicate a wolf shifter is standing just inside the woods. Nyx is safe.

I sigh with relief. I blow a kiss out the window to Nyx

Then I close it.

After all, I wouldn't want any evil spirits sneaking into my room.

I sit hard on my creaky bed. My chilled hands cool my warm face.

I can't stand Oscar. He knows he's good-looking. He thinks that makes him special, but it doesn't. Not to me at least. Maybe he can charm the others, but I'm onto his game. I don't know what he's up to, but if he's in cahoots with Lexus, it can't be good.

Oscar's good looks have to work overtime to make up for his lack of brains and talent. He's nothing like Lexus. Regardless of what I think about her, I have to admit that she's extremely cunning. She knows how to manipulate almost everyone she meets, including Oscar and, unfortunately, my father.

Lexus has Oscar at her beck and call. She's convinced him that he should be my future husband. Oscar has taken her bait, hook, line, and sinker. The thought of marrying him is completely revolting.

Luckily, she can't easily control me. But she can control Oscar. The spell I cast on him won't last longer than a few days. Hopefully, I can just cast another one if he tries to bother me again. I'd hate to have to rearrange his beautiful face with my fist should he poke his nose back into my room.

I growl pretty good for a witch. Nyx would be proud.

I've got to get out of here. I can't stand it anymore. Lexus is always watching me, and when she isn't, one of her minions is.

A fist clenches around my heart. Oscar almost caught Nyx in my room. Nyx could have been in terrible danger. I have to be more careful. There's no way that Oscar just happened to be passing by my room. Lexus was waiting for me to sneak out. She was probably going to have Oscar follow me. I have to watch out for both of them, and there may be other witches involved too. I can't trust anyone at the Academy.

I take a deep breath to try to calm down.

When I think about Nyx's visit, I smile briefly. He was sweet to come and check on me, especially when it was so dangerous. He knows the witches at the Academy are being trained to hate shifters, but he came anyway. There's a lot of tension between witches and shifters. With Lexus at the helm, this place is especially dangerous. If Lexus knew he was here, she'd have the other witches tear him to shreds.

"This war is so stupid."

I slump on my bed and scream into my pillow because I'm fucking stressed. My best friends are shifters. I couldn't stand to lose any of them. It would tear my soul apart.

Only a few witches are trying to start this war. Lexus is their ring leader. However, most witches want peace. The war between shifters and witches was settled decades ago. We've been living in harmony for many, many years except for the occasional brief skirmish.

Hopefully, the war will never start, and everyone will be able to live in peace again. There's absolutely no reason for a war to break out except for idiotic old prejudices and misconceptions and turf disputes. Still, Lexus uses anything she can to rile the witches to train for her battles.

I close my eyes and try to relax against my pillows.

Images of Nyx's naked body pop into my head. I almost wish he hadn't covered himself. His body is art. His face is ruggedly handsome, unlike Oscar's pretty mug. And Nyx has a good soul. He may look like a badass on the outside, but he's nothing but sweet and kind to me.

Before Oscar interrupted us, Nyx leaned closer to me. I know he was about to kiss me. I wanted that kiss more than anything I've ever wanted. Stupid Oscar ruined everything.

My hands clench.

Lexus is doing a better job at ruining my life than she might think. I haven't forgotten Lexus' so-called warning about my safety. She seemed overly concerned about accidents that happen at night—accidents like my mother's. I don't want to say it aloud, but my gut says that Lexus had something to do with my mother's nighttime death.

Would Lexus actually try to find a way to hurt me and make it look like an accident? I wouldn't put it past her. She thinks she can control my life. Well, she's dead wrong. I stay at the Academy because of my father. Even though he's clueless about Lexus, I still love him. Outside of Nyx, Remus, and Torak, he's the only family I have left. My father wants me to stay at the Academy because he thinks I'm safe here... if he only knew.

What will happen to me when Lexus finally decides she's had enough of me because she can't control me? Will I have an accident? Or worse yet, will Nyx, Remus, or Torak have accidents? Or will Lexus murder them because I made a mistake? I'm sure she could make it seem like they were the aggressors. What if Lexus hurts them because they're trying to protect me? I can't stand the thought of that either.

I throw a pillow in frustration. I hate it here. This is hell.

I'm constantly watched everywhere I go. Lexus' threat looms over my head like a dark cloud ready to burst.

I even have someone lurking outside my door in the middle of the night to make sure I don't sneak out to see my friends. I can't even get a bit of fresh air without someone spying on me.

Do I leave?

Unfortunately, I don't really have any place to go. I don't have any other family to run to. Where would I go?

Nyx, Remus, and Torak have their own houses. Would I put them in danger if I stayed with one of them? No one here would have to know where I went.

There must be some way to sneak out of the Academy undetected. I just have to wait until no one's looking.

When, though? Someone's always watching.

Except when I'm in my room.

I get up, walk to the window, and look out.

If Nyx can get in, surely there's a way to get out. I sneak out every night. I might not be able to take everything with me, but I'm not trapped here. I could leave if I had someplace to go.

I lay on my bed and consider my options. I like Remus' house the best. He has an awesome shop attached to the front of his house called Thyme and Country. He sells herbs to witches for spells and to shifters for food and medicine.

The best part is that he has a field of lavender behind his house. It smells divine. It's so relaxing to go out to there and just sit among the blooms. When I'm out there,

I don't have to worry about anything. It would be so amazing to be able to go out there anytime I wanted.

A whiff of imaginary lavender teases me.

Would Remus let me move in with him? It's a crazy idea. A crazy idea that I'd consider if it meant getting out of this hell. I'll have to ask him what he thinks. Maybe tomorrow I'll sneak out to go see him.

I snuggle beneath my silky sheets and warm comforter. The promise of escape distracts me and my thoughts drift back to Nyx. What if Oscar hadn't interrupted us? Would Nyx have kissed me? He'd leaned in so close that I could feel his warm breath on my face. His beautiful brown eyes, the color of milk chocolate, had fluttered shut. I could almost taste his mouth as he'd licked his bottom lip. His left hand had cupped my cheek and his thumb had touched my lips.

I indulge in the fantasy. The kiss would be tentative, gentle at first. Then gradually, it would deepen. His hands would cup my face. I'd wrap my arms around his naked body. He'd be so firm beneath my hands. I'd touch every muscle as I caress his back.

And then what? Would he gently lay me on the bed and continue kissing me? Would he take charge? And then sensing my body's response, would he make love to me? Would he press his body into mine and make love to me until fireworks exploded between us?

It may only be a fantasy, but it just feels so right.

My body and my heart don't want to heed my brain's warning that I could ruin our friendship. I almost found out tonight if I'd be ruining or improving it. Damn Oscar. Damn him. And damn Lexus for sending her little puppet to "protect" me.

I can't live like this. I can't live knowing that every little move I make is being watched. Could that evil witch even be spying on me in my own room?

As the thought pops into my head, my skin crawls. It's like a thousand tiny spiders are walking all over my body. Goosebumps pebble on my arms.

"I'm done. I'm leaving," I whisper.

Satisfied with my decision to talk to Remus tomorrow, I exhale. I clutch my pillow and wish I could hold Nyx tonight. I just hope I can get out of here. If Lexus finds out I'm leaving for good, there's no telling what she'll do.

CAPTIVE OF THE WOLF PACK:
CHAPTER 5

REMUS

I n the warm glow of golden sunlight, I squat between rows of verdant herbs in my garden behind Thyme and Country. A wide-brimmed hat protects my eyes from the sun's vital yet dangerous energy. I smile as I consider this duality in light of my current task.

I learned long ago how to help plants thrive. To care for my many herbs, I have to regularly pinch and prune them. In the process, they're able to flourish, which is why they're so coveted by the witches in Bonfire Falls.

Much like the sun, gardening is all about contrasts, seemingly dichotomous elements that combine into a whole. The phenomenon doesn't limit itself to gardening, by any means.

Who would have thought Nyx, Torak, Iris, and I would form such a strong bond? Talk about dichotomous elements.

I grin. We're an odd bunch, but somehow, it works.

With a palm-sized pair of clippers, I carefully snip off the spiny leaves of a rosemary plant. Rosemary is hardy and doesn't have to be pruned to live, but in order to thrive, one has to put in extra effort. I don't mind. I treat the plants with respect, and they grow faster and stronger because of it.

I pause when a busy ant clambers out onto one of the spines I intend to prune. With a chuckle, I bend the stem down and shake it gently until the red insect falls to the ground. It scampers away to join its friends. Even ants have a place in the garden.

I resume my activities until a bell draws my attention. It only chimes when someone pushes the button at the entrance to my shop, which is situated in a huge room at the front of my house. The shop is attached to the house on one wall, but it's essentially a separate space. There isn't a door connecting the shop to the house. The shop has its own door.

My brow furrows in confusion. It's too early for customers. Witches, obviously, prefer to do things at night. Who could it be?

I stand and dust my hands off. I adjust my belt buckle and gardening pants before I head into the house. On my way through the living area, I remove my hat and pause at a mirror to finger comb my hair. I quickly don a green apron with Thyme and Country emblazoned across it in large yellow script. I put on my best customer service smile and head toward the shop.

Oddly, no one is visible outside the front door. Perhaps it could have been the mailman?

At the entrance, I flip the sign from closed to open. I'm about to step inside when I spot someone out of the corner of my eye.

Iris?

My eyes widen. She's the last person I expected to see today.

She's standing next to the corner of the shop so that

she's partially hidden by the wraparound porch. A suitcase sits next to the rustic rocking chair I keep on the porch for tired customers.

Iris' brows furrow as she frowns. While she's clearly happy to see me, she still seems apprehensive. She hasn't said a word, and she's constantly checking the road.

"Iris?"

Her frightened gaze snaps to my puzzled one. I check her over as she approaches me. She seems no worse for wear, other than her fear.

"I didn't know where else to go," she whispers.

"Did you leave the Academy?" I can't keep the shock from my tone.

"I—can we go inside?"

"Of course. Come in."

I grab her luggage and usher her back to my house and into my sun-bathed kitchen. After setting down her luggage, I quickly fill a tea kettle and set it on the stove.

"You can sit anywhere you want."

She takes a seat at the kitchen table. She's usually never this quiet. It worries me to no end.

As the kettle heats on the stove, I use a mortar and pestle to grind some dried lemon verbena leaves into a powder. The herb is good for upset stomachs and also functions as a mild sedative. I hope the tea will calm her anxiety. I add a pinch of chamomile for good measure.

Once the kettle whistles, I pour water into an artfully painted porcelain cup. I place the silver infuser into it and reach for a glass jar of thick amber honey.

To put her more at ease, I engage her in small talk.

"It's best to put in the honey right away so it has a chance to melt into the hot water." I add two teaspoons of the viscous liquid to the cup and stir it around a bit. "Some people prefer to wait, but then the honey doesn't mix well, and it settles at the bottom. This honey comes from the hive I have out back. It's great for allergies and easier for your body to metabolize than granulated sugar."

I realize I've begun to ramble and hurry across the kitchen to hand her the drink. Iris takes it, but her hands shake terribly. The cup rattles against the saucer beneath it.

She's clearly terrified.

"Hey." I take the teacup and saucer and place them on the table. Then I gather her into my arms and hold her close against me. Her arms encircle my waist, and she seems to take comfort from the gesture.

Even in my human form, her scent intoxicates me. She smells like wildflowers after a thunderstorm. Iris feels good in my arms, as if she's right where she's supposed to be.

We break contact, and I can't mask my concern. "What's wrong?"

"I—I've decided to leave the Academy." Iris crosses her arms over her stomach and glances toward the road. "I can't stay there any longer, but I have no place else to go."

"You can stay with me. My house has more than enough space."

She smiles, but it quickly twists into a worried frown.

"It could be dangerous." She purses her lips; her lovely face draws into a frightened grimace. "Lexus will be so pissed, but I can't take it anymore. I'm sick of her long-winded, bogus tirades about how evil shifters are. It's not true."

We come together in another embrace. I gently stroke her hair as I hold her close. After a few blissful moments, Iris stares up at me with her big, beautiful eyes.

"You're one of my best friends in the world." She sighs, able to relax at last. "There's no evil in you."

Then she nestles her head against my chest. I'm glad she can't see my worried scowl.

You'd better believe there's no evil in me, well, except when I think about her. All kinds of dirty, naughty thoughts come up when I picture myself with Iris. I can't understand how she doesn't realize how much I want her.

For years, I've harbored a desperate, intense desire for her. For a long time, I've been wanting more. Selfishly, desperately wanting more than her friendship. I long to tell her how I feel, but so far, I haven't. If I do, I'll cross a line that can never be undone. I may lose her friendship, and the thought of that scares the heck out of me.

I also have to consider how a romantic relationship with her would affect Nyx and Torak. Our little pack of four, a witch and three shifters, has been an unlikely success story. I don't want to be the one to ruin it. If Iris and I become romantically involved, it would change the entire dynamic of our group. Nyx and Torak are my best friends. I don't want to piss them off and lose them too.

Still, it's hard not to kiss her. Iris's body against mine is something I've dreamed of. Now here I am, in the middle of the scenario I've invented and replayed over and over in my mind for so long.

I want to kiss her so much that I ache inside. I summon every ounce of self-control and force myself to step back.

I won't kiss her. I won't cross that line. Not yet. I'll help her because she needs me, not because I want something from her.

"Come on." I pick up her suitcase and motion for her to follow. "I'll show you to your room."

As I lead her from the kitchen to the living area, polished wooden floorboards creak under our footsteps. In the living room, a rarely used television sits on an entertainment center. Most of the room is bare but for the country-style art on the walls. Two comfortable stuffed chairs flank an equally homey sofa, all upholstered in brown suede.

"This is the living room." I stop. "It's a good place to sit and drink tea. I have cable, but I don't watch it much. Feel free to use it whenever you want."

"This is cozy." Iris examines the room and smiles. "Thank you so much."

"It's nothing." My cheeks flush. The memory of her touch has me so flabbergasted I can barely function. "Ah, there's also a sound system hooked up to my streaming service. Say 'Hey, Bamboozle' and tell it to play whatever you want. Come on, I'll show you the bathrooms."

"Bathrooms?" Iris's brows arch. "You have more than one?"

"Well, not exactly." I lead her down the hall toward the staircase and motion toward a half-open door. "That's the half bath. There's a toilet and a shower, but no tub. Upstairs, there's a master suite with a bath and shower. Your room also has a full bathroom. You can use which-ever one you want."

"Great."

I can scarcely contain my excitement. My secret crush —and best friend—has officially moved in. Hopefully, Nyx and Torak won't be too jealous.

I lead her up the stairs to the upper floor. Upstairs, it smells like my homemade lemon cleaning oil. I love the fresh scent much better than traditional cleaning prod-ucts which are filled with chemicals. My wolf can't stand the smell of bleach, but it loves lemon. It thinks we're about to have lemon pie. Every once in a while, I'll indulge the beast and make a fresh lemon pie just to appease him.

I push on the door to the guest bedroom and we go inside.

"This will be your room." I pull open the drapes, tie them back, and raise the blinds. The room is bathed in warm sunlight.

A vase with slightly wilted daisies sits on a three-legged nightstand in the corner. I make a mental note to replace the flowers.

Adjacent to it, there's a queen-sized bed with a plush down comforter and a full complement of pillows. The only other furniture is a vanity and a stool. Another door is set into the far wall. I open it to reveal the en suite bathroom.

"You have a bathroom all to yourself." I open another door inside the bathroom. "This will be your walk-in closet. I've got some stuff stored in there, but you can move it around if you need more room."

"This is wonderful." Iris' smile is warmer than sunlight. It penetrates deep and heats my blood. "You're so good to me."

"You can have anything you want in the house." I clear my throat. "I mean, you know, food or tea, or whatever. My house is your house now."

Iris breathes a sigh of relief as she pulls me into a warm embrace.

My house is your house now.

I love the way that sounds. While Iris won't share my bed, she will share my house. There may not be a romantic relationship between us, but this is a huge step in the right direction. Now that she's living with me, I may be able to shift our relationship from friendship to something more... maybe even love.

I just hope Nyx and Torak won't be too angry.

CAPTIVE OF THE WOLF PACK: CHAPTER 6

IRIS

For the first time in years, I feel safe. I love my new bedroom. I've been here for a couple of days. When I woke up this morning, I didn't even want to get out of bed, so I'm sitting in bed watching birds flit around on tree branches by my window.

I can finally breathe and enjoy the sunshine without someone watching my every move. I can finally sleep at night without the threat of imprisonment. I know that if I open the bedroom door, creepy Oscar won't be there.

Remus' house is small yet cozy. The lemony scented air helps me relax. It's also energizing. I like the open, airy feel of this place. It's completely different from the dark, ominous Academy which felt like it harbored evil within its walls. I'm so glad to be gone from that prison. I should have left a long time ago, but I was scared. Not anymore.

Since my arrival, Remus has made sure I have everything I need. He's the perfect housemate. He even massages the tension from my shoulders and brings me flowers. For the first time in a very long time, I have a home and a family. Maybe not in the conventional way, but nothing about my life has been conventional.

I'm just happy to be safe. I don't have to look over my shoulder for Lexus or one of her witchy minions, but I'm still scared Lexus will somehow make good on her threat. I'm afraid she'll cause me to have an "accident".

What terrifies me even more is the possibility that Lexus will hurt my friends to get back at me. I wouldn't put it past her. My friends are shifters, and she loathes shifters. It would be a double bonus for her to do something evil to Nyx, Remus, and Torak. Since Remus has given me safe haven, Lexus would probably go after him first. She wouldn't show any mercy toward anyone helping me. I have the distinct feeling she views me as one of her possessions, and she's going to want me back.

I still don't have any proof that she hates me or that she's evil. All I have is a gut instinct that's telling me there's something vile about her. I have to trust my gut. I can't question it even for a second. It's too dangerous.

She keeps pushing for a war between witches and shifters, even though no one else really wants to fight it. No one has been strong enough to stand up to her. I'm not strong enough either, but I hope someone stops her.

She teaches witches how to strip shifters of their ability to shift. It's terrifying and heart wrenching to see it happen. That seems like more than enough evidence to prove she has a dark heart—if she even has one. Sometimes I doubt it. She's more like the evil stepmother from the old fairy tales than the kindhearted mother figure she wants me to believe she is. But I'm on to her. She can't fool me.

Unfortunately, my evil stepmother took it upon herself to pick a man for me. Oscar. As if you could call him a man. He's nothing compared to my shifter guys. They're all real men, while Oscar's still a boy trapped in a man's body. I'd rather eat raw toads than marry that idiot.

Does Lexus think she has me fooled? She's very shrewd and rarely underestimates those who oppose her. I'd give almost anything to see the look on her face when she finds out I'm not at the Academy. She's going to freak out when she realizes she has no control over me anymore. I may not have as much worldly experience as she does, but she's underestimated me. I'm smart, and I have common sense, which is more than I can say for Oscar the Dolt.

Lexus may have used her beauty and charm to manipulate my father, but I see through her charade. I see her dark spirit. I'm not so naive as to believe her lies.

I've escaped, at least for now. I'm safe here with Remus. Even though I haven't told him much about why I left the Academy, I know he's extra cautious and watchful for anyone or anything out of the ordinary.

Remus.

I inhale. He really is the perfect man. He's been absolutely wonderful. Not only is he letting me stay with him, but he's also allowing me to help him with his herbs. I have a lot to learn about these plants, but he's a great teacher. What else could he teach me?

My mind goes to a dark and sexy place. With that gorgeous body, I bet he could teach me all kinds of things. Butterflies dance in my stomach. I try not to picture him shirtless, but it's no use. Earlier in the day, he was outside, shirtless and sweaty. I've never seen him so sexy. I could hardly focus on what he was trying to tell me about various herbs. I could listen to him talk about plants all day long.

His presence puts me at ease. He doesn't even have to talk. When he puts his hands on my shoulders or gives me hug or looks at me with that quirky, sexy smile of his, I melt. There's nothing more relaxing in the world than being in his presence.

Even though shifters don't have magic, I swear Remus has the innate magical talent of being able to make everyone around him happy.

I catch him watching me now and again, but it's not creepy, not like when Oscar would stare at me. No, with Remus, it's sweet. I'm filled with warmth when he looks at me. I can tell Remus cares about me. He loves me as a friend—or maybe something more. A couple of times, I thought he was coming close to kissing me. He never did, but I think he wanted to.

It makes me think of Nyx. If Oscar hadn't interrupted us, I'm sure Nyx would have kissed me. Ugh! I want to find Oscar and stab him right in the eye. He's such a jerk.

I take a calming breath.

What if Remus actually kisses me? I bet his kiss would be as delicious as Nyx's but different. Kind of like strawberry milk versus chocolate milk. Nyx would be chocolate for sure, sensual and enticing. Remus would be strawberry, sweet and natural. And what about Torak? Certainly not vanilla. Something else. I'm not sure what, but I want to find out.

I chuckle. I should probably get out of bed, but I like sitting here thinking about my guys, especially Remus. How can I think about anything else when he's around all the time?

He has a classically chiseled face, watchful eyes, and a beautiful mouth. His face often has dirty smudges on it since he works with plants, and his hair is charmingly scruffy. Sometimes his hair even has bits of dirt or leaves in it. He'll often push his hair out of his face while he works. For some reason, seeing him a bit dirty makes him even sexier.

I decide to get out of bed and finally start my day. After quickly dressing, I join Remus in his shop. We work together for several hours. Business is brisk, so we don't have a lot of free time to talk.

At least four girls have come into his shop today for no reason other than to talk to him. He doesn't even notice they're attracted to him. He's the consummate professional as he answers their questions, rings up their purchases, and moves them along. I'm glad he doesn't notice them flirting with him, because I'd hate to have to claw their eyes out. He's mine, even if he doesn't realize it yet.

I love to watch him work. His arms and chest are muscular from years of hard work and herb gardening. The afternoon is so hot that he takes off his shirt. Beads of sweat glisten like diamonds on his brawny chest. It's all I can do to not cross the room and lick up one of those droplets just so I can find out what he tastes like.

What would happen if I slept in his room instead of mine? Does he sleep naked? He'd probably be an amazingly gentle lover. He'd take it one step at a time, and he'd guide me down a path I've never traveled. I've never been with anyone before, but I'd let him be my first.

Even though Nyx, Remus, and Torak all make me want to explore that part of life recently, I'm still a little nervous about it. I've never even had a true kiss. Lexus would always set up my dates so that they wouldn't amount to much.

These thoughts I have about Nyx, Remus, and Torak are simply a reaction to my body's response every time I'm near them. I have to stop thinking about them like this. It's the only way to save our friendships.

I'm about to head into the main house when a bunch of noise comes from the driveway. I recognize Torak and Nyx's voices, so I jump to my feet and run outside. I hug Torak, then Nyx. They start pulling snacks and my favorite cherry cola out of the trunk of Torak's car. It's all my favorite stuff. I never knew they paid such close attention to what I like. It's too sweet of them.

"How did you know I was here?" I ask as I lead them into the main house.

"We're stalking you." Torak waggles his eyebrows at me.

Remus wanders into the kitchen. "I called and told them where you were. I know they're worried about you."

"You guys are awesome. I'm a lucky girl to have best friends like you." I smile.

Torak notices there's a lot more junk food than Remus' table can handle, so he grabs another one.

It's one of the many things I love about Torak. He's always thinking about potential problems and how to solve them. If he faces a particularly difficult problem or he's bothered by something, he plays his guitar. He also plays it when he's happy and wants to have a good time. I wonder if he brought it with him.

Torak's also incredibly sexy. His tight black T-shirt outlines his well-sculpted arms, chest, and stomach. His hair is a little long, perfect for running my fingers through it. Not that I've done it, but I want to.

I envision my hands in his hair, his gorgeous face dipping down toward mine, our lips melting together into a burning passion. His tight pants show off his masculinity. He has an incredible behind, muscular legs, and of course, he's wearing his signature pair of cowboy boots. He never leaves home without them.

I lick my lips and hope no one else notices.

Nyx tells everyone where to put everything. It's almost a shame his sexy body is hidden by his clothes. The top button on his shirt is undone and reveals a little tuft of hair on his chest. My fingers desperately want to feel that chest hair to see if it's as wiry as it looks. The hint of scruff on his face fits his alpha personality.

I do love a man who takes charge. He can definitely take charge of me.

I sip the soda with a smile and lean back against the couch cushions. My leg rubs up against Remus' and my heart beats so hard I'm sure everyone in the room can hear it.

Casually, he drapes his arm over my shoulder. I lay my head against his chest. Remus is the most laid-back person I've ever met in my life. No matter what's thrown at him, he sits back and calmly analyzes the situation before he acts. If there's a conflict, he scrutinizes both sides before he takes a stance. He's my rock. I can always count on him.

Right now, he's a bit dirty from working in the herb garden. I have a sudden urge to kiss away the smudge on the tip of his nose. I picture us on a blanket together among the lavender blooms, making sweet love for the first time.

I'm startled out of my stupor as Nyx snaps his fingers in front of my face.

"Is anyone home?"

I jump a little and laugh. "Sorry, I was lost in thought."

I lift my head off Remus' shoulder. He still has his arm around me.

"Apparently!" Nyx laughs. "Either that or you were in a coma. Want to share your thoughts with the rest of us?"

"Girl things, which makes you absolutely unqualified to hear them."

"Glad you noticed I'm a man and not a girl."

"It's hard not to notice all three of you are men."

The playfully wicked smiles that spread across their faces are mirror images of each other. Even though they're all very different men, one could get easily confused and think they're all brothers. In a way, I guess they are brothers. Not only because all three are wolf shifters, but they've been together since we were all very young. Sometimes blood isn't thicker than water, which is definitely the case with my guys.

"So, why'd you decide to move in with Remus?" Nyx asks. There's an edge to his voice, and I'm not sure what to make of it. "If you were going to run away from home, I was hoping you'd move in with me so I could have a full-time chef and a maid to clean up after me."

Everyone laughs.

"Remus' place seemed like the right fit," I say with a shrug.

All three men turn their heads instantly toward me. I blush.

"I mean his herb shop and his lavender field are so nice. It just seemed like the right place to go." I stop talking because I really don't know why I chose him over the others. Probably because Nyx still runs "errands" for a dangerous motorcycle club, and Torak's place is never quiet because he's always picking a new song on his guitar.

Nyx, Torak, and Remus all nod as if they understand, although I could swear Remus looks disappointed by my answer.

"Seriously, though. Why'd you suddenly decide to leave the Academy?" Torak asks.

I hesitate. What if I tell them my thoughts about Lexus and they all think I'm crazy?

But will they think I'm crazy? Really? These guys are my friends. They know I'd never say anything bad about anyone unless I was absolutely sure it was true. I might not have proof that Lexus is evil, but I'm sure she is.

"I'm afraid of Lexus. I'm pretty sure she is evil." Nyx, Torak, and Remus don't say a word. They all look confused. Nonetheless, I continue, "Lexus is training witches to stop shifters from shifting. Also, she can force a shifter to shift. She's teaching other witches how to do it."

It's hard to miss the looks of shock and disbelief on their faces.

"I promise you it's true. I've seen witches do it before."

Their expressions would be funny if the situation wasn't so serious. If anyone besides me told them this story, they wouldn't believe it. However, since they trust me, they take my word for it.

Remus unintentionally jerks his arm up from around me. He stands with Torak and Nyx, and they all stare at me as they think about what this could mean for the shifters.

Nyx's voice shakes with anger. "We've got to tell the pack elders. If these witches can force us to shift, then every shifter needs to know about it."

Even though all three men are very independent, they're still members of the wolf pack. It's their duty to protect the pack at all costs.

I nod. I'd expected this reaction. I want to protect them, so I knew I had to tell them. I don't want anyone in this stupid war to get hurt.

"Did Lexus teach you the spell? Can you do this magic you told us about? Can you force a shifter to shift?" Nyx's voice sounds harsh at the thought that someone could control him in such a way.

All three stare at me anxiously.

"I've done it once. It freaked me out so much I never tried it again."

"You need to come with us to the wolf pack den in the woods. You have to show the elders the magic spell so they'll believe us. They have to be warned."

Remus and Torak nod in agreement.

My heart drops into my stomach. I'm terrified of going into the woods to talk to the wolf pack elders. I glance at Nyx, Remus, and Torak, and it dawns on me. I'll do anything to protect them, and they'll do anything to protect me. I'll be safe with them.

I nod sharply. "We must warn the pack."

CAPTIVE OF THE WOLF PACK:
CHAPTER 7

IRIS

Nyx, Remus, and Torak waste no time. As soon as they learn of Lexus' plans, they immediately take action. This cozy chill session quickly transforms to a strategy meetup. Even Remus, who usually is more laid back, is adamant we go immediately to warn the other shifters about the danger. The sooner they have the information, the quicker they can figure out how to protect themselves from my stepmother's dark magic.

We decide to go to the wolf den and talk to the elders after dark. The darkness might keep Nyx, Remus, and Torak out of sight while in their wolf shapes and hide the fact that I'm with them. We can't alert Lexus to our plans.

I don't want to go into that forest. I know we have to, but I don't want to. I'm terrified someone or something may hurt Nyx, Remus, and Torak.

"The elders will listen to you. I promise," Remus says. "They'll listen to you after you show them the magic spell that Lexus taught the witches at the Academy. None of the shifters want war. They want to be left alone."

Remus knows I'm terrified, and he tries hard to comfort me. However, this time, it doesn't work. Or maybe his charms do work, because I'd be a complete basket case otherwise. At least he has me calm enough that I can function.

Besides, if my guys believe me even after I've told them something so unbelievable, then I have faith in them. I know neither Nyx, Remus, nor Torak would ever lead me into any kind of danger. If they say the elders will listen to me, then the elders will listen to me. No question about it.

We spend the rest of the afternoon in Remus' living room. He closes his shop for the day, and we plan our actions for the night. Although none of the men want to show they're anxious, I know they are.

Nyx paces around the room, sits for a couple of minutes, and then he jumps back up to pace again.

Remus sits still as he stares into space, lost in thought. More than once, I assume he's fallen asleep with his eyes open. Then he moves, and I know he's awake.

Torak strums his guitar. Normally, I love to hear him play. He's so talented and can play almost anything for any mood or occasion. Today, I barely hear him.

An uninterrupted line of "what ifs" dance through my brain. I try to focus, but I can't.

Remus sits on the couch next to me again. I lean into him as I try to breathe. In through my nose for four seconds, hold it for four seconds, out through my mouth for four seconds, wait four seconds, and repeat. Remus taught me this breathing exercise years ago. I use it all the time.

Even though Remus seems to be completely absorbed in his own thoughts, he slips his arm around my waist. It takes all I have to not climb into his lap, wrap my arms around his neck, lean against his chest, and lay my head on his shoulder. I'm content to snuggle against him for now, but my desire for him gets stronger every day. Soon, I won't be able to resist kissing him.

While I count breaths, I notice how good Remus smells. He doesn't use cologne or anything else. It's his natural scent, woodsy and herbal. Despite my anxiety, I enjoy being so close to him.

After dark, Nyx, Remus, and Torak turn into their wolf forms. They're very handsome wolves. To relieve my tension, I playfully scratch each one between the ears and tell them they're good boys. All three howl, and Torak nips playfully at my hand. Before my mother's death, I had a dog. Scratches would start between the ears, but he would slowly walk forward until the scratches were on his butt.

"Would you guys like me to scratch your butts too?" I ask in a baby voice.

I'm not surprised to see all three turn their butts toward me. My best friends are smart asses, but those asses will have to scratch themselves.

Too soon, we're serious again. It's time.

I climb onto Nyx's back. He takes the lead through the dark forest to the wolves' den. Even though I know none of my guys would ever let anything happen to me, I'm afraid. Not only for myself, but for the guys too. I'm scared to death something bad will happen to one or all of them. I worry more about their safety than mine. It should be the other way around, but it isn't. I have magic, they don't.

Remus and Torak flank us to guard us. They're on edge and constantly survey the woods around us as we fly through the forest.

This is a bad idea. This is a very bad idea.

It's so dark out. I don't know how the guys can see the path without any light to guide them. There's no moon out. Even if there was, the trees are so dense no light could shine through them.

Unseen eyes watch us from everywhere. I can sense them even though I can't see them. I know they're out there. The goosebumps on my arms and the churning in my gut confirm it.

Are the unseen enemies shifters? Or has Lexus figured out where I am? I don't know which is more dangerous.

Actually, I do. I fear Lexus and her followers a lot more than I would ever fear shifters.

Since there's still technically peace between witches and shifters, I can enter the forest. However, it's an unwritten rule that no one goes into the wolves' territory without permission. This isn't a rule I wanted to break.

Finally, I can't take it anymore. I tug on Nyx's ear, and he stops. I hop off, and Nyx turns into his human form. I'm so scared I don't even stop to admire the sexy naked man in front of me.

Remus and Torak stay in their wolf forms and stand guard. They move close to us, and their fur brushes against me. I lay my hands on their backs to steady myself. But I can see they're uneasy over the situation too.

"I'm worried. Are you sure we should tell the other wolf shifters about the magic spell? What if the information makes them so angry that they decide to start a war?"

"It's not the shifters who want war." Nyx does his best to reassure me. "We told you, the elders and other shifters want peace. But if Lexus gets aggressive, we need to be prepared to stop her. You know how powerful and determined she is."

I nod.

"If we tell the other shifters, they'll at least have time to figure out how to defend themselves if the witches attack."

"But shifters can't defend themselves against this type of magic. It's a very dark magic. Shifters don't have *any* magic, let alone dark magic."

"They can come up with a plan to protect the shifters from attack. Although shifters aren't magical, they're very intelligent and cunning."

Nyx and I are so intense in our discussion that we don't notice we're surrounded by wolves until several step out of the darkness. Dozens of wolves come out of the forest and stare us down. My knees buckle. I have to grab Nyx to stay on my feet.

No, no, no. This can't be happening. My guys don't stand a chance against all of them. We'll be torn to pieces.

One of the wolves shifts into human form. Despite my terror, one ridiculous thought flies into my head—he definitely isn't as sexy as Nyx, Remus, and Torak. I almost laugh at how stupid it is to debate the sexiness of the wolf who's about to eat me.

I cling tightly to Nyx's arm while Remus stands next to me and Torak stays behind me.

In a deep baritone voice, this incredibly huge man informs us that Argus would like to have a word with us. Although his statement is phrased in a very polite manner, it's clear it's not a polite request. It's a command.

"Who's Argus?" I ask.

"He's the alpha of the wolf pack." Nyx whispers in my ear. His eyes are still on the other wolf, who crosses his arms. The man's stance indicates he means business. I wouldn't mess with this guy. He looks like he's ready to kick all of our butts.

"We're on our way to see Argus anyway. We don't need an escort." Nyx sounds bold and shows no intention to back down.

"Perhaps I wasn't clear enough. You're Argus' captives.

We'll escort you to see him. He'll decide whether to free you or not. Who knows? You could remain captives." He says it so nonchalantly that it sends a chill down my spine.

I hyperventilate. This is exactly what I was afraid of. I can't catch my breath. My heart thunders at a million miles an hour. It feels like a baseball is lodged in my throat. My entire body trembles with fear. I've never fainted before in my life, but I'm about to pass out now.

I shouldn't have said anything. I knew I shouldn't have said anything. I put everyone in danger when I told Nyx, Remus, and Torak about the magic spell. They're good, honorable men. Of course, they want to protect the shifters and warn them of the dangers, but at what cost?

Nyx rubs my back. "It'll be okay. I promise. Please don't be afraid. You know I'll rip the throat out of any wolf who tries to touch you. None of us will let anyone touch you."

I know he means it too.

He pulls me in close for a quick hug and then he shifts back to wolf form.

Remus and Torak brush up against me before they take their place on either side of Nyx as guards.

My heart slows. I can breathe again. My legs have calmed enough that I can mount Nyx. I place my hand on Remus' back to steady myself so I can swing a leg over Nyx's back.

The pack closes in tightly around us and barely leaves us any room to move. The spokesman shifts back into a wolf, and we journey through the forest together.

To know Nyx, Remus, and Torak have my back reassures me. I know with my three guys around, nothing in the world can hurt me.

After my mother's death—or murder—my world became very isolated. I couldn't count on my father because of his infatuation with Lexus. Without these guys, I'd have no one to turn to. Their protection and loyalty mean more to me than they'll ever know. I don't know what I'd do without them. I'd be lost.

As we travel, my thoughts shift.

It's hard to miss the strength of Nyx's body as we run through the forest. He carries me on his back like I'm no heavier than a feather. He's not even out of breath. His wolf form mirrors his human form—strong, handsome, and sturdy. His muscles between my legs, despite my fear, pulse a familiar heat throughout my body.

I don't know how I could possibly be turned on at a time like this, but I am. I crave Nyx's naked body against mine. How would it feel? How would if feel to have his naked human body clamped between my legs? Maybe I'll never have the chance to find out.

Remus and Torak run beside us. They're equally hot. Their movements show off how strong they are. Their muscles ripple from their front legs, through their chests, across their backs, and down their hind legs. Would riding them feel any different from riding Nyx? Would they feel the same in bed as they feel when I ride them in wolf form?

I want to run my hands over their bodies and explore every inch of them. I want to know what it would be like to kiss Remus. To kiss Torak. To kiss Nyx.

The three of them are so incredible. They're so different, and yet I love them because of their differences. Each is perfect in his own way. I know they could make me feel things I've never felt before. If only I could share my most secret fantasies with them.

I love them all so much. What if I didn't have to choose? I want all three. And not just their bodies, but their hearts too. Now I might never have the chance. I should have acted when I could.

My fantasies are abruptly cut off by reality. Nyx, still in wolf form, carries me deeper into the forest. If I can't convince Argus we have good reason to trespass in the woods without permission, then we'll be in serious danger. It's up to me to protect all of us. I just hope I don't screw this up.

CAPTIVE OF THE WOLF PACK:
CHAPTER 8

IRIS

As we travel into a part of the forest I've never been through, tension shrouds us like a wet wool blanket. It's getting harder and harder to catch my breath. Inky darkness swallows us like a black hole. Even a magical light orb wouldn't penetrate the dark void that stretches through the forest. I don't like it here, and I already never want to come back. The sooner we can get done with this meeting, the better.

The closer we get to the wolf den, the more nervous I get. Nyx senses my anxiety and twitches his ears to reassure me. I practice controlling my breathing again. I remind myself that I'm a grown woman who is strong. I'm not a scared little girl. If I pass out and fall off of Nyx during our journey, I'll lose any credibility with the pack.

Eventually, my breathing slows, and my head clears. I stay calm by replaying what the guys told me. The shifters want peace. The pack leader will listen to me, especially if I can prove that what I'm saying is true. I trust Nyx, Remus, and Torak. They'd never do anything that would put me in danger.

But what if I can't perform the spell? I've only tried it once. What will happen when I fail?

I sit up straighter. I can't fail. I won't fail. Even Lexus admits I'm a powerful witch. That's why she wants to control me and why she wants Oscar to marry me.

Besides, with Nyx, Remus, and Torak standing beside me, there's no way that I can fail. Their faith in me and their support give me strength and power. I can use that to strengthen my magic. I can do this.

The rational side of my brain banishes the frightened side. The men give me strength and power. Because of them, I can stand strong. Because of them, I'm able to do my part in preventing war and saving the shifters from Lexus' evil.

I'll make Argus and the other shifters believe me. If I have to, I'll perform the spell to show them that Lexus' dark magic is danger not only to them, but to all shifters.

My love for Nyx, Remus, and Torak steadies me. I smile as I picture each of their faces. They've always been there for me, no matter what. They've helped me get through the death of my mother and the dark days at the Academy. They'll help me get through this. Nyx, Remus, and Torak are my true family.

As tension drains out of my body, Nyx twitches his ears at me again. It's amazing how in tune he is with me and my feelings. Sometimes, it feels like we're one. I guess we are, in a way, since my soul feels connected with all three of them. It's almost as if we can communicate our thoughts and feelings without even talking. I wish I was telepathic, but I'm not. It's a skill I'd love to develop some day.

We start climbing up the side of a mountain using a path hidden by trees. Branches snap and leaves rustle as we maneuver our way along. The path is narrow, and we all have to walk single file. Nyx is sure-footed, and never slips. I'm grateful that it's dark, because I'm not particularly fond of heights.

Soon, we arrive at a small opening in the mountainside which is partially hidden by trees. It's just large enough for the wolves to squeeze through. No one would ever be able to see it from the base of the mountain or from anywhere on the path leading to the entrance.

Two wolf guards meet us at the den entrance.

Several of our escorts, including the leader, turn into human form while the rest stay as wolves. Nyx turns human and grabs my hand. He squeezes it to remind me that he's there for me. Remus and Torak stay in their wolf forms. They'll work together to keep me safe.

The leader of the wolves who captured us enters first. Nyx, Remus, Torak, and I are right behind him, followed by the rest of our escorts. Nyx holds my hand tightly. His warmth chases away the chill from the damp cavern walls.

We travel through an endless maze of cave-like passages. It'd be so easy to get lost in this maze, but the wolves know exactly which passages to take.

Finally, after what seems like miles, we arrive at a great stone room. I gaze about in awe and amazement. Torchlight glitters off multi-colored gems which are embedded in the walls around the royal room. Crystal stalactites hang from the ceiling, creating beautiful, deadly daggers.

A stone dais sits at the end of the room. Argus, an older man with graying hair, rests on the throne. His stately countenance leaves no doubt that he's the leader of the pack. His very presence demands respect. Thoughtful wisdom gleams in his eyes.

Dozens of shifters gather into the room, until it's very crowded. Apparently, it's highly unusual for a non-shifter to be brought into the den, let alone the throne room. The leader, who so *politely* issued the invitation to speak with Argus, walks up to him and bows his head. He speaks quietly to him.

Argus nods. He looks at us and then addresses Remus and Torak. "Would you be so kind as to turn into your human forms so we can discuss the purpose of your visit?"

Argus' request is very polite, but once again, it's obvious that it's not a simple question. It's a command that Argus expects them to obey.

Remus and Torak shift. Remus stands on one side of me and takes that hand. Torak stands behind me and puts his hands on my shoulders. Nyx remains on my other side, holding my other hand. The message is clear. These men support me and stand behind me, no matter what.

Nyx, the alpha of our little pack, speaks in a clear, strong voice. "I am Nyx. This is Remus, and this is Torak." He points to me. "This woman is Iris. She's a witch and she's come to warn the shifters of a grave threat."

There's dead silence in the throne room. Every shifter seems to want to hear what we have to say. All eyes are on us and Argus.

Argus looks at me. His grey eyes show wariness and curiosity but also kindness and fairness. Still, I'm nervous as I begin to speak. There's a slight tremor in my voice as I address Argus and the rest of the shifters. Remus and Nyx squeeze my hands to reassure me, and Torak tightens his grip on my shoulders to remind me that he's there. His hard body presses up against me from behind.

"My stepmother, Lexus, is the head witch at Dark Magic Academy. She has many witches in training for the upcoming war between shifters and witches."

Argus frowns. "I'm aware of the Academy and what's taking place there. While it's disconcerting that they're preparing for a war with us, I'm not sure why you came to tell me this. I'm not even sure there's going to be a war. Many shifters and witches are working hard to prevent it."

"Sir, Lexus wants a war. She'll do anything in her power to create one. They're training to fight you. But there's something else..." I breathe deeply to calm my nerves. Remus and Nyx squeeze my hands again to give me courage. Argus waits patiently, intently staring at my face.

"There's an evil spell that I fear poses a great danger to all shifters. It's a spell that you can't fight." I pause, knowing that what I'm about to say will sound unbelievable. Argus waits patiently. "There's a spell that can force shifters to change form. The spell can also prevent shifters from being able to shift."

The entire room erupts at this news as everyone shouts in disbelief. Argus merely lifts his hand, and the room quiets.

"I find this very difficult to believe. I don't see how it's possible."

"I understand, sir. If I hadn't seen it myself, I never would've believed it. But I swear to you, it's true."

"What proof do you have?" His voice is still quiet and calm, but now there's an edge to it. An edge that proves there's still danger lurking inside the pack leader.

"Sir, may I cast a spell on you to prove that what I say is true?"

"Yes, you may." He smiles as if he's placating me.

I step away from my friends and move closer to Argus. He sits, unmoving in his chair. I close my eyes and focus on Argus and my intent. I repeat the spell silently. Argus is fighting me, trying to resist the spell. I picture his resistance as a brick wall. Little by little, I pull the bricks out of the wall, destroying his internal protection. I push harder, and finally, there's a large grey wolf perched on the throne, staring at me in bewilderment.

He continues to fight me, trying to turn back into human form, but I hold the spell for a few minutes, showing him its evil power. Once he's shifted, preventing him from changing back doesn't take much energy. It's simply my will keeping Argus in his wolf form.

No one in the throne room moves. Every shifter is frozen, unable to comprehend what's happening in front of their eyes. Even Nyx, Remus, and Torak are unmoving and unblinking.

When I release him, Argus stares silently at me. The disbelief in his eyes is replaced by a hint of fear.

"Where and how did you learn to do that?"

"As I told you, my stepmother is training witches to use their magic to defeat shifters in an upcoming war, a war she wants to start. She hates shifters. I've been living at the Academy since I was a little girl. I was trained there as well. Lexus taught me and every other witch how to use this spell against shifters."

Rage burns in Argus' eyes. "The Academy must be destroyed." His thunderous voice echoes around the stone room.

"If you and the rest of the shifters are to be safe, it must be." I'm amazed at how calm my voice is. I'd hate to see so many people hurt in such a battle, but for the sake of the greater good, the Academy and all those who know this spell must be destroyed. If one person from that Academy survives, shifters will never be safe, and peace will eventually give way to war.

Argus looks at me with a mixture of gratitude and confusion. "Why did you warn us? Aren't you in putting yourself in danger by warning us?"

"I am. But warning you and the other shifters is more

important. I don't want war in Bonfire Falls. I want peace. Most of the other witches want peace. I want to help stop Lexus from destroying our world."

"You must go into hiding until this issue can be resolved and we can destroy the Academy."

I smile, touched by his concern. "Sir, I'm already in hiding. I escaped from the Academy, and I'm living with Remus now."

He nods in approval.

"What are your plans for destroying the Academy?" I ask.

"I need to meet with the leaders and elders of other shifter clans, including the bear clans. Together, we'll decide what needs to be done. All shifter clans will have to come together and decide how to eradicate the Academy. We'll all have to set our differences aside and work together to stop Lexus."

I nod gravely. "If we destroy Dark Magic Academy, we might be able to avoid this stupid war and have peace between us again."

"I hope so. Thank you for coming to see me. You've risked a lot to come and protect us from this great evil. I grant you safe passage back to Bonfire Falls.

"Thank you." I turn to leave but stop and face him once again. "I just want peace. Some of the people I love most in this world are shifters. I'll do anything to protect them."

"I'm sorry I didn't believe you at first. Please accept my apologies."

"Thank you."

Argus nods and we're dismissed. The leader who'd brought us here approaches us.

"Follow me." His tone is completely different than the one he used earlier.

He leads us back out of the maze. Although I am sure that Nyx, Remus, and Torak know their way around, I'm grateful that Argus is providing us with extra protection.

Remus grabs my hand and gives me a soft smile. "Are you ready to go home?"

Home. That word has never sounded better, and it's never had so much meaning before. Remus' house is my home. It's where I belong.

"Yes, I am."

Remus shifts into wolf form, and I mount him. I'm finally safe. It's all because of Nyx, Remus, and Torak.

CAPTIVE OF THE WOLF PACK: CHAPTER 9

NYX

As Remus and Torak tidy up after breakfast, they move around like busy bees flying from one flower to another. Plates clatter in the sink. The sound echoes dissonantly through Remus' kitchen. They laugh and whip each other with dish towels. I sit back and watch from the kitchen table.

Like the good old country boy that he is, Remus has laid out quite the spread. We had sausage and scrambled eggs as the main course, with biscuits and gravy as a side. There's a plate of peach preserves and a pile of sourdough toast waiting for me to eat them. A tray of butter sits in the center of it all.

The scent of maple bacon and freshly brewed coffee should be enticing, but all I can think about is Iris. I haven't finished my plate because I'm too busy staring at her through the window.

As she strolls through the lavender field in a home-spun country dress, I can't stop thinking about how beautiful she is. The light blue color of her dress truly emphasizes the splendor of her eyes. Framed by golden sunlight, Iris is a true vision of beauty.

A gentle morning breeze teases her hair. Lavender stalks dance on the wind. Her expression is a dark contrast to the beautiful day. Her shoulders are slumped, and a sullen frown darkens her beautiful face. The gravity of the situation has really got her down.

I want to comfort her right now, but there's more to it than that. My desperation rears up again—it's hard to fight this desire. It's so wrong to want her at a time like this, but I do. I'm hard as steel and the only thing I want to eat right now—is her.

To be honest, I woke up early, hoping I'd have a chance to be alone with her. I've wanted her, for as long as I can remember. Not when we were really young, of course, but as we got older, she was all I could think about.

Last night, seeing her in action made me want her even more. She's not only beautiful, but she's incredibly brave as well. Her ability to stand up to Argus without displaying so much as a whiff of fear stunned me. As I reflect back on it, I can't believe she was so fearless before him. Or if she was afraid, she kept it well hidden.

Either way, she has nerves of steel, and I can't help but respect that.

Iris is impressive. I knew she was a kick-ass woman, but after seeing her last night, my crush for her is burning on a whole new level. I can't stop thinking about how much I want her. I want her to be my woman.

"Nyx, are you finished with your breakfast?" Torak stands next to me. He reaches for my plate of half-eaten sausage. His eyebrows rise in query, and I nod my head. He looks kind of goofy wearing one of Remus' spare Thyme and Country aprons.

"I'm done. Thank you." I rise from the table and put on my jacket. "I'll go check on her."

I leave the two of them to finish their domestic duties and tromp out into the backyard. The lavender field stretches out before me. A light breeze causes a fresh wave of scent to envelop me.

Iris strolls through the purple field at a leisurely pace.

The turf crunches under my boots as I walk briskly along the dirt row between plants. It doesn't take me long to catch up.

"Hey."

She turns to face me. A sad smile creases her lovely face. Her beauty is dazzling, even with the gloomy expression on her face.

"What's up?"

"I wanted to see if you're okay."

Iris turns away and stares out at the lavender stalks. She idly reaches up and brushes away a windblown strand of hair from her face. Her body leans forward as she walks, as if she's bearing a heavy burden.

She's too young and too innocent to have to suffer through trials like the ones that have been thrust upon her.

"Maybe I'd feel safer if the Academy never existed." She sighs, shakes her head, and turns her somber gaze toward me. "I know that sounds terrible."

I nod. We walk through the lavender together. Right now, the best thing I can do for her is listen and let her get these dark feelings off her chest. She's a good friend, and I'm here for her.

But she's so lovely, it's hard not to stare. I long to pull her into my arms and whisper that everything's going to be okay. But I don't know if it will be okay. Only time will tell.

Our passage disturbs a flock of birds. As they take flight, their wings beat the crisp morning air and they caw madly in terror.

My nose twitches a bit as I take in their scent. My wolf thinks those birds are good to eat, and if I were in wolf form, I might have tried to catch one.

Iris watches the birds as they take flight. A slight smile spreads across her face.

For a moment, I believe she's feeling better, but when she speaks, there's a bittersweet wistfulness that causes me to wince.

"I wish I could do that—just fly away from all my problems."

"Yeah, I know what you mean." I stare at the birds as they arc through the bright blue sky. Sunlight catches their black feathers and reveals dozens of other colors around their bodies. "Sometimes, when I'm on the highway, I think about driving away from it all, so I don't have to deal with life."

She nods. She seems a smidge less depressed, but she isn't smiling yet. I want to see her smile. It's the only thing I want today.

"I hope Argus can come up with a way to destroy the Academy once and for all. I'll gladly use my magic to help him, if it comes to that," she says.

The idea of my sweet Iris going into battle against the dark arts sends a bolt of panic through me. Anyone who even thinks about hurting her is dead. Pure rage rises up to choke me. My fists clench.

"I don't think you should get involved." We pause in our stroll, turning to face one another squarely. "I don't want you to get hurt."

She seems surprised but not angry. She smiles, and my heart absolutely melts. I'd die for that smile.

"You're so sweet. I'm glad you weren't busy with the club so you could have breakfast with us."

"Well, I was supposed to go on a run." I'm a bit apprehensive, but I try not to show it. The motorcycle club is pissed at me because I didn't go on a scheduled run. I had to pull the family card to get out of going. Iris is my family, so the club let it slide. "I told them I couldn't go last night. I wanted to be with you when you went to see Argus. I want to make sure you're safe and protected at all times."

"I feel so safe with you." She lays her hand on my forearm and the light touch sparks fire in my core. Desire runs fast and hot through my shifter veins. "You're protective and understanding. And you cheer me up when I'm down. Not many guys are supportive like that. Honestly, I don't know what I'd do without you."

Suddenly, she moves forward and flings her arms around my body. She nestles her cheek against my chest. I'm stunned for a moment, but then I quickly put my arms around her. I've waited a long time to feel her body pressed against mine.

It feels so good, it hurts.

I've wanted Iris for a long time, and I think she wants me too, but I'm still hesitant to do anything about it. I don't want to ruin what we have by chasing an impossible dream.

I could hold on to her forever, but I might not get the chance again. The moment is perfect for our first kiss, but do I dare?

The tension between us is thicker than honey, but she's my friend. She's been my friend for a long time, and that's been totally cool with me. I'm selfish for wanting more from her, but I can't keep denying my heart's desire.

I can't help myself. I gently nudge her chin up so that our gazes lock. There's a long pause while we stare into each other's eyes. I get lost in her eyes. They're so full of sweetness and innocence and light. Sometimes I feel like I'll be consumed by my need to claim her as my mate.

My gaze drops to her lips. She inches closer. When our lips meet, I groan.

Her lips feel amazing. They're so soft and warm. I taste maple syrup on her lips, and a hint of something more. She isn't pulling away. She's leaning into me, fisting my shirt in her hands. Pulling me closer.

We continue with slow, gentle kisses. There's no tongue, not yet. Just a gentle exploration of each other. But the longer we kiss, the hotter it gets.

I fall into the kiss and slip my tongue between her lips. She melts against me with a deep sigh of pleasure.

She's so sweet, so innocent. I should be happy with this hot make out session, but I can't help but want more. Our bodies are pressed together. Surely, she must have felt my erection by now, but does she want more?

To test her intent, I slide my hand down her spine, then lower. I firmly cup her butt and pull her even tighter against me.

She laughs softly and pushes me away.

"We should get back before they come looking for us." She looks up at me longingly and then pecks me on the lips one last time.

She squeezes my shoulders, then turns and strides back toward the house.

I stand there for a long moment while I watch her walking away. My heart sinks with disappointment because she me cut off.

I'm Nyx. I don't normally get cut off.

But I'm a real man, and a real man respects a woman's boundaries. Besides, the kiss was so hot, incredible, and mind-meltingly awesome, that I'm bizarrely satisfied. She may not have commented on our sudden and intense make out session, but that kiss definitely had substance.

I can wait until she's is ready to take the next step. Hell, I'd wait forever for her.

Besides, right now she's busy with her evil witch step-mother. Maybe once all this drama with the Academy is over and done with, she'll be ready to talk about what's happening between us.

I can only hope.

CAPTIVE OF THE WOLF PACK: CHAPTER 10

IRIS

L evitation spells are second nature to me now. They weren't at first. On my first day at the Academy, I was the only witch who couldn't levitate. I felt so stupid that I spent every night for two weeks in the practice rooms—the ones with shatterproof windows and padding on everything—to perfect the simple spell.

Now I don't even have to look at my target to successfully pull it off. I stare into space as I trace the spell symbols in the air with one hand and hold my wicker basket in the other. The snip of the levitating gardening shears and the gentle wisp of the herbs as they land in the basket tell me I'm on track.

My lips still tingle from Nyx's kiss, even though that was hours ago.

I've come into the garden to distract myself. Obviously, it doesn't work. One glance into my basket tells me I've gathered herbs I don't need.

Seriously, the last thing I need to make is a fertility potion.

With a deep sigh, I cut herbs for protection spells instead.

Remus' garden is a work of art. Aside from the vast gardens at the Academy, I've never seen such an impressive collection. He even has mugwort, and it's one finicky plant.

I levitate a snip into my basket.

A lot of witches underestimate the importance of herbs. Indeed, it's not as flashy as sparks of lightning from your fingertips or thought manipulation, but herbs are literal lifesavers. It's much easier to hide caches of protective herbs around a property than it is to continuously cast a protective barrier.

Plus, it's easy to tell someone to shove off via flowers. Oleander, begonia, and basil.

"Hey," a deep voice says.

Apparently, I'm too focused now because I didn't hear him come up behind me.

Before I realize it's him, my fight-or-flight brain shoots a blast of wildfire. Remus dodges smoothly. His sage plant does not.

The garden is immediately filled with the musky scent of burnt sage.

"Well, at least we don't have to worry about bad spirits," he says wryly.

I quickly cast a cooling blast of frosty air at the plant. All the leaves that didn't crumble to ash are charred and useless. "I'm so sorry. I'll replace it, I swear."

"Don't worry about it. Sage is easy to grow. I've got plenty of seeds to spare. Sorry I scared you."

"You don't need to apologize." A smile spreads across my lips the moment I lock eyes with him. I can't help it. Something about Remus evokes a smile. "It's silly that I'm so jumpy in the first place."

"To run away from the Academy and a warmongering stepmother would make anyone jumpy."

"Don't try to make me feel better." I smirk.

"Too late." His smug smile is so sexy it makes my heart flutter. It should be illegal.

"That's not the only thing that has me on edge. Have you seen the ravens?"

"I've seen one or two. What does that have to do with anything?"

"They're Lexus' spies." My lip curls up into a snarl.

"Wow. I mean, I know ravens are smart, but are they smart enough to be spies?" Remus rubs the back of his neck and squints up at the bright blue sky. I follow his gaze to check to see if any big black birds are circling above us.

"You know how most witches have familiars?"

"Little animal buddies? Sure."

"Familiars have a magical link with their witches. Lexus has that too, but she's crazy good. She can summon multiple familiars, and their loyalty is unshakable. She can even join minds with them if she needs to."

I'll bet Lexus uses the ravens for their memory. She would've used hawks if she wanted to share vision directly, or maybe a cat.

"That's intense."

"You can say batshit crazy. That's what it is. It's batshit crazy."

"Ravenshit crazy."

I snort out a laugh.

"You know what's really ravenshit crazy? Your ability to make exile seem like a country vacation."

"I do what I can." He closes the distance between us and gently grips my shoulders. His hands are warm and heavy, but their weight is pleasant. Solid.

He leans down a bit to look me in the eyes.

"Everything will work out." He sounds so sure, I almost believe him. He's clearly trying to give me peace of mind. I can't make myself contradict him.

He leans back and frowns.

"You'll still have that little line between your brows no matter what I say, won't you?" He presses his thumb between my brows. I scrunch them up on a reflex.

If my eyebrows are tense, imagine how tense the rest of me is. My shoulders feel more like boulders. I should risk a trip to the massage studio in Bonfire Falls. If I do magic with tense muscles, I'll look like a stooped hag from a fairytale before I'm forty.

I self-consciously lift a hand and press it into the space between my shoulder and the curve of my neck. There are a lot of things that should be rock hard. My muscles shouldn't be.

"Are you all right?" Remus gives me a weird look.

"Yeah, why?" My brow furrows again. Damn it, I have to work on that.

"I poked your forehead, and then you went all quiet and squished your shoulder."

"Oh." I shake my head. "My muscles are tense. I'm so scatterbrained lately. I guess I let myself get too in-my-head, you know?"

"I know a cure for both of those things."

"What?"

"Relax." There's that sexy grin again.

"Very funny." I roll my eyes.

"Maybe some good news will help you relax."

I perk up.

"News? You've had news this whole time and you're only telling me now?" God, why am I such a motormouth?

Is this what stress does to a person? No wonder I've avoided it for so long.

Thankfully, Remus doesn't think my string of word vomit sounds insane. He laughs.

"Argus wants to meet with you in a few days."

"How is that supposed to make me relax?"

"You'll get to tell him we have other witches to fight this battle with us."

My nerves cause some kind of delay in my brain. It takes a moment to process Remus' second statement.

"You found witches to help us?"

"Minerva and Azealia. Do you know them?"

"I do." I smile.

I should've thought of them sooner. It's no secret Minerva is a friend of the Bear Clan and an insanely powerful witch, and everyone knows the story of Azealia. Her power is nothing short of legendary.

I've never thought I'd get to meet her in person. We aren't friends or anything, but ever since she and Minerva became friends, Azealia has been to some of the Bonfire Falls social events. Rumor has it she's a beast at bingo night.

"If we intend to wipe the Academy off the map once and for all, those are two witches we want on our side," he says.

I nod in approval.

"Look at that. The little wrinkle is already smaller."

"Really?"

"No. You still look as tense as a loaded spring trap." He chuckles.

"That'll probably stop once this whole mess is put to bed."

"Probably?" Remus arches one strong brow.

"No promises."

We fall into a comfortable silence. I magically pluck the last of the herbs I want while Remus gathers leaves from that poor sage plant.

When I stoop down and group the herbs together in neat little bundles by plant species, a thought occurs to me. I straighten and stare at Remus with my mouth open. I struggle to find the right words to voice my sudden barrage of thoughts. He must sense my stare because he turns to face me.

"You look like you swallowed a garden beetle," he says.

"It's so strange. Did you ever think we'd be a part of something like this? To topple the Dark Magic Academy is to basically launch a revolution."

"It's a lot to wrap your head around. I never expected to be a part of something so major. I always thought you would, though."

"Me?" I shake my head. "You can't be serious."

"I am. You've always had fire in you. Even though the circumstances aren't ideal, I'm glad I get to watch you put that fire to good use."

I blush.

"That's one way to look at it." I glance down at my feet in an attempt to hide my goofy smile. "I never understood Lexus' deep hatred of shifters. Or anyone's, for that matter."

"All the witches I've ever met, with the exception of one or two, are good people. When we first learn to control our shifting powers, we're taught to always be cautious around witches, but I never understood why. Every injury I've suffered has been from a shifter."

I remember my first lesson about shifters. "The instructors at the academy made all shifters sounds like brainless savages that would tear our throats out the moment we let our guard down. I believed them until I was, like, ten. Then I realized everything they said was basically hateful lies. But why go to that trouble? The war was already fought."

"Grief, stubbornness, and bad blood make for a toxic mix. It's not just the witches. This illogical hatred is in some of the shifters too."

"So illogical that a witch and a shifter can't even be lovers." The thought is voiced and out of my mouth before I can rein it in.

"That's nonsense." The ferocity in Remus' voice startles me. "The war's over. There's supposed to be peace between witches and shifters. Find me one good reason why a shifter and a witch can't be lovers."

Words catch in my throat. There are no good reasons. He and I both know this.

"I'd pay good money to see someone try to take you from the witch you want to be with," I say.

Remus steps closer. "You'd pay for a bloodbath."

That's the most aggressive thing I've ever heard him say.

As I gaze up at him, I'm not sure if my heart beats ten times faster than normal or if it stops completely. I know he means what he says. Remus may outwardly appear to be the most laid back of our little band, but he's still a wolf, and wolves have teeth.

A hazy sensation washes over my body. A thrill runs up my spine and causes me to shiver in a way that might be mistaken for fear, but it's something else entirely. A pang of longing and desire for Remus pops up that's so sharp, so sudden, it nearly takes me to my knees.

His intense gaze darts to my parted lips. I'm not sure who moves first, but the next thing I'm aware of is his lips pressed against mine. My hands go to his arms and grip the sleeves of his worn leather coat.

My fingers dig into the solid muscles that lurk beneath. Every inch of him is hard and taut except for his mouth. It's never occurred to me his lips would be so soft.

I consider what Lexus and the other elder witches would think of this. The fact it's so forbidden only makes me like it more.

"What was that for?" The smile on his lips reaches all the way to his eyes.

"I've wanted to kiss you for ages."

"You're the witch I want to be with." His voice rumbles through his chest. My knees go weak as if I'm a maiden in one of those Greek tragedies. Oh my God, I've swooned. Somehow, Remus has turned me into a swooner. "I waited so long because I didn't want to risk our friendship."

"Our friendship..." I murmur.

Suddenly, it feels like icy water has been thrown over me.

Remus and I are friends. Lexus knows this. She hates him enough as is. What will she do to him if her ghastly raven spies discover he and I are something more?

"You don't want to risk it." His strong brow furrows.

"It's not that. I just can't make a decision like that right now. My head's not in the right place. There are so many other risks to consider. If Lexus ever finds out, she'll skin you alive, make your coat into a hide, and deliver it to me in person."

"My God."

"The messed-up part is that I'm not exaggerating."

Remus' expression softens. He tucks a stray lock of hair back behind my ear.

"I understand that you're not in the right mind to make a decision." His hand leaves my hair to rest on my shoulder. The weight of it steadies comforts me. "If you ever need to talk about what's going on in that wonky head of yours, you can come to me. Always."

"Thank you." I can't think of the right words to fully express my gratitude. "Even if you think my head is wonky."

He plants a kiss on my forehead. It's not romantic or sexy, but it's meant to reassure. It's exactly what I need.

"Now that you've mentioned those ravens, I'll walk the property and see if I can scare them off," he says.

"Be careful. Who knows what kind of spells Lexus has put on them? I'm headed inside to dry these herbs. If I do it right, we can use them tonight."

He pulls me in for a hug before we go our separate ways.

Once I'm alone, my thoughts shift to the kisses I've shared with Remus and Nyx. Yes, I've fantasized about both of them, but I've never thought it would happen, especially with everything else going on.

Remus' kiss felt warm and familiar. Nyx's felt like a ride on a wild animal, but I don't think that's a bad thing.

If someone were to ask me whose kiss I prefer, they'd wait an eternity for the answer. My attraction to both men is undeniable.

Memories of kissing their delicious lips sends my heart into a flurry all over again. My cheeks flush, and I stumble over my feet as I walk.

I need to get it together. Now is not the time to lose focus. Lexus could show up to incinerate the house with all of us in it, and here I am with thoughts about which man is the better kisser.

Remus said he wants to be with me. I admit I like the idea a lot. Yet I also feel something for Nyx. I don't fully understand what it is, but it's strong. If I were forced to choose between them right now, I couldn't do it.

My foot catches on a stone hidden beneath the grass. I stumble. The herb basket slips from my fingers, and its contents scatter over the dirt.

"By the witches' moon, pull yourself together. They're just men. You don't need to lose your head after a single kiss."

Even as the words leave my mouth, I know it's not true. They aren't just men. They're something more. They're *my* men. When all of this is over, I'm going to have to choose between them. I don't want to do it, but I don't see any other way. How can I expect them to share me? They'd have to be crazy in love to agree to that proposition.

CAPTIVE OF THE WOLF PACK: CHAPTER 11

TORAK

Usually, the lavender field behind Remus' house is one of my favorite spots to write songs. The brilliant purple stalks always get my creative juices flowing. The scent relaxes my mind and allows lyrics to pop up naturally. But today, my process isn't going so well.

It's a beautiful sunny day, and the purple flowers contrast nicely against the clear blue sky. Bright sunlight warms my skin. Butterflies flutter about the field and float in the occasional breeze. Bees buzz from one flower to another, and birdsong accents the insect sounds of the day. It's a perfect day to write songs.

But for some reason, my fingers seem clumsy on my guitar. None of my chord progressions feel right, and all my lyrics sound weak and clichéd.

Several pages of my notebook are full of crossed-out lines about flowers and bees and who knows what else. All are very lame, heartsick teenager lyrics.

I'm supposed to have this song over to Gareth Desharp's people by next week so they can get into the studio to work on his new album, but I can't find an angle. He wants an inspiring, original, powerful love song. And right now, I can't string together one chorus. It's a bit of a problem for a professional songwriter, especially when the client is as big a star as Gareth Desharp. A hit song for him would be a huge boost for my career.

Every time the melody and lyrics start to flow together, my mind strays back to Iris. Whenever I muse on the concept of love, I picture her smiling face.

I wish I could push aside my feelings because we're such good friends. It's not right to lust after close friends who trust you so much, but at the same time, I can't change my heart. I just wish it wouldn't interfere so much with my professional life.

It's not very professional to pine after your best friend like a pup.

As much as I try to focus on my writing, I can't help but wonder how she'll hold up with all this conflict about to boil over. The wolf in me wants to protect her, to tear apart all who would threaten her. The man in me wants to hold her, stroke her hair, and tell her everything will be all right.

As my fingers slide across the frets, they find their own way over the strings. They ring out a slow, haunting melody that sounds like it has potential. Lyrics follow close behind, and lines come in, half-formed, but good.

My moon, I am the wolf
    Howl longingly for you
    Feel your push and pull

·   ·   ·

I PAUSE to scribble furiously in my notebook. I will my hand to move as fast as it'll go to keep up with the lyrics that stream forth in waves now from my subconscious.

With the opening lines written, I try the melody again. I start the progression a few frets higher this time, slide down the neck and match my lyrical cadence to the chord changes. It sounds good, but I shouldn't write about Iris. The concept of unrequited, forbidden love is the only thing I'm able to articulate right now, and Iris is the inspiration.

The first couple of stanzas are ready. I run through the chord progression again and lose myself in the performance. My head's awash with the scent of the lavender and my heart's afloat with love.

MY MOON, I am the wolf
> The only way I can show love
> Is to howl for you

IN MY VEINS, I feel your soft pull
> It's enough to keep me on the run
> But I'm no fool

EVERYONE ELSE HOWLS for you too
> After all, you're the moon
> Everything with blood
> Feels your push and your pull

I OPEN my eyes as the last chord echoes across the field. Iris stands right in front of me with a smile on her face.

"Hey." A rush of heat makes its way from my chest up my neck and into my face. "How long have you been there?"

"Long enough." She smiles a sweet, impish smile. "That was beautiful. Like really, incredibly, beautiful. Did you just write it?"

My blush intensifies. "Uh, yeah, it's for a really important client. It's not finished, though. You weren't really supposed to hear it. I don't usually share works in progress."

"Well, I guess it's a good thing you didn't notice me here then, huh?" Her mischievous grin spreads wider across her face. "Lucky for me, you were lost in your own world."

"Ha, yeah. I guess you got a free show." My embarrassment fades slightly as we fall into a familiar back and forth. "But next time, I'll have to charge you. Can't work for free here."

She laughs. "So, who's the lucky lady?"

The blush returns. "Oh, it's not about anyone in particular. Just a project for my client. Radio always wants more generic love songs."

I want to tell her she's the woman, the inspiration. That she always has been. And that practically every song I've ever written has been about her in one way or another. But I know I can't tell her.

We've been friends for too long. I can't ruin our dynamic. To disrupt it would terrify me. But not telling her the truth about how I feel is also unbearable.

"Oh, come on," she says. "I don't buy that. I heard the way you sang it. That wasn't some generic, meaningless love song. You should've seen yourself. I could see the pain on your face, hear the longing in your voice."

"There's nobody. Really. Just some lyrics that came into my head."

"Nope, no way. Come on, just tell me who it is." She shoots me a devious, conspiratorial grin. "I have to know so I can go punch her in the face and tell her what an idiot she is not to want you."

I know it's probably not a good idea, but I can't live with my secret emotions for one more second.

"It's you."

She looks surprised, naturally, but not taken aback or appalled, or offended, as I feared she might. I even see what I hope is the hint of a smile tug at the corners of her mouth.

"What?"

"It's about you." My gaze drifts away from her, scared of what I'll find on her face. I stare out over the lavender field as I will myself to be calm. "You were the inspiration. You're the moon."

She's quiet. I chance a peek at her face. She looks at me intensely.

"I love it. It's beautiful. I totally get it what it's like to want something so much that you're afraid you're going to burst." She surprises me when she sits in front of me and envelops me in a tight hug. "You're so talented. I'm so lucky to have you in my life."

Her breath is hot on my neck. I can feel her gentle heartbeat against my chest. My heart pounds like a bass drum. My embarrassment has shifted and blossomed into a full-body blush now. Blood rushes simultaneously to my crotch and my head.

But for the first time, I don't see my feelings toward Iris as inappropriate. To hold her like this feels completely natural. It feels right. We fit together like two pieces of a puzzle, and I never want to let her go.

Her breathing deepens. The wolf within me calls out as I sense her passion. The man within me calls out too. Both aspects desire one thing—her.

I shift my head slightly to angle my mouth toward hers. As she clutches the back of my shirt, she shifts her head too. Her fingers press gently into my back and neck.

My hands slide along her back to search tentatively for a signal. I pull my head back, and our eyes meet. Her gaze darts to my mouth. Her lips part and our faces seem to be drawn together by some inextricable force.

When our lips meet, a current of energy radiates from my mouth into the rest of my body. Her mouth opens like a blooming flower. Her tongue reaches out delicately. My long wolf tongue responds instinctively to flick against hers as our mouths move in passionate concert.

My hands find their way to her round bottom. I squeeze her against me. She groans and wraps her legs around my waist. My cock jerks hard and desire burns in my belly.

She slips one of her hands inside the unbuttoned portion of my shirt to run it across my hairy chest. I growl in response.

Our mouths open wider and our tongues glide across each other as the kiss takes on a hungrier tone. We press against each other hard now, almost desperate with desire. I run one hand underneath the back of her shirt while the other slides up her stomach toward her chest.

Her hand drops down to my waist to search under my shirt and down into my waistband. My body calls out for her. It screams with the intensity of pure desire. I want to lay her down and surrender to passion amongst the lavender stalks.

But before she can grab my fully erect cock, before I can caress her breasts or bite her neck or undo her clothes, she pulls away. She pulls her hand out of my waistband. She rests both hands on my chest and gently eases back.

We both take shaky breaths. I lick my lips, still hungry for her. She gazes at me, and I see the same hunger reflected in her eyes.

"I wish you didn't have to sell that song. I know it's your job, but I love it so much. I wish it could be ours."

Before I have a chance to respond, she turns and hurries away from me through the lavender field. I'm too stunned to call after her, struck dumb by what just happened.

We kissed.

I can't believe it. After all these years, I kissed Iris. Or she kissed me?

I don't even know what happened, but damn, it was hot. She's flat-out sexy. It'll take a long time to get rid of this aching erection, but it was so worth it.

Still in shock, I sit and think about her.

She's one of the kindest, most genuine, most good-hearted people around. She's one of my favorite people to spend time with, and if I'm being honest with myself, I've pretty much always been in love with her. But I've never really thought it could work out between us—until now.

We've always had so much fun together, but usually, we hang out with Nyx and Remus too. I've never wanted to screw up our friendship before, and even now, the possibility worries me. All four of us have been so close for so long. I would never want to do anything to change that. But for Iris, I don't know. Right now, I would risk almost anything to kiss her again.

All of this is a moot point until all this witch-versus-shifter conflict is resolved. The threat to shifter-kind really worries me. Iris also has a lot to deal with since her evil stepmother is the root of all the trouble. We don't have time for drama in our personal lives until we neutralize these witches.

If they succeed and take away our ability to shift, they might as well kill us. A shifter without their animal aspect is incomplete, a shell of their former self. I don't know what I would do without my wolf inside me.

I can't imagine losing the bond I feel when I'm around other shifters. I can't fathom losing my ability to hunt with my pack. How would I defend myself if I lost the instinct that raises the hair on the back of my neck when something is off?

I will never allow that to happen.

Shifters and witches must unite to burn the Academy to ashes. We'll tear it down brick by magical brick, if necessary, and shred all who stand in our way. And when Iris' stepmother and her lackeys lie in pools of their own blood, we'll howl at the night sky in triumph and run free through the forest as we were born to do.

And then, with that settled, maybe Iris and I can figure out where we stand. I'm scared to redefine our relationship. I know we'll always be close friends, and I'd never do anything to jeopardize that, but maybe we can be more than just friends. Maybe I can finally show her how much I really love her.

CAPTIVE OF THE WOLF PACK:
CHAPTER 12

IRIS

My head is in the clouds. Ordinarily, that's not a problem. However, today, I've already shattered a mug and upended a little side table in my carelessness. Maybe I'd be safer outside at this point.

I go into the woods behind the house and walk toward Remus' beehives. They're the kind that allow him to collect honey without hurting the hive. It's a job he has to do every few days, so I'm hoping he'll be happy to have the extra help. He's been so sweet to me; I want to find ways to give back to him too.

He hasn't been able to give his store his complete attention because of me. The least I can do is help him restock his honey supply.

I plan on collecting a little extra so I can make honey cakes later this evening. The Bear Clan loves honey for obvious reasons, but my wolves will appreciate a sweet treat too.

My wolves. Listen to me. I sound like a crazy person.

Who am I kidding? I *am* a crazy person.

I've kissed all three of them. I've never been ashamed

of the fact that I'm a sexual being with sexual urges, but I'm still a virgin, for heaven's sake. I've never done anything like this before, and I seriously doubt there's a how-to book for this situation.

I should write one.

The thought makes me laugh.

Aside from the sweet, golden treat of honey, this walk also provides me with an opportunity to figure out what to do about the guys. I need to stop thinking about it, but I can't. They're on my mind all the time.

This obsession with them isn't like me. I pride myself on my level-headed nature. I couldn't have coexisted with someone like Lexus without having a stable head on my shoulders. She watches me like a hawk. She's been that way from the moment she entered my life. To learn to be sneaky required careful thought, and I'm a master at it.

Well, maybe not.

A master at careful thought doesn't kiss her three male friends who she happens to be in exile with. This situation is a ticking time bomb. If I'm not careful, it could end in disaster.

Lost in thought, I miss the turn to the hidden deer trail that leads toward the beehives. My mishap isn't a total waste of time because I find a small patch of belladonna.

With a snort, I recall the day I'd considered squeezing the toxic juice of the berries into Lexus' tea. At the time, I believed myself incapable of it. Now, I'm not so sure.

I carefully pluck some berries, wrap them in a strip of cloth I brought along to wipe honey from my fingers, and double back on the forest path.

The deer trail is overgrown and looks like it hasn't been used in a while. The deer had likely found somewhere else to live after it discovered that a wolf shifter had moved onto the land.

I follow the faint trail, ducking under low-hanging branches and carefully stepping over roots. The buzzing of bees is audible long before I see the hives. Fuzzy balls of black and yellow curiously dart around me. Right now, they mean me no harm. However, I'm certain that'll change the moment they realize I'm after their treasure.

I set the basket down and breathe. Bees are so little. It doesn't take much magic to affect them.

With an incantation and a wave of my fingers, all of the bees gently settle down for a nap. So long as I don't accidentally squish one, they won't be harmed while I collect honey.

I grab several jars from my basket and approach the hives. A few stragglers buzz toward me in alarm. I quickly put them under the sleeping spell.

I've never harvested honey from this type of hive before. It's basically a box with several vertical trays that can be lifted out. It allows the hive to stay intact while I collect honey.

It takes me a few tries to figure out the best way to do it, but before long, I have one jar filled to the brim with golden honey. I cap it and begin again with the next jar.

Once I figure out a system, I let my mind wander once more.

My thoughts first drift to Remus and his kind eyes. I know he wants to be with me.

What would it be like if it was just us in the house?

He'd probably swoop me up in a tender embrace the moment I walked through the door. He'd kiss me until I was dizzy. We'd make dinner together, laugh over a glass of wine, and then fall into bed tangled up in each other. And there'd be candles. Lots and lots of beeswax candles.

Remus seems like the candle type.

He'll be gentle, patient, and overgenerous in bed, just like he is in his daily life.

Nyx, on the other hand, will be wild. I'll be putty in his hands, completely at his mercy, and I'll give myself over to him willingly. He's an expert, after all. I can practically hear myself scream his name while I grasp the bedsheets.

The honey jar slips through my fingers. I tighten my grip before it drops completely.

Where Remus is familiar and safe, Nyx is adventurous and dangerous. Not that he'll ever do anything to put me in harm's way. To be with him would be like dancing with fire.

And Torak. Just the thought of him elicits a wistful sigh from my lips. I've never met a more talented musician. He should be on a world tour, adored by all.

Though, if he was, I'd be terribly jealous. It breaks my heart that he doesn't believe in himself the way I do.

I struggle to find the best way to describe what I imagine him to be like in bed. I finally settle on transcendent. He'd take me to otherworldly places I can only dream about.

A relationship with any of them will be incredible. I can see myself happy with each of them. I ought to be relieved I have three perfect options, but it only makes things more of a challenge.

How can I ever pick one?

I can't.

They're all so perfect, I can't possibly make a choice, even if it makes me a terrible person. Don't they deserve more than that?

I start to think I shouldn't pick any of them out of fairness and respect, but the thought of it pains my heart to the point where it physically aches. Why can't I just have them all?

My body goes rigid as a realization strikes me.

Maybe there's a chance I can have them all. All four of us have known each other forever. We get along so well, and I have strong feelings for each of them. We could make it work, couldn't we?

As I pack up the last of the honey jars, I resolve to ask each of them about it. I have to get them alone first. It could work. Maybe. I won't know until I ask them.

I try not to let myself get too excited or hopeful. What I'm about to ask is crazy. I doubt they'll agree to share me. Even the thought sounds ridiculous. But I have to try. I can chalk my crazy idea up to stress if they get upset with me.

As I walk back to the house, my plan seems less and less outrageous. By the time I'm out of the woods, I've convinced myself it's possible to have all three.

"I'm home with honey."

"The phrase is 'Honey, I'm home,'" Torak shouts back from the garage. I follow his voice and find all three of my guys in the garage. Remus had it converted into a workshop and he makes all of the items for his shop in here.

"Very funny." I place the basket filled with honey jars on the wooden table in the center of the garage and remove one jar for myself.

"What do you plan to do with that?" Remus asks.

"It's a surprise." I grin.

"I hope you're thinking what I think you're thinking." Nyx gives me a wicked smile.

"If it involves honey anywhere other than a cooking dish, you're wrong." I roll my eyes and head back into the house. I store the spare jar of honey in one of the kitchen cupboards.

When I return, the guys have started an assembly line to purify, refine, and infuse the honey for Remus' store.

"What's in the pouch?" Torak jerks his chin toward the basket.

"I found belladonna in the woods, so I took some. It might come in handy."

"Good idea." Nyx turns to me. "Torak and I heard some witches are on the lookout for you."

"What?" I almost upend the basket in my surprise.

"Don't worry." Torak glares at Nyx. "From what we can tell, no one knows you're here."

"Are you sure? Lexus sent ravens after me. How do we know she doesn't know?"

"She would've done something by now, don't you think?" Remus finishes with a jar and moves to the next.

"Maybe. Or she'll bide her time." I pace the short length of the garage. My heart beats frantically under my ribs. "I hate this. I hate not to know what goes on in the world around me."

"I know." Remus' words are quiet.

Torak suggests I move somewhere else. Remus stops his work and slowly turns to face Torak.

"Why?"

Torak explains how people are always in and out of the store.

"She's never in the store," Remus says.

"I know, but she's outside around the house. Someone could see her." Torak makes a good point, though I'm always careful not to get too near the store. When I first moved here, I thought it was safe, so I helped out in the store. But after a few days, I reconsidered it, and I've stayed hidden ever since.

"She's safe here." Remus growls and moves closer to me.

I'm not sure if he realizes he's put himself between me and Torak, as if Torak's a threat to me. I place a hand on his shoulder. His muscles are tense but relax under my touch.

"Is that what's actually true or are you trying to just keep her to yourself?" Torak doesn't back down.

"I can keep her safe and you know it."

"What if there's a better way?" Torak asks.

"She can't move now. It's too risky." Nyx agrees with Remus.

"Exactly. She stays here." Remus gives a nod of finality.

I'm happy at Remus' home, but I don't want my guys to fight over me. Tempers are about to flare, and I don't want to make it worse. I especially don't want Torak to feel like we're ganging up on him. I don't want him to be annoyed with me when I ask him if he'll share me with Remus and Nyx.

The thought makes me blush. I turn away so none of them will notice. Now is definitely not the time to bring something like that up.

Torak finally yields. "If someone in the store spots her and trouble comes to your doorstep, it's on you."

"I won't let that happen." Remus squares his shoulders and goes back to the honey, which effectively ends the conversation.

"I went to see Argus." Nyx speaks up out of the blue.

"What?" Both Torak and Remus turn to look at Nyx. Looks like the conversation's not over after all.

"Before you both flip, I have good news." Nyx raises his hands in mock self-defense. "Argus has made progress in rounding up witches and shifters to help us shut the Academy down."

"That's great." I smile. The corner of Nyx's perfect mouth curves up into a smirk that makes my breath catch in my throat.

"Argus also wants you to join us when the time comes, but I told him no." Nyx gives his head a little shake.

"What?" My brow furrows. "Shouldn't I be involved in that decision?" I expect both Remus and Torak to say something, but they're silent.

"Given your relationship with Lexus, I figured it might be too difficult. That doesn't mean I believe you aren't capable in the witchcraft sense. I know you're a powerful, talented witch. But a fight against family is something no one can prepare you for."

My expression softens as Nyx explains his reasons.

"I've never truly considered Lexus family. But you're right. I hadn't given much thought to what it would be like to take her down. She was supposed to be a mother to me. She turned out to be the opposite, but she's still my father's wife."

"That might make things awkward at the family reunion," Nyx says wryly.

"Tell me about it." I chuckle. "Still, it feels like it's something I have to do. I appreciate your concern, though."

"Your well-being is my top priority," Nyx says. It's not a line. He's being genuine and sweet.

Remus chimes in. "Her well-being is top priority for all of us."

"Thank you." I blush. "But if that's true, I need all three of you to play nice."

"Wolves never play nice." Torak smirks. "But I see your point. We aren't much help to you if we can't agree on anything."

"Glad you see the brilliance of my logic." I preen.

"How about you use your brilliance to heat this honey?" Remus hands me a jar. "It'll take the infusions better when it's warm."

"You got it." I walk to the stove and gently stir the honey until it's not gloopy. Remus is right. When I sprinkle in crushed anise seed, it doesn't clump up at all.

"As much as I enjoy Easy Bake Honey Shop, I have to dip out for a few hours." Nyx leaves his chair.

"Where to?" Torak glances up from his task.

"I haven't been home in a few days. I want to get the mail and check on a few things."

"How mysterious." I can't help but tease Nyx.

"My air of mystery keeps people guessing." Nyx's sly smile sends heat rushing to my core. If we were alone right now, I'd kiss him again.

I return my attention to the honey until a thought occurs to me.

"Hey, Nyx?"

"Yes?"

"Do you mind if I tag along?"

All three heads turn to look at me with equally confused expressions.

"What? As much as I love Remus' house, I'll go stir crazy if I don't leave for a while." There's some truth in my statement, but it's not the whole truth. I want to be alone with him, and this is my best shot at making it happen.

"We just spent an hour concerned about your safety." Torak laughs. "Now you want to go walk around town?"

Remus agrees with Torak and insists it's not a good idea.

Nyx refuses to let me tag along. He echoes Remus' and Torak's concerns.

"Please." I give Nyx a pouty lip.

"Don't make that face. You know it's not fair."

"Which is why I use it. To go out for a little bit, even just an hour, will be good for me. I can't be at the top of my magic game if I stay cooped up here all the time."

Torak considers my reason. "We all get antsy when we can't run wild as wolves every so often."

"What if we go at night?" Nyx offers an alternative. "Nothing I have to do needs to be done in daylight. If we go late enough, we probably won't run into anyone."

"That's fine with me." I turn to Remus and Torak for confirmation.

"It's up to you." Remus shrugs.

"I know, but I don't want to do anything you won't like," I say.

My words make Remus smile.

"If time away from the shop will make you feel better, then I want you to go," Remus says.

"I'm good with it as long as you're careful you're not followed," Torak says.

Once again, I'm struck by how lucky I am to have these three incredible men in my life. They've been my dearest friends for longer than I can remember, and, if I do this right, they might become more than friends. It's going to be a long afternoon, but I'm excited to finally be able to spend time alone with Nyx.

CAPTIVE OF THE WOLF PACK: CHAPTER 13

NYX

The incessant throbbing between my legs has nothing to do with my Harley as I ride down the twisted road toward my house. Rather, the catalyst is an extremely hot, sexy young witch who has her arms wrapped so tightly about my midsection that I can barely breathe. As if her lithe, warm body pressed up against me wasn't bad enough, I can feel her supple breasts through the thin fabric of our shirts.

I don't know if Iris is aware of how much I want her right now, but I certainly am. It's all I can do to pilot these seven hundred pounds of steel and not send us to Road Rash city.

I take the turns with a little less speed than I would if I didn't have a passenger. Regardless of my views about the maneuver, Iris seems to find excitement in it. She shifts position and leans in close. Her helmet brushes against my shoulder.

I'm damn glad I have that extra helmet because I'd never let her ride without one. I'm not stupid, and I wouldn't her risk her life like that. I'd rein in my lust and wait until I had a second helmet with me.

When Iris asked if she could come with me tonight, it was hard not to freak out. I was so damned excited, but I played it pretty cool for the first few hours. Or, at least I thought I was playing it cool. She'd noticed how antsy I was getting. She'd whispered that I wouldn't have to wait much longer.

That's what I like about her. She cuts through the bull-shit and says exactly what she's thinking. She's not like other girls who play stupid games and are always trying to keep you guessing. She's up front and honest. I love that. It makes life so much easier.

For days, all I've thought about is that intense make out session in the lavender field. I've kissed plenty of women, and yet none of them ever meant much to me. They didn't ignite a fire inside me the way Iris did the morning she kissed me. I'll never forget that kiss.

Every time I smell the scent of lavender, I think of her. I even bought some of those girly sachet things to put in my dresser drawers. My wolf wants to roll around in that scent, and I don't blame him, because I want to roll around in it too.

Honestly, all I want to do is get her naked and into my bed. The thought of her warm body pressed tight against mine makes my cock so swollen that my pants feel like a prison.

Still, I don't want to rush it. I have a hunch that if I do, I'll break everything we've built over years of friendship. I want to move things forward, but slowly, so I don't scare her away. I've waited a lifetime to be with her, I can wait a little longer.

Trying to make love to her at Remus' place was impos-sible. Although my herbalist friend has an expansive house, with all four of us there, it seems a lot smaller. I love Remus and Torak like brothers, like my pack, but there are times I wish I could get her alone. Now I can.

The fact that she suggested a trip out to my place makes my heart hammer in my chest. She clearly wants to be alone with me too, but why? I think she wants to kiss me again, but I won't know for sure until we get home. I can hardly wait. I can't help but get my hopes up that maybe something will happen. But I have to wait for her to make the first move.

We zip through a tunnel bored straight into the side of the mountain. The yellowed fluorescent lights make little buzzes as we pass beneath them. They fall into rhythm with my heartbeat. Ahead, the blue sky beckons, along with my hopes and dreams.

When we leave the mouth of the tunnel, I lean the bike into another tight turn. Iris squeals and hugs me even tighter. A smile stretches across my face even though I know she can't see it.

I slow the throttle as we take a steep decline because there's a set of old mining tracks at the bottom. It's a pretty rough crossing. If I were with a different woman, I would be tempted to take the tracks fast to excite her. But with Iris, I just want to be careful. No matter what, her safety is paramount to me. I would sooner boil in a vat of liquid silver than see one hair on her head harmed.

At the bottom of the hill, we skip over the old tracks. The suspension I put in last summer gets a good workout. Iris gasps but no longer seems afraid. That pleases me very much.

I accelerate toward a steep hill that leads up to my place. It isn't paved. If I don't have good momentum at the start, we won't make it. There's not enough purchase for the bike to go from a dead stop.

We flash up the hill as trees zip by at a rapid rate. We crest the hill, and for a moment, Iris gets a hint of what lies in store for her.

A misty valley comes into view. A blue ribbon of water snakes through it. I love the way moonlight ripples across the river.

As we pass through another tunnel, it disappears, only to reappear on the other side.

Once we're out of the second tunnel, we exit the gravel road. I pull onto my driveway. It's paved, nearly a quarter mile long. My house is concealed by several large trees. She won't be able to see it until we're almost on top of it.

My home comes into view. Three stories of rugged yet polished postmodernism, with a huge garage where I can work on my bike, and more than enough space to entertain. It sits on the edge of a ravine where it overlooks the same river we saw from higher on the mountain.

My living room has a great panoramic view of the valley. I like to sit by the window and watch the sunset. One day, I hope Iris will be able to see it too. I hate that we had to sneak out of Remus' house under cover of darkness, but I understand why it was necessary.

I pull the hog to a stop in front of the garage and put down the kickstand. Unfortunately, this means that Iris won't be holding onto me anymore. Once she gets off the bike, a strange emptiness lingers. Without her warmth against me, the chilly night air seeps into my skin.

"Wow." She whistles as she admires the house. My spare helmet is tucked under her arm. Even with her hair matted down in places, she's still beautiful. "This is your house? It's wonderful."

"You haven't seen anything yet." I hold out my hand for the helmet, and she places it in my palm. After I secure it to the back of my bike, we head around the garage to the house. "Welcome to Casa de Nyx."

Tall elm and oak trees surround my home like sentinels. They protect us from harsh sunlight and road noise. There's a stump as wide as I am tall about midway through my yard. I hate it because it's so hard to mow around the damn thing, but I sometimes wonder if I should turn it into a natural picnic table.

Iris' head is on a swivel as she takes everything in.

"It's so peaceful here." Her smile is as radiant as the sun. Again, I'm struck by how intense my desire is and how far it goes beyond physical need. I need more than just her body; I need her heart and soul too.

"The wolf in me loves this valley." I close my eyes and let the breeze wash over my face. I inhale the tasty scents of the lush greenery. Somewhere, a forest owl hoots twice after it catches its prey.

"I love this valley too." She takes in a deep breath, and a bit of tension seems to drain from her.

Right now, the troubles of Dark Magic Academy and her wicked stepmother Lexus seem quite far away, almost as if they belong in another life. We don't have to think about any of that. It's just Iris, me, and the wind.

We arrive at my front door. I unlock the deadbolt then throw the door wide open. I gesture grandly at the foyer, which features a polished marble floor. I went for luxury when I was designing this place.

In the living room, a stone fireplace sits ready for use. Well-cured wood is stacked on either side of it. The stairway sweeps gracefully up the wall toward the second floor.

"This is incredible." She turns and punches me in the arm. "You nut. I can't believe you never brought me out here to see this place. You've been keeping it all to yourself."

"Yeah, I'm a jerk like that." We both chuckle and stare at each other. Tension builds in the silence until I have to say something to fill it. "It's way more space than I need, but I've always hoped that one day my wife and kids would live here."

She smiles, and her cheeks flush. Maybe she imagines herself as my wife. I know I do. I can't help myself. It seems so right, so logical, and so perfect, that she would be my wife.

I used to seduce women for sport, but Iris makes me want to be a one-woman man.

Does she think of me in the same way? Does she see me as a husband material?

When we kissed, she definitely seemed into it—way into it—even if she did cut me off.

I mean, she kissed me back, right? That means something.

I know it.

All I want to do is tell her how badly I want her. All I can think about is how I much I want to make love to her all day and all night.

What's wrong with me? I've turned into one of those whiny losers who pines for women and writes them unintelligible non-rhyming poetry.

It isn't fair. I don't like to talk about my feelings. I don't even know where to start, but I want to say something. I want to tell her how much she makes my heart ache.

She stands there, waits on me to do or say something, so I gesture toward the steps.

"Let me show you upstairs," I say lamely.

As we head upstairs, cherry-stained boards creak under our feet. Iris reaches out and playfully rubs the antlers I found in the forest. She pokes her index finger with their blunted tips.

Upstairs in the second living room, a massive picture window overlooks the misty valley and magnificent river. It's a spectacular sight. No matter how many times I see it, I have to stop for at least a minute to appreciate it.

Iris' beautiful eyes widen, and her mouth drops open. She walks across the room until her nose is nearly up against the glass. She stares in wonder at the magnificent view.

"I picked this spot to build my house so I could look at this every day," I say.

"Oh, it's so beautiful. How can you ever bear to leave this wonderful view?"

"There are some things that are even more beautiful in this world." I reach out and brush the backs of my knuckles across her cheek. Her skin is so soft it nearly drives me insane.

"I could live in a house like this." She smiles up at me.

Suddenly, I want to kiss her again.

Slowly, I move in. My inner fire burns, and my wolf strains against his ethereal leash. As I hold her face gently, I lean in and kiss her fully on the lips. Like last time, she eagerly responds.

Our lips melt together, and we kiss for several minutes before I explore her mouth with my tongue. She gives as good as she gets, and soon, I'm breathless. She's so innocent in her exploration of my mouth, yet so sensual at the same time.

My arms wrap around her waist and I pull her closer. She embraces me. Her hands clutch at my broad shoulders.

I went too far, too fast, last time, so now I need to go slowly and gently. I don't want to rush her.

My hands linger lightly on her back above her waist. I love the feel of her skin beneath my fingers as I trace the sweet curve of her back. I literally find every part of her desirable. I want to touch and lick and kiss everywhere at once. It's killing me to hold back, but I manage to do it —barely.

Soft moans escape her mouth. Slowly, I trace kisses down her cheek to her neck. When I reach the hollow of her throat, she gasps and clutches me tighter.

I slide my hand down her back and around the sweet curve of her butt. She moans and tilts her head back, encouraging me to continue.

On instinct, I grab her around the waist and lift her into my arms. She goes with the motion and wraps her legs around my waist. I move forward until I reach the wall. As I press her up against it, I smother her with kisses. Her nails dig into my back as I move my mouth down to her throat once more, and my hands fumble with the buttons of her jacket.

When my mouth isn't occupied, I mumble sweet nothings to her.

"I want you so damn bad."

"I want you bad too." There's a note of regret in her voice, enough to make me pause and look her in the eye. She looks away before looking back at me. "I'm... I'm not ready to be tied down to one man. But I love being with you."

It's a knife to the gut, but I shrug and try to play it cool.

"Hey, that's okay." I continue to unbutton her jacket. "If you want no strings attached, I can do that. Sound good?"

"Yeah." She smiles and squeezes her thighs tightly around my waist.

Right now, I'd agree to pretty much anything. I'm happy she's okay with my suggestion. I definitely want strings at some point, but we're still trying to figure this whole thing out. It might kill me, but she's helping me develop the patience of a saint.

Suddenly she yanks open her shirt to reveal her soft, perfect breasts. I groan. This can't be happening, but it is. She's giving me the hungriest look I've ever seen. I know exactly what she wants, and I'm going to give it to her. She may not want strings yet, but by the time I'm done with her, she'll want to be all tied up in them.

CAPTIVE OF THE WOLF PACK: CHAPTER 14

IRIS

I'm not supposed to want Nyx, but I do—desperately. Desire consumes me as I stand in the middle of his living room. He's holding me in his arms, and I'm drowning in sensation. I've never wanted anyone so badly. I've never needed anyone like this before. I was never the kind of girl who would come up with elaborate fantasies about my first time. I never really thought about it much until recently. And now that it's going to happen, I want it to be perfect.

For a split second, I hesitate. Nyx is one of my best friends. Am I really going to go through with this? Am I going to give my virginity to him? Once we cross this line, there's no going back. I'm burning up for him, and he's clearly ready to take me to bed, but should we? Do we dare?

My body aches with longing. I don't know why I'm hesitating other than... Well, I'm nervous.

"I've never done this before," I murmur between kisses.

"Do you want me to stop?" He immediately stops and takes a step back.

"No. I want you." I'm never this blunt, but I can't dance around my feelings anymore. I can't deny the over-whelming need to be with him. Perfection is overrated anyway.

"Come here," he whispers softly before extending his hand toward me.

I rest my hand in his. I need him to take the lead, and he does. He pulls me in close. Our bodies are pressed together. My arms weave around his neck. His arms slide around my waist.

When his lips meet mine, white-hot energy streaks through me. I fear I'll burn so hot for him that I'll acciden-tally singe something.

"Keep me away from the drapes."

"What?" He laughs against my mouth and gently bites my lower lip.

I can control my magic most of the time, but I feel totally out of control right now, and I love it.

As I roll my hips, I press myself the rock-hard length of him. A new kind of insatiable hunger overcomes me. I want to see him, to feel him, to touch him—everywhere.

"You're more maddening than a Wolf Moon," Nyx growls in my ear. "Are bed sheets fine, or do I need to keep you away from those, too?"

"No." I moan between kisses. "Bed sheets sound great."

He lifts me off the floor. Our kiss doesn't break as I lock my legs around his waist. As he carries me into the bedroom, I part my lips to let his tongue melt against mine.

The bedroom is dark. Moonlight streams in from the

window to cast an otherworldly glow on his bed. My belly flips. My pussy is damp and tingly.

"Ready?" A devilish grin flashes across his face.

"For what?" A shiver of anticipation races down my spine.

"For this." He releases his hold on me. I freefall onto the bed with a squeal. He laughs softly before crawling across the enormous bed to join me.

"What else you got?" I'm lying on my back, propped up on my elbows. I lick my lips.

"What else do you want?"

"Everything."

"I can do that." His sexy grin makes my nipples pebble.

Wearing only a bra, jeans, and panties, I'm on my way to being totally naked. He's in no rush. He spreads leisurely kisses across my lacy pink bra before dipping to lick a trail over my belly. My entire body clenches when his lips stop at the top of my jeans.

He gives me a coy smile as he slowly pulls the zipper down. Goosebumps cover my exposed skin. I want him to get rid of all our clothes as fast as possible. I just want to feel him everywhere.

After pulling my jeans over my hips, he sucks in a breath.

"You're so beautiful," he whispers.

"You've seen me in a bikini."

"Mm... but not in your panties." His throaty growl reverberates against my pussy. My hips arch and he takes it as an invitation to remove my panties.

I slip out of my bra. Suddenly shy, I cover my breasts with my hands.

"No," he murmurs. "I want to see you."

He gently grabs my wrists and pulls my arms apart.

His gaze feasts on my body. My cheeks burn. I've never been so exposed, so vulnerable before.

"I don't know why we waited so long," he says.

"We don't have to wait anymore. I want you, Nyx. I want you to be my first."

He groans and buries his head between my breasts. I stroke his hair before sliding my hands down his back. I love the feel of his muscles under my fingertips.

His head tilts up and our gazes lock.

"I want to taste you."

I swallow and nod.

"All of you."

"Okay," I whisper.

His mouth is molten lava pouring down my body. His lips graze one taut nipple before capturing it. As he teases and torments my tender flesh, I whimper and dig my nails into his back. I never knew I could feel like this. I never knew I could be so aware of every inch of my body. Even my toes tingle with energy.

As he drags his lips from one nipple to the other, I moan. I want to make him feel this good, but he's covering me, and I can't reach anything but his back and his hips. I don't know what to do.

"Relax," he says. "Just let me love you."

I'm trembling like a leaf in a storm. I'm overwhelmed by the feel of his mouth on my belly. He traces a ring around my belly button before sliding lower.

Hot breath caresses my pussy. He looks at me and our eyes meet. There's passion, desire, and concern in his gaze, as if he's checking to make sure I'm okay. I'm more than okay. I couldn't even imagine feeling better than this.

As he kisses my inner thighs, damp heat coils in my core. Swirls of red energy spiral tighter. When his mouth brushes my moist lips, I press my shoulders back into the bed. Sharp sparks of electric energy burst to life as his lips nudge me open.

I spread my thighs, not caring about what I look like, only how I feel.

He hooks his hands under my thighs and pulls me forward onto his mouth and into a state of ecstasy. His tongue strokes along my delicate folds before delving deep. I moan and grab the sheets. They twist in my fists.

As he licks me, I writhe. I can't hold still. It's too much, too intense, too perfect.

"Oh, Nyx!"

He gently traces one finger around my wet entrance all the way up to the sensitive bud at the top of my pussy. My back arches off the mattress. His lips capture my clit and I'm soaring. I can hardly drag in a single breath. He strokes me higher, pushing me toward a precipice.

I want to jump. To fly. To sing with pleasure.

As he slides his tongue deep into my glistening center, my head rolls from side to side. I rock my hips against his mouth to urge his tongue deeper. When he pulls away, I cry out in protest. Then, he parts my pink petals. His tongue invades me once more to twirl around my clit.

I can't see straight. A low, guttural growl rolls across my lips.

For the first time in my life, I feel what it must be like to be feral. All of the trappings of culture and humanity mean nothing. I don't care about pursuing what's right or resisting what's wrong. I just care about Nyx and what he's doing to me with his perfect mouth.

I soak up pleasure as I ride his tongue. When he lets out a moan, it sends vibrations through his tongue directly into me.

"Oh my god." My voice is high and breathy.

My legs begin to tremble. Every inch of me starts to

tingle. He grabs my hips to hold me steady while he uses his clever tongue to drive me hard into an orgasm.

I scream as sharp waves of ecstasy break over me.

As I ride the rolling tide of pleasure, he lays his cheek on my thigh. He's watching me, but I want him to do it. I want him to see what he's done to me.

"Was that okay?" he asks playfully.

"Better than my vibrator."

"Good. I was hoping I could beat that machine."

We both laugh.

I sink into the mattress as he crawls up my body. He props himself up on his arms, hovering over me.

"Don't get too comfortable, I'm not finished with you yet."

"Oh really?" I grin.

He hops off the bed and does a sexy strip tease for me. *Magic* is definitely the right word for his little dance.

Tremors from my orgasm still rip through me, but I'm already eager for more. I can't tear my gaze from the gorgeous length of his cock. It's thick and long. Maybe too long.

I scrunch up my nose.

"What?" he glances down at his rigid cock.

"It's so big."

And so is the smile on his face.

"I want to touch it—you," I quickly amend. I don't want him to think I'm only after his cock. This isn't even about sex; it's about finally acknowledging what we really feel.

He lays on the bed beside me.

"Have you ever touched a man before?" he asks.

"Not... No."

"Here." He grasps my hand in his and guides it toward his erection.

As I wrap my fingers around him, I'm shocked. It's like velvet over steel.

"What?"

"It's so hard and soft at the same time."

He grunts a response. His eyelids droop and he fixes me with a gaze that spurs me forward. I slowly stroke his length. He's hot in my hands and soon a drop of precum glistens on the tip.

"Rub it around," he urges.

I brush my thumb over the tip, then bring it to my lips. I have to taste him.

He's salty and musky. It's the most irresistible scent I've ever smelled. I want to taste all of him, so I scoot down until my lips are inches from the head of his cock.

His hands are in my hair, holding it back. As I lower my lips to his plump head, I inhale. The subtle scent of lavender soap invades my senses.

I part my lips and flick my tongue out to touch the tip. He groans and his hips flex.

Encouraged by his response, I suck him into my mouth. I use instinct to guide me. My tongue runs down the seam along the underside of his cock. My jaw aches from being spread so wide, but it's worth it. His eyes close and his mouth forms a tight "O".

As I suck him, he hisses. I stop. His eyes fly open.

"Why did you stop?"

"You hissed."

"Because I don't want to come right away."

"Oh." I silently congratulate myself as I resume sucking.

It doesn't take long before he grabs a fistful of my hair and pulls me away. Before I can react, he has my on my back. He's between my thighs and his cock is pressed against my entrance. We don't need condoms because shifters can't catch diseases, and I'm on the pill. It's the one thing the stepmonster did right.

"Are you ready?" he asks.

"Make me yours."

His eyes go dark with desire. He rubs the head of his cock across my lips. I grab his ass and try to pull him down.

"Relax, sweetie," he whispers.

"You're torturing me."

"You've been tormenting me for years. I'm allowed a few moments to torment you," he teases.

"You're wicked."

"Yes, but you already knew that."

Before I can say anything more, he pushes the head of his cock slowly into my core. When he meets resistance, he thrusts hard.

I gasp. A sharp sting steals my breath.

Then, he's moving inside me.

Every inch of him fills me so completely. I tighten around him as he slowly pulls back before plunging back in. He's in complete control, and I adore every second of it.

As he grinds into me, my pussy flutters. The tension's back, and I'm spiraling toward another orgasm. I'm on the brink, ready to explode, and he's just getting started.

"Nyx, please," I beg.

"Not so fast," he growls. "I'm going to make you come over and over until you'll never think about anyone but me."

My heart clenches because I wonder if he's right. Will making love to him take away my feelings for the other guys?

Before I can delve into the question, Nyx rolls us so he's on his back and I'm straddling him.

"Ride me."

"Like a horse?"

"Uh, yeah, basically."

I rise slightly before coming down. It's awkward and feels strange but good.

"Am I doing it right?" I ask.

"Hell yeah."

Buoyed by a fresh wave of confidence, I rock up and down. He's so deep inside me, I can hardly believe I can handle it. My breasts sway as his hips buck and he bounces me on his cock. Each time my nipples brush against his chest, it adds a new element to my pleasure.

He plays with my breasts, pinching and nipping at my nipples. I love it. I never knew it could feel this good.

"You're the sexiest woman in the world," he says.

I grin. Damn right I am!

An orgasm builds within me. Nyx must recognize the signs because he leans closer and whispers to me. "Say my name when you come."

That alone almost sends me over the edge. When he slings one arm around my waist to hold me up so he can brush my clit with his free hand, I come apart in his arms.

"Oh, Nyx." I cry out as stars explode behind my eyes.

"Say it again."

"Nyx."

As I tighten around his cock, he reaches his own height of pleasure. He pulses into me over and over until I'm slick with his release.

I collapse on top of him. He holds me close as I shiver.

"Just keep riding it," he whispers.

I don't know if he means the orgasm or his cock. I couldn't possibly move right now if I wanted to, so I just relax against him. I lay my head on his chest and listen to his rushing heart.

Slowly and with great care, he slides out of me and

settles me on the bed. It's far too hot to get under the blankets, so I lay back against the pillows.

Nyx curls me against his side before wrapping his arms around me.

"Are you okay?"

"I feel like I've died and gone to Heaven."

His chuckle rumbles through his chest.

"Are you too hot?" he asks.

"You're warm, but I'd rather overheat than not touch you." I'm still out of breath. My head swims, yet if he asked me to go again, I'd agree without hesitation. "You're going to be my new addiction."

"That's my goal." He presses a kiss into my damp temple.

Would that still be his goal if he knew I also feel the same for Remus and Torak? I thought making love to Nyx might change everything. It changed how close we are, but it didn't change my desire for the other guys.

A wave of guilt washes over me. I should've talked to him before we had sex. It's my fault. I couldn't resist him. Everything about him is so damn sexy.

"What's with the face?" His lips graze my ear and it sends shivers down my spine.

"What face?" I ask, even though I know what he means.

"You look like you're thinking, and if you're coherent enough to think straight, then I've done something very wrong."

"Believe me, you've done nothing wrong." I trace my fingers down the smooth, muscular planes of his chest.

"Then, what's with the face? You've clearly got something on your mind."

There's no way around it now. I can't lie to him. He deserves to know exactly where my heart is. I hope I don't ruin what's between us before its even had a chance to begin.

"I've fallen for you," I say before I can second guess myself. I glance at Nyx in time to see his expression brighten. A megawatt smile eclipses the rest of his features.

"I've fallen for you too." His hand snakes around to the back of my neck. He pulls me in for a kiss that I'm more than happy to drown in until he pulls away. "Wait, then why did you make that weird face?"

"Weird?"

"Beautifully weird. But still weird. But, seriously, why the face?"

"I've fallen for you." I begin again, but this time the words get stuck. "But I've also fallen for Remus and Torak."

The light in his expression dims. I wish I'd kept my mouth shut. I'm insane to think this could ever work. Nyx is going to hate me forever.

"What does that mean for us?" He doesn't sound thrilled, but that's better than it could have been. Small victories.

"I'm not sure. I didn't think we'd get this far."

"Well, we did. You must know I'm crazy about you. If you tell me what you want, I'll do my best to give it to you."

"You say that now."

"Come on. Tell me." Nyx gives me a gentle nudge. There's laughter in his voice, so this must not be as bad as it seems.

"I want to be in a relationship..." My words get stuck again. Seriously, why is this so hard? I'm past the point of no return now. I can't be a chicken about it. "With all of you." I finish with a wince.

"Oh." I can't tell if Nyx is surprised, angry, or in a catatonic state.

"What do you think?" The silence is unbearable.

"This is uncharted territory for me."

"Really?" I'm embarrassed by how shocked I sound. It's no secret Nyx is one of Bonfire Falls' most notorious playboys. He never settles down and certainly never commits. This arrangement should be right up his alley.

"You may have noticed I'm kind of a lone wo—"

"If you say lone wolf, I'll leave," I say in jest. "That's too much of a cliché."

"I'm the original lone wolf, sunshine. I can never be a cliché," he jokes back, but he's not enthusiastic. "My point is, I don't like to share."

"That's understandable. I could never expect you to agree to something so weird. I'm awful to even suggest it. You deserve better than that."

Nyx silences me with a kiss.

"You didn't let me finish." His eyes are warm and soft. "Remember how I said I'm crazy about you? I mean it. Even if I can only have a piece of you, I'll take it."

I'm so shocked it takes me a moment to speak.

"Seriously?"

"Seriously," he says.

I snuggle closer to him. Relief washes over me as it finally hits me that he has agreed to share me.

"Have you talked about it with anyone else?" he asks.

"No. You're the first one. The first for, well, everything."

"I'm glad I could be your first." He wraps his arms around me and squeezes me against him. "Is it selfish to hope Remus and Torak hate the idea so I get you all to myself?"

"No." I laugh. "But if they agree, do you promise to play nice?"

"When have I ever played nice?" He snarls playfully and gently nibbles my earlobe. Goosebumps ripple down my body. My skin is still flushed and sensitive.

"Never," I say breathlessly as he kisses a trail down my neck toward my breasts.

"If the other two agree, I'll be respectful," he finally says. "I won't fight, scheme, or otherwise try to steal you so I can keep you all to myself. I promise."

"Okay." I smile at the sincerity in his tone.

"Good. Are you ready for round two?"

"Already?"

"As long as I have you to myself, I'm going to take full advantage of it."

I grin. If he wants to make love to me all night long, I'm ready. Who needs sleep?

CAPTIVE OF THE WOLF PACK:
CHAPTER 15

IRIS

I'm glad I can escape the tension in the house to stroll through Remus' lavender field. Ever since I slept with Nyx, everyone has been on edge. It's mostly my fault because Nyx and I made love all night, which left me exhausted. I fell asleep immediately after we finished. I hadn't planned on staying the night, but I did. And... I forgot to call Remus and Torak. They were worried sick. And let's just say it was more than a little awkward the next morning when we returned to the house.

Torak and Remus were pissed.

Nyx and I should have called them. I don't blame them for being mad. I haven't told them why I spent the night, but I'm sure they have their suspicions. I want to talk to both Torak and Remus separately about my feelings, and I need to do it soon. If I wait too long, it might be too late.

They claim they're only mad because they thought something horrible had happened to us. However, something tells me there's more to it. If they were only worried about my wellbeing, they would've calmed down the moment I walked in the door. Torak and Remus are still bothered by something. It might be jealousy because I spent the night alone with Nyx. I haven't spent the night with either Remus or Torak yet, but I hope I'll be able to work things out with them.

Remus barely says a word to me now. I've tried to make conversation over the last few days, but all I get are one-word answers or grunts. He's never been like this before. I don't know what to do.

Hence the lavender.

I might pick some, make it into a tea, and then make them drink it. That would calm everyone down. Nyx and Torak aren't particularly fond of tea, though. Maybe I should bake a cake instead. Or ice cream? I don't know.

I linger in the lavender fields long after my basket is filled. I don't want to go back to the house until I know what to do next. I can't stand how things are between me and the guys, especially now that I need them more than ever.

When the sun starts to dip below the tree line, I know I have to go back. Remus will only be more upset with me if I stay out after dark. In the dark, it's harder to avoid Lexus' spies.

The lights in the house are dim. I expect Nyx and Torak have both left to go to their own homes. Torak has slowly moved instruments over to Remus' place, but I know he likes to escape to write songs every so often. Nyx is trying to give us space, so he only comes over for a few hours during the day.

There's a light on in the workroom. Remus must be in there to prepare items for Thyme and Country.

Good. This'll give us a chance to talk.

I enter through the side door. In the workroom, the

scent of lavender is overpowering. Apparently, Remus also decided to use the plant to calm himself down.

He's bent over a boiling pot where he's mixing lavender essential oil with other herbs. Delicate perfume bottles are off to the side. He'll fill them later.

He looks over his shoulder when he hears me. He gives me a nod and turns back to his work.

"Great minds think alike." I give a lame chuckle. He says nothing in response.

"Can I help?" I try again. "You know, in case you're worried about broken perfume bottles."

It's been known to happen. His hands are so big, and the funnels are so small and flimsy. The bottles aren't cheap either.

"I'm fine."

"We both know that's not true." I set the basket of lavender on the table in the center of the garage. "Talk to me. Please."

He stirs the herbal mixture in silence. I'm about to give up and go into the main house when he finally speaks up.

"You scared the hell out of me the other day. When you didn't come home, I was sure I lost you. I thought Lexus had finally caught up with you. Do you have any idea how horrible that was for me?"

"I can't imagine." My tone is quiet with guilt. "It was an accident. I'm so sorry."

"I know it was an accident." He takes the Ashwood spoon out of the pot and sets it aside before he turns to face me. "It's okay. Accidents happen, but that doesn't undo the fear I felt."

"I know. Please tell me what I can do to make things right between us. I'll do anything."

"Nothing's wrong between us." His expression softens

into a smile. "It's me. My worries sometimes get to me. That's all."

"Share your worries with me. You've taken on my burdens. Let me take some of yours."

"It's nothing." He shrugs. "Sales have dropped this week. People in town have bought extra water, non-perishables, and even weapons. Bonfire Falls knows something's up, and they want to be ready for it. No one wants to spend anything they don't have to spend. My shop is a luxury. I've always known that."

"I'm sorry." I chew my bottom lip.

"Why? You didn't drive my business away." He frowns.

"Didn't I? If I didn't start this whole thing with Lexus, we wouldn't be in this situation." I suck in a shaky breath as I wonder how much better things would be for Remus, Nyx, and Torak if I'd minded my own business.

"Don't do that." He sighs. "Don't take on that guilt. This is all Lexus' fault. If you hadn't gotten involved, no one would have known about Lexus' plan to destroy shifters. We're on the brink of war. There's bound to be some backlash."

"That doesn't make me feel any better about it."

He lowers the temperature of the stove and covers the pot with a glass lid. It'll need to cool before it can be bottled.

He walks over to me and pulls me in for a hug. I lean into him and inhale his scent. Sometimes I wonder how wolf shifters don't go crazy from their heightened sense of smell. Remus' scent drives me crazy.

"None of this is your fault." He strokes my hair. "I'll take away your garden privileges if you say it's your fault ever again."

"That's mean." I pull back and mock glare at him.

"I can be very stern when I need to me."

"Is that so?" When he gazes down at me, something shifts in his eyes. Playfulness is replaced by an intensity that makes me go gooey inside. My breath hitches in my chest, and my lips part. Remus doesn't hesitate. He dips his head and presses his lips to mine.

I expect a sweet, tender kiss like the one we've previously shared. Instead, I get a burning kiss filled with passion. It's enough to make my knees weak. He wraps his arms around me to hold me up. Our chests are pressed together. My knee slips between his legs.

"I have another confession," he whispers against my mouth.

"Tell me."

"I'm jealous." He marks my neck with a trail of kisses.

"Oh?"

"You spent the night alone with Nyx. You've never done that with me."

"How do you know what I did? Did he tell you?"

"He didn't have to tell me. It was all over his smug face."

"I told him not to gloat."

"He can't help himself."

"Well he needs to try."

"Right."

"Don't think about him." I stroke his clenched jaw. "I'm here with you. I live in your house, not his. I consider your house my home now."

"Even after what you did with him?"

"Yes. I wanted to talk to you about it."

"I don't want to talk about it right now." His lips meet mine. He pulls me hard against him. I can feel his stiff cock through his jeans. His kiss is demanding and possessive. I love how aggressive he's being. He's usually never like this.

I'm not sure what I expect. He backs me up until my butt hits the workbench. My ass hits the lavender basket, tipping it over and spreading fragrant clippings across the table's surface. Some lavender falls to the floor. As I'm trying to maintain my balance, I step on one by mistake. A fresh explosion of fragrant lavender fills the air.

His hands wind into my hair. He pulls hard enough to force my head up. Once again, he covers my neck in kisses.

"I'm making a perfume for you." His breath tickles my ear. It sends a shiver through me. "I want you to wear it so I can smell it every time I'm near you."

"I—thank you." I don't know what to say. He's gone from not talking to me to putting his hands all over me. He still doesn't seem to want to talk, but we need to. We can't avoid this conversation forever. "Don't you have questions about Nyx?"

"We can talk about that later," he growls. "Right now, I don't want to talk."

He takes me by my shoulders and spins me around, so my back is to him. He pushes my chest against the table. I'm shocked and so turned on that I'm already wet.

As he runs his hands down my back, I moan. One hand travels farther down to squeeze my ass, while the other slides around to grab my breast. He caresses me roughly. I never expected him to be like this, but I like it. Maybe I've underestimated him. Maybe he's wilder than I'd expected.

I reach around to press my hands against the stiff bulge in his jeans.

"Look what you've done." He grinds his bulge into my hand. "You make me so fucking hard."

I like this side of Remus. I can't believe it's taken me so long to experience it.

"Take your clothes off," he commands.

Holy hell's bells, yes!

I do as he tells me. As I slowly strip, I enjoy the hungry way his eyes ravage my body. His predatory, possessive gaze sweeps down from my breasts to my pussy. He doesn't even attempt to hide his lust.

I glance at the door. It briefly occurs to me that I don't know when Nyx or Torak will be back. I just as quickly realize that, right now, I don't care.

"Now what?" I ask.

"Bend over the table."

How did I miss this about him? He's so dirty. I thought Nyx would be the kinky one. Boy was I wrong.

I bend over the workbench. It's built for someone of Remus' height, so I have to stand on the tips of my toes. Fortunately, most of my weight is supported by the bench.

Remus moves closer. He uses his hands to spread my legs.

"You're so beautiful and perfect."

"Thank you."

"But you've been a bad girl." His tone is dark and dangerously sexy.

Without warning, he gives my ass a little smack. I jolt. A fresh wave of desire makes my pussy clench.

He rubs my stinging ass lightly. The sensation is the most erotic thing I've ever felt.

"I've been very, very bad," I whisper.

"Yes, you have. Do you need a spanking? Because I think you do."

My whimper of need is the only response he needs. His hand strikes my ass. I gasp and spread my legs wider.

"More."

He whacks my ass with open-handed slaps until I'm burning hot and ready to do anything to please him. I never expected him to awaken my submissive side, but he has. He's teaching me things I never knew about myself.

Without warning, he slips one finger inside me. I groan as he slides it in and out.

"You're so wet already."

"I need you."

He reaches forward to gently move my head so I can see him from the corner of my eye. He gazes at me as he licks the finger he's removed from my center.

"You taste as sweet as you look."

My brain can't bring forth any coherent words, so I sigh and lay my cheek on the table. I crush more lavender in the process. Remus removes his shirt and unbuckles his belt. The moment I see his cock, I instinctively arch my back in invitation.

"I know what my little witch wants." He strokes his huge cock.

"I want you."

The change in our dynamic blows my mind. For all the years I've known him, I've only ever seen his easygoing, always-down-to-meditate side. Never in a million years would I have imagined we could be like this. I always saw him as the type of guy who would give a woman a rose petal fantasy of slow, sensual sex. I'm glad I was so totally wrong. I like this much better than a rose petal fantasy.

"Hang on tight, baby," he croons.

He pushes his cock into my slick folds. I reach forward to grip the edge of the workbench as he buries himself in me to the hilt. He doesn't yield. He sends sensation after sensation of pure, primal pleasure through me. I'm overwhelmed by him. There's no one else I'd feel safe enough to surrender control to, but it feels so right with him. It's perfect.

He leans forward so his mouth is against my ear. "You like it deep, don't you?"

"By the Goddess." I groan and arch my ass against him.

He slides deeper still. With each thrust, I let out a cry and crush another sprig of lavender. The scent is all around us now, and it mixes into our hair and settles onto our damp skin.

Remus pounds into me hard enough to make the workbench slide forward with each impact. He slips his hand beneath the workbench and finds the apex of my dripping core. With movements that are gentle in comparison to what he's doing with his cock, he teases my clit.

"Damn it." I cry out.

"Don't hold back now. Come for me."

I do as I'm told. My orgasm rips through me and, apparently, inspires his own. He howls as he comes. Heat floods my center as he thrusts deep and buries his cock inside me. I pulse around him, milking his cock for every last drop.

Later, he slides out of me. I nearly fall when he's not supporting my weight anymore. He scoops me into his arms.

"Come on, sweet witch." The tenderness is back in his voice.

"I had no idea you were so naughty," I murmur.

"I'm only naughty for you."

"I'm honored," I say in a teasing tone.

He smiles. "Let's get you somewhere where we can relax."

He carries me into the main house. Thankfully, we still have the place to ourselves. He brings me into his room and settles me onto the bed. The room is cold, but he covers me with blankets before I begin to shiver.

He lays beside me and pulls me into his arms. We lay in comfortable silence for some time before thoughts of Nyx and Torak start to creep into my mind.

I should bring it up now. Remus deserves to know everything.

"I know you have something to tell me." He intertwines his fingers with mine.

"You must be a mind reader."

"I know you." He kisses the back of my hand. "You've clearly got something on your mind. I'm pretty sure I can guess what it is."

"You can?" I laugh nervously.

"You like Nyx. And Torak too." His words are so blunt I struggle to respond.

"I—"

"You've slept with Nyx already, right? That night you were gone. That's what you were doing, right?"

This is it. The moment he starts to hate me forever.

"Yes." I have to be honest with him now.

"I knew it." He doesn't sound angry at all. In fact, he sounds almost satisfied that he guessed correctly.

"What?"

"Look. I care about you a lot. I've never felt this way about anyone else. And I know you care about me too.

"But?"

"No buts. I know you care for the other guys too. It took me a while to get used to the idea of sharing you, but I want you to know I'm okay with it. I'm willing to share if it means I can be with you from time to time."

"I don't know what to say." I can barely speak above a whisper.

"You don't have to say anything. Just let me hold you." His smile is so warm and caring, I fear I'll cry.

"You amaze me."

He tucks my head under his chin and strokes my hair. I don't know how I got this lucky. I thought he was going to hate me, but it's anything but that. I don't want to speculate about how much he cares, but if he cares enough to share me with Nyx, then he must be head over heels for me.

But I still need to talk to Torak. I don't want to wait too long. He's just as mad as Remus was, but I hope he'll be as understanding. I won't know until we talk, but I hope it goes well.

CAPTIVE OF THE WOLF PACK: CHAPTER 16

TORAK

Out in the garden behind Remus' house, I pluck absentmindedly at my guitar. I play a nondescript melody just to keep my hands occupied. It's a beautiful, warm day. Birds chirp and insects buzz through the fields. A thick, hairy caterpillar inches slowly across a broad sunflower leaf towards its brilliant yellow flower.

My mind has been on Iris since our kiss. For the most part, it's been great for my career. Songs have been pouring out of me. Lately, I can't sit for ten minutes before lyrics will start to coalesce in my head. But, it's not all good. I'm tormented by painful longing. The memory of her soft lips on mine twists my heart into a knot. I keep replaying the kiss over and over in my mind while I stare off into space with my mouth hanging open. The other day, Iris caught me like that while I was sitting at the kitchen table.

"What're you daydreaming about?" She'd fixed me with those warm, bottomless eyes. A lazy smile spread across her face.

It killed me not to tell her my thoughts were about her, or more specifically, about our kiss. I wanted to drag her into my arms and press her body against mine. I wanted to kiss her and caress her and tell her everything I've kept locked in my heart. But Nyx was also in the kitchen making a sandwich. So, I lied.

"Oh, nothing. Working out some lyrics in my head." My heart flinched at the untruth. It begged to be unburdened, but I couldn't do it, not with Nyx in the same room.

She'd tilted her head and had scrunched her face doubtfully. I wonder if she ever thinks about the song I wrote for her, or about how hard she'd kissed me when she'd heard it.

I thought she was going to say something, but she kept glancing at Nyx. Then Remus came in from the shop to complain about an ornery customer and the moment was lost. With Remus and Nyx both there, it didn't seem like the best time to express my undying love for our mutual childhood friend.

Although, they don't seem to care about blurring the friendship line with Iris. Nyx and Iris seem to have gotten closer recently. Ever since they spent that night at his house, they've whispered in each other's ears and have laughed conspiratorially. I've even seen them kiss when they thought no one was around. It made my chest go tight, my stomach flip, and my hands clench into fists. I had to dart outside to not howl and snarl at them.

And it's not just Nyx either. She and Remus have gotten closer lately too. The other day, they came out of Remus' workshop giddy and disheveled. Then they'd shared a quick, passionate kiss before they'd gone their separate ways.

I've never cared about anyone the way I care about Iris. Even though she's clearly into the other guys, I still think our bond is magical. When she's in the room, I'm drawn to her like a magnet. I can't seem to pay any attention to anything else. When we're apart, she's never far from my mind, and when I allow myself to think about her, the music seems to flow forth naturally. It's true what they say about heartbreak, it's good material for art, but I can't let this ache go on any longer. I have to let Iris know how badly I want her.

I set my guitar down and head toward the house. I will myself to be calm and strong, but when I step into the kitchen, I freeze. Iris is pressed up against Nyx, who is leaning back against the marble counter. His hands are on Iris' back. Their mouths are locked together.

My heart sinks, and the words I'd wanted to say disappear down my throat. A prickling heat climbs up from my churning stomach. I'm not sure if it's rage or grief, but I know if I don't get outside right now, I'll either scream or cry.

Nyx's eyes go wide when he sees me over Iris' head. He pulls away. Iris turns around, confused. She opens her mouth to speak, but I dart out the back door before she has a chance. I stomp along the path through the herb garden when the back door clangs open.

Iris' call makes my heart leap despite my anger and confusion. I don't know what I'll say if she catches me, so I push on toward the center of the garden.

"Wait." She jogs along the gravel pathway.

I run toward the gazebo at the center of the garden. I catch myself on the railing at the back of the gazebo, my breathing moderately heavily from the brief exertion. Iris sprints in behind me a few seconds later.

"Hey, you okay?"

"I'm fine. Don't worry about me. I needed some air." I try to avoid eye contact so she doesn't see through me, but she's so damn beautiful that it's impossible not to look.

"You're not a very good liar." She smiles at me sympathetically.

"I'm fine. Really."

"No, you're not." She crosses her arms and gives me a skeptical look.

"Fine." I turn away to hide my shame. "I guess I don't like to see you all over Nyx. Or Remus. I know you're an independent woman. You can do what you want. It's just that..." I trail off, reluctant to continue.

I plop down on the gazebo bench. She walks over and sits next to me. Warmth radiates from the point on my leg where her knee touches me.

"I'm sorry, I didn't mean to hurt you," she says.

"It's okay." Tears threaten to spill over. Disappointment grips my chest like a vise. "I-I assumed we had a connection. But it's all right. I'll get over it." With great effort, I stare away from her beautiful eyes for fear I'll lose control of my emotions and drown in my longing.

"No, you were right. We do have a special connection. I hate that I hurt you like this. I've wanted to talk to you. I just never found the right time. That's completely my fault, and I'm sorry about that." She places her hand on my thigh.

Hope blooms within me. "So, you do feel it?"

"Of course I do. But I'm a little confused." She bites her lower lip and hesitates.

"Confused about what?"

"Well, I sense a strong connection with you. I do. But it's also that way with Nyx. And Remus." She looks away, shame apparent on her face. "I guess that's why I was so nervous about talking to you about us." She turns back to me. Determination and passion burn away the shame.

"I'm in love with you. With all of you. And I wasn't sure how you'd feel about that. Sometimes it seems like maybe I'm asking for too much."

Relief washes over me. My chest loosens and my heart slows.

"No way. Nothing is too much for you. The whole world would be only a fraction of what you deserve." I take her hand in mine.

"I don't know..." She gnaws on her bottom lip. "What's so special about me? Why do I deserve so much?"

"Are you serious? You're incredible. You're my muse. You've always been my muse. I didn't realize it until recently, but I can't remember the last time I've been this inspired. I've written more songs in the last three days than I have in the last three years. Every time I envision you, my heart soars, and lyrics pour out of me. I sit and daydream about you, and melodies seem to stitch themselves together. I need you. And if that means I have to share you, then I'm more than happy to share."

She stares at me with tears in her eyes. A slight smile brightens her face.

I lean in. She meets me halfway, and our lips touch in an explosion of electricity. We dance the tips of our tongues together briefly before we slide them deep together. I gently guide her hand up my thigh to my hard cock, which bulges against my jeans.

I ache for her.

She sighs into my mouth as she caresses the outline of my cock. I slip my hand up her thigh under her skirt. Her skin is hot, and a damp heat radiates from her pussy. I brush my fingers over her wet panties and my cock jumps.

I slide one hand to the back of her neck. I pull her mouth hard against mine. With my other hand, I gently massage her pussy through her lace panties. Wetness drenches the thin fabric. She opens her legs a little and moans softly.

I slip my fingers beneath her underwear and slide them up her wet lips toward her swollen clit. When I touch her, she lets out a little whimper and her body pulses against my fingers. She unbuttons my jeans and slips her hand inside my boxers. As she strokes up and down my hard shaft, I grit my teeth against the need to come.

As I kiss down the side of her neck, I rub my finger in little circles over her clit.

"I want you so bad," I groan.

"I want you too."

"You're so wet."

"You do this to me." She spreads her legs even farther and moans when I slide two fingers deep into her wet pussy.

"You're so hard." She squeezes my shaft. "I need you inside me right now."

Her hot breath against my ear sends a shiver down my spine. For a second, I fear I might come, but I quickly gain control of myself.

She grabs at my waistband. I raise my butt off the bench so she can work my pants down toward my ankles. I stroke her wet pussy as she leans over and takes my cock into her mouth.

"Oh, shit." I wasn't expecting that.

She slides me all the way down her throat. When her lips wrap around the base of my shaft, I throw my head back and groan. As she bobs her head up and down, she moans onto my cock. Her hips move back and forth involuntarily as I massage her g-spot.

I grab her hair and pull her off me, so I won't come in her mouth. I press her lips to mine again. Our kiss is sloppy and wet.

"I need to be inside you. Now."

I hoist her onto me. She throws her leg over to straddle me. I pull her panties to the side and guide my cock toward her delicate pink pussy. She shudders when I caress her clit with the head of my cock.

"Put it in, please."

I slide her down onto my hard shaft. She cries out and her eyes roll back. I wrap my arms around her, hike up her skirt, and grab her ass firmly in both hands. She rocks back and forth on my cock.

"Oh, my god, you feel so good." She grabs my hands and squeezes them so hard it hurts. Her eyes are closed, and her expression is saturated with pleasure.

I rock her back and forth faster now. I lift her shirt so I can caress one soft, perky breast. I flick my tongue across her other nipple. She moans loudly. She pulls her shirt over her head and tosses it aside.

"You're so sexy." I concentrate on relaxing my muscles. I don't want to come too quickly.

"Oh, my god. Yes, like that. Faster." She drops one hand down to caress her own clit. "Oh, my god. Fuck, I'm going to come. Oh, my god. Oh, my god, I'm coming." Her low, guttural moan is positively feral. I have to fight not to come inside her.

Her pussy spills juices all over my cock. She contracts and convulses as she continues to rock back and forth sporadically. I can't hold back.

I grunt as I thrust deep and explode inside her. I grab her hips and pin her down on my lap. My cock jerks until I'm empty and completely satiated.

As I lie back against the cool wood, she rests her head on my chest. I'm still inside her and it's exactly where I want to be.

"That was amazing," I murmur.

"So amazing."

I can't believe what just happened. I just made love to Iris. I thought for sure I would be the odd man out in our little foursome, but it turns out there might be room for me in her life after all. I don't care if I have to share her with the other guys. As long as I can have her, that's all I need. She's what I need, and I never want to let her go.

CAPTIVE OF THE WOLF PACK:
CHAPTER 17

IRIS

With the four of us all under one roof, it's not often I have any time alone. The good thing is that I don't often want to be alone. Remus, Torak, and Nyx are absolute angels. Naughty, sexy, kinky angels, but angels nonetheless. Their constant companionship keeps me sane as preparations to deal with Lexus and the Academy continue to develop.

It's been some time since we've heard from Argus, so we've developed a routine while we wait for word. Thyme and Country runs as if nothing is amiss. Sales have gone through the roof lately, which means a steady stream of work for all of us. I guess people are getting ready for the war by stocking up on magical herbs now.

Usually, two people work in the shop and two people make products in the workshop. However, the shop is so busy today that Torak left the workshop to help in the store. Remus must be thrilled by how many customers he has now. I wish I could go help him in the shop, but I'm still in hiding.

Everyone seems to need something from Thyme and

Country. Wreaths, in particular, fly off the shelves. Witches even use levitation spells to snag them before others can get to them.

The citizens of Bonfire Falls know something's up. Orders for the sold-out protection wreaths are piled an inch high on the workbench. Torak is supposed to help me make them today, but it looks like I'll have to handle it on my own.

I don't mind. Every now and again, the silence of an empty room is nice.

I smile as I bundle lavender to be dried.

Through a small window, I can see the three of them working together in Thyme and Country. They snap and bicker with each other in a playful manner. We've become a family now, and it's more than I'd ever hoped for.

The sound of fluttering papers grabs my attention.

I set up a special slot in the wall so that orders can immediately be transferred from the store to the workshop. Now no one has to leave the shop to deliver orders to the workroom. As much as I would love to see one of my darling men pop into the workshop to drop off orders, the slot is way more efficient.

I flip through the order slips and notice the influx of demand for oils. The desired ingredients for at least twenty new orders are all for protection. Yep, the locals know something's up.

The timer on the dehydrator chimes. Another batch of lavender is finished. I take the old bundle out and put a new one in.

Some witches view the use of modern inventions as cheating. Those witches like to make things more complicated. Why wait three days for herbs to dry when I can get the same result in two hours?

With a frown, I stare at the sheer number of orders

piled up. I'm damn good at wreaths, oils, and herb caches, but they all take time. The last thing I want is to cost Remus a sale because I'm too slow.

On top of the orders, I still need to find time to go out and pick fresh basil. Yesterday, we completely ran out. Remus had to take the cooking basil from the kitchen to fill the orders.

I meant to pick more last night, but I got too caught up with prep for the today's wreaths. Had I known I'd be this swamped, I would've gone this morning. Instead, I'd enjoyed a lovely breakfast with the men.

Basil is used in many protection spells because it's easily obtained, but it can be substituted. I'll have to dip into the less common herb stocks to do so. I never like to do that. I'm always worried I'll use a rare herb as a substitute only to desperately need it for a very specific spell later on.

I slice fragrant buds from their crunchy stems. I attach them to the wreath bases I made last night. I set three aside to make special wreaths for Remus, Torak, and Nyx as a token of my affection.

I still haven't decided what I want to add to their wreaths. Some herbs are obvious choices like coriander for love and fidelity and bellflowers for gratitude. I've considered rose buds, but that seems too obvious. Although Remus, with his lover's soul, might like them.

Three lavender wreaths are done. I'm ready to sprinkle them with essential oils to enhance their effects when the side door opens.

"Are you guys finally going to give me some help back here?" I ask with mock consternation.

When I don't hear an answer or any other sounds of movement, I get up to investigate.

Lexus is standing in the doorway, dressed in a sleek

black pantsuit and stilettos tall enough to be considered lethal weapons.

My blood runs cold.

"Hello, darling." She puckers her ruby red lips and blows me a kiss. I hate it when she calls me darling. She knows this. "I've looked all over for you."

"So I've heard." I step backward until I bump against the table in the center of the room.

"Have you? And you didn't make yourself known to me? Your mother clearly didn't teach you manners."

"Leave my mother out of this." I grit my teeth. "Besides, when you married my father, you were supposed to take over the motherly role. I suppose my manners are proof of your shortcomings as a mother."

I shouldn't mouth off to this woman. I don't want to fight her here. Not now. I'm not ready. I need Remus, Nyx, and Torak with me—preferably a whole legion of shifters too.

I can't do this alone.

"You're panicking." A wicked smile spreads across Lexus' too-smooth face.

I can tell she uses anti-aging spells. Those are notoriously difficult and cost a great deal of magic if the caster doesn't want to murder someone to make them work. With Lexus, either scenario is equally likely.

"No, I'm not panicking."

"It's okay if you are." Her voice turns sickly sweet. "I know this has been an overwhelming time for you. I've come to tell you it's all over."

"Define *over*."

"You can come back to me now." I can't tell if Lexus is mocking me or if she genuinely doesn't understand how thoroughly I despise her and everything she stands for.

"I appreciate the offer, but I have to decline. I've

started my life over. I'm comfortable. Thank you for your concern."

Lexus cackles like one of those fairytale witches that give us all a bad rep.

"That's adorable. You're in the stuffy garage of a glorified doghouse. What kind of life is this? An abysmal one. I can see that for myself."

Anger flashes through me, but before I act on it, Lexus advances towards me.

"A war is brewing, darling girl. It'll make the last war look like a skirmish." She speaks as if I'm a child.

"You're wrong."

"Don't play dumb. It doesn't suit you. It's time for you to join our side."

"I won't pick sides in a pointless war. I won't have any part in this insane hatred between witches and shifters." I lift my chin in defiance.

"At what point did I ask you to choose?" Lexus smirks. "You'll return to the Academy to fight alongside the other witches."

"No."

Lexus lifts a finger to silence me. Her black nails are filed to look like claws.

"You should let me finish. Join the witches, or I'll kill your little pets."

"I'd like to see you try."

Lexus is powerful. I can't deny that. My wolves will put up one hell of a fight if it comes to it. Despite Lexus' power, she's still only one person.

"Believe me, darling. You have no idea how much I want to spill the blood of those brutes. How could you betray your kind like this? Can you imagine my shame when I discovered you here?"

I choke back a laugh. Of course Lexus would feel shame over this.

"Which one are you fucking?" She lifts her brow with a crude smile. This catches me off guard. "Come on, I'm not stupid. Those animals are only good for fighting and fucking. You haven't been fighting them."

"They aren't animals. They're people."

"Please. Let me let you in on a little secret. My girls have perfected their training. Their power is stronger than ever, and so is mine. We're strong enough to wipe out all of the shifter clans now, and we'll kill anyone—human or witch—who stands in our way."

"You don't have enough pupils to be that strong."

"That's where you're wrong. All my students have learned how to force a shifter to change. We can make each and every one of them into puppets."

The color drains from my face.

"You're insane." Fear reduces my voice to little more than a squeak. I know Lexus well enough to know that she doesn't bluff. My false bravado slowly slips away from me, and my hands tremble.

"I'm insane to want my coven to achieve greatness?" Lexus asks. "The superiority of witches has been set aside for too long. We were given our gifts for a reason. Why should we confine our true power? Why should we have to live equally among beasts?"

"True power allows peace to flourish."

I glance at the clock on the wall. Remus usually closes the store for lunch in about twenty minutes. However, since it's been so busy, I'm not certain he'll close at all.

"That's what the weak say when they realize how powerless they are." Lexus rolls her eyes. "I won't pretend we've always gotten along. Honestly, I would've preferred it if your father didn't have a child when I married him.

But I'm no fool. You're powerful. I'd even call you talented. You lack refinement, but that's easily remedied. Don't you understand what I'm offering? A chance at greatness."

"I don't understand anything about you."

"I offer you the world." Lexus' eyes widen. "You'd have power. All the power you could ever want. I'll teach you secrets only I know. Secrets I refuse to share with other students. I already have Oscar ready for you. I've been giving him extra training. He's a powerful warlock who worships the ground you walk on. Your children will have more natural ability than even I was blessed with. How can you prefer mangy mutts to everything I'm offering?"

"I'd try to explain it to you, but you wouldn't understand."

"We're in agreement there." Lexus nods. "Deep down, you know I'm right. There has to be some small part of you that wants what I offer. Listen to that part of you."

"Even if that part of me did exist, I'd rather die than listen to it."

Lexus' ample chest sags with disappointment.

"No one can say I didn't try." She says this to no one in particular before she looks at me once more. "My patience has run out. It's time to leave."

Lexus flicks her bony wrist. Her thin diamond bracelet sparkles in the light as she casts a spell. I'm too slow to block it.

White ropes of pure energy wind around me. They pin my arms to my sides and lock my legs together. A scream rises in my throat, but dark energy forces it down.

I can't alert anyone that I'm in trouble.

"If this is all it took to make you cooperate, I would've done this years ago." Lexus grins.

With another flick of her wrist, I levitate off the floor.

The tips of my toes bump against the ground as she forces me forward.

My fingers are still free. I attempt to weave several spells to loosen my magical restraints, but nothing works. Lexus' magic is too powerful.

She leads me out the side door and away from the back of the house. She must've cloaked us from sight somehow. We're definitely visible from the road, but no one sees us.

To quell my panic, I convince myself that this is the best outcome. Lexus has admitted I'm powerful. She won't kill me. Not right away, at least.

Remus, Nyx, and Torak are safe. They're my best hope for rescue, but I don't want them to have to fight Lexus without me. For now, they're alive and out of Lexus' sight.

I know she plans on taking me back to the Academy, so I'm not surprised when she leaves in that direction.

Before long, the black spires of that horrible building poke through the trees. She takes me in through the dungeon entrance. I used to dare my classmates to come down here in the middle of the night. I'd always believed that the use of the dungeons had stopped centuries ago, but the bodies in some of the cells tell a different story. There are other people down here.

I'm so terrified she'll lock me away that I sigh in relief when she takes me up the stairs to the main floor. She uses the servants' staircase to bring me to the dormitory. The hallway is empty as she levitates me into my old room.

With a thrust of energy, she launches me against the wall. I land hard on the stone floor. My muscles protest as I struggle to right myself. Stars swim through my field of vision, but I still sprint for the window.

Lexus quickly blocks it with a lattice of thorny vines. I

realize I have no idea of the full extent of her power. We're far above the ground, yet somehow, she's commanded plants to grow right through stone.

"I'd intended to remove the restraints, but I see now it's pointless," she says.

I stare at her with wide eyes.

"Dear me, you've got quite the bump on your head. Lie down and sleep it off. You have plenty of time for a nap."

With a snake-like smile, she shuts the door. The lock clicks into place. The hum of magic lingers in the air. She's added a secondary lock, a magical lock, to my door.

It's only when the click of her heels fades away that I move. I go to my bed. Sitting down is a struggle, but I manage it.

Now that Lexus has moved away, her magical restraints start to weaken. They'll disperse eventually, but magic this strong takes time to wear off. Not that it matters. I'm trapped here with or without the restraints.

My best option for escape is get through the vines that cover the window. They will shred my hands to pieces, but it's the only way out.

I consider it for a second, then give up. Even if I managed to get through the tangle, I'd still have to figure out how to climb down the slick stone walls. I'd never make it. I'd fall and break my neck. No one would ever know what Lexus did because she'd say I jumped to my death. She's such a good liar, even my father would believe her.

Trapped and desperate, I think about my guys. I'm glad they were spared from Lexus' wrath, but they won't know what happened when they realize I'm gone. I didn't leave any sign of struggle. They might think I left on my own volition. They have to know I'd never leave them, right?

CAPTIVE OF THE WOLF PACK: CHAPTER 18

NYX

I t's hard to stand here at the checkout counter of Thyme and Country and keep a smile on my face. Numbers aren't my thing, and after hundreds of transactions, my brain grows numb. Normally we would have stopped for lunch already, but there are too many customers. I hope Iris isn't working her hands to the bone. I was hoping I'd get to go back to the workshop to help her make wreaths.

A snotty middle-aged witch with a short haircut approaches me. She wants to see the manager because we're out of rose hips. A scowl darkens her face. There is no joy in this woman whatsoever.

"I'm sorry, ma'am, but this is all the rose hips we have left." I spread my hands and try to evoke friendliness with my smile. "I can't wave a magic wand and make more appear."

"Wave a magic wand?" She sneers. "Is that supposed to be a slur against me because I'm a witch? That's it. I demand to speak to the manager."

"Of course," I mutter. "I'll go grab Remus right now."

I turn to get away from the shrew and almost run right into Torak.

"Where's Remus?"

"He's in the parking lot helping a lady put a seventy-pound bag of nightshade soil into her trunk." His brow furrows. He glances behind me at the angry woman at the cash register. "What's up?"

"Just a bitchy customer."

"Another one?"

"Yep. People have their tail feathers in a fucking fluff today. Watch your back around these witches." I tap him on the shoulder and head out to the lot.

I catch Remus as he closes the trunk and makes pleasantries with the elderly witch patron. When he sees me, he can tell I'm agitated.

"What's wrong?"

"Some grouchy customer wants to see the manager." I point my finger at him. "That's you."

"Right." Remus smiles at the elderly witch, then heads for the store. "Go ahead and lock up. We're closing in five minutes. I need a break."

"Hell yeah." I clap my hands and eagerly go to do his bidding. I can't wait to see Iris. It's been a long day.

When I get back, Remus has sweet-talked the crazy lady into purchasing a substitute herb for her potion. She leaves with a smile on her face. I have to hand it to him, he's smooth.

After the last customer leaves, Torak and I take care of the dirty work while Remus counts down the cash drawer. People in Bonfire Falls are on edge, and with good reason, but it's good for his bottom line.

Once the store is properly stocked, cleaned, and closed, I take a quick peek into the workshop. It's empty.

She probably gave up on us and went into the house to get some food.

I'm the first one into the main house. I check the living room. There's no sign of Iris. The TV is off. A cup of tea sits on the end table. When I pick it up, the ceramic is cold. My heart sinks, and I sense that something's amiss.

I move through the house as I call her name. The kitchen is empty. By the time I get to the upstairs bedrooms, I'm in a frenzy.

"What's the matter?" Remus yells from downstairs

"Iris isn't here." I stop at the top of the staircase. "I don't think she's been here for hours."

"Calm down. Have you checked everywhere?" Torak asks.

"Everywhere but the garden. Come on."

We search the herb garden and the lavender field. She's not in either spot.

"Are you sure she wasn't in the workshop?" Remus asks.

"I only took a quick look. Maybe she was hiding behind something as a joke?"

I lead the way as we head back to the workshop.

Inside, our eyes are immediately drawn to a crushed lavender wreath on the floor. My hands clench into fists as Remus walks over and picks it up.

"Something's wrong," he says. "She never would have left a wreath on the floor like this."

"We were right next door," I say. "How could anything have happened without us knowing?"

"Lexus." Torak's tone is dark with fear.

I glance around the workshop but find no evidence of foul play.

"You might be jumping to conclusions. How did that witch sneak in here and snatch her without us knowing?"

"She's a witch." Torak gives me a look as if he thinks I'm an idiot. I just can't accept the fact that Lexus might have her.

"If Lexus took her, then Iris is probably at the Academy." Remus sets the wreath aside.

"Then that's where we're headed," I say.

I turn and shove my way past Torak. Low growls escape me in anticipation of the upcoming battle. The thought of sweet Iris in the clutches of that old harpy makes my blood boil. I have to save her.

"Wait." Torak catches me by the arm. I allow him to stop me, but I give him a menacing glare. He lets go of my arm and clears his throat. "You can't go off half-cocked. We need a plan."

"No time for a plan."

I'm about to leave, but Remus calls after me. "Hear him out. What do you plan to do, attack the Academy by yourself?"

"If I have to."

"Stop walking," Torak snaps.

I stop and give him my full attention. "All right, let's hear it."

"Thank you." He rubs his chin and his eyes seem to focus on a spot in the distance. "Argus plans to attack the Academy. Let's hope he's gotten enough pieces in place to pull it off because we can't wait anymore. We need to do this now."

"We need to go see him," I say. "Right now."

We exchange glances. There's not an ounce of doubt in any of our minds. We'll do whatever it takes to get Iris back.

Torak and Remus stop to take off their clothes, but I'm in such a rush I barely slip out of my jeans before I start to shift. My T-shirt rips to shreds. Only a ragged strip clings to my flank as I lope into the dense forest.

Trees flash by as I dash through clumps of moss. I fly past clusters of mushrooms growing off the side of hollowed-out trunks. Fading sunlight flickers through the trees to cast shadows onto the forest floor.

My nose detects more than my eyes ever will. Rabbits scuttle out of my way. I scent their fear, but they have nothing to worry about. I'm hunting far bigger prey today.

We splash through a rushing river and dash up the edges of a steep ravine to take the most direct route to the wolf den. Our fear for Iris makes us much more determined to struggle over every harsh incline. I picture her face as I fight through thick brambles that cling and tear at my fur.

Torak and Remus are somewhere behind me in the woods. I'm not stopping to wait for them. They'll catch up eventually.

At last, I break through the tree line and come upon the wolf den. Argus and several others sit outside as they tend a fire and pass around a bottle of scotch. Their conversation stops when they see me. I shift back into human form and step into the firelight.

"You seem on the verge of panic, boy. Speak," Argus says.

"It's Iris." My eyes meet Argus' gray ones. "She's been abducted by Lexus and taken back to the Academy. We have to attack now."

"Now?" Argus' eyes narrow. His hands go to his hips. "This kind of thing must be carefully planned. I've set things in motion, but it'll be days before I'm ready to attack the witches on their home turf."

"We don't have days," I yell.

Argus' eyes widen. He takes a step back. I'm shocked to realize how ready I am to fight him over this.

Torak bursts out of the woods and lopes up next to us before he transforms. He grimaces with the final pains of transmutation and then stands by my side.

"It's true. We can't afford to wait any longer. Every second we wait puts Iris in even more danger. We must attack as soon as possible."

Remus joins the group and stands beside Torak. There's a bramble still entangled in his hair. He brushes it out while he addresses Argus.

"We know Lexus' plans to destroy the shifters somehow involve Iris. If we let her remain in the Academy's possession, Lexus may complete her task and wipe us all out, or at least permanently remove our ability to shift."

Argus strokes his gray beard thoughtfully and regards us. I still want to run to save Iris right away, but I'm able to hold myself back.

Finally, Argus speaks.

"Very well. We cannot allow our enemies to use our allies to further a foul endeavor." His eyes flash to mine. The old wolf smiles a toothy smile, a hunter's smile. "And besides, this young cub will piss himself if we don't go soon." He waves a hand toward me. I ignore the insult, only because I need his help.

Argus turns to address the pack members who have ventured out from the cave to find out what all the screaming is about.

"What say you, pack brothers? Shall we gather the army I have amassed these last few weeks and go on the hunt?"

The pack howls. Their voices join in a chorus that reverberates off the trees and echoes through the woods. Argus joins in the howl, and soon, so do the three of us.

"All right, then." Argus turns to address us once more. "We'll gather in the town square of Bonfire Falls in three hours."

"Three hours?" I'm exasperated. Why can't they sense the urgency of this matter?

"Silence." Argus glares at me until I'm compelled to take a step back. "Three hours is the fastest I can pull this off. Unless you want to challenge me for leadership of the pack, you will wait."

I could probably take him, but I don't want the responsibility of running the pack.

"We'll meet you there in three hours," I say.

Argus nods before barking orders at the pack.

Remus, Torak and I shift back into wolf form and head to Remus' house. Fortunately, there's not much time to kill after we make it back. We get dressed and grab weapons. I spend the last forty minutes seated on my Harley in the Thyme and Country parking lot, arms crossed over my chest as I wait on the others. Waiting is killing me.

Remus finally comes out of his garage mounted on his four-wheeled ATV. It's quite useful on his farm, and now he'll ride it into war. Somehow, it seems appropriate.

When Torak putters up on a red scooter, I can't help but sit there with my jaw on the ground. I stare. Mr. Rockstar rides a scooter.

"Are you serious?" I shake my head in disbelief.

"Don't be a jerk," Remus calls me out. "It gets great gas mileage, and it's easy to park."

"Yeah, and it's a great way to remain a virgin."

"Hey, I'm not a virgin."

"Don't remind me."

"Asshole."

"Let's go."

We rumble out of the parking lot and hit the highway. Well, Remus and I rumble. Torak's scooter makes a high-pitched whine. It's embarrassing.

Remus and I are kind of assholes about it too. We speed way ahead of him and force him to do crazy stuff to keep up, like take a hill too fast. He flies a good four feet in the air. Sparks fly from the scooter's chassis, but Torak keeps it straight. When he sees me grin back at him, he flips me the bird. It would be fucking hilarious if I wasn't so freaked out about Iris.

We pull into the center of Bonfire Falls. I'm shocked to see how many people Argus has gathered. Of course, most of the Wolf Clan is here, but there are also quite a few of the Bear Clan present. The Dragon Clan is missing, of course. Pussies are still up the mountain, hiding. They wouldn't come down unless they were being directly threatened. I hate those guys.

Then there are the witches. Lots of witches. I'm surprised so many of them share Iris' views on the Academy. I guess the use of dark magic goes against their beliefs too.

Argus rumbles in on his huge chrome motorcycle and raises his arm in the air. Everyone mounts up and falls into formation behind him.

Some of the witches double up with the Wolf Clan. Since Remus' ride is a four-seater, he gives a lift to three of them.

One of the other witches begins a chant. A black void opens in the middle of the street and a skeletal horse strides out. Its nightmarish whinny sends chills down my spine. The witch leaps into the saddle and then joins the army. Fire sparks from its hooves as it gallops.

Soon, we're racing down the highway toward Dark

Magic Academy. I should draw a measure of strength from my pack, but inside, I'm terrified. What if we're too late to save Iris? What if I never see her again?

I've told her I love her. She needs to know that I've always loved her, and I'll love her forever. If we survive this war, if I get to see my sweet Iris again, that's the first thing I'll say to her.

CAPTIVE OF THE WOLF PACK:
CHAPTER 19

IRIS

As I predicted, the magical restraints eventually wear off. My limbs ache from being held in place for so long. I stand in the center of my old room and stretch. The restraints were one of about a dozen problems I needed to solve. One down, and about a million to go. I don't know how I'm going to get out of this place, but there's got to be a way.

I'm not sure how long I've been here. Lexus conveniently removed all time-telling devices from my room. Either that, or that klepto witch Zarina, who lives two doors down, broke in and stole my stuff. I've been here long enough for my fear to shift into anger.

Lexus is a terrifyingly powerful witch. Now I have to fight her on her own turf, and I'm all alone. Lexus threatened to kill the men I love, so in a way, I'm glad they're not here. No matter how scared I am, I can't let her win. She'd kill my guys out of spite. I'll do violent, unspeakable things to her before I let her harm Remus, Nyx, or Torak.

Have they figured out what happened to me? They're smart guys, and wolves are excellent hunters and trackers.

No doubt they've picked up my scent. My heart wants to leap out of my chest when I imagine that they're on their way to me now. But if they're on their way here, that means they'll have to face off against Lexus and her pupils. I can't let them do that alone. I have to get out of here.

I pace the length of my room as I try to come up with a plan. I try the doorknob even though I know it's locked both physically and magically. I thought maybe the magical lock had worn off, but it hasn't.

I charge at the door, slamming my shoulder into it until I'm on the brink of dislocating my shoulder. The door is just as locked as it was ten minutes ago and now my shoulder hurts.

Brilliant, Iris. Absolutely brilliant.

I weave a small healing spell to dull the pain, but it won't stop the bruise that's already developing.

I turn to my desk and scour the drawers for anything useful. I find a pair of scissors and attempt to cut through the vines over the window. The vines are so strong they fracture the scissor blades.

"Damn it." I throw the broken scissors across the room.

I stand in the center of my room directly across from the door and take a deep breath. I don't want to use too much magic to escape. I want to save my energy for fighting, but it looks like I don't have a choice.

I start with the obvious spell, a firebolt. I blast the door, but it's been fireproofed. I laugh at the irony. Years ago, I pointed out to an instructor that wooden doors made locks pointless once the school taught us how to summon fire. Now I wish they hadn't listened to me.

I turn around and send a firebolt at the vines. It only destroys some of them, but it might be enough. I rush to the window and clear away as many remaining vines as possible. I try to open the window, but it won't budge. It's been magically locked.

"Ugh!"

I run to my bed and tear up part of the comforter. It's thick enough to protect my hand as I punch through the window.

The stained glass was over eight hundred years old. I feel terrible about breaking it, but it's the only way out.

I peek through the hole and look for ledges or footholds that I can use to climb down. Of course, I'm not that lucky. I brush my fingers over the wall. It's slicker than I recall. If I were to climb out, there'd be nothing to stop me from falling straight to my death. I broke that window for nothing.

"Shit."

I can't break through Lexus' spells. She crafted them with dark magic. All witches study dark magic in theory. We learn how to prepare ourselves against it, but we're never outright taught how to use it. It's not uncommon for a witch to learn dark magic from an outside source, but I'm not one of those witches. I have no idea how to craft a dark spell, let alone undo one made by a powerful, evil witch.

If I'm going to get out of here, I need to find something stronger than the blackest magic from the evilest of hearts.

"There has to be something else. I'm missing something. I know I'm missing something."

I look in my closet on the off chance that I'd stowed some contraband items in there. I hadn't.

However, I find an old gift Nyx gave me years ago. I'm ashamed to admit I'd forgotten it. It's one of his leather jackets. His favorite, if I remember correctly. The dark leather is worn and soft. When I press my nose against it, it still smells like him despite the fact that he hasn't touched it in years.

As I run my hands over it, I notice something I hadn't noticed when he first gave it to me. Just inside the right sleeve, where the leather ends and the silk lining begins, is a hand-stitched red heart no larger than my pinkie nail.

I clutch the jacket to my chest and fight the waves of tears that threaten to spill over. I can't get upset now, even if missing him and the others is more painful than I ever imagined. The thought that I might never see them again is enough to make me go insane.

"I will see you again," I whisper into the soft folds of the jacket.

Nyx wasn't the only one to give me a gift. Remus gave me pressed rose petals. The first rose he ever grew, I believe. There could be magic in the petals.

I go back to my desk and open the small compartment carved into the surface. There's a velvet pouch containing rose petals that have turned deep purple with time. Examining the petals, I spot a tiny heart etched into one of them. Coincidence?

Torak gave me something as well. A song. The sheet music is hidden away in my bedside table. When I retrieve it, the heart drawn in the upper right-hand corner stands out clearly. Once I have all three items, magic hums through the air.

At first, I fear Lexus is returning to finish me off, but the sounds of her clicking heels never come.

I take a deep breath to focus my energy. The magical sensation is coming from the gifts. How is that possible? Wolf shifters don't have magic.

I examine the little hearts on all of the gifts. Then it hits me.

I always believed these gifts to be symbols of friendship, but the hearts tell me otherwise. Even though these gifts were given long before I knew I loved any of them, love spells were woven into them.

Love magic is tricky. It has a mind of its own, and it's very difficult to control. Witches learn about it, but no one teaches witches how to wield it. I know enough about love magic to know that the user has to fully understand what it means to love. If they don't, whatever spell they cast will warp into something twisted and wrong. If the user is feeding off the love of someone else, it's even more complicated. Not only does the user have to understand love, but they also have to be truly in love with the original caster and the caster has to truly love them in return.

It's all very complicated.

I've heard horror stories about witches turning to dust instantly from casting a bad love spell. We were always cautioned against it. Love spells are only used by stupid, arrogant witches.

However, if it's wielded correctly, there's nothing more powerful than a love-based spell.

I understand love thanks to Remus, Nyx, and Torak. I love them with everything that I am, and I know they love me too.

I can wield this magic.

I put on the jacket, gather the rose petals in one hand and hold the sheet music with the other. There are many ways that this could go wrong, but it's worth the risk. Lexus needs to be stopped, and I have to see my men again.

While I'm no musical genius, I manage to sing Torak's song. Like everything he writes, it's a work of beauty.

The rose petals grow warm in my hand. No doubt they were planted in magic soil.

Power builds inside me until I fear I'll burst open. I almost lose control over it, which causes a small panic. I think of seeing Remus, Nyx, and Torak again and the magic falls back under control.

With a scream, I unleash the power of love magic upon the door, reducing it to a pile of smoldering splinters.

A pair of pale-faced students run by the door. I almost feel bad for scaring them.

When I step out in the hallway, one of them looks over their shoulder at me.

"You need to take cover," she says.

"What do you mean?" I ask.

"Shifters are in the school. They're here to kill us all."

"Which way?"

She points a trembling hand toward the mouth of the grand staircase. I take off running. The sounds of battle reach my ears. The sensation of magic in the air is so strong that my hair floats in a static cloud around my face.

I reach the final landing and stop in my tracks. The ongoing battle is vicious. Bolts of magic fly across the room. Shifters of all species snap and slash at witches. Blood mars the once pristine marble floors. Some have already fallen on both sides.

Fear squeezes my throat as I look at the dead. Remus, Nyx, and Torak are blessedly not among them. I search for them, but everything is a blur punctuated by disorienting flashes of light.

A ball of fire explodes nearby. I leap down the remaining stairs to avoid it. Someone has spotted me. They must realize I'm not an ally.

I craft a protective aura around myself and move behind the staircase railing.

From my new vantage point, I finally glimpse my wolf

shifters. My heart could burst as I see all three of them fighting in tandem in their wolf forms. Relief loosens the anxious knot in my belly. The battle is overwhelming in every way, but at least I know the men are taking care of each other.

I weave a protection spell around them for good measure. They're all moving so wildly that it takes all of my concentration to hold it.

A writhing bear shifter catches my eye. I realize, with a horrified gasp, that he's shifting against his will. Once in human form and much more vulnerable to magic, he's run through with an ice spike that's almost as large as he is. My heart wails as his body goes limp.

I can't stand here any longer. I have to get in there and help. More than anything, I want to fight beside Remus, Nyx, and Torak, but I must go to where I'm most useful, not where I want to be.

Minerva and Azealia are near the center of the bloodied foyer. They stand back to back, blasting streams of magic outward to devastating effect. They're more powerful than all of the witches in this room combined, with the exception of Lexus, but they're unprotected.

Moving will shatter my protection spell. I don't know that I can make it to where Minerva and Azealia stand without it.

"Iris!" A familiar voice grabs my attention. It's Remus!

Wait, what? I can hear him in my head. He's still in wolf form. How is this possible?

Remus, Nyx, and Torak dash up the stairs to where I am. I grab hold of each of them, letting the battle fade away for just a moment. When I pull away from Nyx, his fur is bloody.

"Don't worry. It's not mine." His upper lip pulls back

over his wolf-teeth in a way that resembles his well-known smirk.

I still can't believe we can communicate while they're shifted, but now is not the time to question it. I'll figure out our sudden ability to be telepathic with each other later.

"Azealia and Minerva need help," I explain. "The protection spell surrounding you will weaken if I move away."

"There's a protection spell around us?" Torak's wolf form snarls.

"Of course. I'm not here to admire the view." I give him a nudge.

"Don't worry about us," Remus says. "Protect the witches. If we lose them, this will be much harder."

"Okay." I set my jaw. "Be careful."

"We'll cover you," Nyx says.

I transfer the protection spell to Minerva and Azealia. It's easier to hold it over them since they aren't moving very much. I bolt into the fray with my three wolves at my side. We tear through everyone who tries to stop us.

Minerva sends out spirals of crackling fire while Azealia unleashes torrents of ice. They nod to me as I stand beside them.

Remus, Nyx, and Torak circle us and keep anyone from getting too close. I whip up swirling air and suck up both Minerva's fire and Azealia's ice, making the tornado from hell. I whip it at our enemies. No one attempts to block our combined magic. They all flee the moment they see what we've unleashed.

All except Lexus.

Her hair is disheveled. Her eyes are wild, gleaming with madness.

"I'll turn you all to dust!" She shrieks and charges us.

Remus snarls and swings around to pounce on her.

"Wait." I call him off. I look to Azealia. "Bind her."

She nods and sends out ropes of energy similar to the ones that Lexus used to bind me, only they're much stronger and, from the look on Lexus' face, very painful.

Azealia brings Lexus closer and forces her to her knees.

"It's over Lexus." I've dreamed of this moment for weeks. I expected to feel more emotion. I thought I might cry. Instead, there's just numbness and ice in my heart. "You've tormented enough people. It's time for you to stop."

"Tormented? I'm your savior!" She smirks.

"Tell that to them." I point to three fallen witches bearing the mark of the school.

"They were weak." Lexus shrugs.

"So are you," Minerva says. "I expected more."

This elicits a thrash from Lexus, though it has no effect on the magical binds.

"What are we going to do with her?" I ask.

"Kill her," Azealia suggests. "She's too dangerous for this world." Azealia's right, but something about her words don't sit well with me.

"No." I hang my head. "I don't want her death to stain our souls. We'll banish her to the shadow realm where she can't do harm."

"You aren't strong enough to send me to the shadow realm." Lexus holds her head high, and a smirk smears across her lips.

"Poor Lexus." Azealia gives her a pitying look. "You have a knack for underestimating your opponents." She turns to me. "I'll lend some of my power."

"I'll lend mind as well," Minerva says.

We join hands. Azealia keeps one hand up to power

the magical binds around Lexus. Their power enters me. I begin the incantation.

Black smoke pours in through the shattered windows. Lexus' eyes go wide. She finally understands she's been beaten.

"Wait. You don't have to do this. I'll go to prison. I'll leave the coven. Whatever you want. Just don't send me to the shadow realm."

"Your heart is a wasteland of ice and darkness. You should live in a place that matches it," I snap.

"Think about your father," Lexus begs. "This will destroy him."

"Don't you dare," I shout. "If anything is going to destroy my father, it's you."

Lexus begs and blubbers until the black smoke surrounds her completely. Faint laughter signals that the shadow realm creatures are prepared to welcome a new resident. Lexus' pleas turn to screams.

The black smoke swirls up and dissipates.

She's gone.

We're finally safe.

IRIS

N ow that I've had more than a few seconds to stand still, I realize how much every inch of my body aches. Using that much magic has physical side effects. I've also been tied up and yanked around today. It's all starting to wear on me.

With Lexus gone, her army falls apart. Witches and warlocks from the Academy walk around with foggy eyes like they've been asleep for one hundred years.

"You don't think Lexus put some kind of mind control spell on them, do you?" I ask Azealia.

"I think that's exactly what happened. Look at them." She gestures to the zombie-like academy students.

"Isn't there a spell or two that will bring them clarity?" Minerva asks.

"There are hundreds, but do you want to make them remember everything Lexus made them do?" Azealia makes a good point.

"Let's get them healed up first," I decide. "Give them a chance to remember on their own. If they don't, we'll give them a nudge. They deserve to know what Lexus made them do. They need to know so that they don't fall victim to another evil witch."

"Are you sure that's the right choice?" Azealia arches a brow.

"No," I admit with a hollow laugh.

"Fair enough." Minerva nods. "We'll start the healing spells."

As Azealia and Minerva cast healing spells over the remaining witches and shifters, I look around the room. It seems less populated than it was several minutes ago. There seem to be fewer witches and warlocks bearing the emblem of the school than before.

"Did some witches leave?"

"It looks like it," Azealia says.

Maybe Lexus didn't have to brainwash all of them. I bet there were some that were all too willing to join her cause. They would've escaped by now. We'll have to deal with them later.

"Iris." Remus' voice rings through the cavernous space.

He, Nyx, and Torak have shifted back into their human forms and are now wearing fresh clothes. I break into a run. My legs are wobbly after using so much magic to open the shadow realm. They open their arms for me as I stumble into them. I'm enveloped on all sides in a warm, safe embrace.

"Are you all okay?" I ask.

My head rests between Nyx and Torak's shoulders. I feel Remus' cheek on the back of my head. Now that they're literally supporting me, I realize how exhausted I am. The men sense it and do what they can to hold me up.

"We're fine," Nyx says.

"Not even a scratch on us," Torak adds proudly.

"I can see a scratch on your arm now." I run my finger along the angry red line in his arm.

"That's a graze, not a scratch."

"Oh, silly me." I chuckle.

"We should get you home," Remus says softly.

"Not yet. There's still work to be done."

"Argus can handle the rest," Nyx says.

"I want to stay here until the job is done," I say. "She was my stepmother. I feel responsible for bringing her into the community."

"You didn't bring her into the community. Your father did that. You know it's not your fault at all, don't you?" Torak's voice wavers with concern.

I bite my lip and look down.

"Sometimes I feel like I didn't try hard enough to stop my mother from driving the night she died." It's the first time I've said as much out loud. Usually, I don't even allow the thought to fully form, but it's always there, lingering at the back of my mind. "If I'd tried harder, she never would've died, and Lexus would've never come here."

"That's utter bullshit," Remus insists. "You're a gifted witch, but you don't have the powers of clairvoyance. You can't be held responsible for not predicting the future."

"None of this is on you," Torak echoes.

"I guess not. And about clairvoyance, did you guys notice I could talk to you while you were shifted?"

"Yeah, it was super weird, but good," Nyx says. "I just hope you can't get into our heads all the time."

I smile and lean on my men until the sharp edges of guilt soften. The grief I feel over the loss of my mother will never fully leave me—I know that—but the burden is easier to bear with them near me.

"There's Argus." Nyx jerks his chin in the direction of

the foyer. The towering shifter briefly surveys the group before calling everyone over. "Let's go."

The men pull away from our shared embrace. Each lays a hand on my back to guide me over to Argus. A crowd of witches and shifters gather around us.

"Well done." Argus greets me with a firm nod. I suspect that's high praise from him.

"What's our next step?" Torak asks.

"The school," Argus replies. "It's time to remove it from the landscape of Bonfire Falls."

"Must we?" a witch asks. Her brow is furrowed and blood smears her cheek. "I know Lexus turned it into a symbol of hatred, but before that, it was a respected school. There's deep history running through this building. Does all of it deserve to be erased because Lexus went insane?"

A bear shifter growls. "As long as this school stands, it will be a symbol of hatred against shifters."

"That's not true," the witch says. "This school has been a home to many. It was a safe place once."

"I understand that some of you have ties to this structure," Argus speaks over the rising din. "Shifters have lost many monuments to war before and believe me, I understand the grief it causes. I don't wish to remove history. I only wish to remove evil. Lexus' evil has seeped into the very foundation. She will always be linked to this realm as long as her power has a resting place."

"We must destroy it," Azealia says. Her reputation has earned her the respect of every witch and shifter in the room. The opposers fall silent. "However, evil can be cleansed. The school should be dismantled, but perhaps we can purify the stones and reuse them." She looks to Argus for his thoughts.

"An excellent idea." He smiles.

My men and I share a look.

"That's a lot of stone to get through." Nyx claps his hands. "We should get started."

"Agreed." Argus nods. "We'll start at the top and work our way down. Work with the greatest of care. Don't break any building materials unnecessarily."

"There's a loose stone in the tower," I say. "It's a good starting point for dismantling. The stones are enchanted into place, but the spell isn't complicated. Most of the students are capable of it."

"Excellent. Let's get to work."

Argus' army breaks off into groups to begin the laborious task ahead of us.

"Are you sure you're up for this?" Remus gently takes me by the forearm.

"I'm a little wobbly," I say. "I can still do the spell to loosen the stones. It's simple. It won't take too much out of me."

"We'll handle the heavy lifting." Nyx winks.

"Everyone's going up to the towers," Torak says. "Why don't we work on the outside structures? The ones that won't collapse if we move them."

"Like the garden," Remus chimes in. "I bet Lexus was growing all kinds of exotic herbs. Maybe we'll find something to use in the shop."

It takes hours to collect a decent amount of stone for purification. The top half of the structure looks like a gnarled skeleton.

With the assistance of some promising students, Azealia casts purification spells.

"Many of these stones are beyond saving." She sighs. "Lexus' evil ran deeper than we thought."

"What should we do?" Argus asks.

"After everything we've taken down, only five stones

have been successfully purified," Azealia says. "I think it's best if we destroy the rest. We can't leave evil like this to putrefy for long. It'll seep into the earth if we aren't careful."

"Very well." Argus gathers the witches and shifters and explains the change of plan.

There's some protest, but in the end, everyone agrees that protecting the earth from Lexus' dark magic is more important than preserving the Academy.

My magic is far from fully regenerated, so I opt out of taking part in the destruction.

Minerva, Azealia, and the rest of the witches gather in front of the structure, palms raised.

"Bring hellfire," Azealia instructs.

Witches weave their spells. Sharp flashes of blazing lighting rain down from the sky. The exposed wood quickly catches fire.

"Bring it together," Azealia calls.

The witches gather their fire into a tight ball. The air pressure gets denser as their power builds.

"Step back," Nyx urges.

All three of them move me away from the structure. They stand in front of me to form a protective barrier. I peek through a gap between Nyx and Remus.

"Release," Azealia shouts.

The fireball explodes, reducing the remaining parts of the Academy to ash. When the smoke clears, there's only a mountain of charred rubble.

"I sure hope everyone got their belongings out." Nyx chuckles.

"I didn't," I realize suddenly. "Most of my things were still in my room."

"Oh shit," Torak exclaims. "I'm sorry, Iris. Was there anything important in there?"

The other two nod in agreement.

"No." I smile. "I took the most important things out already."

I'm still wearing Nyx's jacket. I pull the petals and the song from one of the pockets.

"You still have those?" Remus grins.

"Of course. I used them to break out of my room when Lexus locked me in."

"You finally figured out a love spell, then?" Nyx lifts a brow.

"Yes." I laugh.

"It took you long enough," Remus teases.

"I'm sorry! I thought we were only friends at the time."

"Your mistake." Torak winks.

"Oh, be quiet," I tease. "Come on. Let's check the ruins for anything worth taking."

We don't take more than two steps toward the rubble when someone calls my name.

"Iris."

I don't recognize the voice at first. I turn to find the source. My mouth falls open.

My father stands, hat in hand, near the side of the rubble pile. He looks lost amid the bustle of purposeful activity around him. A few shifters sniff at him as they move past. He smiles but his eyes are nervous.

He's not as tall as I remember him being. His hair is shot with streaks of gray, but he hasn't lost his handsome-ness. The features I inherited are clear. The rest of me is my mother.

"Dad." My voice comes out a croaky whisper.

I've barely seen him since he married Lexus. His job in the city keeps him occupied. I suspect Lexus drew a great deal of funds from his bank account every month. How else did she pay for the school?

"My dear girl." My father closes the distance between us and envelops me in a hug. I'd completely forgotten what it feels like to be hugged by my father. I wonder if that's the product of Lexus' meddling or simply a product of time.

"I'm sorry I didn't come sooner," he says. "I didn't know any of this was happening until just a few hours ago."

"How is that possible?"

"I suspect Lexus censored my messages and phone calls. That's not an excuse. I would've figured everything out if I'd only come home more often."

"I'm not sure that's true." I frown. "We suspect Lexus controlled the minds of some of her students. She might've been doing that to you as well."

"I'm your father." He sighs heavily. "It's my job to keep you safe, and I failed you."

"You didn't know," I whisper.

My father and I used to be close. Mother's death put a strain on our relationship, as grief often does. Lexus took advantage of the wedge between us and turned it into a ravine.

"How could I not have known?" my father laments. "I should've known something was wrong the moment you stopped talking to me as much as you normally did."

"You never could've suspected Lexus would turn out to be this evil," I say. "No reasonable person would've suspected it."

My father laughs shakily and smiles.

"You can stop trying to make me feel better now," he says. "I'm supposed to be comforting you."

"Thanks." I smile faintly. "I'm not in desperate need of comfort like I thought I'd be. Maybe it hasn't hit me yet."

"Just wait until you lie down to sleep tonight." He

sighs. "That's when things always caught up with your mother. It wouldn't surprise me if you're the same way."

"I'm sure you're right." Tonight will be difficult, but it's all right. I know I won't be alone. "What're you going to do now?"

"Get remarried."

"Dad!" I frown.

"Only joking, of course. I'm retiring from the marriage game. Lexus had me like a fish on a hook. I was lonely and grieving. She was beautiful, and the sex was—"

"Oh my god," I shriek. Suddenly, I'm an embarrassed teen all over again.

"I know you don't want to hear about it, but I'm pretty sure that's how she mind-controlled me."

"Okay, that's way too much information." I bury my face in my hands. "Just please stop."

"This is just like old times, isn't it?" My father laughs. "I didn't just come here to apologize for Lexus. I came here to take you home."

"Home?" I repeat. "Are you moving back into the old house?"

"No," he shakes his head. "Bonfire Falls has too many bad memories for me to remain here, even seasonally. I want you to move in with me."

I gasp. "What?"

"Just temporarily, of course. You're welcome to find your own apartment as soon as you feel up to it. I've already printed out a list of stunning lofts I think you'd like. I'll pay for everything, of course. You wouldn't have to worry about that." He's talking faster. He does that when he's nervous.

"I appreciate the offer," I say. "But I actually already have a place to live that I like very much."

"Really?" His brows shoot up. He's trying to mask his disappointment, but I can see it anyway.

"Yes. Remus, who owns Thyme and Country, has opened up his home to me. I help him in the shop." I decide to leave out the rest of the details. It's too complicated to explain to anyone, especially my father.

"I see." He nods.

"Remus has a guest room," I say quickly. "I'm sure he'll let you stay there whenever you want to visit. I'll go up to the city to see you as well."

"I'd like that." He gives my shoulder a squeeze. "I have some legal things to take care of while I'm here. What do you say to dinner tonight after we've both had a chance to clean up?"

"Sounds great." I grin. "My number's the same. Just give me a ring when you're ready."

"Will do. I'll see you later, honey."

My father kisses the top of my head before walking away. He can't get away from the ruins of the Academy fast enough. I don't blame him. Right now, I want nothing more than to leave. I never want to come back to this part of Bonfire Falls again.

"How did it go?" Remus asks as he joins me.

"Better than I thought it would. Dad and I haven't been the best at communicating since Mom died, but now with Lexus gone, I think that'll change."

"I hope so." Remus' smile is warm. I lean into him and breathe in his earthy scent.

"There's nothing useful in the rubble." Nyx appears next to us with a disappointed scowl.

"What were you hoping to find?" I ask.

"I don't know. A golden chalice? A book full of alchemical secrets?" He shrugs.

"At least we got to the garden before that was incinerated," Torak says. "Lexus grew corpse flowers, not that I'm surprised."

"I'm not planting corpse flowers in my garden," Remus says.

"You say that now, but humans will pay out the ass to get a picture of a corpse flower in bloom," Nyx says. "Plant one and then open up your garden up as a tourist attraction."

"Thanks. That's the worst idea I've ever heard," Remus says.

"It's called passive income and it's the best idea ever," Nyx replies.

I laugh. Leave it up to Nyx to cheer me up. He always does.

Remus hugs me closer to his side as we turn our backs on the rubble. All the way home, Nyx and Remus playfully bicker about passive income and corpse flowers. Torak occasionally throws in his two cents as he drives us back to Remus' home on his scooter.

No, not his home, *our* home.

CAPTIVE OF THE WOLF PACK:
CHAPTER 21
IRIS

I t takes a few days for things to feel normal again. Azealia took the purified stones from the ruins of the Academy and turned them into a rather depressing memorial in the town square. Salem has more cheer than that thing.

Argus arranged for a purification ritual to take place once the rest of the rubble has been removed. Remus was asked to provide oils and herb bundles for burning. Every morning since defeating Lexus, I've been in the herb garden gathering sage. There's a lot of evil in that part of Bonfire Falls. It'll take time to cleanse it all.

I still have difficulties going back to the site of the Academy. Remus, Nyx, and Torak never make me come along when they go to help Argus and his followers clean up the rubble. Sometimes I make myself do it. It's silly to be uneasy around a bunch of dirt and charred bits of wood, but I sense simmering evil. I can't wait until it's all gone.

Sometimes, I prefer to be alone.

Shortly after banishing Lexus to the shadow realm, the four of us decided it's time to move to a new house. Nyx's house is the largest and one of the only houses in Bonfire Falls that's been completely modernized. His refrigerator can post on social media. I have no idea why it's necessary, but he has it and it's cool. The state-of-the-art security system is nothing to bat an eye at either.

While the men are off in the woods hauling away fragments of the Academy, I spend a few hours packing up the last of my belongings at Remus' home. Some of his things have already been moved over to Nyx's mansion. I still plan on working in the garden and the workshop most days of the week.

Nyx has decided to stop working all together. Apparently, he's been investing his extra money by putting it toward purchasing rental homes all over the place. He keeps crowing to Remus about passive income. Sooner or later, Remus is going to passively put his boot up Nyx's ass. I'll be there to dispense lectures and kisses in equal measure.

In the kitchen, slapped to the refrigerator, is a bright yellow post-it that I wrote to myself two days ago, but I've already forgotten.

Furniture Delivery at 9 am tomorrow.

That's right! Good god, why would I schedule a delivery that early in the morning?

Remus won't be using much of the house once he moves, but he hates the thought of the space going to waste. Being the gentle soul he is, he came up with the brilliant idea of turning the unused rooms of the house into a sanctuary for orphaned witches.

The beds are being delivered along with dressers and a new sofa. It'll be a little cramped—four to a room if we can manage it—but Remus wants to take in as many orphans as possible. Profits from Nyx's business ventures, as well as the sales from Thyme and Country, will keep the place running.

We've hired some of the kinder instructors from the Academy to care for the children when we're not here. All of us plan on being heavily involved in the lives of the orphans, but we also need alone time.

After one more check, I think I have everything I want to bring to Nyx's house. Now that Lexus isn't hunting me anymore, I like to walk through town. The guys all wish I'd just buy a car. They think it's safer. I will, eventually. For now, I enjoy the sun on my cheeks too much.

When I finally reach the new house, I see several cars and Nyx's motorcycle in the driveway. At first, I think they're home early, but my watch tells me that I'm just late. I didn't think it would take so long to walk here. I hope they won't be too worried.

They're all in the entry room when I come through the front door. Nyx is perched on the armrest of a pristine white couch. He's staring out the window. Remus is pacing the length of the room. Torak absentmindedly strums his guitar.

"Is this what you do when I'm not home?" I laugh.

"No, sometimes we wrestle." Remus takes the box of belongings out of my arms and puts them somewhere out of the way.

"That, I'd like to see." I lift myself onto my tiptoes to give him a kiss.

Torak is still focusing on the song he's composing, but he tears his eyes away from his guitar long enough to give me a kiss.

"How are the renovations coming?" Nyx asks after kissing me.

"The beds are being delivered tomorrow," I say. "Still want to help me put them together?"

"Of course!" All three men have been so helpful and eager to get the shelter up and running, but Nyx has taken it to a whole new level. "We can't bring our children home without making sure they have enough beds."

"They aren't *our* children." Torak laughs without looking up. "The goal is to find families for all of them."

"I'm adopting all of them," Nyx says with determination. "I was born to be a stay-at-home dad."

"Pay up." Remus jerks his chin to Torak who sighs and reaches into his pocket. He pulls out a twenty and passes it to Remus.

"What's that all about?" I ask.

"We had a bet to see how long it would take before Nyx starts calling himself dad," Remus says proudly. "I had bet it would start before the shelter's even open. Thanks, pal." He shoots a mock salute at Nyx.

"Glad I can be of service."

"You're so sweet, Nyx." I grin. "Underneath all that leather and axle grease, you're perfect father material."

"The best part is that I'll be doing it with you." Nyx's smile is so open and earnest that my heart cries out with joy. "I couldn't ask for anything more. I love you, Iris."

"I love you, too." Tears prick at the backs of my eyes. I rapidly blink them away.

Remus' strong hand lays on my back.

"You know I love you, Iris," he murmurs.

"I love you, too. Guys, you're going to make me cry if you're not careful," I warn.

"Finished!" Torak exclaims.

"Finished what?" I ask.

"You'll see." With a sly grin, he stands up and starts

playing a proper song on his guitar. I recognize his style immediately, but I don't recognize the tune.

"Another new composition already? That's amazing!" I sit on the couch between Nyx and Remus. I hold their hands while Torak sings the most stunning love song I've ever heard. I give up on trying not to cry. Remus hugs me close while Nyx dabs at my tears.

When Torak is finished, I leap from the couch and run into his arms.

"That was beautiful. I love it. I love you."

"I love you, too."

"I want to do something special for all of you," I say.

"You don't have to do anything." Remus smiles.

"But I want to. It'll make me happy." Now it's my turn to pace the room. I've come up with a few different ideas, but nothing feels quite right. I want to think of something we can all enjoy equally, together.

The perfect idea strikes me so hard that I take a step backward.

"I know what we can do." I look over my shoulder and give the men a sly smile. I crook my finger. "Follow me, my loves."

I lead the way up the stairs, removing pieces of clothing as I walk. I drop them on the floor behind me like a sexy breadcrumb trail.

Nyx's master bedroom is a thing of beauty. It still takes my breath away every time I see it. There's a Zen waterfall in his room. Sometimes I'll sit and stare at it for hours.

I wait until I reach the bed to slip out of my underwear. By this time, the men have caught up and they are staring. I love the way they're looking at me with lust in their eyes. I've never felt so beautiful.

"I want to do something that will truly bind us together forever. Like a love spell." I smile. "I never want to leave any of you. I want you with me always. I love you all so much."

"We love you, too," Remus says.

"Nyx, do you mind if we use your bed for some fun?" I give a pouty smile that tends to make things go my way. Nyx is already taking off his clothing.

"You know me, sunshine. I'm down for anything you want to do."

Remus and Torak follow Nyx's lead before I can even ask.

"Now, gentleman. It's Nyx's room, so he gets to make the first call. Fair is fair, right?"

"I suppose," Remus agrees, but I can tell he's a little jealous.

"Don't worry, you'll all get a chance to have fun." I wink.

Nyx smirks. "I'm a generous man. I can share."

I lay on the bed and open my legs. Nyx's warm breath tickles the insides of my thighs. When his tongue caresses me, I shudder and squeal to put on a show for the others.

I prop my head up with a plush pillow and let my eyes flutter closed. I rock my hips against Nyx's probing tongue. I'm so into what he's doing that I jump in surprise when I feel two more tongues caressing my nipples.

I open my eyes and take in the stunning sight of the three men I love giving me so much pleasure. The sight of them drives my ecstasy to a new level. I'm trembling against Nyx's mouth before I can stop myself. Silvery sparks of magic, like tiny stars, dart through the air around me as I climax. I've never seen anything like that before.

"You're too good at this." I playfully pout as an orgasm shudders through me.

"Don't worry, love. We're far from finished," Remus says.

He climbs onto the bed and sits upright. He lifts me into his lap to tease my dripping core with the head of his rock-hard cock. I wiggle my hips, silently begging for what I know is coming. He lowers me onto him, grabbing my hips so that I don't have to do any of the work. He just wants me to enjoy it.

We spend a few minutes working ourselves into a good rhythm. Someone moves up behind me. I peek over my shoulder to see Torak. Remus arches my hips back and urges me to spread my legs even more. He holds me against him when I can't keep balanced.

I let out a low, primal moan when Torak gently brushes his cock against my ass. I don't know where he found a bottle of lube, but I'm glad he did. I'm slippery with it by the time he thrusts into my tight little hole. I've never been so stuffed before. The sensation is indescribable.

Once more, he, Remus and I slowly work up a steady rhythm. They fall into sync with each other, ensuring that I'm always filled with at least one cock at any given moment.

"Sunshine," Nyx purrs.

I lazily roll my head in the direction of his voice and open my eyes. His perfect cock is less than an inch from my lips. Without hesitation, I take him into my mouth.

Torak holds my hips steady while he and Remus thrust in and out of my ass and pussy. Remus reaches up and gently strokes my cheek before grasping the back of my neck. I let him hold me steady while Nyx's thrusts his cock in and out of my mouth.

Incapable of moving and filled in every way imaginable, I let my eyes close and my body relax. As my three lovers make love to me in unison, Torak plants kisses on my shoulders. Nyx lovingly strokes my hair. Remus holds my neck steady and keeps my back straight. I let him carry my weight, trusting him completely.

My hands roam from man to man. I can feel the difference in their skin, their hair, and the way their muscles curve and flex.

My hands wander to my breasts. I rub my thumbs over my erect nipples. Torak's chin rests on my shoulder so that he can admire the view. Remus grows harder inside me. He loves watching me touch myself. I'm not sure if Nyx can see me from where he is, so I moan along to his cock.

"Are you going to come for us, love?" Remus murmurs in my ear.

I try to say yes, but it comes out as a breathy whimper. Remus thrusts faster, prompting the others to pick up their pace. There's something warm bouncing off my skin, like a little electric shock. I open my eyes as more of those dazzling sparks flying around all of us.

Another orgasm tears through me. If it weren't for Remus, I wouldn't be able to hold myself up. They start to slow their thrusts.

"No," I cry out. "Don't stop. You can't stop until you come. You all have to or else the spell won't work."

"Don't have to tell me twice." Torak chuckles as he buries his cock deep in my ass once more. He plunges into me with more vigor.

Remus is quick to follow suit.

I open my mouth as wide as possible to take Nyx's cock down my throat.

Remus is the first to climax. I clench around him, savoring the sensation of bringing him pleasure. Nyx is next, then Torak finishes with a violent shudder.

As Torak's cock twitches in my ass, Remus reaches

between my legs and strokes my clit, prompting another orgasmic wave of sparks. I gather the energy into the spell that will bind us together forever. We may not get married in the conventional way, but a magical marriage is far more important. It's forever.

Every nerve in my body is alive and thrumming. Each little touch feels so delicious, I'm on the verge of another orgasm. I ride their still-hard cocks with abandon until my energy's coiled tight and spirals together with theirs.

I explode, blasting the energy in every direction to let the whole universe know these are my men.

I'm delirious with pleasure as orgasms continue to roll through my body. It's not until the cool silk of Nyx's pillow embraces me that I realize that they've moved me so I'm lying down.

"Did the spell work?" Nyx whispers in my ear.

I'm too exhausted to speak, so I simply nod.

"Didn't you see those sparks?" Torak asks. "I think that was the spell."

"Those little stars were real," I murmur, already half asleep.

"You did it. You bound us together forever." Remus' gentle fingers brush hair away from my cheek.

I sigh. "I love you all."

Remus moves so that my back is pressed to his warm chest. Nyx settles down in front of me, his heartbeat gently thumps against my chest. Torak lounges near my legs and lays his head in my lap. I run my fingers through his hair.

"I couldn't ask for anything more perfect than this," I whisper. "I can't wait to spend forever with all of you."

"You'll never be apart from us," Nyx whispers.

"We're in this together," Remus adds.

"Always," Torak finishes.

I know their love is real. It took a long time for us to realize that we were meant to be together, but now we know. We'll spend the rest of our lives loving, and laughing, and maybe even raising little witches and shifters together. I can't see the future, but I've found my family, and I know I'll never be alone again.

CAPTIVE OF THE DRAGONS:
CHAPTER 1

ARIADNE

The weighty crack of thunder shakes the walls of my parents' house. The shockwave flings pictures that clatter on the floor. One hits close to where we cower beneath the sturdy legs of the kitchen table. It's my college graduation photo. The glass plate has shattered, and my face is cut lengthwise.

I hope it's not prophetic.

Father peers through half-lidded eyes out toward the street. His wizened lips peel back from his teeth when he speaks.

"That was close." He sits back onto pea-soup-green linoleum. His expression is grim. "I never expected the war to get to the center of town."

"There's a powerful witch out on the battlefield, about a hundred yards due east." My parents turn to me and astonishment twists their expressions. I shrug. "Lightning magic travels far."

My father's face scrunches up as if he's trying to understand. He pretends to understand, but never really will. It's not his fault, he's a normal man amongst the shifters and witches of Bonfire Falls. It doesn't matter that he's only human. My mother and I love him as if he were a god. He belongs here as much as anyone who wields magic.

For the longest time, we've grown blasé about the impending war between witches and shifters. In the non-magical world, the threat of nuclear war is the only good comparison. It's a possibility that hangs over a person's head, it's serious and deadly, but it doesn't affect day-to-day life very much. It's like that here too. Magical warfare was always a threat, but now it's real.

Bonfire Falls is being consumed by chaos and violence. It's so terrifying that several days ago, I left my comfortable home to stay with my parents. My mother isn't as powerful a witch as I am, but between us, we've managed to strengthen the protective wards that keep this house together.

Outside, magical warfare darkens the streets. Right now, someone could lay dying on the same sidewalk where I learned to ride a bike. A friend I went to school with could be bleeding out, and there's nothing I can do to save them. I don't want to think about it, but when the walls shake and sorcerous lights flash outside of the kitchen window, what choice do I have?

"Sybil must be out there." My mother's face is fixed with a thin-lipped grimace. "She's one of the only witches powerful enough to use lightning magic."

"She uses more than just lightning magic." I can't help but grimace. "Sybil uses dark magic to enslave shifters. It's just wrong, and I'll never join anyone monstrous enough to use that type of sorcery."

My father scoffs, which draws our attention.

"Who cares if she's messed with the minds of a few

shifters? Sybil and her cronies are the reason we have a war in the first place."

"That's not entirely true. There are zealots on both sides who won't be happy until there's blood." Another crack of thunder rattles the house. My voice is tinged with bitterness when I speak. "I suppose they've gotten their wish now."

"If only there was a way to stop it." My mother sighs, her careworn face droops with misery. "I'm afraid that if this doesn't stop soon, there won't be a town left."

That's my cue. I share the other reason I wanted to see my folks. "I have a plan, but you guys won't like it."

Dad's jaw sets hard. I can already tell he'll shoot down whatever I say. My mother seems worried, but she's also confident enough in the woman she raised to give me the benefit of the doubt.

"I should go to the other side of the mountain and ask the Dragon Clan for help." I speak in a rush because I'm scared. I want to fill space so they can't raise their objections yet. "They wanted peace so badly that they retreated to the mountaintop to live in solitude. Surely, they have a vested interest in ceasing a full-blown war between witches and shifters."

Dad laughs ruefully, his eyes narrowed to slits.

"The Dragon Clan? What kind of help will those cowards give us?"

"Do you know how dangerous the forest is?" Mother shakes her head. Her eyes are full of tears. She won't allow them to fall. "Not to mention it's a war out there. You can't go. It's just not safe."

"Your mother's right." Dad nods authoritatively, as if his word is the law. "You need to stay with us until it calms down and the war stops."

"*If* it stops." I keep my tone neutral, but I scowl. "I can't just stand by and watch while witches and shifters destroy Bonfire Falls and our home."

Mom and Dad exchange a long, silent gaze, and then turn toward me. My mother licks her lips before she speaks.

"It's too dangerous."

"But I have to stop this."

"It's too dangerous, and that's that." Father pounds his fist on the floor for emphasis, as if we haven't had enough loud noise for one day. "You'll stay here until this bloody business is settled."

There's no point in trying to debate this with them. My parents are both stubborn as mules. So, I hold my tongue. We sit in silence until the sounds of battle grow distant.

Eventually, my father goes out to "scout the perimeter". He returns to tell us it's safe—for now.

"Still, it's probably best not to leave the house." He pats my arm and tries to give me a reassuring smile, but there's a lot of fear in his eyes.

The sun sinks below the horizon and darkness comes to Bonfire Falls. Despite the relatively early hour, everyone goes to bed by mutual agreement, as if we could sleep. And perhaps, magically, the conflict will be done by morning. Although, I highly doubt that. It feels more like the beginning of a war, not the end of one. I can't trust that it will be over any time soon. We need help and the dragons are our only hope.

Once my parents are asleep, I slip out of bed and prepare for my journey up the mountain. They're not wrong about how dangerous it is, but I have to try to stop this war.

It takes about twenty minutes to get fully dressed in the rugged jeans, long-sleeved shirt, and hiking gear I'll need to navigate the forest. The dragon village doesn't have any roads that lead directly from Bonfire Falls to its gate.

I can't understand why they even have a gate. Why would they need one when they eschew modern technology? They can fly right over it. But I guess it's what they use to keep people out. They don't like intruders, so going there is a huge risk, but it's one I'm willing to take if it means saving my family and our town.

It will be an arduous journey for me to get to them. My mastery of lightning and fire magic won't help much as I bushwhack my way through the wilderness, so I pack accordingly. Luckily, Dad took me on a camping trip when I was young. I still have this stuff squirreled away in my closet. I'm glad I never threw it out.

I feel a bit guilty when I raid the pantry for a handful of Dad's dried beef sticks. I don't want to starve up there if I get lost. And even if I do find the place, who knows what dragons eat? I just hope they won't see me as a tasty little snack. I don't want to end up charbroiled.

After I finish packing the supplies, I turn my attention to the other vital accouterments: magical gear. Simple herbs and plants, when employed properly, can be just as effective as spells and enchantments. Fortunately, my mother has maintained a prodigious garden behind our house.

As I head outside, the neighbor's dog starts barking wildly. I cringe and quickly cast a spell to make him sleepy. It will wear off soon. It's just enough to keep him silent while I work.

As I pick my harvest, I glance at my parents' bedroom window. They didn't stir. They're going to be furious when they find out I've left, but I just hope they will understand why I had to do it.

With everything I need, I head to my parents' room.

Their door is closed. I stand outside of it and for a second, I consider staying. But I can't. Someone needs to coax the dragons down the mountain. It's the only way we'll be able to stop this war.

I head outside and stand in my parents' front yard. I'm too scared to take the first step. Even though it seems like combat has died down for the night, I know it's not over.

"It must be done," I mutter.

The sounds of a skirmish across town spur me into action. I begin a brisk walk for the edge of town where civilization ends, and the forest takes over. The battle continues, but it's not near me. I'm grateful that I won't have to deal with that too.

A snuffle and heavy ruckus stops me dead in my tracks. I'm next to a large home surrounded by a dense wall of shrubbery. A big, burly object sits on the other side of the greenery.

I force myself not to panic. After all, it might not be a shifter. It could be another dog.

But what if it's a shifter? I'm not here to fight them, but how will they know that?

Of course, I can use my magic to defend myself, but that will escalate the conflict instead.

Branches snap as whatever is on the other side begins to claw its way through. I backpedal a few paces. My hands go up defensively in front of me. My fingers are alight with a crimson glow as I summon my magic. I don't want to hurt anyone, but I can use a minor spell to generate a smoke screen.

Black smoke billows and cascades out of my hands. I sweep my arms in wide arcs and blanket the street with its impenetrable inky essence. The creature I assume to be a shifter manages to break through the shrubbery, but now there's only a wall of darkness. Best of all, the cinder and ash will block its sense of smell as well as its sight.

I close my fists and dispel the nimbus of flame, because there's plenty of smoke screen now. I double back, head to the end of the block, then cross between the fences.

The only place to walk is in the concrete gutter designed to catch the runoff from heavy rainfall. I slog through dead leaves and inches of mucky water, but it keeps me off the main street. It also leads right to the edge of town in a relatively straight line.

I say goodbye to my pristine hiking boots. They're already spattered with a black foulness that will never go away, but at least my feet are dry.

As I prowl behind the homes of people I've known my whole life, I come across a house damaged by the combat. Half of the roof has been blasted away. Tiny fires dance around the structure. I can only hope that no one was home when the eldritch storm hit.

I call upon my magic, hold my hand out with my palm upward toward the fiery house. As I close my fist, I will the hungry flames to quench themselves. The fire smolders and whimpers until I snuff it out.

Perhaps I can't protect this family from the chaos of war, but at least their home won't burn to the ground. I continue my journey along the concrete gutter and feel a bit better. Eventually, the houses grow sparse and I can walk on dry ground.

As the houses of humanity retreat, the trees grow more numerous. Soon, the paved road winds a hundred feet to my left and I leave behind the only signs of civilization.

Just when I'm about to leave Bonfire Falls behind and

melt into the forest, I realize I'm not alone. As I silently curse, I spin on my heel and hold up my hands. I summon bright globes of white, hot energy.

A wolf shifter crouches nearby, poised for an attack. His mouth is open, but his lupine eyes seem cloudy and distant.

"Don't worry, he won't hurt you."

I nearly jump out of my own skin at the sound of Sybil's voice. She strides up, regal and darkly beautiful in her deep purple gown. Silver earrings, bracelets, and necklaces do more than just enhance her mature beauty, they are thickly enchanted with protective magic.

I can throw my biggest fireball at her and it will barely stir her lustrous, midnight black hair.

Sybil stops next to the wolf shifter and deigns to put a hand atop its furry head.

"These shifters are so much less disagreeable once you domesticate them, don't you think?"

"I'm afraid I don't use that kind of magic." In spite of my fear, I can't keep the note of derision out of my tone.

Her mouth stretches in a toothless smile. I get the impression she's both mildly annoyed and utterly unconcerned about my opinion.

"To each their own." I shrug.

Sybil's dark, impressive eyes narrow to slits.

"Where were *you* when your sisters risked their lives to protect you from the blight of the barbaric shifter clans?" she asks.

My heart pounds in my chest. Magic wells up around her. I realize she can smite me to a mote of dust on the spot.

"It's my parents." My voice shakes. All my earlier bravado flees. "I take care of them."

Sybil relaxes a bit, but her gaze is still full of suspicion as she eyes me up and down.

"You're not just on a casual stroll." The wolf shifter she pets growls menacingly. "Where are you off to at this time of night?"

I want to crumple up and die on the spot, rather than face her wrath. But I manage to hold it together. I even manage to keep the quiver out of my voice when I speak.

"To the forest to gather herbs." I gesture toward the mountain. "My parents need them. I go at night because there's less of a chance I'll get caught up in the war."

She nods, her body posture changes as she relaxes. No longer poised for a fight, she looks toward Bonfire Falls as the distant rumble of unleashed magic reaches our ears.

"The war will be brutal, but we won't lose. With your magic on our side, there could be a lot fewer dead witches. You should join us."

There's a note of admonishment in her tone, so I tell her what she wants to hear.

"Once my parents are well enough to manage on their own, I'll join the fight." I lick my lips and try to sound gung ho. "Those shifters won't know what hit them."

"That's the spirit." Sybil smiles, but again, it's mirthless. I can't imagine that woman ever feels joy other than when she's burning the flesh off a shifter. "Go, gather your herbs, get your parents back to full strength. Then come and find me. I can find many uses for a witch of your talents."

"I will."

Sybil turns to leave, her mind-slaved shifter wolf in tow. I don't dare believe I've really duped her until she actually disappears into the thick forest.

I head deeper into the forest and put Sybil literally

and figuratively behind me. I don't know if she really bought my story or not, but at least she let me leave.

Right now, she's the least of my worries. The dragons can be even more dangerous than Sybil, and to navigate this forest at night bears its own hazards, even for a witch like me. But the dragons are our only hope for peace, so I bury my fear and march into the dense woods.

CAPTIVE OF THE DRAGONS:
CHAPTER 2

BLAZE

I n the dark and quiet midnight hour, I amble past houses made of red cobblestones. Whenever sleep eludes me, a walk relaxes me more than the blank walls in my bedroom.

After enjoying six cups of coffee earlier today, I've probably had too much caffeine. Oh, well. One day I'll actually listen to my friend Ember's lectures about too much caffeine and its effects on a dragon shifter's sleep patterns at night. He won't touch the stuff after noon. That's his cut off and he sticks to it. I, on the other hand, insist on sipping coffee throughout the day. It keeps me alert and ready for any potential danger. We haven't had conflict for years, but there's a stillness to the air that portends a coming storm.

Most of the time, I grab a torch before I stretch my legs with these nightly walks, but tonight the bright moon and constant blasts of magic from Bonfire Falls light my way. I suspect the magical attacks signify another war between the shifters and witches. It has been a century since the last war raged down in that town. They can't seem to hold onto peace for any length of time, at least not lately.

They need to find peace like my people have. I shake my head and grimace in disgust at the sounds of combat that drift up the mountainside.

I only hope this show of their inability to get along doesn't make its way to my dragon enclave. We aren't interested in the war. The other shifters and witches only seem to care about overpowering each other. That kind of greed sickens me.

As I turn around in front of Mr. Sandston's Apothecary store, I scrape my boots against the loose rocks that form a path to the door. Mr. Sandston's business borders the forest. It's close to a rarely used trail that leads deep into the forest. I can't venture into the woods without more light to guide my way. I don't want to bump into a tree.

I should try to catch a bit of sleep before dawn. An early start is required since I have a new client who keeps pestering me about the sword I've been working on for him.

As a blacksmith, I get to do what I love. I'm my own boss but dealing with irritable people isn't my favorite part of the business.

A shadow moves near the edge of the forest. I glimpse the silhouette of a woman. She breathes heavily as she slowly makes her way through the moonlight. She hasn't spotted me lurking in the shadows. Her gaze darts from side to side. Fear lingers in her eyes. I'm intrigued. What is she doing here?

God, she's beautiful. She's radiant, almost supernaturally stunning.

Oh shit, she's a witch!

"Fuck," I mutter under my breath. What the hell does she want?

Her blue eyes are wary, but strength and determination radiates from them. Her expression almost makes me hesitate to interrogate her. Then, the rumble of magic from Bonfire Falls sends a sudden flow of anger through my blood. She'd better not try to pull a fast one on us. If this is a trick, I'm about to find out.

I step out of the darkness into a pale shaft of moonlight, directly in front of her.

"Who are you? Why the hell are you here? You don't belong here." I huff the words into her face. I tower over her, hoping my intimidation will force her to answer honestly.

This woman doesn't seem as scared as I hoped she would be, so I grab her arm. She stands straighter and gazes directly into my eyes. The hint of defiance in her gaze heats my blood.

"My name is Ariadne and I'm from Bonfire Falls. I need help. I'm looking for the dragon shifters' village. If you can point the way, I'll leave you alone."

I loosen my grip. An amused smirk spreads across my lips.

"My name's Blaze. Why do you need our help?" My crisp reply is short, but she's got my attention now. I narrow my eyes at her, since I've already figured out what her next words will be.

Magical warfare sparks in sky above Bonfire Falls. Devastation briefly crosses her face, so quickly, that I wonder if I'd imagined it.

"Shifters and witches are at war down there. Can't you see that? There isn't a lot of time before they kill everyone I know and love. I'm here to ask you for help."

She's a brave little one—I'll give her that. To come up to the enclave all alone, especially given the situation that

Bonfire Falls seems to be in, took guts. I admire her courage.

"What are we supposed to do about it? Fight the shifters off for you?"

"Yes... No. We only need your help." She grunts and looks a little frustrated. "We need the dragons' firepower. It's the only way to stop the bloodshed. Not all of the witches and shifters want war. It's only a small group within each clan, but it's enough to ruin everyone's peace. I want them both to stop this nonsense. They could destroy the whole town over nothing."

"Are you serious?" I try to breathe calmly, but it's useless. My mouth starts to get hot. I need to spew fire, but I hold it in. This gorgeous woman wants us to step into the crossfire of those imbeciles and put all of us in danger. They don't deserve our help. "How dare you come here with your problems. I can't believe you expected us to help you fight a ridiculous war. We're safe up here, far from your peasant squabbles. Go home, little girl."

The glow of the moon illuminates her hardened jaw. Passion and anger glisten in her eyes. Ariadne's too beautiful to be in the crossfire of war, but her actions might endanger my own people. I can't allow that to happen.

I don't care how beautiful she is, there's no way dragon shifters would join the fray. Those witches and shifters got themselves in this mess, so they'll have to figure a way out on their own. This doesn't concern us.

She presses her lips tightly together.

"I'm out of options," she says. "What else am I supposed to do? My parents are down there with the other innocent people who aren't a part of this war. I know you don't like to interact with our town anymore, and you live in isolation, but I have no one else to turn to. Please. You have to help me."

Her voice starts trembling over her words. Some of my tension and anger drains away. Her emotional speech sways me. She only wants to stop the war, yet I can't put my own people in danger for any of them.

I glance toward our silent village. It's too late to alert the others. There's no real reason to wake anyone until morning. However, the dragon council needs to be informed of this situation. We won't step in, but the council should be alerted to possibility of danger from below. If Ariadne managed to make it to our enclave, other witches may try to ask us for help too. We need to send the message back with Ariadne so she can tell her people that we have no intention of helping them.

The moon hides behind a cloud. There are only a few more hours until sunrise. This can wait. The only question now is, what will I do with her? I can't let her run around the village asking everyone for help. She's bound to be burnt to a crisp if she wakes the wrong dragon. She's no threat to me, but others might not see her the same way. I must keep her safe until morning.

I can't trust that she'll agree with my decision.

Should I hold her captive until morning?

If she stays at my house until daybreak, it will be safer for her, and for us. After all, she's still a witch. She seems to be on the side of good, not evil, but it could still be a trick.

"Come with me. We'll go to my house." I snag her arm and tug when she resists. "It's pointless to wait out here in dark. You can stay with me for the rest of the night."

"Will you help me then?" Hope echoes in her words as she hurries to keep up with my pace. She's far shorter than I, so she's forced to scurry alongside me. I slow my pace slightly.

"No." My voice is more rigid than I'd intended. A

heavy sigh escapes before I can hold it in. "I don't want to get involved in this war. I won't risk of the lives of my people. Maybe this war is killing innocent people, but that doesn't mean that stopping it with dragon fire will be easy. Some of us will die. Innocent people from my enclave will die. It's inevitable. We only want peace up here on the mountain. We don't want any trouble from witches or other shifters. Your people could destroy the entire enclave."

"What? That's it? You won't even consider it? A simple *no* is your answer? Have you looked at the chaos down there?"

"I'm sorry, but that's not our concern." I shrug my shoulders.

I harden my expression to conceal my emotions. Her story does sound terrible, but that doesn't mean much to me. The world is full of pain and suffering. It's not our place to fix it.

"You don't have the balls to face witches and other shifters. You're too scared, aren't you?" Anger darkens her beautiful eyes. Sparks of magic glimmer in their depths.

I laugh at her audacity to bravely say all of this to my face. A woman this fiery would probably be wild in bed. I try not to let the idea linger too long in my head, but her soft skin is pure temptation. The scent of rose petals wafts off her hair. My imagination goes crazy with lustful scenarios about what we could do once she's alone with me. These thoughts are ridiculous, of course. She's given me no indication that she's interested in anything more than just our help. I quicken my pace and push away the strong urge to kiss her rosy lips.

"I thought dragon shifters would want to help us. I had no idea you'd prefer to sit on your asses while innocent lives are being destroyed by the greedy leaders of

Bonfire Falls." Her voice grows louder and more confident.

"You don't know a goddamn thing about us," I snap back. "Now, let's get to the house so we can get some sleep before I send you back tomorrow morning."

She spins out of my grip and starts to run.

"Fuck." I quickly chase her and snatch her forearm.

Instead of giving in, she performs fire magic. I dodge her blast and quickly shift into my dragon form. My enormous blue-green wings expand to fill the space before I flap them to take flight. I hover over her and glare at her with vibrant green eyes.

Ariadne's mouth hangs open. She stands transfixed, too surprised by my dragon form to cast any more defensive fire magic. Apparently, she's never seen a dragon shift before.

I breathe fire into the sky, a warning not to fuck with me. I can be fierce if I need to be. She doesn't stand a chance against me when I'm in my dragon form, but I don't want to do that to her if I can help it.

Her shoulders sink as she seems to give in. The utter defeat in her eyes almost makes me sorry for her and the situation she's in. I shift back into my human form and grab my shredded clothes. I do my best to cover myself as I lead her along the jagged rocks to my humble home. It's not much, but my father built it when he started a family with my mother thirty years ago. It's been my home since they passed away a few years ago.

As I take my boots off at the door, I begin to doubt my decision to take her into my home. Can I trust her not to sneak out in the middle of the night?

For some unknown and illogical reason, I trust her not to kill me in my sleep. Yet, I don't know what she would do in the village without me by her side. Maybe this has been her plan all along, to get me to take her in, only to escape once I'm asleep, so she can commit unspeakable horrors in the center of the village.

I eye her with suspicion as she removes her boots. At least she's being polite about not tracking dirt into my home. Still, I can't trust her.

The safest option might be to hold her captive.

Better safe than sorry.

I snatch her hand once again and lead her into my bedroom.

"You'll sleep in the living room, right?" Uneasiness rattles her voice. She squeezes my hand tightly.

I open my closet and grab a rope I used during last month's rock-climbing adventure with my friends, Copper and Ember. We could just fly up to the top, but we enjoy the challenge of climbing. I'm glad I have the rope handy.

When I take the rope out, however, Ariadne wriggles and claws at my arm.

"Stop!"

"Let me go." She tries to pry my firm grip off her arm, but there's no point. She may have magic, but I'm still stronger than her. She twists and turns her arm to slip free, but nothing works. "You don't have to do this, please."

"I'm not going to do anything." I'm offended that she would even consider it. I'm not that kind of guy.

I sigh and tie the rope around her wrists and then the bed frame. I make sure it's not too tight. I don't want her to get rope burn, although with the way she's flailing, it might happen anyway.

She struggles with the rope, which only tightens around her dainty wrists.

"What the fuck! Let me go! I'm only trying to get help so I can save my family and my home before it's all destroyed." She continues to pull and twist as she tries to break free.

"Stop struggling. I'm not going to touch your hot little ass."

She stills at my joke. Her gaze is murderous. I highly doubt she's as intrigued by my body as I am by hers. She's probably planning on slaughtering me. And I don't blame her. I can see why she's scared, but she has nothing to fear from me.

When she starts to whisper under her breath, I grab another line of rope and use it to gag her. I can't risk having her cast a spell on me.

"Calm down. Morning is just a few hours away. I'm doing this for your own good," I say.

She glares.

I pull the covers around her small frame and tuck her in. Hopefully she won't get too cold tonight. I need to put more logs in the fireplace to warm the house. It's coldest right before dawn.

I lean over her and check to make sure she's secured, but that nothing is too tight.

Instead of another frown, her breath quickens. Interesting, maybe she isn't as offended by my ass comment as she pretended to be. Is it lust or anger that drives her swiftly rising chest? Maybe I'll never know, but for the first time in years, the stir of desire is hard to resist. If I sleep near her tonight, I may be tempted to find out if she's as aroused by me as I am by her. Maybe I'm reading too much into it, but her gaze has darkened, and she watches me though lowered lashes. This could be part of her magic. She could be trying to seduce me with her witchy ways.

I back away so I don't forget we're not on the same side. She's a witch, and I'm a dragon shifter. We have nothing in common. To think that she has anything but scorn for me is a trick. She could be getting into my head to twist my thoughts.

A chill runs down my spine.

"I'll sleep in the living room. Goodnight."

I quickly close the door.

She won't be able to escape my bedroom since there's only one way out, and that's through the living room. I can keep watch and get a good night's sleep without being tempted by the curvy witch in my bed.

Of course, if she attempts to escape tonight, I'll burn her to a crisp. That will solve both problems. But I'd hate to lose all those luscious curves.

Damn.

It's been a while since we've had any new women in the village. I can't think of the last time I've ever seen a woman as gorgeous as Ariadne. Her fiery nature makes her even more irresistible. Too bad she's leaving in the morning, but I'd love to see how she is in bed. Under other circumstances, I'd let her seduce me. But not tonight. There's too much at stake.

CAPTIVE OF THE DRAGONS:
CHAPTER 3

ARIADNE

The gentle light of dawn wafts in through the window of Blaze's bedroom, a welcome but annoying phenomenon considering I'm still tied spread eagle to his bed. I can't move my eyes out of the blinding shaft, so I keep them shut. Hopefully he's not the type who likes to sleep in.

I didn't get much sleep last night. For starters, it's quite difficult to sleep when your movement is restricted. Several times, my eyelids grew heavy, and I drifted off. But then I would try to roll over and the ropes would cut into my skin. Wide awake once again, I lay in the darkness, seething. He was smart to gag me too because I would have been out of these ropes in a heartbeat if I'd been able to whisper an unbinding spell.

A flash of anger hits me. Blaze is such a jerk. First, he said he wouldn't help, then he wouldn't let me talk to his people, and to top it all off, he tied me to his bed. In other circumstances, I might have welcomed being tied to his bed. He may be a jerk, but he's an incredibly hot jerk.

I can't stop thinking about what he said, something about *not* touching my "hot ass". I didn't get a creepy vibe from him at all. I guess I'm lucky in that I found a dragon who respects women. Well, maybe that's not the right word considering I'm still tied to his bed.

No matter how angry I am with him, I can't deny the effect he has on me. However, just because I find him attractive doesn't mean I'll cut Blaze one ounce of slack. Dragon shifter or not, to treat someone like this is barbaric. I'm tied down like an animal and he's denying me the basic right to pee. I'd cross my legs if I could.

"Blaze!" I try to yell through the gag. The resulting sound is unintelligible, but hopefully loud enough to get his attention.

Footsteps sound, coming my way. I tense. As I hear Blaze's approach, my bound hands form into fists.

He steps into the room. His eyes are still blurry with sleep, but he somehow manages to look gorgeous anyway. Ugh, why are the hot ones always such a pain in the butt?

In his defense, he only glances at my breasts for a split second before we make eye contact.

"Are you hungry?" he asks as he pulls the gag out of my mouth.

I'm so dazzled by his appearance that it takes me a moment to register what he says.

"Yes. I'm also thirsty and need to pee."

He stares at me with what may be a hint of amusement, then reaches down and unties the rope around my ankles. While the unties my wrists, I lie there and take in his scent. He smells like the air after a lightning strike, with a smoky undertone that isn't unpleasant in the least.

His skin is warm and quite close to mine. If my mission weren't so dire and urgent, I might be more distracted by his unparalleled good looks.

Once I'm free, I sit on the bed and stretch. I stare at him pointedly. "Where's the bathroom?"

"To your left down the hall. It's the first door on the right." He points at the hallway. As I rise, he attempts to help me up, but I slap away his hand. His brow furrows. "I only wanted to help, witch."

"Like you 'helped' me last night?" I glare at him and carefully rise to my feet. "I can manage on my own, thank you."

I leave him there with his jaw hanging open. He probably doesn't have people who give him sass very often. Most people wouldn't talk like that to a dragon shifter, but I'm too pissed off to care.

I expected a smelly outhouse, but instead, I'm greeted to the sight of a well-kept white marble bathroom. It's luxurious and completely unexpected. I thought the dragons lived in a medieval village with primitive huts. His house would fit right in amidst the homes in Bonfire Falls.

Once I've answered the call of nature, I can't help but stop in front of the massive silver mirror hanging on the wall. My disheveled appearance is as bad as I'd expected after my traipse through the woods. Being manhandled by a dragon shifter didn't help. And then of course, I was tied to a bed all night. There's not much I can do other than comb my fingers through my hair and wash my face.

I'd been so intent on packing magical goodies and survival supplies, that I'd forgotten basic amenities such as a hairbrush.

I come out of the bathroom, and Blaze suddenly straightens up and seems a bit nonplussed. Perhaps he was listening at the door. After I cock an eyebrow at him, I clear my throat.

"I'm hungry."

"Oh, yes, of course." He shakes his head and gestures grandly. "Please, come this way."

"No way." I cross my arms over my chest and glare defiantly up at him. It's hard to stay mad when he's so hot, but I manage. "Last time I turned my back, you ended up dragging me off to your lair and then you tied me to your bed for an entire night. You go first."

Disappointment and a bit of guilt flash across his face, but he recovers quickly.

"As you wish." He turns and walks ahead of me down the hallway.

His muscular back is a magnificent sight. He's only wearing a pair of jeans low and loose on his hips, which gives me a great view of everything from the waist up. Bear and wolf shifters have great bodies, but they're nothing compared to a dragon shifter's physique. God, why does he have to be so hot?

He leads me out of his house and onto the cobblestone streets of the village. All around me, dragon shifters come out of their homes and greet each other cheerfully. There's a placid tranquility about their demeanor that is sorely lacking in Bonfire Falls.

Even before the war broke out, tensions have always run high between witches and shifters. With the Dragon Clan, however, it seems as if everyone trusts everyone else. No one is looking over their shoulder. No one seems to be on alert for anyone who might be dangerous.

As we fall into the throng of shifters, I'm the subject of many curious stares. Perhaps I'm walking with the clan leader? He must have some kind of power here because no one questions my presence or speaks to me, but I have a feeling that will change soon.

"Did you tell anyone why I'm here?"

"No." His voice carries a note of finality. "I've decided not to discuss this with anyone. You will leave today."

"What? Why not?"

"There's no point. They won't agree to join the fight. It's not our fight. It's yours."

My lips twitch because I want to snarl a snarky response, but I hold myself back. I'm too hungry to think straight. The smell of delicious food draws my attention. A delectable scent hits my nostrils and my belly rumbles audibly.

"Patience, witch, you'll be fed soon enough." A wry grin spreads across his face.

"Go to hell. And I told you, my name is Ariadne. Not *witch.*"

"Ariadne." He carefully forms his mouth around my name, almost as if he fears he may mispronounce even the slightest inflection or syllable. "That's a good name."

"Hmph."

"Good to strike fear into the hearts of your enemies."

If I roll my eyes any harder, they'll probably fall out of my head. He's a lost cause. If only he weren't so damn easy on the eyes. Even when I'm mad at him, I find him gorgeous.

Ahead of us, I spot the source of the wonderful smell. The dragon shifter villagers are all filing through the double doors of a structure nearly half the size of the school where I teach.

We follow them through the door. I'm greeted by the sight of nearly a hundred villagers sitting at long tables. They're eating communally. They really are one big happy family. Bonfire Falls could take a lesson from this enclave.

Once I get over the sight of so many dragon shifters, I'm awestruck by the incredible spread of food. It's being served buffet style. Nearly every type of fare is available, from simple green vegetables and fruits, to stacks of pancakes drizzled with thick amber honey. Platters laden with greasy, steaming sausages sit near the end of one table.

My mouth waters as one young villager seizes a link still too warm to handle. He promptly takes a bite. Tears form at the corner of his eyes and he opens his mouth to let steam out. Apparently, the fire-breathers can't handle hot food. Interesting.

Sausages aren't the only type of protein. There are platters of ham, bacon, and thinly cut pork chops. It's like an all-you-can-eat diner, except this is all high-quality food that has clearly been freshly prepared.

"Come." Blaze leads me to the front of the food line.

I take up a ceramic plate with a lovely painting of a field of daffodils in the center. As I Follow Blaze's lead, I take a bit of everything because it all looks so good.

Around me, the dragon clan continues to stare, but no one speaks to me. Perhaps they'll wait for a sign from their enclave leader. Part of me just wants to shout, *"Hey, there's a damn war on the other side of the mountain. Maybe you should get off your asses and help put an end to it!"*

I hold my tongue out of politeness. From what I've been told, manners and courtesy go a long way with the dragons.

And who knows what Blaze might do if I holler? He might slap a hand over my mouth, drag me back to his bed, and then tie me down again. It takes me a moment to banish that thought from my head. It appeals me more than I'd like to admit.

Just as I'm about to take a golden-brown blueberry muffin, someone with a melodious, relaxed voice speaks.

"I do hope you enjoy my humble breakfast."

This new stranger stands on the opposite side of the buffet table. A thin white apron struggles to cover his thickly muscled chest. His smooth, high cheekbones are stretched into a friendly smile, and curly hair is tucked into a white plumed chef's hat.

I'm not about to miss this opportunity. He may be just a food service worker, but he's the only dragon shifter who's spoken to me other than Blaze.

"This is hardly what I'd call a 'humble' breakfast." I gesture at my already heavily laden plate. "Are you the cook?"

"I am." He offers a little bow. It's hard not to stare because he's insanely, unbelievably hot and doesn't even seem to realize it. "I am called Ember. I prepare the meals here. Well, me and my wonderful team."

"Nice to meet you, Ember." I offer my hand for a shake. "I'm Ariadne."

Blaze grinds his teeth with impatience.

"Nice to meet you, Miss." Ember's hand is huge. Mine nearly disappears inside of it. For a cook, he's in fantastic shape. "I hope you enjoy your stay in our little village."

Blaze clears his throat and steps closer to me.

"She's leaving." His hard stare seems lost on the jovial Ember. "Right after breakfast."

"Really?" Ember turns his expression of disappointment my way. "That's too bad. I'd love to show you around the village. There's a lot to see here."

"That sounds like a lovely idea." I smile as I pop one of the sausages into my mouth. It's crispy and spicy and as wonderful as it smells. Around a mouthful of Ember's sausage, I continue to speak. "You can show me around after we eat."

Ember seems nice enough. Getting a tour from him will be a great way of getting out from under Blaze's watchful, judgmental gaze. And who knows, maybe Ember will agree with me that the war needs to be stopped. He might be a powerful ally. The guy who feeds the village is probably pretty influential around these parts.

"She's with me." Blaze's voice is low and rough. I scowl at him as Ember turns an inquisitive, but somewhat envious stare my way.

"Are you really with him?"

"No," I say. Blaze flinches at my denial. "Absolutely not. Your great clan leader wasn't exactly very cordial to me last night. He tied me to his bed and wouldn't let me leave or talk to anyone."

"Wow. He did that?" Ember turns toward Blaze and looks at him askance. "I never knew you were into that whole 'taking women captive' thing."

"I didn't take her captive." Blaze's voice rumbles through the hall. Many shifters look our way. He leans in closer and lowers his voice to a whisper. "Okay, I did kind of take her captive, but you have to understand, she's from Bonfire Falls."

"Bonfire Falls?"

"Keep your voice down." Blaze's voice is an angry snarl. "Apparently, there's a war tearing the town apart. Ariadne's people are caught in the middle. Keep it between us, or you'll start a panic."

Unfortunately for Blaze, and perhaps fortunately for me, his stage whisper isn't nearly as subtle or covert as he'd intended. As he fills his plate nearby, a man stares at us with his jaw hanging. He nearly stumbles into his fellow villagers as he hastily finds a table to eat at. He whispers to his friends, and soon, the story is passed around the dining chamber.

"See what you've done?" Blaze stabs his hand at the room, which is filled with anxious, hushed conversation.

Most of the village glances our way. More whispering continues until a woman with long, frosty hair stands. She shoves her wooden chair under the table with a shrill screech, and points directly at me.

"Who are you, and why do you bring talk of war to our peaceful village?"

Her query is taken up by the disorderly throng and they begin to swarm us. They would probably try to rush me if Blaze wasn't standing behind me with a protective hand on my shoulder. I shake his hand off and stand.

"I'm here because I need your help." My voice cuts through the din. The dragon shifters quickly silence themselves. At least they're polite in this village, well except for their jerkface leader. "War has come to Bonfire Falls. Blood literally flows in the once peaceful streets."

"Why would we care about what happens in Bonfire Falls?" The old woman's condescending tone carries an undertone of fear. "We moved away from their petty squabbles ages ago."

A murmur of agreement rolls through the villagers, many of them nod their heads.

"But you're not separate." I spread my hands out, palms up in supplication. "Your history is tied to ours. We all live on the same mountain. The war could easily cause you harm whether you want to get involved or not."

"Bah. I say she's full of rubbish." A man stands up and skewers the crowd with fierce blue eyes. "Witches won't dare take a stand against the might of the Dragon Clan. We have no stake in this war."

"Right." Another man stands. "Who cares if the lesser shifters and witches kill each other? It's not our concern."

"Wait, please." My voice falls on deaf ears. No one wants to listen to me. It's as if the entire village has shunned me. Even Ember refuses to meet my pleading gaze.

I've failed. The Dragon Clan doesn't want to help, and without their aid, I fear Bonfire Falls is doomed.

CAPTIVE OF THE DRAGONS:
CHAPTER 4

COPPER

My eyes flutter open as the tickling sensation on my nose overwhelms my exhaustion. I must have fallen asleep at my research table. Last night, I was up until the early morning hours, well past my normal bedtime, because of the wondrous celestial phenomenon I'd witnessed—a red comet. As far as I know, no one else has ever seen one in the modern era, but they have great prophetic significance.

That's why I'm now using my cedar desk as a pillow.

My gaze focuses on a furry gray mouse which is sitting on the table. The little fellow sits on its hind legs, holding a nub of cheese left over from my late-night snack. His black nose twitches.

"Hello, little friend." The mouse doesn't respond until I raise my head off the table. Then it skitters away, dropping noiselessly from table to floor. "Well, goodbye then."

A piece of paper sticks to my face. It crinkles as I pull it away. I stare at what I've scrawled across its surface. It's barely legible, but it seems to be about the comet.

"The comet!" I stand too fast and my head spins.

I need to tell Blaze and Ember right away.

Glancing out the window, I surmise that it's already well into the late morning hours. I'm late.

I leave the paper on the desk and I race out of the study. Taking the steps two at a time, I nearly stumble in my haste. The time it takes to put on a pair of boots seems to stretch on forever. And wouldn't you know it—the laces are knotted! I have to get an awl to loosen them.

"Today of all days," I mutter.

Bursting out the front door of my home, I run halfway down the cobblestone street before I realize I'm still wearing the same clothes from yesterday. I also didn't bother to brush my hair or do anything to fix my devastatingly awful morning breath.

"Whatever, nothing's as important right now."

I run past Blaze's forge and then quickly return to it. He keeps a barrel of water to quench the ironwork he hammers day and night. He refills the barrel from the stream before breakfast, so the water is fresh every day. That big bastard can haul a sixty-gallon barrel of water on his shoulders like it's nothing. I wish I could do the same without first shifting into dragon form, but what I lack in brawn, I more than make up for with my mind. Brute strength is good for some things, but a strong mind is better for others.

Exultation rushes through me when I peer into the barrel. Yes! It's filled with fresh water.

Holding my breath, I plunge my head into its depths. Cold, so cold. I should've tested it first. Still, I tough it out, hold my head beneath the surface, and give it a good shake.

When I pull back out, I swish a mouthful of water and

spit it back out. There, clean enough. Maybe I should do this every day.

But it's not every day that you get to tell your best friends about a prophetic comet.

I race toward the dining hall. I smile and wave at passing villagers but have no time for any other pleasantries.

At last, the door is in reach. I start shouting before I even have it all the way open.

"You won't believe what I saw last night!"

Ember twists his head toward me and his smile melts. Blaze stands next to him. The walking mountain of muscle seems agitated. His face is a mask of worry.

"Oh, good, you're here, too." I walk across the mostly empty dining hall while talking a mile a minute. "Do you remember how I said that the Omicron meteor shower was going to be particularly brilliant this year, provided one had the telescope necessary to see it? Well, I was on my roof, scoping out that distant galaxy, when I happened upon a great crimson smudge of light in the sky."

Ember opens his mouth as if to speak. He glances to his left, then presses his lips together. I follow his gaze and glimpse the arm and shoulder of a third person hidden behind Blaze. I don't know who it is, but it doesn't matter. Nothing matters except for this comet.

"My first thought was it must be a comet. But there's no comet due to visit anywhere close to our solar system for at least three more years. So where did it come from? Red comets are unheard of, but then I discovered that it is, in fact, a harbinger of great doom. Doom which could come in the form of..."

My voice trails off when I come all the way around Blaze's side. I spot the third member of their party. She's not a villager. I know everyone, and I'd definitely remember her if I'd met her before. My tongue turns to lead as I drink in the sight of her beauty. Not even the Pillars of Creation, a magnificent, distant nebula, could compare to such a wondrous sight.

This strange woman is stunning. Her eyes glimmer with a sense of purpose that could be good or evil. She's driven by something, that's for certain. I shouldn't stare at her, but her beauty takes my breath away. Even in her mud-stained hiking garb, she's gorgeous.

"I thought there was no such thing as red comets," she says.

I'm stunned by the sound of her voice. It's as smooth as honey, and yet it possesses the same charged aura that the sky gets right before a storm.

"I—Who?" Turning my gaze between Blaze and Ember, I desperately seek some clue as to the identity of this wonderful new creature. Is she single? Have my good friends have already staked a claim to her?

Ember smiles and gestures to the woman.

"This is Ariadne. She's—"

Blaze interrupts. "She's a witch."

"A witch?" My heart sinks. The universe itself has betrayed me. This lovely woman is completely off limits. "No."

"Yes." She offers her hand and smiles. My anger melts away. Maybe she doesn't spend a lot of time witching. I take her hand in mine and marvel at her supple skin against my own. "I'm Ariadne. Nice to meet you... um?"

I stand there shaking her hand awkwardly for several seconds before I realize that she's waiting for me to tell her my name.

"Oh, I'm sorry." I clear my throat. "I'm astrologist the

Copper. I mean, I'm Copper the astrologist. Pleased to meet you."

Ariadne tilts her head and looks at me quizzically. "Did you fall into a lake?"

"What?" My gaze drops to my soaked shirt which is clinging to my body. That's when I recall my unwashed body, unbrushed teeth, and the tangled mess of my hair. "Ah, why—no."

I clear my throat again and try to casually brush my wet hair back.

"So, ah, what brings you to our village? You're not planning on putting a hex on us, are you?"

Ember smirks while Ariadne scowls. Even with her face scrunched, she's beautiful.

"I'm not here to hex you."

"Too bad, I was hoping you'd hex me and have your way with me," I say.

Ariadne's lips twitch into a smile. If I didn't know any better, I'd say she's checking out my chest, which is clearly visible through my now-translucent shirt. But I'm probably just seeing what I want to see.

Her smile fades and her eyes darken.

"I'm here because my town, my students, and my parents are in danger. There's a war in Bonfire Falls between the shifters and a cabal of dark witches led by a woman named Sybil."

"War?" I blink several times and then gasp in realization. "That's what all of the rumbles from down the mountain have been. I thought there was mining going on or something."

"I wish that's all it was." She glances out the window, toward the likely direction of her home of Bonfire Falls. Now I understand why she seems so driven.

"Well, you may have come to the wrong place." The look of disappointment on her lovely face makes me regret speaking. "I mean, I'm sorry to have to be the one to tell you, but the Dragon Clan would never help witches. Never in a thousand years."

Ember sighs and shakes his head in agreement. "He speaks the truth, I'm afraid. The Council of Elders will never agree to help you."

Blaze's rumbling baritone joins the discussion. "We don't have magic and we don't have modern firearms or other types of weaponry. We have fire, but the risk to dragon lives is too great."

"We really are a peaceful bunch." I can't help but feel badly for her. If only there were a way we could help.

Ariadne bites her lower lip. She stares out the window as another distant rumble from Bonfire Falls reaches our ears.

"I understand." She sighs. "I'll go home, I just—I hope it's still standing when I get there."

She's close to tears but is holding them back. This woman is very strong and she's very brave. She risked the difficult trek up the mountain to beg potentially hostile Dragon Clan shifters for aid. I admire her courage.

I eye my fellow dragons. "Can I speak with you two outside for a moment?"

"Sure." Ember turns to Ariadne with a sheepish expression. "Would you excuse us for a bit, please?"

"Of course." As Ariadne watches us leave, sympathy wells in my heart. I can't imagine what it would feel like to be helpless in the face of evil.

Once we're outside and the door swings shut, I address the Ember and Blaze. "We have to try and help her."

"Have you lost your mind?" Blaze holds his hands out

imploringly. "I want to help her just as much as you do, but we don't get involved with witches—ever."

"You've spent so much time staring into the heavens that you've forgotten our history." Ember shakes his head sadly. "Witches are the reason we had to come up the mountain in the first place. Ariadne seems nice, but still—"

"No, it's *you* who's forgotten our history." I cross my arms over my chest and stare at him. "The French had a 'wait and see' attitude in World War II and they wound up being conquered by Germany. When the first colonizers came to Africa, their allies were tribesmen who wanted to remove native rivals."

"What's your point?" Blaze snarls.

"My point is that war never stays in one place. It will creep up the mountain like a plague, flattening trees and blackening the earth until we're surrounded by devastation. And then what will happen? Will they just leave us be in our quaint little village? Or will they go for the valuable natural resources this place has to offer?"

My words hang in the air while my friends ponder them. Ember opens his mouth, then looks to Blaze and closes it.

"What are you thinking?" I ask.

"I'm thinking you're right," Ember says.

"I wonder how bad the fighting truly is." Blaze looks toward Bonfire Falls. A grim scowl darkens his face.

"There's only one way to find out," I say.

Blaze nods. "I'll fly down there and see what the situation is. If it's as bad as Ariadne makes it out to be, we should try to convince the others to get involved. Copper's right. The war could come up the mountain. If it's bad, I'd rather fight it down there. I don't want magic up here destroying our village."

Ember looks to me. "Can you keep Ariadne occupied while I prep for lunch and Blaze does recon?"

"Of course." And get to spend time with that lovely woman? Don't twist my arm.

We head back inside and report our plan to Ariadne. She's a bit shocked that Blaze is willing to risk flying down the mountain to Bonfire Falls. Cautious optimism plays across her magnificent face.

When Blaze leaves to prepare for his journey, and Ember goes to attend to his duties, I'm left alone with Ariadne.

"Would you like to see the village?"

"Yes, I would." Her smile is radiant enough to melt iron. I'll have to keep her away from Ember's black-smithing studio.

I lead her out of the dining hall into the street. I point out structures like the council meeting chamber and the apothecary.

"We should stop and get a healing salve for the rash on your wrists."

"It's not a rash." Ariadne's face twists into a sneer. "He —" She cuts herself short.

"He what?" I prod.

"He went and—never mind, he's helping me now. That's all that matters. So, you're an astronomer?"

"Yes, that's right. I'm an astrologer and an astronomer. I can show you my workshop if you'd like."

"That sounds interesting." The sincerity and wonder in her tone make my belly clench. She's the kind of woman I've been looking for my entire life. Why does she have to be a witch? Fate is a cruel mistress.

As we walk toward my workshop, I try to make conversation. I'm curious about her life in the city down the mountain. I've never been to Bonfire Falls. I've flown over it just to stem my curiosity, but I've never walked its streets.

"You said your students were in danger. Does that mean you're a teacher?"

She nods.

"Yes, I teach at the integrated school in town." She sighs. "I'm sorry, I know you're trying to take my mind off my troubles, but I'm really worried about my parents. I'm an only child and they don't have anyone else to take care of them."

I gently grab her hand and hold it. "I promise we'll help you if the war is bad enough. The others may be reluctant, but they're not stupid. They will realize that fighting a war in Bonfire Falls will be far easier than fighting one up the mountain. They don't want war in the village."

"I guess it depends on what you consider 'bad enough'," she says with a sigh.

I nod and give her hand a light squeeze.

"Trust me. If it's bad enough, I'll make them fight for you."

"Why?" Her gorgeous eyes meet mine.

"Because I won't stand by while innocent people are being killed." A ghost of a smile lights her face. I turn and point toward my home. "That's my place."

"I can't wait to see it."

I get her settled in the living room before heading into the kitchen. I stack wood in the stove and light it. A cup of herbal tea will help to steady her nerves. It's not much, but it's all I can do for her until Blaze returns.

After I set the steaming cup before her, she takes it in both hands. She delicately blows the top, sending small ripples across the water. When she brings the rim of the cup to her feminine lips, I stifle a groan. I can think of any number of places I'd rather she put her lips right now. I can't think of the last time I've wanted a woman so much. I hardly know her, but I know enough to want her in my bed. It's an impossible dream because she's a witch and I'm a dragon, but then again, red comets are supposedly impossible too.

CAPTIVE OF THE DRAGONS:
CHAPTER 5

ARIADNE

W arm sunlight beams through the window of Copper's study, glinting off the delicate metal flanges of his Copernican armillary sphere. With the slightest touch of my finger, I send it spinning in a tightly coordinated but beautifully intricate dance.

Copper stands near my side, patiently allowing me to prod and poke at every little bauble and gadget in his study. Dad once told me that seeing into a man's study meant seeing into his mind and how he saw the world. Copper is a man of interests, both mundane and arcane, judging from his study, and he's highly organized about both.

"You seem rather taken with that piece."

Copper's velvet smooth voice startles me out of my contemplation. I shift my gaze from the sphere to his gorgeous face.

"It's so precise, yet so lovely." We watch as the spines bearing the planets slow their movement. "What is it for, exactly?"

"It was a model of the solar system before good telescopes had been invented." Copper runs his nail along the golden edge of Mars. "Unfortunately, it's a flawed model. Copernicus believed that the universe must be perfect because God is perfect. But he was wrong, at least when it came to solar system."

"Our solar system isn't perfect?"

"No, there are no perfectly symmetrical orbits around the sun. All the planets pull and tug at each other, and there's a gradual slowdown of their velocity so minute that it's only observable over millennia." Copper stops speaking and grins. "I'm sorry. I shouldn't force you to listen to me ramble when you're here on such urgent matters."

"It's all right." I smile at his smooth and youthful yet sage face. He's insanely attractive, but he's also correct about my urgent business. My hometown is literally on fire but while we wait for Blaze, listening to Copper speak is a great distraction. "I kind of like the way you ramble."

His smile stretches wider. I've certainly pleased him, and that also pleases me for some reason.

A knock at the door startles us out of the moment.

Copper's face wrinkles with a micro flash of annoyance before he goes to answer the door. A moment later, he returns with Ember in tow. The town's resident food maestro takes my breath away. Are all dragon clan shifters this remarkably sexy?

I keep my cool and force myself to remember why I'm here. I'm not here to hook up with hot dragon shifters, I'm here to save my town.

"Ember, was it?" I smile at him with as much nonchalance as I can muster. "What brings you by?"

"I'm honored that you remembered my name." He offers a bow with enough flourish to make my smile genuine. "I'm just here to make sure that my good friend Copper is safe and sound. I thought he might need some protection from your witchy enchantments."

"My witchy enchantments?" I laugh and raise an eyebrow.

"I'm doing just fine, brother." Copper claps a hand on Ember's shoulder—his finely chiseled, well-developed shoulder. "She hasn't cast a love spell on me yet, so I'm safe."

Together, they look even more extraordinary. These two sexy as sin dragon shifters are making me hotter than a midsummer's night. Maybe I should use an enchantment spell to live out my naughtiest fantasy.

I silently chide myself. Now is not the time to be drooling over men. But it's hard to ignore the sizzling tension between the three of us. Our mutual attraction is frivolous, unless I turn it to my advantage. Should I flirt with them just to get their help to stop the war? Are they even single? How do I find out without sounding obvious or desperate?

After a brief internal debate, I decide to help save Bonfire Falls by any means necessary. I reach out and run my fingers over Copper's shoulder. It's the exact same place his buddy Ember touched him.

Instantly, I have his attention. He focuses those magnificent eyes on me.

"If a love spell will get you to help me save Bonfire Falls, then that's what I'll do," I say coyly.

Ember steps back, his eyes widen. Copper, on the other hand, offers me a shy smile. His gaze drops to where my hand caresses his shoulder. He doesn't recoil from my touch. After all, I'm not the plague-ridden, wart covered witch of fairy tales.

I take my hand away and laugh heartily. Copper seems a bit disappointed, but Ember relaxes.

"It's a joke, guys. Come on, my specialty is fire and lightning magic, not sex magic."

"You might want to keep her away from the food." Copper winks at Ember. A wry grin is etched into his lovely face. "She might enchant the whole town and turn us into her personal dragon shifter army."

"I would never try to enchant an entire village...but I might try to enchant a couple of men..." I glance from Copper to Ember, then back. Their eyes speak volumes about what they might want to do to me if I did cast a love spell. And honestly, I can't say that I object to any of it. Unfortunately, I don't mess with love magic. That's just asking for trouble.

Love magic is incredibly messy. It conjures the attention of dark forces. It tends to explode into tragedy under the best of circumstances. And when it really goes wrong, it's an epic disaster. Azealia, a powerful witch who only recently returned to Bonfire Falls, could confirm that based on personal experience. I've heard her story, and now I know not to mess with love spells.

"I'm afraid we can't do much until Blaze returns and reports." Copper seems genuinely apologetic. "After that, we might be able to help."

"Yes, we need to find out what he discovered before we make any moves," Ember says.

He's slightly more relaxed, but he still keeps a bit of distance between us. Perhaps he's afraid I'll cast a love spell on him. I smirk, because given the chance, I doubt he'd turn down the opportunity to be my love slave.

"I see that you have things well in hand here," Ember says. "I'm off to prepare the next meal. I'll see you later, Ariadne."

"I'm looking forward to it." I grin.

His gaze darkens with desire before he turns and walks away. I get a splendid view of his tight butt as he heads for the door. I hate to see him go, but I love watching him leave.

I turn to face Copper. He scratches his back with a sheepish expression.

"I'm afraid, with all the excitement of the red comet, I didn't have a chance to take a bath today. Would you like to go with me to the river?"

"If I say no, will you tie me up?"

He turns bright red.

"Blaze tied me up."

"What?" His eyes narrow.

"He didn't hurt me," I quickly say. "He was just afraid I'd get loose and cause havoc in the village."

"I trust you to stay in my house, but you should come with me. The water is pure and clear, and I guarantee that you'll find it very refreshing."

"What? Do I smell?" I try to discretely sniff myself. I am rather ripe, after all I did walk through a burning village, traipse through the woods, then I spent the night tied up. I've been wearing the same clothing since yesterday morning. I probably do need a bath. "Okay. Let's go. Besides, there's not much else we can do until Blaze gets his grouchy, scaly butt back here."

Copper laughs, though he shakes his head in admonishment.

"That's not entirely fair. He has a lot of weight on his shoulders, but he always means well even if he comes across as gruff."

Gruff? That's one way of putting it. "So, where's the river? Please tell me it's not a long hike."

"It's not long at all."

As we walk out of the village, we climb across rugged terrain which acts as a barrier to the dragons' village. I'm glad I had the foresight to wear hiking boots, because at times I'm clambering over rocky outcroppings and sliding down shale which breaks free from the surrounding mountain.

Copper handles the journey with the grace of a shifter. Even in his human form, I can see a bit of his dragon lurking within. He seems like he'd be content to sun himself on one of these rocks, while contemplating the nature of the universe.

He straddles a deep fissure in our path and offers a hand to help me across. I accept, and he softly tugs me toward him. His strength is amazing, but so is his gentleness when he releases my hand.

"This seems like a lot of trouble to go through just to take a bath." I wipe sweat out of my eyes with the back of my arm. I cock an eyebrow. "Don't tell me you do this every day."

"Well, normally, we would be in dragon form and we'd fly over all these obstacles." Copper smiles. "But I don't mind the walk, really. It gives me time to think."

"About what?"

"Nothing." His cheeks flush a bright pink.

"Come on..." I bump my shoulder against his. "You can tell me."

"It's really nothing," he mumbles.

I let it go. I love teasing him, but I don't want to push my luck. He's still a dragon who could burn me to a crisp in an instant.

After a few more minutes, we come around a dense copse of pines. A babbling stream rolls down the mountain over a small waterfall into a beautiful oasis. The water is white and frothy before it spreads out into the icy-clear splendor of the oval-shaped swimming hole.

A red-breasted bird bathes itself in a shallow depression in a rock near the edge of the stream. The spray of droplets forms a rainbow over the falls. I've never seen a place so beautiful and peaceful.

"Wow, the walk was definitely worth it!"

I step up to a relatively still section of the pool and gaze at my erratic reflection. I turn to find Copper staring hard at me. His tongue flicks at his lower lip, but he's unaware that he's doing it.

Casually, I reach down to my waist and grab the hemline of my long-sleeved shirt. The sweat-dampened fabric proves difficult to wrestle from my body, but I peel it off over my head and fold it neatly before I place it on a dry rock near the water. I may be a bit curvier than the average girl, but I'm proud of my body.

Copper's mouth drops open. His gaze rakes across my scantily clad form.

I don't acknowledge his attention, instead I unlace my boots. Once my feet are bare, I unbuckle my jeans and slide them down to my ankles. The simple black bra and thong I'm still wearing don't leave much to the imagination.

I step into the water and grit my teeth at the difference in temperature. Although I'm hot from the hike, it takes a moment to get used to the freezing runoff from the snow-pack. I slowly wade into the water until it reaches my waist. I lean back and sit on the rocky bottom, fully submerging myself to my neck.

It's a marvelous experience, almost as marvelous as watching Copper strip. I can't take my eyes off him as he shimmies out of his shirt. His shoulders and chest are wide before tapering down to his narrow waist.

His six-pack abs draw my gaze until he slips off his pants. His slender yet muscular hips flare out into well-developed thighs, and again, there's a feral and draconic allure about his manner and appearance.

Soon, he's only wearing a white undergarment. It's similar to men's briefs, but with a cute line of buttons that are pushed out by the bulge under the fabric. I'm not simpering virgin, but damn, he's huge! And once that fabric's wet, I'll be able to see every inch of his cock.

Now it's my turn to blush.

He doesn't seem to notice. Instead, he picks up a small bar of soap, then steps into the water. His face scrunches up as he tries to adjust to the sudden drop in temperature. He slides into the water until his elbows rest on a submerged stone. He keeps his head above the surface.

"See? Isn't it relaxing?" he asks.

"Yes, it really is."

"Here." He hands me the soap. When I put it up to my nose and sniff, I catch the strong aroma of lavender. "I made it myself."

"It smells heavenly. Is that your job in the village? Are you the resident soap maker?" I rub the bar between my palms to work up a lather. I rise until the water is knee-high before applying the lather to my torso.

"Soap maker? No." He can't help but stare. I admit that I'm reveling in his attention. "I'm an astrologer and an unofficial mediator. When tensions run high in the village, I'm the one who calms people down."

I splash water on myself to rinse away the sweet lavender foam. His gaze never leaves my body, so I slow and make a show of it without making it obvious. I like this power I have over him. I don't need magic to make this man want me. It's been a long time since I've thought about a guy as anything other than a friend. But with Copper... I can envision something more between us.

When I'm done, he takes the soap from me. His hand lingers in my own for longer than necessary. He finally stands, and I do my damndest to keep my eyes above his waist, but it's hard not to steal glances at his perfect cock. It's got a slight upward curve and it's thick enough to make me shiver. Now I'm wet from more than just the water.

"If you're good at getting people to calm down, then you're exactly what we need in Bonfire Falls." I avert my gaze so it's not any more obvious than it already is.

"We'll see what Blaze says."

We're standing close, very close. The heat from his skin warms my own even from inches away. He finally sets the soap on a rock. I can't help but take another glance down. He's hard and thick and temptation is clawing at my soul.

Copper's gaze intensifies. His eyes go dark with desire. I gasp as hands close around the small of my back. He jerks my body against his own. For a long moment, he gazes into my eyes, as if savoring the sight of me, and then he mashes his lips against mine.

His kiss consumes me. I'm on fire and there's a chance he'll reduce me to ashes.

My hands involuntarily go to his chest, as if to push him away, but instead, I slide them down his pecs, over the hard knots of muscle in his abdomen, toward the place I really want to touch him.

I return his kiss, melting into him and tasting his hot breath as it mingles with my own.

His hands grip my back and slide up my spine. When he runs his fingers through my hair, I moan against his lips. We're both practically naked and I can feel every inch of his arousal pressed against my belly.

My lips part. His tongue presses against mine before slowing to explore my mouth.

How far is this going to go?

As I wrap my fingers around his cock, he pushes me away. I don't know if I should be disappointed or grateful, or maybe both.

"I'm sorry." He shakes his head, as if trying to escape a mind control spell. "I didn't mean to do that. You're just so... so damn *hot*."

"I'm glad I won't have to cast a love spell on you now." We both laugh, but then the smile drains from my face. "I hope I didn't freak you out. I didn't mean to get so carried away. I really need your help back at Bonfire Falls."

"This won't change anything."

"Are you sure?"

"Let's just keep it between us though. I wouldn't want Ember or Blaze to get the wrong idea."

"I understand." I don't really, but I'm dying from embarrassment and just want to change the subject. "There is something I don't understand..."

"What?"

"Why are the other dragons so afraid of getting involved in the war? Aren't you all big, powerful, fire-breathing beasts?"

"We are." His grin is back. "But we're also students of history. Three hundred years ago, the shifters settled onto this mountain. Witches came shortly after that, but they didn't just want to live in peace. They wanted more—more land, more control over the region. So, they started the first war."

The cheerful sunlight splashing off the rippling water seems utterly at odds with the grim story Copper weaves. We stand there in the water while he recounts the old tale.

"The war with the witches lasted over a hundred

years. Many dragons were killed, even after we figured out how to dodge the witches' magic. Finally, we were able to fight back. The witches saw that we were worthy adversaries who would never back down, so peace accords were achieved. But after all the death and suffering, the dragons retreated to this side of the mountain. They wanted peace, so they were willing to give up their homeland. We've had peace for over two hundred years. It's not something we're willing to give up without good reason."

"I understand why your people are reluctant." I place my hand on his powerful forearm again. "I really do, but I'm afraid that the people who control the war in Bonfire Falls are too power hungry and greedy to be happy once they have claimed my town. Whoever wins, whether it's Flint and his shifters, or Sybil and the witches, whoever wins will come up the mountain. They will want to conquer your dragon clan too."

"I know." He smiles sadly and places his other hand over mine. "I just hope Blaze comes back with enough proof to make the others take action."

The wind stirs our hair and a chill runs down my spine. I head toward the banks of the river where my clothes are sitting. Copper follows me. We dress in silence.

"We should finish up and get back to my house. Blaze will return soon, and then we'll figure out what needs to be done."

As we finish dressing, I can't help but steal glances at his masculine form. He's incredibly sexy—practically irresistible—and he's the last thing I should be thinking about right now. I should be thinking about my parents and all of the innocent people in Bonfire Falls. I hope Blaze returns with news that will convince the dragons to help us.

CAPTIVE OF THE DRAGONS: CHAPTER 6

ARIADNE

The heat in Ember's kitchen draws forms beads of sweat on my brow. The delicious aromas emanating from the stovetop more than make up for a little perspiration. Besides, watching him work is quite entertaining. Copper stands near my shoulder as we lean on the counter and observe a true kitchen master ply his craft.

"The secret to a good sear is to make sure the pan is really, really hot." Ember takes the ebony lid off an iron frying pan, and a rush of steam expands toward the ceiling. "Copper, will you hand me that plate of peppers?"

Copper picks up a ceramic plate laden with diced green and red peppers. Ember takes it from him without looking his way and expertly scrapes the peppers into the hot, greased pan. The pan hisses, sending up more steam as Ember carefully arranges the pepper chunks so that each one is in direct contact with the metal.

"Won't you burn it if you don't stir?" Copper asks.

"Of course not. I'm not trying to cook it—I'm trying to sear it. You form a seal on the outside to keep all the juices in while it grills on top of the fish. Ideally, you only flip them over once for the whole process."

"Hmmm." Copper nods. "I guess cooking requires just as much methodical attention to detail as stargazing."

"I would say it requires more." Ember grins at Copper, who chuckles mildly at the friendly jibe.

Once the peppers are properly seared, Ember drains them in a wire mesh basket. The basket handle is intricately carved and depicts a dragon head and neck. I can't help but express my admiration.

"That's beautiful work."

"It is, isn't it?" Ember takes a moment to grin at me before he returns his attention to the cuisine. "Blaze made it for me."

"Wow, I didn't know he was that skilled."

Ember reaches into the basket and takes out a crimson shred of pepper, partially blackened by the sear. He pops it right into his mouth and nods, a satisfied smile spreads over his handsome face.

"Perfect. There's nothing like a fresh pepper. You don't know what you're missing in the city, eating supermarket food."

"You guys don't have a grocery store?" I turn to Copper for confirmation. He nods and gestures toward the rear of the house.

"We grow all of our food in the garden behind the dining hall or forage it from the woods. The food that goes into our bodies is all natural—no pesticides, no genetic modification."

Perhaps that's one of the reasons the dragon village is inundated with hot guys. Copper, Blaze, and Ember are definitely a cut above what is typical in Bonfire Falls, but I have yet to see an unattractive person in the village.

Ember switches out the pan for a grill plate and rubs a

generous slab of lard onto its surface. The heat melts the lard until it's transparent. He selects a boned, scaled trout from the large basket sitting in the sink.

Ember lays the fillet onto the hot grill with precision. The smell that wafts to my nostrils makes my belly rumble before it's even half cooked. Ember then adds a fat slab of goat butter on top of the fillet before he arranges another one on the grill.

Once the fish is properly grilled, he lays down a bed of peppers and places a fillet on top of it. With a flourish and a warm smile, he presents the plate to me along with a knife and fork.

"For me?" I eagerly take the plate and set it before me on the counter. Ember uses a knife and fork to cut off a slender bit of ivory meat. He spears a few chunks of pepper on the tines, then offers the fork to me.

I lean forward, open my mouth and slowly take the dollop of heavenly delight off the fork. The fish melts in my mouth. The peppers explode with enough flavor to be interesting, but not so much it that drowns out the entire entrée. Before I can even stop it, a low, sensual moan erupts from my half-full mouth.

Ember's eyes glaze over with sudden heat.

Was my moan that sexy?

He holds my gaze with his own as he feeds me another slice. I never take my eyes off his as I take the offered bite and chew it slowly.

The way he's staring at me right now makes me weak in the knees. I want him as badly as he wants me. Selfishly, I want us to have some time alone. I should be concerned about Bonfire Falls, not hooking up with men, especially incredibly hot, sensual men who can cook like this. But I need a way to distract myself while I wait for Blaze to return.

Outside the kitchen window, a shadow flashes over the sun-splashed village center. Copper and Ember glance out too. Their faces are inscrutable. Ember almost sounds regretful when he speaks.

"Blaze is back."

Sure enough, a moment later, Blaze's scaled dragon form drops into view. His wings are flared out to slow his descent, but he still lands hard against the dirt. His neck cranes about smoothly with a kind of grace that should never come so easily to such a massive creature.

His dragon body shimmers as he assumes human form. In a moment, the dragon is gone, replaced by an incredibly sexy shirtless man with fierce eyes. Even the annoyed scowl scrawled across his lovely face doesn't diminish his beauty.

A pretty young villager with long blonde hair braided down her back offers Blaze a towel to dry his sweaty body. He accepts it with a smile. A stab of jealousy jabs my chest until I notice the troubled look in his eyes.

Blaze speaks to the girl for a moment. When she points toward the dining hall, he trudges toward us immediately. He comes through the back door to join us in the kitchen.

"Welcome back." Copper says cheerfully. "You should try some of this fish. It's scrumptious."

"Later." Blaze's jaw is set hard. His eyes are full of anger. "We need to talk."

"All right." I sit up a bit and prepare to give him my full attention, which isn't hard because he's so damn easy on the eyes. But Blaze shakes his head.

"No, not here." He glances out the window, where the young village girl is speaking with the townsfolk. "Outside, in the garden, away from prying eyes and ears."

Copper, Ember, and I pick up on his somber mood.

Grimly, we follow the blacksmith's huge muscular back outside into the bright sun. The smell of growing vegetation permeates the air as we walk deep into the garden. When the noise of the village is somewhat muted, Blaze stops and turns toward us.

"How's Bonfire Falls?" I ask when he doesn't immediately speak.

"Bad." He glances in the direction of my hometown. His gaze is hard and unwavering. "Very bad. There's open warfare in the streets and many of the buildings are burning."

I put my hand in front of my mouth to restrain a gasp. What if my parents' house is on fire? I should go to them.

As I start to walk away, Copper puts a hand on my shoulder and squeezes reassuringly.

"You can't rush off," he says. "Let's hear what Blaze has to say before we do anything."

I nod and let Copper put his arm around my waist. Blaze's eyes narrow and Ember cocks his head slightly.

"I tried to speak with the leader of the bear clan, a man named Flint." Blaze's eyes form angry slits. "It didn't go well. He refused to see me."

"He didn't even talk to you?" Ember frowns, stroking his chin thoughtfully. "Certainly, he could at least hear you out. It's not as if we're witches—no offense, Ariadne."

"None taken." I turn toward Ember. "What did Flint have to say?"

"Through one of his minions, he made it abundantly clear that he has no more use for dragon shifters than he does for witches." Blaze bares his teeth in a spiteful grimace. "If I'd stayed a moment longer, he probably would've sent his pack out to attack me. His mind is full of hate and violence. I don't think he wants peace."

My heart sinks with disappointment. I should have

expected this outcome based on my own dealings with Flint. He's a jerk on the best of days. However, I'd hoped that Flint would've been more receptive to a fellow shifter.

"What about the leader of the witches?" Ember asks. "Did she see the light of reason?"

Blaze's jaw clenches tight, and his hands rasp into fists. His limbs tremble with barely contained rage.

"That, that—" He glances my way and clears his throat. "That *woman* was even less hospitable than Flint's furry ass. Not only did she refuse to listen, she actually attacked me with her sorcery."

Hot anger boils up inside me. How dare Sybil try to hurt him!

Her enchantments can enslave the very souls of shifters. Blaze was lucky to have dodged the worst of her magic.

"Are you all right?" Ember claps Blaze on the shoulder.

"I managed to escape unscathed, but now I'm truly worried." Blaze sighs and seems to deflate. "I fear that Ariadne is right. Neither of those militant zealots will be satisfied with just one war. They'll likely come up the mountain once they destroy their current enemies. There's too much anger in their hearts. They won't stop after they've claimed Bonfire Falls. They'll come for us next."

"Not everyone wants this war." Blaze turns his gaze on me as I speak. "Sybil and Flint are psychopaths. They don't care who they hurt, even if it's their own people, so long as they annihilate the other side."

Copper lets out a frustrated grunt.

"If only those two didn't wield so much influence over the people of Bonfire Falls," Blaze says.

"There must be a solution. You know them better than we do. Any ideas?" Ember asks.

"Maybe there's a way to cut their network of power, like cutting the strings to a spider's web until it all sags and falls to pieces," I say.

"Brilliant." Blaze snorts and stares down his nose at me. "How do you propose we go about that?"

"I don't know." My brow furrows. I glare at him because I can't deal with his negativity right now. "I was hoping maybe you guys might have some ideas. Some of you are smart."

Blaze blanches.

"Perhaps I could do some divination," Copper says. "That red comet must have some significance. I might be able to find a clue as to how we should proceed."

"What good is staring up at the night sky?" Blaze scoffs.

"I don't hear you coming up with any ideas, blacksmith."

"Fine, here's an idea." Blaze's eyes light up with eager excitement. "We simply kill Sybil and Flint. Cut off the heads and the beasts die."

Ember shakes his head.

"I don't know if that would work. More death might drive everyone to fight even harder to avenge the fallen."

"What if we make it obvious that it was the dragon clan who did the deed?" Blaze arches an eyebrow. "Then they won't turn vengefully against each other."

"No, but they might turn vengefully against us." Ember sighs. "That's what we want to avoid. I'd rather die than see any of the buildings in our village on fire."

"Killing an elder shifter and a powerful dark witch wouldn't be an easy feat either." Copper rubs his chin.

"Ariadne says that Sybil has potent, evil magic at her disposal. How do we go up against that?"

Blaze growls and thumps a meaty hand off his chest. "I'll kill her myself."

"Didn't you fly away from her with your tail tucked between your legs?" Copper asks in a far too innocent tone.

Blaze glares at him, but Copper just grins back.

"Maybe we're all missing the point." We turn our attention to Ember. "Violence isn't the only way to solve a problem. What if we gather the warring factions together for a big peace summit? I'll cater it. Once they have a belly full of delicious food, they'll be much more amenable to a compromise."

"Oh, yes, that's a wonderful idea." Blaze rolls his eyes. "We'll kindly ask the whole town to stop blowing the shit out of each other long enough for us to set a nice dinner table."

"Don't be rude. We're all on the same side here." I put my hand on Blaze's forearm for emphasis. The muscles play beneath my fingers as tension flows through his body, but he does close his mouth for the moment.

"She's right." Copper's distant gaze is directed toward Bonfire Falls. "Whatever's going on in Bonfire Falls might be far away now, but that doesn't mean it doesn't affect us. It affects all of us in the village. It's only a matter of time before they come for us too."

"This is a huge problem." Blaze's nostrils have ceased flaring, and his eyes have lost their wild zeal. I like him better this way, though I have to admire his passion. "It's bigger than us."

"Are you thinking what I'm thinking?" Copper asks.

"That the council should hear of this?" Blaze asks.

Copper nods.

"I concur. This will take wisdom beyond the years we four possess," Ember says.

"Excuse me." Three hot men turn their attention toward me. It's hard not to be flustered by their intense gazes. "What council are you talking about?"

"The council is made up of thirteen of our eldest and wisest members." Blaze's tone is reverent. "They are the most respected people in the village. They should decide how to proceed."

"They've seen trouble come and go." Copper nods sagely. "They'll know what to do, though I fear they'll debate the matter endlessly before they reach a consensus."

"Then it's settled." Now that we have a plan, I feel better. "We'll let your council decide. If they're as wise as you say, then they should have no problem recognizing the need to get involved."

The three of them agree. They're all trying so hard to help me. Blaze has literally risked his life to try and help quench the fires of war, and I know that Copper and Ember would do the same in a heartbeat. I'm grateful to have met such powerful allies. They're not only powerful, but honorable and courageous as well. Their loyalty gives me warm and fuzzy feelings in my heart. I haven't known them that long, but they're already getting to me. I love being with them, and I can tell they like being with me too. I don't know if our fast friendship will ever lead to anything more, but I'd like it to.

I still can't understand why all three of them are single. I'd crawl naked over broken glass to claim any one of the trio as my lover. Hopefully it won't come to that, but I'd be willing to do whatever it took to get any of them into my bed.

Having to choose seems like such a tragedy, but what

if I didn't have to pick just one man? What if I could be in a relationship with all three of them? Would that even be possible?

I shake my head as we head back into the village. I should be focused on presenting information about the war to the council, but instead, I'm trapped in fantasies about the future. It's hard to think about anything else when I'm in the presence of three powerful, sexy dragon shifters, but I must focus. The fate of my Bonfire Falls depends on garnering their help. If I fail, my town will fall, and war will come to the dragon village to kill us all.

CAPTIVE OF THE DRAGONS: CHAPTER 7

BLAZE

The dragon council has held every meeting in the center of the village there since we established our enclave on this mountaintop. As I walk next to Ariadne, Ember and Copper flank us. It feels as if we're trying to protect Ariadne from the rest of the world, but I know she doesn't really need our help to protect herself. Her strength and courage are powerful, and I have no doubt that she'll be able to use magic to defeat an enemy, but that doesn't stop me from wanting to lay down my life for hers. She could probably take on one or two witches alone, but not a whole army. That's why she needs us, and that's why I must convince the council to join the war.

The sunset causes pink rays to shine in Ariadne's dark hair. She never stops being beautiful. Although she appears calm and determined, her hands shake as we march across the cobblestones. The urge to take her hand into my mine is overpowering. I shove my hands in my pockets. Now isn't the time to try to touch her.

And why would I want such a thing?

I shouldn't care so much about helping her but I do.

Her sweetness and innocence are irresistible. I try to stop wanting her, but it's impossible. My feelings grow stronger every moment that she's by my side. I won't stop until her people are safe. Yes, I want to protect the enclave too, but Bonfire Falls must come first. All of my attention will be directed there until the war is over. I hope the dragon council agrees with what must be done.

We reach a beautiful Douglas fir cabin. It looks small and homey from the outside, yet once you step inside it feels luxurious. Tall windows let in the sunlight and high ceilings give it an expansive feel.

Our boots click across the hardwood floors. Several rooms are almost always available for various village and dragon council meetings. Right now, they stand empty, but I expect them to be filled soon enough.

I lead us past the two-hundred-year-old chimney, and down a long, narrow hallway. Near the end of the hall, I open a door to reveal Maria, secretary to the dragon council. She's sitting at a very organized desk, scribbling on a piece of paper. When she finishes, she looks up at the four of us with a bright smile.

"We are here to see the dragon council." I return her smile. Maybe it's a little too flirtatious since Ariadne frowns at me, while Ember snorts, and Copper rolls his eyes.

"One moment, please." She scoots her chair noiselessly across the floor and knocks softly on the council's door.

"Come in!" A gruff male voice calls.

She walks into the room and closes the door behind her, leaving us in her office. I've only been inside the place a few times, but it's familiar enough.

While we wait, Ariadne keeps peering at all the deer heads on the walls. Her nose wrinkles and she tilts her head to the side. I'm not sure if she's disgusted or curious as to why the dragon council has so many of them in here. I really don't know the answer either.

Maybe it's to intimidate those who enter?

The door leading to the meeting room creaks open to reveal the thirteen men and women who hold equal weight on the dragon council. There's no ultimate leader among them. The choice was made many years ago to maintain harmony amongst our people. We don't let greed or power get in the way of caring for one another, not like the witches and other shifters in Bonfire Falls.

"Okay, they're ready for you." Maria waves us in with another brilliant smile.

"Thank you."

As we enter, I admire the long pine table in the center. Ages old wooden chairs line each side, but the council only sits on one side.

"Please, have a seat." Sierra, one of the council members, nods her head at us. I've seen Sierra around the village, but I've never spoken to her until now. We all take a seat in one of the six chairs on the opposite side to the dragon council. "What is this impromptu meeting request about?" Her words are polite, yet her voice is wary. She eyes Ariadne as if to assess whether Ariadne's a threat to the council.

I clear my throat, which seems loud in the suddenly quiet room.

"You're probably aware of the war in Bonfire Falls due to the constant blasts of magic. Ariadne came to ask for our help. The war between witches and shifters is far from over. Innocent people are dying in the streets of Bonfire Falls. I've seen it with my own eyes. We can't let any more innocent people die because of a few power-hungry shifters and witches. We need to intervene on their behalf."

A wooden chair creaks, almost breaking my concentration. I shift in my seat, lean back, and try to figure out how to say this the right way.

"At first, I didn't think we should concern ourselves with the fate of the people of Bonfire Falls. But I went down there myself and, quite frankly, it's worse than anything I could've imagined."

As I lean my arms against the table, I gaze into each member's eyes. I hope they can feel my passion for justice.

"Earlier today, I shifted into my dragon form to scout the area. It's a complete mess of burning buildings. Dead shifters lay in the middle of the street. I've never seen anything like it. I even tried speaking to each of the warring leaders, but neither of them would listen to what I had to say. They refuse to discuss this matter."

I pause as thunderous explosions in the distance replace the once eerie stillness in the room.

Huffing out a breath, I continue.

"I know we don't usually get involved with their disputes, but I've got to say that this time, we need to get involved. This time it's different. I'm worried that if we don't step in now, this war will get out of hand and it will come to our doorstep."

The council members all speak at once.

Jameson, an older gentleman with a full head of white hair, hold up his hand to silence them. Their chatter slowly stops.

"Continue," he says.

I nod in acknowledgement.

"Thank you. I know this might be a lot to take in, but I suggest we need to act now. We should come up with a plan to defuse this nonsense. We can't let another night pass. We can't risk waking up tomorrow with our enemies at our door."

Another series of blasts erupts from Bonfire Falls, yet the members don't seem concerned. They're too calm. It's been too long since we've fought a war. They've forgotten the violence and the bloodshed of war. If only they'd seen what I've seen.

They murmur and whisper once more. Their voices are too quiet, so it's impossible to catch much of what they're saying to one another. All I'm able to understand is random words like "witches" and "war."

Ember, Copper, and Ariadne all look at me with worry in their eyes.

Some of the members keep shaking their heads. This doesn't look good for any of us.

Jameson briefly holds up his hand. The room is once again quiet. They all nod at one another, in silent agreement.

Maybe that's a good sign.

"The decision is made," Sierra says. "The council disagrees with your opinion that we should take action tonight. However—"

"But, Sierra—" I try to interrupt her, but she cuts me off.

"However," She glares until I sit back. "We will think on this some more. What you've told us here tonight requires thoughtful consideration. We won't make hasty decisions, especially when it comes to war."

Ariadne jumps out of her seat.

"Are you kidding me? More people will be dead by morning. Time is of the essence. Don't you think?" She points toward where another explosion rips through the air. "You have to help them."

Ariadne's breathing fast and hard, a flush reddens her cheeks.

Sierra puts her hand up to quiet Ariadne's outburst.

"We haven't participated in a war in over 200 years. The witches and shifters in Bonfire Falls make it a habit to of seeking war and trying to gain power. We're not like that. We have no need for power, and we avoid conflict unless we're provoked. As council members, our job is to ensure the safety of everyone in the enclave." Sierra quietly looks at each of us in turn. "We will think on it and render a verdict when we're ready."

Her voice is stern, but Ariadne is still flustered. I know that's not the answer Ariadne wants, but at least they're going to think about it. It'd be better to take action right away, but I know they need to think it over for the sake of our people.

"Thank you for your council." I push back from my chair and pull out Ariadne's.

"But—"

I usher her out of the room before she can say something that will make the council render an immediately negative decision.

"Goodnight, Maria," I wave as I guide Ariadne out of the council's chambers.

"I know the dragon council will do the right thing." Copper puts his hand on Ariadne's shoulder.

"It might not seem like it now, but I know they will help everyone in Bonfire Falls who isn't a part of the war," Ember says with confidence.

"Yeah, I know you're right. But I don't want anyone to suffer or die in the meantime, especially not my family." She rubs her hand against her forehead. "I just hope they're safe."

"I could go check on them," I offer.

"No. It's better that we wait," she says.

"Hopefully the council will render their decision soon. You can stay with me for the night." I wrap my arm around her shoulder.

"Are you going to tie me to the bed again?"

Her frown makes me feel bad for tying her up last night, so I try to lighten the mood.

"Only if you want me to." I grin while the other guys roll their eyes at my lame joke.

"I guess I can stay another night at your place." She shrugs her shoulders.

"We'll meet you at breakfast tomorrow," I say to Copper and Ember. They nod and after a moment of hesitation, they head toward their respective homes.

Ariadne and I take our time walking back to my place.

My stomach rumbles. I get the munchies at night. It's a habit I can't seem to break.

When we arrive at my home, I head straight for the kitchen.

"Do you want some cookies? I have some stashed around here somewhere. I need to eat something." I find my stash of sweets in the cupboard.

"I love cookies. What kind do you have?" She tries to peer around me to see what I'm unwrapping. I show her the chocolate chip cookies Ember makes when the mood strikes.

I set several on a plate and hand it to her.

As she takes a big bite into the chocolaty goodness, a moan escapes her rosy lips.

God, she's beautiful.

Lustful thoughts seem to come out of nowhere. I turn away and add some logs to the fireplace. No one in the village has electricity, so this fire is our heater. It gets chilly at night, especially with days like today when the evening gets cold fast.

"Wow! These are delicious. Did you make these?" She says through a mouth full of cookies. Her cute curiosity almost makes me lie to her.

"No, Ember made them. I ask him to make them when I want a sugar rush." I laugh and try to ignore a tinge of jealousy. I make a mental note that I should learn to bake.

"When it gets this cold, I usually sleep in front of the fireplace. We could sleep there tonight. It should keep us warm." My voice is husky and betrays the undercurrent of desire in my tone.

She brushes at the crumbs clinging to her shirt and pants. It takes her a while to answer. A contemplative look crosses her face before she turns back to me and straightens her shoulders.

"Okay." She doesn't seem overly excited by or averse to my proposed sleeping arrangements. I don't know how to read her response. But then again, maybe there's nothing to read.

I pull the hideaway bed out of the couch before tossing some blankets and pillows onto it.

"I don't have a nightgown," she says.

"It's... that's okay. I could give you one of my shirts."

Or, you could just get naked!

"Thank you."

When I come back with a shirt, I find her underneath the covers. I strip off the shirt I'm wearing and climb in beside her.

"I—Could you close your eyes while I change?" she asks.

"Sure."

I smash my eyes closed, but the urge to peek is killing me. I manage to keep them shut until she's done.

"You can open them."

She's got the blankets pulled to her chin and her eyes are wide. I'm alarmed by the twinge of fear in them.

"You're safe here," I say.

"I know." Her nervous giggle fills the room.

The only way to stop staring is to turn my attention toward the fireplace. I watch the flames crack and hiss. Sparks fly up the chimney.

I risk a glance in her direction. I can tell by the sudden silence, and the serious look on her face, that she's worried about her family.

"I know I didn't make the best first impression, but I'll try to help your family. I need the council's approval because I can't win the war by myself. I need other dragons by my side."

"I know. I understand. These are your people." Her words are spoken so softly that I almost don't hear them.

She gently leans against me. I put my arm around her. The scent of lavender wafts from her skin. I want to press my nose into her hair and inhale her essence.

When will this obsession with her end?

It doesn't seem like my attraction for her will ever go away. I haven't been this instantly attracted to anyone in a long time. I sense that she might be romantically interested in me too, but I could be wrong.

Should I try to kiss her?

Her response will reveal how she truly feels about me.

Then again, is now the right time to test our relationship? She's already got so much on her plate. To try to distract her from her worries is just a selfish excuse. This has nothing to do with the war, and everything to do with my desire for her. But, if the kiss does go well, then she can take comfort in my arms. Even if it's only for a little while.

A shiver rakes through her body.

She's cold.

Ariadne's too polite to tell me that the room is still too chilly.

"Do you need another blanket?"

"No, I'm fine."

"You're shivering." I run my hand up and down her arm. After a few minutes, her skin warms beneath my fingers.

I gaze down at her. The urge to kiss her is stronger than ever.

She peeks up at me through lowered lashes.

I close the distance gradually, making sure she has enough time to stop me from kissing her. When our lips touch, she responds immediately by twisting around on the bed and moving her arms around my shoulders.

My lips tingle and blood surges straight to my cock. I stroke the curve of her hip lightly at first, but then grow bolder. I suck her bottom lip into my mouth, biting gently then sweeping the tender skin with my lips and tongue once more. She moans and gasps as my tongue slides between her lips. I taste the sweet nectar of her mouth, and I'm instantly drunk on it.

Her groans send hot spears of need into my shaft. My cock hardens so fast that it takes my breath away. I've never needed anyone like this.

My hands shift into her hair. I hold her head in place as I claim her mouth and beg for more with my lips and tongue.

I break the kiss and tilt her head sideways. I nibble her neck and cup her breasts in my hands. I flick her nipples though the shirt until they peak against my thumbs.

"Wait. Wait." As she pulls away, I release her and sit back.

"I'm sorry."

"No. It's... It was as much me as it was you."

Both of us try to control our breathing. I want to say something, but I don't know what she needs from me right now.

"I'm very attracted to you, but my life is complicated right now." She moves back into her original spot on the bed.

"Have you had complicated relationships before?" I take a chance and reach for her hand. She laces her fingers into mine.

"Every relationship is complicated." She pauses, as if trying to find the right words. "I haven't dated in a while. I've had some terrible relationships in the past, and I haven't been involved with anyone for a while. I'm not sure I'm interested in a relationship right now, especially with everything happening in Bonfire Falls."

"I understand." I give her hand a light squeeze. "It's too bad we met this way. I wish it had been under different circumstances so I could get to know you more."

"We could still get to know each other—with our clothes on," she quickly adds.

Before I can stop it, laughter bursts from my lips. My arm goes around her again and she cuddles close to me. I won't deny that I'm disappointed that we can't take this relationship further tonight, but I understand. She has too much on her mind and making love to her will only complicate things.

But that kiss! It was so incredible that I'm willing to wait for as long as it takes. Maybe she'll be ready for something more once the war in Bonfire Falls has ended. Until then, I'll be the man she needs, and I'll do whatever it takes to help her people find peace.

CAPTIVE OF THE DRAGONS:
CHAPTER 8

ARIADNE

Chilly wind whips across the mountains to dampen the warmth of the rising sun. Long shadows stretch across the village. I'm standing outside the council building with my arms crossed over my chest. I try to stand in the direct sunlight as much as possible as I await word from Blaze. He went in without me. He thought I might "fly off the handle". I told him I might fly a broom right up their butts if they didn't make a decision soon. That was the final straw and Blaze left me outside to wait.

I stomp my foot. What in the world could be taking them so long? Don't they care about everyone who's dying in Bonfire Falls?

"Heartless, fire-breathing jerks," I mutter.

More than once, I've had to stop myself from using a spell to bust the door open. I just want to know what's going on. Is that too much to ask?

I try not to think about what Flint might do to my parents if he found them hiding in their home. My mom's a witch, which is all he would need to know. He's determined to kill every witch in Bonfire Falls, and if he's not stopped, he will do it.

Sybil is just as bad. Her pursuit of dark magic has made her even more twisted and vile than before. She favors the dark side, which she utilizes to enslave shifters. She could enslave witches too. A witch can absorb another witch's powers, but it will destroy her soul in the process. I wonder what's left of Sybil's soul. By now, I wouldn't be surprised if evil forces had fully claimed it.

The sun rises a bit higher and helps to banish the chilly air. My breath no longer comes out in white puffs, but my nose is still numb. I put my hand over my face and breathe hot air into my palms.

Suddenly, Blaze shoves the door open. I jump as he stalks out. His lips are thin with worry. He runs a hand along the back of his head.

"The *wise* council has decided they can't come to a decision yet." His mouth is rigid, and his words are clipped.

"Seriously?" I shake my head in disbelief. "But they had all night."

"I know, but they claim to need more time. I believe they are going to vote soon."

"Soon?" I struggle to contain my exasperation. "How soon? An hour? Two?"

"I wish I knew." Blaze walks toward his home, and I fall into step beside him.

"How much longer do we have to wait?"

"I don't know. An hour. Maybe more."

I sigh heavily. Blaze stops and turns to me.

"I feel the same way. The elder council is very wise, and they seldom make mistakes, so I trust they'll come to the right conclusion, but we need to wait. Please be patient for a little longer."

"Are you sure they'll make the right choice?"

"I'm sure." He grabs my hand and gives it a soft squeeze. "Please trust me."

"I do."

"Until they come to a final decision, I can't stand around waiting. I have a bunch of work to do. Between the excitement of your arrival, and my trip to Bonfire Falls, I've had no time for my workshop. I need to complete one of my projects soon. Come with me and I'll show you how hard I can pound metal." His impish grin is back.

"Sounds impressive." Since we have to wait anyway, I might as well see what he does all day. "Lead the way."

His workshop is similar to a mechanic's garage. The outer doors slide open to allow plenty of airflow through the space. The ground is dirt. Fresh rake marks form a pattern in the earth. I'd expected to find the floor littered with hunks of metal, but it's very orderly.

Several shelves and cabinets line one wall. I've never seen some of the equipment before, but I do recognize some of the items. There are iron brands, crucibles, and hammers in all shapes and sizes. I venture closer, but he tugs me back toward him.

"Don't touch anything. This stuff is dangerous."

"Okay."

When we reach his workbench in the center of the room, he releases my hand. I step back as he strips off his shirt. His muscled chest flexes as he slides a heavy leather apron over it. He stokes the coals under his forge, sending a cloud of black smoke curling up toward an open window in the roof.

"Your workshop is impressive. How did you become a blacksmith?"

"I've always loved fire—more than a typical dragon—so it seemed like a natural fit. We encourage young dragons to pursue their passions, and luckily, mine turned into a life-long job."

"Do you get a lot of work from the others?"

"Plenty. I'm behind right now, and I'm never late with my projects. I need to work hard to catch up."

Blaze picks up a cloth-wrapped object from his work-table. He unwinds the cloth to reveal the gleaming metal of an ornate double-edged longsword. Its handle is absent. There's a thin bar and crosspiece, but they don't look very comfortable. I can't imagine trying to maintain my hold on it while swinging it through the air.

"Will that be a sword?"

"Good eye." He cocks an eyebrow. "I wouldn't think that a witch from the modern world would recognize a partially forged sword."

I shrug.

"I've seen all the *Lord of the Rings* movies. The neighbor kids played *Dungeons and Dragons*. Swords aren't missing from the modern world, but it looks like it's missing a part. Doesn't it need a handle?"

"It does, and it will have one by the end of this day." He rewraps the sword and then picks up a heavy block of dark metal. He slides it into his forge and begins the heating process. As he does, muscles ripple along his back.

I could stand here and watch him work all day. Depending on how long the council takes, I may end up doing exactly that.

"I don't want you to get bored as you watch me work."

"Not possible." I give him a salacious smile.

He chuckles.

"And, as much as I'd love to have you around, I can't have you distracting me while I'm playing with molten metal."

"I'll be quiet. I won't interrupt," I promise.

"I'm sure you won't, but you distract me anyway." He smiles. "Could you help Ember prepare breakfast? It might take your mind off the council's decision, and it will give me time to work."

"I thought you didn't want me near your food." I tease. "You were afraid I'd cast a love spell on the village."

"You've already enchanted me. Now I have nothing to fear." He winks and turns back to his work. I turn molten at his words.

I've enchanted him?

The thought fills me with pleasure. Part of me wants to stay and watch him forge the sword, but Blaze seems to be quite busy, so I decide to go and help Ember with the morning meal. I look forward to more time with the village's handsome chef.

"I'll see you later."

"I look forward to it," he says.

As I walk through the gradually awakening village, I'm struck by how peaceful it all is. No car alarms, no cell phones, no exploding magical balls of fire. I can see why the dragons aren't willing to give up this life. Why give up this tranquility to join a war that has nothing to do with them?

I do understand why they're not eager to join the fight, but I just hope they realize that the war could come up the mountain sooner rather than later. If Sybil or Flint manage to gain control of Bonfire Falls, nothing will stop them for coming for the dragons' village next.

I replace fearful thoughts of death and destruction with thoughts of Ember. To watch him in the kitchen is an oddly satisfying experience. His food is extraordinarily tasty. It's because he pays attention to detail.

Is he like that in bed too?

I find Ember in the kitchen pantry. He's cursing as he opens one ceramic pot after another in search of something which clearly eludes him.

"What is this now—thyme? Why do I have two pots of thyme? Same reason I have three pots of turmeric root." He casts his gaze to the ceiling and sighs. "All I want is one single, solitary pot of tarragon. Just one."

"Good morning, Ember," I say cheerfully.

Ember jumps. The pot flips out of his grasp and does a full rotation in the air. Thyme twigs spill everywhere. He manages to catch the pot in his palm but uses a tad too much force. The jar flies into another arc. Ember catches it once more and, this time, manages to hold onto his prize.

"I'm sorry." I bend over and pick up a sprig of thyme. "I didn't mean to startle you."

"It's fine." His warm smile warms me from the inside out. He bends over to assist me with the retrieval of his precious herbs.

"Look." I hold up two handfuls and grin. "I have too much thyme on my hands."

"Well, put it back in the pot then."

I stare at him for a long moment before I sigh. I brush the thyme out of my hands into a trash bin. "It was a joke. You know what, never mind. What did you need? Tarragon?"

Ember's face scrunches as he goes back to his desperate search.

"Yes, tarragon. Without it, I can't make my fabulous crustless quiche. And I can't bear to tell the villagers we won't have crustless quiche on crustless quiche day. It's expected."

"Calm down, hon." I put my hand on his back and give it a pat. He's not as big as Blaze, but he's still well built. "Do you want me to get you some from the garden?"

"Would you?" His eyes light up, and he turns to take my hands in both of his own. "I mean, if it's not too much trouble. Would you like me to show you where it is?"

"I'm a witch. I can find an herb." I gently pull my hands free from his.

"Oh, right. Thank you. I don't know where my jar of tarragon went, but fresh is better anyway."

"I'll be back in a flash."

As I leave, we smile at each other. I keep the door open for a few seconds longer than necessary just to get one last glimpse of his gorgeous face.

He may be frazzled right now, but I bet he pays a lot of attention when he's intimate. I wonder if I'll ever know for sure, but boy would I like to see what he's like in bed. I don't know what's come over me since coming to the village. These men have had such a powerful effect on me that I can't help but wonder if we're fated to be together. In time, I'll know for sure, but for now, I can only hope to have some kind of future with them.

As I stride into the garden, the breeze stirs my hair. Plants dance in the wind. The fragrant aroma of dozens of different herbs fills my nostrils with their earthy scent. Birds sing merrily in the trees as they flit from branch to branch in an ancient courtship ritual.

Someday, I'd love to live in a place like this. It's not that I don't like my own home—far from it—but, I appreciate their simpler way of life.

Maybe they don't have electricity, or hot running water, or cell phones, but they don't seem the lesser for it. If anything, their strong sense of family and community more than makes up for any lack of technological sophistication.

They work hard to take care of each other, and I hope that will include me too. I know I'm not a part of their community, but they seem to truly care for people. So I can't imagine they'd turn their backs on the innocent people in Bonfire Falls.

I spot the tarragon, a spindly plant with long spiny leaves. When I reach out to touch the fragrant green herb, it shivers in the wind.

"Thank you for your gift." I pluck enough of the herb for two handfuls, but I'm careful not to take too much from one plant so it will continue to grow. "I promise it won't go to waste."

I find both French and Spanish tarragon, so I harvest some of each. My mother has always liked Spanish tarragon better, but I don't, because I hate the black licorice aftertaste. However, in the hands of an expert chef like Ember, I'm sure it will taste better. I gather some sprigs of it for good measure.

When I return to the kitchen, I watch Ember vigorously beat a yellow slurry with a whisk. His eyes light up when he sees the twin fistfuls of tarragon I've brought him.

"You're back. Is that my tarragon?"

"I brought French and Spanish." I walk up beside him. "Do you want me to just dump it in?"

"Wait a minute." His face is a mask of concentration. He leans close to my hands and carefully sniffs each pile of leaves. "Put the French tarragon in the bowl. We'll save the Spanish for tonight's dinner."

"Yes, chef." I drop the correct version of the herb into the slurry. He beats it with expert precision.

When it's ready, Ember tilts the bowl and drizzles a perfectly uniform stream of eggs, cheese, and herbs into a pie dish. He fills another and then another. It takes over thirty dishes to satisfy the entire village. I'm impressed by his quick hands. They're strong and firm. My breasts tingle with the need to be touched by him.

To distract myself from lusty thoughts, I jump in to help. I open oven doors and hold filled pans while he fusses with seasoning.

"Too bad you're a witch, because you'd make a great cook."

"What does being a witch have to do with anything?"

"Can't you just conjure up anything you want to eat?"

"Not exactly, but I know a few tricks." I bat my lashes and close the oven door with a thrust of my hips. He laughs, and his eyes twinkle. "I can even make homemade scones."

"Really?" He rubs his chin and grins. "Scones are hard to get right. Think you can whip up a batch of wild blueberry scones?"

"Do you have a spare apron?" I grin and put my hands on my hips.

He tosses me a folded cloth bundle, and then I get down to business.

Scones require cold cream. How will I get that? Ember reveals they have a cold cellar which utilizes an underground stream to keep their perishables at around forty degrees.

I take the clay pot of cream, lift the lid, and give it a suspicious whiff. There's a definite grassy note to it, which is different from the type I buy in stores, but it's far from spoiled.

Ember stands to the side and marvels as I toss a mountain of flour into one of his massive mixing bowls. Sugar and a wee bit of salt join the mix, and then I use my fingers to cut in the butter.

"I usually use a fork for that." His tone holds a note of admiration.

"I do, too, if I don't want to get my hands messy. But, this works much better. It's easy to get the butter into very small pieces. What you want is loose, wet crumbs. Like this."

I show him my handiwork. He whistles in appreciation.

"That's a good, even texture, all right."

"Thanks." I form the dough into an inverted volcano, then pour in three cups of thick goat cream. With a wooden spatula, I work the cream into the dough until it's a smooth consistency.

On my cue, Ember dumps a large bowl of freshly picked wild blueberries into the mixture. I turn the batter out onto a massive cookie sheet, then brush a generous amount of cream on top. The whole thing goes into the fire oven, but I'm worried about how it will turn out.

"I'm not sure about the time in this kind of oven."

"Trust your nose." He gestures toward the cream pot. "Are you done with that?"

"Heavens, no. If you want perfect scones, you have to brush them with cream a couple of times while they bake."

"I see." He regards me with new admiration. Maybe he likes me as much as Blaze does, but for different reasons.

We talk about baking while we wait for the scones to finish. When they come out of the oven, they're the perfect shade of golden brown. It's a torturous wait as they cool, but soon, I'm able to present Ember with a plated triangle of blueberry scones.

"Here." As I break the tip of the triangle, a hot blueberry bursts. The fruity blue liquid stains my skin. As soon as I lift the piece to his lips, he opens his mouth. I press the treat between his lips. His eyes sparkle before closing. A low moan rumbles in his throat.

"It's perfect." His gaze meets mine. As he licks my fingers, his pink tongue delicately teases my sensitive skin. "It's the best thing I've ever eaten."

I want to kiss him so badly. It's terrible that I feel this way with the war and everything, but I can't help my attraction to him. I lean in, and so does he. When our lips meet, I sigh into the kiss. I've been waiting to do this since the moment we met, but this is the first chance we've had.

I can't help but compare each of the guys' kisses. Copper's were passionate and earnest, while Blaze's kisses were wild and primal. With Ember, I fall into a slow, steady rhythm. His fingers delicately stroke my hair, while his other hand holds the small of my back.

He's so adorable that I want to eat him alive, but I instead of losing myself in the kiss, I match his pace. It's slow and sensual and perfect.

We pause to smile at each other. Then we're back to sharing soft, butterfly kisses. As he takes me in his arms, I sigh with contentment.

"Even if the council doesn't vote your way, I'll still do whatever I can to help you," he says.

"Thank you, Ember."

He gives me a gentle kiss before releasing me.

"Let's go." He grabs a platter of quiche. "It's time to serve breakfast."

Ember is a delight as he serves his fare to the villagers. He takes time to speak to almost everyone. I follow behind him with more trays of quiche. At first, the villagers regard me with suspicion, but once they see Ember by my side, they relax.

I can't stop thinking about the kisses we shared. He's

more tender and affectionate than Blaze and Copper, but it's not better. It's just... different.

I step back from the table and dip my head to let my hair partially cover my face. I don't want anyone to see my worried frown. I didn't come up here looking for love, and I certainly didn't expect to find it with three different men at once, but that's exactly what's happening, and I don't know what to do about it.

CAPTIVE OF THE DRAGONS: CHAPTER 9

COPPER

After washing down a delicious quiche with a mug of coffee, I wait for Ariadne to finish eating her breakfast. We're the only people left in the dining hall because she'd insisted on helping Ember serve everyone. We both told her that she didn't need to work, but she wanted to help. She's so sweet and considerate, unlike some members of the dragon village who can't be bothered to lift a finger to help anyone else out. She'd make such a great addition to the village.

Whoa! Where did that come from? She's only here to get our help, not to move in. Although, the more time I spend with her, the more I want her to stay. It might not be possible, but after that kiss we shared, I can't imagine watching her walk away from the village, and from me.

Ember's in the kitchen cleaning up after breakfast and Blaze is working in his shop. I'd told them I would keep her company while we're waiting on the elders to make a decision. It's no trouble, I'm happy to have her all to myself.

She finishes her plate of scrambled eggs and bacon, and then wipes grease from her mouth with a napkin.

"That was delicious."

"I heard you picked the herbs for the quiche."

"Yep. I love Ember's garden."

A twinge of jealousy gnaws at my heart.

"Since the council's not ready yet, I was thinking we could go for a walk and get some fresh air. What do you think?" she asks.

"Sounds good to me."

A slight smile curves her lips as she gets up to add her tray to a pile of dirty dishes. I follow her out into the morning sun. Birds chirp overhead, and kids kick a ball around in the mud. It's a typical day in the village, despite the blasts of magic coming from the direction of Bonfire Falls.

She's oddly quiet as we amble across the cobblestones. Her expression is one of interest. She seems fascinated by what I'd consider a mundane morning. I hope she doesn't think we're backward in our ways. We take pride in our community. Our peaceful life is enough for us, but would it be enough for her?

I bite the edge of my lip and continue walking by her side.

Morning fog clings to the tops of oak and cherrywood trees. Sunlight pours through the branches, creating unique halos around the village.

When we sit on an old wooden bench near the edge of the forest, a thick ray of sunshine lands on Ariadne. She squints against the light. I can't stop staring at her. She hypnotizes me.

As she glances my way, my heart skips a beat.

She's so beautiful.

A sudden blast of magic echoes from Bonfire Falls.

Ariadne gasps and chews on the edge of her lower lip. I want to kiss her fear away, but there's no point. Until the council makes a decision, we're stuck in limbo.

Before I can offer any comfort, she jumps to her feet to pace back and forth in front of me.

"Waiting is killing me," she says.

"I know. It's hard for me too." I stand and wrap my arms around her. "Don't worry. They will make the right choice."

"When?"

"I don't know."

As she presses her face into my shoulder, I hold her even closer. I don't know how to take away her fear, but I do have ways I can distract her from it

"Would you like a tarot card reading?" I ask.

"I'd love that. Thank you." She gives my cheek a soft kiss.

"Let's head on to my place. My tarot cards are there."

"Okay." She holds her hand out, and I take it.

As we head back into the village, we pass a few townsfolk who stop to say hello. Wariness still clouds their eyes when they look at Ariadne, but they seem to be more accepting of her. Given enough time, I know she'll be able to win them over.

When we arrive at my place, I start a fire. Although she won't admit she's cold, it doesn't take a genius level intelligence to figure it out. She's been shivering and rubbing her arms the last few minutes. Shifters almost never get cold, so I guess that's one way we're very different.

"I'll do the reading here." I point at the kitchen table. "Let me get my cards."

"I've only had my cards read once before."

"How did it go?"

She makes a face. I guess it didn't go that well.

"Hopefully today will be better." Her lovely lips form a slight pout. I'd much rather kiss her than do a reading right now, but honestly, I'm curious about what the cards might reveal.

I head into my bedroom and grab my favorite deck from a shelf in the closet. The deck is tucked away in a carved, wooden box, and the cards are wrapped in a purple velvet cloth.

When I return to the kitchen, her eyes light up.

"Wow, very fancy." She's leaning over the table, peering into the box as I set it between us.

"Someone who comes to me for readings gave it to me." I pull the deck out of the box and unfold the velvet cloth. I lay it on the table, then set the cards on top.

"A woman?"

"Huh?"

"I bet the person who gave you the cloth was a woman." She grins.

"Maybe." I smirk.

"I bet she likes you."

I love this teasing side to her.

"She's ninety-three years old," I say. "Far too young for me."

"Too young?" Her giggle is pure magic.

"I like my women older and more refined," I say in a snooty tone.

"I'm sure." She rolls her eyes.

"Shuffle the cards." I hand her the stack. "Be sure to concentrate your energy into them."

"I will." Her eyebrows knit together as she concentrates.

Little blue sparks of magic flitter into the cards. I didn't expect her to literally send her magic into the cards, so now I'm not sure if I should touch them.

When she sets the deck on the table, the magic flutters away. I guess they're safe to touch now. I don't know for sure, since I've never read for a witch before, but I'm about to find out.

I gently grasp the deck. Since I don't immediately combust, I figure it's safe enough. I lay ten cards, face down, on the table, using a standard Celtic Cross reading.

The first one I flip over is the High Priestess. The card depicts a woman in a long robe with a unique crown on her head. A moon and little stars light up the black background.

"This first card represents the present. So, this card is who you are right now," I say.

Ariadne nods as I turn another card over and lay it on top of the High Priestess.

When I glance down at it, I'm not sure if I should continue with the reading or not. The crossing card is meant to reveal the immediate challenges one might face. In this case, the Tower card represents radical destruction. This is very bad, considering there's a war going on in her hometown. This might mean the war could directly affect her in some negative way. Of course, it's not overly specific, so I don't know exactly what it means. But regardless, it's not good.

Is the card trying to warn her about her parents or is it trying to warn her specifically? Does this mean she'll be in danger if she goes back to Bonfire Falls? Have her parents already been killed? Are they in immediate danger?

"What's wrong?" she asks.

"The Tower card represents chaos and destruction."

"The war," she whispers.

"Yes. I can't tell you what it means specifically, but the war will greatly impact your life."

"But how?"

"I don't know. I only get a general sense of what's to come, nothing specific."

"I want to know the rest." She holds her head up and waits for me to continue.

"The next card represents the best outcome related to the challenge you're about to face." I take a deep breath before flipping it.

The Temperance card stares up at us. An angel pours liquid from one golden mug to another. My knotted muscles relax.

"It's the Temperance card. It means peace, harmony, and balance." A slight smile spreads across my face. "That's better than the last card. The outcome of the challenges you face should be resolved peacefully."

"I hope that's true," she says.

"So do I."

"This next card depicts the immediate future." I lift the card to the left of the first three main cards. "The Five of Wands represents conflict. Everyone is arguing, but nobody's listening."

"That's what it's like in Bonfire Falls right now. No one wants to negotiate anything. There are too many witches and shifters willing to help their greedy leaders. Peace will never come if all they want to do is fight."

"It's unfortunate, isn't it?"

Her eyes soften as she nods in agreement.

"They shouldn't be fighting each other. We're all magical creatures in one way or another. Everyone in Bonfire Falls needs to band together in case humans ever attack again. That should be their only fear. We may have lived in peace for centuries, but all it takes is one attack from humans to ruin our world." The passion in her voice stirs my soul. She's the kind of leader they need in Bonfire Falls. Not leaders driven by greed or vengeance, but leaders driven by love.

I place my hand over hers, trying to comfort her as she closes her eyes.

"Keep going," she whispers.

"This one is your recent past." I tap on the card to the right of the others. Flipping it over, the Two of Swords shows us the image of a blindfolded woman in a white robe, holding two crossed swords. "The Two of Swords can mean a passive-aggressive relationship."

"Ugh, that sounds like my ex." Her tone is bitter as she runs her fingers through her hair.

Should I ask about her past relationship? Would it be too personal?

My curiosity gets the best of me.

"You don't have to answer if this is too personal, but what happened with your ex?"

"I had an ex who made it seem like everything was always my fault. Eventually, after being with him for far too long, I kicked him out of my life and moved on. But I can't believe I was in that relationship for as long as I was. He treated me like crap the whole time."

"I'm glad you got rid of him. He's an idiot for treating you as anything less than a princess."

"Are you serious? You think so?" She gives me a skeptical look.

"Of course, you're a very special woman. Any man would be lucky to have you."

Her face softens and her cheeks flush. I'm guessing she hasn't received a lot of compliments lately.

"Anyway, I haven't dated much since then. I don't like drama."

"I can understand that. My last girlfriend was totally unhinged. She'd get jealous if I even dared to glance at another woman. She needed to know where I was every minute of the day. I couldn't breathe when I was around her, so I had to end it. I've been burnt out on relationships ever since."

"Would you ever consider dating again?"

"If the right person came along, I would." I cover her hand with mine and give it a soft squeeze. I can't stop thinking about our kiss the other day. My gaze drops to her red lips and it takes everything in my being not to climb over the table to kiss her again.

"We haven't finished the reading. Do you still want to see the rest of the cards?"

"Please," she says.

We continue the reading, going through more card meanings and possible explanations for them. When we reach the last card, I turn it over.

The Lovers.

"It must not have anything to do with the war." A light blush forming on her pale cheeks.

"It could be leftover energy from the kiss we shared," I say softly.

"I liked kissing you." she licks her lips.

"You did?"

"Mm."

"Come should how much you liked it." I'm half teasing, half-serious, but she's in my lap before I can take another breath. "Oh!"

"Kiss me, Copper."

I wrap my arms around her waist and hold her securely. She leans in slowly, gently pressing her lips to mine. My heart kicks against my ribs. Her sweet, sexy kiss is ruining my control. I want to sweep the cards to the side and lay her on the table. I want to slip off her clothes and kiss every inch of her.

Her arms go around my neck. I part her lips with my tongue, and she moans into the kiss. She's everything I've ever dreamed about and more.

Diving into her warm mouth, I caress her tongue with mine before lightly sucking on it. I gently glide my hands up and down her back. I kiss her with an all-consuming passion. My cock throbs inside my jeans. I try to ignore my violent need to claim her, but it's nearly impossible to control.

When I lift her into my arms and set her butt on the table, she pulls away.

"Copper?"

"Yes?" I murmur.

"We should stop."

I groan and press my forehead into the valley between her breasts. She strokes my hair.

"I love kissing you, but with the war going on..."

"I know," I groan.

"When it's over, I'll be able to think about relationships again. But not now."

"I understand." I do. But having to wait for her might kill me.

"We should check in with the council to see if they've made a decision. I know it might still be too early, but I need to check." She tries to stand, but she's pinned between the table and my body. "Copper?"

It kills me to back away, but I do.

"I'll go with you." I stretch to try to relieve the tension in my muscles. As I move, my shirt hikes up to reveal my lower abs. Her gaze is fire on my skin.

"I should go. Alone. I'll be fine. I'll see you later." She skitters toward the door then stops. She rushes back to give me a quick kiss on the cheek before heading out into the village. Then she's gone, leaving me hard, and alone.

I sigh.

As I place the cards in a pile and fold the purple cloth around them, I wonder what The Lovers card means.

Will we be lovers someday?

I hope so, because she's perfect for me. She's beautiful and sweet and kind. She's got the most tender heart of anyone I've ever known. She was even brave enough to face a whole village of dragon shifters to save her family. But until her family is safe, we can't be together. I understand her reasoning, but I don't like it. I wish the damn council would hurry up and render a decision because I'm about ready to go into battle without them. If I have to die to save her family, I will. She's captured my heart, and the only way to get hers too is to win this war.

CAPTIVE OF THE DRAGONS: CHAPTER 10

ARIADNE

Warm sunshine splashes across the stone shingled roofs of the dragon village. As I stand beside the council chamber, I silently wage a battle against my darker impulses. I want to burn this place down and force the council to fight for me. Of course, if I do set their village on fire, I highly doubt they'd fight willingly. Patience was never one of my strengths.

I bang on the door. Maria opens it and informs me that the council has once again failed to reach a decision. Before I can respond, she closes the door and locks it.

"Dammit!"

Attracted by the sudden increase in my body's natural electromagnetic field, bits of dirt lift off the ground near my feet. Without realizing it, I've summoned lightning magic. Sparks appear between my fingers. My hair stands on end. A dust cloud coalesces around my body.

I have to calm down. My anger won't serve anyone. In moments like this, I can see how easy it would be to let the darkness suck me in. I have to resist so I don't become a dark witch like Sybil.

Fortunately, my mother trained me to control my magic. Using slow breaths, I'm able to relax my body and my mind. Within seconds, the energy dissipates. I'm left covered in dust.

"Great." I spit dirt out of my mouth. The foamy wad is brown. "So gross."

I need a bath. The spring Copper and I visited the other day seems like the perfect place to wash this mess off me. I remember the way, and the rough terrain is less bothersome this time, possibly because I know what to expect. Or maybe it's because my mood is so different from the last time I was here.

When I reach the stream, its beauty overwhelms me. The crystal-clear swimming hole is gloriously free of other people. Since no one is around, I take everything off before diving into the cool water.

As I splash my face, the water's inherent magic refreshes me. I take a drink to satiate my thirst, then spend the next few minutes paddling around the pool.

I'm so sick of thinking about the council that I decide to ignore them for now. Every time I try to think about them, the water around me steams. Rather than boil myself alive, I turn my thoughts to something that won't send me into a fit of rage—my men.

Blaze is a force of nature, all fury and passion. He puts maximum effort into everything he does, whether he's arguing his point, or pounding away on a bit of stubborn metal, he's relentless. His warrior exterior hides the artistic craftsman within, and I can't help but wonder, would he be so relentless, and passionate, and creative in bed?

A smile spreads across my lips. Yes, I bet he would be

all of that and more. He would probably sweep me up in those massively muscled arms and drag me off to his bed, like a caveman. Now that I've had time to get to know him, I'm not quite as miffed about the way I was treated on my first night in the village. After all, the dragons are very superstitious when it comes to witches, so I guess I can't blame him for tying me up and gagging me.

Is it wrong that I want him to do it again? Only this time, I want him in the bed with me.

A part of me is thrilled by the thought of being tied up by a powerful alpha male. I'd let him have his way with me for sure. I know Blaze would never force himself on me, but it's fun to imagine all the sexy things he might do if I let him.

But as much as I want him, I can't banish thoughts of the other guys from my mind.

Copper wouldn't be the kind of lover who would simply take me. He'd be a full-blown partner in the exploration of pure pleasure. Or at least, that's what I'd like to believe based on our single make out session. He's very sensitive and intuitive about how people feel. And the way he looked at me when he revealed The Lovers tarot card still drives me wild. Sex with Copper could probably last all night and involve lots of sensual cuddling and spooning, which I'd totally love.

Last but certainly not least, there's Ember. His methodical precision and attention to detail in the kitchen will translate well into the bedroom. I bet Ember has a dog-eared copy of the *Kama Sutra* with notes written in the borders. I wouldn't be surprised if I found it in his nightstand.

Thinking about the three of them makes me wonder, if the war wasn't about to tear my whole world apart, which guy would I choose?

It's a ridiculous question. If we do go into battle against Sybil and Flint, then there's no guarantee I'll survive to even make a choice. I'll sacrifice anything to keep my parents safe. I already feel like I've been with the dragons for too long. It's only been a few days, but it feels like an eternity has passed. If I wasn't so sure they could help win the war, then I wouldn't bother waiting on a decision from the council. But if they do agree to help us, then we'll end the war swiftly and without many more deaths.

A sharp report from down the mountain shakes a flock of birds from a nearby tree. A chill runs down my spine. Instead of continuing to indulge in mindless fantasy, I decide to head back to the village.

Dressed and ready for a new distraction, I head toward Blaze's workshop. I him shirtless and covered in sweat and soot from the forge. His pectoral muscles ripple beneath his shining, sweat slicked skin. His hands are clad in thick gloves, and he holds a glowing red bar of iron with a pair of forceps. He smashes a massive square-headed hammer against the iron, which sends up sparks into the air. I'd love to have those powerful, capable hands control my body like he so expertly controls the iron.

He stops for a moment to suck in a great breath of air. His chest expands, and smoke trails out of his nostrils. His cheeks bulge and redden before he leans forward and unleashes a white-hot stream of fire. The metal bar nearly liquifies.

As he returns to hammering the bar, more sparks fly. I'm wet just watching him work like this. I could watch him all day and not get bored. He's the most masculine guy I've ever met. He's pure sexiness and I literally want to lick his sweaty abs.

I'm amazed that he can breathe fire in his human

form. How does he do it? He wears dragon scale gloves to protect his hands, but what about his lungs? Perhaps he's fireproof in human form, but only on the inside. Does he have to eat sulfur to replenish his fire breath, or is it an ability with no limits? I have so many questions.

He hasn't noticed me standing just outside the door to his workshop, so I continue to watch him work. Occasionally he breathes more fire to keep the metal hot enough to work. Eventually, he hammers out the iron bar into a longer, flatter shape. It's awesome to watch, especially as the crude iron bar grows to resemble a shape I recognize. It's another sword.

There are many more iron bars of a similar shape waiting for their turn. Why is he making so many weapons for a supposedly peaceful village? Does Blaze know something I don't know about the council's decision? Did they decide and he didn't tell me?

"Blaze?"

"Hey." He wipes sweat out of his eyes, then smiles. He dips the blade into a bucket of water, then sets it onto a rack to cool.

"I'm not interrupting you, am I?" I gesture toward the lined-up bars of iron. "Don't let me keep you from your work."

"I'm trying to get ahead."

"Of what?"

"The council will make the wisest decision, which is to get involved in the war. There's no other way to guarantee peace in the village." He wipes his grimy hands off on a cloth and uses another to clean his face. "Are you bored?"

"Just admiring the view." I give him a lascivious smile.

He grins and almost imperceptibly flexes the muscle in his torso.

"Is that so?"

"Mm-hum."

"I'd be happy to show you more any time you want."

My heart skips a beat. Damn it, why does he have to be so breathtakingly hot? I want to see more. I want to see a lot more.

We gaze at each other for several seconds. I can't resist him, so I take a step forward. He eagerly comes to meet me in the middle of the forge. My hand rests on his firm, but smooth chest. His heartbeat thumps against my palms.

He puts his hands on either side of my face and tilts my head slightly before moving in for a kiss. I part my lips in eager anticipation.

This, of course, is also the exact moment Copper and Ember arrive. We hear their voices a split second before they come into view from the street.

"—should have used quail eggs in the batter. That's how you get the right texture," Ember says.

"What makes quail eggs so special?" Copper pulls up short and stares at me and Blaze. His eyes narrow. "What's going on here?"

Although Blaze and I had broken apart as soon as they'd walked into sight, our obviously flustered appearance gives away exactly what was going on, or at least what was about to happen before we were interrupted.

"What can I do for you, stargazer?" Blaze puts his hands on his hips and glares at Copper.

"You can tell me why you were forcing yourself on our guest—again."

"No, no. He wasn't—"

"Forcing?" Blaze sputters as he moves a few steps closer to Copper. "I wasn't forcing anything."

"He wasn't," I mumble.

Ember chuckles and elbows Copper in the ribs to get his attention.

"Maybe not this time. It's not like when he dragged her off and tied her to his bed," Ember says with a smirk.

"Right. I'd forgotten about that particular incident," Copper says. "How do we know you weren't about to drag her off again?"

"If I were, it wouldn't be any of your business, and she wouldn't be minding it at all." Blaze puffs his chest.

"Okay, guys." Copper steps between them and holds out a restraining palm each way. "We're all friends here, and we all want what's best for Ariadne, right?"

"Right." Blaze nods firmly but doesn't stop glaring at Ember.

"Of course." Ember cocks an eyebrow at Blaze.

"Then there's nothing to worry about." Copper grins at both of his friends. "She's only one woman. We'll have to be patient and let her decide who she wants to spend time with. We shouldn't be fighting over her like she's a piece of meat."

"I'm not a tri-tip, boys," I joke to break the tension.

Blaze laughs. Copper and Ember join him.

They spend the next few minutes ribbing each other and play-fighting.

They're all jealous of each other, but they're also good friends. They usually get along really well, so I'd hate to be the reason their friendships are hurt. But maybe they don't have to fight over me, and maybe it's possible that I don't have to choose between them. Poly relationships aren't unheard of in either shifter or witch communities. Maybe they'd be willing to share me. It's a crazy dream, but who knows, it could come true. I just have to gather enough courage to ask them.

I can't just blurt it out, I must test the waters with each

man individually. I need to find out how they feel about sharing me. If they're not into it, then I will have to choose, but I really hope it doesn't come to that.

As I start to wonder how I'll accomplish this feat, we hear the rapid patter of running feet. A young villager stops just outside the shop. He bends over and puts his hands on his knees. He takes several deep breaths before he speaks.

"You're to bring the witch to the council immediately. They've made their decision."

I gasp. Blaze, Ember, and Copper look at me.

"Really? They've finally made up their minds! This is wonderful news," I say.

Copper pats the boy on his shoulder. "Take a few more breaths before you answer, but did the council happen to tell you anything about their decision?"

The boy shakes his head rapidly. My shoulders slump. No news. That doesn't mean it's bad news, but I wish I didn't have to wait another second to find out what they've decided.

Blaze shows the boy where to get a drink of cool water. I can barely contain my nerves. The council has finally rendered their long-awaited decision. But what do they have to say? Will the Dragon Clan help us, or will I be forced to watch my town burn?

CAPTIVE OF THE DRAGONS:
CHAPTER 11

ARIADNE

I stride with purpose toward the council chamber. Ember, Copper, and Blaze rush to catch up and fall into step beside me. My heart beats faster than a rabbit's. The Dragon Clan council has finally made their decision. Will they help Bonfire Falls, or will they leave us to burn? While I hope the Dragon Clan will help stop the war while there's still a town left to save, I'm fearful they'll decide to do nothing.

I don't wait to be ushered in. Instead, I shove the door open and stride boldly into the council's chambers. These people have made me wait long enough. I can't help but notice many of them, close to half, give me a scornful cold shoulder. It doesn't bode well for the decision they made.

One of the elders clears her throat.

"The council has reached a decision. We thank you for your patience in what must be a troubling time."

"That's an understatement." I cross my arms over my chest and stare back defiantly. They've made their decision. It doesn't matter if they like me anymore. "So, what is it? Or do I have to wait three more days for you to finally tell me?"

The elders seem rather nonplussed by my attitude, but my male companions are utterly shocked. Ember claps a hand over his mouth and stares at me as if to say, *what have you done?*

Copper looks from me to the elders, as if one of them will strike me down.

Blaze, on the other hand, lets out a sharp bark of laughter.

"She's bold. Perhaps you'd better tell her your decision before she unleashes her magic on you."

The elder's mouth twitches.

"It is the decision of this council that the Dragon Clan will render aid to Bonfire Falls."

Despite my earlier bravado, I nearly faint with relief. My parents will be saved. If they're still alive.

"Thank you." I don't know if it's proper or not, but I offer a deep bow to the Dragon Clan council of elders. "I know this wasn't an easy decision to make, so thank you."

"We only want peace." The elder woman's mouth stretches into a thin, mirthless smile. "But in order to preserve that peace, we must deal with the violence that ails your fair town. The majority of us agree on this."

"The majority?" I arch my eyebrow, and then glance at the rest of the council. No wonder so many of them seem angry. "How much of a majority?"

"The council voted seven to six in favor of helping Bonfire Falls."

My stomach bottoms out as I realize how close my town came to disaster. Seven to six? I hadn't expected so much resistance. I suppose I'd always assumed the Dragon Clan were somehow chivalrous and would eagerly ride off to battle for a just cause. I couldn't have been more wrong.

After seeing my town consumed by warfare, I can't blame the Dragon Clan elders for their hesitation in offering assistance. But what I'd said before, about how neither Sybil nor Flint will be satisfied with Bonfire Falls, was true. They will try to take the entire mountain. It's in the dragons' best interest to stop the war become it comes to their village.

"So." I clap my hands together. "When do we leave? Are we going to go in groups, or would you prefer to sneak up on Sybil and Flint?"

The elder dragon holds up a restraining palm. Age lines form channels on her wizened skin. A spider's web of blue veins stretches from her wrists to her fingertips.

"Calm yourself." She spreads her arms. "We will fly to the aid of those who do not seek war under the leadership of Sybil and Flint. But we must have time to prepare. It has been many moons since we fought in battles, and we are ill equipped to do so at present time."

"How much time?" My eyes narrow, and my voice drops a few octaves when I speak.

Copper puts a hand on my shoulder, but I shrug it off.

"Several days, at the least."

"Several days?" My heart pounds, and my knees go weak. I've had to wait so long already, and now they expect me to wait even longer? "No, we have to leave now. People are dying in the streets right now. We don't have several days. We don't have several hours. We don't have a single second to spare. We must go now."

The elder coolly regards me, but her eyes have a merry twinkle. Perhaps she likes my spunk, or maybe the hysterical girl from down the mountain amuses her.

"We cannot leave now." She gestures toward Blaze. "As

skilled as our blacksmith is, even he needs time to forge more weapons. Our arsenal hasn't been maintained very well, for we have no use for weapons here on the mountain."

"Don't you breathe fire?" My own voice grates on my ears. I know it's not totally fair, but I desperately want to help my family and my town right now. "What do you need weapons for?"

Another elder, this one a male, clears his throat.

"Dragons are more than a match for wolf or bear shifters. However, our fire may not be of much use against witchcraft. Surely you don't expect us to go into battle unarmed?"

Well, he put me on the spot, didn't he? Now I'll sound like a total bitch if I try to insist we leave right away. Part of me still wants to argue, but in my heart, I know they're right. It wouldn't be prudent to go off into battle unprepared.

I'm still terrified that we'll be too late for my parents. However, my family has prepared for this war for a long time. Even though we'd hoped it would never start, all the signs were there. Discontent has been brewing in Bonfire Falls for years. It was only a matter of time before war broke out.

My mother has cast dozens of protective spells around our home. By now, my parents are probably hiding in the basement where we've stored several weeks-worth of food and water. They may not have the most comfortable time down there, but they're probably still alive. If it weren't for their careful preparations and foresight, I wouldn't be able to wait a single second longer. But unless Sybil or Flint discovered their hiding space, my parents should still be safe.

I take a deep breath and let it out slowly.

"Fine." I can sense the guys relax behind me. "We'll leave as soon as your preparations are complete."

Besides, what's another day or two at this point? I'd rather have the firepower of a hundred dragons behind me, than try to stop the war myself. I'm just not strong enough, which is why I need them. I can wait because waiting will ensure victory.

"We will begin our preparations with great haste." The elder woman nods to me before turning to regard Blaze. "Will you require anything of us to make our armory anew?"

Blaze grins and rubs his chin. He seems to like the idea of the elders' reliance on him for something so important.

"I'll need a few of the stronger boys to fetch water from the stream. I'll handle the rest."

"Then you will have all the assistance you require." The Elder woman gestures toward the exit. "If you will all excuse us, it has been very long since we waged war. We must discuss our strategies."

"Thank you." I give her another quick bow because it seemed to go over well the first time. The elders are too caught up in strategy to acknowledge our exit.

I wait until I'm outside in the warm sunlight before I finally give voice to my frustrations.

"Fuck!"

Ember puts his hand on my shoulder and gives it a gentle squeeze.

"You were great in there."

"Thanks." I reach up and squeeze his hand back. "I guess there's not much to do but wait."

"I'll be in the workshop." Blaze cracks his knuckles. "Hopefully the kids they send me can follow simple directions."

By mutual unspoken agreement, we all march back to Blaze's house. I suppose I'll stay there until the dragon clan is ready to fight. It's hard not to feel frustrated. After all, I waited for so long, and just when the waiting seemed to be over, I'm forced to sit through another delay.

As we reach Blaze's workshop, the village springs to life. News of the upcoming battle has spread. All around us, the village prepares to fight in the war. Young people gather in the streets to practice drills and formations. Others stand in a circle, taking turns shifting into dragon form. They compete to see who can do it the fastest. Even those too old or too feeble to fight gather to discuss how to defend the village.

I'm shocked by how quickly everyone is moving to embrace the council's decision. I wonder if they all knew the council would agree to join the war effort. Why else would they be so quick to gather?

"Everyone's getting ready." I pause as a group of children runs past us. "I hope I've done the right thing by getting your people involved in this war."

"You followed your conscience," Copper says. "As long as you do that, even if you make mistakes, you'll still be on the right path."

I smile at him.

Blaze heads toward the workshop and we follow.

"Speaking of preparations, we can't go into battle without weapons," Blaze says.

"Forge well, my friend." Ember clasps his hand, and they have a moment. It's sweet, but it also makes me wonder if perhaps we could make an unconventional relationship work after all.

"Everyone's doing something to help, and I'm just standing here." I sigh and rub my eyes with the back of my hand in frustration.

"I've got an idea," Copper says. "Why don't you practice your magic? We'll need it."

"Excellent suggestion," Ember says. "I know where you can practice."

"I'll catch up with you later," Blaze says as several boys join him outside of his workshop.

Ember and Copper lead me through the village until we reach a path that winds into the woods. After a long walk, we come upon a ravine that plunges down the mountain.

"What is this place?" My voice echoes back to me from the shadowy passage.

"A spot where we can practice our fire breathing and not burn down the village," Copper says.

"Or the forest." Ember indicates we should walk down the steep path. "It widens up and gets sunnier further in."

The walls hem us in for several minutes, but true to Ember's word, they eventually retreat as a forty-foot-deep ditch comes into view. The ravine terminates in a sheer rock wall that's covered in old soot. A half dozen wooden poles, which appear to have been blackened by fire, stand like silent sentries. Ember points to the wooden staffs.

"Those totems are practice targets. Don't worry, they're covered with a resin designed to resist flame."

"You know," Copper gives Ember a half-smile. "I don't think I've seen Ariadne use her magic yet."

"I haven't, either." Both of them turn their gazes on me, as if they expect a show.

My lips spread in a cocky grin. My boys want to see a show? I'll give them a show.

I concentrate power into my hands to summon my magic. Sparks of energy dance between my outstretched fingertips, and the static charge they create makes my hair stand on end. Ember and Copper take a few steps back, their jaws wide open.

I pick out the closest totem and continue to build the energy until my whole arm shakes. Then, with a cry of effort, I release the lightning bolt I've stored up. A white-hot flash briefly flashes between my hand and the totem. It splinters into a thousand pieces, while the resulting shockwave caused by a powerful release nearly bowls over my dragon companions.

I turn a smug smile on the men.

"Incredible." Ember picks up a splinter of wood from the totem which has landed near his feet. He blows out the tiny flame at the end of it.

"Understatement." Copper smiles at me and chuckles. "Got any other tricks?"

"Any other tricks?" Ember's mouth is wide open as he scoffs at his companion. "Like she needs any."

"Lightning and fire are my specialty." I make little flames dance at my fingertips, a simple enough manipulation of my magical energy. "But now that you mention it, I have been working on something for a while. Something special."

"Oh, let's see it." Copper's as eager as a pyromaniac child at a fireworks stand. I laugh at the way he bounces from foot to foot.

Ember rubs his chin thoughtfully, but he doesn't turn down the chance to see more of my magic.

"All right." I turn away from them and plant my feet shoulder length apart. Over my shoulder, I address them again. "You might want to step back further. This spell is dangerous, and I don't have full control of it yet."

Ember and Copper take a few more steps back, but they never lose the eager gleam in their eyes. I take a deep breath, hold it for a moment, and then slowly let it out through my nostrils until a placid calm envelops me.

Then I summon up my magic once more. This time, I don't build up a massive charge in my hand for a lightning bolt. Instead, I hold my hands at chest height and concentrate on making the energy burn bright, not hot. This creates an electromagnetic field which sucks in dust and debris and creates a miniature maelstrom between my palms. The whirling ball spins at a high velocity and increases in size as more mass joins the spin. Sparks of electricity dance throughout the dark vortex, which seems like a miniature black hole.

Then comes the tricky part. I charge all the particles until it's emitting near constant flashes of light. Finally, I summon fire magic to ignite the swirling maelstrom.

I pretend the furthest wooden pole is Sybil.

Threaten my family?

Destroy my town?

I'll show you what power is.

Now!

A scream tears out of my throat as I send the flaming ball of death away from me. As it travels toward its target, the ground is scorched beneath it, and more debris is swept up into its swirling mass. By the time it reaches the target, it's ten feet in diameter.

The ball strikes, releasing the charged electricity in an explosion that vaporizes the wood. A thunderous crack nearly knocks all of us off our feet. The rapidly expanding fireball flashes hot over our heads. I doubt any of us would still have hair right now if we'd still been standing.

Smoke obscures our vision as bits of wood and rock rain down around us.

Copper whistles, while Ember is struck speechless.

"Geez, I don't think you need to practice anymore," Copper says.

My confident smile is in direct conflict with the fear gnawing at my gut. A stationary target is easy to hit; a witch wielding dark magic is an entirely different matter.

I hope I'm truly ready for this battle. Until now, I've been so focused on getting the dragons' help that I haven't been thinking about the fight to come. But now it's all I can think about. I'm putting not only myself in danger, but my men too. If we fail, we will have lost everything, including our chance at love.

We can't fail.

CAPTIVE OF THE DRAGONS: CHAPTER 12

BLAZE

Loud chatter echoes in the dining hall as everyone devours Ember's famous lasagna. After I chew the last bite of mine, I take a sip of my glass of water to wash it all down. Although I took a double portion, I want more. I glance at the buffet tables, but the trays are empty. I sigh. I should have asked Ember to make an extra tray just for me. This is my favorite dish, so I'd happily munch on leftovers all night.

Ariadne's plate is almost finished as well. A splash of pasta sauce is stuck to the corner of her lip. I cover my mouth and try to hide my smile. She looks adorable, and she's oblivious to the sauce that settles along the crease. I hold in a groan of arousal, but part of me wants to lick it off, to taste the sweet flavor of her skin.

"You have a little something right here." I point to the side of my own lips with a sly smile.

She tries to wipe the wrong side.

"Did I get it?" She tilts her head to the side.

"No." I try to hold in a laugh and cough in my fist instead.

She huffs and finally smears the sauce, yet she doesn't get it all off.

"Here, let me." I lean over the table and wipe it away with a swipe of my thumb. I suck my finger to taste the spicy sauce.

The lighting in the dining hall brings out the gold swirls in her bright blue eyes. I've never noticed them before. There's so much more that I want to know about her, but we never seem to have enough time with her. I want more than just a few days; I want a lifetime.

Am I in love with her?

I don't do love. Hell, I don't do relationships. The closest I ever come to a relationship is when I've got a willing woman naked in my bed. It's just sex, though. That's all it's ever been. But with Ariadne, it's different. I want more than just a quick release. I want her love.

After dinner, Ariadne and I say goodnight to Ember and Copper. As we leave the dining hall, loud explosions echo from Bonfire Falls. Ariadne jumps and grabs my hand. I pull her to my side and wrap a protective arm around her. As long as she's with me, she'll be safe. I want her to know that.

All around us, villagers shoo their children into their cottages. Smoke drifts up from brick chimneys. Candlelight flickers in windows around the village as the villagers get ready for another cold night.

I hope to stay warm tonight by getting Ariadne into my bed. She'll be staying the night at my place, and I can't help but be excited. Even if nothing happens between us, we'll still have more time to get to know each other. She's more fascinating than any other woman I've ever known. She awakens my passion and desire in way that no other women ever could. I've never wanted just one woman before, but I want her, and only her.

Inside my place, we sit on the couch and cuddle by the fire. Cookie crumbs fall between us while she shares more about her life in Bonfire Falls. I can see why she's desperate to save her town. Bonfire Falls sounds like the perfect place to raise a family. I don't know why that's on my mind, but ever since I met her, all I can think about is settling down with a family of my own. She's changed me, and now all I want to do is make her happy.

God, listen to me. I sound like a lovesick fool.

But maybe I am.

How could I resist falling in love with her? I'm not about to let her slip through my fingers. I won't give up on our relationship. It's not moving as fast as I'd like, but there's a lot going on. I understand why she's hesitant to commit to anything other than the war, and I know I can't rush anything with her. For once, I'll have to be a patient man. It's hard, but I'm trying.

"I love being here with you," she says.

"Me too." I lace my fingers through hers and kiss the back of her hand. "The last few days..."

"I know."

"It hasn't been long."

"It doesn't have to be... not when it's real."

I lean in and she meets me halfway. Our lips burn as they meet, and I swear I feel her magic shimmering into my body. I cup the side of her face and tilt her head slightly. She sighs into the kiss. I swipe my tongue between her lips, and she melts into me.

She's all fire, and passion, and I can't help but burn for her.

Her moan of pleasure shoots straight to my cock. With each whimper that escapes those sweet lips of hers, I grow harder. She presses her breasts against my chest. Her arms encircle my neck. One hand feathers through my hair, while the other clings to the nape of my neck.

A groan vibrates in my chest.

This is heaven.

I could kiss her all day, but my impatience is hard to contain. She seems to feel the same way, because her fingertips slip underneath my shirt. Her palms slip up to my chest. She tugs at my shirt.

"Take this off," she demands.

While I pull it over my head and throw it over my shoulder, she starts to yank her shirt off. She unhooks her bra and tosses it away. My hands caress her breasts. She shivers.

"Are you cold?"

"Not anymore."

I trail kisses along her jaw and down her neck. She drops her head back to make room for me. I'm greedy as I try to devour every inch of flesh. I can't seem to get enough of the intoxicating scent of roses along her neck. I kiss and nip until her skin flushes.

"Oh, God. That feels so good." Her moans make me want to please her even more.

My belly clenches as her hands wander along my pecs and my abs. Her mouth is hot against my bicep. She's dragging her teeth across my skin and it's killing me.

I scoop her up and carry her to my bed. As I set her down, her gaze locks with mine.

"Undress me."

I swallow and obey her command. After pulling her pants free, I drop to my knees beside the bed. I kiss the inside on one thigh, then the other. Her scent is the most powerful aphrodisiac in the world.

Her panties are in the way, so I slip them down her sexy legs. After tossing them aside, I gently push her thighs apart so I can see her. All of her. She's lying on the bed with her arms bent so she's propped high enough to watch me.

Our gazes lock. I kiss and lick the inside of her thigh, spreading tight little circles across her skin until I reach her damp pussy. She moans as my tongue swipes up the length of her. When I grasp her tight little nub between my lips, she shudders.

"Blaze." My name is a whisper on her lips.

I stroke her pussy with long, luxurious licks until she's writhing against my mouth. With deft strokes, I coax her closer and closer to the pinnacle of ecstasy.

"Please," she moans.

With dizzying speed, I vibrate my tongue against her clit. She clamps her thighs around my head and screams, thrashing and twisting as pure pleasure enslaves her.

I pull back to give her space.

As I climb onto the bed, she drops her head to one side to watch me.

"I haven't come like that in... ever."

"Ever?" I grin.

"Ever."

I smile and trace spirals around her nipples. They're small and pink, but her breasts are big enough to fit in my palm. I raise one hand and pluck a nipple to gauge her reaction to the simple stroke. Her back arches, so I play with her nipples until she turns and pulls me toward her.

"Don't make me wait."

"Mm."

I replace my fingers with my tongue.

"Oh, wow."

Her amazement brings a smile to my face. I can only hope to give my woman as much pleasure as possible.

My woman?

I shouldn't get ahead of myself.

I kiss a line from one breast to the other. With my teeth, I cling to one perky nipple. I bite down enough to elicit a whine of pleasure from her glistening lips. She hangs her head back. Her eyes close, but her mouth hangs open in a silent cry. I lap at the sensitive spot and suck gently to lessen the occasional nip.

"Fuck. How can you do that with your mouth?" She whimpers and grips my shoulder harder.

"You're not the only one with magic." I can't help but tease her.

As I continue to kiss her breasts, moans of pleasure slip from her rosy lips. Her hands pull at my jeans. I quickly kneel on the bed and unbuckle the belt. I strip my boxers and toss them aside.

Naked and erect, I'm ready to plunge into her, but she reaches for me instead. She wraps her delicate fingers around my shaft and now it's my turn to whimper.

Her caresses are soft at first, but she quickly grows bolder. She tugs at my cock until I'm close to coming in her hands.

"Wait."

I pull free and crawl to cover her body. She arches against me.

"Make love to me, Blaze."

I can't seem to focus on anything but her pleasure. Even my own takes a back seat to hers.

That's never happened before.

I rub the head of my cock against her slick folds. She gives me an exasperated look. I grin briefly before slowly pushing inside her.

"Oh, Blaze." Her eyes flutter closed.

I grit my teeth as her velvety body clamps down

around me. She's wet and tight and perfect. And, she's mine.

We move as one, pushing and pulling and flowing together until we can't hold back any longer. I angle my hips to press against her tender core and she wraps her legs around my back. I know she's close by the way her lips fly open.

"Come for me," I whisper against her ear.

She does, exploding all around me while I struggle to maintain some semblance of control. It's useless, and I'm dragged into the swirling abyss of pleasure. My body clenches as I pulse into her, filling her with everything I've got.

When we finally relax, her eyes open and tears well in the edges.

"What's wrong?" I ask, concerned that I hurt her.

"Nothing."

"Talk to me." I roll onto my side and pull her into my arms.

"I have nothing to give you."

"I'm not asking for anything, not yet."

"But you want more?"

"I want everything." I kiss her softly. "I want you."

"Everything's so messed up right now."

"With us?"

"With my life."

"I know."

"I'm not looking for a relationship right now," she says.

"I understand. There's too much happening." A small stab of disappointment pierces my heart, but I know that I just need to be patient until the war is over.

"My home is falling apart. Until all that's resolved, I can't think about a relationship."

"I know, and I'd never force you to make that choice."

"I wish my life was normal right now because I love being with you." She breathes softly against my neck, then looks down at the warm comforter. I pull it up to cover us.

"Hey," I gently touch her chin to lift her eyes to meet mine. "I love being with you, too. If you're not ready for more, I can handle sex only." When she smiles, I continue, "Maybe we can explore a relationship later, but for now, I don't want to pressure you into anything. Being with you is enough for me."

"You're too perfect."

"Don't forget it." I tap the tip of her nose and she grins before snuggling closer.

"Blaze?"

"Yeah?"

"Do you think we'll win the war?"

"I do," I say with confidence. "We're dragons. Although we haven't fought in any recent wars, protecting our own is what we do. We'll fight to the death to defeat our enemies. And right now, that mean anyone who's causing trouble in Bonfire Falls."

"You're amazing."

"Give me ten minutes and I'll be amazing again." I waggle my eyebrows.

"Seriously?"

"Oh, yeah."

Excitement flows through me. My energy returns and I know I'm going to make this the best night of her life. I want to leave her sweaty and breathless in my arms at the end of the night. Then, she won't have to worry about the war, at least not for tonight. It might not be much, but it's the best thing I can give her right now.

In a few days, we'll charge into battle, but until then, I intend to make her as happy as possible. When the war's over, I intend to claim her as my mate. Until then, I'll do everything in my power to make sure she knows what her life will be like if she chooses to stay with me. I can tell she has feelings for the others. It kills me to admit it, but I'd be willing to share her with Copper and Ember, as long as I get my fair share of time with her. I don't like to share, but for her, I'll do anything. Anything to keep her by my side.

CAPTIVE OF THE DRAGONS: CHAPTER 13

ARIADNE

Hours later, I'm still in bed with Blaze, mostly because I'm sure I'll never be able to walk again. Not that I'm complaining. He's a beast between the sheets and I can't get enough of him. He trails his fingers over my shoulder, dipping to caress my breasts.

"Would you like a snack?" he asks.

"That sounds amazing, but I don't think I can eat any more cookies."

"How about peanut butter and jelly?"

"On white bread?"

"Fluffy white bread. Ember made it yesterday. He gave me one of the extra loaves."

"He's such a good chef." Blaze stiffens beside me. I kiss him softly. "Don't think about him when I'm with you, I don't."

"It kills me to know that they care about you too. But... I want you to be happy."

"When I'm with you, I'm the happiest woman in the world."

"And when you're with Ember and Copper?"

"They make me happy too," I confess. "But I already told you, I can't think about relationships right now."

"I know." He slips out of bed and pulls on a robe. "I'll be back with sandwiches. Would you like some tea too?"

"Do you have any more blackberry tea?"

"Of course."

As he leaves, I lay back in his bed. A fire still crackles in the stone fireplace in the living room. Even without the fire, I could burn up being so close to Blaze. My center is molten, and he's stripped me of my defenses. I couldn't resist him if I tried. But I don't need to resist him, not as long as he's willing to take what little I can give him right now.

He returns with a plate of sandwiches. I don't know why he's made so many. Maybe he's extra hungry. He should be after expending so much energy making love to me.

As he sets the plate on the nightstand, I bite my bottom lip.

"If you keep looking at me like that, I'm skipping the snack." He removes his robe before joining me in bed.

"We wouldn't want to get crumbs in the sheets."

"No, we wouldn't."

His lips are on mine and I glide my fingers into his hair. His rough, callused hands scrape against my back. I shiver in anticipation. No one has ever turned me into a puddle of need before. But I need him, desperately.

"Are you trying to seduce me?"

"Do I need to try?"

"You're so cocky."

"And you love it."

"I do."

He covers me with his body and pins my hands over my head.

"Tell me what I'm thinking," he says.

"I can't read minds."

"If you had to guess?"

"I'd guess you're thinking about salami."

"What?" He pulls back and rests his butt on his heels.

"I'm kidding."

"Now you're going to get it."

He leans down to trail smoldering kisses across my neck and breasts. My nipples pebble against his lips. My moans echo off the walls. I'm sure half the village has heard my cries, but I don't care. Let them hear. Let them know that I'm his, and he's mine.

My belly quivers as he kisses the curve of it.

"You're so beautiful. I love every inch of you."

Love? Does he mean love, love, or is he just blurting out whatever comes to mind?

I want to ask him, but I don't want to ruin his gentle exploration.

"Stop thinking," he whispers. "We only have what's happening right here and now."

"I worry about the future."

"Worry about where I'm going to put my tongue next." He grins before lowering his mouth to my pussy.

"Oh, God." My eyes go wide.

"Are you still worrying?" he asks.

"What?" My brain refuses to form a coherent thought.

"I thought so." His smug smile disappears as he licks my trembling slit.

My cries of passion fill the room. I sink my fingers in his hair and pull him closer. I'm shameless in my need. I can't even count how many orgasms this will be, but he seems to have an infinite supply of naughty tricks to keep me coming. How have I missed this my whole life?

"Oh, Blaze. Lick me."

"I am licking you," he murmurs against my clit.

"Oh, fuck. You know what I mean."

He returns to relentlessly lash his tongue against my tender bundle of nerves. I lose the ability to speak as he keeps me just shy of coming again.

"Tell me what you want," he whispers.

"Make me come, dammit!"

He finds the perfect spot and uses his deliciously evil tongue to push me over the edge.

I scream.

My whole body shudders.

"I want to feel you." He changes position and now it's his cock inside me, thrusting past my spasming muscles to claim me completely.

I'm euphoric as he grinds his hips against mine. Lost in absolute pleasure, I keep coming and coming until I'm sure I'll die.

"You feel so good," he groans.

I squeeze him tighter.

"You're a woman of many talents."

My throaty laugher is cut short by my low moan. I surrender everything to him, and he takes it with greedy delight.

Locked together, his thrusts grow rapid and his growl is feral. He's consumed by lust and I revel in my effect on him.

"Come for me," I murmur.

He comes with a roar, fulling me with hot spurts of pleasure. When he finally stops, his entire body quivers. He clings to me and doesn't seem like he'll ever let me go. And in a way, I don't want him to ever release me. I want to lay in his arms forever and forget everything but the way he makes my body hum.

Eventually, he rolls onto his back. I cuddle against him

with my head on his shoulder. The war in Bonfire Falls seems so far away. All I want to do is lay here with Blaze and feel this wonderful afterglow. I could fall in love with this man. I'm half in love with him already.

I want to tell him how I feel. Once the fighting is over, I want to explore this blossoming relationship. But he's not the only man I care about. I want relationships with Copper and Ember too. I don't know if he'd be willing to share me with them, but I need to know.

"That was amazing," I whisper.

"You're amazing." He kisses me on the top of my head, and I snuggle up even closer.

"So... I've been thinking..." I don't know what to say next, so I go silent. Blaze waits for a long moment before he prompts me.

"About what? The war?"

"About what will happen after the war. With us, I mean."

"Well, we could always do more of this."

"Yes, of course."

"Whatever you need to say, just tell me." He props his head on his hand and looks at me intently.

"I want more of this." He laughs, and I gently shake my head. "No, I don't mean just the sex. I want to be together. I want to be with you."

"Nothing would make me happier." His hand snakes around my shoulder. He squeezes me tightly against him.

"That's great." I take a deep breath and then take the plunge. "How would you feel about an open relationship. I mean, not really open. But multiple people."

"Multiple people." His body stiffens against mine. I worry I've pushed him away, but then he relaxes. "I've never really considered it. Polyamorous relationships aren't unheard of in our enclave, but it's rare that it works out." His tone seems to be more thoughtful than hurt or confused, which gives me hope. "I've never been in that kind of relationship."

"Do you think you could do it?" I can't keep the anxious tone out of my voice. "Could you share me with Copper and Ember?"

"Copper and Ember. Why am I not surprised?" He chuckles, and I relax. "I hate sharing, but I'll do anything for you. If having you means I have to share you, then that's what I'll do. I'm just glad it's Copper and Ember, and not some other guys."

"You three are my guys, my only guys. I know it's strange, but I just... I care for you all equally." I sigh and press my cheek against his warm chest.

"I know. I could see it in your eyes."

"You could?"

"I know you, Ariadne. You're too much woman for one man to handle alone. I mean, I'd be up to the task, for sure, but I wouldn't mind letting Copper and Blaze take on some of the responsibility of keeping you satisfied."

"Really?"

"Really." His expression grows serious. "We all care about you more than you could know. We've never talked about it, but I can tell the other guys would be willing to die for you."

"No one has to die," I whisper.

"I hope not. But the war is far from over, and it's going to be dangerous. You should speak to the others about how you feel. We'll need all the motivation we can get before we head into war. If they know you care about them too, then they'll fight even harder."

"You think so?"

"I know so. They're my best friends. I know them.

They're good men and they'll take good care of you. That's the only reason I'd ever agree to share them with you."

"Thank you."

He kisses me softly before settling back into the sheets.

That went much better than expected. When I'd first started to explore the possibility of a relationship with all three men, I'd anticipated a great deal of resistance. I'd expected most of that resistance to come from Blaze. He's so alpha compared to the others. But if he's willing to share me, then maybe the others will also agree to this arrangement. I need to know that they feel the same way. And the only way to do that is to ask them.

CAPTIVE OF THE DRAGONS: CHAPTER 14

ARIADNE

I roll over onto my side to snuggle up to Blaze, but he's not in bed. The sound of muted hammering reaches my ears, and it dawns on me that he's hard at work in his workshop. He's putting in so much effort to help save Bonfire Falls. I know he cares about me, but what he's doing is above and beyond anything I could ask of him.

As I sit up in bed, the memory of last night rushes back. I can't keep the grin off my face. Making love to Blaze was even more amazing than I'd dared to imagine. He's so full of passion. It's almost animalistic in a way, yet I don't fear him at all. He'd never do anything to harm me. He cares for me deeply, and although he didn't say he loves me yet, I think he does.

I slide out from under the sheets and pad into his bathroom. My skin is still alive with the memory of his fiery embrace. I can still taste him on my lips.

I run through my morning routine. Blaze gave me one of his extra toothbrushes on my first morning here, so I use that to clean my teeth.

When I'm finished, I stretch before searching for my clothes. I find most of them in the living room near the still-burning fire. Blaze must have added more logs before he left. He's so sweet, always making sure I have exactly what I need.

I sniff my clothes. They could use a wash for sure.

I'm about to pull them on when I notice a dress draped over a straight-backed chair in his bedroom. A note is pinned to it.

I HOPE YOU LIKE IT.
 ~ Blaze

As I FINGER the soft fabric, a smile spreads across my face. The dress is long and flares out from an empire waist. It's the perfect shape for me. The bodice has stylized images of flames and has a cute, lace-up neckline.

I toss my soiled clothes into a pile in the bathroom. I'll wash them later.

Once I slide the dress over my head, I realize it's very snug across my chest. Even with the ribbon laced up as high as it will go, I'm displaying more cleavage than would be appropriate in most settings. I wonder if Blaze did this on purpose. I shake my head and smirk. He's so perfectly naughty.

I use the silver mirror in his bathroom to inspect myself. I twirl so the skirt flares out. The fit is flattering enough, but I don't look like myself any longer. I'm a sexier version of myself. It's not a look that I'm used to, but I like it.

As I pull on my black hiking boots, I chuckle. They clash terribly with the dress, but what can I do? If I'd known it would take so long for the dragon clan to get their shit together, I'd have packed more clothing.

When I exit Blaze's home and stand on the sun-drenched street, the hammering grows louder and more distinct. As much as I want to go to him and hold him in my arms once more, I know he needs time to complete his important task.

Since Blaze will be busy for some time, I decide to check in on Copper and see what he's up to.

As I head through town, several villagers do a double take. They're not used to seeing me dressed in such a feminine way. While most of them are friendly enough, a few cast suspicious glances my way as I pass. The vote had been quite close. I'm sure many members of the dragon clan would rather not get involved in the war. I understand their reluctance, but I'm trying to save my town.

I reach Copper's house and politely knock on the door. A few moments later, it opens. Copper grins.

"It's so good to see you again." He takes my hand and kisses it tenderly. As his gaze runs up and down my body, approval shines in his eyes. "You look ho—great."

"Thank you. I feel great."

He steps aside and gestures for me to enter. Inside, his workstation is cluttered with unrolled scrolls, voluminous leather-bound tomes, and many different tools and artifacts. I can only guess the function of some of them.

"What's all this?" I gesture at the crowded worktable.

"I'm working on a birthday astrology chart for a dragon clan baby who came into this world last night." He chuckles lightly as he stares at the grand mess. "I suppose I've gotten a bit carried away, but I do enjoy my work."

He leads me into his den. A pair of comfortable chairs are partially turned toward each other. A table holding a half-melted red candle sits between them.

"Please, sit." He gestures toward the chair on the left. "I didn't see you at breakfast."

"I slept in." My face reddens when I remember why I was up so late last night.

"I saved some sausage and toasted bread." Copper retrieves the items from his pantry. "This should make a good snack. Would you like some wine?"

"So early?"

"It's almost noon."

"Oh, well then, I'd love some."

I wait while he lays out an impressive spread of spiced venison sausage, dark and crusty bread, and a wedge of yellow cheese. He uses a bone-handled knife to cut the sausage into thin slices. He uses them to assemble a sausage and cheese sandwich.

"I hope you like it."

"I'm sure I will." I take a bite. It's gloriously salty.

He pours two tall glasses of white wine and sits in the chair opposite my own.

"This is imported from France."

"How do you get things from so far away? I don't see any computers."

"We don't have power. We trade with people in a town on the other side of the mountain."

"Interesting."

"They want fresh food from the forest, and we want wine and other items we can't make ourselves. It works out."

The wine is dry, but its pleasant warmth spreads throughout my chest, and soon I don't care about its lack of sweetness. After only half the glass, I already feel giddy. Or maybe it's the company that has made me this way. I'm excited to talk to him about our relationship, but a little scared too. What if it doesn't go well?

Copper dabs at his lips with a handkerchief and sets his wine glass down carefully. He leans across the table and places his hand on top of mine where it rests on the arm of the chair.

"How are you holding up?" His somber yet affectionate expression warms my heart.

"To be honest, I'm worried." I sigh heavily. My shoulders curve inward. "I try not to think about it. I've tried to find ways to distract myself, but I've been less than successful."

Copper tears his gaze away from my chest. I can't blame him for looking. It's certainly being pushed up and out by the bodice. The ribbon lacing is doing a less than adequate job of concealing it.

"If I can do anything to, ah, help distract you— anything at all—please, tell me."

There's an opening if I ever saw one. I'd love to jump into his lap and make love to him right here and now, but I don't want him to think I'm too forward.

"Thanks." In the search a way to break the tension, I inquire about the astrology chart. "So, how do you make a birthday astrology chart?"

"Oh! I'll show you." He jumps up to retrieve the unfinished star chart.

When he returns, a smile of pure excitement covers his face. There's such a joyful quality to his personality. I really enjoy being with him. Just being in his presence makes me happy.

I listen intently as he explains the various charts and diagrams which led to his findings. Most of it goes over my head, after all, I'm the girl who slept through *Cosmos*, but he's so eager and so passionate about his work that I'm not bored. I'm just a bit confused, but he does his best to explain it anyway.

Eventually, we end up back in his study while he finishes up the chart. I sit and wait, content to watch him work.

"It's finished." His eye sparkle with mischief. "So, what else can I do now to distract you?"

Our gazes lock, and something primal passes between us. His chair scrapes the floor as he stands and turns to face me. Before I can say anything, he takes me in his arms. I let out a little gasp of surprise when he pulls me against his muscular chest, but I don't protest or try to escape. I'm right where I want to be.

When our lips meet, he sighs. His kisses are so tender and so sweet. He's so focused on me that I'm overwhelmed by his rapt attention.

"I'm glad you came to me."

"I missed you."

"Even though you were with Blaze last night?"

"I—"

"I'm sorry. I shouldn't have said that. You don't have to explain anything. You're here now, and that's all that matters." He slides his hands down my bare upper back. "This dress is..."

"Something," I finish.

"You're so beautiful." His breath is hot against my throat. "I want to kiss every inch of your body."

"Copper," I sigh as I lace my fingers into his hair.

"I need you." His strangled voice sends tendrils of erotic need straight to my pussy.

"You have me."

I gasp when he gently nibbles on my earlobe. The hand on my back slides lower until he grasps my rear tightly. He tugs me even closer to his body.

How can I be this lucky? Am I really about to have sex with a second hot guy within a span of twenty-four hours?

Part of me wants him to take me roughly on his desk, but I'm also enjoying this slow, sensual seduction.

"You're so sexy," I whisper.

"No." He suckles on my ear lobe, and I dig my nails into his back. "You're the one who can melt iron with a look."

"That's just magic."

"You're magic. I know you're a witch, and you've probably cast one of your witchy spells on me," he teases. "But being with you..."

"Shh." I put a finger to his lips. "Be with me."

His hot mouth leaves a trail of smoldering kisses down my neck. The press of his lips against my throat makes my breath come faster. Meanwhile, his hand slides down to my waist. He gathers the fabric of my voluminous dress into his huge hand, and slowly expose my bare leg.

"Oh, God." As Copper's smooth palm caresses my outer thigh, my body thrills to his touch. I grab his hand boldly and put it between my thighs.

A grunt escapes his throat as he strokes my moist center. He grows more insistent with his kisses and his hands. His tongue slides between my lips and he takes control as I submissively melt into his embrace.

I throw my arms around his neck and squeeze him tightly to me. I moan as he probes my slick pussy. As he strokes my quivering lips, I spread my legs to give him better access. He takes advantage and pushes one finger into me, then another.

Copper leans his head forward. With his teeth, he grabs the ribbon that ties my dress closed. He grins and gives the ribbon a tug.

"You're so bad." I laugh as he pulls the ribbon loose.

The neckline flops open. He tugs the dress down further to expose my naked breasts and then puts his hot mouth on my nipple. A low moan escapes me as Copper gently kisses both breasts before burying his face between them. I toss my head back, loving the way he sighs against me.

His fingers are insistent against my clit. I grind against him, wanting more.

"Take me, Copper." My voice is husky and filled with hunger.

He kisses me deeply, then gathers me into a tender embrace. As he turns me around, he's sensual but firm. My back is facing his chest as he bends me over his worktable.

"I've wanted you since the moment I met you." He tugs down his zipper with one hand while he throws my skirt up around my waist with the other.

A light breeze tickles my exposed pussy. The windows are open and although the one in his office doesn't face the village center, anyone could still walk by and see us. The thought excites me. I never expected Copper to be so wanton.

I risk a glance over my shoulder. He's naked. His swollen cock juts up from his fist.

"Turn around," he commands.

I comply and spread my fingers wide against the table. My back arches and my ass lifts. I spread my feet wider on the floor. I want him inside me so desperately. I can hardly wait.

But I don't have to.

A sharp cry rips from my throat as he pushes his cock all the way inside me. He's just as big as Blaze, maybe bigger. I've never felt so stretched, so full, and it's profoundly amazing. I didn't think anything could be better than last night, but the way he's taking me, with rough thrusts that shove the table forward, it's simply mind-blowing.

I rest my cheek against the desk. He thrusts into me over and over until I'm pushed up on my tiptoes. He grabs my thighs and pins me to the table. He thrusts faster and harder. The table rattles and I hope it can hold up under the force of our bodies against it.

Tools bounce off its surface and clatter to the floor. Papers rustle and whoosh as they paraglide around the room. Soon the table has scooted all the way against the wall, and every time he slams his hips into mine, the table thumps loudly against the plaster. I'm sure anyone walking by would stop to see what all the fuss is about, but I don't care.

I scream as he drives me to a thunderous orgasm. I claw at the desk as he fills me up with his own release. He collapses across my body, panting. As he kisses the back of my neck, our heavy breaths echo off the nearby wall.

When he slips out of me, I feel the loss all the way in my soul. I want to be bound to him forever, not just because of how hard he can make me come, but because I truly care for him. I'm falling for him, just like I'm falling for Blaze, and Ember. And I need to tell Copper the truth about how I feel.

He carries me into his bedroom and lays me on the bed.

"I got carried away," he whispers as we spoon.

"It was perfect."

"Have you been with Blaze and Ember?"

His question shocks me, and I don't want to answer. I don't want to hurt him with the truth, but I won't lie to him either.

"Blaze. Not Ember. How did you know?"

He laughs gently and turns me to face him. He caresses my cheek with the soft pads of his fingers.

"I can tell you like them, too, but it doesn't matter to me."

"It doesn't bother you?"

"No." Copper hugs me close and sighs. "I want you any way I can get you. If sharing you is my fate, then who am I to question it?"

Relief spreads through my body, and I snuggle closer to him. He's making this so easy, almost too easy. Will Ember feel the same way? Could I possibly be that lucky? I need to find out before we leave for Bonfire Falls because there's no telling what will happen once we go down the mountain.

CAPTIVE OF THE DRAGONS: CHAPTER 15

EMBER

On my way back from checking on the herbs in the garden, I spot Ariadne sneaking out of the back of Copper's small cottage. In the late afternoon sun, I glimpse the flush along her cheeks, and the strands of her hair sticking to her skin. With a frown, I sniff in her direction and catch a whiff of Copper's scent all over her.

I suspect she's also sleeping with Blaze because they're constantly flirting, and Ariadne always sleeps at his place. The way they look at each other when they think no one else is watching also confirms my suspicion.

But she's having sex with Copper, too?

My shoulders droop with disappointment because we haven't been intimate. We've kissed, but that's it. Now, I'm not sure if she cares about me. If she's off having sex with the other guys, where does that leave us?

Am I jealous?

Yes, I'm jealous. It's a foreign sensation that weighs heavy on my heart, but there's no denying what I feel.

Why doesn't she want to have sex with me? Am I lacking something that the other guys have? I wouldn't say we're similar in every way, but we're all friends. We share a lot of the same values, hopes, and dreams. I may not be as brawny as Blaze or as esoteric as Copper, but I'm one hell of a chef. I know she enjoys my cooking, but I guess that's not enough for her.

A stab of pain pierces my chest. I can't stand the feeling of being left out. It's as if they've all abandoned me.

She doesn't see me standing beside a giant evergreen tree.

Should I confront her?

Before I can decide on what to do, she's already halfway to the edge of the northern woods. She must be heading toward the river.

I push my shoulders back and brace myself. It's time to have an honest chat with her. I've been holding back my feelings for days, but now I have to tell her exactly what's on my mind. Because if I wait too long, it might be too late. I've seen the pile of weapons outside Blaze's workshop. It grows by the hour and it won't be long before we leave for Bonfire Falls. If I wait too long, it will be too late.

As I follow her down the mountain to the river where we bathe, I try to come up with a way of approaching the subject. I can't exactly tell her that I know she's sleeping with the others, but not with me. Ultimately this isn't about jealousy or envy, it's about us, Ariadne and me. There's something brewing between us, I just know it. But how do I talk to her about what's in my heart without sounding like a jealous fool?

Branches and vines hang in the path that leads to the swimming pool. As I push the last one aside, I glimpse her in the river. She's already naked and looks sexy as hell.

When I reach the edge of the river, her back is to me. Her pale skin glistens in the remaining rays of sunlight. Wet locks of hair tumble down her back.

I hold back a groan. My cock hardens in response to her erotic display. I've only caught a glimpse of her, and yet I'm ready to join her and make her mine—if only she'll agree.

A stick cracks under my shoes before I can call out to alert her of my presence.

"Did you decide to join me?" She calls over her shoulder.

As she turns, her dazzling smile drops. A small gasp escapes her pink lips. "Ember?"

"Expecting someone else?" I try to stamp down my disappointment.

"Yes, and no." Her beautiful smile returns, which confuses the hell out of me.

Isn't she anticipating a visit from Copper or Blaze, instead of me?

"I assumed you were waiting on Copper, since you came from his place." I try not to sound too bitter, but my gruff voice betrays my jealousy.

"So, you know?" Her smile fades.

"I know... about both of them."

"You're right, I've slept with both of them." She pauses and pulls her luxurious hair into a knot at the nape of her neck. "Well, are you going to join me? The water isn't too cold, not that you couldn't handle it."

Is she playing with me? Or is she serious?

"Join you?"

"Please come talk to me. I've been wanting to get you alone."

"Really?"

"Yes. And I'm hoping we could talk now."

Her small plea is all it takes for me to strip. I frantically fold my clothes before splashing into the water. I keep my boxers on since I'm not sure where our relationship stands. I don't want to make her uncomfortable by making assumptions.

The cool water feels good on my sore feet. I've been standing in the kitchen all day, baking bread and cooking food for the coming battle. I could use some relaxation time. However, I'm anything but relaxed as I swim up to where she treads water.

She doesn't say anything right away. I wonder what she wants to talk about. She probably wants to clear the air about the kiss the other day.

Does she regret it?

Maybe she wants to tell me she's in a relationship with Blaze and Copper. It would kill me if they didn't want to include me too, but maybe there isn't enough of her for all of us.

Whatever the case is, I'm not ready to let her go. I'll still be her friend, if that's all I can have. I would be heart-broken, but at least I'd still be able to see her.

"You look good, all wet and sexy." Her eyes twinkle. "But you're staring."

"I'm sorry, I—"

"Relax." She moves stealthily through the water. My heart thumps faster in anticipation. All I want to do is hold her close and kiss her soft lips again. I just hope she still wants me.

I take a deep breath and slowly exhale.

"So, what did you want to talk about?"

She clasps my hands in hers. There's nothing sensual about the simple gesture but touching her sets my blood aflame. I yearn for her with the passion of a thousand star-crossed lovers. She's my Juliet, but I'm afraid she's surrounded by Romeos.

"I needed to tell you that I'm falling for Blaze, Copper..." My heart stops. "And you."

"Me?" I grab her hands tighter. Excitement courses through me.

"I want a relationship with all three of you, but I'm not sure if you'd be interested in sharing me with the other guys."

"They're my friends."

"I know, and I wouldn't dream of breaking up your friendships. I feel terrible for even asking, but I have to know if you feel the same way I feel about you."

"Which is?" I ask because I still can't believe she wants me too.

"I want to be with you. All of you."

I grin like a fool because it's easier to keep this stupid smile on my face than it is to express how much I want her in my life.

"Ember?" She cocks her head.

"If a relationship with the other two guys is what you need, then I'm in. I haven't wanted anyone else in years. You're an incredible woman. You're beautiful and smart and brave. I can tell you care deeply about your family and the other innocent people in Bonfire Falls." I pull her into my arms. "And right now—if you'll let me—all I want to do is worship this sexy body of yours."

"I'll do more than just let you," she whispers in a low, sexy voice. "I want you just as much as the others, if not more."

"Because you've never been with me before?"

"I don't know what I'm missing. Show me."

Before she can utter another word, my lips crush against hers. My kiss is raw and scalding. My need to possess her sears my soul. She mine. She's finally mine. And although I have to share her, I don't mind. I'd do anything for her, even let her be with Copper and Blaze. At least I know they'll treat her well.

When I release her hands, she hooks them behind my head. With our arms out of the way, I press her body against mine. Her breath quickens, and when I part her lips with my tongue, she tastes like spring water. I could drink every bit of her and still want more. I'll never get enough of her.

Our tongues melt together, and I can't seem to get enough. She's just as wild. Her kisses aren't tender by any means. They're boarding on feral, as if she's been holding back just waiting for me to come to her. I shouldn't have waited, but now I don't have to, not anymore.

As she wraps one leg around my waist, I grab her ass and pull her tight against me. She hooks her other smooth leg behind my back, and she clings to me. The heat from her pussy seeps past my boxers to warm my swiftly hardening cock.

"Ember?"

"Mm?"

"I've wanted you since the day we made quiche together."

"Why didn't you say anything?" I ask, exasperated.

"I wasn't sure where you stood."

"But I kissed you."

"I know. I was a fool."

"But now you're here, and you're mine. So less talking and more kissing." I arch a brow and she laughs. I love the sound of her voice. It's melodic and hypnotic at the same time.

Her gorgeous breasts are just below the level of my mouth. I dip to kiss her soft mounds. Her silky flesh glides under my tongue as she angles to push one nipple into my mouth. I pinch the little pebble between my teeth. She gasps and rolls her hips against my erection. It's pure torture, and I'll endure an eternity of it to make her happy.

As I grasp her other nipple, she moans. When I suck it hard into my mouth, a cry falls from her lips. Her hand grabs my short hair. She pulls hard, while pushing her breast deeper into my mouth.

"Lick me everywhere, Ember." Lust fills her voice as I pluck and blow on her wet nipple. Goosebumps ripple across her skin. The way she responds is intoxicating.

I sweep her hair off one shoulder and start to trail a path of kisses and nibbles across her skin up to her neck. I suck harder and swirl my tongue against her salty skin.

"Please, please." Her whimpers and pleas are burning through my control. I fight the urge to plunge into her pussy. But I don't like to rush, I like to take my time.

"You taste better than anything I've ever baked. Sweeter and more refined."

"Refined?" She arches an eyebrow. "If I asked you to make love to me on that grass over there, would that be *refined* enough for you?" She points toward a grassy spot alongside the river.

I laugh. So much for going slow.

As I carry her to shore, she releases her clamped legs and stands. I scoop her into my arms and gently lay her down in the grass. I cover her body with mine and prop myself up on my forearms. Her legs wrap around me once more. My boxers are the only thing separating my arousal and her sex. I wriggle out of them.

Naked, pressed skin to skin, I reclaim her lips. As our

kisses grow more frantic, she arches against me. I'll never have enough of her supple lips. She's rendering me useless to any other woman. I'm hers, for as long as she wants me.

The tip of my tongue slips along the pale skin at her throat. The setting sun provides enough light to reveal the pure lust in her eyes. I could look into her eyes forever, but my restraint is fading fast.

As I string kisses along every inch of her belly, my hands touch the smooth skin of her thighs and hips. Her moans echo through the forest. My journey continues along the top of her thighs where I lick and nibble her quivering flesh.

I drag my lips across the top of her pussy, teasing her, never touching exactly where she wants it most. I'm evil like that.

As she curses and grabs a chunk of grass, I can't keep a smile from forming on my lips. She twists the grass and pulls it up by its roots.

"Want me to stop?" I tease.

"Hell, no. Don't stop. Please, don't stop." She props up on her elbows and glares.

I grin wickedly before delving into the delicate folds of her pussy. Her wetness drives me crazy. Her scent is a drug, and I'm an addict.

Gazing back up at her, I watch her reaction as I plunge one finger between her folds. She grunts with pleasure, her eyes flutter closed, and a vibrant flush colors her cheeks.

Fuck, yeah.

She's gorgeous and all mine.

At least in this moment she is.

Her legs begin to tremble as I stroke her. Her back arches off the grass and she claws my back.

"Now, please. I need you." She exhales loudly.

A wild passion overcomes her. She pushes on my chest and flips us over. I gasp in surprise as she straddles my thighs. And when she lowers herself down onto my cock, I'm stunned. She's completely taking over, and I love it. I'm genuinely enchanted by her and her confidence.

She closes her eyes as she tests herself on my length.

As I grip her waist to guide her with my hands, she shivers.

"Oh, Ember."

"You feel so good," I groan.

She rocks her hips, gradually increasing her speed as she grabs her breasts. She twists her nipples and groans up at the night sky. Twilight comes to the mountain, and the chirp of crickets fills the air. We're all alone in this perfect oasis, doing exactly what I've been dreaming about. I've wanted this for so long. I can hardly believe it's really happening.

Her constant bouncing is bringing me far too close to the edge, so I flip both of us over. I cushion her head against my hand. She smiles before kissing me long and hard.

I grasp her thighs, lift them up as I reposition my cock, then I thrust back into her with a hard smack.

"Yes, harder." She moans and grabs her breasts again, pinching and twirling her nipples. Watching her play with them drives me crazy. I slide in and out, picking up speed. Her inner muscles clutch my shaft.

Fuck, this is incredible. I've never felt like this with a woman. She's driven me mad with her passion.

Her inner channel starts to tighten as her climax approaches.

"Oh my God. Oh my God!" She screams as she comes on my cock.

She pulses around me and pushes me over the edge with her. I'm lost in her softness and her heat. My entire body shudders as I explode inside her. I cling to her until the last flutter of orgasm leaves my body.

Puffing heavy breaths against her forehead, I drop to my elbows and hunch over her shoulder. Slowly, I pull myself out and lay down beside her. She twists her little body around, throws her leg over mine and uses my shoulder as a pillow.

Another smile forms on my face. My eyes close while I let my breath return to normal.

As I come down from the high, I sigh against her temple with relief. She wants me in her life, and after the war is over, I want to build a life with her.

But then, doubt start to fester in my mind. Does she want a relationship with all three of us? Is this temporary, or will it become something more, something permanent?

It could happen, provided she wants a life with us.

Her eyes are heavy with sleep. She's so adorable that I wish we didn't have to leave. I wish we could spend the night out here away from everyone and everything that's fighting for our attention.

My hand feathers through her hair as we lay there, enjoying the night sky.

"Do you think you're ready for a relationship with three dragons?" I'm not trying to ruin the moment; I just need to make sure she really wants a future with all of us.

"Yes. I want a future with you, and Blaze, and Copper, but I want to wait until the war is over." She gazes at me with love in her eyes.

"I hope it ends swiftly."

"Me too." She frowns and bites her lip.

As I kiss her fears away, she melts against me once more. We need to return to the village soon, but I'm not ready to leave yet. I don't know when I'll get her alone again, so for now, I want to stay right here, loving her and kissing her until the last possible second. The future is coming, and I don't know what it will entail, but I do know one thing for sure: I'm in love with this woman and one day, Blaze, Copper, and I will make her our mate.

CAPTIVE OF THE DRAGONS: CHAPTER 16

ARIADNE

Whether you're a witch or not, there's something magical about the hour just after dusk. A magnificent lavender sky spreads out over the dragon village. It's almost too serene given the coming battle.

High above me, three winged shapes bank and dive in a tight formation. They fly high enough that the last splashes of golden sunlight reflect off their iridescent scales. My men are beautiful in their dragon forms. Their power and grace combine to make them formidable warriors.

We've just received word that we'll attack at midnight. I can't wait for this to be over. I've been maintaining a confident façade, but inside, I'm terrified. We have to win this war, because if we don't, Bonfire Falls and the dragon village will both fall to dark forces.

I can't let that happen.

It's been several days since the dragon clan agreed to go into battle with me against the forces amassed by both Sybil and Flint. In that time, I've spent nearly every waking hour with one of my three men. We're growing closer with each passing moment. I've learned a lot more about Copper, Ember, and Blaze in these past few days. All is well between the four of us, and we're settling into what could become an amazing life together. That is, if we can stop the war and survive. The four of us have been combining our efforts to prepare for the coming violence, each tailored to our individual talents.

I think we're ready.

I hope we're ready.

Because in a few hours, we're flying to Bonfire Falls to end this war.

Ember and I have been spending a lot of hot days in his kitchen—and some even hotter nights in his bed. After some squabbling, we've worked out a sleeping schedule. Eventually I'd like for all of us to sleep in the same bed, but I'm not pushing it yet. I want them to get used to the idea of sharing me before I add any additional stressors.

Several days ago, Blaze pointed out the fact that an army travels on its stomach. The dragons will need a lot of food to fuel their powerful bodies, so Ember and I have made certain there is plenty available. We've made portable, hardy, and yet scrumptious fare for the dragon clan warriors. I have no doubt they'll be well fed.

Copper has been ardently exploring the stars, while hoping to discern some tidbit of prophecy that might aid us in the coming war. The red comet comes out at night to slowly travel across the sky. We watch it warily, and with great concern.

Aside from our fear of the coming war, I've truly enjoyed the nights I've spent in his arms. I've sat with him as he pored over a multitude of scrolls and books. Of course, we've had to take breaks from all of that exhausting study, and I'd like to think I've helped to keep him from becoming too tense.

While stargazing, I've witnessed many falling stars. According to Copper, that can be a good omen, or a harbinger of tragedy. I prefer to think of them as a sign that I'm fated to be with my three dragon men. Maybe it's wishful thinking, but I cling to it anyway.

Fate can be a cruel mistress. There's no guarantee that we'll achieve everything we want to achieve, but we're ready to die trying. Which is why every moment with my men is precious.

Blaze has been working day and night at his forge, creating dozens of newly minted weapons for the soldiers to carry into battle. Apparently, he tailors each weapon to its wielder. Some dragons like their swords to be long and straight for hacking. Others prefer a delicately curving blade called a scimitar, which is supposedly one of the deadliest weapons ever made. That's why the hilts for each blade are different weights, lengths, and shapes. He'd explained this while we snuggled naked in his bed one night.

As the dragons swoop across the darkening sky, Blaze is at the head of the triangular formation. Night comes quickly in the mountains, but I can still clearly see their forms as they sail through the air. Despite their muscular, scaly bulk, they fly with grace.

Blaze twists in the air, and rolls into a steep dive. With his claws, he grips a massive sword with a blade as long as my body. He wields it as if it were made of plastic rather than fifty pounds of steel.

He swoops toward a battalion of dummies. He's so low that his wings brush the dirt, but he doesn't falter. Three of the training dummies fall to the swift swing of his sword. He darts past them before the timbers even hit the ground.

After gaining altitude, he tucks his wings and dives to buzz me on the ground. I duck. My hair dances wildly in the wind. After he passes, he climbs back into the night sky. I could swear that his laughter is raining down from the heavens, but I was always told that dragons can't speak when they're in their dragon form.

I grin. I love that he's still playful considering what we're about to face.

Copper and Ember flash by a moment later. Both of them manage to take out their own wooden practice targets. I find the strength, grace, and beauty of their draconic forms to be as magnificent as their human bodies.

I am in absolute awe of the strength of my men, particularly Blaze. He moves with such liquid grace for someone so massive. Funny, I never would've imagined that something with scales could be sexy, but he is. All three of them are, and I find myself enjoying the sight of them flexing their might on the mock battlefield.

Blaze leads the trio for another pass. This time, they squeeze themselves into a tight formation. With Blaze acting as the head of their spear, they sweep through the rows of training totems, severing faux limbs and reducing the timber bodies into thousands of splinters.

I tilt my head back so I can watch them climb back into the dim sky. They rival the stars in their beauty.

Suddenly, Blaze banks hard. He turns his body into a graceful, curving dive. He plunges from the sky like a bullet. A faint whistle follows him as his body cuts through the air. When it seems as if he's about to impact the ground, he suddenly flares out his enormous black wings. They billow out with air and slow his descent until he floats to the ground.

Before my eyes, his dragon snout shortens into his familiar, handsome human face. Part of my mind wonders where all his extra mass goes when he shifts between forms. There are many theories on the subject, some more researched than others, but ultimately, no one really knows.

Blaze trudges across the practice field, sheathing his massive sword into his equally massive scabbard. He walks toward me with a determined look in his eyes.

"Are you ready for tonight, my love?"

"Yes, I'm ready." I hold up my hand and witch fire dances between my fingers. "I'm ready to do my part. The dragon clan shouldn't have to take on all of the risk to save my town."

He nods, then cocks his head to the side.

"Are you sure you aren't at least a little bit nervous?"

"Of course I'm nervous." I laugh and shake my head. "Truthfully, I want to get this over with so we can enjoy being together without war and destruction hanging over our heads."

Blaze puts his hand on my shoulder. His gaze is gentle.

"That's what I want too." He looks up at the sky. A few stars peek out from the rapidly darkening purple canvas of night. "I wish I had Copper's gift for reading the stars. It would be nice to know if we'll win or not."

"We're going to win." I only wish I was as confident as I sound. I put my hand on top of his and squeeze it tightly.

He leans forward. I meet him and surrender to his kiss. It's the only comfort I can take right now. There's no time for anything else.

When we finally pull apart, he holds me at arm's length. A serious, somber light glistens in his eyes.

"We'll be leaving in two hours." He caresses my cheek with the back of his hand. "Don't worry. The dragon clan has made you wait long enough. We're ready for battle, and we will win."

"I hope so."

"I want you to ride on my back when we go into battle tonight."

"Ride you?" I let out a bark of laughter. "Are you serious?"

"Of course I'm serious." Blaze grins. "Imagine unleashing your magic while riding a fearsome, fire-breathing dragon. It will be legendary."

I consider the idea for a moment. Yes, it would be rather epic to ride into battle on a dragon. And it's not like I haven't been riding Blaze quite a bit lately, although that was while he was in human form. This would be a completely different kind of riding, but it could be just as fun. Well, if we weren't getting blasted with magic at the same time. It will be dangerous for sure, but it might be worth the risk.

"All right, I'll ride on your back when we go into battle." My eyes narrow and I jab my finger into his chest. "But remember, if you drop me, I can't fly. So, I'll be splattered all over the ground."

"I won't drop you." His grim determination fades and is quickly replaced by curiosity. "I've been meaning to ask you something. Are witches really unable to fly?"

"Some witches can. Those that control the element of air. I control fire, so I can't fly. However, there is a legendary potion that will give a witch the power of flight. But, it's not something I'd ever try to create."

"And why is that?" He tilts his head to the side quizzically. "It seems like being able to fly would offer a tremendous strategic advantage."

"I'm sure it would, but the potion comes at a high price." Suddenly I can't look him in the eyes. I'm not proud of some of the darker aspects of witch culture. "The ingredients aren't rare, but to obtain them leaves a stain on your soul."

"What sort of ingredients?"

I sigh and cross my arms over my chest. I shiver even though it's not cold.

"The base comes from the distilled and reduced fat from a young child who died in agony, preferably by fire."

Blaze's jaw drops open. His eyes go as wide as Ember's dinner plates.

"That's fucked up. Who would do something like that?"

"Sybil would." My jaw clenches. "An alternative option is a bone from a living victim. Dark magic's lure is potent. You'd be surprised by what some witches have done to increase their power."

"You would never—"

"Of course not." I'm offended that he would even attempt to ask me that question.

"I'm sorry. I know you'd never try it. I don't know why I even said that. Don't worry, I won't drop you."

"I might be able to use some magic to cushion my fall, but it's not a risk I'd be willing to take."

"And I wouldn't want to risk it either. I'll keep you safe." He kisses me again, and I believe he means it with all of his heart.

The next two torturous hours pass like molasses through a colander. Weapons are distributed to the warriors. For a while it's a wild, jubilant scene as the villagers send their blades through practice arcs. A few sparring sessions commence out of nowhere, which forces crowds of people to suddenly jump back as the dueling dragons spark their blades together in mock combat.

After the clash of steel against steel fades, there are other supplies to be distributed. Each warrior gets a parcel of the food Ember and I prepared.

When the preparations are complete, the council of elders gathers to address the winged battalion. The elderly woman, who serves as the council's spokesperson, eyes each and every warrior individually before speaking.

"For hundreds of years, we have lived in peace on this mountain. I know that many of you did not want to become involved in this war. I know that many of you think it is not our affair."

As if to add emphasis to her words, the rumble of a distant explosion from Bonfire Falls echoes across the mountain side.

"But it *is* our affair. We have secluded ourselves, but we are still a part of this world. Are we going to let innocent blood be shed when we can stop it?"

"No!" A rousing chorus of denial rises over the milling horde of warriors. More than one weapon is stabbed toward the starry sky in defiance.

"Are we going to strike fear into the hearts of our enemies?" she yells.

The warriors roar in acknowledgement.

"Go out and fight as if our village depends on it, because it does."

As the crowd clamors with excitement and determination, the elder smiles. She turns to leave. Her work is done.

Blaze approaches me in this human guise. He hands me a red scale mail shirt. It's like chain mail but without the added weight. I slip it over my hiking gear.

He gazes at me, dressed like a warrior, and I'm not

certain he likes the idea of seeing me charge into battle. He gathers me into a crushing embrace and passionately kisses my mouth.

"After our glorious victory, we will celebrate any way you like."

"I'd like that very much." I peck him on the lips again and then hold him tight.

Reluctantly, we break off the hug so he can shift into dragon form. He drops to all fours and lowers his spine so I can climb aboard. I'm amazed by how smooth and warm his scales are. There's a scale ridge where his head and neck meet. It makes a convenient hand hold.

I'm scared and nervous, but I'm also ready to get my life back. Blaze's muscles bunch up under my rump just before he launches us into the air with a prodigious leap. His wings snap out and flap powerfully, raising us higher into the sky.

Behind us, the other dragons shift and take flight. I squeeze my legs tightly against Blaze's sinuous back and watch as the ground fades beneath us.

Finally, after so much waiting, we're going to the aid of Bonfire Falls. I'm ready to fight to reclaim my town. It's the only way I can keep my family safe and secure a wonderful future for myself and my dragon men.

I'm ready.

CAPTIVE OF THE DRAGONS: CHAPTER 17

ARIADNE

As silhouettes against the full moon, we glide through thin mountain air on leathery wings. We're headed toward the shifter clubhouse on the outskirts of Bonfire Falls because we're hoping they will be the easiest to defeat.

Wind whips my hair back into wild disarray, but I don't care. If I were a dragon shifter, I'd be flying all of the time. I don't know why I haven't asked my men to take me flying at night. If we all survive this, I want to fly across the night sky as much as possible.

Blaze's scaled muscles ripple between my thighs. His expansive wings propel us even faster with each powerful downbeat. Copper and Ember flank us on either side. Their dragon forms are slightly smaller than Blaze's but they're still impressive. If I fall, it's going to be a long drop, but with my three dragon men by my side, I have no doubt one of them will catch me. I've never felt safer.

We travel over rocky mountain cliffs and dense forest. It's a strange feeling, seeing a flock of birds from above.

The birds squawk and make a terrible racket, probably terrified by the massive flight of dragon shifters.

Tonight, the dragons hunt much larger prey.

Or maybe not. Even though Flint has behaved like a total ass, the dragons still want to give him a chance to surrender peacefully. I don't see it happening, but I can't blame the peace-loving dragon clan for wanting to avoid a fight.

Besides, I can see the logic in it. Facing down Sybil is going to be tough, and if we can convince the shifters to join the fight against her, our odds of victory go up exponentially.

Blaze beats his wings hard, leading the cadre in a sharp upward arc to take us over the final ridge. I spot Flint's war camp on the other side.

For a moment, everything is a blur as Blaze buzzes the upper branches of the pine forest. Then we clear the cliff, and I'm shocked at the sheer number of followers Flint has amassed. There are so many of them that the clubhouse can't hope to house them all. Dozens of orange campfires blaze in the night, providing warmth against the chilly mountain air.

At first, we aren't noticed. Blaze flies less than two dozen feet above the heads of the sentries at the camp perimeter. Their gazes and guns rotate everywhere but up.

As we fly over the horde of shifters, I begin to worry that the dragon clan is outnumbered. Since Flint lives in the clubhouse at the center of the war camp, we're going to be surrounded by his people. If things get ugly, we'll be in serious trouble.

When we see the shifter army for what it really is, I don't see vicious men and women who only want to kill. Many are frightened or wounded. Nearly all seem exhausted. The fighting has raged on for weeks. Perhaps it won't be too hard to convince the shifters to join our cause or give up the fight altogether.

We land inside the fence guarding the clubhouse. We're met with nothing but the hardened stares of seasoned campaigners. These men are soldiers by trade, and they aren't likely to experience the battle fatigue of the rank and file.

Still, they're wary enough of the flight of dragon clan warriors that they don't immediately attack. They do surround us, some shifting into bear or wolf form, while others point automatic weapons at us.

Reluctantly, I dismount. Blaze shifts into human form and stands tall. The bear and wolf clan members part to allow Flint's passage. His hard gaze doesn't falter. He's not impressed with our warriors, but I detect a hint of wariness.

Flint stops a dozen feet from Blaze and tucks his thumbs into his belt. The action reveals twin chrome-plated automatic pistols in quick draw holsters. He sneers at Blaze before he speaks.

"What are you doing here, lizard?"

"Flint, we're not here to fight." Blaze sticks his massive sword into the dirt, and holds his hands out, palms up.

"Then you came to the wrong place." Flint and his shifter minions laugh. "This is a war camp. We're here to make war, not peace."

"The war is tearing up Bonfire Falls. Are you too blinded by your lust for power to see it? If this war doesn't stop soon, there will be nothing left of that town." Blaze's words hang in the air for a moment. Flint's lined face screws up into a mask of twisted rage. He can't deny the truth in the blacksmith's words.

"Attack!" Flint's bellow carries across the camp. The shifters surge into action. Flint draws his pistols and takes aim on Blaze. Someone screams *No*, and it takes me a moment to realize it's me.

Quick as a flash of lighting, Blaze snatches up his blade in both hands and sends it into a spin. I've never seen the dragons really unleash their full potential before. I never dreamed he'd be so fast. Bullets ring off his blade, which was forged in dragon fire and is stronger than a diamond. Flint's magazines go empty, and Blaze ceases his furious flurry. He glances my way and begins to shift.

"Get on my back. Quickly."

All around us, the dragon clan are returning to the air. I hop onto Blaze's back. The dragons form a line to defend the perimeter while their companions take flight. The wolf shifters' teeth and the bears' claws are unable to snag warriors who are so nimble and deadly.

Once most of the dragon clan is back in the air, the remaining dragons breathe fire. Suddenly, we're in the eye of a firestorm. The dragons keep the flames coming. Their cheeks bulge and their bellies go hollow. Wolf and bear alike have no choice but to retreat before the inferno, giving the remaining dragons time to get back into the air.

Blaze and I are still on the ground when a new threat emerges. A wolf shifter, who'd flattened himself against the earth to avoid the flames, springs to his feet. Much of the fur on his back is missing. The exposed skin is blackened and charred, but he's already beginning to heal. Blaze's back is turned away from the shifter. My dragon's about to leap into the air and I don't have time to use my magic before the wolf reaches us.

The wolf shifter's salivating, snapping jaw is less than ten feet from us. Suddenly, a sheet of white-hot flames envelops him. Copper breathes out the flame. I've never seen the gentle astronomer looking so fierce and determined. He's not going to let the shifters hurt us.

When Copper's breath is exhausted, he speeds off to gain altitude for another diving attack. Bullets whizz through the air, but he dances through the hail of deadly lead, dodging and weaving as he flies.

We take flight, leaving the smoldering, charred ruin that used to be a wolf clan shifter on the ground. Blaze's powerful wings beat air against the scorched shifter, and it dissolves into a million specks of ash.

While gunfire whizzes through the air around us, Blaze raises us into the sky. A sudden sound, reminiscent of rain hitting a tarp, blasts the air around us. Blaze winces. I look to my left to where his wing has several bleeding wounds in it. The bullets have a hard time penetrating his dense scales, but the thin membranes of his wings are vulnerable.

His angry roar nearly bursts my eardrums.

He maintains our flight with hardly a stutter, soldiering on. He might not have been hurt badly, but he's bleeding. Rage boils in my belly. Flames burst from my hands. The fire transforms from orange to white to blue as I pour my magic into it.

"Blaze, bank hard to your left." My shout barely reaches his ears above the din of battle and the rushing wind. "Give me a shot."

He lets out another roar that splits the air. Even the most fearless bear and wolf shifters hesitate in their struggles. The men firing on us with the automatic weapons pause their barrage just as Blaze heads into a curving turn.

The action tilts his body to the left. His massive wings move out of my way. With a scream of fury, I point my hands at the shifters and let loose the energy I've been building up.

Twin beams of deep blue flame shoot from my hands.

The fire magic is so hot that it ruptures the very air and sets off the loudest thunder crack I've ever heard. I pay no heed to the sound.

Pouring power into my hands, I sweep deadly beams across the line of shifter artillery. Everything they touch is instantly engulfed in flames. A sonic boom reverberates across the mountainside. The men's weapons melt into pools of red-hot magma. There's nothing left but a charred stain on the mountain when men once stood.

"I'm glad you're on our side." Blaze's voice vibrates my whole body.

"You can talk?"

"Of course."

I smirk, so he was laughing at me earlier today. I bend over and kiss his serpentine neck.

"Those shifters shouldn't have hurt my man."

"Remind me never to cross you."

"As if you ever would."

Blaze's draconic laughter joins my snickers as we arc into the air to prepare for another dive.

The dragons use their speed and ability to fly to keep their distance from the shifters. From our viewpoint up here, the fight is hardly fair, but they brought this on themselves.

Blaze swoops down and I'm able to destroy most of the guns. Their bullets were the only real way to hurt the dragons while they're in the air. Without guns, the fight is as good as over.

Or so I think.

Just as we make the turn for another run, a massive chunk of moss-encrusted limestone smashes into a dragon clan shifter. He spirals to the ground and lands in a twitching heap.

As several more boulders join the barrage, I look for

the source of the attack. There are a dozen bear shifters who've formed a line and are hurling every bit of debris at the dragons they can reach. Stones the size of golf carts, fallen logs, and even a motorcycle fill the night sky. Their superior strength must make the task easy.

In the center of the bear shifter line stands Flint. In his bear form, he's absolutely terrifying. He's nearly fifteen feet tall. Enormous muscles bunch beneath his thick coat of fur. The curved claws rasping the rough edges of boulders are the size of my forearm.

"Sweet mother of mercy." My heart sinks. How can anyone stand against such a daunting foe? He flings boulders like they're river pebbles.

"Let's get him." Blaze dives right toward the line of bear shifters, weaving between their deadly missiles with deft grace. We pass less than ten feet above Flint when Blaze unleashes his fiery breath.

Flint holds a boulder the size of a Volkswagen beetle between himself and the sheet of flame. I turn my head back as we pass over, dreading what's coming next even as I attempt to summon magic to stop it.

Below us, Flint takes the massive boulder in his paws and twists his torso. He unfurls his body like a coiled spring and sends the chunk of mountain sailing right toward us.

I summon a lightning bolt, hoping to at least deflect its impact. It does nothing but scorch the surface. Blaze takes the boulder right in the midsection, exploding the air out of his lungs and sending me flying off his back.

"Shit!"

The scorched earth rushes up to squish me into paste. There's no time to use magic to even slow my descent. It seems an eternity has passed, but it's only been a few seconds since this free fall started.

Then, Blaze is diving to save me. His wings tuck to streamline his form so he can cut through the air and catch up. His claws reach out and grab my shoulders. The long talons pierce my skin, but the pain is welcome considering the alternative.

He goes into a wild spin. I cling to his talons. At the last moment, he pulls up to avoid splattering us against the mountain.

Blades of grass tickle my toes as we barely cheat death. At some point my boots fell off. I'm just happy to be alive.

"Get Flint!"

"Are you okay?"

"I'm pissed off!"

Blaze beats his wings and soon we're charging straight at Flint. The line of bear shifters who serve as living catapults have mostly fallen to dragon fire and dragon steel. All around us, dragons have asserted their dominance. The shifter army falls back.

But Flint is still dangerous. He throws himself to the ground to avoid a blast of fire from Blaze's maw.

As we pass overhead, Flint's paw snags Blaze's tail.

I scream as we're thrown to the ground. Blaze takes the worst of it, thudding hard on his belly and getting the wind knocked out of him again. I go on a bouncing, tumbling, bruising ride across the torn battlefield and come to rest hard against a basketball-sized stone jutting up from the earth. A sharp pain drives into my side, and every breath makes it worse. I think I might have broken several ribs.

Copper flies down to attack Flint with his scimitar, but the cagey bear shifter uses his massive claws to deflect the whirling blade. Flint clamps his jaws onto Copper's sword arm and flings him to the turf. As I struggle for breath,

Copper bounces a dozen feet away and lands in a moaning heap.

Flint screams as a blast of fire lashes across his back. He turns to face Ember, who lands and brandishes his sword, which resembles a giant meat cleaver. Flint's back is to me, and he's been terribly wounded by the fire. Bits of charred skin are hanging off his body. However, he's already healing. I've never seen a shifter recover so quickly. It's almost as if he's in league with a witch who has cast a healing spell on him.

I glance around but don't see any witches in the area. There's no magic but my own. I don't know how he's achieved this level of healing so swiftly, and it's terrifying.

Ember can't land a hit on Flint either. The shifter flings him across the clearing.

My vision dims. I struggle back from the precipice of unconsciousness and attempt to gain my footing. Clasping one hand to my side, I silently cheer on Ember.

But my heart sinks as I realize that Flint is a better fighter. Ember attacks again, but I can tell he's beginning to tire. Flint manages to strike his temple with one massive paw. Ember goes down. His eyes are barely open and blood trickles down his face.

Blaze struggles to rise but has barely managed to lift his head off the ground. Flint strides over and plants his foot across the back of Blaze's neck, forcing him back to the turf.

Flint's horrifying gaze falls on me. His jaw opens wide. I'm shocked to realize he could fit almost my entire body inside his gaping maw. He's going to kill Blaze. And then I'm next.

Screaming in rage and terror, I throw everything I have at Flint. Lightning arcs out of my left hand, while a continuous gout of blue-hot flame pours out of my right.

Flint dodges the attack by bounding away from Blaze's prone form.

The pain in my side grows worse, and I have to cease my attack. A groan of agony escapes my clenched teeth as Flint gallops on all fours across the battlefield toward me.

I only have one chance. Summoning up my remaining strength, I clasp my hands in front of me and build up a massive charge of electricity.

My hair stands on end.

My primal scream splits the air.

Flint's massive jaw opens wider, showing the pink of his throat.

A bolt of pure white lightning streaks out of my clasped hands, shooting directly into his mouth. His eyes go wide, and his skeletal system flashes into view as the tremendous energy courses through his body. He's held airborne by my energy for several seconds before he collapses in a steaming heap.

I run to Blaze's side. He shakes off his injuries, which are already beginning to heal. His wing isn't even bleeding any more.

"Come, my brothers." His voice rouses Copper and Ember who climb back to their feet. "Let's finish off the bear and wolf shifters once and for all."

I glance around the battlefield. It's almost over. The dragons have backed the remaining wolves and bears into a huddled mass in the center of the camp. They're being held at bay by bouts of flame and sharp steel.

"No, Blaze." I clasp his forearm. "Don't do it. Please, give them a chance to surrender."

He lets out a low growl, but then turns to address the miserable mob of defeated shifters.

"Listen up, furry ones. If you want to live, you'll join us in the fight against the witches—*only* the witches under

Sybil's command. If you help us stop the war, we will grant you your lives." Blaze points his sword to the heavens and unleashes a geyser of flame into the sky. "Let any of you brave enough to accept my offer rally behind this blade."

One by one, the shifters come forward and fall into line behind us. I can't stop smiling, even though the side of my body is in agony. We've won a major battle.

But the war isn't over yet.

ARIADNE

Blaze flares out his wings to slow our descent as we land in the Bonfire Falls town square. My heart sinks with despair at the sight of so many buildings in ruins. The pharmacy has been burnt to the ground, while city hall's marble dome stands fractured in two. Some of the dark, twisted forms among the rubble are possibly bodies, but I'm afraid to take a closer look.

In the center of the square sits a circular fountain roughly the size of a tractor wheel. The water only jets up about six to seven feet, but it has a nice colored light show at night. Many residents grumble about it because you have to drive around it and take turns to avoid a traffic pile-up, but it's a landmark that no one wants to see destroyed.

That's why I sigh in despair at what Sybil has done to it. Instead of a cheery light show, the fountain is sputtering thick, viscous blood. That sort of thing happens when you practice dark magic. Fields go barren, women miscarry, rivers turn to blood, that sort of thing. Usually the effects are temporary, but she must've worked some foul magic. This level of evil takes unimaginable power.

Sybil walks into the circle. She's flanked by two wolf shifters. Perhaps one of them is the same shifter who stalked me on my way out of Bonfire Falls. It's hard to tear my eyes away from the witch standing between them. Her eyes have taken on a sickly amber hue. The black veins on her face stand out in stark relief to her ghostly skin.

"Ariadne." She smiles at me. A cold shiver runs down my spine. Her sinister gaze takes in Blaze, Ember, and Copper. "And you've brought your men. How delightful. Killing you alone would have posed no challenge whatsoever. I've had my eyes on you in the dragon village. The night I ran into you sneaking out of town, I knew you were up to something."

"Stop this war, now." My voice quivers a bit with fear, but I stand firm. The presence of my dragon men gives me strength. "Even now your army of dark magic is being defeated by the combined might of all three shifter clans. It's over."

"What do I care if you kill those petty bitches?" Sybil shrugs. "I don't need them. I don't need anyone. Look at this fountain, witch. Isn't it beautiful?"

"It's sacrilege." My hands clench into fists. "What have you done?"

Sybil examines her fingernails nonchalantly, and then buffs them on her bodice.

"Nothing but trifling feats, darling. A few dozen shifter sacrifices to the Darkness has been more than enough to give me all the power I need. In time, I'll wipe *all* shifters from the face of the Earth."

A few dozen? My knees go weak, but Copper's claw steadies me.

"You're bold, considering you're far outnumbered." Blaze grips his sword in both hands.

Sybil smirks and dismisses him with the flick of her wrist.

"Give up while you still can." Ember steps forward and brandishes his weapon.

"Enough. Let's take her out." Smoke trails out of Copper's nostrils and he flexes his wings.

Before I can shout a warning, the three of them charge forward. I don't like the way Sybil just stood there and let us approach. She's way too calm for a small woman with three gigantic dragons bearing down on her with blood-stained weapons.

We're missing something. Something important. I just don't know what it is.

Sybil draws a rune in the air. The smoking shadow hangs in place, neither moving, nor dissipating. I don't recognize the rune, so I hesitate for a split second.

While I'm trying to decide what to do, she speaks a single word of power in a dark and guttural tongue. The rune expands into a moving wall of darkness. It envelops the three charging dragons. When it diffuses and silver moonlight once again reveals the square. Copper, Ember, and Blaze all lie unconscious on the pavement in their vulnerable human forms.

"Pathetic." Sybil casts a predatory smile at me. "As for you, my dear, I think I'm going to enjoy swallowing your soul and gobbling up all of that sweet, delicious power."

My jaw sets hard. Blazing flames envelop my hands. The witch fire extends until my arms are covered in blue flames.

Spreading my arms wide, I focus my power, shaping it to obey my will.

With a shout, I bring my arms together, flinging the

flames toward her. They expand in mid-flight to form a rushing wall of fire.

The twin wolf shifters barely get out a brief yip before they are incinerated, but a translucent black aura flickers around Sybil, and my fire is deflected.

She glances at the two charred corpses by her side and chuckles.

"You must be dreaming if you think such low-level fire magic can touch me."

I do my best not to let despair show on my face. That had been one of my more potent spells and it hadn't so much as singed a single hair on her head. I'm still holding back my most powerful magic, but I'd at least expected my attack to drain some of her energy.

Panicked, I throw lightning bolts with both hands. Sybil remains still as a statue as the energy crackles about her shield. When I stop the attack, panting and weary, the ground about her is blackened with scorch marks from the lightning, but my foe is unscathed.

"Is it my turn now?" Sybil smiles sweetly. "We shouldn't be fighting each other, my sweet. We're twins in spirit, opposite sides of the same coin."

"I'm *nothing* like you." My voice is guttural when I shout my denial.

Her eyes widen, and I sense her amusement growing.

"Oh, really?" She bats her eyes at me and smirks. "Do you not yearn for the love of three dragons?"

My jaw falls open. How did she know that? Although she'd admitted to spying on me while I was in the dragon village, how could she know what's in my heart?

A sudden stab of pain slices through my head.

"Stop it." I hold my head in my hands, trying to will her out of my consciousness. "Stay out of my head."

"I know everything I need to know about you. I know

your secrets. I know about the time you burned down Mr. Cleary's barn because you were practicing forbidden fire magic. You weren't even old enough to use it, and yet you did. Why?" Her voice throbs in my head, much louder than humanly possible. "Because you're drawn to the power. You're just like me."

"Please, stop." I don't want her digging into my memories and cherry picking all of the times I've failed to live up to my parents' standards.

"You're a spoiled, arrogant, *greedy* witch." Sybil laughs. I fear my skull will fracture under the thunderous sound of her mirth. "Look at you, not satisfied with one lover. You must have three."

"Don't talk about them." My voice comes through gritted teeth, but it sounds stronger. I'm pushing her out of my head. It's not easy, but it's working, and suddenly she doesn't seem to loom so largely in my mind. "I've made mistakes. Everyone has. But you? You're a murderous monster."

Her mind battles to take over my own. We're fighting for dominance. If she manages to take over my mind, she'll be able to control me and she'll use my magic against my men.

I bend at the waist. My hands clench my head. I summon every ounce of willpower I have.

"Get. Out. Of. My. *Head*."

A sharp sound akin to glass breaking reverberates through the air. Sybil stumbles back, holding her own head. A trail of black blood leaks from her nose. Her eyes narrow to mere slits. Black lips peel back from ivory white teeth as her face becomes a mask of rage.

"You think I'm a monster?" She holds her hands close together in front of her chest. An oily globe appears between her fingers. It ripples like a soap bubble. "Monsters kill pretty young women, don't they?"

I'm not about to let her throw that thing at me, whatever it is. With a cry of anger, I send a streak of lightning with my left hand while the outstretched fingers of my right hand produce a jet of fire. Sybil ducks into a crouch, displaying more nimbleness than I'd expected, and my attack misses.

She thrusts her hands at me, and the oily bubble shoots my way. I have no time to summon fire, so I hold up my hand. The bubble splashes against my palm and washes over it, spattering over my face. Like a sinister amoeba, it morphs its mass to fully cover my head, cutting off my air. It smells like dried blood and urine, and it's packing my nostrils and mouth. My hands scrape ineffectually at the gooey substance as Sybil laughs, her voice sounds like it's coming from underwater.

"I always thought the best death was the one longest suffered. I'll enjoy watching you die, Ariadne."

I fall to my knees, struggling in vain as the revolting blob chokes me to death.

As my vision dims, I call upon my magic in a desperate bid to save myself. I produce a low flame across both hands and move them closer together. It takes a moment, but soon, the bubble peels open like melted plastic. I gratefully snort in air.

Sybil sneers, and hurls twin bolts of dark energy from her hands. I barely get a defensive barrier off in time to stop it.

While my fire burns hot, her eldritch beams are as cold as the dark side of the moon. Steam rises into the air where our energies meet.

"You can't keep this up forever." Sybil's boast sounds a bit strained as she grits her teeth together.

"Neither—can—*you.*" I push back against her power, but my flames are soon quenched by her dark magic.

"Fall, little witch." Sybil walks forward, intensifying her attack. "*Fall.*"

I'm losing. She's just too powerful, and I can't hope to stand against her. Of course I'm afraid of dying, but what really drives me to despair is the thought that after she's done with me she'll likely finish off Blaze, Copper, and Ember. Or make them her slaves, like the wolf shifters. I'm going to lose everything if I lose this battle.

"Give it up, you little fool. There is no greater magic than the power of death itself," she kisses.

No. She's wrong. There is a form of magic that can transcend even death. The magic of love, the most powerful magic of all. This isn't the dark, manipulative love magic used by some witches. This is the pure magic of true love itself. Maybe I'm not doomed. Maybe there's a bright future awaiting me, one filled with love and happiness.

I can't stand against her for my own sake, but for the sake of the three men I love. My parents are also counting on me. I sense their vibrant life forces coming from our home. They're still in hiding. They're still safe, for now. But I must end this fight with Sibyl to have any hope of ending this war.

I find new purpose. Her relentless assault has driven me to one knee. Gradually, straining from the effort, I stand. Sybil is only a few feet away. Her face twists with hatred, but she can't move any closer.

Screaming, I expand my fire shield until it forces her energy back and envelops Sybil entirely. Her shield holds, but she's thrown off balance enough to cease her attack.

"You stupid witch. You think that's enough to defeat me? I'm not finished yet." A sneer mars her sinister face.

"Neither am I."

I pull my hands back near my solar plexus, the energy nexus of my body. Magic pulses through my being, fueled by the love I feel for my men and my parents. If I can harness this love and propel it into my magic, then Sybil won't hurt them ever again.

Lightning sparks around my hands as I create the same electromagnetic field I'd accomplished in the training ravine. Only this time, my target isn't a wooden practice totem. Sybil's brow furrows in confusion as she watches my magic at work.

"What are you doing?" Her voice is the hiss of a serpent. "I don't know that spell."

"I'll teach you."

I open myself up and unleash every ounce of my power. Last time, I'd created a moderate-sized maelstrom of swirling debris and barely contained energy. This time, it expands to the size of a truck and keeps going. I'm forced to raise my arms over my head to keep it from touching the ground.

Sybil drops to a crouch and tries to scurry away to avoid being dragged into the swirling nexus.

I ignite the maelstrom. I hurl the magical shitstorm right at her desperately scrambling form. The street melts into molten lava as the fireball shoots toward her.

For a few moments, she's visible as a silhouette in the center of the blazing cyclone as her shield manages to fend off the deadly energy. Then the shield flickers and sputters away.

She gets out one final scream before she bursts into flames.

The fireball rolls on, melting the foulness of the fountain away and demolishing what's left of city hall. A long, heavy rumble of thunder reverberates for almost a minute as I sink to my knees in the street, heady with my unlikely victory.

For a time, I just lay there and pant. I won. I defeated a witch consumed by dark magic. I can't believe it.

Blaze staggers to his feet them helps me to mine. I throw my arms around his neck and hug him for all I'm worth. Then Copper joins the embrace, and then Ember. We're all just standing there holding each other while what's left of the town burns around us. The sounds of warfare stop. The other witches who fought with Sybil are nowhere to be seen. They've fled the town, hopefully never to return.

Approaching footsteps makes us all wary. My dragon men brandish their weapons. I summon fire into my hands as a hazy figure appears in the smoke.

"How could she have lived through that?" Ember's voice holds a heavy note of fear, which is mirrored in my heart.

That *was* my best shot. If Sybil survived that—

My mother steps into view. I sigh with relief.

"Mom." I run across the cracked pavement and gather her up in my arms. She's lost a little weight but seems otherwise unharmed. A moment later, my father joins us. I hug them so hard that I never want to let them go.

Blaze clears his throat, and I sheepishly break the embrace with my parents.

"Mom, Dad." I gesture at the men. "These are my—my mates. The big hulking one is Blaze. The one with the dimples is Copper. And the guy comparing my looks to Mom's is Ember."

"I am not." Ember holds up his hands in supplication to my parents. "I swear."

"Nice to meet you." A radiant smile lights up my

mother's face. I think she's charmed by these handsome men.

Dad seems suspicious, but he holds his tongue while I make introductions.

"I told you not to run off," Dad finally says.

"I'm sorry. I knew we needed help, so I went to the dragon village."

"You could have been killed."

"But she wasn't." Blaze hooks an arm around my waist and pulls me close. "She's a warrior who rides dragons into battle. She's a legend."

"I wouldn't go that far," I mutter.

"Your father and I are just glad to have you home at last. We were so worried."

I wince, and glance back at my dragon men.

"I'm sorry that I worried you. I just wanted to help."

"And you did," my father acknowledges. "Welcome home, honey."

"Actually, well, I'm not staying."

"Why not?" Mom asks.

"I'm going to stay in the dragon clan's village for a while. We have some things to work out."

"I guess that's for the best. It's going to take some time before the town is rebuilt and things return to normal." My mother sighs. "Besides, I have the feeling you're in good hands."

I flush. She has no idea how good those hands are, and right now, I want them all over me.

**CAPTIVE OF THE DRAGONS:
CHAPTER 19**

ARIADNE

T he normal morning sounds of the dragon village are absent when I awaken in Blaze's bed. No one is thatching a roof, or milking goats, or preparing a fishing line for the myriad of crystal-clear streams which crisscross the mountain. It's silent. Peace has finally returned to the mountains. Bonfire Falls is safe, and so is the dragon clan. After the events of the previous day, the entire village is enjoying the well-deserved opportunity to sleep in.

When I originally imagined all three of my guys taking me to bed at the same time, sleep was nowhere on the menu. But when we'd returned from Bonfire Falls, we'd all been too exhausted to do anything but sleep.

Right now, I'm nestled up with Blaze on my right side, Copper on my left, and Ember lays between my thighs with his head in my lap. We're all naked. We'd crawled into bed with the intention of staying up all night, but after a minute, we all agreed that our sexy celebration could wait until morning.

After a gloriously peaceful night's, what I want right

now has everything to do with being in bed, and nothing to do with being asleep.

A cheeky grin plays across my lips as I consider the three slumbering dragon men. Which one should I wake first?

Ember's soft breath warms the inside of my thighs, and he mumbles a bit in his sleep. I think I hear my name. Should I awaken him and make his dream reality?

Blaze's massive chest provides part of the cushion on which I lay, and his arm is tucked up around my shoulder. The blacksmith of Dragon Village is the true alpha of the group, but does that mean he gets to be the first in line for our morning romp?

Copper lays on his stomach. His arm is flung across my midsection, and his fingers are splayed around my navel. He's the sweetest of the three, but do I want dessert before dinner?

Maybe I'm going about this in totally the wrong way. Maybe I should just wake them all up at once.

For a time, I lay pretending to consider my options, but really, I'm just enjoying being here with my men. I can't believe I've gotten this lucky. Any one of them would have made my life complete, but to have all three? Sometimes I wonder when I'm going to wake up from this wonderful fantasy come true.

Eventually, I realize there's no use in pretending I'm going to do anything other than wake them all at once.

Using my magic, I summon the flame effigy of a rooster, which perches on the footboard of Blaze's bed. With a flap of its fiery wings, it extends it throat and opens it maw. It crows a bit louder than I'd been expecting. I guess I'm projecting my impatience for cock of the non-flaming variety.

The men stir and gradually gain their senses.

"That was an epic battle for the ages." Blaze smiles and squeezes me tighter.

"Indeed." Copper nods his assent. "I've finally figured out why the red comet was streaking across the night sky."

"Oh?" I tilt my head.

"It prophesied the arrival of our warrior goddess."

"Oh, don't flatter me." My cheeks redden at the heartfelt compliment.

"Yes. Ariadne was most impressive last night when she was saving all of our asses." Ember stretches and yawns, and his speech is garbled by the act.

"Did you not see the way I burned our enemies?" Blaze glares at him, a miffed frown crosses his lovely features.

"I did." Ember grins mischievously. "I also saw you get blasted back into your human form and lay there moaning and stunned while our resident pyro witch roasted Sybil with the biggest damn fireball seen since the dinosaurs got wiped out."

Copper holds up his index finger and clears his throat.

"Actually, they didn't all get wiped out. They turned into birds."

"Oh, come on." Blaze points at the flaming cock on the baseboard, which I have yet to dismiss. "You're telling me that a skinny chicken's great-great-great grandfather was a T-Rex—Hey! Your bird is scorching the wood."

"Oh, I'm sorry." I hold up my hand, fingers extended and palm facing the bird. When I close my fist, the flaming cock snuffs out as if smothered. I wince at the sight of the little black bird tracks now charred into his headboard. "I'll get you another one."

"No need." Blaze shrugs as if it does not matter. "We'll just build another bed—one large enough to accommodate all of us."

"A new day is dawning over Bonfire Falls. They'll enjoy peace for the first time in months." Copper glances out the window at the morning sun.

"I hope it doesn't take them long to clean it all up," Ember says.

"They have magic on their side. They'll be able to restore a lot of it within days. Some things may take longer, like that fountain." I wrinkle my nose for a moment before smiling. "I think we should celebrate our glorious victory."

"How should we celebrate?" Blaze asks.

"I could cook a huge celebratory feast." Ember perks up immediately.

"We should consult the stars and see if a celebration would be in alignment with our best possible destiny." Copper rubs his chin thoughtfully.

"Guys." I put my face in my palm. "That's not what I meant."

"Then what do you mean?" Blaze arches an eyebrow at me.

When I grin, light dawns in his eyes. He leans his head in and kisses my neck. My eyes flutter shut, and I tilt my head back, enjoying the amazing feel of his lips on my sensitive skin.

Copper's hands slide up my belly to cup my breasts. His massaging of the tender, pliant mounds sends tendrils of fires through my whole body. I have to be careful not to set the whole bed on fire.

Ember takes advantage of his position to roll onto his belly and push my thighs apart. He inhales deeply and a delighted grin spreads across his face.

"I know what I'd like to eat for breakfast."

"Oh God." His sexy grin makes me instantly wet. His

tongue flicks faster than a butterfly's wings and without warning, I'm wracked with my first orgasm.

Blaze feathers kisses down my neck, then moves out to my shoulder. I wonder what he's up to. Isn't he moving in the wrong direction?

He takes my wrist, caresses the skin softly, and then holds it up to the headboard. Soon I feel the familiar braided cord which had once bound me to the bed. He never took it off, it seems.

Once I realize he's tying me the bed, I laugh softly. When my hands are secure, he moves down to tie my ankles apart.

"You've wanted this from day we met, haven't you?" I challenge.

"Maybe." His grin betrays his nonchalance.

Copper squeezes both of my breasts together which places my nipples mere inches apart. He takes advantage of this and runs his hot mouth and tongue all over my sensitive nubs. The way he just manipulates my body and makes it do what he wants is a huge turn on.

Ember continues to lick and suck my pussy. He uses his soft lips to press against my clit. I'm already well on my way toward another orgasm, or maybe I just haven't come down from the first one.

Now that Blaze is done tying me down, he moves back onto the bed. The springs squeak under his massive weight. He kneels near my head and shows me his massive, rock hard cock.

"Is this what you want?"

I look up at him with half lidded eyes. Ember's pussy licking and Copper's wickedly sexy mouth make me come, and I'm too caught up to respond to Blaze.

An orgasmic scream rips from my mouth. I'm unable to speak as my body quivers in ecstasy. I thrash as far as the ropes will allow. My body arches toward the ceiling as much as possible with Copper still laying across my chest and kissing my tits.

"Since you can't tell me how much you want me, show me," Blaze says.

I try to put my mouth on the purple head of his throbbing cock, but he moves it away teasingly. I laugh, enjoying the game. I just want to worship his cock. Blaze straddles my face, allowing me to kiss from the bottom of his shaft down to his balls.

Blaze lets me suck him for several minutes before pulling his cock away. I whimper at the loss of it.

He walks around to the base of the bed. It takes a moment for the guys to coordinate their efforts, but I'm quite impressed at the way they're all working together so hard to please me.

Copper moves up from my breasts and kisses me on the mouth. I crane my neck, trying to mash my lips into his. Our tongues swirl in each other's mouths.

Ember pivots his hips to the side and changes position so he's eating my pussy from the top. My scream echoes off the bedroom wall as I come yet again.

His face is still conveniently out of the way of Blaze's cock. Blaze presses the head between my slick pussy lips. I let out a long, animalistic groan when it fills me completely.

Copper slides his tongue deeper into my mouth.

They're all controlling me, yet they're using that control to induce the most wonderful sensations I've ever known. It's odd, but I've never felt safer or more cared for than I do right now, tied to the bed and at their mercy.

At last, overwhelmed by the trio's ministrations, I come hard. I scream, thrash, and quiver wildly as they watch with delighted smiles. It pleases them that they've pleased me.

While I float in post orgasmic bliss, they untie me. Copper strokes my hair out of my face gently and smiles down at me as I lay prone on my back.

"Did you have a good time?"

"Have a good time?" I scoff. "You make it sound like it's over."

I reach out and wrap my hand around his rock-hard shaft. I rise into a sitting position and climb into his lap, facing him. He raises up my hips a bit and maneuvers his cock into position. As I slide down his shaft, my eyes squeeze tightly shut. He lowers me slowly until I'm seated in his lap.

He embraces me around the small of the back, helping to hold me steady. I grind my hips into him, swiveling them just the way I like it. Copper gasps, his face is strained as he tries to hold himself back.

Sitting at the foot of the bed, Ember grins from where he's watching us.

"Damn, Copper, are you fucking her or is she fucking you?"

I turn a half-lidded gaze on him and speak intermittently between thrusts.

"Shut—up—you're—next."

Blaze's rumbling chuckle fills up the room and he slaps Ember on the back loudly.

"Better get yourself ready, huh?"

Ember grins sheepishly, and then wraps his hand around his cock, intently watching my face as I bounce up and down in Copper's lap. The thought of him jerking off to me is intoxicating.

I arch my back. My hair brushes the floor while Copper holds me steady on his lap. My legs wrap around his waist and the new position lets him drive his cock in even deeper. The head directly hits my g-spot, and I come in a screaming, thrashing orgasm.

Copper pulls me into his arms, and we share a lengthy embrace.

I peer over his shoulder at Ember and grin.

"You didn't think you were going to get off easy, did you?"

He shrugs, cocking his head to the side.

"Well, I'd hoped that I wouldn't."

I kiss Copper before crawling off his lap. He lays back and smiles as he watches me move towards Ember.

I crawl on around the bed on all fours until I'm directly in front of Ember. Positioning myself so my head faces away from him, I lift my ass in the air, then lower my face to the mattress.

"What are you waiting for?" I wriggle my ass around in circles as Copper and Blaze chuckle.

Ember eagerly crawls onto the bed, kneeling behind me. I arch my back as he eases into me until he's balls deep. He grips my hips.

"Are you ready?" His whisper is low and husky in my ear.

"Oh, yeah."

Ember's steady, low grunts accompany each powerful yet smooth stroke. My hands twist in the sheets as my loud moans split the air. He slams his hips into me ever faster, until our mutual cries of passion fill the air.

I grind my rear into him, desperate to have him as deep inside of me as possible. Finally, I scream as my body is wracked with one of the biggest orgasms I've ever experienced. He roars as he comes, and we tumble into a mass of writhing limbs.

Soon, all four of us are cuddling on the bed together.

For a long time, we just lay there, basking in the afterglow of our wild passionate tryst.

"I love you," I murmur. "All of you. I love you, Blaze, and I love you, Copper, and I love you, Ember. I can't choose so please don't make me."

"You don't have to choose. You can have us all. I love you." Blaze strokes my cheek and kisses me softly on the lips. "I don't care what strings come attached to it, I want to be with you."

"I love you, Ariadne the fire witch." Copper snuggles up next to me with his head on my belly. "It was in the stars all along, if I'd bothered to look."

"I love you, and I don't care if I have to share." Ember smiles at me and brushes an errant strand of hair out of my eyes.

I feel so warm, and so content in this moment. Perhaps we have a lot of things to work out, such as where we're going to live, but I know we can work it all out.

Because love really is the strongest magic in the world.

CAPTIVE OF THE DRAGONS: CHAPTER 20

ARIADNE

Dad pulls his four-doored sedan onto the grassy shoulder of the dirt road we've been following as it winds through the mountains. Thanks to aerial recon, we know this is the closest you can get to the dragon clan village by driving. It will still be a half-mile trek through wilderness, but Blaze found a game trail I can follow the rest of the way.

"Well, this is it." I exit the car, and the old familiar back seat that I'd ridden in since I was a child. I'm going to miss it, and my parents, but the time has come for me to start my new life. I'll visit them from time to time, and of course they will always be welcome in the village.

"Are you sure you only needed to pack one bag?" My mother frowns as she exits the passenger side and stands next to me on the road.

"The village is quite efficient. They produce everything I need, so why pack what I don't need?"

My father harrumphs from behind the steering wheel.

"I still don't know how you can live without electricity.

If I can't watch the Vikings play or watch *Jeopardy*, count me out."

"Your daughter is about to move out of town, and you're going to just sit there in the car?" Mother throws up her hands and glares at my father from outside the car.

Dad breaks out in a sweat, and he stumbles over his defense. "Ah, well, you know, it's been a rough couple of months, and anyway my corns—"

"Don't even mention your corns. You get out here and give your daughter a hug and tell her you love her this instant."

Driven by finely honed self-preservation instincts, my father hastily exits the car. He joins us on the shoulder of the road. He gives me a tight hug and kisses the top of my head.

"If those boys don't take good care of you, tell me. I'll give them a good thumping."

I laugh and squeeze.

"They're good to me, Dad. But thanks."

"You take care." My mother joins the embrace, and we stand there as a family for a sweet moment.

Then it's time to leave.

I linger next to the car even after my parents have gotten back inside. My heart is heavy as I watch them drive away, but it won't be long before I see them again. I could never turn my back on my family.

As dusk rapidly approaches, I depart. I hum as I hike through the woods. This is it, the start of my new life with Ember, Blaze, and Copper. I couldn't be happier, even though I will miss my parents. Luckily, they're just on the other side of the mountain.

It's good to have a hometown to return to from time to time, but the fact of the matter is that I no longer belong in Bonfire Falls. I've found where I truly belong in the world, and it's with the dragon clan in their village on the mountain.

A smile spreads over my face when the first whiff of Blaze's forge fire reaches my nostrils. I'm almost there. I'm almost home to my men.

This time when I come out of the woods, I don't have to worry about running into an angry dragon. The clan has accepted me into their fold. Several villagers wave to me as I walk through town toward the new home Blaze, Ember, and Copper have constructed for us. I wave back.

All is peaceful once again, both in Bonfire Falls and here in the village. It had taken some time to clean up after the war, both figuratively and literally. City Hall has been temporarily set up in an unused wing of the segregated school I used to teach in. The teacher who took my spot truly loves the kids, both the witches and the shifters. I'm glad she'll carry on the tradition of teaching acceptance of all kinds of people.

I come around the side of the dragon clan council meeting chamber and spot my new home. When I'd left to visit my parents, it hadn't been complete yet. My mouth gapes open at the sheer size of it. It's huge and dwarfs the homes the four of us lived in before.

Blaze has moved his forge to the southern corner of the structure. Although I can't see him yet, I can hear him hammering away on a project. A gracefully arched dome sits atop the middle of the home. It's a planetarium for Copper to practice his celestial divination. Ember, of course, still cooks in the communal dining hall, but he has an expansive private kitchen on the first floor of the house. He plans to experiment with tasty new recipes and let me have the first taste of everything he creates.

As I approach the ornately carved front door, it swings open. Copper appears. He's carrying a mass of star charts and scrying devices in his arms. His eyes widen when he sees me. He gives me one of his charming, dimpled grins.

"Welcome home." He sets everything he's carrying down. When he spreads his arms wide, I abandon my pack in the dirt. I throw my arms around him in a tight embrace. Our kiss lingers as we continue to cuddle in each other's arms.

"Thank you." I reach up and stroke my hand across his cheek. He's so incredibly handsome. I can't wait to get naked with him again. With all of them.

"So, were they able to find a replacement for you at the segregated school?" Copper tilts his head to the side and quickly adds. "Not that anyone could replace you, of course, but I mean, did they find another teacher?"

"Yes, they did." I sigh. "There's not much industry in Bonfire Falls these days, so there were a lot of qualified candidates to choose from."

The sound of quick footsteps draws our attention. Ember comes outside, dusting flour off his hands.

"Is that Ariadne?" He steps into the sunlight and his eyes light up when he sees me. "I missed you."

I go to him and we kiss. He tastes sweet, like he's been baking blackberry pies. I hope that's true because I'm famished.

Copper seems to be happy that I'm happy, and not the least bit jealous. As we navigate this polyamorous relationship, his ability to keep the peace will be essential. I doubt we'll squabble much, but he'll be there to smooth things over if anyone gets their scales in a twist.

Ember holds me at arm's length and gives me a warm smile.

"Can I give you the grand tour?"

"I'd be delighted."

We link arms. Copper and Ember lead me across the

threshold. I whistle at the sight of the bright and airy open concept first floor. Downstairs consists of a kitchen, dining room, den, and a study for me to practice my witchcraft. New, heavily polished wooden furniture with goose down cushions decorates every room. Apparently, members of the community donated the furniture to help us start our new life together. It's very sweet of the villagers to be so welcoming.

A spiral staircase winds up to a second floor.

"This is wonderful." I sigh, while I take it all in. "It's so spacious. I can't believe I get to live here. It's like a dream."

"Wait until you see upstairs." Copper tugs on my arm. "Come on."

The skylight in his observatory casts oddly geometric shadows around the room, which makes his devices seem even more mysterious. He has nearly twice the space he had before, but he's managed to fill it with all kinds of books and star maps.

"This is amazing."

"I ordered a telescope from a guy I trade with. Soon, we'll be able to look at more than just stars, we'll be able to see constellations far out into the universe."

"I can't wait."

"Neither can I. Can I show you the bedroom?" He grins and my belly clenches with desire.

The three of us head into the bedroom. A massive circular mattress dominates the room. There is with plenty of space for the four of us to lay on it together. There are also four doors which lead to walk-in closets in each corner of the room, one for each of us.

"This looks like heaven." I can't resist diving into the middle of the mattress and rolling around.

"Is it comfortable enough?" Copper asks.

"Yes." I stretch out and can't help but imagine all the ways we could use this bed.

I blush when I see that there are ropes dangling from four quadrants of the bed. I'm sure that was Blaze's idea. Dirty dragon.

"Come on." Ember offers me his hand and assists me as I climb off the bed. "Let's go tell Blaze that you're here."

I'm surprised when we don't head for the spiral staircase but instead walk down the hall. At the end of the hall, there's a door which leads to a balcony. A separate outdoor staircase spirals up to connect the ground floor to the balcony.

"This is amazing." I step out and enjoy the sights and sounds coming from the village below.

Copper comes up beside me and puts his arm over my shoulder. Ember joins me on the other side. I lean into him and squeeze him tightly.

Below us, the hammering stops. Blaze peers up and wipes sweat from his eyes. The late afternoon sun is right in his eyes, so he can't quite see us.

"What's going on up there?" he asks.

"Blaze, I'm home." My voice is sweet as honey as I wave at him slyly.

"You're back." He drops his hammer and takes the stairs two steps at a time. He rushes up and sweeps me into his arms with a crushing hug.

"Stop, you're all sweaty," Copper says.

"Yeah." Ember adds. "And you're getting soot all over her clothes."

"All the better to get her out of them while they're clean." Blaze places me back on my feet, then plants a smoldering kiss on my lips. The taste of his salty sweat is intoxicating.

"How do you like the house?" Blaze asks.

"I love it." I break away from his embrace and gesture at the grand home. "I can't wait to show my parents. You know, they want to come up next week for the Dragon Festival."

"That's a wonderful idea." Copper squeezes my shoulder and smiles. "I can't wait to show them around our village. Who knows, maybe they won't want to leave."

I laugh at that idea and place my hand on top of his.

"My dad would never be able to do that. He'd die if he couldn't see the Vikings on a regular basis. Though he'll probably like your homemade meals."

"I'll prepare a feast for your parents, one that will make them never want to leave." Ember offers a bow and I laugh.

"I know you will." I take a deep breath and feel tension across my chest. There's something I need to say to them. "Guys, I hope you're ready for our life together. As in really, really ready. Because it's about to get real."

"Really?" Ember laughs at his own joke, but Blaze and Copper glare him into silence. He clears his throat and speaks once more. "I'm ready for our new life. I love you."

"I love you too." Blaze nods sincerely and crosses his arms over his chest. "I want a new life with you, with all of you."

"And I love you too, my fiery witch." Copper takes my hand in his and kisses it. "I'm ready for whatever our new life holds."

"That's good." I nod, as I build my courage. "That's good, because I have some major news."

"So, tell us already." Ember laughs.

"Well, I wanted to wait until the Dragon Festival, but I can't hold it in that long." I take a deep breath and then blurt, "I'm pregnant."

For a split second their eyes widen in shock, and then

they all exchange gazes. I'm not sure what to expect, but I'm fearing the worst. Will they fight over who is the biological father?

"That's great." Blaze pulls me into his arms, then releases his grip as if he's afraid to break me in two. "A baby. I can't wait to teach our child how to melt iron."

"When did it happen? It had to have been after the battle, or the next day. Let's see, carry the two—does that make your due date in September? No, October. Wouldn't it be a fine coincidence if the baby were born on Halloween? A witch's child born on Halloween is perfect. I have to get to work. I have to make a star chart and forecast the baby's future." Copper abruptly ends his long-winded speculation. The rest of us try not to burst out laughing at his exuberance.

"You know what?" Ember asks. "This occasion calls for one thing and one thing only—cake."

Our chorus of laughter echoes across the village. Joy builds inside of me until I'm ready to burst. I've always wanted a family of my own, but it never seemed like it would happen. And now, it has. I have not one, but three heartfelt relationships, and a child on the way. Despite how traumatic the journey was to get to this point, I'm the happiest woman in the world. I can't wait to spend the rest of my life with my dragons.

CAPTIVE OF THE VAMPIRES:
CHAPTER 1

AZEALIA

Dawn. When life rests in balance, light and dark both hold sway over the world. Stars rest on the gentle curve of one horizon while the first delicate pastel hues of morning make themselves known above the tree line. Cold and warmth reconcile. Birdsong weaves with silence. Within these few small hours, everything knows peace. At this time, magic is at its strongest.

I step through the ankle-high blades of grass and let a shiver pass through my body as dew clings to my bare legs and feet. I should be used to the chill. My skin has touched the bare earth countless times yet, with each new moon, the brisk sensation takes my breath away.

To the east, the sky sleeps in deep blues. The most pristine diamond stars lay in a scattered blanket, but their weave across the morning sky fades with the change from midnight blue to soft yellows and pinks. The air is still, no breeze stirs my hair.

It's beautiful. A perfect morning.

I turn my face to the sky and smile as I wander to the back of my garden. The path winds among rows of flowerbeds, past the smooth glass walls of my herb garden, past my sunflowers, and past my apple tree. They all brim with energy and they seem to reach towards the blanket of sky above them.

Rosemary for healing.

Lemon balm and chamomile for sleep.

Mint and sage for protection.

I know them all by name and purpose. Dozens of plants with dozens of uses, but there is only one reason I'm out on this particular moonless night.

The bush waits for me, beautiful and strong at the back of my garden. Its tallest branches stretch over my head as I admire it. Slender, bell-like flowers hang from its limbs, each delicate bloom open to the magic beneath them, deep in the earth. *Datura.* A cousin to *Belladonna*, nightshade. It's a potent hallucinogen I use in some of my strongest spells and potions, easily one of the more powerful plants in my garden. Some witches call it *Devil's Trumpet* for the way its flowers lean away from the sky. Others call it Thorn-apple, to describe its spiky, unfriendly fruit. Still others call it Moonflower, for on moonless nights it blooms brightest and its petals swell with magic. It's highly toxic if not prepared by a witch. Fortunately, I know exactly how much to use for various purposes.

Magic is simple, in theory: It's comprised of two halves, Light and Dark. Light magic is the power of positive energy and intent, willpower and desire that never comes from a place of hatred or willingness to harm. A spark that breathes life back into a wilted plant, the gentle flicker of energy that brushes shut a wound or softens a bruise. Words of support and kindness spoken at a memorial. Bright, joyous laughter.

Dark magic is precisely the opposite of Light. The

power of negative energy and intent, emotions that stem from places of anger, hate, fear. It is energy used to harm other things, to dominate and control. It lashes out with fury, shapes a strong will and bladed words into a spell that cuts cleaner than the keenest of razors. Where the Light mends, Dark maims. It is violence in its purest form.

In my years, I have encountered magic used in countless different ways. During holidays, to celebrate life with bright, spiraling colors. During funerals, to protect and bless the remains of a lost loved one. I've seen it in conflict, though the use of magic to harm others is discouraged.

I've seen magic used in life. And in death. I've learned to balance these forces, to truly understand that both magics complement each other. Negative and positive, neither could exist alone. Both are strong individually but when used together, in balance, they are a force that is nearly unstoppable.

I am a witch, and I am unstoppable.

I stand in front of the datura bush and reach for a flower. My fingers brush the plant. Its energies dig deep into the earth, into the stone and soil. After a moment, those waves of energy seem to reach back into me. The tiniest bits of its magic intertwine with mine in a sort of greeting. Sensations of bright summer mornings pass through my mind in the span of a heartbeat. I feel the primal comfort of warm sun after a chilly night; the familiarity of an old friend's embrace.

Hello again, it seems to say.

I respond with a greeting of my own, a subtle pulse of my magic as I touch a different leaf. An image of the gentle fog that clings to leaves on early spring mornings pops into my mind. The featherlight caress of a warm autumn breeze wraps around my body.

"I come on a night with no moon," I breathe into the darkness. "Asking for a gift, freely given." The plant's energies curl around its leaves. It wraps barely visible tendrils around my fingers as it absorbs my intent. "For protection," I continue. "For clarity."

The air around it ripples. The bush reaches into itself, into its deepest roots and tallest branches. It searches and curls. My attention is drawn to a cluster of three flowers. Yes, these are the ones I'm meant to take tonight. I'm full of gratitude, and I let the sensation wash over me as I move to pluck the plant's gift.

A rustle pulls my attention skyward. A section of stars blinks off and on again. I frown as my eyesight adjusts to the darkness. A black shape passes in front of the stars, blocking them from sight. It's some sort of bird.

Now that I've noticed one, others appear. Two, then three. Four, five, six? Nine, ten. I lose count as they settle on the fence and my fruit trees. There must be a hundred birds or more.

I turn in a careful circle. Cold realization freezes me in place.

Crows.

Icy fingernails of dread dig into my scalp. They scrape across skin and down my spine. Time seems to slow before everything leaps into perfect clarity. My heart beats against my ribs.

Turn around, my mind screams. *Run. Find the safety of walls, of a roof, anything!*

My limbs refuse to listen.

Without thinking, I clench my right hand into a fist. The tips of my fingers tingle. I latch onto that energy, that magic, and pull it deep from within me.

Another wave of unease washes over me. I push it away and focus on calming myself. The sense of calm radiates out, and with a flick of my wrist, I cast a spell that spins discs of light into the air above my head.

A bird caws behind me—a wholly unearthly sound. The anxious shiver that passes through me is reflected in the spell, spawning large circular eyespots on each swirl of magic.

Crows are cowardly, nothing to be afraid of.

They travel in numbers, but they're skittish and easily spooked. If the light doesn't scare them away, I hope the eyespots will. A bird would never ignore the bright-eyed predators swirling above them.

Around me, there is nothing but silence. No shuffle of wings, no rattle of crows calling. The spell frays at the edges, then spins into nonexistence.

I release the magic and stare into the sky. I focus on one bright star, then another, then another, encouraged by the lack of anything crow-related, until a dark wing passes in front of my face.

The birds are still here.

There is no hesitation this time. My flight response takes over. As I stumble backwards, my feet tangle in the dew-damp hem of my skirt.

"No!"

I fall backwards and hit the ground hard. The rustle of coarse black feathers passes over my head. Before I can scramble to my feet, a crow lands heavily on the grass in front of me. It caws loudly, tilts its head to one side and then the other. The wicked curve of its beak, and the bright silver shine of its eyes entrance me.

Wait...

Curiosity shatters the veil of fear that shrouds my mind. Morbid curiosity gets the better of me. I lean forward a hairsbreadth and direct my magic to illuminate the area. I'm enveloped in pale, warm light when a horrid realization washes over me.

Every bird turns to look at me with swirls of silver in their eyes. It's a side effect of possession caused by strong, dark magic. But I'm the only witch in Bonfire Falls with the ability to cast such powerful magic. The magnitude of ability needed to sustain a spell like this—not to mention over the sheer number of crows—is something very few witches are capable of.

So, who watches me from behind this myriad of eyes?

A sharp pinch at my ankle snaps me back to reality. I flinch from a bold crow who pecks at my bare legs.

"Shoo. Get away."

As dozens of birds break the quiet sanctity of my garden, I push to my feet. I leave the datura behind since there isn't time to retrieve it.

The dusty rustle of their wings and the click-snap of sharp beaks and claws serrates the air. They swoop down to pull at my hair and flap their wings in my face. As I duck, shield myself, they peck at my arms.

I stumble up the porch steps. I can't find the doorknob. Where is it?

When my fingers finally find cool metal, I twist the knob roughly.

I dash inside. The door slams behind me, and the deadbolt as it slides into place. Beaks and claws scratch at the window near the top of the door. I take a few steps back to distance myself from it.

The glass will hold. It will. It's survived thunder and rain, and hailstones heavier than these birds. The glass will hold.

But after a full minute of flailing birds, I'm not so sure.

Suddenly, the commotion subsides. My gaze is drawn to the motionless body of a crow which is laying on the ground outside. Its neck is bent at an angle that no living thing can hope to maintain. One wing is dislocated and ugly. It must've hit the door when I shut it, unable to reverse its inertia in time.

Poor thing, part of me thinks, the part of me that hates to take life in any form. But as I stare, bile rises in my throat and my gaze hardens. *It deserved that. Filthy, disgusting, treacherous—*

From the corner of my vision, it twitches. Did I imagine that? No, it wasn't a trick of the light. It moved. But how? It's clearly dead.

As I struggle to comprehend its sudden movement, the crow's body warps in terrible ways. It attempts to get back onto its feet, but it overbalances and crumples onto its shattered wing. Its head swings on the end of its limp neck, like a morbid pendulum come to haunt me. Ripple after ripple passes through its feathers as if worms crawl incessantly beneath its skin. It finally gets one foot under itself, then the other. Each joint and tendon cracks and pops into place as it reassembles its body. Until very recently, I'd assumed it was very, very dead.

"I was right, it is dead. But that isn't stopping it."

Like a puppet dangling on invisible strings, it continues to twitch and snap and jerk in awkward, clock-work-like movements until finally it stands. Its head snaps back into its correct position. The bird looks around, sizes up the glass door, then stares directly at me with those blank silver eyes.

I slide away from the door. I push myself back out of sight and hide behind the sofa. I cradle my head in my hands, wondering what will rid the crows from my house. I can't focus. Every few seconds, the thought of that crow pops back into my head. It haunts me. It might be stuck in my mind forever.

Three loud knocks on the glass snap me out of my

trance. I startle. Crows can't knock. At least I don't think they can.

I hesitate before risking a quick glance around the corner of the sofa. The glass door frames a bulky silhouette. The man's face is unrecognizable in the dim morning light, but I know who he is. Only one person visits this early. Bastian.

"Why are there so many birds outside? There must be one hundred crows in your garden. What in the world's goin' on?" he yells through the glass.

I swallow the fear that bubbles as I unlock the door, but the crow on the porch is gone. Bastian enters. When I slam the door shut behind him, he fixes me with a sideways glance, one eyebrow raised in question.

"Is this one of your spells?" His voice rumbles low in his chest. If a mountain had a voice, this is what it would sound like—deep and gravelly. Every other sentence ends in a near-growl.

The deadbolt slides home. I'm safe. Safe from the flock of silver-eyed crows—at least for now.

The bulk of Bastian's body blocks most of the view of the outside. I immediately feel a bit better with him here.

I shake my head and wet my dry lips with the tip of my tongue. "I don't know," I admit with a shrug. "They showed up when I went outside."

Liar.

All at once, the crows burst into flight. The air fills with raucous calls and I swear I can understand them.

Liar. Liar.

Dozens of them lift from their perches around my garden, scattering leaves and feathers in their wake. I turn to watch them fly past the windows, silhouetted against the rosy morning sky. One hops onto the windowsill, taps tentatively at the glass, and watches me. It glares at me. A chill runs down my spine and I whisper one word into existence, a name.

"Adrian?"

The bird fixes me with its unblinking silver stare, then hop skips into flight after its brethren with a gravelly croak. I realize it's also possessed, so it couldn't be Adrian.

Not Adrian. Breathe.

"Hey, there. Easy. It's okay," Bastian says. The warm rumble of his voice subdues my panic and dampens my fear. I pull a blanket over my shoulders and walk over to the kitchen table. Bastian stands behind me. He's facing the window, as if on guard.

As I pull the blanket tight, his arms encircle me. They're strong, warm and protective. I focus on his strength and rest against his chest. His presence calms me. It's been ages since anyone has held me like this, ages since Adrian.

"Who's Adrian?" Bastian asks.

I glance at him.

You can read minds? Since when can you read minds?

He gives my shoulders a little squeeze and gestures at the window where that crow had been. "You were lookin' at that bird like you'd seen a ghost. You said 'Adrian' like the thing could understand you."

Ah. He can't read minds. Good.

"Adrian is... someone I knew a long time ago."

Bastian doesn't reply. He merely squeezes me into a gentle hug, which is exactly what I need right now.

"What's on your mind?" he asks.

I hesitate for a moment, then decide to tell him the truth. "I've been having dreams. Bad dreams. Nightmares of things to come." I pause to gather my thoughts. Bastian gives me another encouraging little hug, the barest squeeze of his arms. Words come easier because I know I can trust him. "In my dreams, I see a storm cloud, rich with magic and darkness. It looms over everyone. Over the whole mountain. It starts small, but it grows bigger by the day. It gets closer, and closer. I don't know what it means, or what it could be warning me about, but..." I glance towards the horizon, hoping to find comfort in the newborn pink light, but dread is my companion.

Bastian murmurs quiet, reassuring words.

"Something is coming," I whisper. My body yearns for the comfort of Bastian's arms. I sink into his embrace and nestle against his broad chest. "Something is coming for me..."

CAPTIVE OF THE VAMPIRES: CHAPTER 2

BASTIAN

I'd heard rumors about Azealia for years, both before and after she'd ended her self-imposed exile. According to the people of Bonfire Falls, she was a cursed witch hiding in a cursed forest. A legendary woman filled with unspeakable power. But once I'd met her, I stopped believing the stories. Azealia is kind and gentle. A woman who eats toast for breakfast while sitting in her garden. A woman who takes in fallen birds and nurses them back to health. She listens to what people say about her but carries on anyway. She's a woman who's been alone for years. I don't understand why she's so intent on living a solitary life. She's fierce, powerful, and beautiful—the woman I want standing beside me.

A worthy mate, my bear grunts silently.

I've never seen Azealia afraid before, but she's clearly terrified.

"Something's coming for you. What does that mean?" I ask.

She rests her cheek on my shoulder. I stroke a hand

over her wild red hair. "I don't know. I've never seen a threat like this before."

My grip strays from her shoulders. I gently remove the blanket from around her shoulders. My grip strays and I glide my fingers over her soft shawl. "You've lived so long, sometimes I forget. It's hard to believe there's anything you haven't seen."

She pulls away and twists to look at me with those deep hazel eyes. "No one can see everything."

"No, of course not."

She moves to the bookshelves on the wall nearest her garden. Her fingers glide over old leather tomes.

"It sounds like you have unfinished business with Adrian?"

She freezes. Her spine forms a rigid line. "At this point, I have history with many, many people."

"It sounds like you mourned for him." I'm not ready to let it go. Something about this Adrian guy is upsetting her, and I don't like to see her so rattled. I move a few steps closer. She pushes her hair behind her ear. It's something I rarely see her do. "I'm sorry, for your loss."

"I didn't lose him. He left. He made his choice."

"And it wasn't you?"

She plucks several books from the shelf before turning to face me. Her chin juts up. "I don't think we know each other well enough for this conversation."

"We've known each other for years."

"And yet you already know more about me than I've ever known about you." She crosses to her table and drops her pile of books onto it. She sits before grabbing a book and flipping to a random page. All that long, curly red hair falls over her shoulder. She pushes it back behind her ear with a sharp little flick of her hand. Outside, the wind rises, whistling through cracks in the windowpanes and doors.

"I've always answered your questions," I say.

She trails her finger across the paper, flips to a new page, and then traces down the page again. The writing looks like an ancient language. The letters are actually pictures. Her fingers tap against the tabletop. "Of course. But maybe I should have asked you more personal questions. Or maybe not. The greenhouse could build itself if I asked the panes of glass to move, but I prefer your company."

"I'm glad I could help. I know you could have constructed it with magic instead."

"It would have been exhausting." She flips her first book shut and floats it back over to the shelf with an absent-minded flick of her wrist before cracking another one open. This book looks like it's in cuneiform, or some other writing that doesn't use modern letters.

Outside, darkness creeps over the pale sunrise. Thunderheads gather faster than should be possible.

"You can ask me anything you want. I didn't realize you wanted to get to know me more. I thought you just wanted me for my muscles," I tease.

She tuts at the book, or maybe at me, but the other corner of her mouth ticks. She waves her hand to light candles to read by. There's no electricity this deep in the forest. "You're talkative today."

"I've never seen you scared before. You ran to me."

"Indeed."

When she doesn't look up, I glance out the window at the angry sky. My bear urges me to protect our mate. Well, prospective mate—which is the same thing as far as he's concerned. I have no idea what I need to protect her from, but I always listen to my bear's keen instincts. He's kept me safe through more than his fair share of shit.

She finally looks at me. Flames from the hearth dance in her eyes. "I'm no stranger to fear. And touch is always a comfort." There's a long pause as she reads through some Hebrew. "Especially yours."

"*Especially* mine?"

Her head snaps up and her freckled cheeks pale. Outside, huge drops of rain splash against her windows. "That's enough with the questions for today."

I swallow my curiosity and return my attention to the storm. It too fast to be natural—it's linked to her. Her fear, her anger, or maybe something else.

Strong, my bear reminds me. *She's so strong.*

Strong enough to control the weather?

My bear grunts in agreement.

Azealia holds a scroll, but her eyes flick from it to me. She blows a harsh breath out, and thunder rumbles.

"If you want my help, if you want me to shelter you from whatever's coming, you only have to ask." It's on the edge of my lips to tell her that I'd do anything for her, but I think that will just scare her away. She may be a powerful witch, but her emotions are clearly out of control.

"Stop!"

She's beautiful when she's agitated. Her curls lift away from her as her power rises. She seems lighter, almost floating in the chair as her eyes snap to mine. Her power is a vise on my lungs. Fire burns through my blood.

Beautiful, my bear says. *Strong.*

"I'll protect you."

"I said *enough.*"

Thunder rolls through the sky again, and lightning

strikes. I close my mouth as sparks jump between her fingers.

Glorious, my bear says.

And intimidating.

"I'm sorry. That was out of line." I run my fingers through my hair. This is why I've never told her how I feel. She's so powerful that she could smite me with magic without a second thought. The storm outside is just a fraction of her capabilities. I know she's my perfect match, but for the life of me, I don't know how to bridge the gap between hired help and fated mate. But I'll be damned if I don't figure it out. And soon. I can't let her slip away from me.

"It's all right." She blows out a breath. The power circling in her drops. The rain outside falls more softly. She returns to her bookshelf. Tomes and scrolls float behind her and into place. She kneels to rifle through her bottom shelves.

"I care about you," I blurt. I can't help but push through my nervousness. We've never had a conversation even close to this intimate before. I can't let it drop. I want her to know how I feel.

She sighs, exasperated. "Please don't start."

"It's the truth."

She looks up from the floor. Firelight catches on the ring she wears on the fourth finger of her left hand. Is it from Adrian?

My bear growls in my chest. The beast can't stand the thought of her being with someone else, and neither can I. I've heard rumors about her secret past, but I want to know what really happened. I want her to tell me why everyone in town is so terrified of her power.

She stands with her next haul of books, three or four are suspended by magic.

"Play a game with me," I say.

She sets the books on the table. "A game?"

"I used to play it with my sister while we picked berries."

"I need to research the crows—"

"It's called a secret for a secret." I lay my hand over hers and give it a gentle squeeze.

Her eyes meet mine, and her lips part slightly. Outside, the rain becomes a gentle rhythm. Without the thunder and lightning, the room feels smaller. The fire's warm, and its light makes her eyes shine like gems.

"All right." She sits in a chair and folds her arms across her chest. "You start."

"My secret is, I see those pretty eyes of yours in my dreams sometimes. They're looking at me like you are right now."

She gasps and looks away. "This is a bad idea."

"A trade's a trade." I grin. "Fess up."

She twitches her mouth to the side a bit, while keeping her gaze away from mine. Stays silent for so long that I don't think she's going to respond. But she does, which surprises me. "My secret is, sometimes I make too much food on purpose so that you'll join me for breakfast."

"I know."

"You do?" She glances at me through lowered lashes.

I take a step toward her. "My secret is, I can see the weight of years of solitude draining you, and all I want to do is kiss away your pain."

A blush rises into her freckled cheeks. "This *was* a bad idea."

"Say stop and we'll stop," I whisper before gently pulling her into my arms.

A shiver goes through her. She lifts a knuckle to stroke

the edge of my jaw. "My secret is, I haven't been touched like this in years."

I spread my fingers across her back and tug her a little closer. She's soft, curved, and draped in silky shawls. Her wild, red hair shimmers across her shoulders. Her pretty, hazel eyes finally meet mine and I'm suddenly bolder. "My secret is, I'd touch you more, if you told me you wanted it."

A puff of air bursts from her lips. Our gazes lock. "Is that what *you* want?"

Before I can tell her that it's exactly what I want, a knock sounds on her front door. I tighten my grip on her, but she slips out of my embrace and the moment is lost. I want to kill whoever's on the other side of that door.

"Wait, it's not safe." I hurry toward her, but she doesn't listen. Instead, she tugs the door open.

Fortunately, it's Mason from the local wolf pack. He's second in command behind their Alpha, Kael, who has been after Azealia for years.

Damn him.

They talk briefly. I cling to the faint hope that maybe that moment between us will come back when the door shuts. Instead, she invites Mason into the house. We exchange pleasantries.

"Just one moment and I'll grab it for you." She drags a small trunk out from under her apothecary cabinet, levitates it with magic, and drops it into the wolf shifter's waiting hands.

He thanks her, hands her a roll of notes tied with ribbon. She unwinds the cord, checks the contents.

"This is too much," she says as she gives him half the notes back.

"I really appreciate the help," Mason says.

Her rosy cheeks go sheet white. Her eyes go wide. The

wild flapping of crow wings fills the air and a bird's talons aim straight for her face.

My bear's roar vibrates out of my throat. I'm by her side in a heartbeat. I grab the bird and fling it out the door. It thuds into the doorframe and something cracks. It hops away, but not before fixing its mean, silvery eyes on me. It drags one bent wing on the ground behind it as it goes.

"What the hell was that?" Mason asks.

"Go home. It's not safe here." I hustle him out of the door and slam it in his face. Through the window, I watch him shift. In his wolf form, he grabs a strap around the trunk with his teeth before dashing into the forest.

Azealia's hiding in the furthest corner from the door. Her eyes are wild, and her breath comes in big heaves. She shakes while tears run out down her cheeks. All of the candles blow themselves out. The fireplace is snuffed like it was doused with water.

Suddenly, a flash of bright blue lightning blinds us. A thunderous sound reverberates through my bones. Through the blasted-open door, I see the tree explode. Wood chips burst in every direction. Limbs snap off to pummel the ground. Azealia shouts something and the door slams shut. Half the tree slams onto the roof of the cottage. Rain hammers the roof. The repeated thud of something hitting the wet earth captures my attention.

Smoking, black bodies fall from the sky.

"Crows," I whisper.

Ten or twenty birds fall in the wake of the lightning strike. One by one, they shake awake. They spread their sizzling wings and take flight into the rain.

That's not possible.

Magic, my bear spits, disgusted. *Their eyes were not their own.*

I turn toward Azealia. She's fallen to the floor. I kneel next to her, gather her close and hold her as she shivers. It doesn't take long, thirty seconds, maybe a minute, before she relaxes. She's strong, my mate.

"I'm sorry. I'm so sorry, it's the crows. All these crows."

I run my hand over her hair and draw her into my chest.

"It's Adrian. It's him, the curse, the crows," she moans.

I hush her and pull her into my lap. The wall supports my back. "I'm here and I'll never leave you. You're all right."

"It's my secret, it's been a secret for so long. I'm sorry."

"Shh, this isn't a game. We don't have to play."

"I want to. You need to know what happened." Her tears dry as she struggles to compose herself. "I want to tell you about Adrian. Will you listen?"

I nod, while keeping her close. Her tears start again, but outside, the rain quiets.

In starts and stops, she tells me the story of Adrian, her lover. About how she found him kissing another girl, a younger girl, in a meadow, centuries ago. The despair of betrayal still burns her soul. She'd thought Adrian was her other half. She was wrong. So, she cursed him.

She'd laid a curse on his wretched heart, and on the woman's soul. She'd turned her man into an omen, a crow, and the girl into a trout, intentionally sending them into separate worlds so that they'd never to meet again.

When the village had heard what she'd done, they'd looked at her with hate, so she'd run. And run and run, deep into the woods to this cottage. This isolation. These cursed woods and all their pain.

"I can't let that happen again," she whispers. "I can't— let you get any closer. I'm sorry." She pushes at me and tries to get me to let her run away again, but I'm not letting her run, not this time. I hold her tight and refuse to let her go.

"I'm not him," I murmur against her hair. I try to convey my strength and warmth with my touch. I place a gentle kiss on her forehead.

"It's ok. You're all right. I'll never hurt you like that."

As she quiets, I stroke her hair.

"I'm so tired and it's barely morning," she says with a sigh.

"I'm staying with you, whether you like it or not. I'm staying right here where I can keep you safe."

"I can set magical wards if I need to. I can take care of myself. I've been doing it for years."

I hush her again. "You're dead tired, and you need sleep. I'll protect you. Let me stay."

"I can't let you in."

"I'm already in."

She sighs and snuggles into the safety of my arms. I meant every word of what I said to her. I'd die to protect my mate. There's no way in hell I'm leaving until I'm sure she's safe.

As I lift her into my arms, she wraps her hands around my neck. Her eyes stay closed as I carry her across the cottage into her bedroom.

After I set her on her feet, she drops her shawl and starts to work on the ties of her skirt. The soft skin of her belly is briefly exposed. I stifle a groan.

"Thank you for being here." Her eyes are heavy with the need for sleep, but her lips part and she catches my hand. She presses a kiss to the center of my palm. Fiery need burns straight to my core.

My bear urges me to den down with her. He sees that soft strip of skin and demands that we claim our mate, but I can't. Not yet.

I push my bear's urges away and help her settle into bed.

"Go to sleep. Everything will be all right."

She mumbles something I can't make out, and then she's asleep. The soft rise and fall of her chest soothes my own fears. I don't know what we're up against with those crows, but it's powerful and driven by dark magic. I don't know how I'll protect her from someone strong enough to scare her, but I'm damn well going to figure it out. She's my mate, and I'll stop at nothing to protect her.

CAPTIVE OF THE VAMPIRES: CHAPTER 3

AZEALIA

The sun is high in the sky by the time sleep releases me. I shuffle out of bed, feet bare, with a fresh shawl wrapped around my naked form. Embers burn in the hearth, but Bastian is nowhere to be found. His strong, earthy scent still lingers. He must have left when he heard me get up. I don't know why he didn't stay, but I'm glad I'm alone. I need time to think.

The shawl I wore early this morning is folded neatly and is sitting on the coffee table. A note sits atop the shawl.

Nothing suspicious, Bastian's sprawling handwriting covers the page. *Crows took off once you were asleep. I have some things to take care of at the den today. But if you need me, hold this charm in your hand, and I'll come.*

I lift the note and see a curved tooth, likely from a bear, tied intricately to a leather strap. I slip it over my head. The cord is long enough to leave it nestled between my bare breasts. As I admire it, warmth spreads throughout my body.

I gesture at the hearth, and a fire springs to life. It

feasts on the bits of wood still left. I feed several logs into the fire and flames rise. I shake out the folded shawl and wrap it around my shoulders. It smells of Bastian. My nipples tighten as I breathe in the scent of him. I remember the warmth and strength of his arms last night, bands of protection.

"My secret is, I'd touch you more, if you told me you wanted it."

I shiver at the memory. It was wrong to start that game. I should know better than to give my secrets away. Love isn't a game, and I'm not in love with Bastian. My traitorous heart might long for him, but I know better.

I glance at the note. This time, I notice words I hadn't seen before. *My secret is, it'd be a pleasure to continue our game tonight.*

Pleasure is underlined.

I cast the note into the fire, ignore the spike of heat that lances through me at the thought. By all the gods, it's been too long since I was touched or pleasured. Bastian would consume me if I let him.

As I cast my mind back through the years, and then the decades of loneliness, a blush rises to heat my cheeks. I stamp down the temptation to clutch the bear tooth. It would bring him to my door, and I could take him into my bed.

I shake my head. No. It can't be done. I need to focus on the crows.

After searching through my books, I find nothing. The few books in my library don't contain any answers which would explain the attack.

Bastian's note burns in the fire. My irritation rises with the flames. I know where there are more books— hundreds more books, shelves three times as tall as a man. But the books are guarded by a particular wolf—Kael.

He was a young challenger for the position of Alpha when I knew him 20 years ago. He was just a young man with a mean streak and a need for control. As he rose through the ranks of the Bonfire pack, we'd clashed and argued over various issues. We even fought when he tried to move his pack onto my land. His attempt to intimidate me into an alliance didn't end well for him. I kicked him off my land and told him never to return unless he wanted me to turn him into a worm. The years have doubtlessly made Kael worse.

Nonetheless, I need answers.

Outside, crows perch on the ruined tree near the cottage door. My stomach fills with dread, banishing all thoughts of lunch or tea.

I want answers. I want this resolved.

I wave a hand to summon my clothes. As I dress, I steel myself for the fight to come.

Bastian must have cleared the path to the cottage as he left this morning. The limbs of the ruined tree are stacked at its base. A murder of crows watches from atop it. I consider a spell of disguise but think the better of it. If the witch possessing the crows thinks I'm unafraid, then I'll be at a distinct advantage when we inevitably meet.

It's not a long walk through the woods, maybe three or four miles. The crows fly and squawk behind me the whole way.

I stop to confront them. Silver eyes peer back at me, and a shiver of dread runs down my spine. If they attack, there's nowhere to hide.

The birds hop and glide from tree to tree in slow tandem with my steps. The woods feel wrong, foreign, devoid of birdsong. An eerie silence and the sense of something dark and evil is pervasive.

They follow silently. Whoever sent them has clearly

tasked them to watch anyone that comes or goes from the cottage.

Maybe I shouldn't go back.

And where would I stay? With Bastian, on the other side of the mountain with the Bear Clan? No. That's dangerous, deadly, especially now that heat burns between us. The strength of our bond has developed throughout the years, and now I see the inevitability of it. If I were ever to love again, I could love Bastian.

But it's not to be.

And what about Kael?

I laugh sharply. He'd keep me chained in the den, if he could. When I knew him, his need for control had regularly outweighed his propriety.

Control is less about an iron fist, and more about the confidence that your commands will be followed. It's a nuance Kael has never understood, but one that every magic user must master. That knowledge creates a wide chasm between us.

The den is past the next cluster of aspens. A turn in the path leads to a beautiful, massive complex set into the side of the mountain. I remember, centuries ago, when the wolves decided to move out of the caves and begin to build. I'm not sure anyone has ever been through all the rooms. It's a labyrinth. Each generation added a new piece of the puzzle. The den has had construction in progress since I first discovered it. Before my exile, they'd come to me with stones or trees. They needed my spells to give their building materials greater strength so that they could carve tunnels through the mountain.

Something rustles in the underbrush off to my right. My heart kicks. My stomach drops. What else could this enemy have summoned? What other creatures can they control?

A low, lupine growl sounds. A blur of grey bursts forth from the brush. I throw a hand over my head to summon a shield. Facets of quartz rise from the ground on all sides of me to form a protective barrier.

The small, wet nose of a wolf pup smacks into the crystal. The little one folds like an accordion, then bounces off and falls to the ground on its tail, legs splayed. It looks at me in confusion.

"Come here, you little brat," a gruff voice calls.

Kael strides through the underbrush. His strong shoulders are bare. His focus is on the two wolf pups that trail after their intrepid—sibling?

Are these Kael's cubs?

He pauses when he sees my shield. I stare at the full expanse of his tanned skin. He's completely bare. The crystals refract a rainbow of colors across his naked flesh. Blues shimmer across his rugged face. Greens cascade across his thick neck and broad shoulders. Yellows trace a trail of dark hair that stars just below his belly button and down his toned stomach. Oranges splay across the vee of his hips like worshipful fingers. And then red that leads down, down, to the culmination of those hips in a thatch of dark hair, the strength of his thighs, and the thickness of his—

A blush in full power sprints up my cheeks. I reach out a finger, shatter my crystal shield into a hundred pieces, and banish the shards before they can hit the ground. A wolf pup trots up to my leg to beg for attention.

"Christian, knock it off."

Kael strides over, clearly unconcerned about the lack of clothes. I refuse to gaze upon his back as he bends to scoop up the pup.

"This one has too much energy." He tucks Christian under one arm before scooping up the other pups in his other arm. As Christian's siblings squirm for freedom, my heart melts.

Kael settles a hand under Christian's fat little stomach, lifts him to eye level. "You behave or I'll give your chicken bone to Carmen tonight."

The top puppy under his other arm stops its wiggling. Her ears prick, eyes brighten, and her pink little tongue lolls out happily. *Carmen, then.*

Christian settles in with a sad whine. Kael eyes him and then lifts his chin. Christian gives it a little lick. Kael smirks, sets him at his feet, and Christian sits quietly.

I've never seen Kael so relaxed. So soft. Not that there's an inch on him that's particularly soft.

"To what do I owe the pleasure of this visit?" he asks with more than a hint of sarcasm. "From the head witch, no less."

I purse my lips and look into the trees. "I'm not the *head* of anything. You could stand to put some clothes on."

"I didn't pack any for my shift. Why, does it bother you?" A devilish grin forms dimples in his cheeks.

"Of course you didn't," I grumble.

"What I do on my land's my business. Isn't that the line you gave me way back when?"

My teeth grit. "Apparently, courtesy's *still* not one of your virtues."

"Courtesy's a cheap form of deference. I'm Alpha here, and you're the most powerful witch around. We're equals, so why should I be overly courteous? What do you want?"

Kael drives me mad, in more ways than one. He's disrespectful, rude, and a hard ass. And he's never once been afraid to treat me like an equal—a rarity I've found only a handful of times through the years. For that, I grudgingly accept him as an equal, but I haven't told him so. No, that would stroke his ego far too much for my liking.

"I'm here to *respectfully* request you let me use your library."

"You've got your own library—dammit, knock it off Carina."

After he pries one pup's ear out from between the teeth of the other, he drops the two wolf pups to the ground. Carina yips, jumps on Christian, and they start to tussle. They roll into a mud puddle.

"And now you need a bath. Your mom'll be so pleased." He passes me Carmen and barely looks to make sure I've got a hold on the pup before prying the other two apart by the scruffs of their necks. I very pointedly don't study his backside as he bends. Instead, I force my attention to the sweet, gentle pup flopped over my forearm. She looks at me and licks at my chin.

Kael's eyes are sharp as he watches that little motion. "You want the library? Help me."

He strikes off around a curve in the path, dirty pups in hand. Mud drips from both of their fuzzy backsides.

There's no way to escape the view of *his* backside, as we march through the door of the wolf den. There's not a speck of mud on the floor. It looks as if it's been freshly swept.

He shouts for his second. Mason, a strong man, tall with blonde hair and green eyes, and built like a whip, appears. He's fast and light on his feet. He tuts when he sees the messy pups.

"Take *these* guys to Hima, would you?"

Mason grabs them gingerly. Carina squirms, gets her muddy little paws all over the front of his shirt. He gives a deep, tired sigh. "She's asleep right now. She had a rough night last night." He lifts Carina to eye level. "Unsurprising, with you around. Nursery?"

"I don't want the mud in there. Go find Viren, tell him he could stand to spend more time with his kids."

Not Kael's pups.

He shakes some mud from one of his hands. "Baths are time, right?"

Mason nods. Carmen wiggles in my arms and yips until I put her down. She trots behind Mason and whines softly to say she wants to be carried too.

Kael's tone is judgmental, but his smile and his eyes are soft. "They're spoiled brats. They're the only pups we've had in the last few years. Everyone gives them whatever they want."

"Clean clothes by the fire, boss." Mason's shout rings in the tiled hallway.

"Follow me," Kael says.

I follow him to the hearth.

"So, why the sudden need for the library?" He yanks a pair of pants off the line before the fire and slides them on.

"I'm interested in the possession of animal groups."

Kael's head snaps up. "Possession of groups? Like a pack?"

"A flock of birds, maybe."

"What for?"

"I imagine that it would make finding things easier if one had control of many pairs of eyes."

He cocks his head. "Birds hunt worms and bugs, not the plants you use."

"There are uses for all forms of life in magic."

"Are you going dark on me?"

My teeth grit. "Not all magic used to control things is

dark. I'll thank you not to pretend you've got a nuanced view of the craft."

"I've got a nuanced view of who should and shouldn't have information that could harm my pack."

"When have I ever failed to help your pack? I sent Mason off with potions yesterday. For dirt cheap, I might add."

His eyes harden. "Then we'll pay your full price. We don't need your charity."

"Pay me in kind. Let me use the library."

He studies me. His eyes dart from my shoulders to the set of my jaw, to the strip of stomach exposed between my skirt and shirt. Likely an effort to size up the level of threat. He must realize I have no intention of leaving without access to the library.

"Fine. Follow me."

He leads me to a library. It's lit by orbs I'd spelled for him years ago. They float across the tall stone ceiling. Mirrors are hung everywhere to reflect the light. Ladders lead up to the higher shelves. Fireplaces burn at a safe distance from the delicate pages, and tables and chairs litter the open spaces between the stacks.

"Back wall, north side is your best bet. It has a lot of old witch tomes, and some grimoires. The only other section that's useful will be by the door—animal behavior. But I don't think that's what you're here for."

"It's not. But thank you, I'll remember."

He nods. "I'll be back to collect you before dark. No visitors when the moon rises."

"That's fine." I'm already focused on the books before me. I turn the corner and disappear into a row before he even gets out the door.

The hunt is long. I search titles, turn pages, climb

ladders, read in more languages than I've had occasion to in decades. There's plenty on the possession of humans, demonic possession, some on the sale of souls, the sale of bodies, how to raise and possess the dead. But it's always one being at a time, and nothing on how to possess animals. All sources say that fusing a single human mind with an animal's can be done but linking it to many creatures would drive the witch mad. The spell would break immediately.

I slam my last book shut before pushing my agitated hands through my hair. Nothing, nothing, nothing.

I don't even know a witch who would want to hurt me. Or one who could manage to do it.

Adrian is the only one who comes to mind, but I'd never felt his curse break. He might be dead already. I've no proof that my magic made him immortal, only a fear that sits like a stone in my heart.

Someone clears their throat at the end of my table. I nearly jump out of my skin. Lightning sparks from my fingers to the ground in two great blue flashes

"So, you kicked up that nasty storm, huh?"

I meet the deep amber warmth of Kael's eyes. He's in a deep blue shirt and dark pants that hug his hips.

"What?"

"It's dark, and you've clearly been here all day." He gestures at the books scattered on the table, tossed haphazardly, the pages of crumpled notes, the scorch mark on his floor from the lightning. "You hungry?"

Starving, but I don't want to admit it. I don't want to owe him anything, so I stay silent.

"That's a yes then. All right. Get your shit, come on." He turns his back to me and moves toward the door.

"What?" I scramble to follow.

He looks back over his shoulder. "No wonder you're

getting nowhere. You can't think on an empty stomach. Bring your stuff, I'm taking you to dinner."

"That's not necessary—"

"No. But it's what I've decided." He gives me a hard look. "Now come."

I don't like his tone, but I don't like the empty pit of my stomach either. I fix him with a hard look, gather my few useable notes along with my shawl, and follow.

CAPTIVE OF THE VAMPIRES: CHAPTER 4

KAEL

I've never seen her like this before. Azealia's the most powerful witch in this town, maybe in the world. I don't know for sure because the world's not my purview, but if you need something in Bonfire Falls, something no one else can give you, you go to her. Everyone knows it, not many like it. But there's no denying her power. She's got the bite to back up her bark.

She's been stuck in my head since she denied my pack rights to her land, maybe 20 years ago now. She'd handed my ass to me. I've still got a damn nasty scar from one of her hexes, right over my heart.

Figures.

My wolf had been pissed off. He's always mad about lost fights. It comes with the territory when you're Alpha of the pack. No one should be stronger than me, but in some ways, she is.

I'd wanted to bind her to me right then and there, even with my ass in the dirt. She'd towered over me. Red hair lifted in her power, skirt wrapped around those lean hips, shirt torn by claws, chest touched with blood. A Valkyrie. A swift and brutal vengeance.

Not my usual game. Women are great packmates, as well as great bedmates for a night. Beyond that, I haven't had use for a mate. But Azealia... Azealia will be my mate, one way or another. She's a powerhouse, an equal. Someone who can help me with my plans for this town, this mountain, and more. We've been in the shadows too long, and she's got a light to her like I've never seen.

I shake my head at that. I could do without the poetry, but she brings it out in me.

"What?" She looks confused. A little suspicious still.

"Nothing. It's a little further."

She looks to the path ahead of us. It's the main road through town. Bonfire Falls isn't a big place. It's comprised of one town square, dozens of residences, and several shops. There's only one decent restaurant in town. She has to know where we're headed by now.

Shifters and witches are peaceful, but tense with each other. My pack, the bear clan, and the dragon shifters are allied, but the bonds of alliance are tenuous. The need for power is strong. We've all figured it's better not to pile on top of each other. And the witches? Well, we all remember the wars. We remember what the witches did when some of them chose to embrace dark magic.

The town proper is neutral ground. We all keep it that way. The central fountain, specifically, can never be claimed by any faction. It's where leaders hold meetings. I've been there, tense, bored, and watchful, for far too many of them now.

Azealia never comes. She's been silent and hidden for years. But we all know the stories and, even without magic, we feel the unwelcoming vibrations from her patch of woods. It's better to never venture into her territory uninvited.

She glances at the trees on either side of us before scanning the buildings ahead. Her brow knits. If she's concerned about something, we all should be worried. I don't know why she's scared, or why she needed my book. But I've seen her drop ten wolves with a wave of her hand. She won't even break a sweat.

I have no idea what could be worrying Azealia. Something's clearly got her on edge, and that's bad news for me, my pack, and all of Bonfire Falls.

We make it to the edge of town. Her stomach growls like a cornered wolf.

"It's not far."

"'Not far' would have been my cottage."

"Does your cottage have wild boar stew that's good enough to make you cry?"

She raises an eyebrow. "Someone bothered with a boar hunt?"

"I brought it down myself."

She scoffs, and her chest swells with it. "Well, you've always been—what would the word be? Pig-headed?"

The woman's a spitfire. No one's insulted me in years, and here she is, casual about it. I want that fire. I want her.

I open my mouth to tell her. Better to be blunt about this.

A howl rises from the woods, less than a quarter mile away. One of my pack, Marcus. One of our fastest.

She turns to the sound. "Better answer that."

I wouldn't trade my pack for anything—but I'd trade the interruptions.

I brush my hand along the soft skin at the small of her back as I step past, toward the woods. "The restaurant's five doors down. Timothy's the head chef. He's one of ours. Ask for him, tell him I'm on my way. He'll treat you well."

Her lips part a bit as I run my thumb down her spine. She pulls her shawl a bit closer around her. She mutters something about how I'm the one who's supposed to treat her well.

I slide my hand to her hip and pull her back against me before I go. "His stew will make you moan, but I can make you scream."

She sucks in a breath. I scent the warm spice of her as it rises from the side of her neck.

She pulls away, faking offense. "In frustration, maybe."

"You can't deny that we're equals. There's no reason to deny what's burning between us."

A blush rises in her cheeks. I catch a glimpse of how she'd look in my bed, before I dart into the woods, ears trained for Marcus. She pushes out an angry little sigh as I go.

She can deny the tension between us all she wants, but it's still there. And one day she'll come to me for more than just books.

Marcus isn't far, a hundred feet past the tree line, already part way through his shift. I let him catch his breath before I demand a report.

"There's been a murder."

The trace of heat in me, the scent of my mate in my nose, drops, cold taking its place. "Who? Where?"

"Brinda. She didn't check in after her patrol."

"You sent out a tracker?"

He eyes me, a little insulted. "Of course."

"She was—where? Northeast boundary last night?"

"Yeah. Sir, she was still shifted. There was no blood."

The wolf growls inside me, hackles raised. *Witchcraft.*

Dead shifters always change back into their human form. It's for our protection, to keep our secret. It's something only powerful magic can overcome.

Azealia's magic is that strong, that deep. And she's been on the hunt for possession information. Could she have done this as some sort of twisted experiment?

"Are you saying she died without wounds?"

"No, sir. There were wounds. But no blood left in her—"

Both of our heads shoot up and swivel. Storm clouds gather over town, thunder crashes through the sky. A downpour starts out of nowhere.

The scent of magic, huge magic, lances through the air. Electric. Like Azealia had been.

I've smelled it before in the land wars. It's Azealia's magic, freed. And on the tail end of it, the smell of *blood.*

Her blood, my wolf says. *Our mate's blood.*

My suspicion about her involvement is forgotten. I run. Marcus is hot on my heels. We make it to the edge of town in seconds.

There, two doors up from the restaurant, is Azealia. She clutches a nasty gash in her chest. A blood red stains mars the creamy shades of her full skirt. Blood spatters the thin top wrapped around her. Her shawl's ripped.

She flings blades of magic, red as her own blood, at her attacker. I see her dip her fingers into the wound.

Blades of her own blood? Holy shit!

My wolf growls his approval. I take him off his chain and feel him under my skin. He's ready to shift at a moment's notice. I catch Marcus' gaze and point her way. He corrects course and heads toward her.

Azealia's practically immortal. If she can still move,

still breath, and still fight, she'll be fine, even without his help. But I'm not taking any chances.

The man in front of her, pale, mid-battle through her magic, won't last once I sink my teeth into him.

I charge, snarling. Five steps later, I jump at him. He's too focused on her with no awareness of his back. His mistake.

I pull a partial shift, call up my wolf's claws, his snarl, and his teeth. I sink my claws into the attacker's back and chest. With a sharp snap of my jaw, my teeth sink into his icy flesh. I lift him and throw him back twenty feet.

He's cold to the touch. He smells wrong. Like he's already dead.

He will be dead soon, my wolf assures me.

The attacker's eyes dart to mine. The irises are bright red.

Never seen that before.

It doesn't matter. I charge. The strange man struggles to get up. His face is spooked, but his motions are so fast they almost blur.

I swipe a razor-sharp claw at his face. He dodges. He's almost too fast to see. My claws only graze him. The blood that comes out of him looks—old. Too dark, already a little clotted. The wounds heal almost immediately.

The fuck?

He hisses, bares his teeth. He chucks a dagger toward me before turning to run. I dodge to the side before giving chase.

Damn, he's fast. Too fast for two feet. I call my wolf and force a change mid-step. It hurts like a bitch, but between one step and the next, I go from two feet to four.

I'd trade the interruptions of my pack in a second, but not the power. There are perks for Alphas, always.

My wolf's a huge beast with yellow eyes and dark fur that fades to a grey on the base of his legs and his muzzle. He stands about as tall as my shoulder, when he's on all fours. Bigger than even me.

He growls and lunges for our prey's leg. He locks his jaw into the cold meat of it and shakes. A snap of bone tears through the air. The attacker screams.

My wolf's meaner than me, too. He refuses to let up. Instead, he jerks the man like a rag doll.

The man's scream rises to a screech, high and painful. It gets louder, louder, until it slices into my wolf's ears. We drop him and stumble back.

What the fuck? Are our ears bleeding?

The attacker drops. He drags his legs for a few steps before it snaps into the proper angle again. He runs at full tilt toward the fountain in the center of town.

We make a break for him, sprinting at top speed. He still manages to put distance between us. I push my wolf. The ringing and the pain in our ears fade. My wolf ramps up the speed, paws light on the ground.

One of Azealia's blood blades slams into the attacker's side. It throws him bodily into the fountain. I see a flash of rib and a spray of blood before he falls under the water.

We charge harder. We jump the side of the fountain and plunge our muzzle into the water. Snapping, and snapping again, we try to get him, but he dodges and blurs away. He reappears ten feet away, right at the edge of the fountain. His eyes track back to Azealia, almost like he's forgotten me.

Mine track back to her as well. We're maybe a thousand feet away now. I snap back to the attacker. He's coiled. His thighs tense to move forward.

Fuck you.

We lunge and manage to get our teeth sunk into his arm this time. We shake him until we hear the bone in our mouth crunch and his shoulder snap. We toss him back toward the center of the fountain, away from our mate.

He hits the streams of water that spray from the top of the central post, and there's a sound like a collision. The water stops for a second, waves of impact ripple away from him. Then he slides down the path of the streams like they're bars on a cage.

What the fuck is going on here?

Doesn't matter, my wolf growls. We stalk in front of him, putting us between the prey and our mate. Our hackles rise; our teeth are bared. The attacker stands, hisses. His teeth lengthen in his mouth, fanged and sharp. His red eyes start to glow, and his nails sharpen into claws.

Is that a fuckin' vampire?

He steps forward, blurs left, right, left again, and too fast to see, he stabs his claws into our chest, lifting us off all four feet.

The pain is sharp. Red. It's been a long time since someone landed a good hit on me. He's clearly not practiced with wolves my size, because he's off a few inches from where my heart is. Either that, or he's not in this to kill me. And that's his fucking mistake.

We snarl, swipe at his face and catch him in the side of the head. One of his nails caught a lung, I can feel it when I suck in a breath. His head snaps to the side, nasty blood darkens his pale complexion. I swipe again, kicking at him with my hind feet. He stumbles back and lets me fall to the ground.

Those nails hurt more on the way out than they did on the way in. There's a burn to the wounds, a nasty, radiant heat.

Poison?

I step forward, and my legs already feel weaker.

Fuck.

My wolf snarls, pushing my consciousness down. He's all instinct now. All rage. He raises his muzzle, and the vibrations rise in his throat, coiling around him.

He howls a call, a command. Six, seven, ten, then more howls answer, scattered across the mountainside.

My pack. The strength of wolves has always been in numbers.

The attacker's eyes dart around. He seems to be counting the number of howling wolves. A grimace overcomes him. With a nasty snarl, he blurs left. My wolf charges.

It's a fucking trap, don't!

He's to the right and past us before my wolf can change course. Size isn't on his side in this instance. The water blurs out of the attacker's path. He's up and over the wall of the fountain, almost back to Azealia, before my eyes catch him.

My wolf snarls and sprints toward our mate. He's out for blood now, for a kill, and his speed increases until he's almost a blur too.

I need him alive. I need information to protect her.

He doesn't hear me. He's too far gone.

There's a blur of brown and white. A wolf, smaller than me, but fast, so fast, slams into the attacker's side. It knocks him out of his headlong rush at my mate.

Marcus.

My wolf snarls, awash with rage. It's his kill, and he feels challenged by the interference.

Don't.

He growls, adjusts course again, and springs. He hasn't decided if his target's the prey or our packmate before he's in the air.

I let him go too far. I gave him too much freedom and control.

Fuck, stop!

My wolf is pure heat, pure rage, with snapping teeth and a taste for vengeance. He lands on our prey and blood fills our mouth.

CAPTIVE OF THE VAMPIRES:
CHAPTER 5

COBALT

F rustrated, I press my lips together in a terse line. "I don't like it," I say to my empty shop, hands on my hips. "I don't like it, and I don't know *why* I don't like it." Before me, an arrangement of scarves sits across a chair, a wholly uninspired cloth heap. They wait expectantly, eager for me to do *something* with them—but what is that *something?* Inspiration rests just out of reach, tantalizingly close, but I'm unable to grasp it.

Colors, rumbles a voice from inside me. My dragon flicks his tail, and I catch an image of him as he idly inspects a collection of attractive rocks. *Rearrange them by color, perhaps. That will look nice.*

I push up my sleeves. *It's worth a shot, I suppose.*

It takes some time, but once the first few pieces are set, I understand what my dragon means. The arrangement goes swiftly after that, and before long I step back to admire our creation: A pinwheel of fabric, soft cotton scarves of every shade fanned out in a brilliant nova of color. And it feels right. Like everything is where it should be, now. *Thank you for the suggestion.*

It's good. My dragon growls approvingly, content at this display. *It flows nicely,* he says. I can't help but agree with him. Autumn reds and oranges sweep softly into yellows and spring greens, while blues fade from a sky-hue to a deep, warm indigo. It's beautiful.

"Glad to have that finished," I say with a grunt as I scoot the chair across the floor towards the window, where it will sit on display for anyone who passes by.

I sense her a moment before she enters the shop, a blanket of light that rises like a wave above the shore. Her presence is like nothing I've known before—sunlight and silk, cherries and gold. With her nearby, I'm unstoppable. I can do no wrong. She inspires me like nothing else. She's the song in every breath I weave into my fabrics. She's the sun, the moon, and the stars. She's—

She's bleeding!

My dragon snaps to attention, eyes wide and wild. I'm at her side in an instant.

"Azealia? What happened?" She stumbles and I swing an arm across her midsection. "It's okay, it's all right. I've got you. I'm here." Something soaks into my pressed linen sleeve, and my dragon rears his head, hisses in equal parts revulsion and alarm. I reach for a cloth reflexively and grab pieces of fabric from my new project to use as makeshift bandages around her wound.

Heal her, my dragon presses insistently. His claws score imaginary furrows beneath him. He savages the air in helpless frustration. *Help her. Without her we are nothing.*

I know!

Magic swells to life, eddies of light that swirl on my palms, not from my dragon, but from the blood of my half-witch lineage. The spells are already at my lips, ready to spring into life, eager to mend, and to heal.

"What happened?" I ask again before laying a gentle

hand on her shoulder to direct her towards a comfortable seat. Her frame relaxes at my touch, but a shape outside the window catches her eye and suddenly her muscles tense beneath my palm. She surges upright and her fingers stretch towards the glass.

Magic pools at her fingertips. Fibers of gold and gray weave into a tight ball that hurts to look at.

A spell? She's too weak.

There is already blood on her face, a trickle that traces a wet trail down her lips and chin. Whatever spell she has prepared, it's sure to take a great amount of energy from her, energy that she can't spare.

"Forgive me," I breathe as I lift a gentle hand to her brow. "I'm doing this for you."

Heat and light bloom between my fingertips and her temple, and the fury in her eyes fizzles. Her body sags, but I catch her before she falls and set her onto a cushion.

Rest.

Some small part of me can't help but be lost in the grace of it all. Fire flickers hot and fierce in her eyes; her fan of hair is a wild blaze in the wake of her spell. Teeth bared in a snarl of defiance. Even now, wounded and blood-soaked, she's beautiful.

My muse, the song on my lips, the light of my—

The window behind us shatters as someone is tossed through it. Innumerable shards of glass shimmer and gleam as they scatter across my shop. It's like a rain of diamonds, and in that split second, she looks like an angel of war. A thousand points of reflected light skim off her skin, highlight the bow of her lips, the curve of her cheek, and the curl in her hair.

My dragon surges to the forefront of my senses. He pulls me back to reality as the figure stands behind me, sending glass to the floor in soft, bright impacts.

A threat, my dragon roars. *A threat to our muse.*

We turn from Azealia as my dragon bursts forth. My skin ripples, turning into sheets of hard steel-blue scale. Bones and tendons pop and click. Clawed feet land heavily on broken glass, but dragon's scales are more than enough protection. And even if the glass had bled us, our pain is meaningless next to Azealia's.

The target of our ire scrambles out through the open window frame. My dragon's gaze snaps to him. Several hundred pounds of scaled fury lumbers into the street in pursuit, a storm of claws and fangs. The distance closes between us. My dragon snakes out his neck, but the offender dodges to the side, barely evading the snap of steely jaws.

There's a snarl, and a sudden blur of gray from the corner of our vision. Our target hits the ground. A wolf rests top on him, pinning him to the street.

The figure is still, then rises in a burst of action and shoves the huge beast away in an attempt at freedom. The wolf dashes forward before my dragon can react. There's a scuffle, a flurry of tangled limbs, and then the target is flung farther into the street.

My dragon's eyes sharpen. Sparks fly from between his teeth.

An opportunity.

He takes it.

Fire and fury climb from deep in his chest as he digs wicked sharp claws into the ground. Razor-pointed teeth part in an eager grin, and the air around us shimmers with heat.

The figure climbs to his feet and stares in captive horror as my dragon coils and strikes. He only has a moment to scream before blue-hot fire pours from behind my dragon's fangs to devour the unlucky figure.

I'm furious.

How dare anyone harm her! My dragon snarls.

Our minds roar in tandem.

This man threatened her with mirror-knives of glass, and soaked the heathen ground with our angel's blood? How. Dare. He.

There is only ash when our rage finally dies, a pile of dust where the threat had been. My dragon's flames fade. The heat-shimmer around us disperses. In a huff of accomplishment, we clear smoke from our snout.

My thoughts turn back to Azealia.

Is she all right? We must return t—

Another snarl, and a burst of motion. A wolf slams into my shoulder. I stagger to regain my footing. A fire sparks within my dragon's chest once more and he bares his fangs in challenge. We're both more than prepared to crisp this threat as well. If they so much as breath of ill intention towards Azealia, we'll burn this wolf to death.

Surprisingly, the wolf doesn't advance. It only crouches and convulses.

A shifter, some part of me recognizes.

My dragon remains tense and ready to spring into action at the slightest provocation. We watch as fur recedes for skin, claws make way for fingers, and growls turn into—well, his words are still growls.

"What the fuck?" he yells at me, predatory in his approach. He turns away at the last second, then heads towards what remains of the intruder.

My dragon huffs, catching the wolf's scent. It's Kael, the Alpha of the local wolf pack. Neither my dragon nor I care much for him because he's an egomaniac and far too aggressive for our taste.

"You killed him! What were you thinking? He could have answered questions!" Kael pauses his tirade and glances back at me. "Hey, are you even fucking listening to me?"

An irritated snarl bubbles from deep within my dragon's chest. He lunges forward, a posture, a challenge, but I push his presence down and shift. The street is damp from earlier rain and unpleasant on my bare feet.

Let me out and there will be no discomfort, my dragon insists. He wants to fight, and yearns to rip and tear this loud, inferior wolf to pieces. But I take a deep breath and square my shoulders. My reply is calm and lacks my dragon's ire.

"I was worried about Azealia," I begin. "If someone comes through the window of my shop, I'm going to defend it. And her as well." Kael rolls his eyes, but I continue. "Perhaps if you had taken care of the problem in a timely manner, I wouldn't have needed to involve myself. But you had to toy with your food, didn't you? Throw it around a bit, toss it through a window or two while Azealia bleeds to death, covered in glass?"

"That's enough," Azaelia's voice snaps from behind me. She must already have shrugged off my sleep spell.

Something behind Kael's eyes turns hard. He snarls, approaching me with his hands balled into furious fists, like he's about to throw a punch. "You think I don't care about her? That's what you think?"

He's not quite as tall as me, but I'm thinner, and more agile. Kael is built to fight like a mountain. I'm built to fight like a violent wind.

Kael's a jackass, my dragon grumbles.

I don't point out that they're both eager too eager to brawl. There's no doubt in Kael's eyes how much he wants to hit me, and my dragon is itching for the wolf to throw the first punch. But the wolf doesn't swing. Not yet. Would I be able to win that fight, I wonder?

A sharp prod to the chest snaps my thoughts to the present. Kael scowls at me, lip curled in disgust. "I said, are you even *fucking* listening to me?"

"I said enough!"

We both flinch as Azealia's voice sweeps past us and a strong breeze gusts through the street. I turn and see Azealia standing in the doorway of my shop, one hand on the frame for support, with her hair haloed behind her in a cloud of copper red.

An angel.

But her eyes burn, and she glares first at Kael, then me. I falter beneath her gaze, fold like a leaf before a storm as she fills her lungs with words meant to berate, to scold.

An angel of wrath.

"You." She turns on Kael, eyes hard and voice even. "You don't get to order everyone around. Not everyone around here is part of your pack. Cobalt acted as he thought was best, and you don't get to fault him for that." She glares as the wolf attempts to interrupt. Kael must think better of it because he goes silent beneath her fierce gaze. "Alpha or not, you need to calm down. And put on some clothes." Her tone is an obvious dismissal, and though pride sparks dangerously hot in Kael's eyes, he turns and stalks off, shifts back into his wolf and vanishes around the corner.

"And *you*—" That single syllable passes through me like a death sentence, and I dip my head in shame. "You left me unconscious. You knocked me out during a fight and left me alone. Passed out and unprotected, Cobalt." Each accusation is a blow upon my back, a whip that scorches my failures into my skin. I remain bowed, reverent, until she sighs. Her fiery eyes soften. "Don't do it again." she says, then turns and walks into the shop.

Although my heart laments at the razor-sharp words she has for me, I can't help but be caught in the glory of her. Even with her clothes torn and bloodstained, she's still a beacon of strength and power.

The silence stretches for several moments as I reflect on what she said.

We failed her, my dragon grumbles.

We will not fail her again, he assures me. He's coiled and broody. *Attend to her.*

I will, I silently tell my dragon.

I follow her inside, grab a scarf from the floor and shake it free of glass shards before I tie it around my bare waist.

She sits in a chair, eyes closed. Her cheeks are flushed, perhaps from exhaustion or perhaps from exertion, maybe both. Either way, the color gives her face the type of glow I find enthralling. Even when pushed to the limit, she's flawless.

I kneel at her side, an assortment of fresh cotton rags in hand. Without a word I begin to pick glass shards from her hair, and wipe blood from wounds that have already started to mend. I'm nervous, my dragon is nervous. Have we fallen out of her favor?

She'll be mad at us for days, my dragon says.

When I reach to tuck her long hair behind her ear, she smiles. Her face is radiant and bright and strong, and suddenly I know that things will be okay.

Inspiration hits me. It compels me to move to a shelf where I remove a long cut of fabric which is covered with symbols and shapes that bend and whirl in the light.

It's luminous. Just like her.

"This is for you."

I offer Azealia the fabric. She takes it with a curious quirk of her brow. "What's this?"

"A shawl," I grin, proudly. "It's one of my latest pieces." I gesture at the symbols as they dance in and out of the weave. "These are—"

"—protective charms," she finishes, tracing the design with a delicate touch.

I nod as warmth blossoms across my face. I'd spent a full week painstakingly weaving protections into the cloth, strong charms to keep the wearer safe and to heal them. It's one of my best works.

It's only natural it belongs to her now.

She takes it and hangs it around her shoulders. She twists it around her torso so it accents the rise of her breasts, and my breath catches in my throat. It looks incredible on her, better than I could have imagined, and I'm lost in poetic bliss again.

She stands, pulls the shawl around her, and smiles. "Thank you." Light catches in the cloth and dances off the inset charms. "I should head back and get some rest. But you and Kael, could you visit soon? I'd like to talk to you both about something."

Kael or not, if our angel needs me, I will be there. "Of course. Whenever you want. What do you need me—us —for?"

She looks out the window as the last scattered bits of ash are blown away by the breeze. There's a look in her eyes that I can't place. Something distant.

Something afraid.

"I need your help."

CAPTIVE OF THE VAMPIRES:
CHAPTER 6

AZEALIA

I leave Cobalt to clean his storefront and Kael to clean up his packmate. My magic is more useful for finding answers than it is to ease the burdens of men who don't deserve the help. I'm angry at both of them, so angry.

If Kael could cede control for a moment and ask for help instead of demand answers or apologies, this whole mess could have been avoided. And if Cobalt could focus, for even the briefest moment, we might still have the attacker to question.

The sky rumbles. In the distance, lightning strikes.

Calm yourself.

I carry a tuft of hair in my hand, ripped from my attacker when I pulled him away from my neck. At least not every part of him was lost. There are plenty of things to be done with someone's hair, plenty of answers to be found. I wave my hand over it, snap, and send it ahead to my cottage, where I know it will be safe.

Tonight is the closest I've been to death in centuries. I need to heal. To think. Cobalt's charmed shawl has stopped the flow of blood from my wounds, but they aren't closed. I ache, and I hurt all over.

My stomach growls like a hungry monster trapped in a cage that won't yield. I need to get home so I can get out of these clothes. The eyes are still watching me. I can feel them, even as I check the trees behind me. Silvery eyes glow in the coming darkness, so I hurry my step.

My fingers go to the charm Bastian left me. I trace the intricate weave of leather that holds it to the cord. I miss him, his care and his steadiness. Kael is strong and unafraid of me, and Cobalt is worshipful, and concerned with my happiness. But Bastian would never leave me during a fight. I clutch the tooth, call him.

Bastian.

A pulse of magic flares from the charm. The intricate swirls engraved in the tooth glow a bright green. A tug at my navel directs me toward the bear clan's den.

Behind me, the caw of a crow and the rustle of wings sound. Three crows take flight, as if following the energetic line connecting Bastian and myself.

No.

The ability to see magic, to trace it like that, is rarer than rare. It's an art I had to work to master for over ten years, one I haven't taught anyone else. If whoever's in control of the crows has learned it as well then this enemy is more dangerous, and more of a threat than I thought.

Torn between seeing Bastian and finding out the truth about who is after me, I decide to head home. Bastian's with his clan, and he'll be safe as long as he doesn't respond to my call. I send a silent plea for him to stay home. I don't know if he'll listen, but I hope he heeds my warning.

I need answers. About the attack. About the crows.

About how to protect these three men, all of whom I care for.

More than care for.

The thought is pushed out as I press through the last half mile to my cottage almost at a run.

I check the bowl on the long, sturdy oak table where I do my craft. The tuft of hair has settled into it, right where I charmed it to appear. The runes on the bowl hum faintly, ready for work.

Yarrow, and quartz. A Dragon's Blood stone.

After settling the kettle over the fire for tea, I wrap my hair atop my head. From a huge cabinet on the hearth-adjacent portion of the room, I collect brown bottles of herbs and tinctures—willow for foresight, and chunks of amethyst the size of my fist. I also gather moon water, mugwort, and dried datura.

I need to scry.

I carry an armload over to the table as Bastian ducks through the doorway, broad shoulders set and eyes wild as he searches the room for me.

Oh, thank god.

His eyes catch mine, and there's a moment of friction between us. I told him to stay home, but he didn't listen. However, I'm grateful that he's here.

"Are you all right?" He checks me over, running his hands over my arms and torso. "You're bleeding!"

I set the bottles down, realizing that I never changed out of my dirtied, bloodied clothes.

"What cut you?" He eyes the bottles.

"It's from the attack."

He goes stone still, his emerald eyes wide. "The attack?"

I shut my eyes, angry with myself. He hadn't known. "It's nothing. I'm all right."

"Don't damn well tell me it's nothing, you're bleeding and—are those claw marks?"

He tugs the hem of my shirt and it pulls at the edges of the wound, where dried blood has fused it to my skin. I gasp, watching as the wound starts to bleed again. I look past Bastian to see Cobalt's gift dropped on the floor by the front door.

"Please, leave it."

"Like hell."

He gets his arms under my arms and legs, lifts me, and carries me over to the hearth. The kettle begins to scream where I'd forgotten it over the fire. He quiets it.

"Now don't you start with me. You've been attacked, and I'm going to see to you."

His accent grows thicker, his movements more agitated. As he lumbers around in search of rags and a bowl for the hot water from the kettle, he bangs around in the cabinets. He cusses a little when he can't find what he's after. "Where's your mending kit?"

I gesture toward my cabinets of supplies. Three jars float out toward me. He watches their path suspiciously.

Bastian has always cared for me, but not as much for my magic. There's a reason I ask for his help with labor-related tasks, rather than spells.

He makes his way over to me, snatches the jars out of the air as they start to unscrew their own tops. "That's enough of that. Save your strength."

He settles behind me, pours the hot water from the kettle over a bit of cold water in the bowl, enough that the steam stops, and it reaches an approachable temperature. He leans me back against his chest, takes one of my hands in his and begins to wash the dirt and blood off me.

"I can banish the mess away."

He shushes me, running the warm rag up my arm gently. I settle back against the breadth of his chest.

He works on me slowly, up my arms to my shoulders, down to my collarbones, and over my jaw and my lips. He soaks the rag, then uses it to soak my top, trying to get the dried blood to release the edges of the wound.

"It's deep, that cut."

"There might have been poison, on his claws."

His teeth clench and his jaw groans under the pressure. His hands remain gentle on me as he soaks the fabric wrapped over my breasts to the point of transparency. As the water cools, my nipples harden. I know he can see them. He settles me closer to him. The warmth of him, the size of his body, and the little protective rumbles he lets out, lull me into a sense of peace.

He manages to unwrap the fabric from around my ribs with only a little pain on my end. I show him which poultices to use on what, and in which order, and the process starts over again. The fire warms the room, and the heat between us rises.

My eyes begin to close as raised voices make themselves heard on the path outside my cottage. Kael and Cobalt.

Kael struts through the door, backwards, with his finger raised. He's mid-argument with Cobalt. A faint wisp of smoke drifts from the dragon shifter's nostrils.

"Stop it, both of you."

They turn to look toward my voice and then their eyes catch on me, top bare, with Bastian curled protectively around me.

The room stops like I let out a time spell. All three of them freeze. The tension rises and rises.

Ridiculous, all of them. All of this.

I grab Cobalt's shawl from the floor by my foot and

wrap it around myself. "Thank you, Bastian, you've been... thorough."

The tension spikes higher.

Wrong thing to say.

I snap my fingers, and the jars of medical poultices reseal themselves before snapping smartly back onto the shelves. The fire flares and logs fly to the hearth to feed the flames.

The roof groans a little as my magic settles the house. The men stand there, staring at each other.

Useless posturing.

They couldn't be more different, honestly. Cobalt is lean, wily, with almost silver hair chopped in a scruffy cut, and a clean-shaven face. There's a softer look to him, a more exotic one, and those beautiful blue eyes of his are visionary. He sees hope and beauty in the world in a way that makes me want to create that world he sees.

Bastian is a beast of a man, as huge as his animal might suggest. He's strong, so strong, with powerful muscles from a life of labor. His hair and beard are thick. They're a rich, beautiful brown like the crisp edges of a baked apple. Like the bark of a redwood tree.

Kael's skin is darker, tanned from a life lived outdoors. He's got scars, small reminders of challenges won. They make him look rugged, dangerous, as does the tone of his musculature. Built for speed and strength, escape and pursuit. A hard man with amber eyes, a strong jaw and the air of absolute authority about him.

Heat rises in me. The intensity of each of their stares melts me to the core. I'm pulled toward each one of them, but for different reasons. Any of them could take me away from the fear and the pain of the attack. With a single touch, any of them could distract me.

Or all three.

They'd never agree to that.

But think of the power you could generate. Together.

I don't have time to fantasize while so many questions remain unanswered. The thought of Adrian weighs heavy on me. The sting of that betrayal is still sharp. Sharper than my desire for these men.

"I need your help to stop the crows and the attacks before it gets worse for me, or before my unknown enemy threatens Bonfire Falls."

"I can protect you," Cobalt says.

"Like you protected her today?" Kael gestures towards my wounds with his chin.

Bastian's on his feet before I have a chance to intervene. "And where were you when those crows lit after her yesterday, huh? All this talk around town about how she's your girl, but I don't see you around here, ever."

Kael growls again, teeth bared, but it's Cobalt who takes the most offense. He turns on Kael, breathes out a faint wisp of smoke again. "As if Azealia would lower herself to the likes of you—"

"You watch your mouth, Scaley, I'm not done with you for earlier."

"Earlier?" Bastian's tone demands an answer. "What do you mean earlier?"

"The wolf's mad that I protected her—"

"—that you *torched* the one fucking lead we had."

"All of you, stop!"

They turn to meet my eyes again, all three with their hackles up. A wave of want washes through me, but I push it down.

"I asked you here for solutions, not more problems. If your plan to resolve this is to fight amongst yourselves, get out." I wave my hand, and the door swings wide.

No one moves to go.

"The attacker is not the issue. I'll scry with the hair I stole, but I need silence. I don't need bickering. Your senses are keen, but they won't let you track magic."

They grumble but remain quiet.

"I need help catching one of the silver-eyed crows. We learned last night that they're hard to kill. My magic doesn't do much."

"I can get the pack out to hunt them." Kael eyes me. "We'll canvas the woods and bring one of them down."

"Like a retriever."

Kael's eyes snap to Bastian's, but Cobalt interrupts him. "Leave it, bear. Or can't you do what she asks?"

"You think birds are the most important part of this, when she came home bleeding and scared for her life—"

"Thank you." I shout over the top of them. "I appreciate the pack's help, Alpha."

I see Kael's eyes heat when I call him Alpha. He steps over. "Do you want guards tonight?" His tone is softer, pitched lower. More intimate, as the other two men boil in their respective corners.

Bastian growls. "She has me."

"My wards are enough. I wouldn't sleep well with people on the property."

He nods, ignoring the other men. As he pulls a ring from his pocket, I gasp. He slides it onto my hand. It's silver and depicts the head of a wolf. I'm stunned by its beauty.

"This has been charmed to sound my pack's howl. If you need help, tap the head and it will call me. I need to go organize the pack."

I nod, too stunned by his gift to respond. It's a comfort to have an ally in Kael.

He leaves. Bastian and Cobalt watch him the whole way.

"You need to consider this attacker more seriously," Bastian says.

"He's dead. I'll have any answers he can give me when my ritual's done."

"Baby, please—"

"No!"

I say it too harshly. The cups in the cabinet shake and the windows rattle. Eventually I control my emotions and silence falls once again.

Bastian looks at me. There's a touch of fear in his eyes as my magic pulses. That touch with Kael might have made me too authoritative. I fed off his energy, which is dominant, to say the least.

"The crows are the focus. I could use you on the hunt," I say.

He nods and swallows. When opens his mouth to offer to stay tonight, I shake my head. "I know what time of year it is. You still have coming-of-age rituals to finish with the bear clan tonight. Your people need you."

"You're my people too."

Our eyes meet, hazel to deep green, and there's a moment of pure desire. I remember his note, and a powerful craving washes over me. I imagine the power of him under me, in me, tucked into my room, in my bed, myself wrapped in his arms and secure, us together.

"Go. I'm fine." I arrange myself behind my worktable, distracting myself with ingredients and runes as he eyes me.

In time, he leaves. There's silence, for a moment, and then Cobalt shuts the door, closing us inside.

He's watchful. He waits. I know he has questions. He saw much more in that exchange than he'll ever let on. Cobalt's like that, obsessed with beauty, smarter than even he gives himself credit for. He moves to the hearth and puts another log on the fire. I finish my last grind of ingredients with my mortar and pestle.

"Can I stay to watch you cast a spell?"

I meet those intense blue eyes of his. I know he's always liked the sheer creation of my magic. It's the witch half of his blood. There's no fear in him, only delight in creation.

I gesture to the stool opposite me, but he raises a hand. He digs in his satchel to pull out charcoal and sketch paper.

He never lets me see what he draws, but he almost always draws when he's here.

"May I?" he asks.

"Of course."

As the ground crystals thrum to life, magic rises. I'm focused only on my power. Everything else falls away. I trace the energy in the individual strands of hair and try to trace their signature.

Thin cords radiate from each strand. Cords track back to ancestors, to places he's been, to people he's cared for, and to everything and everyone he's ever loved. I need to pull the one that leads back to his master.

There are flashes of blood and of pain. There's a tiredness, an endless march of time, an endless hunger, an emptiness, a void of loneliness, cold, cold, so cold, and then—

Eleonore.

He gives that name such reverence, such care, softness, and attention. His master. His... queen?

Sharp pain stabs my fingertips. My eyes glaze over as flames jump and twist in the bowl before me. I yank my hands away, but not before blisters bubble on my inflamed skin.

The bowl containing the hair flies toward the hearth.

When it hits the flames, it explodes. Cobalt jumps back while brushing embers from his hair.

The fire snaps out.

Silence as deep as interstellar space settles over the room.

Outside, a crescent moon touches the horizon. I wipe a bit of blood from beneath my nose. I've never had a spell end like that before.

Fatigue washes over me.

Eleonore. Who the heck is that? A witch? Does she have something to do with the crows? Is she the one controlling them? And why does that name sound vaguely familiar?

And where's Cobalt? He's gone. The ripped shawl from earlier today is draped across the chair he was sitting in. The tear has been mended. On the seat is a sketch, rendered in charcoal, and comprised of blurred lines.

It's me, bare-breasted, wounds styled as scars, hovering maybe six inches off the floor. My eyes are rolled back in my head, all whites, while my hair floats wildly in the air. The shawl he had gifted me is draped over my shoulders. It's alight with runes and sparks of magic. My materials are all suspended in the space around me, and smoke wafts from my open mouth. Magic. Words of power in a hundred different languages cover the rest of the paper.

It's beautiful. Terrible. A witch in her full power, one to be in awe of. Cobalt must have exaggerated, because this woman, she can't be me.

CAPTIVE OF THE VAMPIRES: CHAPTER 7

AZEALIA

The wolves gathered in my garden look at me with suspicion in their eyes.

I bite my bottom lip as I twirl the wolf's-head ring on my right hand. I've faced packs larger than this—even *this* pack when it was larger—but it's been a long time.

And Kael hadn't been their Alpha the last time we'd fought.

He's standing about two feet in front of me. In wolf packs, power dynamics are important. If we are to gain the wolf's trust, then Kael needs to be in the Alpha position. What we're about to ask his pack to do is dangerous, so they will need to be in agreement before we can proceed.

I need to be quiet and let him have control. It doesn't escape me that these are mated behaviors. That this is how shifters mark out who belongs to who. It hadn't been worth the argument. It doesn't matter what Kael's pack thinks of me, or what he thinks of me. I'm still being followed by possessed crows, so finding out who's behind it is the only thing that truly matters.

And that name—*Eleonore*. It still haunts me, although I don't know why. Not yet. I need more information, and I need his pack to help me get it.

"You'll feel cold, until the spell settles," Kael says as he continues to explain the spell I want to cast on them. "Then, you'll be able to see colors you can't normally see. You can follow them with your eyes like your nose follows a scent. Azealia will tell us which trails are the most important ones to track."

Mason raises a hand and waits to be acknowledged before he speaks. "Has she done this before?"

"She demonstrated it this morning. Now just on me, but on the Bear and the Dragon too."

That had been the other stipulation—that Cobalt and Bastian stay separated from the pack. It's been a long time since the shifters last warred, but tensions between Shifter Clans—like all tensions in Bonfire Falls—remain high.

I'm surprised by how many pack members came to my house. Kael had made it clear that he only wanted volunteers. I'd expected a handful of wolves to meet us, but most of his pack is here. Several had approached me to thank me for potions I'd whipped up over the years. Although I never spent much time with the pack, I never turned away someone in need of magical assistance.

Kael glances over his shoulder and nods at me. It's my signal to begin. I step to the side and loosen my tongue for the Norse incantation.

He gestures the first group of five wolves forward. There's a girl in the group who can't be more than seventeen years old. She's strong through the arms and shoulders, with sharp eyes and an easy smile.

"Will the spell hold after we shift?" she asks.

I nod, and she gives me a wary smile.

I'd been up all night trying to find a way to give my

second sight to the wolves. The magic needed to stick through a shift, without making the wolf lose their mind in the process. It hadn't been easy, but right before dawn, I'd finally figured it out.

I breathe in, then out, and in again. As I reach for the well of magic in my center, I let my vision go dark.

"Með eyur minn sjá knátta þú—"

My fingers dance, pushing and pulling threads of magic, weaving the ability to see energetic traces in with the wolves' other senses. A rainbow of colors and sparkling runes dances over the wolf shifters. The magic settles into their skin in whorls of light and power.

I don't know what it looks like from the shifter's perspective. I've never seen myself cast before. Not since Cobalt's sketch last night.

For a moment, my hands falter. Letting Cobalt see me unleash my power is one thing, but allowing all of these strangers to witness my frightening magic is another.

Now is not the time.

I stamp down my embarrassment. The crows are far more important than my fear of being seen as a monster by the others. I shouldn't care what they think, but after living in exile for so many years, I can't help but wonder what they whisper behind my back.

It takes a full three minutes to cast the spell. The chant is intricate, and the motions are precise. Toward the end, my strength starts to fade. I can feel how little time I've spent resting over the last few days. The memory of the blood that leaked from my nose at the end of scrying last night washes through me. The metallic scent envelopes me. I nearly gag but manage to regain my control.

There are still twenty-six more wolves to go. I'd never expected so many to come. The kindness of the pack is... I don't have words. *But by the gods, maybe I should have slept until this afternoon.*

By the time we're through the last batch, I'm tired, so very tired. My muscles shake. My bones ache. Kael is behind me. His hand rests lightly on my hip to steady me.

As the wolves disperse and depart, unease settles over them. Their fear is palpable. I don't blame them. We don't know what we're up against.

They shift before following a muddy trail out of my garden. As they pass through the unseen barrier around the house, a faint, transparent shimmer of gold closes behind them. Beyond it lie the cursed woods where an evil witch made her home centuries ago.

That *evil* witch is me, at least that's what the people of Bonfire Falls think. After today, perhaps the pack will change its mind about me. Kael seems to have laid claim to me. But fear dies hard.

My knees tremble. That was the largest spell I've ever done. My physical and magical reserves have been spent. I haven't needed to store magic in decades, but I have a feeling I need to start capturing reserves soon.

Kael catches me by an elbow, steading me. "You're all right. I've got you. They're gone. You can lean on me."

He soothes me with his presence and his strength. I let him guide me to the bench in my night garden. We sit among star jasmine and honeysuckle blossoms. Lazy afternoon sunlight seeps through the trees to charge the plants with fresh power.

As I sit there and regain my energy, he keeps his eyes sharp, flitting his gaze from place to place. He's protective. Watchful. Strong.

"I wanted to thank you," I say.

He quirks an eyebrow at me.

"All these people—I never expected so much help. Especially with my reputation."

He blows a breath out through his nose. "Your reputation is part of the reason we're here. When you're the smallest cub in a pack, you make friends with the biggest wolf in the den."

"So, who's the biggest wolf, and who's the smallest cub in this scenario?"

"Does it matter?" He's looking at me with something akin to reverence, but Kael would never revere me.

His gaze drifts down to my mouth. My lips tingle.

"You're wrong about what people think of you," he murmurs.

My breath catches. Color rises along my cheeks. I clear my throat and look down at the closed buds of the flowers to my right. I stroke a finger along the petal of a star jasmine, and it blooms, followed by ten or so blossoms around it. The scent is light, as beautiful in the daylight as it is in the starlight.

I clear my throat, unsure of how to move forward with him. I'm not sure how to handle him when he's soft like this. The way he looks at me is tender, and it terrifies me far more than when he comes at me as a growly wolf.

"I spent so many years alone... my tongue ties easily in a knot."

Kael's fingers brush my hand, and I meet those warm amber eyes. "Words are cheap, but action is rare. The pack is grateful for the help you've given us over the years."

"Sometimes I think I should have stayed alone here with only the trees to keep me company."

"A lonely life."

"Yes," I admit.

While he watches me, I force myself not to look at him. I keep my eyes down, and my voice silent. He tangles our fingers together more firmly, while blowing a breath out.

"We're not like most people. Our ability to command power makes us special. It's a burden, and a responsibility. It means we can hand down orders and make difficult decisions, but it also means that sometimes we need to get away from everyone. Solitude is a virtue. Sometimes when I'm on a peak, howling at the moon alone, I feel completely at peace."

"I understand."

He tugs my hand over to his thigh. He spreads my palm and traces the lines from my fingertips to my wrist. "It's hard to stand on the peak of anything. Begin a leader is a never-ending job. All people see is you standing at the top. They don't see the long climb it took to get there or see what it takes to maintain your position."

Those little strokes of his fingertips across my palm light a fire in me.

"But I see you, up there, on the mountain. Alone." He looks to me, as if peering directly into my soul. "I see everything."

I lean toward him, drawn in by the longing which rolls off him in waves. His powerful words have touched my heart, and I can't resist him. With him, I can be real. I don't have to keep up appearances or pretend that I'm not lonely. He understands me.

We're an even match.

"Yesterday, I wondered if those cubs were—"

"Mine?"

I nod, but I'm not sure why it matters. I've been alone for so long. Is opening my heart to him really worth the risk? What if we're both standing on separate mountains, unable to cross the valley between us? We'd be just like

Adrian and his lover, separated forever, never to meet again.

Perhaps I cursed myself when I cursed them.

"Why did you wonder if they were mine?" he asks.

I can't touch that. I can't touch him. I tug my hand gently, trying to get it away. Trepidation rises in me. He stops his fingers at the edge of my wrist, tapping twice to get my attention. I can't look at him. His lifts my chin and forces me to meet his eyes.

"There's no one else on this peak with me. Only you," he whispers.

I can't breathe, not while he's looking at me this way. I search for something, anything to dispel the sense of free fall, this closeness. Somehow, I always knew we'd end up here, close enough to kiss, but still separated by the great divide between us.

"Is that why you're such an ass all the time? Because I'm the only one strong enough to question you?"

"Am I an ass?" The corner of his mouth lifts again.

"You could be kinder." My voice is nothing more than a whisper.

"Kindness invites pain. Control invites strength." He draws me closer.

"That's a hateful truth."

"It is." His gaze is intense but lacks its usual predatory gleam.

My tongue slips out to wet my lips. I know what's coming, and I'm powerless to stop it, even if I wanted to stop him, but I don't. Goddess help me, I don't want to push him away, even though I know I should.

"Maybe we could be strong and kind, together."

As he brushes the backs of his knuckles across my cheek, I turn into his caress with a yearning I haven't felt in decades. He trails a hand down my arm. We're less than a breath apart. The urge to lose control, to burn through all this tension, to let all this heat between us finally ignite, is nearly unbearable.

I don't know who moves first, but our lips meet. His hand dives into my hair and he pulls me closer. His lips are so soft, his hands so strong. The heat of him, the power—I'm overcome.

I lay my hands on his chest, grip the soft linen of his shirt, and cling to him. My fingertips spark, and little shocks of energy flash against him. He flinches and leans back.

"What was that?"

"Magic."

I tug him closer, wanting his lips against mine once more, but he resists. As he pulls away, lightning strikes, flashing down my spine and out through my feet. My hair crackles and lifts. The scent of jasmine and honeysuckle intensifies, mingling with the scent of *Kael*. It's hot and sharp, an assault on the senses.

My magic reaches out, twining around him in little arcs of desire, and power. Other tendrils curl out like roots to nestle into the rich soil beneath us. I open my eyes to see my night garden in bloom. It's beautiful.

His eyes go wide with wonder, only to darken once again with near-feral desire. He growls and dips to nip at my shoulder. One of his hands makes it way to my hip. With the tips of his fingers, he caresses the soft skin of my stomach. My nipples bud as our skin sparks together.

Flashes of golden light and silver—

My eyes dart to a glint of silver at the corner of my vision. Three crows perch on the long branch of a willow tree. Their silver eyes are trained on me. The air stills. A strange twilight encircles the garden.

The hands on my skin become narrower, with longer,

more delicate fingers. Kael's full lips thin. His teeth sharpen. I see a flash of golden hair, like the hair I'd stroked and braided centuries ago.

Adrian.

I shove him away.

Kael's amber eyes flash. His black hair flies in every direction as he stumbles backward. The confusion on his features is so different from the smug look on Adrian's fading face. I shake my head to dispel the hallucination.

"I'm sorry. I can't do this."

Kael catches my hand before I can turn to go. When he sees the fear in my eyes, his jaw firms. His shoulders straighten, and his grip intensifies. He won't let me go so easily, and for that, I am grateful.

"What just happened?"

"Adrian. He was here, but he wasn't. Like a vision from the past."

"He's not here."

"It felt so real."

"But it wasn't." Our gazes lock once more. He rubs his thumb over the back of my hand, just once. "When you're ready to come down off that mountain, you let me know."

The tears threaten to spill from my eyes. I nod and release his hand. He doesn't understand that I'll never be ready. The specter of Adrian will always be there. Not because I still love Adrian, I don't. Not even close. But because I let a man destroy my heart once, and I just can't do it again.

CAPTIVE OF THE VAMPIRES:
CHAPTER 8

BASTIAN

My body burns like fire as I shift from human to bear form. Bones crack and re-align, muscles ripple and deform, while shaggy fur sprouts from undulating skin. Dropping heavily to all fours, I join the search for the possessed creatures who dared to hurt Azealia.

While the others rely on Azealia's spell to find her tormenter, I prefer to rely on my trusty old snout. A hundred different scents play across my palette, and filtering through them would normally be a daunting task, but I'm determined to find out who's trying to hurt her, and why.

Above me, in the crooked limbs of a pine tree, a pregnant squirrel stows away nuts in a hollow. Heavy musk from a forest fox in heat lingers upon the low foliage, mixing with the aroma of decaying vegetation. The criss-crossing trails of the wolf pack are strong here as well, but there's one major odor which is distinct from all of the rest.

The hair which Azealia had managed to steal from her attacker had a peculiar smell about it. Without being able to really put my finger on it, the best description I can come up with is old, dusty, dead things. Like long after the rot is over, when all that's left is withered skin hanging loosely over jagged, broken bones.

My bear form lopes alongside a rushing, narrow river. Moonlight reflects off the flowing water, creating an aura which is totally at odds with the smell of death and decay. On any other night, I'd use the light to help me fish in the river. But not tonight.

Suddenly, the scent I've been searching for assails my senses. My wet nose sniffs at the ground, and I finally detect the path taken by the musty, dead-smelling thing.

I turn my shaggy head toward the trail I'd followed to get here. By my estimate, I'm roughly a mile away from Azealia's cozy little cabin. I could go back and tell the others what I've found, or I can follow it deeper into the woods. Until I know what we're up against, I don't want to bring the others into it, so I continue sniffing and tracking the creature.

The sounds of a wild chase occurring in the woods echoes throughout the trees. The noise of howling wolves, followed by the deranged cawing of the bizarrely affected crows, creates a cacophony which I ignore. I have perfect confidence in the pack's ability to bring down its prey. I'll let them deal with the birds while I track the real threat.

As I continue to inhale the putrid scent, my fur stands on end. Something is very wrong with this creature. It should be dead, but it isn't. It's unnaturally alive. But how?

My bear paws tear into the ground as I increase my speed. Rough-barked trees speed past in the gloom, their branches gaunt and sinister in the night. As I dodge between their grasping lengths, I trample smaller one. Thatches of fur catch on the sharpest of them, but I ignore the sparks of pain as my fur is ripped out.

The smell grows stronger. I'm on the right track, but I slow my pace, moving with caution. I don't know what I'm going up against, but whatever it is, I've never encountered it before. It would be fooling to rush headlong into a fight before knowing what I'm dealing with.

Heavy pads on the bottom of my paws absorb the sound of my passage. In the wild, you might be mere feet from a grizzly and never know it unless the bear wants you to. I use my natural stealth now, because I don't want to let the undead thing know I'm coming.

What if it has a keen sense of smell also?

My predatory senses are on high alert, so I approach the creature from upwind. I still haven't seen it, but it's close.

The musty earth smell of a cave reaches my nostrils. The scent I've been tracking rolls out of the cavern in putrid waves. I stop at the edge of the forest, just inside the tree line. The yawning blackness of a cave's mouth beckons me. Whatever I've been tracking is in there, but do I dare go in alone?

I pace back and forth in front of the entrance. Whatever attacked Azealia must be inside. Anything powerful enough to mess with her must be bad news. Should I go in alone, or should I tell the ancient and powerful witch about my find?

Eventually, I decide to risk going into the darkness. It would take some time to return to Azealia, valuable time during which the thing I've tracked might escape. I can't let that happen.

As I pad into the mouth of the subterranean space, the smell of decay and rot is strong, much stronger than I'd expected. My bear snuffles and shakes his head. It wants to leave. I fight the urge, and together we spelunk even further into the musty gloom.

It's obviously an old, natural aqueduct which used to funnel an ancient stream through the mountains. Smooth stones lie under my feet, while dangling stalactites hang ominously overhead. I recall seeing a movie once where someone got impaled by a falling stalactite. Or was it a stalagmite? I always get those confused.

The scent of death is overpowering. I come to an area of flattened dirt where something had laid down to rest. Something foul. Something... rotten.

Dead things aren't supposed to move around. Is my nose finally going out? Have I reached an age where my ability to track has started to fade? Or maybe I've gone crazy, and I'm wasting my time in this godforsaken place.

I gradually get a hold of myself. No, there's something here. I'm certain of it. The smell might be unnatural, it might be something I've never encountered, but that doesn't mean it's not real. Something attacked Azealia. Something that smelled like death. Until I find evidence to the contrary, I'm going to operate on the assumption that I'm not alone in here.

After thoroughly exploring the tunnels, I don't find anything of interest. I decide to make my way back out to the forest. When I reach the threshold, a pine-scented breeze ruffles my fur. I'm so relieved to be out of the darkness, that I almost miss the sound of something approaching through the underbrush.

Silently, I creep to a nearby bush and crouch low, concealing myself in dark shadows. There is nothing I can do about my scent, but at least I'll be in a good position to perform an ambush.

The wind shifts direction. I catch a whiff of fear tinged

sweat. For Azealia, it's an odd combination, but I'd know her particular scent anywhere.

She careens into the meadow. Wind catches her tangle of red tresses and blows strands across her face. A few leaves and thin twigs have ensnared themselves in those crimson locks, but she doesn't seem to notice them. Instead, she's staring into the mouth of the cave with her big, green eyes.

As I shift back into my human form, my pack slides from shoulders. I quickly change into my human clothing.

Azealia hears me rustling in the brush.

"Who's there?"

She stands with her body sideways, and her arms spread wide. Her left hand glows a violet hue of protective magic, while a sickly yellow phosphorescence covers her right hand. It's probably some sort of poisonous spell. I drink in the sight of her at her full power. She's Goddess incarnate, and she's about to blast my dumb ass.

"It's me, darlin'." I crawl out of the brush and straighten my plaid flannel shirt. She relaxes. The magic nimbuses fade into nothingness. "What's wrong? You look like the hounds of hell have been nipping at your heels. Have you been running this whole way?"

"I'm—" She heaves a heavy sigh. "I used datura and had a vision. I'm concerned about the birds. That's all."

Now, I reckon I know Azealia about as well as anybody can know a reclusive hermit, but I can tell that she's holding something back. She's keeping something from me. It should bother me, but it doesn't. I know Azealia wouldn't hide what she's really thinking without a good reason, so I let it drop.

"Want to see what I've found?" I ask.

"The birds?" Her brow furrows in confusion.

"No, I haven't been tracking the birds at all."

"Bastian, that was the whole point of this organized hunt."

The look of disappointment in her eyes makes my heart die a little. "I'm sorry, but this was important, too."

"If you weren't tracking those possessed crows, what have you been doing?"

"Remember when you showed me the hair from the attack?"

"Yes."

"Well, my bear told me that there was a weird scent to it, like the smell of death, and old rot, and decay. Not fresh, juicy decay, but meaty death, like yesterday's road-kill. Old, dry death, like an ancient tomb."

Azealia purses her lips and her posture changes to one of weariness. She wipes sweat from her brow and sits down on a nearby log. I don't think she's physically tired, it's more like mental fatigue.

"What you're saying doesn't make much sense, Bastian. Are you saying that I was attacked by something dead?"

"Well, there's dark magic, right? Maybe someone tried Voodoo and raised a zombie or somethin'?"

"Oh, stop." Azealia flashes a brief smile. "Voodoo isn't the dark, menacing thing you believe it to be. That's all just myth and rumor."

"But there are spells that revolve around dead stuff, right?"

"There are some necromantic spells, but I would have detected the use of them. This isn't Voodoo related."

"Huh. Well, I don't know if it's a dead thing or not. All I know is that the scent led me here." I gesture toward the cave. "To this place."

"Have you gone inside?"

"Only fifty feet or so. I'll go back in with you if you want." I hold out my hand.

After a moment's consideration, she takes it, allowing me to pull her to her feet. We hold hands all the way to the threshold where she abruptly stops. She raises her hand and a yellow nimbus surrounds her fingers. Using this as illumination, she steps into the cave and I follow a step behind. Her free hand traces yellow light through the air, and then sends a ball of fire streaking off into the deeper recesses of the cavern.

"What was that?"

"A tracing spell. If someone is using necromancy magic, I'll find out."

I show her the spot where the undead thing had sat down for a time.

"What could it be?" she muses.

As we consider it, I notice that she still has some leaves still stuck in her hair.

"Hold still for a second."

"What's wrong?"

"You got some leaves stuck in your hair."

I step behind her and start plucking debris from her gorgeous hair. As I fumble with detangling a stubborn stem from her tresses, she leans back into my body. It's an unexpected intimacy that sends both my hopes and my heart rate soaring.

When my hand brushes the last vestige of the leaves from her hair, she turns around and places her hands on my chest. Her eyes are shimmering with hope, and with longing. I can't resist the pull between us.

Leaning over, I gently kiss her lips. My hands slip around her waist, and slowly the kiss becomes something more. Her mouth is sweeter and more intoxicating than

I'd ever dreamed it could be. And now I don't have to hide how I feel any longer. It's finally happening. We're finally exploring this energy between us.

I back her into the wall. She melts into the kiss, clinging to my shirt and letting soft moans slip from her lips. When she hooks her leg around my thigh, I press toward her, pushing my growing erection against her belly. Her hands slide to my ass, and her lips part. As her tongue invades my mouth, I let out a low growl of pleasure. She smiles.

Of course, that's right when the stupid wolf pack decides to kick up a monstrously raucous howl. It's a predator's howl, a howl of success on the hunt.

Azealia startles. Her body stiffens in my arms. We stare at the entrance for a moment, and then a sudden commotion from deeper in the rock catches our attention. Hundreds upon hundreds of dark, winged shapes come bursting out of the rear of the cave. They don't attack us, far from it. Instead they nimbly dodge around us as we stare in amazement.

I've never seen a bat up close before. They're so little and furry, but with huge teeth, abnormally large teeth. They don't look right. Something's not right about them. But the sheer number of them keeps me from overanalyzing their odd appearance.

Their squeaks and clicks make my ears ring, but it's an awesome sight to see the entire profusion of them circling around and bursting into the night air.

I glance at Azealia. Her eyes are wide and shining. Her lips part and a sigh of wonder brushes over my skin.

When all the bats have fled, she gently disentangles herself from my embrace. I feel the loss of her all the way into my soul. We'd finally had a moment alone, together, and now this.

As she moves toward the mouth of the cave, the wolves continue to howl. Our moment has passed, and all I can do is admire the curve of her hips as she walks into the moonlight. With the taste of her still on my lips, I sigh and follow her outside.

CAPTIVE OF THE VAMPIRES: CHAPTER 9

COBALT

Golden light from the setting sun blankets Azealia's garden in a magical glow. I'm standing by her side, watching the wolves pad away. They're taking their stony Alpha with them, leaving me alone with my mate. Earlier, Bastian, the beastly bear shifter, had left to talk to his clan about the birds. I can't stand that brute of a man. He's not right for Azealia, but he wants her. I see it in the way his gaze slides across her body. Kael looks at her the same way, which is too damn bad because he can't have her. Neither of them can. She's mine.

Azealia's delicate fingers wrap around the handle of a birdcage. Confusion knits her brow. She whispers an incantation to weave threads of magic around the cage to contain the evil inside. Wildly beating wings thrash against the metal bars. The wolves had captured our prisoner earlier today. It's a silver-eyed crow, and it's almost mad with the desire to escape. Azealia has charmed it into silence, but it's still violently assaulting the enclosure.

I don't pay much attention to the crow because

Azealia's beauty is captivating. I notice everything about her—the plumpness of her irresistible lips, the delicate pink of her tongue that flicks out to moisten them, and the way she cocks her head as she studies the bird.

She's still wearing my gift, the wrap made of blue linen with small stars woven in. The cloth snuggles against her hips, and drapes across her breasts. I envy that fabric and wish it were my hands caressing her body instead.

"Have you seen anything like this before?" She asks as she turns to me.

"Anything like you? No. You're glorious." I give her a confident smile.

She looks up, lips parted, expression innocent, and then a hint of color pinks her cheeks. She smiles. "You're as sweet as ever."

Now it's my turn to flush.

She reaches out, smoothing her small hand across my stubbled cheek. I haven't shaved since yesterday. After being up all night while working on her gift, I didn't have time for much more than a quick shower this morning.

"The feathers seem standard, but there's a very peculiar iridescence to them." I nod toward the bird. "They'd look stunning on a cloak, or a fascinator."

"A what?"

"It's a style of hat."

"I'm sure crow feathers are excellent materials, but have you seen a *possessed* animal before?"

"Oh, no. Never. My mother was a witch, but she never dabbled in possession. She'd always emphasized the importance of free will, even for animals."

"It's a very rare skill. I've never met another witch who could wield possessive magic. I'll have to keep researching this type of sorcery. It might lead me to the culprit behind the attack."

She touches the hollow of her throat, a spot she strokes frequently when she thinks. My new gift for her was designed to fit perfectly in that spot. However, she seems to have acquired a different necklace. It's a carved bear claw which has been woven into a leather strap. It's crude and devoid of any skill, clearly made by an amateur.

That's a mating token, my dragon snarls. My belly twists as his eyes and throat begin to glow with molten fire. He's ready to unleash his fury, and I can hardly contain him. *The bear must have given it to her. Bastian.*

I shake my head slightly as my dragon urges me to leave and find Bastian so we can burn him to a crisp. I would never act on that impulse because I can see that Azealia has a deep friendship with the bear shifter. Letting my jealousy go unchecked will only hurt me in the long run. She'd never forgive me if I killed her friend.

Tell her about the gift, my dragon urges.

"I have something for you."

"More gifts? But you just gave me this gorgeous shawl yesterday. I still need to find a way to thank you for that. The charms you wove into it may have saved my life."

Pride rises in me like liquid gold, and my dragon gives a roar of conquest. *The sweet silk of her gaze is more rewarding than anything I could have asked for.*

"I don't know about that, but thank you, nonetheless." She chuckles while squeezing my hand.

Did I say that out loud?

Yes, my dragon snickers.

"I'll always welcome a gift," she says softly.

My heart swells until it's nearly too big for my chest, or maybe that's just my dragon resting on my ribcage.

"It's at my shop. I'll get it. Don't go anywhere."

"I'll be inside working on a scrying spell."

I release my dragon. My bones snap and shift. The dry

rasp of iridescent scales sliding across each other fills the air. My wings spread wide, and I take flight toward my shop.

A few minutes later, I arrive there. I shift back into my human form so I won't break anything. I just repaired the window this morning, and I'm not in the mood to have to fix more broken glass right now.

I find the necklace exactly where I'd left it, sitting on my worktable. Bits of metal and string cascade down from the design's focal point—a blood-red Jasper cabochon. The semi-precious stone is streaked with veins of deep black and rich gold. It's as large as the palm of my hand.

With my claws, I'd carved a spiral pattern of runes into the stone. I'd bound my own magic to it through a blood incantation. If she needs me, she can call me using this necklace, and when she's wearing it, I'll be able to find her anywhere.

After wrapping the gift in a satin-lined wooden box, I grab several long lengths of twine which I'll use to secure the package.

Standing in the street, I shift into my dragon form. My claws are unwieldy, but I manage to bind the gift box to my neck. I want to leave my claws free in case any of those possessed crows try to attack me. I could easily defend myself against one or two, but if the entire flock of hundreds comes at me, then I'll need to be ready to maneuver without worrying about dropping the gift.

When I arrive at her home, the last rays of sunlight are illuminating the trees around the cottage. For now, the branches are free of crows. I find my discarded clothes folded neatly on the porch. I shove her gift into the pocket of my pants.

As I dress, I spot Azealia through the cottage window. She's gathering glass bottles and other supplies. When she sets them on the kitchen table, the caged crow squawks in protest at its captivity. Since she's busy, I don't want to interrupt her. There's something I've been meaning to do anyway, and it's better that I do it when she's inside where she's safe in case my magic goes awry.

I set her gift on the porch before heading toward the edge of the forest. The golden shield she's placed around her cottage is beautiful and powerful, but something compels me to reinforce it. She deserves peace, beauty, quiet and veneration, not these wretched attacks, or the invasion of these unknown, hostile—

Intruders are kept out by spell work, not poetry, my dragon says.

He's right.

After asking the trees' permission, I break sturdy branches off several cedars. I carry a whole armload toward an open space between the cottage and the garden. Using an axe, I cut the broken limbs into stakes and leave them in a pile. I need one more item.

In her garden shed, I locate the twine she uses to tie bundles of herbs together. It's sturdy enough to weave, and it should easily hold my knot magic.

Using what's left of the setting sun to guide my path, I pound a circle of stakes around the cottage. I wrap the twine around the first stake and begin using knot magic to reinforce the protective spell. Every few feet, I tie another magical knot, infusing it with protective intent as I work.

When I'm done creating the powerful circle of protection, I stand back to survey my work. It's beautiful and humming with power, like Azealia.

"You're beautiful to watch," she calls, startling me.

I turn to see her posed in the doorframe. Her arms are crossed against the cold. She has that blue starlight fabric wrapped around her hips and only my shawl to cover her breasts. She stuns me, captivating me with her beauty. A deity to be worshipped, venerated—

"I never would have thought of it myself. Where did you learn it?" she asks, and when I continue to stand there, stunned by her beauty, she frowns. "Are you all right?"

She smells of worry, my dragon growls, faint smoke trailing from his nostrils.

"Yes, I'm fine. I'm sorry."

"No need to be. This is deeply intricate work, and you've been at it for hours."

Have I?

I glance up. The moon is high in the sky. "I suppose I have."

"Did your mother teach you?" She beckons me into her cottage. It's colder than it should be. Her fire's gone low in the hearth.

"She taught me when I was a boy." I move toward the woodpile to gather a stack of logs to feed the fire.

I'm rewarded with a quick smile. "Your mother was an incredible weaver. She made the best cloth on the mountain. What happened to her was a tragedy. She was taken from us far too soon." Azealia's tone is laced with sadness.

I nod as my chest constricts. To distract myself from the pain, I try to arrange the firewood in a way that will generate the most warmth. I breathe fire and the kindling catches. Flames lick higher as I stand back to survey my work.

Azealia lays her hand on my forearm. Her pale green eyes catch mine. I can't look anywhere else but at her, not that I'd want to. She's trying to comfort me, but the ache never goes away. My mother was killed by another witch for her power. I rarely talk about her, and I don't want to remember what I saw. I can't fall back into that abyss.

She slides her hand up to my bicep and her gaze drops to my mouth. The memory of kissing Azealia sparks flames of desire deep in my core. I wonder what she thinks about the kiss. I step closer, my most painful memories forgotten.

"This is the gift I went to fetch." I pull the box out of my pocket.

"You spoil me." She laughs, and her cheeks color.

I present my creation in the palm of one hand. She looks to me and then at the box. With a small wave of her fingers, the lid opens on its own. When she sees the necklace, the light that washes over her features astounds me.

"I've never seen anything so beautiful," she whispers.

"Neither have I." But I'm not looking at the necklace, I'm looking at her.

Our gazes lock. For a moment, the world stands still.

When she turns and lifts her hair, the scent of honeysuckle fills the room. I lift my creation and settle it into the perfect hollow of her throat, above the *mating* charm that *bear* gave her.

I clasp it, settling the cold chain onto her skin and appreciating the delicate shiver that passes through her. She lets her hair fall. I brush it over one of her shoulders, just to touch her, just to catch that scent again. I let my fingers trail softly down the side of her neck.

I lean closer, drawn in by the warmth of her. My lips graze her shoulder, and her scent consumes me. She shivers, leaning back to cradle my head as I kiss her again. She turns to face me. I slide my hands into her luxurious hair and dip to kiss her waiting lips. She moans and wraps her arms around my shoulders. I delve into the kiss, parting her lips with my tongue, searching for something only she can give me. I've never wanted like this before. I've never needed anyone, until her.

As the kiss smolders, she slides her hands under my shirt. My belly clenches, not because her hands are cold, but because she's setting off little sparks of pleasure with her fingertips. I can't imagine how good it would be to make love to her. I don't know if I'd survive it, but even if I perished, lost in the ecstasy of her, I'd die a happy man.

A loud crash shatters the air. Something smashes into the barrier just past her house. I glance out the window at the thin ribbon of gold around her property. It shudders once, then again, and again. Ten, twenty, thirty impacts.

Azealia screams as the magic of her ward breaks and a swarm of bats flies in, each with bright, blood red eyes. They flap wildly, blocking out the stars, and then almost as one slam into the magic of my string barrier.

Their shrill screeching deafens me. I slam my hands over my ears. Azealia does the same, falling to the ground near my feet. A flash of light as bright as the sun blinds me. The bats hiss. The smell of burnt flesh seeps through the cottage walls. With another painful screech, they depart, wisps of smoke trailing in their wake.

I drop to a crouch next to Azealia. Small trails of blood dribble from her nose and ears. She looks dazed and disoriented. The backlash of magic from her broken ward might have caused a concussion. But more than anything, she looks afraid.

Azealia's the most powerful witch in Bonfire Falls. It would have taken an extremely powerful force to crack her ward. Powerful, and deadly.

I draw her close. She curls into me, and clings to me. Fear turns her eyes a deep forest green. Smoke trails from my nostrils like incense, and I send up a prayer with it to the gods. If I'm to keep my mate safe, I must find this monster.

CAPTIVE OF THE VAMPIRES: CHAPTER 10

AZEALIA

It would have been easier to get Cobalt to leave if I hadn't clung to him like a newborn baby. The backlash of magic from my fallen ward stuck me hard enough to steal my breath. I need to be alone. I need time to think. And I can't do it with his arms around me. When he's holding me, all I want to do is surrender to his strength. I want to steal it for myself, but I'd never do that to him. My heart would fracture if I ever tried to betray him like that.

"The bats were lost," I say in a shaky tone.

"Lost?"

"They use echolocation to find their prey. They would have sensed the ward. They never would have flown directly into it."

"I'm staying with you tonight."

"No. You should go and warn the others. Something is coming for me. Something dark and terrible." I shiver.

"I'm not leaving you." He helps me to my feet. "Don't send me away."

"Cobalt," I gaze into his luminous eyes. "I can't concentrate when you're here."

"I'll be quiet. I'll sit by the fire and I won't bother you unless—"

"Please!"

"Are you sure?" He asks with a frown.

"Yes."

"The necklace, I imbued it with—"

"It's a locator charm. I know. Thank you."

"If you need me—"

"I need you, but not in the way you might think," I murmur.

The air around us thickens. Part of me wants to keep him here with me, but I can't. I wasn't lying when I told him I can't focus when he's here. I'm too caught up in thoughts of what his gorgeous, artistic hands could do to my body.

He kisses me before he leaves. I watch him through the window as he shifts and flies away. I trust him to tell the others what just happened. I can sense his jealousy when Bastian and Kael are near, but I can't think about that complication right now, not with everything that's happening.

I set a bowl of moonlight-charged water on the table. I stare into its depths. Willing my eyes to stop seeing this world, I open my third eye. Using a faint trail of energy from the captured crow, I travel on the ethereal plane toward my nemesis. I can never reach her, but I know her name. I saw it when I was scrying.

Eleonore von Schwarzenberg.

Images of Europe from hundreds of years ago fill my head. German cathedrals and Prussian military uniforms parade across my mind's eye. A tomb sealed over with heavy stone vibrates malevolence. Red eyes peer in my soul. Fangs that drip with blood—*A vampire!*

That's it. That's who, or what, I'm dealing with.

Dressed in aristocratic clothes, she exudes money and power. A powdered wig curls intricately around her face and shoulders. A corset nips her waist into narrow submission. Silk brocade falls to form the elaborate folds of her dress. Early eighteenth century, if I'm not mistaken.

But this is an old vision. She wouldn't look like this now. If my long years have taught me anything, it's the need to blend in with the passage of time. Someone would have noticed her failure to age in the *lifetimes* she's been alive if she hadn't changed her appearance. And because of this, she could blend into today's society. She could be anyone, anywhere. She could be in Bonfire Falls right now.

Icy fingers slide across my spine. I don't know how to kill a vampire. They've never infested Bonfire Falls, and I would know if they had because I've been here for centuries. As far as I know, they're a European scourge. They haven't troubled this side of the Atlantic since they were snuffed out in the early seventeenth century.

Is that what attacked me yesterday? A vampire?

I need more information. My eyes burn, my bones ache, and I desperately need to sleep, but I carry on. The urge to pull a sleeping potion from my medicine cabinet is set aside. There will be time to sleep after the threat is gone.

Or maybe when, at last, I am dead.

I pull my books down, pouring through each one. Assyrian, Turkish, and Babylonian, the language doesn't matter, I've learned them all.

A vision of Kael as he plays with those baby wolves pops into my head. He'll make a good father one day. He's tough and demanding, but that's his nature, not an indication of vindictiveness.

Stop it.

I decipher Old Norse, with tales of Cold Ones who haunted villages further north than I've ever been. Their stories are haunting and at times, terrifying.

Each time my mug is low, I charm my kettle to make more tea. The steam that wafts from it reminds me of the smoke that filters out of Cobalt's lungs when he's angry.

Focus.

I read, and read, finding so little it frustrates me. Garlic does nothing to stop vampires; apparently, it's an old wives' tale. Severing their head only stops them for a time. I search for more ways to kill a vampire, but there are conflicting descriptions. Nothing makes sense, so I change direction and focus on animal possession instead.

Unfortunately, I don't find anything useful, only horror stories meant to scare children. The terrible descriptions of their powers will keep me up tonight. Sleep will be but a distant fantasy. I wish Bastian was here. The bear shifter's powerful embrace always makes me feel so safe.

Enough of that.

When my books fail me, I look out the window toward the moon. It's an hour from dawn, maybe less. I need sleep. I need peace.

I make my way to my room, stripping my clothes as I do. With a wave of my hand, I levitate logs and pile them into the fireplace. Effortlessly, I relight and stoke the fire.

As I lay on the bed, I sigh. I should have let Cobalt stay. I could call Bastian with the claw necklace or go to Kael. Maybe I'm being too greedy, but I want all three of them. I care about them all, but for different reasons.

I know there are witches who take more than one

consort. In an effort to amplify their magic, I've seen witches form triads. The more bonds there are, the more powerful they become. However, I've never seen shifters in similar arrangements. Each partner must be equal to all the others in the group, otherwise it won't work. So how could I ever expect my guys to agree to share me?

Bastian cares about me in a way that makes me trust him. He's steady, firm, a rock when I need someone by my side. But I can tell that my magic scares him. He's in awe of me, but he's also slightly afraid of me.

Kael, on the other hand, is a strong and powerful leader. I'd never have to hide my magic from him the way I would from Bastian. In addition to that, I wouldn't have to live up to Cobalt's lofty expectations. With Kael, we'd wield enough power to keep crows at bay, to vanquish bats, maybe even destroy vampires. Together we could stop the endless wars that have nearly destroyed Bonfire Falls. But as much as I want him, I can't ignore the others.

Carefully, so I don't accidentally summon him, I trace the runes on the necklace Cobalt gave me. He's beautiful, gentle, and so creative. He looks at me like I've hung the moon and the stars, and he worships me like it's my due. But sometimes he can't come down from that lofty place in the sky. He's not grounded enough.

Each man has positive and negative qualities, and yet together, they give me everything I need. If I had to choose just one guy, it would be impossible. I couldn't do it. I can't pick one over the others.

But what if I could have them all?

Call them, the lonely part of me says. *You can summon them all, bring them here, and make them love—*

I'm out of my bed before I can finish the thought.

Love.

Absolutely not. Not after what Adrian did to me. Not

after his betrayal. I vowed never to fall in love again, so why am I indulging these feelings for my guys?

A headache pierces my skull.

Have you forgotten the pain? The betrayal? No. Never again.

My nose wrinkles in disgust.

I can't stay in the house a second longer. Clouds are gathering outside in the predawn light. I remember what Kael said about the storm that gathered last time I was upset. I need to be outside in fresh air. I need to ground and center myself before I start a mountain thunderstorm.

Barefoot, I dart into my garden. I focus on the soles of my feet, trying to ground some of my panicked energy. I'm so caught up in my emotional turmoil that I miss the sound of paws in the dirt until it's too late.

Low growls vibrate the air as wolves close in around me. They're so large that they must be shifters. They're not wild wolves. I freeze under the predatory gaze of their silvery eyes. One wolf springs out from the underbrush. I don't react fast enough, and it pins me to the ground. Its muzzle is inches from my face. Its hot breath bursts across my nose and the putrid scent of death assaults my senses.

All around me teeth snap. Snarls sound. Claws scrape at the earth. There are five, six, seven of them, all converging on me. One grabs my wrist and shakes it in a death grip. Another grabs my ankle.

I scream.

As their teeth sink into my flesh, I fling my arms up and push at them with my magic.

Nothing happens. None of my spells work.

I reach into their minds, past the haze of silvery eyes, and find nothing but the drive to kill. It consumes them, drowning all other thoughts in a layer of red, like the blood that spills from me, like the eyes of that vampire.

A burst of magic explodes from beneath my skin. It fires out in every direction, tossing the nearest wolves back thirty feet or more, ending their lives in a flash. The scent of smoldering fur fills the air. I struggle to stand as a constant stream of magic flies from my fingers. Thunder rolls through the heavens. Lightning strikes once, twice, each time illuminating the angry sky.

"Go!" My voice booms.

The remaining wolves turn tail and run, and so do I.

CAPTIVE OF THE VAMPIRES: CHAPTER 11

KAEL

My eyes snap open in the pre-dawn darkness of my room. Loud voices shatter the morning calm. My wolf is agitated, upset that I took so long to awaken. As I get out of bed, a few empty bottles roll off the mattress and clatter onto the floor. It only takes a moment to shimmy into a pair of jeans before I head into the main hallway of the den.

Various members of the pack stick their lethargic heads out of their rooms. They nod as I walk past them. They remain in their rooms. As pack leader, it's my responsibility to deal with any threats to the den. I will only summon them if this disturbance is something I can't handle alone.

The closer I get to the entrance to the den, the louder the voices get. My eyes narrow. Whoever is causing this ruckus is disrespecting our sleeping time. One of my pack's guards is arguing with a woman. I recognize Azealia's voice and I'm ready to light into her as I turn the corner.

"What the fuck is your deal—Azealia?"

The threat turns out to be no threat at all. Azealia, her clothing and skin torn and bleeding, shoves past the guard to get inside. She throws her arms around my midsection even as I take in the sight of her blackened and bloody feet.

"Did you run barefoot all the way here?" I ask, unable to keep the shock out of my tone.

"They're coming! You have to fight them!"

Azealia casts frantic glances over her shoulder. I don't see anything moving in the forest, and I can't smell anything either. Still, something is seriously wrong here.

Several wolves from the pack head toward us.

"I'll handle this." I dismiss them with a wave, and they return to their rooms.

I don't know what the hell's going on, but I don't want them to see her like this. She has an image to uphold and although I don't care about her disheveled state, the others might see it as a sign of weakness. I can't let that happen.

Carefully guiding her through the halls, I take Azealia to my room. She's never been so deep in the den before because we don't typically let humans past the entrance, but she's clearly in need of my help.

I settle her onto a comfortable sofa and hurry to make a cup of coffee. I place it in her hand, but she doesn't move. She's staring at the floor, at nothing, and it's almost as if she's stuck in a trance.

"Azealia?"

"They had silver eyes."

"The birds? Did they attack you again?"

She shakes her head but doesn't speak. I assess her wounds, giving her time to calm down. I'm not a medic, but I can handle non-life-threatening injuries. I manage to clean her wounds before applying gauze and non-stick bandages to her feet.

"Who did this to you?"

"Wolf shifters." Her eyes narrow, and there's a hint of accusation in her tone.

"What? From my pack?" As my hands fist, my blood begins to boil.

"I don't know." Azealia shakes her head, and squeezes her eyes shut. "It all happened so fast. They had the same silvery eyes as the crows."

As pack leader, I'm responsible for whatever my followers do, good or bad. I know most of my pack is here at the clubhouse, but there are bound to be others out dealing with their own affairs.

"Will you be okay for a moment?" I ask.

"Yes." She gazes into the coffee as if scrying for answers.

I hate leaving her alone, but most of the pack is within earshot. If anything happened, I'd know right away. And nothing can get past the guards I have stationed at the entrance to the den. For now, she's safe.

After leaving my room, I knock on the next door over. There's a bit of noise and then footsteps. The door opens and a bleary-eyed girl stares at me in confusion.

"Good morning. I need to speak with Mason."

He comes up behind her, towering over her. He's six and a half feet of solid muscle. Tattoos cover most of his arms and he keeps his hair longer than the lead singer of an 80s hairband.

"Hit the mattress, babe, I'll be back in a few." He gives the girl a pat on the ass. She winks at him as she squeezes past him.

"What can I do for you, boss?" Mason leans against

the doorframe, sticks a cigarette in his mouth, and lights it.

"I need you to do a head count of the pack. Account for every member, not only their current whereabouts, but find out what they were up to last night."

Mason straightens. He might be a playboy, but when it's time for business, he's as solid as they come. "Sounds serious. What happened?"

"Azealia's here. She was attacked last night, and she was wounded."

"Again?" Mason goes into his room and slips on a pair of faded denim jeans. He continues to dress, the cigarette in his mouth bobs as he moves.

"Yes, again."

"Was it the birds?"

I take a deep breath. "It was wolf shifters."

"No." Mason goes slack jawed; the cigarette butt dangles from his mouth.

"She says so, and I have no reason to doubt her. You know that she'd never lie to me."

"Yeah, I guess not. All right, head count, and find out where everyone's been."

"Also, Azealia thinks they may have been possessed like the crows were. It's possible that if it was some of our pack, they might not be aware of what they've done."

"Gotcha, boss man. Consider it done."

With that business settled, I return to Azealia's side. She sits on the sofa, both hands around the mug. I sit next to her and drape my arm over her shoulders. As she leans into me, she buries her face in my chest.

"It's all right. You're safe here. Mason is looking into it. He'll find out if anyone from my pack was a part of the attack." I gently stroke her hair. "I'll protect you. You're here, you're mine, and you're safe."

"I'm yours?" She pulls her face away from my chest and gives me a quizzical and mildly annoyed look. "When did this happen? I was certainly never notified." Her tone is teasing, but strained.

"You've been mine ever since you came to me for help all those years ago. Remember?"

Her mouth stretches into a warm, nostalgic smile, but her gaze seems far away. At least she's not stuck reliving her recent trauma.

"I remember things a little differently. I came to you for help with that reality television crew." She shakes her head slowly.

"*Paranormal Happenings.* Those idiots thought they would solve the enigma of the Bonfire Falls witch."

"They certainly were persistent. I've never seen such determined people. Even after blundering around in the woods for weeks they wouldn't quit."

"Ironically, the more you tried to deceive them with magic, the more certain they were that something paranormal was going on." I chuckle and pull her in close for another hug.

"Then there was that poor director of photography who fell into a ravine."

"I took care of that for you, though. No one connected it to you in any way."

"And I'm grateful to you for that. You protected me from myself."

"Haven't I always been there when you needed me?"

"Yes, you have." She settles in against me and her hair tickles my nose. I inhale her sweet scent. It's heavenly.

"I wasn't the leader of the pack back then, but now that I am, I'll do whatever it takes to protect you."

"You've always been the heart and soul of this pack."

"Yes, but back when we first met, Athos was Alpha."

My teeth gnash as I remember the old pack Alpha. He was a filthy man, both in body and in soul. As soon as he'd started to develop an unhealthy interest in Azealia, I'd begun making plans to take him down.

"I'd rather not hear his name." She shivers. "He didn't know how to take a hint. The more I pushed him away, the more he wanted me."

"He thought that being an Alpha meant that he could take whatever he wanted. But that's not what being the Alpha is all about."

"What *is* it about?"

"It's about taking care of the pack, period. It's about putting their needs above my own. Their safety becomes more important than my safety. Their bellies should be filled before mine. Athos used to know that, but somewhere along the way, I guess he forgot what it means to lead."

"He didn't forget. He didn't care. I'm sorry you two fought because of me."

My fingers brush over a scar on my belly, a scar left by the claws of the old pack leader.

"It was inevitable. As long as he put his needs first, he was a danger to the pack. You were the straw that broke the camel's back, but his downfall was inevitable."

"The pack is much better off with their new Alpha. In my humble opinion, of course." Her radiant smile melts the wall around my heart.

"Oh?" I put my hand on top of hers and squeeze gently. I'm amazed by how soft her skin feels against my own. These aren't the weathered hands of a terrifying witch. These fingers have woven spells to heal and to help others. I'd do anything to protect the owner of these hands from harm, even if it meant risking my own life to do it.

"Yes." Her gaze meets mine, igniting a fire in my belly.

"And why is that, oh great and powerful witch?" I tease.

"Besides being adorable?" She pinches my cheek playfully. "You're also capable, intelligent, and you put the welfare of the group above your own. In short, you're a great leader. I'm glad that I'm your friend."

"You know you're more than just a friend, don't you?" My voice is husky with the sudden need to make her mine. My wolf wants to bite her, to mark her, to lay claim to her. The desire is nearly overwhelming.

"Do I?" She pauses to flick her tongue across her lips. "Am I more than just a friend?"

My arms encircle her waist and I pull her against me.

"You're are mine. From the moment we met, I knew you'd be mine one day."

"But you waited, why?"

"You weren't ready."

"And I am now?"

"Are you?"

She bites her bottom lip. A playful and mischievous smile crosses her lips, and I can't hold back any longer. I cup the back of her neck and pull her close.

"If you're not ready, tell me," I whisper, her lips a breath away.

Her response is a soft brush of her lips across mine. I groan and pull her into my lap. She gasps, parting her lips and allowing me to kiss her with every fiber of my being. With her in my arms, I'm whole. She's what I've been waiting for my entire life. But she wasn't ready before. She seems to be ready now, but I can't help but wonder if this an expression of gratitude in exchange for my protection.

Is the heat between us a small flame with no real fuel,

or is it the spark of a wildfire destined to set our hearts ablaze?

As the taste of her fills my senses, I explore the soft curves of her mouth. Her sensual body is flush with mine, and I can't hide my response to her. I need her desperately. I've waited for so long, but I can't wait another second. Claiming her is all I can think about, and it's the only thing I could ever want.

"Kael?" she whispers.

"Mm?"

"Is this crazy?"

"What we're about to do?" I pull back so I can look deep into her eyes. I'm terrified that she's going to ask me to stop, but I would. I'd do anything for her. "Tell me what you want."

"You. I want you. I've always wanted you."

I scoop her into my arms and carry her to the bedroom. After kicking the door closed, I tumble onto the bed with her. Her hands pull at my clothing. She yanks my shirt off. Suddenly wild, she flips me onto my back and pins my wrists to the bed.

"I've waited a long time for this," she whispers.

Her eyes glow with desire and she's literally the most beautiful thing I've ever seen in my life. I'm stunned by her beauty and her power. She's the perfect match, and she wants me. It's all over her flushed skin and it's evident in her hungry gaze.

As she lowers to kiss my naked chest, I pull her shirt over her head. I'll have to deal with her skirt later, but for now, I'm granted a stunning view of her voluptuous breasts.

Carefully cradling her breasts in my palms, I sweep my thumbs across her nipples. They form taut peaks against my flesh. She shivers with pleasure, and little goosebumps pop up on her arms.

As she reclaims my lips in a passionate kiss, I surrender to her. In all other aspects of my life, I maintain complete control. But when I'm with her, I lose myself. I give her everything. And I love every second of it. I love her. And I'm going to show her exactly how much I want to make her mine.

CAPTIVE OF THE VAMPIRES: CHAPTER 12

AZEALIA

He's consuming me with kisses, and I'm ready to dissolve into his love. I writhe against him, pinning him to the mattress, holding his hands above his head. Sparks shoot between us, little shocks every time a new part of our skin touches. His eyes meet mine. I see his wolf there, primed and ready to spring. The beast is ready to be unleashed, and I want him wild and free.

I want to see him finally snap.

And I do, as he flips me over and covers my body with his. Without hesitation, he glides his hand up my thigh and grabs my skirt. I lift my hips and shimmy out of it.

Lying naked beneath him, I'm struck by how huge he is compared to me. I've never considered myself a fragile little thing, but compared to him, I'm positively dainty.

I hook a leg over his hip. He growls and presses his body into mine. His jeans are rough against me, so I unbutton them and yank down the zipper.

He moans as my fingers slide against his naked skin.

As he works his hips out of the pants, his cock springs free. It's weighty in my hand. Hot, hard, and all mine.

This need to possess him overwhelms me. And I don't mean possess him with magic, I mean to capture his soul. He's already said I belong to him, and if I'm being honest with myself, I do. I'm already his. But that terrifies me. For so long I've been completely alone. Am I ready for this?

The growl he lets out is pure desire. My core pulses and I know without a doubt that I want this, I want him.

He drags his teeth up my shoulder, across my neck, and up to my ear. "You make me want to give you everything."

"All I want is you."

"Only me?"

I hesitate. I can't let myself think about the others, about Bastian and Cobalt. They're not here with us right now, not physically anyway, but the specter of those relationships threatens to ruin the mood.

"I don't care about the others," Kael whispers. "I know I'm not the only one you care about."

"It's just that—" He silences me with a kiss.

"Don't think about any of that right now. Just think about me."

"I can't think of anything else," I say truthfully.

And with that, I'm caught up in his passion, because when we're together, he has a way of tearing past my defenses. Even if I'd wanted to think about the implications of making love to him, I couldn't do it, not when I'm in his arms. So for now, I simply surrender.

I shiver as he nibbles the lobe of my ear. He's being cautious, testing my resolve.

"Don't hold back," I murmur.

His deep, throaty laugh turns my sex molten. I melt

into the sheets as his hot breath trails down my throat. He nips and kisses and licks a trail down to my breasts.

When he captures one nipple between his teeth, I let out a little sigh.

"Such a pretty sound," he whispers against my skin. "I want to hear you moan for me, cry out my name, tell me that you're mine."

"I am."

Magic sparks and snaps between us. He hisses, holding onto his sanity by the most tenuous thread. A dark part of me wants to see him break so that I can put him back together again. We're the same in so many ways. We've been broken by life, by the deaths of those we've loved, but we've never given up on living. Maybe because we both knew one day we'd come together like this.

My nipples tighten and my breath comes harder. Whatever reverence is left in his kisses dissolves into pure lust. He's driven by a single-minded focus, and I want what he wants.

His teasing, tormenting kisses travel lower, across my belly and toward the soft mound over my pussy. Pictures and furniture start to shake as frenetic energy builds. Clouds gather outside and the crack of thunder shakes the walls of his room.

"Please," I whine. The sound is desperate, not at all like me.

"You've waited this long, a few more minutes won't hurt." Although his tone is teasing, there's a bite to it, as if he's trying to exact seductive revenge for making him wait for all these years. I can't blame him for being frustrated. I've been frustrated too. But now that we're together, I'm almost desperate in my need to become one with him.

His lips drag across the thatch of hair over my pussy. I

prop up on my elbows to watch him. He's unapologetic in his leisurely exploration.

"Do you want me?" I demand.

"Can't you see that I do?" His mouth claims my damp lips and I drop back against the bed in shock. "Can't you see that I want to taste every inch of you?"

I moan as his tongue sweeps across my clit. A skylight above his bedroom gives me a view of the night sky. Outside, lightning flashes. Inside, little arcs of electricity jump from his lips to my pussy.

"Did you mean it?" he asks between licks.

"Mean what?"

"I want a partner. I want an equal... I want a mate." He stops and leans on his forearms. His eyes never leave mine.

"A mate?" I swallow back my fear. I told him I'm his, but... his mate? That's an eternal bond that, once forged, can never be broken.

"I want someone willing to be my mate."

"You could have anyone."

"I only want you."

Thunder rumbles, lightning flashes, and the bed starts to float. All my fears about relationships come raging back. My heart skips wildly in my chest. To bind myself to someone else, to mate with them... well, that would be a formidable bond. One that would be impossible to break. We'd be locked together for lifetimes, destined to replay our love story over and over again. Unless it wasn't love. Then...

I shudder.

"I can't."

"There's nothing you can't do."

The bed rises another foot. Outside, the storm rages. Sparks snap between us.

"Stop being afraid of this. Of us."

He doesn't let me respond. His lips are wild and savage on my delicate folds. I'm caught up in a tornado of sensation. And this time, he doesn't let up. He pushes me harder and faster toward the abyss and I'm utterly helpless to resist because he's right. I am afraid of what it would mean to truly become his mate. And until I can let go of that fear, I'll never be able to fully give myself to him.

"Please," I whimper.

His growl against my clit sends me soaring. We levitate off the bed. His hands grip my hips, while his tongue continues to ravage me. A particularly rough stroke of his tongue has me screaming out his name.

"You're mine, Azealia."

I'm lost in waves of pleasure as we crash onto the mattress. He knees my thighs open and when he surges into me, I'm lost. I cling to him as he pushes his rigid heat deeper and deeper until I'm filled with every inch of him. I can hardly hang on as he moves with maddening precision. It's like he already knows me, inside and out. And he knows exactly how to make me burn for him.

He's thick, hot, and he goes on and on. I drop my head into the mattress. My eyes roll back and guttural sounds of feral pleasure burst from my lips. I'm lost to him. Utterly possessed by him, and he's not nearly done with me.

"I've loved you from the moment we met," he growls into my ear. "And I swear I'm going to claim you."

"Kael, oh, God!" I shake apart, lose everything but the thread of his voice.

"That's it my love, come for me. I want to feel you shatter."

I do, fracturing into a million tiny pieces. But it's not enough for him.

He reaches between us and strokes my clit. I undulate

toward his touch. He's inside me, not just my body, but my heart and soul too. I can deny it all I want, but we both know that I belong to him, and he belongs to me.

I rise to meet him every time he pushes his thick cock into me. I pull on his hair, and he sinks his teeth harder into my shoulder. His bite is deep, and it'll scar, but it's a true mating mark, an Alpha's claim.

I'm his. By all the gods, I'm his, marked and claimed forever.

Make him yours.

I push him to the side, and we roll until he's on his back, and I'm straddling his hips. I sink back onto his cock, letting him fill me completely.

As I ride him, another orgasm rips through my body.

"That's it," he whispers. "Take what you want from me. Take everything." He's beautiful, almost feral, the wolf inside him shimmers across his face.

Our eyes lock, hold, and the bond completes. As his breath becomes mine and our souls melt together, he throws his head back and howls. The cords of muscle in his neck stand out, gorgeous and strong under all that tan skin. His dark hair is a tangled mess on the pillowcase, and I can't resist marking him too. I lean down and sink my teeth into his shoulder to give him the same scar he's given me. He cries out more from shock than from pain. The feedback of magic is instantaneous. It's a blood bond that will keep us together forever.

His thrusts become raw and needy. I lose track of everything but the sparks of pleasure emanating from where we're locked in the most intimate embrace. His breath catches in his throat as an explosive orgasm rolls through me. He follows me into a sea of pure ecstasy and together we drown in the sensation of complete bliss.

I collapse against him and he holds me close. He's still inside me, and I never want to let him go.

"Now you'll always be mine," he murmurs.

I freeze. I have to tell him about my feelings for Bastian and Cobalt. Keeping this secret will kill me. This is not the way I'd intended to tell him, but I must be truthful if I'm going to honor our bond.

"You're mine..." I begin slowly. "And I'm yours... but I'm not *only* yours."

He rolls me onto my side. We're facing each other and I read more than just concern in his furrowed brow. He's upset. I don't want to hurt him, but we can't move forward together until we talk about the other guys.

"You want that bear? That dragon too?" he asks through clenched teeth.

"They're mine like you're mine."

"Bullshit." He moves to leave the bed. I scramble to straddle him and pin him in place. Anger and desire burn in his eyes. He's already getting hard, already trying to probe my slick heat.

"It's not bullshit." I keep my voice low to try to calm him.

"You're my mate. *Mine.*"

"I'm sure they'd say the same. It's not that simple, but it's not that complicated either." His jaw clenches and he looks away. I gently grasp his chin and turn his face toward me. "I'll still be yours... I'd just be theirs, too."

"That will *never* work." Kael scoffs.

I hook my feet under his thighs and slowly drag my pussy up and down the length of his shaft, careful not to let him inside me.

"You're not going to distract me."

He's glaring at me as I palm a breast. With one hand, I pinch at one nipple, while my other hand trails down my stomach toward where I'm spread open. I stroke my clit, and my knuckles brush his cock. I play with myself, already close to the edge.

"It's what I want. You told me to take what I want," I say with a sigh.

"I meant *me*, and you know it."

I lower myself onto his cock, drawing him inside me inch by excruciating inch. There's so much heat between us that he's sucked into the vortex. His thick cock stretches me until I'm filled with the full length of him.

"You're trying to trick me," he grunts.

"It's not a trick, or a game, or a ploy. You're mine, Kael. And you've already made me yours."

He makes an angry little sound, a snarl with the snap of teeth. He tumbles me onto the bed and pins me beneath him. He thrust deep, stroking into me with possessive, dangerously sexy strokes.

"You're *mine*," he growls.

"And you're mine. Nothing will ever change that. No one will come between us." He pounds me into the bed, and I'm lost in the pleasure. Rough and demanding, he's desperately trying to hold onto me, but he can't, and he knows it. He knows I belong to all three of my men.

"Look at me," he says. My eyes snap to his. He's stone-faced, full of his own power and determination. He thrusts deep. The moan that slips from my throat makes him smirk. "Don't you think I can satisfy you?"

"You do."

"But you need more? More than any one man can give?"

"Oh, yes." I've lost track of the conversation, but he doesn't seem to notice. I'm caught in a salacious fantasy. Six hands. Three mouths. Tongues and cocks in every place imaginable. "I'm yours. I'm greedy, I need it, fuck, please—"

"My needy fucking mate." He grinds his cock against my clit and it's more than I can take.

I come so hard my muscles seize. My nails claw down his back. He roars, coming deep inside me. His teeth dig into my shoulder, mingling pleasure and pain. Together our power is infinite, magical, and as we crash back to earth, I just know everything will work out for us. It has to, because he's got a piece of my soul now, and I know he'll never give it back.

CAPTIVE OF THE VAMPIRES:
CHAPTER 13

AZEALIA

My head pounds as Kael's voice rises. We're standing in the great room of the wolf pack's den. He's been yelling at the pack for the last five minutes. It's only been twenty minutes since I left his bed, but he's making me reconsider our relationship already.

"Why didn't you scent her before she made it to the den? We have enemies in our territory," he snaps. "Where the hell were you when my mate needed protection?"

His mate? I'm barely his mate now, and certainly not in a traditional sense. But the title doesn't seem to surprise any of his wolves—no one bats an eye.

"There's no fucking excuse for this. What binds this pack together?"

As one they raise their eyes to him, their voices joined. "Unity."

"And what is the death of this pack?"
"Division."

Kael crosses his arms, cracks his neck, and forces his

shoulders down to a calmer position. "Now what the fuck do we know about these other shifters?"

Mason steps between Kael and the rest of the wolves. "Ten wolves are unaccounted for. Most of them live in town, and they wouldn't have gotten the summons yet."

"Get them here. Now." Kael points at me. "The scars of their claws and teeth are on what's mine."

"I am not a possession." My tone is low and filled with warning.

"You're my *mate*!" He spins to face me. The full force of his fury and fear are evident in his eyes.

Lightning crackles between my fingers. My hair lifts from the back of my neck as power arcs through me. I know if I speak, it will be with the rumble of thunder. I roll to the balls of my feet.

The stakes are too high for this. I can't unleash my frustration right now. Not in public. Later.

"I will do what I deem necessary to protect you," Kael's voice booms.

Above us, one of the charmed glass orbs shatters. Shards cascade down between us. The door behind me flies open, slamming into the stone wall. Some of the wolves startle. Kael's eyes dart to the ceiling, over to the door, and then back to me.

I turn and leave without a word.

Outside, clouds roil and churn, blotting out the sun. Pine needles jab at the cuts and bruises on my feet. I cast spells to heal myself. I should have done so last night, but Kael distracted me from everything, including my pain. The bond between us took me to a place of pure pleasure, so I forgot everything that came before it.

Maybe that's over now. If he can't keep his temper under control, I'll need to find a way to sever our connection. I've lived too long and have fought too hard to let a man dictate my life.

I check the trees. They're devoid of crows. The woods are quiet, the calm before a storm. If this vampire has the power to possess shifters, then we're all in danger.

"Sweet Jesus, darlin'. Thank God you're all right."

Bastian charges out of the trees, undeterred by the blackberry brambles in his way. His eyes are wild; his pace frantic. He runs his hand over my hair before pulling me into his arms. My anger toward Kael drops away. It's replaced by sadness. Tears well in my eyes because with Bastian, there's no need to pretend to be strong.

"Let me see you. Are you hurt?" He runs his hands over my arms and shoulders, stopping to look at the still-pink wounds as my healing spell finishes. His breath is fast, and his heart hammers against his ribs. I lay a hand on his bare chest and send a calming spell into his body.

"I'm fine." My shaky voice betrays me.

"I found wolf tracks all around your cottage and saw their charred remains. Your blood was everywhere. I followed the scent trail to get here. What the hell happened?"

"Shifters. There was an attack—we're not sure if they were Kael's." His bear lets out a growl. When he steps toward the door of the den, I push against his broad chest. "Don't. Whoever it was, they were possessed, just like the crows. It wasn't their fault."

He glares at the den. His jaw twitches. His gaze is intent, as if he's weighing his options. If he decided to force the issue, there's no way I'd be able to stop him physically, perhaps not even magically. Bastian is a force of nature when it comes to my safety.

"You scared me." He cups my cheek and draws me closer.

"I'll be okay. My magic will heal me."

He takes a breath, then lets it out slowly. His hands rest lightly on my hips. The nearness of him is so comforting that I can't help but lean into his chest. He slides his hands around my waist and closes the distance between us. A soft, sweet kiss brings us together.

His lips are pure magic, and his hands are strong and warm. I want to sink into his protective arms and make sure he never lets me go.

"That's a hell of a goodbye kiss, darlin'. I guess I missed my chance, lettin' you go this long." He sees the confusion and the hurt in my eyes. "You smell like Kael. I've got to say, I'm jealous. I'd probably pitch a fit if you weren't hurtin'. I wanted you all to myself."

"Bastian, it's not like that."

"I always knew you'd choose; I'd just hoped it'd be me."

"I'm not with Kael—"

A growl sounds from the doorway to the den.

Kael's standing in the doorway. Some of the larger wolves in his pack form a line behind him. His shoulders tense when he sees how close I am to Bastian. With his hands on my hips, and my hands on his chest, we look like lovers. We look like everything Kael doesn't want us to be.

Kael's teeth snap. His eyes glow with a mixture of anger and betrayal. He flicks his hand forward and wolves pour out of the den. Ten, twenty, thirty, maybe more. It's not his whole pack, but it's a majority of them.

When they're gone, he continues to hold my gaze. Anger darkens his eyes because I've shamed him. I let his pack know that I'm not entirely his. I don't belong to him, no matter what he might choose to believe.

I straighten my spine and move out of Bastian's arms. I

don't watch his pack shift. Instead, I hold Kael's eyes, refusing to look away first.

He glances toward the woods. He strips, leaving his clothes in the doorway of the den. In a flash of light and fur, he shifts. As inky black, amber eyed wolf gives me a hungry look before snarling at Bastian.

"You're being rude," I snap.

He huffs and takes off into the woods behind his pack.

"Leave him be. He'll get over it eventually." Bastian takes my hand, then draws me toward the trees in the opposite direction. I don't have the strength to resist him. I let him draw me into the woods, with no thought given as to where he might take me. We wander for half a mile before he lets out a little growl.

I freeze and scan the trees.

"What is it?" I whisper.

"There's nothin' wrong out there. I'm just... I'm mad at myself is all."

"About what?" My heart slows to a normal rhythm.

"I stayed up all night, chasin' that dead smell. I was still in my bear form when I passed out in your greenhouse. I slept through the whole attack, and I was probably still there during most of your...your *time* with Kael. I didn't even notice you were gone until you missed breakfast in the garden." He shakes his head. "I'm a shitty protector, a damn fool."

"I never feel safer than when I'm with you." I tug his hand, stopping us just inside the tree line at the edge of a meadow.

"Don't say things like that unless you mean it."

"I mean it." I draw him closer, settling his hand on the small of my back.

He sets his forehead against mine. Our breath mingles as we stand in the shade of an ancient pine.

"Help me understand what's goin' on here. You've got another man's smell on you, his mark on your shoulder, and you're comin' to me for love and comfort."

"I don't want to choose. I don't know how this works, or if it works, or how to move forward, but I can't lose you. I can't lose him. I can't lose Cobalt. I want—"

He stops me, kissing me until I'm breathless and overcome with desire. We may not have shared the mating bite the way I did with Kael, but we're just as bound. I'm falling for him. Or maybe I fell a long time ago. It doesn't matter now. I'm in the arms of one of the men I love, and that's the only thing I care about.

His kiss is filled with longing. I slide my fingers into his hair and stroke his head. When we finally break apart, his eyes are radiant with love.

"I don't care who else you want, darlin'. Let me have this. Let me keep you close. Let me keep you safe. I want to take care of you."

"I want that. I want you."

A deep, rich vibration rumbles in his chest. My nipples tighten, and my breath hitches. I guide his hand to the tie which is holding my skirt together. He works the knot gently, my sweet bear shifter, the man I've loved for so long. I let years pass, knowing that he was waiting for me. I gave up time we could have had together because I was too afraid to let myself feel again. And now that's all I seem to be doing—feeling. And I can't stop it. I can't deny my feelings anymore.

"I've wanted this for so long," he murmurs as my dress slips free.

I moan in response. For a brief moment, I wonder if we should let ourselves get so vulnerable out in the middle of the forest, but I'm sick of hiding. I don't want to wait another second. I need him here and now.

He's out of his clothes before I have a chance to help him. Naked and warm, pressed chest to chest, we embrace. His lips find mine and I'm lost in a kiss that intensifies with each passing second.

Time stands still when he fully claims my mouth. I part my lips and the stroke of his tongue over mine electrifies every cell in my body. I'm coming alive again in his arms. With Kael, we came together in a sort of rough desperation, but with Bastian, there's a wistfulness to the kiss that is so endearing, I can't help but kick myself for pushing him away for all these years.

As his kisses trail down to my throat, I entangle my fingers in his hair. His lips mark me everywhere except where Kael bit me. Bastian skips over that tender spot and moves down to nuzzle my breasts.

The rasp of his tongue and the way he's holding me break my heart wide open. I'm in love with this man, and I want him to know how much he means to me.

"Bastian," I cradle his cheeks in my palms. "I'm sorry I made you wait."

"You were scared. I get it. But I don't want you to ever feel like that again. I swear to you, I'll make sure you always know how much I love you."

"You love me." It's a breathless statement, and it's all that I can manage. I knew he loved me, but this is the first time he's said it. He's making it real, and it's terrifying, and exciting, and I can hardly contain my joy.

"Of course I love you. No man in his right mind could possibly do anything but love you. You're a queen among peasants." His lopsided grin brings me to my knees. "Come here."

As he lays me on the soft grass, my hair fans out around my face. He brushes a few errant strands to the side before kissing me again.

"Now let me love you the way I've been wanting to love you," he whispers.

He slides between my thighs and trails his fingers across the smooth flesh. As his head dips between my legs, I sigh. His mouth is hot against my sex. His tongue lays languid strokes across my swollen lips.

Warmth pools in my core. He's awakening a part of me Kael hasn't touched. Where Kael's hard, Bastian is soft and gentle. It's not bad; it's not better; it's just different.

As he glides his tongue along my slit, I moan and arch my back. With greater access, he delves into my pussy, finding and teasing out every part of me until I'm spread wide and desperate for release.

Tension builds and builds until I'm writhing beneath him. He grips my hips and mutters something about not moving. But I can't stop. My hips arch and retreat, searching for the perfect angle, the exact spot that will send me to the moon, and then he finds it.

"Bastian!"

I'm lost in pleasure as rolling waves of pleasure carry me into a state of pure ecstasy. He kisses up my body then settles between my thighs. His thick cock is hot against my wet center. And then he's moving inside me, claiming me with one, long stroke.

Fully seated, he kisses my lips. My salty sweetness is still on his tongue, and the erotic scent mingles with the taste of him.

His gentle thrusts drive me wild. This isn't a fast, rough coupling like last night, it's slower and far more sensual. While one hand holds him up, his other caresses my breasts. He takes one plump nipple in his mouth and sucks until I'm gasping.

The spiral of need coiling in my pussy tightens until it's ready to spring free. I can't take the luxurious thrusts anymore. It's too intense. Too intimate. Too overwhelming.

"Bastian, please."

He hushes me, and then strokes a hand down my hip. He grips my thigh, dragging my leg around his back. I hook my ankles behind his waist.

Deeper now, he's taking me further than I've ever been before. I've never floated in a realm of such extravagant beauty. His face is rugged, and sexy as hell, while his eyes are half-lidded and filled with tenderness. And he's all mine.

I crash into my orgasm. It shakes through my core, stealing the strength from my bones. I go limp, while he goes impossibly hard. His eyes close and his mouth clenches. He groans and drops his forehead to my shoulder.

As he pulses his own release, he kisses and licks the place where Kael had marked me, as if accepting that connection. I want to weep at his acknowledgement. He's not asking me to choose, not the way Kael did. And for that, I'm even more in love with Bastian.

When he's spent, he leans on his elbows to look down at me.

"You're the most beautiful woman in the world, and I can't believe you're willing to share yourself with me."

"Because I love you." It's still terrifying to open my heart like this, but I can't see any other way to move forward. I need him and he needs me. Together, we could have something special, if we can work out an arrangement with the other guys.

As much as I care for Bastian, he's not the only man I care about. I can't deny my feelings for the others, but Bastian isn't making me choose. Thank all the Gods for that.

"Don't go back to your cottage. Let me take you somewhere else, somewhere you'll be safe." He means the Bear Clan's den, but the mere thought of it brings to mind Kael's rage, and Cobalt's pain.

"I need to go home. I need time alone, to think."

"Now's not the time to be without protection. You need me. You need us. I'd never ask you to pick one of us over the others, but I won't let you be alone right now. Not until we deal with the possessed crows and violent wolves. I know somewhere safe we can go. It's not the Bear Clan's den, but Kael won't like it."

He's asking me to trust him, and I do. So after a quick dip in the river, I get dressed then lace my fingers into his, and follow him into the forest.

CAPTIVE OF THE VAMPIRES:
CHAPTER 14

COBALT

I'm stretched out in my bathtub, trying to have a lazy day, when someone starts knocking on my door. I'd hoped for some relaxation after a hard day in my shop. Instead, someone seems hell-bent on ruining my night.

"Calm down, damn it. I'm coming." I drag myself from the gloriously warm water and reach for a towel. I dry off hastily, which causes me to drip water all the way from the bathroom into the living room.

At the last moment, I realize I'm naked and quickly wrap the towel around my waist. I knot it securely before opening the door.

"What is so damn important—Azealia?"

She's standing on my porch with her arms crossed over her chest and eyebrows knitted together. I start to go to her when all of sudden, a hairy mountain of a man injects himself between us.

"Cobalt, let us in. Now," Bastian says.

"Why?" My eyes narrow. Something's different, but I don't know what yet.

Azealia leans toward Bastian. Her hand rests on his forearm. The familiarity between them is like a stab to my heart. So, there's been a change in their relationship. Just my luck.

"Please. It may not be safe for us out here," she says.

"Of course, come in." I step to the side. Bastian's barrel-chested form barges right in. He doesn't even wipe his boots first.

While I'm glaring at the tracks he's making in my lovely butterscotch-colored carpet, Azealia comes in behind him. She hugs me tightly. I am gratified to see her wearing the necklace I gave her. It nestles in the hollow of her throat, glittering in the twilight.

"What's going on?" I pose the question to Azealia, but the burly bear shifter answers.

"Please forgive this sudden intrusion, but she needs a place to crash for a few days. A safehouse, if you will."

I'm jealous of their newfound intimacy. I want to be that close to Azealia. If she's in trouble, she should have come to me first. At least she's here now.

"I'll take care of her."

"Hey, do you have any food?" Bastian's nose wriggles. He glances in the direction of my open concept kitchen.

"Neither of us have eaten since last night," Azealia says.

"Ah, sure." I shrug and gesture toward the kitchen. "You're welcome to whatever you can scrounge."

"Great." Bastian stomps off toward the kitchen

As he starts to rummage through my cabinets, I turn to Azealia. I'm dying to ask her about the obvious change in her relationship with Bastian. My dragon wants to breathe fire all over him, but of course that's not an option.

Are you sure? my dragon asks.

Quite sure. Now calm down, I'll speak to Azealia.

Why is she with that beast? Why isn't she our mate?

Let me handle it.

"Azealia..." I take her hand in mine. "You know you've always been my muse, right?"

"Right..." She cocks an eyebrow at me. A nervous smile flitters across her face.

"Well, I—"

A furious pounding at the front door interrupts me. Again.

"Who could it be now?" I grumble.

Azealia blows out a frustrated sigh. "It's probably Kael. I'll let him in."

"Kael?" For a moment, I stare at her back as she heads for the door, but then I dash ahead and open it myself.

The wolf pack leader stands there. His body trembles with nervous energy. I get the feeling he loped here in wolf form, and he hasn't quite made the change all the way back. His arms are still awfully furry.

"Cobalt!" He glares me up and down. "Why the fuck are you naked?"

"Nice to see you, too. If you must know, I was taking a bath when all of the sudden my home became ground central for a gathering of witches and shifters."

"Azealia?" Kael cranes his neck and spots her in the living room. "Out of the way, dragon, let me in."

"Not so fast." I anchor myself there in the doorway, taking it up so he can't move past me. "You can't just barge into my home."

"I can do whatever the hell I want. Now get out of my way." He growls at the end, and his teeth seem particularly pointy. But he's not the only one who can get in on that act. Steam vents from my nostrils. My own dental work skews toward the reptilian.

"This is my home. My studio. You'll not set foot in here without my approval."

"This is the last time I'll be nice, little dress maker."

"You can ask nice or you can be an asshole, but either way you're not coming in unless I want you to."

Kael cocks his head to the side. He's teetering in the balance between man and wolf. Shit's about to get physical when Azealia's gentle touch on my shoulder stops both of us.

"Cobalt, please let him in."

I could never refuse her, so I step back from the door and gesture grandly for Kael to enter.

"Please, make yourself at home," I say sarcastically.

He crosses the threshold, smirks at me, and then stalks over to Azealia. The oaf towers over her. She doesn't back down an inch. She crosses her arms and glares right back at him.

"How could you just run off and disappear like that?" he asks.

"Excuse me?"

"You heard me. You ran off with a random bear shifter after you'd come to me for help. Why would you do that to me? What if the other wolf shifters attack you again? I told you I'll take care of you. And... I was worried."

Azealia's gaze softens for just a moment, then grows hard again.

"Why would you go and tell the entire pack that I'm your mate? And anyway, you're not my owner or my Alpha. You don't get to dictate what I do or who I spend my time with."

"Azealia was attacked by wolf shifters?" I ask.

No one pays any heed to my question. Instead Azealia and Kael continue to trade barbs back and forth. I quickly realize two things: she spent the night with him, and she has some sort of intimate relationship with him now. It's like a punch to the guts. She's started relationships with the other guys, but what about me? I care about her far more than these other two ever could.

"Hey!" Kael, Azealia and I turn toward the booming voice. Bastian leans over the island in the kitchen. "I object to being called some 'random bear shifter.' Damn, Kael, we've bumped into each other dozens of times at the bar. Yesterday being one of those times. I bought you a PBR."

"And I forgave you for that shitty beer, you cheap bastard."

"Kael, there's no need to be insulting," Azealia says.

The wolf pack leader throws off her restraining hand. He takes a step toward Bastian. "You're just pissed because when Azealia needed help, she came to me first."

"I'm sure it was just a matter of convenience... or desperation," Bastian says dryly.

"Or she knew who could take care of her, and it wasn't you," Kael snaps.

"Shut. Up." My voice reverberates throughout the room. My entire body trembles. Steam pours from my nostrils. They watch as I stalk across the room to snatch a feathered fedora—don't ask, it's for a client—and thrust it in the middle of the room.

"This." I give the hat a shake. "Is the talking hat. You get it? The talking hat. If you have the talking hat, you can, guess what?"

"Talk?" Bastian's eyebrows are raised and his lips quirk.

I glare at him and snarl, "Shut up. You don't have the talking hat, therefore, you can't talk."

"But you asked a leading question, it would have been rude not to—"

My hard-eyed stare forces Bastian to be silent. "Right. Now you get it. The only person that gets to talk is the one with the talking hat. That should cut down on the shouting and fighting. Deal?"

"Great." Kael snatches the hat out of my hand. "I'll go first. So, does that mean that as long as I'm holding the damn hat, Bastian can't say anything back if I call him a dingleberry factory with bad breath?"

When Bastian growls, I reach for the hat. "No, that's not how it's supposed to work."

Bastian strides over and takes the hat into his massive hand. "So, does that mean that Kael can't say shit if I tell him he's a nasty, sawed off little runt who spends all his time licking his own balls?"

"That's not the point—"

Kael grabs the hat back from the bear shifter and sneers at him. "Hey, look, I have the hat. And it's a good thing, too, because Bastian's flapping jaw was about to put him in a world of hurt."

"Oh, is that a threat, little puppy dog?" Bastian takes the hat back as Kael smiles ruefully. "You think that you're strong enough to protect Azealia? You're so little and scrawny, I bet you couldn't protect a gingerbread house from a cat high on the nip."

Kael takes the hat back as Azealia hides her face in her palms. "I can protect Azealia just fine, and she knows it. That's why she came to me for help. She knew that you were probably out shitting in the woods."

Bastian snatches the hat back and growls. "Oh, bear jokes. Nice. You know, I could knock that pretty face right off with one swipe of my bear's claws."

"Oh, do tell." Kael grabs the hat, but Bastian refuses to release it. "You're too big and clumsy to catch me."

"Dream on. I'd have your innards slopping to the ground before you could howl.'"

"You're just compensating because you have a millimeter peter."

"What? Who said that? I've been told that it's quite substantial."

"That's just what a guy with a small dick would say."

"You want to see it? I'll back up my talk. Can you?"

Suddenly, Azealia's hand's on my wrist. She drags me away from the rapidly escalating fiasco in my living space, takes me into my bedroom, and shuts the door. She places her back against it and sighs in relief.

"I'm so tired of both of them."

"I'm surprised to hear you say that."

"What's that supposed to mean?" She fixes me with an incredulous stare.

"It means you've gotten rather close to Kael and Bastian in recent days, haven't you?"

I didn't mean to make it sound like an accusation, but my ego got in the way. Realization flows over her lovely face, and she comes to my side. She takes my hand in hers and smiles at me. For a moment I forget all about the dick measuring contest in my living room.

"Well, out of the three of you, you're the only one who's given me jewelry." She fingers the tracking amulet I'd labored to make her.

Suddenly, my brow is covered in sweat. How can she have this effect on me? As my cheeks burn, I strive for some way to regain my perceived lost dignity.

"Ah, well, you know if I'd known you were so into collars, I'd have given you one years ago," I say, trying to keep my tone light.

She's so beautiful. Light shines in her emerald eyes. Finely detailed freckles dot the canvas of her soft cheeks

"You're gorgeous." I blurt out the words before I can stop myself.

Her smile grows wider, and her eyes light up with the glow of pure happiness. I didn't realize that she would be so pleased by my declaration.

"Thank you. I know you want me, Cobalt. And I want you, too. Regardless of what's going on between me, Kael, and Bastian, I need you to understand that I feel the same way toward you. It's complicated. But that's me."

"You're not complicated, you're perfect."

"Far from it."

"To me, you're a goddess." It seems like the perfect time to kiss her, so I do. The softness of her lips against mine sends a rush of pleasure throughout my entire body. My dragon is practically singing inside me.

She deepens the kiss, opening herself to me. I take full advantage and slide my tongue across hers. She sighs and wraps her arms around my shoulders. We forget about the two idiots in my living room and focus only on each other. They don't matter anymore because she wants *me*. She wants *us*. And if I have to share her with those morons, then that's what I'm going to do. Anything for my Azealia. Anything for my love.

CAPTIVE OF THE VAMPIRES: CHAPTER 15

AZEALIA

The next morning, I wake up in Cobalt's bed. I smile slowly as I turn toward him. He's gone. I sit up and glace around the room. A folded note sits on the nightstand on my side of the bed. It's from Bastian, which is strange. When did he come into the room? And is that why Cobalt's missing?

I unfold it and read Bastian's message. He's on his way to warn the Bear Clan about the vampires. I have no doubt we're dealing with the ancient evil. Why they've come to Bonfire Falls is beyond me, but we have to get rid of them.

Hopefully, his warning will be taken seriously. Although a shifter's senses are generally weaker than mine, this vampire has caused a huge disturbance in the balance of our town. The shifters should all realize we have a menace in our midst.

Bastian also mentions that he's seeking out the wisdom of the Bear Clan's elders. Some of them are descendants of an ancient and highly esteemed line of brown bears. Surely, they will possess valuable information that can help us in the fight against the vampire queen.

I fold the note and store it in one of my skirt's pockets for safe keeping. I wish I'd gotten a chance to say goodbye before Bastian took off. And Cobalt didn't even leave a note. I hope he wasn't disappointed in last night. It was magical, perfect, everything I've ever wanted. I just hope he felt it too.

After spending a few minutes practicing my morning meditations, I swing my legs over the side of the bed. When I stretch my arms, my joints pop and crack in the best way possible. My muscles expand and contract as I lead them through fluid motions taught to me by ancient priests in a faraway land.

I grab my clothes off the floor. I haven't changed since yesterday. Even with a cleaning spell, they're a mess. I doubt Cobalt would mind if I borrowed one of his shirts, so I slide it off a hanger and slip into it. The fabric is soft and luxurious. The shirt is so long that it brushes my knees. It may as well be a dress, which is good because his pants would be huge on me.

As I head out of the bedroom and into the living room, I spot Kael pacing near the front door. My heart does a little flutter. He may be an arrogant asshole sometimes, but he means well. He just needs to learn how to calm down.

"Is everything all right?"

"You're awake."

"Were you here all night?" I can't stop a blush from creeping up my neck.

"Yeah." His eyes narrow as his gaze sweeps up and down my body.

"I—"

"Those shifters aren't from my pack. They're from another pack on the other side of the mountain."

Relieved that he's not going to berate me for the loud sex I had with Cobalt last night, I sit on the couch.

"You must feel better now."

"Yes, and no." Kael rubs his chin. "If it were my pack, I could whip them into shape and eliminate the threat in one swift move. I can't control the other pack. I can only fight against them."

"I wish I knew exactly what we're dealing with." I run a hand through my hair and try to untangle the knots caused by a night of endless lovemaking. "There are very few witches who can take control of an unwilling shifter. Most witches who are dark enough to do such a thing band together and pool their power to make it happen."

"So, the vampire's powerful. We already knew that."

"Yes, but we might have to prepare for the fact that the vampire is as powerful as you or me. Maybe even more so."

"I don't like this," he snarls.

"I know." I place my hands on his shoulders and allow some of my soothing aura to seep into him. Kael immediately takes a step back.

"What the hell was that?"

"My attempt to keep you from getting all riled like you were last night." I roll my eyes. Sometimes he's so exhausting.

"You're right. I'm sorry." He slips an arm around my waist and pulls me against him. His voice softens but he doesn't loosen his grip. "I know you must be on edge with everything that's going on. I should be more sensitive to that."

"Thank you." I nod. "I'm worried about this vampire. She might be more powerful than me."

"You have nothing to fear." He tucks a lock of hair behind my ear before stroking his thumb down the length of my cheek.

I rise onto my toes to kiss him. It's meant to be a soft kiss, but the moment our lips touch, fire streaks through me. He tightens his grip around my waist.

"Where's Cobalt?" I ask.

"In his workshop. I never would have left you in bed alone."

"Maybe he needed to work."

"As long as he stays away, I don't care what he's doing."

Eventually I'm going to have to figure out how to get these guys to accept the complexity of our relationships. But for now, I surrender to Kael's kisses.

As his tongue parts my lips, I welcome him. I pull his hips against mine and let out a soft moan as his cock stiffens. The tension between us melts away, as does the rest of the world.

I almost cry out in protest when he pulls away. My desire is fully alive now, hungry and wild. I want him again. I don't think I could ever get enough of him.

"If I allow myself to keep going, I'll have to drag you into Cobalt's bed, and I don't want the stink of that lizard on me." His eyes burn like embers as he rakes his gaze over my body.

"You're going to have to get along."

His growl is low and deep.

I shake my head.

"I have to rally my pack. If we wait too long, we might lose any lead we've gained on the vampires."

"You're right." I'm miffed that he doesn't want to talk about getting along with Cobalt. I lean back against the wall to steady myself. "Since that's more important, go." I wave him off.

"We'll continue this later." He leans in and pecks me on the cheek.

When he's out of sight, I flop onto the couch. Bastian's with his clan doing something productive. Kael's on his way to meet with his wolves to do something productive. And Cobalt's being productive downstairs in the shop. I need to do something helpful too. I can't let the men do all of the work, now can I?

My first thought is to return to my cottage alone. Yes, the vampires might be powerful, but I'm still the most powerful witch to ever exist. That must count for something. But I don't want to do anything stupid like try to go up against the vampire alone. I'm going to need help.

Cobalt strolls into the room.

"Hey, sweetie," he murmurs as he brushes a kiss across my lips. "You're up."

"You left me in bed alone."

"I didn't want to wake you. After everything you've been through, I figured you needed some time to recuperate."

"Oh." I stand corrected.

"I'm hungry. Want to go to the café in town with me?"

"Sure."

After Cobalt changes into clean clothes, we walk arm in arm down Main Street in Bonfire Falls. I'm still wearing his shirt, and nothing else, but I don't care. I want everyone to know that he's mine and I'm his.

The cute shops and friendly small-town vibe cheer me up. As we walk through the central park area, I smile at children playing and at young couples holding hands. Oh, to be so young and naïve again.

"I can't believe I stayed away from this place for so long. I'd completely forgotten how charming it is." I sigh.

"It's a shame that we've had to struggle so hard to maintain peace the last few years."

"Indeed."

Halfway down Main Street, we stop at a tiny café. A huge window display is filled with trays of baked goods. Two bistro tables are set outside in the sunshine. Both are currently empty since it's between breakfast and lunch. I settle myself into a chair and Cobalt sits in the one across from me.

As soon as my tea and Cobalt's coffee arrive, I lean toward him.

"I want to talk about the vampires," I whisper, even though no one's around. "I want to find them and stop them."

"We all do." He places his hand over mine.

"Do you have any theories as to where they might be hiding?"

"Vampires and dragons aren't as different as one might initially assume. If I were part of a secret vampire horde, I'd seek out a secluded cave. I told Kael and Bastian as much, though who knows if they listened."

"Bastian and I were in a cave not too long ago."

"Maybe the vampires were in there also."

"It was filled with bats."

We lock gazes and a chill shimmies down my spine. Were those bats shifted vampires?

"That would be the first place I'd look," Cobalt says. "But I wouldn't go alone. If you want to go back to that cave, I'll come with you."

"I never want to return to that place."

"Then you don't have to."

After we finish out brunch, he leans across the table and presses a gentle kiss to my lips.

"What was that for?" I ask in a breathless tone as he pulls away.

"You're too lovely to resist." He grins. "I hate to run, but I have to get back to the shop. If you decide to go hunting for vampires, call me first."

"I will," I assure him.

He looks back over his shoulder three times as he walks between the café and his shop. I smile and wave each time.

Instead of heading directly home, I decide to stop at the Bonfire Falls Library, which is located on Main Street. I pick up a several volumes containing vampire lore. They may not be as accurate as the books in the Wolf Pack's library, but I may be able to glean something from them. Perhaps I'll find out more about Eleonore. I'm sure she's the vampire we're dealing with. Or at least one of them. I really hope it's just her, and not an entire clan of vampires.

Instead of tempting fate by investigating the cave on my own, I head toward Cobalt's shop. He finds an over-stuffed chair and drags it into the workroom so he can keep an eye on me. I open the first book and continue reading until the sun sinks low in the sky. Before nightfall, Bastian and Kael arrive at the shop.

"Good, you're all here." I close a massive leather-bound tome and set it on the small table beside me. "I found some interesting information on Eleonore."

"And?"

"She's unbelievably ancient. So ancient that when she was in her prime, people were too afraid to even speak her name. For centuries, people used her story to terrify children into good behavior. I'm not sure why she's been quiet for so long, but one thing is clear. Every text I've read has mentioned her obsession with power."

"That would explain why she's after you," Bastian says. "She's probably trying to take your power."

"The question isn't—why is she so power hungry? The question is—what are we going to do about it?" Kael insists. "I can take my pack out now and scour the forest until we find her. She may be powerful, but I don't know of anything that can survive being torn apart by a wolf pack."

"No," I protest. "I don't want to put any more innocent people in harm's way."

"We have to do something," Kael says.

"We can take her to the dragon village at the top of the mountain. There isn't a more fortified place in all of Bonfire Falls," Cobalt says.

"The dragon elders will never let a wolf and a bear shifter into their stronghold. They haven't let anyone in for centuries," Bastian points out. "Although they did let that witch in recently."

"Ariadne," I offer.

"Yes, her. She married three dragons," Kael says.

"You're right. They'll never let *you* in, but we have to think about what's safest for Azealia, and the dragon village is fortified and defendable," Cobalt says.

"We could set a trap at her cottage," Kael says.

"We moved her here because we couldn't protect her at the cottage," Cobalt says, exasperated.

"Enough." I close my eyes and lay my palms flat on the table. A headache pulses between my temples. "I can't deal with any more arguments today. We'll revisit this in the morning when we're all rested."

The three men must read the tension on my face because they stop arguing almost immediately.

"You're right," Bastian says. "We'll think more clearly when we're all calmer."

"Agreed," Cobalt says. "She'll stay with me."

"I'm staying too," Bastian and Kael both say.

"Take the bedroom again tonight," Cobalt says. "I'll sleep in the living room with the others. You need your rest. We'll guard you while you sleep."

"Thank you," I dip my head. "I'm going to bed. Please don't fight tonight."

"We won't," Kael promises.

"Of course not." Bastian reaches out to squeeze my hand before I go back upstairs.

As I prepare for bed, I just pray we'll be able to go forward as a harmonious unit. None of us will be safe if they keep snapping at each other's throats.

I slip into a feverish dream. The dark, ghastly face of death peers at me from just outside the bedroom window. I struggle to pull away from the image, but I'm trapped.

Magical bonds slither around my forearms and corset them together. I can't move. I can hardly draw a breath. I open my mouth to scream. A small, strangled noise comes out right before a magical gag clamps across my mouth.

The shadows come to life around me. I'm surrounded by vampire minions as silent as the night itself. I'm powerless to help myself as they gather me up and spirit me away.

CAPTIVE OF THE VAMPIRES: CHAPTER 16

COBALT

Morning sunlight slashes through the bedroom window. The glittering remnants of one of Azealia's bracelets catch my eye. I carefully step toward it. After retrieving it from underneath the edge of the bed, I sniff it. The scent of death and decay assaults my nostrils. I jerk it away from my nose. The vampires. They took her.

Down in the living room, Kael and Bastian are arguing about who's to blame for Azealia's disappearance. My nose wrinkles in disgust. Fighting will only waste time. We need to band together to rescue her.

"No, man. This is your fault!" Bastian's booming baritone blares out the window. "You were being an ass, and you drove her away."

"I was being an ass? Me? You're crankier than a toddler!" Kael hollers.

"Stop being such a little shit. You're just as much to blame as the rest of us," Bastian says.

"No way. I was trying to protect her, and I was doing a

good job until you and Cobalt decided to butt in," Kael snaps.

"She came to us because she knew you were too hot-headed to help her. You only think about yourself and what you want. What about what she wants?"

It's hard to tune the two of them out, especially since they haven't stopped screaming since we discovered she was missing.

I rearrange the broken pieces of bracelet into some semblance of their original configuration. If only it were so easy to fix broken relationships. I don't know how any of us are going to get along if we can't set aside our differences and come together for Azealia. She's been clear about what she wants, and while I don't exactly like it, I'd do anything for her. If they others aren't willing to do the same, then they don't deserve her.

I carefully fold the broken pieces into a handkerchief and then shove it into my pocket. In order to abduct Azealia, someone would've needed to use some pretty potent magic. Why didn't any of us sense it? Her abductor was stealthy enough to avoid our shifter senses, but how?

Hopefully Azealia still has the tracker charm I gave her. She's extremely intelligent, so she'll know what to do with it so that I can find her. All I have to do is use my string magic. The only question now is—do I tell the two idiots downstairs?

If I don't tell them, they'll be out of my way. If I do tell them, they might rush off halfcocked and ruin the element of surprise. These vamps are tricky. A direct attack will never work. We need to sneak up on them. I don't know if Kael's capable of stealth. Bastian, maybe, but I don't want to risk her life by trusting them to keep their shit together long enough to save her.

My decision is made for me when I hear the telltale

snarls and growls of shifted beasts. I head downstairs in time to see Kael streak out of the front door on all fours. A second later, Bastian lopes behind, intent on catching the smaller beast.

I glance out of the open door. They're heading toward the woods near the edge of town. Good. At least I won't have to deal with them directly. Hopefully they can work their bullshit out and come back united.

Unless...

Oh shit! They're probably heading for the cave. Bastian had found a cave filled with bats. The scent of death was strong there, and vampires can turn into bats, so naturally that would be the first place they would look.

I can beat them to the cave if I shift and fly. It's just one advantage I have over them.

As I step outside, the shift begins. My flesh ripples and undulates as my dragon claws its way to the surface. The moment I take flight, I let out a roar which shakes the windows of the houses down the street. I beat my wings to gain altitude, and soon, I'm flying high over Bonfire Falls. The darkened streets flash by as I head toward the forest.

When I spot Kael and Bastian in the woods, I buzz over their heads by a few feet. They both look up and snarl. I spot a clearing near the center of the woods. As I land there, my feet pound the earth. To make sure they notice me, I spread my wings and unleash a burst of flame toward the heavens.

Both shifters screech to a halt in front of me.

"Out of the way, fly boy." Bastian brandishes his six-inch-long claws. "Azealia's in danger, and I don't mind going right through you to get to her."

"What's with the fire?" Kael lowers his wolfen head to the ground and growls menacingly. "Do you want them to know we're coming?"

"You're going in the wrong direction. Idiots," I snap.

Bastian cocks his head to the side and lets out a chuff.

"How do you know that?" Kael asks.

"Because, I gave Azealia a tracking necklace. I can use it to locate her no matter the distance. And it says you're heading in the wrong direction."

"You gave Azealia jewelry?" Kael's tone is heavy with both recrimination and jealousy Funny, considering he took her to bed first.

"Let's not make this another pissing contest, okay? If you two will give me a moment to cast a spell, I can lead us right to Azealia," I say.

"I suppose it's better than blindly wandering around the woods," Bastian says.

While they settle on to their haunches, I close my eyes. I open myself beyond the four dimensions usually experienced by corporeal beings. I focus on the energy between the worlds. Every known color is represented here. In addition, there are a few that defy description. I focus on Azealia and locate a reddish umber strand. When I open my eyes, the beam isn't so brilliant, but I can still detect it. I grunt when I realize that the path will take us toward Azealia's cabin.

"Well? We're waiting!" Kael huffs.

I bite back a snarl. "I have her trajectory. Can you keep up?"

"Try and stop me."

"Hah. What the wolf said," Bastian says with a smirk.

My wings beat frantically, and I rise into the air. I take off at a good clip, but not recklessly. I want plenty of time to spot any ambushes along the way. These vampires are smart and resourceful. I can't forget the silvery gleam in the crow's eyes. Every animal in the forest could be possessed by them. No one is safe anymore.

In order to avoid the trees, I have to fly above the others. I continually cast glances at the ground to make sure they're keeping up. They're doing well enough. I just hope they aren't burning through all their energy.

When we reach the vicinity of Azealia's cabin, I land. I stalk through the woods, carefully avoiding the overgrowth. The bushes are thicker here, which makes it harder to focus on the energetic string, but I can still track it.

Maybe Azealia already escaped the vamps and made it back home. Perhaps I was mistaken, and there was no foul play. It would explain the lack of any magical disturbance while we were sleeping. She may have run just to get as far away from Kael and Bastian's bickering as possible.

As soon as the other guys arrive, we circle around her home. The string passes through it, but comes out the other side, and continues into the woods beyond.

"Shouldn't we check to see if she's home?" Bastian asks.

"No." I turn to face Bastian and curly shake my head. "The trail leads back into the woods. She's not in there."

He grunts but doesn't question me further.

We leave her cabin behind and continue deeper into the woods. Bastian suddenly stops in the middle of the path. I turn to face him, as does Kael.

"What is it?" I ask.

"Trouble? Can't you smell it?"

After a few seconds, the scent grows strong enough that I can also detect it.

"It's coming from the North," Kael says.

"And the South," Bastian says.

"It's everywhere." I back up into the center of the path. Our backs form a triangle. "Be ready."

"I was born ready."

"Shut up, Kael."

A furry creature bursts through the foliage. It's a bear, all snarls, and claws, and fury. Its eyes are silvered over, just like the birds had been.

Bear shifters march in from every direction. Their humongous furry forms block the sunlight. The closest one swings its sharp claws at Kael, but the nimble wolf shifter dances out of the way. Kael snaps his jaws about the bear's forearm and hurls it to the ground.

Bastian is larger than these possessed bears. He uses his greater mass to full effect and tosses two shifters against a nearby tree. Another beast latches onto his back with iron jaws. Bastian roars and claws at his attacker.

Before I can assist him, a possessed bear shifter charges me. There's no time to move. His claws struggle to penetrate my glittering scales. My talons strike at his flesh and rip away chunks of fur. We fight like rabid savages, while howls and savage snarls echo through the trees.

I snake my serpentine neck around and bite the bear firmly on the back of its neck. In seconds, he's gone. I toss him to the side. There's no time to celebrate because Bastian is being overcome by three large shifters.

Kael is running from half a dozen more. He leads them on a zig zag path through dense trees. They're running with careless intent and smash into the trunks. Kael's using their size and lack of agility against them. For now, he's winning, but if he slows for even an instant, or snags himself on the dense underbrush, he's history.

Since Bastian's in worse shape right now, I leap toward him. After inhaling deeply, I breathe a wall of fire to engulf the vicious bear. The disgusting scent of burning hair and flesh reaches my nostrils. I twist away from shrieking beast.

Bastian roars in pain as one of his attackers sinks its

jaws deep into his flank. Kael is cornered, unable to stay out of the way of the whirling claws of his attackers. They're both in trouble, and I can't decide which one to save, so I decide to save them both.

With a nimble bound, I leap into the air. I beat my wings twice for speed, and then spew fire at the bear shifters who are attacking Kael. To my surprise, the bears continue to fight even as their flesh melts from their bones. I've never seen anything like it. Obviously, we're dealing with powerful magic. Could the vampires be stronger than Azealia?

Kael and I strike out in every direction with tooth and claw. I add the occasional burst of flames to keep the bears at bay. Eventually, we stop giving up ground, and we're able to press the bears back until they lie dead or dying at our feet.

Bloody, bruised, but still in the fight, the two of us charge toward Bastian. He has managed to kill one of the three shifters who were attacking him. The other two have him pinned down and are snapping at his hide. Kael and I each tackle one of his attackers from behind. Between the three of us, we manage to put down the final two shifters.

"Is that all of them?" I ask.

"Yes, no thanks to Bastian." Kael seizes the opportunity to lash out at his rival.

"What are you talking about? You ran away like a coward," Bastian says.

"First of all, I was retreating—temporarily—until I found a suitable battle ground. Second of all, maybe I could have employed more aggressive strategy if you didn't have to struggle against a couple of bears."

"A couple? There were at least seven on me," Bastian says.

"Guys, settle down," I say.

Without responding to me, they shift back into human form and glare at each other. Kael tries to tackle Bastian but can't budge the big man. He keeps his arms wrapped around the bear shifter's midsection anyway. Bastian lifts his clasped hands high overhead, and then brings them down on Kael's back. I wince at the sharp impact, but the stubborn wolf won't let go. They fall over and roll around on the forest floor. If they keep this up, we'll never find Azealia.

"Enough!" I release a tremendous dragon roar. The sound reverberates across the mountainside. Kael and Bastian are still on the ground, but their gazes are firmly fixed on me.

"We all want Azealia to be safe. All of us. We have the same goal. Can't you idiots see that?" I ask.

They sheepishly climb to their feet but refuse to look at each other. Kael opens his mouth to speak, closes it, and then shakes his head.

"I love Azealia," he whispers.

"I love her, too," Bastian says.

"I love her as well. Obviously, we all do," I say.

"Well, I'm not giving her up for a bear or a scaly lizard."

"I'm not giving her up for a scrawny puppy dog."

"Guys!" They turn to glare at me. "There's no point in fighting because Azealia's made it clear that she doesn't want to have to choose between us. She wants all of us equally. Why can't we be happy with that?"

They're silent. We might not like the idea of sharing, but none of us want to give up Azealia either.

"Fine. If no one interferes in my relationship with her, then I don't see a problem," Kael says.

"Me neither," Bastian says. "We can each have a relationship with her. I'm sick of fighting anyway."

"Me too," Kael admits.

I relax slightly, glad that we've finally had a chance to clear the air. All of the fighting wasn't helping the real problem. Someone, or something, still has Azealia and we need to get her back.

"Let's see where the magical thread takes us," I say.

"After you," Kael says.

I know he hates to give up control to anyone else, so maybe he really is willing to change. Maybe he will work with us to make sure Azealia's safe and happy. That's all any of us really want, or at least I hope we're in agreement in that regard. I won't know until we find her. And with any luck, she's close, and she'll be easy to rescue.

But as the thread winds through the forest, my heart sinks. We're heading toward the cave that Bastian and Azealia found. The smell of death is all around us. Whoever, or whatever, we're facing is inside. And it has Azealia.

CAPTIVE OF THE VAMPIRES:
CHAPTER 17

AZEALIA

Something hard and knobbly digs into my back. Half awake, I try to roll away from it but soon realize I can't move. I can't move at all, and as soon as my eyes snap open, I know I'm in trouble. The attack comes back to me. I remember darkness, and fangs, and the metallic scent of blood, but after that—nothing. I must have lost consciousness.

I'm bound to a large stalactite by tough silk cords. My restricted arms are stretched out above me; my legs are spread wide and tied to the cave's wall. It's a humiliating position.

Sharp pain brackets the corners of my mouth. My throat is dry. Someone has stuffed a wad of cloth between my lips. It's been tied with a tightly knotted length of twine. I'm unable to speak, so I can't cast a spell to free myself.

A cluster of bats hang from the ceiling. The mass of hairy, pointy-eared bodies writhes above me, wings flapping, fangs slick with saliva. One of them detaches from the ceiling and dives toward the ground. Its sickening cry sends chills down my spine.

As I turn my face away, I shudder. For a moment, I wonder if it's sick, or dying, but then a marvelous transformation ripples through its furry form. The body grows many times larger before morphing into a human. A man. His features retain a great deal of the frightening, primal aspects of the bat. His nose is snubbed and resembles that of a pig; his eyes are black. His ears are abnormally large and flick back as he turns away from me.

The man barely spares me a glance before walking out of the room. He's probably on his way to inform my captors that I'm awake.

I take the opportunity to study my bonds, which have been magically enhanced. Given time, I could probably unravel the tangle of both enchantment and cord, but I have a feeling time is a fleeting luxury.

My thoughts linger on the vampire—because that's what he must be—and his transformation. That must be how the vampires are getting around Bonfire Falls without anyone noticing. I'm sure I'm in the same cave where Bastian and I were surrounded by bats. I have no idea how long they've been lurking here, but I have no doubt I'm being held in their lair. At least now I know why there are so many bats on the mountain.

The sound of footsteps spurs me to struggle harder. Using both my muscles and mental magic, I try to budge the bonds. Unfortunately, I don't make any progress before I have to stop.

My kidnapper makes an appearance.

Imagine a dark, churning sea, beautiful and deadly, and yet somehow irresistible. That's my first impression of Eleonore, the vampire queen. Her ash-gray eyes possess a sinister cast, like that of a feral animal, but her countenance couldn't be more regal. She carries herself with the forgotten grace of past monarchs. There isn't a trace of humility or irony in her manner. Clad in a long, slinky black dress, she exudes a seductive yet menacing aura. Her hair is bound up in an elaborate braid, like you'd see in a classic European painting.

As she stares at me, her red lips part to reveal a toothy smile. What could this creature possibly want with me?

"Do forgive me for the gag, my sweet Azealia." Well, she knows my name. That's probably not good. "After centuries of existence, one does get terribly fatigued when listening to the commentary of one's prey. Do you have any idea how many times my food has begged for freedom? Or threatened me despite their ludicrously helpless state? Too many to count. Maybe all of them."

I'm too afraid to move. It doesn't take much effort to look appropriately fearful of this beautiful but deadly woman.

"I digress. You're probably wondering why I've kidnapped you. It's all about delicious, delicious power. But, I'm sure I'm preaching to the choir—" She chuckles. "You are quite strong, perhaps the strongest witch I've ever dined upon."

Did she say dined upon?

As my panic rises to new levels, a whimper escapes, only to be muffled by the gag.

"Oh, poor darling." Eleonore smiles, displaying her dreadfully sharp fangs. "I'd apologize for feasting upon you, but we both know that would be a blatant lie. Instead, I'll assure you that your death will be for a worthy cause—for my greatness. The world has changed. I'm no longer the potent, feared monster I once was. Now humans have guns that spit out a barrage of bullets in a second, and they have bombs which can rival the sun's ferocity. In order to ensure my position as the most powerful being on earth, I have to take measures some might consider... extreme."

She laughs ruefully.

"Your blood, the blood of the most powerful witch the world has ever known, will give me enough strength to last a thousand years or more. Yes, little witch, tremble in fear, for I am about to take what I am due."

I've heard enough. As I tremble with rage, the force of my magic gathers within my body. With a gagged shout, I unleash the energy in the form of powerful explosions. The bonds holding me to the stalactite are partially damaged. Some threads hang loose, but the rest still hold me in place.

Although the bonds have been enchanted to absorb magical energy, I almost overwhelm them. With another blast, I'm free. I fall to the floor, but as I try to scramble to my feet, trailing ropes slither around wrists and ankles.

Despite my furious struggles, the ropes wind around my body, pinning my arms to my sides. The trailing ends also bind my legs together. I thrash around on the stone floor like an inchworm, deprived of my limbs, my magic, and my voice. I'm helpless as Eleonore simply gestures at me to rise. My body floats up from the floor. My hair lifts in a halo around my head. The vampire queen uses her magic to secure me to the same stalactite. Now I dangle, able to wriggle like a fly caught in a spider's web, but I can't do much else.

I only have one chance to get out of this cave alive. Desperation forces me to trust my magic. I haven't used this much power in a very long time, but it's necessary if I'm going to break free.

Another burst of wild energy courses through my

body. I gather the power into my chakras where I can store it until I reach my full potential. As I continue to summon energy, I fill each chakra, one by one, starting at my root chakra at the base of my spine, and working up to my crown chakra.

Eleonore is either too arrogant or too distracted to notice what I'm doing. She approaches sinuously and caresses my extended legs like a lover. "The femoral artery is the most delicious place to drink. I've tried other arteries, but this is my favorite."

Several bats fly down, landing in their vampiric forms. Eleonore glances back at her hulking minions which lurk in the dark corners of the room.

"Prepare my meal."

I let out a muffled screech as the vampire men suddenly descend upon me. My eyes go wide as their clawed fingers rip and shred the clothing right off of my body. The sudden exposure and increased vulnerability only heighten my terror further, which might not be a bad thing. Wild magic is all about emotion rather than technique. Fury rather than precision. And make no mistake, this additional humiliation has enraged me.

Their pinching fingers linger on my naked body until Eleonore shoos them away with a bestial hiss. She clamps her hands firmly onto my bare leg and opens her mouth. Her jaw seems to unhinge. It's open so wide that I'm momentarily fascinated. I forget about maintaining my power, and much of it drains from my lack of concentration.

Her head descends. A pair of sharp pinpricks herald the end of my life force. As Eleonore drains my blood, I can feel my magic draining along with the scarlet fluid. I have to act. Now.

I stoke the fires of my rage. I use my helplessness and my frustration with the three men in my life, along with the audacity of this vampire bitch, to summon my magic. With a final, ferocious push, the wild magic answers my summons.

Three of my most passionate desires are instantly fulfilled. My desire to contact my men sends out a magical call to them. My desire to be free incinerates the bonds. And finally, my desire to burn the vampire queen off the face of the Earth is answered—sort of. The fireball which engulfs the cave shatters the stalactite and sends a shower of charred bats flying out of the cave.

As I hit the floor in a crouch, flames explode from my wrists. The smoking remains of bats fall like rain, covering the cave floor in a macabre pyre.

When I spot Eleonore, it's hard to believe that she's the same beautiful creature who'd captured me. Half of her skin has been burned off to reveal the charred, underlying muscle structure of her body.

At first, I can't look away from the horror, but then my gaze sweeps up to her seared face. Her remaining eye narrows and her disfigured hand thrusts out in my direction.

"You think that pathetic campfire can kill me?" Her voice is a pained hiss, borne of misery. "Even that small amount of your blood has made me invincible."

"Let's test that theory."

With a sudden surge, I leap to my feet and send the flame whips toward the vampire queen. She stumbles backward, not so invincible now.

A half-transformed vampire drops from the ceiling and lands in my path. With a ferocious snarl, its lips peel back to reveal sharp-as-needles incisors. I snap my wrist and one of the flame whips slashes through the air, passing right through its body. Its bestial eyes widen in confusion before it looks down at its fracturing body. It falls into pieces and the remaining bits quickly sear away, consumed by the magical fire.

Two more swoop down to take its place. I send the whips flying, and the tendrils wrap around both of their necks. With a grunt of rage, I yank backward, and both of their heads are seared right off. The bodies fall onto the cave floor before they are consumed by flame too.

Eleonore is two dozen feet away. A multitude of vampires block my path to her. Rage boils anew within my belly. I become a whirling dervish of fiery death, lashing my fire whips in wide arcs, and destroying every vampire within range.

The cave is soon thick with smoke and the ashes of the undead. But there are too many of them. They aren't frightened by death. Instead, in an effort to protect their queen, they throw themselves at me in droves.

Frantically, I swing the whips around me to create a virtually impenetrable shield, but the sheer weight of their numbers overwhelms my magic. Inch by inch, the dying vampires are getting closer and closer to hooking a claw or fang into my vulnerable flesh.

Eleonore's cackle of triumph is cut short by a sudden roar from the cave entrance. A blast of heat washes over the room, and dozens of vampires scream. Eleonore's head snaps back toward the entrance. Her feral eyes widen in shock.

Help is here!

Rejuvenated by the arrival of the cavalry, I fight on with greater purpose. Eleonore can see that she will lose, so she transforms into a bat. I quickly lose sight of her as she blends into the hundreds of bats that are flying out of the cave.

Bastian, Kael, and Cobalt enter the chamber as I dispatch the remaining vampires. I force them to coalesce into one spinning cyclone of fire and rage. The cyclone expands until it explodes. Sizzling bodies smash against the walls.

I collapse from the effort.

"Azealia!" Bastian—in human form—runs to my side first. As he paws at me gently, worry knits his brow.

Soon Kael and Cobalt are by my side too. They take turns stroking me and caressing me, telling me that I'm safe and that they will all take care of me. I've never felt so alive.

I turn toward Bastian and our lips meet. We kiss with the desperation of long-separated lovers. He pulls me closer and I can't stop thinking about how close I came to death. The press of his powerful body against mine is equal parts comforting and exciting.

Not to be outdone, Kael pries me away from Bastian. I kiss him passionately until his tongue entwines with mine. As the kiss deepens, his hands slide down my naked back to cup my ass.

Cobalt inserts himself between us to claim me as his too. Desire flashes through me like lightning, blinding me to everything but their hands and mouths.

The three men suddenly jolt. As I pull back to find out what's going on, their eyes glaze over with a sheen of silver.

Sheer terror floods me with adrenaline. I jump to my feet and back away. I don't want to have to hurt them.

Kael takes the first step toward me.

Oh no! This can't be happening!

Have I doomed these men because I allowed myself to love them?

There's nothing I can do but flee. As I shove past Kael, he tries to grab me. I jerk away and run. I don't dare look behind me, but I hear them coming. And if they shift, there's no way I'll be able to outrun them.

CAPTIVE OF THE VAMPIRES: CHAPTER 18

AZEALIA

No, no, no, no!

I duck under a skeletal tree branch. I'm too fast and it's too dark to see how big the branch truly is. It nearly takes my eye out. A thin rivulet of blood slips down my cheek as I run blindly through the forest. I don't know where I want to go, I only know that I want to get away. Nowhere is safe anymore. Cobalt will be able to fly anywhere. Kael and Bastian can scent my trail. And the tracker!

I rip the tracing necklace from my neck and toss it aside. Desperate to escape them, I pour magic into my senses. Light from the crescent moon binds to faint starlight to illuminate my path. It doesn't help much, but I can see larger roots poking up from the forest floor now, so I'm less likely to trip.

Branches snap and rustle with the sounds of pursuit. I focus long enough to count the footfalls. They're in human form. Can they even shift when they're possessed? Maybe not. This could be an advantage.

Foolishly, I cast a look over my shoulder to see how

close they are. Their eyes flash silver in the dark forest. Three distinct pairs. I can't tell Kael from Cobalt from Bastian, but that isn't my biggest concern right now. If any of them catch me, I'm dead.

I wish I'd never summoned them. This wouldn't have happened to them. I should've listened to my instincts and handled Eleonore and her vampire horde alone. Maybe I would've died, but at least the men would've been spared.

As I run toward a low branch, I get an idea. I use the tree's limb to swing up its gnarled trunk. I doubt the guys will lose my scent, but this might buy me some time. I scramble up to the highest branch capable of supporting my weight.

Cobalt reaches the tree first. He's glaring up at me, eyes shining like liquid silver. I wonder if he can see me, or if someone else is looking at me through his eyes. I shiver at the thought.

As he climbs the tree, I use a wind spell to fly to the next one. I keep going until I can't see their eyes through the branches. Eventually, I drop back to the ground.

For a moment, I'm alone. But within seconds, they are on my trail again. I have to do something to slow them, but I don't want to hurt them. I know it's not Kael, Bastian, and Cobalt chasing me, but it's still their bodies. Their souls are trapped, but they're not gone. If I kill their bodies, I'll be killing their souls too, and I can't lose them. I can't snuff out the lives of the men I love.

As I run, I cast a sheet of ice behind me. I can't stop to aim properly, but I hope I've created a slippery ice barricade between us.

Unfortunately, their heavy footfalls crunch over the ice, shattering it and rendering it ineffective.

Damn it!

I cast a fireball over my shoulder. My aim is purposefully off the mark. I don't want to kill them. Moon Goddess above, please don't make me kill them. I'd surrender to Eleonore before I let that happen.

My heart pounds so violently in my chest that I fear it'll crack a rib. My fireball did nothing. They're still coming for me. If I'm the most powerful witch in history, then why can't I stop them?

A thought forms in my mind. Under any other circumstance, I would've considered it repulsive, but it might be the only way to save them. If I'm powerful enough to control a shifter in their beast form, then I should be able to force Kael, Bastian, and Cobalt to shift under my control. This might break the vampire queen's possessive hold on them.

I whirl around and throw up an energy wall. It's sloppy and weak, but I don't need it to hold for long. The men crash into it head on. Cobalt summons his magic and lashes out against my forcefield. His magic isn't nearly as strong as mine, but if he weakened it enough, the others would be able to slip through.

Digging in, I harness the darkest powers in my arsenal. Despite my self-inflicted exile, and reputation for being a cold fish, I'm a gentle witch. The spells I cast are largely for protection and peace. To take control of another soul requires dark magic, and while I'm not completely unfamiliar with it, I choose not to practice it. This will stain me, but it will be worth it if I can save my men.

I reach out with shadowy tendrils of twisted magical energy and send them right through Cobalt's chest. His heart wrestles against my magical grip. He struggles and the vampire possessing him fights back, but I win. Even though Cobalt's roaring with pain, I keep going in an attempt to force a graceless transition.

Suddenly scales appear. Wings unfurl. The connection between Cobalt and his possessor severs. I want to weep with joy, but I still have so much to do.

I weave a protective barrier around his mind. If someone wants to take control of him again, they'll have a hell of a barricade to get through.

Now, I have to hold him steady while I transform the other two.

Bastian's next. He's known me for ages. He'll subconsciously recognize the feel of my magic. Hopefully, he won't fight me too hard. I extend another tendril of dark magic towards him.

Is it dark magic if it's done out of love?

He doesn't fight my hold as hard as Cobalt did, but the monster inside him still fights with all her might.

Once Bastian is in my magical grip, I compel him to transition into bear form. When the vampire is successfully pushed out, I weave a protective shield around Bastian.

I steal a glance at Cobalt. He looks dazed, but he's not fighting me. I retract the dark tendril from him but leave the protective barriers in place around his mind.

Kael's going to be the real challenge. I take in a breath. My power, as limitless as it sometimes feels, is waning. I should've tackled Kael first.

When I send a third tendril out, he fights me with all his might. Adrenaline rushes through his body. He can't calm down enough to recognize whose magic is invading him. The pure Alpha power inside him fights anything and everything for control. I can't outmuscle him. I need to try something else.

I attack the link of possession that's directly attached

to his mind. Lashing out with magical strike after magical strike, I drive a spike of magic so deep into the connection that, for a fraction of a second, I see directly into Kael's soul. I sense an unfailing loyalty and an unquenchable thirst for power. My presence is enough to startle the vampire. When the connection weakens, I strike again.

The telepathic link breaks. I shift him quickly, and then weave a protective spell around him. Desperate for more magic to fuel their protections, I drop the forcefield and pour that energy back into the men. I maintain the magic until I feel Eleonore finally retreat.

She's gone.

A moment ago, the forest felt sinister and oppressive. Now, it's become a peaceful refuge covered by a blanket of stars.

My hands are still outstretched toward the three shifters. A dragon, a wolf, and a bear stand before me. Their eyes are as clear as a scrying pool. I retract my control over Kael, Cobalt, and Bastian, but leave the protective spells in place.

"Change back," I say breathlessly. "Make sure your mind belongs to you."

One by one, they shift back. Their eyes are clear. Their limbs move as they direct them to move. I nearly fall to my knees with exhaustion and relief.

"It's gone. There was something in my head. It's gone. What happened?" Cobalt asks.

"I had to take control of you," I explain. "All three of you. I forced you to shift to break the possession. I'm so sorry."

"We were possessed?" Bastian asks.

"Eleonore took over your minds and ordered you to hunt me down. I didn't have a choice."

"We hunted you?" Kael works the muscles of his jaw

and clenches his fists. "Where is she? I'll find her and rip her heart out."

"Take it easy." My breath comes in hard puffs as my energy drains away. "Possession takes a toll on the mind and body."

"So does force-shifting three people. We have to get her home," Cobalt says.

"I'll carry her, it's less physically demanding to ride a bear," Bastian says.

"Good idea," Kael says.

Seeing them agreeing with each other puts a smile on my face. I can't muster the energy to do anything more. After Bastian shifts, Cobalt lifts me and settles me onto his back. Kael shifts as well, but Cobalt stays in his human form.

"They're probably looking for us. If I fly above the tree line with my wings out, everyone will know where we are." I'm not sure if he's talking to me or not, but I murmur in acknowledgment anyway.

Bastian feels like a giant, furry rocking horse as he lopes through the forest. Kael walks alongside us. Every so often, his coarse fur brushes against my arm. Cobalt runs to keep up with the others.

I allow my eyes to close. My magical reserves have been deeply drained. For the first time ever, I'm acutely aware of my limitations. My limbs don't feel like they're attached to my body.

Eventually, the scent of the forest changes. I can tell when we're getting close to my home. Wild lilac perfumes the air, while the sage bush Bastian planted last week soothes my senses.

Cobalt scoops me up in his arms and carries me into my cottage.

"Take me to bed," I whisper. When he sets me down, I add, "Stay with me."

"Now's not the time for that." He moves my hands away from his chest. "You need to rest."

"I need to replenish my power."

Kael and Bastian walk into the bedroom. They're still naked after having shifted back. Through lowered lashes, I look from one beautifully sculpted man to another. My heart aches because I almost lost them. But I didn't. They're here, and my body's eager for their touch.

"Make love to me," I murmur. "Help me regain my power."

Kael doesn't hesitate. He's in bed beside me with his lips on mine. Seconds later, the other two men join. We're in a tangle of limbs and their lips are everywhere. I lay back into the crisp sheets and revel in their love. I need them in my life, and I'm going to do whatever it takes to make it happen. I'm sure we haven't seen the last of Eleonore, but for now, we're safe. We're together. And we're in love.

CAPTIVE OF THE VAMPIRES:
CHAPTER 19

AZEALIA

The next morning, we're back in the cave, looking for clues as to where Eleonore may have gone. I want to revel in the love my guys gave me last night, but I can't, not as long as she's alive. She's a threat to us, to our relationships, and to our future. We can't let her go back into hiding because then we'll never be safe.

"There's nothing left. Everything is ashes. How are we supposed to get a scent?" Kael kicks a pile of ash into the air. It showers down and blows around us like a dust storm.

I understand his frustration. However, I do have a solution.

"Don't worry. There's a trace of her magic still present. I can use that to find her."

"Magic. Hmph." Kael crosses his arms over his chest. He seems upset that he can't contribute to the efforts to locate the vampire queen more directly.

"Take it easy, friend." Bastian puts his hand on Kael's shoulder. "We'd have a hard time tryin' to track flying prey anyway."

Kael still has a sour expression, but his posture relaxes. I'm happy that my men are finally getting along. It seems like they've worked out their issues. They're getting along, and it makes my heart sing.

"I got a good whiff of that nasty fanged monster. I'll know her scent when we do run across it," Kael slaps a fist into the palm of his hand and looks to me. Determination furrows his brow. "I can rally the wolf pack. There's strength in numbers."

"That's a great idea." Bastian nods.

Cobalt's handsome face twists into a worried frown.

"I'm not certain I agree," he says.

Kael's eyes narrow a bit, but he allows the dragon shifter to speak.

"Eleonore has already proven she can easily ensnare the minds of shifters. If we attack her en masse, we might be gifting her new soldiers. Then we'll be up against vampires *and* shifters."

"I wonder how far her control reaches. Miles, at least. And she could have other powers we don't know nothin' about," Bastian says.

"I might be able to answer that for you. When Eleonore bit me, there was a connection. She stole my magic, my memories, my secrets, as well as my blood."

"How does that help us now?" Bastian asks.

"It helps..." I flash a smile at him. "...because the connection was a two-way street. I managed to glean a few tidbits of information from her mind as well."

"What was it like? Being inside her head," Kael asks.

My mouth becomes a thin, tight line as I struggle to recall the chaotic jumble which existed within the vampire queen's mind.

"It's—it's hard to describe. She's been alive for centuries, and like most beings her age, memories are largely nonlinear. However, I did get a general feel for her power. And I know that the scuffle in the cave cost her most of her minions. Only the elite guards survived."

"A scuffle?" Cobalt shakes his head.

"It was all out war," Kael says. "Which is why we need the strength of the pack behind us. Do you want to try fighting her with just the four of us, or do you want the whole pack on our side?"

"Cobalt, I understand your concern, but I would feel better if we had greater numbers backing us up," I say.

"Keep in mind that I can't order the pack into a situation this dangerous. No one signed up to battle a centuries old vampire queen who can ensnare your mind," Kael says.

"Then what are you going to do?" Bastian asks.

"I don't know. Ask for volunteers, maybe." Kael shrugs.

"Then I suggest we head to the den and see who wants to join us," I say.

The men nod, and then Kael gestures toward me.

"I'll shift, and you can ride on my back," he says.

"What?" Cobalt laughs. "Why should she crawl along the ground when she can soar through the skies on my back."

"You'd probably drop her."

I roll my eyes and stroll over to Bastian, who remains removed from their impromptu argument.

"Will you carry me on your back?"

Cobalt and Kael stare at us, their jaws on the floor. Bastian smiles and shifts into bear form. I take handfuls of his shaggy mane and pull myself onto his back. I glare at Kael and Cobalt, hoping that I've made my point.

When we reach the wolf pack's den, Bastian stops in front of the entrance. Several wolf shifters come out to greet Kael. They eye me warily. Thanks to Kael's possessiveness, they consider us their pack leaders. It's an honor that I neither want, nor need. Kael can lead his pack without my input.

"Gather the pack," Kael says. "We'll meet in the great room in five minutes."

When the group is assembled, Kael addresses them.

"As many of you already know, our mountain territory has been invaded by a powerful creature from across the ocean."

Some of them nod, but most of the pack waits with rapt attention.

"This vampire queen—Eleonore—is as dangerous a foe as they come. She's as fast and as strong as we are— maybe faster. Plus, she has demonstrated the ability to take control of the minds of various creatures, including shifters. I can't order any of you into battle with such a monster. Instead, I'm going to put it to a vote. Should the pack help rid Bonfire Falls of this menace?"

The pack breaks into discussion among themselves. As I listen in to several conversations, I can tell things aren't going well for us. The sound level in the room keeps increasing and some of the men are starting to shout.

Kael sticks his fingers in his mouth and a second later he lets out a shrill whistle. The pack members look up and turn their gazes on him.

"Look, I don't blame any of you for not wanting to fight Eleonore. I don't want to tangle with that monster either. I want to kick back here in the den, knock back a few beers, and snuggle up with my sweet honey."

A few hoots go up at that declaration, but Kael holds up his hand for silence. The pack quickly falls into line.

"But you know something? Life's not always about what you want to do. Sometimes, life is about what you have to do. I don't want to go to war today, but I also don't want this undead monstrosity running around Bonfire Falls fucking shit up. This vampire queen is a threat to our way of life, and we have to stop her." Kael walks among the pack, slapping several guys on the shoulder. "So, are we going to cower here in the den while bears and dragons fight this battle for us? Or are we going to go do what we're best at—kicking ass?"

"We're kicking some ass." A burly wolf shifter stands and rips off his shirt.

The pack hoots and hollers, then engages in a pack howl. It's haunting, but at the same time strangely beautiful.

In the end, ten of Kael's warriors volunteer for service. They're all rough and tumble, rippling with muscle and painted with tattoos. I almost feel sorry for the vampires, but not quite.

Kael remains behind with his pack to go over strategy. Cobalt and I head outside where he shifts into dragon form. I climb astride his scaled back and hang on. Bastian shifts into bear form and heads toward his clan. He's going to try to get reinforcements while Cobalt and I go to the dragon enclave.

As we descend through the clouds and swoop down toward the center of the dragon clan's village, many of its citizens look up and wave cheerfully. There's a sense of unity in the clan because they're all coming out to greet us.

Cobalt lands heavily in the village square. I leap off of his back. As he shifts back into human form, a slender, drop dead sexy dragon shifter comes to us. In human form, he's able to shake Cobalt's hand.

"Copper." Cobalt pats him back and they briefly embrace. "How have you been?"

"Quite well. Domestic life agrees with me. Are you well?"

"If I wasn't about to engage in mortal combat with a vampire queen, things would be great."

Copper frowns and tilts his head to the side, but Cobalt waves his concern away.

"I'll tell you all about it soon, I promise. Right now, time is of the essence. I need to see Blaze."

Copper chuckles and gestures behind himself.

"Big guy is at the forge, as usual." Copper turns his gaze to me. "Aren't you going to introduce your lovely friend?"

"Copper, Azealia. Yes, *that* Azealia. Azealia, this is Copper, the dragon village's resident stargazer and oracle."

"You have some skill with prophecy?" I arch an eyebrow.

"I do what I can to help the village. Let me know if you want me to read for you."

"I will."

Cobalt takes my hand and leads me through the dragon village. We head toward a massive house. A plume of black smoke curls up from a workshop. It's been ages since I've been in the dragon village. It's nice to see that it's expanded.

We come upon the forge, marked now by a rhythmic hammering. As we round the corner and enter the open air forge, I spot the blacksmith. His massively muscled back is to us. He raises a hammer into the air repeatedly, bringing it down on a red-hot, glowing piece of steel. It's the beginnings of a sword and even now I can tell his craftsmanship is extraordinary.

"Working hard, or hardly working?" Cobalt jokes.

The big man turns around. His face is contorted into a scowl until he sees Cobalt.

"Welcome back, cousin." The big blacksmith envelops Cobalt in a manly hug. Cobalt winces as his back pops several times.

"Thanks. It's good to see you, Blaze."

"And you as well." The dragon smith turns his golden eyes on me. "And who is this?"

"Azealia the witch, meet Blaze the blacksmith."

"Charmed." I put my hand out for a shake. He stares down at his meaty paw and shakes his head.

"My hands are filthy."

"I'm not bothered by a little dirt."

"Fair enough." We clasp hands, and he has the good grace to be gentle. I get the feeling this man could crush me without trying. "So, what brings you to my forge? I sense an urgency which tells me this is no social call."

"Blaze, you're a weapons expert. We need something that can bring down a vampire," Cobalt says.

"A vampire?" Blaze's eyes go wide. "Those are just legends."

My heart sinks at his declaration.

"Oh, so you *don't* know how to help?" Cobalt asks.

"I never said that. If I remember what my old master taught me during my apprentice days, vampires are can be killed in one of two ways. Either with a stake through the heart or by being burned to death by sunlight. I've heard that fire also works."

"Fire may not be fully effective." I shake my head slowly. "She survived after over half her body was burned."

"Hmm." Blaze holds his chin in his hand as he ponders. "You know, my old master said something about the old, powerful vampires. He said you need to use a stake made of silver and drive it through their heart. Of course, this is only a legend."

"It's as good a lead as we have at the present time." Cobalt cocks his head to the side. "Can you help us out?"

"Give me a few minutes." Blaze grins and sets to work. In less than an hour, he shows us half a dozen spears with silver tips. "Will these work?"

"I hope so," Cobalt says. "Thank you."

"Stay safe, cousin."

"I'll do my best."

After thanking Copper for the spears, I climb back onto Cobalt's back. He's holding three spears in each talon. Our flight is short and uneventful, thank the Gods.

When we return to the wolf den, Kael is still discussing strategy with his ten warriors.

"How did it go?" he asks.

"Cooper made silver-tipped spears. It may be the only way to kill a vampire," I say.

Kael grunts.

"Have you heard from Bastian yet?" I ask.

"Not yet. He can't carry a phone when he's in bear form."

"That's all right. I can send a signal flame to let him know we're all assembled," Cobalt says.

"A signal flame? Won't that alert our enemy that we're coming?" Kael asks.

"It's a magical signal flare," I clarify. "I taught Cobalt the spell. Only you, Bastian, and I can see the flare because that's how I wrote the spell. I've learned a few tricks over the years."

"I trust you, Azealia. If you say it will work, then I believe you," Kael says.

"Thank you."

"Now excuse me for a moment," Cobalt says.

Technically I could cast the spell with less effort than Cobalt, but he needs to learn how to control his magic better. He may only be half-witch, but with practice, he will become more adept than most witches who simply rely on their intrinsic skill.

One of Kael's beefy guards steps out of the line of warriors.

"Ah, I hate to be 'that guy,' but—shouldn't we be attacking a vampire queen right after dawn? Why are we going at twilight?"

I grimace at the fading afternoon sun.

"I wish we had a choice, but we don't. The longer we delay, the more time she has to recover. If we're going to strike, we must do it as quickly as possible," I say.

"All right, fair enough. I had to ask."

"Understandable. Now everyone stay silent while Cobalt works."

I watch Cobalt gather the magical energy into himself. When he's fully charged, he releases it upward in a pyrotechnic blast that only one other person in the world can detect. The plume spreads out hundreds of feet in the air. It should be visible from any part of the mountain, so there's no way Bastian will miss it.

Suddenly an answering flare erupts into the night. It's her, the vampire queen.

"How?" asks Cobalt. "Did I do something wrong with the spell?"

"No." I shake my head. "It's not your fault. It's the bite, the link. Because of that, she's seen our magic, and she knows we're coming."

CAPTIVE OF THE VAMPIRES:
CHAPTER 20

AZEALIA

W e follow her fireball to an old, abandoned building on the side of the mountain, deep in the woods. This place has an aura of death and decay, fitting for Eleonore and her horde. In its glory days, it might've been a ski chalet or a resort. I don't recall seeing it before I went into my self-imposed exile, but then again, I never really left Bonfire Falls until after everything happened. It's a shame I never saw it before it fell into ruin.

Dead ivy clings to dull brick walls. I see the brown, prickly remnants of a hedge maze. The great building's many windows are either cracked, boarded up, or gone entirely. When this is over, I'd like to read the bones of this place. Energy radiates through the ground. I can sense the vampires, but I also sense something else entirely. Residual energy from a long and happy life. My life has been quite long, far longer than the lives of any who once lived here, but I'm willing to bet they were happier. My happiness is new, still in its infancy, and

Eleonore is trying to take it all away. Well that's not going to happen.

"Points of entry?" Cobalt asks as he lands. I hop off his back and head toward where Kael's standing with his pack members.

"Likely underground. All obvious entrances are boarded up and have been for at least a few years," Kael reports.

"We'll go in the old-fashioned way," I say. "Through the front door. Eleonore's powerful enough that she's already sensed us. We may as well confront her head on."

"If she hasn't sent her forces to attack, it's likely a trap," Kael says.

"Of course, it is," I reply. "She didn't live this long by rushing into battle. She outsmarts her foes; she doesn't outmuscle them."

"What do you suggest?"

"We have no choice but to walk into her trap. Stay vigilant. Assess the lay of the building quickly so you can use it to your advantage."

"How do you suggest we get in?" Cobalt asks.

"Break it down." I point at the heavily bolted wooden door.

A good fire spell would do the trick too, but I'm going to need all my strength to fight Eleonore.

Five burly wolves have the doors open within seconds. We spill into what was once a grand foyer complete with dual swooping staircases and a chandelier clogged with cobwebs. There are four stories of rooms and hallways, not to mention whatever might lie beneath us.

As we comb the likely hiding spots, we're forced to split off into smaller groups. The hallways are simply too narrow and too numerous for us to search together.

When we come to a junction of hallways, something

catches my attention. A thread of energy invisible in the air.

"Go on ahead," I urge the others toward the opposite hall. If this magic is what I think it is, it's better that I'm alone when I confront her.

I close my eyes and focus on the energetic signature. It's ancient and wrong. It belongs to Eleonore. She's nearby and she's alone.

As I walk away from the group, I cast a quick spell to keep the others away from this side of the estate. I love them too much to let them walk right into danger. The others can deal with the lesser vampires. The fight with Eleonore herself is mine and mine alone.

At the end of the hallway, a set of double doors shimmers with malevolence. Back when this place was taken care of, the door handles would've gleamed like gold. Old portraits in ornate frames flank the doorway. They're covered in dust and cobwebs, but I can still make out the faces of the subjects. A grand lord and lady. I must be at their bedchamber.

I laugh softly to myself. Of course, Eleonore would choose a place of luxury and leisure to hide. I should've guessed straight away. I throw the doors open. Dark energy whooshes out of the bedchamber. The whispers of long-dead spirits lift my hair.

Eleonore lounges on the plush bed, right at home among the grime and decay. Although half her skin had been burnt off in the cave, she's managed to recover. I waste no time. I launch a fire spell at her. She shimmers out of sight and reappears beside the bed.

"How rude," she tuts. "That's not how this works."

"How does it work then?"

I launch a fireball. She throws up a protective shield. Flames lick at her dress, but it doesn't bother her one bit.

She extinguishes my magic with a cold chill. My breath freezes and hangs in the air.

"We're supposed to banter. Spar with words before we spar with our powers. You should join me. Let me tempt you with all of the wonders of the night." Her voice is deep, seductive, and almost too late, I realize she's trying to cast a spell on me.

"Not interested. I'd rather kill you," I yell as I break the tenuous bond between us.

"Fine You're boring anyway."

Eleonore darts forward with inhuman speed. Before I can react, her marble-like hands seize my throat. From elsewhere in the manor, I hear fighting. Vampire hordes must have ambushed my forces. I'm not worried. They can handle themselves. I just hope the silver tipped spears are enough to kill the vamps.

I summon fire to my palm and press my hand into her face. She shrieks. Her skin browns under my touch. She releases my throat and I dart away. Bloodlust transforms her eyes into molten pools of lava.

Rage makes people sloppy. If I can find a way to use her anger against her, I may be able to get the upper hand.

"I'll kill you," she shrieks as she charges toward me.

I run, but she's faster. Our combat becomes a strange game of tag until we reach the top of the swooping staircase. I miscalculate where she's going to strike next. I lose my footing and grab for anything that will keep me from falling. My hands close around her wrist. She jerks off balance and we both go tumbling down the stairs.

She hits the marbled foyer first. Pairs of battling forces are locked in combat around us. Her vampires and my shifters fight as if their lives depend on it. And they do. Ultimately this is a fight between good and evil. I have no doubt that Eleonore will burn Bonfire Falls to the ground if she wins. I can't let that happen.

While I'm panting for air, I spy one of the pack members driving a silver tipped spear through the heart of a vampire. The undead creature crumbles into ash, then disintegrates before her. I've never been so proud in my life. She's like the daughter I never had.

I glance over Eleonore's still body toward where the rest of the shifter forces are decimating the vampire army. What they lack in numbers, they make up in skill. Eleonore clearly didn't anticipate how many people we could rally to fight against her.

"How few followers you have," I taunt her as she stirs.

"These are cannon fodder. You haven't seen anything yet." She levitates to her feet; I quickly leap to mine.

As we square off, she brings her hands together. A shockwave emanates from her core. More creatures of the night pour in from the windows and other shadowy places.

I rush forward in an attempt to disrupt her summoning spell. She strikes me across the face. Stars explode behind my eyes. I crash into the banister, shattering the rotting wood.

As soon as I recover, I use magic to snap off one of the banister poles. The wooden end splinters into five sharp little points. I swing it at Eleonore, hitting her in the ribs. It's like striking a marble statue. The wood snaps in half. She hisses. Her gleaming fangs glitter in the glint of moonlight shining through a broken window. I launch a pure wave of energy at her. She flies backward, smashing an old table. I'm on top of her before she can get up. Somehow, she gets her foot underneath me and shoves her heel into my stomach, knocking the wind out of me.

As I take in harsh, rasping breaths, I summon a lightning spell. It's not as effective as pure fire, but it keeps her from getting to close while I recover my breath.

"I expected more from you." Her voice is shrill and tinged with madness. She grabs a wooden dowel from the staircase and swings it at me before I can react. I take the hit to my shoulder. It's enough to disrupt the flow of magic.

Sensing her opportunity, Eleonore darts forward. She's nothing but a blur as she crashes into me. She pins my wrists to the floor.

"All that power." She presses her nose into my neck and inhales deeply. "I can't wait to make it mine."

Her fangs scrape against my neck. I can't get my hands free. I can't access my magic like this. After everything, I can't believe this is how it will end for me.

A loud bang echoes through the grand foyer. Something has blown both entryway doors clean off their rusted hinges. The sound distracts Eleonore. I steal a glance as well.

Bastian has arrived. He looks as if he's been through hell, but he immediately joins the fray, tossing vampires out of his way as he rushes toward me.

In the chaos, I manage to free my wrist from Eleonore's grasp. Seeing Bastian kicking so much ass renews my power. My body seems to reawaken. It's not just my energy that's coursing through my veins, it's the energy of my lovers as well. I blast Eleonore across the room.

While she recovers, I gather enough power to perform the most dangerous spell a witch can attempt. As I struggle to hold onto the magic, Eleonore stands. She's oblivious to what I'm doing. I slip between the worlds before she even realizes what's happening.

Let time bend.

Let the past be now.
Let the future be forgotten.

As I weave the very fabric of the universe together, Eleonore goes through her last series of motions in reverse. I scramble her personal timeline until she's lying stunned on the ground. Her eyes are closed; her hands are clasped. I hold her in the space between worlds until I'm ready.

When I allow her time to rejoin the current timeline, I'm standing right in front of her, silver tipped spear at the ready. I allow her personal timeline to start again. She opens her eyes in time to see me shove the silver tip right into her black heart.

Sticky blood oozes from the wound in her chest. She staggers forward, clawing at me with her sharpened nails, but she can't move quickly enough anymore.

"What...did...you...do?" she sputters.

I grab a handful of her hair and hold her in place. Her eyes are mad and wild. I slash the silver across her throat. Eleonore stumbles to the floor, unable to hold herself up anymore. My own magic wanes and fizzles. I sink to my knees beside her. I can do nothing but watch the ancient life drain out of her until there's nothing left. She evaporates into a cloud of sooty smoke.

It's over.

Bastian, Cobalt, and Kael appear at my side as I lose the strength to keep myself upright.

"Are you all right?" Bastian asks.

"I'm fine. Very drained. Not hurt." I can only say two words at a time.

"Keep an eye on her," Kael orders the other two. "I'm going to finish off Eleonore's horde."

He presses a kiss into my forehead before heading back into battle.

Cobalt is on his feet, taking out any vampires that come too close. Bastian sits behind me, holding me up so I can cast meager fire spells wherever they're needed.

Without Eleonore, the vampire horde loses its organization. They grow weaker by the second. I wonder if the vampire queen's death has sapped their will to fight because some vamps simply fall to their knees and crumble into dust.

"I killed her," I rasp.

"I know. We all saw." Bastian runs his hand up and down my arm. That little bit of contact is enough to create a spark of energy. I'm rejuvenated enough to sit up on my own.

"Are you hurt?" I ask.

"A few bumps and scrapes, nothing more," he shrugs it off. I now notice a deep gash on his cheek. It's likely to scar.

"Come here." I bring my palm to his cheek and deliver a minor healing spell to the wound.

"Thank you. Will you be all right if I offer aid to the others?" he asks.

"Go," I urge him.

Soon, all of Eleonore's forces lay dead or dying in the grand foyer. After a few moments, I get to my feet. Her pile of ashes sits in the center of the room. I can't risk leaving even a trace of her magic, so I search the foyer for something to contain her remains. I find a vase crusted over with grime and filth. It'll do.

I gingerly scoop up her ashes and place them inside the container. I'll find a place to bury it on the night of a full moon. The lunar energy will dispel any remaining negativity.

As I move through the foyer, looking for a safe place to temporarily stash the vase, I step over a dead vampire.

"Azealia," a voice rasps.

I'm so startled I nearly drop the vase. I look down at the vampire and gasp.

"Adrian?" Though his face is bloody and sooty, I still recognize the lover who betrayed me all those years ago. "You're a vampire?" I set the vase down and kneel beside him. He struggles to lift one hand. I grasp it.

"No." His body shifts. Suddenly, he's a crow with broken wings. He shifts back to a man with a wince. "I don't know what I am anymore. Year ago, I flew to Europe to get as far away from Bonfire Falls as I could. Eleonore captured me when I landed near her once. She couldn't lift the curse, but she kept me alive for centuries anyway. She tried to cast a second transformation spell, but she never turned me into a vampire."

"Why didn't she kill you?"

"Because I was useful to her." He flickers between his crow form and his human form three times. I realize it's involuntary. With Eleonore gone, he's losing control over whatever gifts she gave him. "I told her about you, about where to find you... and how to kill you. She waited. For years, she waited. And then suddenly, she decided it was the right time to attack."

His words land like blows.

"I wanted revenge for what you did to me," he continues. "But I was wrong. If I'd been the good and decent person you've always deserved, none of this would've happened. It's my fault."

"It's in the past," I say gently. I see death in his eyes. He doesn't have much time left. Despite everything he did to me, and all the pain he caused to the men I love, he deserves to enter the next life in peace.

"I will pay the price for my actions," he vows.

"Go forward with my forgiveness and my blessing." I

move closer to him and take his head into my lap. I run my fingers through his blood-soaked hair. His eyes show only sadness. The pain of betrayal is gone now. So is the love I once felt for him.

"What's going to happen to me when I leave this earth and this body?" he asks.

"I don't know." I can't bring myself to lie to him. "Even I can't answer those questions. But wherever you go next, I hope it will be filled with light and peace. The moon will guide you on your journey into the world beyond ours."

"Thank you," he whispers. One last breath rattles through his chest. His eyes close.

He's gone now.

A tether snaps somewhere within me. Though it's not the joyous occasion I always imagined it to be, I'm free now. Free to love the men worthy of my love.

CAPTIVE OF THE VAMPIRES:
CHAPTER 21

AZEALIA

"Is it bad that I like this place?" I ask as I pick my way across the grand foyer. Last night, I killed Eleonore in this exact spot. After the battle we disposed of the bodies, including Adrian's, but the carpet is still stained with the blood of her fallen soldiers.

"Bad? I wouldn't say that," Bastian says.

"Weird? Most definitely," Cobalt says.

"What's to like about it?" Kael wrinkles his nose as a cloud of dust explodes underfoot. "That probably wasn't regular old dust, was it?"

"Probably not," I chuckle. "And despite the horrors that were unleashed here recently, this place has good bones. Overall, the history of this place is happy. Last night, all I could feel was the evil lurking here, but it was all Eleonore's doing. She probably left traces of evil all over Europe."

"Maybe someone will come along and make this a happy place again," Bastian says.

"I think it should be us," I say.

"Have you lost your mind?" Kael snorts.

"I'm serious. This land belongs to someone somewhere. They clearly don't want it. If this house sits in disrepair for too long, it'll be unsalvageable."

"That information's probably at City Hall. It wouldn't take too long to find out," Cobalt says.

"You're encouraging this?" Kael blinks in surprise.

Cobalt shrugs. "If it's what she wants, then I'm going to make sure she gets it. Besides, she killed Eleonore. She should get a reward for that."

"Exactly," I beam.

"What would you even do with a place like this?" Kael asks.

"Make it a resort?" I shrug. "Cobalt could open a second location here. It'll be a huge hit year-round. Can you imagine this place all covered in snow?"

"The snow will cover the carpet if you don't fix that hole in the ceiling." Bastian points. Sure enough, there's a huge gap in the dome ceiling.

"We'll deal with that later." I say as I wave my hand dismissively. "But first, I want to make sure it's been properly cleansed."

"My pack checked the rooms last night," Kael says.

"I gave the place a once over as well. It was clear then," Cobalt says.

"I want to verify it myself," I reply. "It's not that I don't trust you guys. It's just that an extra layer of caution wouldn't hurt. If there are any other nasty things in here, I'll find them."

"She makes a good point," Bastian says.

It takes a few hours before I'm completely satisfied that dark energy isn't lingering anywhere in the massive building.

"You should charge for your services. That was a lot of work," Bastian says.

"I'll ask them to take a few thousand off the selling price." I grin.

"If it's for sale," Kael grumbles.

"It'll be for sale," I say.

"You sound awfully sure of that. Are you planning on using your tricky witchy magic to make them sell it to you?" Cobalt asks.

"Maybe. Or maybe I'll use my wiles." I wink. "It's seemed to work out for me so far."

"Let's get you and your wiles back to the cottage," Kael says. His eyes hunger for something only I can give him.

"Can I fly with you, Cobalt?"

"Of course," he agrees with a smile.

"Thanks. It's been a while since I've been able to do anything without looking over my shoulder."

"It's nice being able to split up without the threat of death," he says.

"I'm not sure I like splitting up," I say thoughtfully. "I like it better when we're all together."

"I think we're all in agreement there," Bastian says as the three of us leave the building.

Cobalt shifts fluidly into his dragon form. I gingerly run a fingertip over the iridescent membrane covering his wings. He shudders in pleasure.

I climb on with as much grace as I can muster. Riding dragons isn't part of my skill set, but I'm sure Cobalt will give me flying lessons if I ask. I loop my arms around his neck and flatten my belly against his back. His scales dig into my skin, but it doesn't hurt. It's rather nice. I give him a pat to let him know I'm ready for take-off.

"See you back at the cottage." I call to Kael and Bastian

right before Cobalt launches into the air. I let out a squeal of pure delight.

Below me, the other two men shift into their beast forms and take off into the forest. I'm sure they're racing to see who can get home first. They're pretty evenly matched so I don't know who will win, but it's fun to watch them try to outrun each other. It's playful competitiveness, and I'm glad they're finally getting along.

Once Cobalt levels out, I loosen my grip on his neck. As I take a deep breath, crisp, clean air fills my lungs. From this vantage point, it's as if the mountains are cradling the forest in a timeless embrace. The tallest peaks are capped with snow that never melts, and rivers flow down through verdant valleys. It's beautiful, peaceful, and with any luck, it will stay that way forever.

As Cobalt zooms down toward my cottage, I open my palm and wave it to dispel the protective barrier around my home. I won't need it anymore. I'll never need to hide again. I'm sure that, in time, the people of Bonfire Falls will come to know who I really am. Not an evil, fairytale witch, but a woman who'd been hurt, and who found a way to heal herself.

Maybe I'll even start a small magic school. That'd be a good use for the new house. I know Kael's not entirely on board, but once we fix it up, I'm sure he'll love it.

As we land gracefully at the door to my cottage, Kael and Bastian burst through the tree line. They're neck and neck with each other. Kael transforms midstride which gives Bastian an advantage in their race. He pushes a burly bear paw against the door before shifting back.

"I won," he pants.

"No way. I was half a pace in front of you the whole time," Kael says.

"That doesn't matter. I touched the door before you did."

"We didn't specify the winner had to touch the door."

"It goes without saying. It's a race. That's how races work."

I laugh into my palm and shake my head.

"Technically, Cobalt and I won," I say.

"You weren't part of the race," Kael says.

"You didn't ask if I was. You assumed I wasn't."

"I think we should all consider ourselves winners," Cobalt says as he folds his wings against his side and shifts back into his human form.

"That takes the fun out of it," Kael says.

"We all defeated an ancient vampire army and their blood-crazed queen. That's a much larger victory," I say.

"That wasn't a competition. That was doing the right thing," Kael says.

"Boys!" I put my hands on my hips and sigh. "You're all my winners. What else matters?"

"Nothing." Kael's scowl turns into a grin. "You're the greatest prize I can imagine."

"Let's go inside. I'll make some tea."

When I open the door to my cottage, it smells like home. I put on a kettle and bring the water to a boil. By the time I've finished making the tea, the guys have changed back into normal clothing. Too bad because I'd rather having them walk around naked. I grin.

Each man gets a special tea filled with herbs hand selected from my pantry.

"Amazing," Cobalt sighs after his first sip.

"I want to drink this tea every day for the rest of my life." Bastian's already drained his cup. I refill it for him.

"Why don't you?" I ask.

"I..." Bastian hesitates. "I don't know. I wasn't sure if

things would go back to how they used to be before
Eleonore tried to destroy us all."

"Things can never go back to how they were before." I
reach across the table and take his hand in mine. "We're
bonded now. All of us. That can't be undone. What we
have is stronger than any spell."

"You're right," he says as he slips his hand into mine.

"I love you, Bastian. I love all three of you so much.
Sometimes my heart feels like it's going to burst out of my
chest because it's so full of love."

"I love you too, Azealia." Cobalt takes my other hand. Kael
comes up behind me and wraps his arms around my waist.

"As long as you want us, we'll be here," he says.

"So...everyone's okay with the way things are?" I hold
my breath as all three men glance at each other.

"Yes," Kael answers.

When Bastian and Cobalt echo his sentiments, tears
well up in my eyes. One slips down my cheek. Bastian
wipes it away with his thumb.

"There is one little problem," he says.

"What?" The color drains from my face.

"There's only one bed here. A twin bed."

"Oh." I laugh. "I can take care of that. Follow me."

I lead my men into the bedroom. Despite the small
size of my bed, the room is quite large.

"Watch this." I wink at the guys.

I harness the magic within me and use it to manifest
an orb of light. As I add more energy to the spell, the orb
surrounds the bed. The mattress and frame levitate and
start to morph. The brilliant glow generated by the spell is
so bright that the three men have to cover their eyes. I
don't. I'm used to it.

"Open your eyes," I say.

"Wow," Kael says.

"Impressive," Bastian says.

"That's exactly what we need," Cobalt says.

Instead of my small twin bed, there's now an elegant sleigh bed big enough to fit all four of us.

"Try it out," I urge them.

Kael leaps onto the mattress.

"It's like a cloud. I approve." He pulls me onto the bed with him. I lean in for a kiss. The delicious heat from his body warms mine where we touch.

The bed moves as Cobalt and Bastian climb on with us. Bastian's hand strokes my leg.

"I think we need to take our new bed for a test drive," I say between kisses.

"Agreed," Cobalt hums against my neck.

"Come here," I purr.

Their hands, and mouths, and tongues are everywhere at once. In a tangle of flailing limbs, we manage to undress. Locked in the most intimate of embraces, the men make love to me, and I love them in return.

As we crash into ecstasy together, I release a blast of magic which rains down on us, blessing each of us with boundless energy.

"I could get used to this," Kael says as he cuddles my back against his chest.

"Me too," Bastian says as lays facing me, stroking my hip.

"Let's stay like this forever," Cobalt says.

"So mote it be," I whisper.

I don't know what I did to deserve these wonderful men, but I'm not about to question it. Now that I have them, I'll never let them go. I'd go to the ends of the earth for each one of them, and I know in my heart they'd do the same for me. We're bound together by love and we'll be together for eternity.

No woman has ever been this lucky.

To be the first to find out about Liv's next book, and to get special offers and discounts, sign up for Liv's newsletter!

Don't miss the **Curvy Bear Ranch Series.**

Find out more about Liv on her website!

ABOUT THE AUTHOR

USA Today bestselling author Liv Brywood writes paranormal romance. Her scorching hot shifters love curvy women and aren't afraid to show it. They're loyal, brave, honorable, and above all — sexy. Liv's stories are filled with passion, hope, and everlasting love.

To be the first to find out about the next book in the series, and to get special offers and discounts, sign up for my email newsletter!

To find out more about me, please check out my website.

Friend me on Facebook.

Follow me on Twitter.

Email me at LivBrywood@gmail.com